Praise for The Guardians Series

Shortlisted for the B.C. Book Prize for Fiction
(*The Forest Laird*)

"With *The Forest Laird*, novelist Jack Whyte paints a far more complex portrait—one in which William Wallace shines forth not just as an Achilles of the late 1200s, but as a reluctant outlaw, a Latin-speaking kingmaker and a sword-wielding patriot … Whyte opens the novel brilliantly … [and] succeeds in weaving history into the story as it crackles along."
—*The Globe and Mail*

"Whyte's prose is punctuated with moments of tension that contrast perfectly with the book's sombre tone."
—*Winnipeg Free Press*

"Whyte writes with a clear sense of history as an ongoing chess game … [*The Guardian*] is both captivating and transporting."   —*Vancouver Sun*

Praise for the Templar Trilogy

"Whyte's found the key to refreshing the legend and making it live again … The wealth and richness of the historical detail are fascinating. If James Michener is the past master of sweeping epic, then Jack Whyte may well be the future one."   —*Calgary Herald*

"Enough loose ends and cliff-hanging dramatic turns to guarantee an audience for volume two."

— *The Globe and Mail*

"To read Jack Whyte is to surrender to a storyteller of the old school. His writing is firmly rooted in the basics of good storytelling: strong characterization, effective plotting, and excellent writing." — *Quill & Quire*

"A meaty book, full of details you wouldn't expect to find in an adventure so action-packed: what the knights wore, every layer down to their skin, for example, and how ladies of the period prepared their makeup and hair." — *BC Book World*

"This second entry [*Standard of Honor*] in Whyte's Templar trilogy … finds the author in his top form … Whyte gilds the tangled political complications of the late 12th century with a rich trove of Templar lore … Few authors can match Whyte when it comes to epic battle scenes involving blazing heat, choking dust, rearing horses and thousands of sword-wielding knights and Saracens locked in mortal combat."

— *Publishers Weekly*

"[*Standard of Honor*'s] quick rise to the upper reaches of the bestseller list, not to mention signs of strong word of mouth, suggest that Whyte's star is rising even higher." — *Quill & Quire*

PENGUIN

THE GUARDIAN

JACK WHYTE was born and raised in Scotland and immigrated to Canada in 1967. He is an actor, orator, singer, and poet, and was awarded an honorary doctor of letters for his contribution to Canadian popular fiction. He is the author of the Dream of Eagles series (eight Arthurian novels set in Roman Britain) and the Templar Trilogy (featuring the legendary Knights Templar). Whyte's novels are also published in the United States, the U.K., Australia, New Zealand, Germany, France, the Netherlands, Portugal, Spain, Italy, Brazil, and Russia. He lives in Kelowna, British Columbia.

Also by Jack Whyte

A DREAM OF EAGLES

The Skystone
The Singing Sword
The Eagles' Brood
The Saxon Shore
The Sorcerer, Volume I: The Fort at River's Bend
The Sorcerer, Volume II: Metamorphosis

———

Uther

———

THE GOLDEN EAGLE

Clothar the Frank
The Eagle

———

THE TEMPLAR TRILOGY

Knights of the Black and White
Standard of Honor
Order in Chaos

———

THE GUARDIANS SERIES

The Forest Laird
The Renegade

Jack Whyte

The Guardian

A TALE OF ANDREW MURRAY

PENGUIN

an imprint of Penguin Canada Books Inc., a Penguin Random House Company

Published by the Penguin Group

Penguin Canada Books Inc., 320 Front Street West, Toronto, Ontario M5V 3B6, Canada

Penguin Group (USA) LLC, 375 Hudson Street, New York, New York 10014, U.S.A.
Penguin Books Ltd, 80 Strand, London WC2R 0RL, England
Penguin Ireland, 25 St Stephen's Green, Dublin 2, Ireland (a division of Penguin Books Ltd)
Penguin Group (Australia), 707 Collins Street, Melbourne, Victoria 3008, Australia
(a division of Pearson Australia Group Pty Ltd)
Penguin Books India Pvt Ltd, 11 Community Centre, Panchsheel Park, New Delhi – 110 017, India
Penguin Group (NZ), 67 Apollo Drive, Rosedale, Auckland 0632, New Zealand
(a division of Pearson New Zealand Ltd)
Penguin Books (South Africa) (Pty) Ltd, 24 Sturdee Avenue, Rosebank,
Johannesburg 2196, South Africa

Penguin Books Ltd, Registered Offices: 80 Strand, London WC2R 0RL, England

First published in Viking hardcover by Penguin Canada Books Inc., 2014

Published in this edition, 2015

2 3 4 5 6 7 8 9 10 (OPM)

LIBRARY AND ARCHIVES CANADA CATALOGUING IN PUBLICATION

Whyte, Jack, 1940-, author
The guardian : a tale of Andrew Murray / Jack Whyte.
(The guardians series ; book 3)
Originally published: Toronto, Ontario, Canada : Viking, 2014.

ISBN 978-0-14-316913-0 (pbk.)
1. Scotland--History--Robert I, 1306-1329--Fiction.
I. Title. II. Series: Whyte, Jack, 1940- . Guardians series; bk. 3.

PS8595.H947G83 2015   C813'.54   C2015-900287-7

eBook ISBN 978-0-14-319308-1

Visit the Penguin Canada website at **www.penguin.ca**

Special and corporate bulk purchase rates available; please see
www.penguin.ca/corporatesales or call 1-800-810-3104.

To my granddaughter Jessica
and her husband, Jake Strashok,
who is what I have always secretly wanted to be:
a metalsmith.
And to my dear wife, Beverley,
for being herself.

AUTHOR'S NOTE

In my recent travels, meeting and greeting my readers, and even in my daily interactions with people who are not my readers but who know, from various sources, that I write historical novels, one question recurs with frequency: "What *is* historical fiction?"

I've heard this question ever since I first became a published author, but in the past few years the number of people asking it has multiplied so noticeably that I now feel obliged to try to answer it. So let me see if I can.

On the most visible level it's a genre, of course, a recognizable story form that's easy to hang a label upon. (Allow me to digress. Although this genre is growing increasingly popular everywhere in the English-speaking world, it is one of the strangest anomalies of the book-selling trade in North America that the major bookstore chains refuse to recognize it. Readers everywhere are clamouring for it more and more loudly each year, but bookstores appear deaf. There are no Historical Fiction departments in our North American bookstores, and that gives rise to strange bed-fellows. This book you are holding now—very clearly a historical novel—is probably shelved in the Fantasy and Science Fiction section. That is because my first series of books, called

A Dream of Eagles in Canada and the Camulod Chronicles in the U.S.A., offered a speculative but feasible perspective on the probable beginnings of the Arthurian legend, set in fifth-century post-Roman Britain. It was historical, but it was also speculative fiction. Most telling of all, though, it mentioned King Arthur, and so it was designated fantasy and shelved accordingly. But because of that, my last two historical trilogies, dealing respectively with the rise and fall of the medieval Knights Templar and the fourteenth-century Scottish Wars of Independence, have also been consigned to the Fantasy and Sci-Fi shelves, in utter disregard of the minor consideration that they contain no slightest hint of either fantasy or science fiction.)

So what *is* historical fiction? I believe the best of it amounts to a transcription of thoroughly researched records of genuine historical events embellished, emphasized, and made more appreciable to modern readers with one single element of historical commentary that is taboo among academic and classical historians. That element is speculation. Historians know, for example, that King Edward I of England spent an entire night in May of the year 1290 cloistered with Antony Bek, the Prince Bishop of Durham, in a guarded room in Norham Castle on the Scots border, and that Bek left for Scotland the following morning, there to announce himself as King Edward's deputy in arranging the union of the Crowns of England and Scotland through a marriage between

Princess Margaret of Norway, the child heir to the vacant Scottish throne, and King Edward's firstborn son, the boy Edward, Prince of Wales. They know that, but the all-night meeting was behind closed doors with nothing written down for posterity, so they know nothing of what was actually said between the two men that night, and as academic historians they are forbidden to speculate.

That speculation falls within the purview of the writer of historical fiction, who is completely at liberty to put words into the mouths of the participants, with the sole proviso that he or she can say nothing that contradicts the known historical record. And so the historical novelist possesses a power that is almost magical compared with the straightforward recitation of known facts inhibiting the academics: the novelist can breathe life into the otherwise lifeless and unap-preciated protagonists and participants in great historical events, and the really gifted storytellers can transform ancient worlds into reality, enabling their readers to appreciate and understand that their ancestors, the people who inhabited those times and places and lived through great and remarkable events centuries or millennia ago, were people like themselves, facing exactly the same fundamental problems that beset us today, with all our supposed advantages. For then, as now, the problems facing an ordinary, undistinguished man were straightforward and unavoidable—to feed his family and dependents and to keep them safe, with the best and strongest roof over their heads that he could provide—and the role of a responsible woman, in any society, has been unchanged since Eve first smiled at Adam. It is the skill of historical novelists in making those things clear while cleaving as closely as possible to historical accuracy that has led to the recent enormous upsurge in demand for the wondrous stories that are found in historical novels, the genre that the booksellers will tell you doesn't exist.

What most people don't know about, though, is the genuinely massive difficulty in dealing with language accurately, and that, too, increases the demand for accuracy in reporting by the historical novelist. Standard English, as we know it today, became standardized only during the reign of Queen Victoria. Before that there was no such thing as orthography, no formal rules of spelling or syntax. Everyone who was literate was free to spell anything the way he or she thought fit. And even more confusing, less than two hundred years ago people from different regions of the same country—of *any* country—couldn't speak to or understand one another. Every little town and village had its own dialect and its own idioms. In Scotland, for example, the port town of Aberdeen had its own language, spoken only by Aberdonians. Two hundred years ago in Britain, which is where I grew up, Londoners couldn't speak with people from Devon or Cornwall or from Yorkshire or Lancashire or Dorset, and God knows they couldn't converse with Gaelic-speaking Scots or Irishmen or Welshmen. But they all understood their neighbours perfectly, and they conversed fluently in whatever dialect was common to them; and when they needed to, as people always have, they invented bastard languages to permit them to trade with one another. The only means the historical novelist has of dealing with such delicate intricacies is his or her own skill in the manipulation of language and suggestion.

And so I invite my readers, once again, to share my perception, my interpretation, of the world in which my heroes lived in fourteenth-century Scotland. Seven hundred years have elapsed since William Wallace, Andrew Murray, and Robert Bruce fought their campaigns in the name of freedom, but their struggle against tyranny and usurpation is still going on today, around our modern world.

Jack Whyte
Kelowna, British Columbia
August 31, 2014

CHAPTER ONE

FATHER JAMES WALLACE, 1343

I discovered many years ago that Sir Lionel Redvers was the first English knight ever to die at the hands of my cousin William Wallace of Elderslie, and while the discovery pained me at the time, it also gave me a moment of vengeful satisfaction. I have confessed that sin on many occasions but it remains within me unforgiven, for I have never really regretted the satisfaction I derived from it.

Redvers was an undistinguished knight from the county of Suffolk. I only ever met him once, and briefly, and had immediately dismissed him as a nonentity. But within minutes of our encounter he proved how strange are the ways of God, for even a nonentity may be a catalyst. That headstrong, zealous fool changed every life in Scotland and plunged the whole of Britain into chaos because he brought about the deaths of a woman, her small son, and her unborn second child. The woman was in my care at the time and her name was Mirren Wallace. She was William Wallace's wife and therefore cousin to me by marriage.

My name is Wallace, too, and I am a priest. A very old priest. I was born in 1272, which makes me seventy-one years old. Sir William Wallace, Guardian of Scotland, was my first cousin and my dearest boyhood friend. Thirty-eight years ago, on the day he died, he asked me, as his confessor, to bear witness to the manner of his dying and to attest to it should men seek to malign him in times ahead. I swore I would, and that is why I am writing this today, so long afterwards.

For nigh on thirty years I had no reason to recall that promise to Will. From being greatly out of favour with his fellow Scots before his death, he was reborn as a hero during King Robert's struggle to unite Scotland, when the Bruce himself chose to adopt the tactics Will had used against the English, turning the land itself, as well as its folk, to the task of defeating England's plans to usurp our realm. And from the King's open admiration of my cousin's single-minded struggle, a new recognition of Will's worth and integrity grew up in Scotland. I was content.

I have no idea when the substance of his recognition began to change or who set that in motion, and neither have I any doubt that the change continues. It first came to my attention through a chance conversation with an old friend, another priest, whom I had not seen for years. His name was Declan, and we had served together as chaplains to Will's outlawed band in Selkirk Forest many years before, when we were both young. Mere chance threw us together again one night about ten years ago, in the abbey at Dunfermline in Fife, where we arrived separately one autumn afternoon on church business. After dinner that night, reminiscing by the dying fire, my old friend unwittingly destroyed my peace of mind.

We were speaking, as always, in Latin. This is not unusual among priests, since we learn it as soon as we begin to train for the priesthood, and we often find it useful to adopt the language of the Church when conversing privately, particularly if there are others nearby with whom we do not wish to share our thoughts. With Father Declan, though, there was another reason. Declan spoke poorly, even haltingly, in our native tongue, as though he had difficulty finding his words in the common language of everyday life. When he spoke Latin, though, he became another person altogether, his conversation fluid and sparkling with wit and ease. I always took pleasure in that difference.

"This is where I last saw your cousin Will," he said that night.

"In this abbey?" I said, surprised. "I didn't know he'd ever come to Dunfermline. When was that?"

"It was soon after the defeat at Falkirk," Declan said, "but I couldn't tell you exactly when. He was a different Will Wallace from the man I'd known in Selkirk Forest, though. That I can swear to. He looked decades older—haggard and … haunted is what I remember thinking at the time. He spoke to me civilly enough, but I never saw him smile in all the time I was there—he who had always had a smile for everyone and loved to laugh. And then within the month I heard that he had laid down the guardianship."

"Aye," I said, "haunted is a good word for how he looked then. He was a man transformed and disfigured by what occurred at Falkirk. He blamed himself for the debacle and would not be consoled, no matter how passionately we condemned the magnates who quit the field with their cavalry and left him and his men alone on foot to face the English bowmen. He carried all the guilt himself for the hundreds killed in the skirmishes, for he had never trusted the loyalty of the magnates and he believed he should have known they would desert him. He never recovered from the shame of it, though God knows there was no shame in it for him. But it sapped his spirit, and he lost the will to fight."

Declan looked at me with one eyebrow raised. "You seem very sure of that. Did you confess him at that time?"

"No. I offered, but he would have none of it. It was plain to see he had lost all faith in God, in the realm, and even in the King's cause that had sustained him. He had been King John's most stalwart supporter since the outset, even in the face of everything that happened, and he saw Scotland's abandonment of Balliol as a form of suicide—the self-willed death of the realm. He was a man in despair, and I could do nothing to comfort him. All I could do was commend him to his friend Bishop Lamberton, perhaps the single man in all of Scotland he still trusted. Eventually he left on the embassy to France—that was at Lamberton's instigation—and thence to Rome to parley with the Pope and the cardinals on Scotland's behalf, and I did not see him again for four years. Not until the night I visited him and heard his last confession in Smithfield prison."

"But he had regained his faith by then?"

"Aye, he had, and I have thanked God for that. He made a good confession and died in a state of grace, his mind at rest—as far as it could be, knowing what faced him that day. When I left him before dawn that morning, he was the same old Will I had always known and loved."

Declan smiled. "The Will we both knew and loved in Selkirk Forest. But that's not the William Wallace men talk about today."

I shrugged. "That's as it should be. They see him now, too late, as the man he truly was."

Declan looked at me strangely. "No," he said, "that's not what I meant, Jamie. The man he truly *was*? What they're saying today has nothing to do with the man Will Wallace truly was. How can you even pretend to be amused by such a thing? Men speak of him now as if he were a demigod of the ancients, another Finn MacCool, bigger than any living man, greater even than King Robert."

"Finn MacCool would be flattered," I said, smiling at the foolishness of what he had said. "Fond memories play tricks on everyone—especially on those who were not there to share what happened. But I'm surprised to hear the 'greater than King Robert' slur. That's inane. And dangerous. In their cups, I suppose."

"I've heard it said, nonetheless, Jamie. On many occasions and by people who were not drunk."

"Drunk or not, they must have been mad to malign King Robert openly."

My friend turned to look at me squarely, and again I saw that expression of perplexity on his face.

"What?" I said. "You disagree with me?"

A deep cleft appeared between his brows and he stared at me for several moments. "Forgive me, Jamie," he said and sat back in his seat. "I thought you must be aware of what I mean—even though I can't imagine how you can truly *not* know." He drew a breath. "They're changing him, Jamie. Changing everything about him. Will has been dead, what? Twenty-eight years? Most of the folk who knew him are dead themselves. Those who talk about him now are young—not old priests like you and me but plain, very young Scots folk everywhere. They never knew him, never saw him, and they believe what they are being told."

I could feel myself glowering. "Speak plain, man. *What* are they being told? And who is telling them?"

I suddenly saw my friend, whom I had known for so long and who had not aged in my mind, as what he really had become, a careworn, middle-aged priest perplexed by the strange inconsistencies of mankind.

"I don't know, Jamie. I don't know who is behind such talk, or even when or how or where it began. But folk are saying nowadays that Sir William Wallace was a giant. Not merely in his body, which God knows was big enough, but in everything else, too. In his passions and his convictions, his patriotism and his prowess, in the things he did and the things he believed and the things he achieved. They're saying that he was a giant in his virtues, too, a towering, saintly figure, divinely inspired, without flaw and lacking any human faults. They're speaking of him as they would a saint, saying that he had the privy ear of God Himself, and that in the Deity's name he named and publicly condemned this country's treasonous enemies, the Comyns and their like, who abandoned Scotland's cause at Falkirk fight."

I sat open-mouthed, appalled by what I was hearing, yet knowing that Declan would not lie about such things, and as I closed my mouth, swallowing the sourness on my tongue, he spoke on.

"I *knew* Will Wallace, Jamie," he said in a voice that sounded as shaken as I felt. "Not as well as you did, I know, but that last part frightens me near to death when I think of it, for I know how *wrong* it is. Will Wallace was no *saint*."

I have never felt anything quite like the helplessness that filled me then as I sat there, wordless, beside the smoking embers of the fire. It shook me to the bottom of my being, because the truth that rang in Declan's voice was unmistakable and it convinced me that I had been derelict in my duty to protect my cousin's name. I had to swallow hard to moisten my mouth before I could respond.

"I've heard none of this, Declan," I said eventually. "Tell me more, all of it."

And he did, in great detail.

Wallace was being reborn, he insisted, this time stripped of all human frailties and fallibilities and held up to the adoring crowds as a conquering champion who had been sent by Heaven to rally Scotland against its ancient enemies, and who had been betrayed and undone by traitors. Even as I listened, believing what he said, I had to fight the temptation to shout him down and try to make a liar out of him. The clear suggestion underlying everything he told me was that those ancient enemies were the English, and that was monstrously untrue. They had been our enemies for a time, yes, and we had fought a war with them that lasted, off and on, for eighteen years until we bested them at Bannockburn in the seventh year of King Robert's reign. But the people of England had not been our enemies until their aging King, Edward Plantagenet, sensing a weakness in us that did not exist, decided to lay claim to our realm and add it to his own, exactly as he had done earlier with Wales. His barons, hungry for Scots land and wealth, had flocked to support him, but the common English folk had never been our enemies before Edward himself provoked us into war with them.

What was being said now, flagrantly untrue, was obviously aimed at people too young to have known what really happened back in the days when Wallace's rebellion broke out. Older people might have laughed at what they were being told, but most of those older people had died between then and now, and the plain truth known to my generation—that Edward of

England alone was responsible for Scotland's troubles in those days—was nearly forgotten.

Declan asked me, yet again, how I could have been unaware of such goings-on. All I could do was shake my head. I knew, though, that I had simply not been *listening*. I had assumed that my cousin had been redeemed by King Robert's high regard for him, and that therefore I had no further need to worry about him. He had been dead for almost three decades, and the King's esteem had cleared his name of any hint of shame or dishonour. I had believed I could leave him and his memory in God's hands.

I had been wrong.

That evening with Declan was the goad that drove me to begin my history of my cousin as I knew him, and the task of doing precisely that—of bearing witness in Will's memory—has consumed me for more than ten years now. I am realistic enough to know that my puny, unsupported voice can do nothing to influence or interfere with the political ambitions of those powerful but unknown people who are trying to use Will for their own ends. I am also cynical enough to acknowledge that, despite knowing nothing of their identities, their motivation, or their objectives, I could probably point my finger accurately at some who would turn out to be ringleaders. But even were I to do that, who would listen to an old, obscure priest, even though he be cousin to the great Wallace?

By writing instead of speaking out, though, I see a possibility that what I have to say will be read and understood in years to come by others who might heed my words and use them. I have a duty to keep the promise I made to Will, there in the pre-dawn darkness of his prison cell.

The King of England had him hanged in London town in the year 1305, but bade the royal executioners to cut him down before he could die. They brought him back from the edge of death, and then they eviscerated him and forced him to watch his own intestines being burned in a metal dish. And finally they beheaded and dismembered him and sent his body parts to be displayed in various cities as a reminder of the penalty for defying England's most Christian king.

I last set down my pen more than a year ago, unable to continue writing after I had described the inhumanity surrounding the deaths of Will's wife, Mirren, and her unborn child, and the murder of his infant son, another William Wallace. Having written of it, reliving the horror as though it had happened mere days before instead of decades, I simply stopped and walked away, refusing to return to my chronicle. I had no will to pursue the painful memories further. It took me until yesterday to recapture the peace of mind I needed to resume my task, though I doubt even now if peace of mind is the correct term for what I had been lacking. Determination, now that I see it written here, is a more accurate word.

Whatever the right term may be, though, I was spurred to begin again by an unprompted memory of an Englishman, a common garrison soldier called Harald Gaptooth, whom I came to know in a Lanark monastery soon after my encounter with Redvers decades earlier. He was a boorish oaf, completely uncouth, utterly lacking in grace or manners, and coarsely English, but I had paid attention to his tale on the two occasions when I heard it, and I recalled it easily last night and decided, then and there, that I might never find a better point at which to resume my tale.

CHAPTER TWO

THE DRUNKARD'S TALE

Harald Gaptooth would eventually be grateful for having known nothing of what was to happen that night in Lanark town, but even as he began to recover from his injuries he was aware that his own laziness and ignorance had saved his life. He knew, too, that had his friend Bernard of Boothby not been sergeant of the guard that night, he would have been flogged for reporting drunk for duty and being openly mutinous. But he had had no slightest idea, before the world went mad, that anything significant was about to occur; no suspicion that the scene he was witnessing would be seared into his eyes so that he would see it over and over again in the years to come whenever someone mentioned certain things or named certain names. Gaptooth knew none of that. Looking back on the events afterwards, all he would recall was his anger that night, unusual this time because it had a focus, as opposed to the dull, constantly burning anger that consumed him at other times.

He had been angry about being stuck on guard duty when he ought to have been out carousing somewhere on a well-earned leave, safe by a tavern fire on a night that was cold enough for the dead of winter when it ought to have been bright and balmy with the breath of spring. No one had expected snow so late in May. And no one was ready for it, after two months of sunshine and soft weather. Daffodils and crocuses had been blooming for weeks, many of them withered and gone already, and new leaves were bursting their buds on trees everywhere.

And then God, with a malice that denied all logic, had decreed not only that it should snow but that the temperature should plunge within hours and the snow should be blown everywhere by shrieking winds that cut a man to the bone, chilling the marrow at the centre of him.

His commander, the sheriff Hazelrig, a strutting, pride-filled cockerel, had gone off somewhere four days earlier and had not returned by the time the start of Gaptooth's promised furlough came around two days later. That meant that Gaptooth's release had been delayed—that was how Bernard of Boothby, the sergeant, had put it—until the sheriff's reappearance, because the hot-headed fool had taken almost the entire garrison with him and Lanark town was now seriously undermanned at a time when reports of local rebellions and unrest were coming in daily. Two more days had passed since then with no word from Hazelrig, and the sheriff's acting lieutenant, Sir Roger de Vries, was visibly worried.

Then, the night before, a fitful wind had sprung up, blowing out of the northwest, and by dawn a heavy, blustering snowstorm had changed the world. By sunrise, visibility had shrunk to less than a longbow shot, and the sight of snow-shrouded, impenetrable masses of trees looming just beyond the town walls was giving rise to thoughts of being attacked while most of the garrison was absent. De Vries had issued orders that all watches were to be double-manned and changed to a four-hours-on, four-off frequency, replacing the standard six-and-six format. No one was permitted to go outside the gates for any reason, and all leave was cancelled until such time as the sheriff returned and garrison life was restored to normal.

Even before word of these new restrictions was passed, Gaptooth's anger had begun to bubble sufficiently to send him to the nearest alehouse. He set about drinking determinedly as soon as he got there, before noon, and by the time his shift came around, four hours later, he was thoroughly soused, barely able to walk back to his barracks. His friend Bernard, the sergeant of the guard that afternoon, snatched him by the arm as soon as he set eyes on him and dragged him quickly into the lee of a storehouse and out of sight. There he threatened him with hellfire and damnation for being drunk on duty and reminded him of the penalty for being found unfit for guard duty in times of emergency. He sent Harald off with a flea in his ear and a dire warning to wash himself and be sober by the time he showed his face on the parapet walk, lest he find himself arrested and thrown into the cells, where he would, beyond a doubt, be hanged once things returned to normal. De Vries was rattled, Bernard said, probably afraid and certainly unsure of himself, and he would not think twice about reinforcing his authority at the expense of anyone who crossed him.

And so Harald Gaptooth washed his face and head in icy water from a barrel outside the latrines, cursing the weather all the time and shivering like a man with ague as he scrubbed at his cropped, wet hair with a rough towel. Then, wrapped in a heavy sheepskin coat, and with a long muffler made of joined strips of the same fleece wrapped several times around his neck and lower face, he presented himself for guard duty on the tower walk above the castle's main gate.

Sergeant Bernard eyed him with surly hostility but made no reference to what his friend was wearing. He himself wore a heavy, ankle-length cloak of wax-smeared wool that was completely waterproof. Gaptooth had once owned its twin, but he had long since sold it for money with which to drink, whore, and gamble.

"Well," the sergeant snarled, "I don't know how you did it, you ugly turd, but you look sober enough to pass muster. I've given you the bridgewalk post, all to yourself—it'll keep you awake and it'll keep you apart. But if de Vries or any of his people come anywhere near you, say nothing to any of them and for the love of Christ don't let them smell your breath. Otherwise, just stay awake and stay on your feet. Keep that up for four hours and you might escape the hanging you deserve, you sorry whoreson. Carry on."

Gaptooth cursed his friend, because the bridgewalk was the most public guard post in the garrison, exposed at all times to watching eyes, so the sentries up there never had the slightest chance of slacking off for a few quiet minutes. They were on parade constantly, even in the dead of night, trudging incessantly between the man-thick end posts of the great gallows that towered above them, their every move illuminated by the beacons that blazed on either end of the bridge over the town gates that gave the post its name. That night, Gaptooth knew he would be glad of the beacons' heat once they were lit, but two hours of daylight yet remained. All he could do in the meantime was brace himself and keep moving, hoping that the constant pacing back and forth would keep the blood flowing through his veins and stave off frostbite.

There were no bodies hanging from the gallows that day, and Gaptooth was grateful, for even though the chill of the snowy air would have killed any smell of death, Harald, like all his garrison mates, had deep-dyed memories of pacing the bridgewalk beneath a frieze of ripe and rotting corpses in the heat of summer days, and he felt his belly tightening even at the passing thought of it. He had cared nothing, ever, for the people hanged there. They were all Scotch, and merited being hanged for that alone, but he bitterly resented the summer-rotted stench of them, and resented, too, that he and his companions were forced to do duty directly beneath their decaying hulks, breathing in the filth of their stink and walking through the swarms of flies they attracted. Yet where better to place a gallows than directly above the town's main gates, where everyone coming and going would see the dangling bodies and reflect upon the folly of incurring the wrath of English justice? It made perfect sense. Still, every garrison trooper who had ever spent a summer guard watch parading beneath the stinking carrion detested the bridgewalk and the duty of manning it.

The wind grew stronger towards the end of his watch, shrieking with malice and increasing the noise of the two great beacon fires to a deafening roar. He tightened his fleece coat about him and rewrapped his thick muffler more snugly around his neck before marching over to the right side of his post, to stand as close as he could get to the fire in the great brazier, bracing his back against the pillar of the gallows, his spear cradled in the crook of his elbow as he clapped his hands and stamped his near-frozen feet. When he looked up again, his vision distorted by the dazzling firelight, he saw the shapes of Bernard and someone else coming towards him from the far end of the bridge, moving eerily through the whirling snow until they walked into the light from the hissing brazier on that side. They had already seen him marching, knew he was awake and alert at his post, and he felt a surge of gratitude that the wind had roused him when it had, for the man walking alongside Bernard of Boothby was Sir Roger de Vries himself. Harald drew himself fully upright, taking a firm grip on his spear shaft and squaring his shoulders, stooping forward slightly to increase the few inches of distance between his shoulder blades and the pillar at his back. He didn't think de Vries would accuse him of lounging, but he had long since stopped being surprised by the behaviour of any knight.

But the newcomers did manage to surprise him, albeit without intending to. Just as he raised a hand to address the guardsman, Bernard of Boothby leapt silently into the air and spun away to Harald's left, a short, twisting convulsion that sent him over the edge of the parapet and down to the cobbles beneath. A moment later something blasted the spear out of Harald's hand and hurled him backwards into darkness.

When he opened his eyes again Sir Roger de Vries was kneeling on the causeway in front of him, looking up at him from no more than ten paces away, and Harald felt a panic-stricken urge to laugh and look away from the sight of a knight kneeling to him. Then sanity returned and his stomach heaved, for he had no wish to see what he was seeing. Although everything in front of him was blurred by swirling snow and flickering firelight from the braziers, and his eyes felt strange, he had no doubt that de Vries was dying there, on his knees on the bridge, gaping up at Harald with his mouth dripping blood down over his curled beard and onto the rich fabric of his winter cloak, reflecting red and black flickers from the brazier flames. And then as Harald watched, appalled, the knight pitched slowly forward to reveal two long, lethal arrows in his back—unmistakably yard-long broadheads from an English longbow—and Harald felt fear claw suddenly at his bowels. The word *treason* stamped itself into his mind and he turned to spring away to safety and raise the alarm. Except that he did neither, for he could not move.

Fear flared up in him like the beacon at his back. Gasping in panic, he felt his gorge rise in a surge of nausea. He fought it down and forced himself to remain still, keeping his eyes closed and breathing as deeply as he could. He counted to ten, willing his breath to slow towards normal, then did it again, and felt calmer. By the end of his fourth count of ten, he permitted himself to open his eyes.

The knight de Vries lay face down on the bridge in front of him, clearly dead and already dusted with a coating of snow that appeared black around the base of the two arrows. Apart from the swirling snow, nothing else moved anywhere within sight—and it was then that Gaptooth realized his sight was limited. Something was hampering him, stopping him from moving; now he felt pain and an intense pressure beneath his chin. Fighting off another flare of terror, he willed himself to stay calm, and then he peered downward.

It took him several moments to understand what he was looking at, but then he recognized the finger-thick shaft of another English broadhead. It was lodged hard beneath his chin, tilting his head up and backwards and pressing his skull hard against the curving surface of the gallows frame at his back. He could see along the entire length of the angled shaft to the fletching and the deep bowstring notch at the end. He tried turning his head to the right, to pull his chin clear of the arrow's shaft, and an explosion of agony seared the entire left side of his head. He remembered the massive blow that had thrown him back. It had hit his spear! The damn thing must have glanced off and angled upwards to pierce his throat, and he marvelled that he was still alive. A moment later, though, he knew he must be wrong. He could not have lived had the arrow really pierced his throat. Gaptooth was familiar with broadhead war arrows and their wide, triple-barbed, razor-sharp edges, and so he knew that if the warhead had struck him, he would not be capable of moving at all. He would already have bled to death. The lethal arrowhead had missed his throat, and he realized that it had penetrated the thick strips of fleece wound about his neck, piercing them firmly enough to nail him to the gallows post at his back. The pain told him an edge of the broadhead had cut him, somewhere along the jawline, but he felt no strength draining from him and so a clear-thinking part of him recognized that the wound must be a minor one.

And then he heard sounds close by him and he froze just as two men ran by, stooping low and ignoring him completely as they went to examine the snow-covered body of de Vries. One of them pulled the two arrows from the dead man's back, using the full thrust of his thighs to rip them free, then gripped the corpse by the shoulder and heaved it over onto its back. Then he turned and looked over his shoulder. The fellow's eyes swept Gaptooth up and down before he turned back to his companion.

"Get Will."

As soon as the man spoke, Gaptooth became aware of the clamour of voices from the street below the gateway tower, voices he had not noticed until that moment. He narrowed his eyes slowly until they were mere slits and watched as the second man went obediently to the side of the ramp and raised his voice in a shout.

"Will! Up here on top o' the gate," he shouted with a sweep of his arm. "It's me, Scrymgeour. There's a dead knight up here might be the one you're lookin' for." As he moved back to where his companion still knelt over the body of Sir Roger de Vries, he jerked his thumb towards Gaptooth. "Was it you shot that one?" he asked.

The other man glanced over at Harald and shrugged. "Nah. But whoever it was, he was bigger than me, to nail the whoreson to the post like that wi' one arrow, right through the neck, and all. He's a big bugger, but that shot picked him up and threw him like a bag o' beets. Look at the way his feet are crossed. Ah, here's Will."

Harald Gaptooth found himself marvelling at the ways of God. The trick now, he knew, was to keep these men thinking he was dead, and that meant making no movement that might be seen by anyone. Luckily, he knew now how to achieve that, for the Scot had told him how he looked: pinned at the neck to the gallows post by a single hard-shot arrow that was supporting his entire weight, his head and body twisted sideways in different directions and one leg thrown over the other. He inhaled slowly, with great care, and willed himself to remain motionless, his unfocused eyes gazing into the blowing snow beyond the stone parapet.

The Will fellow, clearly their leader, was now standing between his two men, all three of them gazing down at the corpse at their feet. Seeing that they were ignoring him, Harald dared to open his eyes completely and take careful note of the newcomer. The fellow wore a rough tunic, belted at the waist and covered with a thick woollen shawl that was pinned at his shoulder, and his long, sturdy-looking legs were encased in trews of heavy cloth, their lower ends wrapped in the leather cross-bindings of heavy, thick-soled boots with iron-studded soles that left clear imprints in the snow. He was tall and bearded, with an enormous breadth of shoulder and depth of chest coupled with long, heavily muscled arms that would have marked him unmistakably as an archer, had he been English. But he was not English, and clearly he was no archer, for he was carrying a huge sword, the longest sword that Harald Gaptooth had ever seen. He had been holding it reversed at his side as he approached, the elongated hilt pointing downward, the tapered blade stretching upwards over his right breast, but now he leaned on it as he looked down at the dead man, his elbow hooked over the weapon's wide, down-curving cross-guard.

"Ye're sure he's a knight?" The question was an idle one, Gaptooth knew, for the tone of the man's voice indicated that his thoughts were elsewhere.

"Shite, aye, look at him," the one called Scrymgeour growled. "That fancy sword, an' thae spurs. He's a knight, right enough."

"Aye, I suppose. His name'll be de Vries, then. Sir Roger de Vries, Hazelrig's deputy."

The leader turned his back on the dead knight and looked around him, and Gaptooth quickly closed his eyes, not daring to breathe, but the other had no interest in him, for a moment later he spoke again, his voice coming this time from the far end of the bridgewalk parapet. Harald opened one eye with great care and saw the fellow standing there looking down, then turning back to gaze up at the crossbeam of the great gallows overhead. He stood there for a moment and then bent over the bridge, looking down into the street below.

"Shoomy!"

"Aye, Will." The response from below was immediate.

"How many bodies have you down there? English."

A pause, then, "Seven."

"Any alive?"

"No."

"Have some of your men cart them up here. And see if you can find some rope. We'll need lots of rope."

"There's loads o' rope in the wee turret room, there, Will," one of the two men flanking him said. "Coils o' the stuff. They must keep it here for the gallows."

"Aye," the leader growled, then raised his voice again. "Forget the rope, Shoomy. We hae plenty. Just bring up the bodies." He turned back to look up at the gallows again, then spoke to the man Scrymgeour. "Hang this one up there, right in the middle. Take his sword, and ye can keep his spurs, but lash his shield across him so folk can see who he was. Hang the other seven up there, too, on each side o' him. We'll let folk see that Lanark town is no' a welcoming place for Englishmen."

"What about him on the pole? Do we hang him, too?"

Gaptooth's breath stopped in his throat as the big leader glanced at him. "No," he said, "I like him just the way he is. Died at his post, that one, failing to guard the dead men over his head. Let him hang where he is. People will notice him, probably more than the rest."

They all turned away and Gaptooth snatched a cautious breath that was suddenly full of the odour of smoke. The man Scrymgeour cocked his head.

"Are we burnin' the toun?"

The leader, Will, raised his head and sniffed, then stepped quickly back to the edge of the walkway and bellowed, "Shoomy? I said nothing about burning the toun. What's going on?"

"I dinna ken, Will, but I'll find out. If it's organized, d'ye want it stopped?"

"If it's *organized*? Christ Jesus, Shoomy, this is a Scots toun, full o' Scots folk—of course I want it stopped. An' if it's *organized* I want the organizer right here, to look me in the face an' tell me when God put him in charge. Gather up the English that are left alive, but put a stop to any wildfire burnin'. And gin anybody winna pay heed, tie him up and hold him for me."

There followed a brief period wherein the wind sprang up with renewed ferocity, forcing Harald to concentrate hard on not shivering and betraying himself. Scrymgeour and his companion worked hard in the meantime, finding and raising a long ladder to rest against the gallows crossbar and separating heavy coils of rope while their leader stood silent, lost in his own thoughts and seemingly oblivious to the wind. Then a small knot of well-dressed, unarmed men appeared from Harald's right, eyeing him nervously as they shuffled by him. The man called Will saw them but made no move to acknowledge them until one of them raised a hand timorously to attract his attention.

"Maister Wallace," he stammered. "Yer pardon, but are you William Wallace?"

The leader drew himself to his full height and frowned as he closed his fingers tightly on the cross-hilt of his sword so that his knuckles showed white against the darkness of his skin. He looked the speaker up and down, then scanned the small group with him before glancing at Scrymgeour and his companion, who had stopped working and now stood watching. He glared at them until they registered his look and turned away to busy themselves again.

"Who are you?"

"Simpson, Your Highness. Maister Tod Simpson, provost o' Lanark toun. Your men are burnin' our toun, sir. Can ye no' stop them?"

The man Wallace—Gaptooth remembered the name now as belonging to the outlaw Hazelrig had been hunting—sighed and flexed his fingers and his frown deepened to a scowl. "Provost," he said civilly. "Look about you. What can you see? Look up, above your head. That's a gallows, built for hanging ordinary folk like you and me—Scots folk. In a wee while it will bear new fruit—Englishmen. So, as I said, look around you. My men are burning out a nest of Englishmen. That you and yours will suffer by that, I hae no doubt. But you wouldna be having this much grief gin ye'd been a bit less welcoming to your guests. Surely you see that?" He paused, his face solemn, his scowl less evident. "I'm no' saying ye harboured the enemy gladly, mind you. But harbour them ye did, and ye stood by wi'out complaint while they loaded these same gallows, time and time again, wi' your friends an' neebours. You bought your ain comfort by no' complainin' too loudly about the death o' others, but it was a chancy purchase and now the times hae changed. And so ye maun pay now for that comfort ye enjoyed while other folk, aiblins better folk sometimes, suffered and died at the hands o' your guests, and if that means some of your houses might burn down, then so be it. Some would ca' that justice, Provost, so console yersel' wi' bein' yet alive and able to rebuild your toun later on."

He spun on his heel and stalked away, leaving the delegation of townsfolk to make their own way back whence they had come, and Scrymgeour and the other man were soon joined by a large group carrying the bodies of the seven dead Englishmen from below. By the time the beacons were replenished by the raiders, sometime close to midnight, eight corpses swung from the bar above the gates in the freezing wind, and Harald Gaptooth, ignored and untouched, had come to believe that he would, in fact, die there, nailed to the gallows post. But though he was stiff and sore and bruised and chilled to the bone, he was close enough to the beacon brazier for its heat to keep him alive.

By dawn the storm had passed. The snow had stopped, the screams of maimed and wounded men had been silenced, and as far as Gaptooth could tell from where he was, the flames of the burning houses were dying down. Drifting in and out of awareness as he was, though, he could not have said afterwards when it was that he became aware that the Scots raiders had moved on. There came a time when he noticed that he appeared to be alone on the bridge-walk. The creak of ropes above his head told him the English bodies hung up there still, twisting in the little wind that remained, but he could see or hear nothing to indicate that any other living being shared the walk with him, and as the sun began to crest above the trees in the distance beyond the gates he finally dared to rouse himself.

He straightened his legs and pushed the small of his back against the gallows post, and then, braced for the first time in hours, he raised his right hand and grasped the arrow that had saved his life and pushed it sharply up and away from him. The shaft snapped, his bracing leg gave way, and as he fell, the fleece wrappings slid free, spilling him to the ground with fresh, warm blood gushing down from his neck and into his clothing. He landed hard and heard himself cry out at the agony that seared his left side from neck to ankle, and he knew that something in him was broken. But he was alive, and for a while he writhed on the snow-covered bridgewalk, trying without success to move his left arm and shoulder. Then, weary and chilled and sweating with pain despite the cold, he managed to crawl, on his right side, as far as the centre of the bridgewalk before he lost consciousness.

He was found there by the first searchers from the town, and for the rest of his life he would tell anyone who would listen how he witnessed the fury of the outlawed felon William Wallace on the night the Scotch Ogre had first raised his head to ravage Lanark town after killing its sheriff and slaughtering its garrison.

CHAPTER THREE

AWAKENING

When Harald Gaptooth's rescuers discovered that he was still alive they hurried him into shelter, and because he was the sole survivor of the English garrison of Lanark—the few other wounded had died quickly, after lying in the snowstorm all night—they went to great lengths to keep him alive. His wounds were far more serious than he himself had suspected, and the local *medicus*—the title was ironic and the man himself little more than a cattle handler—was afraid that the Englishman would die while in his care, a notion for which he had little stomach. Accordingly, within hours of being found on the bridgewalk, Gaptooth was carried to the newly rebuilt Cistercian priory close by the town, where he was placed in the care of the brethren. It was probably the sole place in that entire region where the Englishman might have found sufficient care and attention to enable him to survive.

I know that, because I was there in the priory with him, recovering from wounds of my own, wounds that I had suffered in an unforeseen encounter with a band of hostile Englishmen while escorting my cousin

Will's wife and family to visit her widowed mother the previous month.

Mirren's father, a prosperous wool merchant named Hugh Braidfoot, had protested against the rapacious taxation policies of Hugh de Cressingham, whom Edward had appointed treasurer for Scotland after the Dunbar battle the year before. Outraged at how Cressingham's crushing greed was destroying the entire country's ability to support the wool trade, the driving force behind Scotland's prosperity, Braidfoot had set out in person in late January that year to bring his concerns for the country's economic welfare, and for the short-sightedness being shown by the English tax collectors, to the attention of Cressingham in Berwick, where the treasurer was stationed. Whether he had met with Cressingham remained a mystery, for by late February it had been established that Hugh Braidfoot had vanished on that journey, never to be seen or heard from again.

His wife, Miriam, whose health had been failing for some years, collapsed and had been confined to bed ever since, and Will had promised Mirren that he would take her home to Lamington to visit the old lady. But at the last possible moment he had been unable to make the journey, and he had asked me to accompany Mirren and young Willy in his stead, along with a small escort of trusted retainers. Expecting no trouble at all, we had ridden into disaster, unaware that Miriam Braidfoot had been revealed to the sheriff of Lanark as the woman whose daughter was the wife of the outlaw William Wallace.

No one was ever blamed for the betrayal, if betrayal it was. People were inclined to blame it on misfortune rather than on anything else, the odds favouring a casual discussion overheard by unfriendly ears in some tavern. A group of locals had been talking about the disappearance of the wool merchant Braidfoot and someone else asked if he was the same Braidfoot whose daughter was wed to the outlaw Wallace. The question had been reported to Sir William Hazelrig, the new English sheriff of Lanark who had been charged with apprehending the Selkirk Forest outlaws. Instead of setting up surveillance on the widow Braidfoot's home, where they might easily have captured Wallace or his wife, Hazelrig had sent one of his knights, Sir Lionel Redvers, to arrest the old lady and bring her from Lamington to Lanark for questioning.

We had met the Redvers party on the road, and Mirren had recognized her mother and run to her as she passed by, carried in a litter. The English had reacted predictably, as had Will's men, and in the fight that followed, Mirren and her young son, Willy, were taken and subsequently killed, as was Mirren's unborn child, and the widow Braidfoot died on the road. I myself was unarmed, but in running to help Mirren I was knocked down and savagely beaten, then left for dead, with several badly broken bones, my teeth kicked out, and my jaw shattered so that I could neither eat nor drink.

I ought to have died there, by the side of that woodland track, and for a long time, ridden by guilt and feelings of failure, I wished that I had. But my companions managed to keep me alive for long enough to carry me to a monastery outside Lanark town, where I found the care and attention I needed. It was there that I met Harald Gaptooth.

He and I must have arrived within days of each other, but I was unconscious when they brought him in and I remained that way for many more days, so I have no memory of meeting him. He was simply there, in place, when I awoke and began to take notice of my surroundings. At first, he told me, I was no more than a sleeping hulk occupying the cot next to his and he ignored me completely other than to complain at first to the brothers about my incessant snoring. They explained to him that my snoring was a result of my injuries, and indeed he acknowledged later that I grew quieter from day to day as my throat and neck began to heal. As my condition improved, he began to talk to me, as I was the only living being in the place with whom he could communicate. The Cistercian brothers of the priory seldom spoke, even to one other.

The truth was that I spoke even less than the monks who tended us, for my jaw was wired tightly shut. My hearing, though, unfortunately for me at the time, was unimpaired.

I have only distant, pain-hazed impressions of what happened in the first two weeks of our shared confinement, but I believe that Gaptooth took quick advantage of my inability to talk back to him, no matter how foolish or offensive I found his opinions to be. Because I could neither shut out his words nor walk away in protest, he accepted that God had given him a captive audience, undoubtedly for the first and probably the last time in his life. I tried hard, in those first few weeks, to accept his never-ending ramblings dutifully as a penance, but Harald Gaptooth's mind was an empty vessel—a dark, featureless, echoing place wherein ideas were smothered before birth and words were rendered meaningless—and his constant, droning monotone brought me close to despair many times.

One evening, he was whining about how he had almost been killed on some bridgewalk and how unfortunate he was that all the world seemed set against him despite his desire to be left alone. I had been trying to ignore his self-pitying monotone when my cousin Will's name snapped me from boredom to eager attentiveness and left me frustrated that I had not been listening more closely, but I could do nothing to interrupt Gaptooth's drone or induce him to begin all over again.

Having heard his story once, though, and despite being unable to remember most of it at the time, I knew that God had sent me to this place for a purpose: to hear and heed Harald Gaptooth's tale of woe. And so I waited, with all the patience I could muster, until the wires were removed from my jaw and I could speak clearly enough to ask him to tell me again the story of his last night in Lanark. He was more than happy to repeat his tale, this time with more frowning thought and effort and far more detail, while I asked questions and soaked it all in like a sponge, knowing that one day soon I would write it down.

I erred greatly in my estimation of when I would write it, however, because forty-six years were to elapse before I did.

After hearing his story for the second time, I experienced mounting feelings of anger and frustration over my own inability to do anything useful. That recollection will be familiar to anyone who has ever undergone a prolonged period of convalescence, when one's mind and spirit are improving measurably from day to day but the physical capacity to express oneself adequately lags far behind. On one such day, when I was feeling at my lowest, the prior himself, Richard of Helensburgh, came to visit me, carrying a sheaf of paper much like the paper on my table today, along with some slender, sharpened sticks of charcoal. The mere sight of him—his friendly smile and the way he raised what he was carrying, brandishing it for my approval— did more for my well-being than anything that had happened since first I woke up and recognized where I was. That had been weeks before, but it felt like years, and now the sight of his gift, which I understood at once would give me back the power of communication, brought tears to my eyes. He noticed them and nodded, as though in commiseration, then laid the paper and charcoal gently on my cot and went to pull the small room's only chair to where he could sit on it beside me.

Most of my pain had finally died away during the previous few days, save for the unrelenting ache and tightness of my face. The padded wooden braces that framed my head had only recently been removed, finally permitting me to move it from side to side, and only a few hours earlier a pair of monks had raised me up to a half-sitting position for the first time—no simple feat, since my entire torso was heavily braced with splints that were tightly bound in place—and I had at last been able to look cautiously about me.

Gaptooth, whom I saw clearly then for the first time, appeared shocked to see me gazing at him, for he himself was not yet fit to do anything but lie on his back and talk. Clearly jealous of my increased mobility but also gratified that I was yet unable to speak, he had been ranting on ever since in his incessant, grating whine. The unheralded appearance of Prior Richard, though, had stricken him mute, and I felt a smile at his discomfiture, despite my inability to move my mouth. The prior, having placed his chair beside my cot, nodded courteously to my companion and then turned to me before Gaptooth could say a word.

"They told me you were better, Father James," he said to me in Latin, "but I am deeply pleased to see you looking so well. You had us sorely worried for a time. Thanks be to God, we have a veteran Knight Hospitaller in our fraternity, a man who learned the art of healing broken bodies in the Holy Wars against the followers of Muhammad. His name is Dominic of Ormiston, and though he remains a Knight Hospitaller he is now *our* hospitaller, being too old to remain with his companions in the order. Now he tends to our few needs and to those of the local populace. He it was who examined your wounds and reset and wired your jaw until the bones could heal."

That was a revelation, for I had believed that my jaw had been irreparably shattered and was therefore locked and useless. I was convinced that the tightness and pain I felt—along with the necessity of being fed with a tube of sheep intestine through the gap where teeth had been knocked from my mouth during the beating—would be a lifelong burden that I must endure as a penance for my sins. Now I blinked in disbelief and raised my hand slowly to my face, fully expecting to feel the knotted ends of wires protruding through my skin. I felt a heavy beard instead, and blinked again in surprise, for I had never been a hairy creature, and the sparse covering I had grown on my cheeks had always been light and carefully trimmed, a minor vanity that had never concerned me greatly.

"The beard surprised you," Prior Richard said through his smile. "Well, it is small wonder, if you but think on it. You have been here now for a month, motionless, your body encased in splints, your arms restrained for your own protection and your head locked in a vise throughout that time. You may not have been aware of the passage of time, for you have slept long and deeply most of the month, thanks to the infusions Brother Dominic fed to you in your broth and milk. Are you comfortable now, this minute?"

I made a humming sound and raised one thumb.

"Excellent. That is a blessing." Prior Richard inhaled

sharply before continuing to speak. "Word came to me mere hours ago that you were better and your arm and head restraints had been removed, and I came as soon as I could. I also thought to bring you some gifts." He waved a hand towards the paper and charcoal. "These will permit you something of a voice again."

I reached towards them, but they were too far away to grasp, and seeing my clutching fingers, Prior Richard quickly bent forward and handed them to me. I propped the pile of papers against one raised thigh while I selected a charcoal stick and examined it carefully, unaccustomed to the flimsy weight of such a thing and knowing, from experience, how fragile charcoal could be. This batch, however, was of superior quality, dense, smooth, and hard. I cautiously set the point against the whiteness of the paper.

Wonderful charcoal, I wrote in Latin.

Prior Richard smiled. "Better than ink for much of what we do," he said. "We have a gifted charcoal burner nearby, a true craftsman, and he uses only the finest wood for this particular purpose because he knows we use it for writing—not for anything permanent, of course, but it serves wondrously well for drafting copies and it saves much precious ink."

I wrote again, my hand trembling slightly from lack of custom with the charcoal. *May I have ink later, as I grow better?*

"Of course. But parchment might be difficult."

No need of it, but why difficult?

That prompted a wry twist of his mouth. "Because

we have no ready source. We are a small priory in Lanark, not a cathedral in Glasgow."

I was growing more confident by the moment. *How will they unwire me, when the time comes?*

Another smile. "By precisely reversing the manner in which your jaw was shut."

Will your Hospitaller do it? Is he here?

"He will, but he is not here today. He has been gone for several days on his regular visits to the people in the surrounding countryside. He has told me, though, that it would take six weeks or so for your jaw to mend, given no further complications."

So two weeks remain?

The prior nodded.

Then he will undo the wires?

"He will. He says the removal will be straightforward. He will simply snip the wires and pull them out. The holes will heal quickly and should not even bleed when we remove the wires. Silver wire, by the way, in case you are thinking of rusty iron."

Will I be able to speak afterwards?

"We believe so. Your jawbone was cleanly aligned and set and you have been healing well. So yes, you should be able to speak as well as you did before."

I hesitated, thinking of when I had first met Prior Richard. He had been travelling through Selkirk Forest with visiting religious dignitaries on their way from England, prime among those John le Romayne, Archbishop of the Holy See of York, when they'd been ambushed by Will and his forest outlaws. I had been there with my cousin that day, having delivered instructions to Will from Bishop Wishart of Glasgow to intercept the English party on the road. His Grace of Glasgow had been forewarned by another bishop in England that the English archbishop was abusing his episcopal immunity and flouting the laws of God and Scotland's realm by smuggling coinage north from England under the spurious auspices of the Church to pay the English garrisons in Scotland. Will, acting in the sovereign name of King John Balliol, had found and confiscated the hoard the archbishop had been transporting.

"This man, John le Romayne, Archbishop of York," Will, prompted by me, said in front of scores of witnesses, "has betrayed his conscience, his brethren, and his vocation, abandoning his vows to the King of Kings in Heaven to win favour of a king on earth, Edward Plantagenet." He waved towards the pile of money chests in the bed of the wagon. "All men, from this day forth, will know that priests are as open to corruption as any other man, their holy orders notwithstanding. No priest has ever been molested in this land while on his churchly business. No priest has ever had his good faith or his goodwill questioned. But no priest will ever again enjoy the privileges this man here has abused. The impiety and treachery of John le Romayne, Archbishop of York, will be commemorated forever by that irreversible loss of an ancient religious privilege."

I saw that Prior Richard was looking at me expectantly, waiting for my next question, and so, without another pause, I asked it, my handwriting strong and confident. *What can you tell me about my cousin Will?*

He read my question and frowned slightly. But instead of answering, he turned to Harald Gaptooth, who lay watching us. "Are you comfortable, Master Gaptooth? Is there anything you require?"

Only when I saw the look of bafflement on Gaptooth's face did I realize that the question had been in Latin and that the other man had likely understood no word of it beyond his own name.

"Wha—? What's that ye say?"

"Your pardon," the prior said, switching to English. "I merely asked if you are comfortable."

"Aye, like enough," Gaptooth answered, his voice as truculent as ever. "I'm fine, save for listening to the two of you jabbering like heathens."

"I am glad to hear that, though I am the sole speaker and hardly heathenish. Forgive me for speaking Latin in your presence but, as you no doubt know, that is the way of priests." He smiled apologetically. "We find it so much easier and more precise to speak the Church's language in dealing with one another, but I will soon be leaving and will bother you no longer."

He turned back to me and smoothly reverted to Latin. "I had to be sure our friend here understood nothing of what we were saying before I answered your question. I fear, though, that I have little good to tell you—and even less of substance, since we hear little of the world outside our walls." He inhaled softly, his eyes gazing into nothingness as he thought about what to say next. "That said, though, I will tell you what little I know." A deep frown marred his wide brow. "You are aware, I hope, that your cousin lost his wife and children?"

I wrote quickly, anxious to relieve him of his doubts. *I was there, at the start of it when they were taken. That is when I received these injuries. Later, before they brought me here, one of Will's men told me they were all dead—and how they had died.*

"And you have heard nothing since then, obviously." The frown on his face had not abated, and his eyes flickered around the tiny room. "We hear rumours here, largely unconfirmed. Some things, however, appear to be true, at least in part … Much has changed here in southern Scotland since that time. An English knight was killed within days of the murders, and I have been given to believe he was in command of the people responsible for the outrage of those tragic deaths. The word was that your cousin himself had slain the man in retribution for the deaths of his family. The English sheriff of Lanark was struck down, too, at about the same time. His name was Hazelrig and he had led a small army—almost the entire garrison of Lanark town—into Selkirk Forest to stamp out Wallace and his outlaws. But he died there instead, with all his men, overcome in their camp in the dead of night."

And then? The raid on Lanark?

His eyebrows rose. "How did you—? Ah!" He glanced again at Gaptooth, who lay glaring at us as he fought uselessly to understand what we were saying. "Our uncouth companion told you, did he?"

I nodded.

"And did he tell you that he is the sole survivor of the English garrison?" He watched my reaction and dipped his head, satisfied that I had not known that. "Unsurprising. I'm sure he himself is unaware of it …"

I waited, but the prior's thoughts were far away, and I reached again to write. *Will?*

He inhaled sharply. "The last I heard was that he had gone south after taking Lanark, leaving it undefended in order to march into Douglasdale, where Sir William Douglas was leading a full-scale attack on the English in his territory." He did not need to tell me of his dislike for Douglas, whose reputation for violence, lawlessness, and turbulence was notorious. "But that is all I know and it is no more than rumour."

"Hmm." That sound, at least, I could pronounce.

"I think it best we get you up and well and back to Glasgow as soon as possible." Prior Richard hesitated. "You yet remain on Bishop Wishart's staff, do you not?"

I dipped my head gently, not entirely certain that was still the case, but he nodded, too, looking slightly relieved. "I had hoped so. I wrote to the bishop with word of your arrival here and the condition in which you had been brought to us, but I have heard nothing in return. Does that surprise you?"

I smiled and shook my head cautiously.

"Why not? I confess it has surprised me."

Busy man. More to fret over than me.

He sniffed, unimpressed, and I added, *He will be glad to know I am safe—and grateful. And yes, I must return to Glasgow.*

"I agree. I will send Brother Dominic to you as soon as he returns. It might be a week from now, or within the hour, or any time in between." He grinned, ruefully, I thought. "Brother Dominic obeys no orders but his own and God's, the only man in this entire place whose duties I cannot dictate. He comes and goes as he pleases, driven only by his own perceptions of his obligations to the sick and ailing. And yet I thank God daily that he is one of us, for his very presence here is a benediction. But I will insist that he examine you as soon as he returns and that those wires be taken out as soon as may be safe." Prior Richard surged to his feet. "And now I must leave you, for despite what you may think of our small place, there is always much to be done here." He raised his hand and blessed me with the sign of the cross, then turned and blessed Gaptooth before leaving.

"You look better," Brother Dominic said by way of introduction four days later, his voice low and deep and unmistakably Scots. Then he looked towards my roommate. "And you do not."

Gaptooth merely gaped at him, and Brother Dominic ignored him from then on, coming to stand at the foot of my cot, where he scanned my face and then my tightly wrapped torso. From the way Prior Richard had spoken of the man, I had known he would be old, and he clearly was, but I had also expected to see in him all the accompanying signs of advanced age: the cadaverous face and stooped shoulders and the ragged, food-stained cassock of an elderly cloistered monk who cared nothing for worldly values or standards of dress.

I could not have been farther off the mark. The man glaring at me now showed none of those attributes. He looked younger and stronger than his years should have dictated; he was burly and deeply tanned, his tonsured scalp fringed with thick, white, clean, and carefully tended hair. His thick black woollen cassock was spotless, as though it had been cleaned and brushed mere moments earlier. A girdle of whitened rope circled his waist, and above it, made of wood and painted starkly white, the distinctive wedge-armed cross of the Order of the Knights Hospitaller hung from a white string looped about his neck.

He stepped around the foot of the bed and came closer, stretching out his hand. I felt him take hold of my face, spreading his thumb and fingers over my jaw, and then his grip tightened, moving my head this way and that as though it were a clay pot that he was contemplating buying. His fingers gripped me harder and I stiffened, waiting for the pain to come, but he ignored my reaction, simply tilting my head to one side, pushing, it seemed to me, against my jaw.

"That hurt?" His voice was a low growl.

I tried to shake my head, indicating that it did not, but he plainly had no interest in my answer. Instead he forced my head around to the other side with one hand while the fingers of the other dug deep into my neck from the back, as though trying to push my jaw forward, and all the while he was frowning fiercely in concentration.

"That?"

I made no move to respond this time, and he released me, stepping slightly back to look down at my chest.

"Cough."

I hesitated, remembering the last time I had coughed. It was not an experience I wished to repeat.

"Cough, damn it."

I coughed, tentatively, and felt nothing.

"Again! Harder this time. Cough hard."

He looked into my eyes for the first time and watched me closely as I obeyed, reluctantly at first and then with more confidence as I began to believe the agonizing pain from my broken ribs had vanished. Four more times he made me cough, each time harder than before. Then he grunted and stepped away to the foot of the bed again, his arms folded over his broad chest, obscuring his white cross.

"I came back this morning and Prior Richard sent for me as soon as he heard. He wants you out o' here an' back to Glasgow as quick as may be. To be truthfu', when I first heard that, I thought he was mad, thought it was too soon. But ye're young an' strong and healthy, for a priest, an' ye've healed well and arena' showin' any pain, so it may be I was wrong. It wouldna be the first time, God knows. We'll get ye out o' that shell about your ribs this afternoon, see how ye fare wi' that. We can aey strap ye up again gin we need to. But gin they're sound, an' gin I'm *satisfied* they're sound, then fine, the jawbone might be mended, too, and we'll think about the wires. But I'll tak nae chances, for once thae wires are out, there'll be nae puttin' them back. An' if they come out too soon, the jaw could break apart again, an' then ye'd really be in trouble. D'ye understand?"

I nodded, trying to conceal the excitement that was leaping in me. I would be out of the rib splints today and I wanted to crow with joy, but I was strangely anxious not to annoy the man in front of me. And he looked capable of being annoyed quickly and effortlessly.

"Fine, then," he growled. "But hear me clearly now, for this is important. Even gin we remove everythin' and all the bones prove sound, don't be thinkin' ye can go runnin' to Glasgow right away. Ye canna. It'll tak at least a week, and like as no' twice that, before ye're ready to leave here." He saw my eyes widen and raised a hand. "Listen to me now. Listen. For one thing, even though ye disagree, ye're too weak to go anywhere. Ye've been flat on your back for more than a month, so your whole body's useless and ye're goin' to hae to learn to walk again. Ye've had enough nourishment to keep ye alive, but nowhere near enough to keep up your strength, let alone to *build* strength. That's goin' to tak time and hard work, just to get back the strength ye had before. An' forbye that, ye'll have to learn to talk again, because your mouth's different now from the way it was before it was kicked in. We'll no' ken how well the jaw's shaped until ye try it—it might hae knitted differently frae what it was. Even if it's perfect, though, ye'll find it different beyond belief at first. Ye've nae teeth left in front, for one thing, so ye're goin' to feel stupit when ye try to say some o' the things ye've been sayin' all your life. Ye'll no' be able to say ess ever again. It'll be eth for you from here on. Can ye whistle?"

I nodded.

"No' now, ye canna. Ye need teeth to whistle. And ye'll hae to cut up your food into bits afore ye try to eat it, for ye canna bite now an' ye canna chew—no' in the front o' your mouth, anyway. Forbye, it'll tak days for ye to learn to stomach food o' any kind, for there's been nothin' solid in your belly since ye took that beatin'." His eyes narrowed again. "Are ye startin' to understand what I'm saying?"

I nodded again, trying to disguise the pain of what I was hearing. My mood had changed, in mere moments, from raging elation to profound dismay as I listened to his litany of all the things I could no longer do.

"I'll come back after nones," he grunted, then swung away and left without another word, leaving me to rail at him in silence for his ill-tempered words and his brusque unfriendliness.

CHAPTER FOUR

THE ROAD TO AYR

It was to be almost six full weeks more before I left the priory and set out for Glasgow, and they were among the most difficult weeks of my life. Everything that Brother Dominic had warned me about proved true. On that first day, and for a week after my restraints were removed, Prior Richard, may God rest his soul, assigned Harald Gaptooth to another room, affording me the dignity of being able to recover in privacy.

My face felt strangely different, because my remaining teeth had been realigned by the resetting of my jawbone. I was appalled by the enormous size of the emptiness where my front teeth had been—the bare gums there felt grotesque. It was I who would be known as Gaptooth from then on, I believed in those early days. At first, no words would come to my lips at all, and later, when they did, I mangled them so badly that I could not bear to listen to my efforts. To call my new impediment a lisp was ludicrous, for the sounds I mouthed were unintelligible.

Of course I soon overcame my difficulties, and my confidence increased rapidly once I realized that people could understand what I was saying. For a long time, though, racking, shame-laden dreams would startle me awake, humiliating nightmares in which folk howled with disbelieving laughter each time I opened my mouth.

The first time I tried to swing my legs off the bed, I discovered that I could not make them move. I had to fight down a flood of despair. I was twenty-four years old, and until my present misfortune I had been in fine condition, strong as a beast of burden despite, or perhaps because of, my priestly calling, for my extra-clerical duties had kept me moving constantly, travelling the length and breadth of southern Scotland in all weathers, and mainly afoot. I knew I could regain my earlier strength, although I did not deceive myself that it would take time.

It wasn't long before I could stand up from my bed without swaying and falling, and I remember well the excitement that filled me as I took my first unsteady steps. Within the week I was outside, walking for almost a full hour one day in the cloisters that enclosed the small priory. The day after that, I went out into the world beyond the gates again for the first time. I walked very slowly at first, no more than a few hundred steps, and I tired quickly, but I was filled with restless joy. A few days later I walked again, counting my footsteps carefully until I reached five hundred paces, then retracing my steps to where I had begun, exulting in the knowledge that I had walked a full Roman mile.

I walked faster and farther every day thereafter, and one day I felt the urge to run, whereupon I quickly discovered the shortcomings of priestly robes. Feeling quite rebellious, I bought a warm woollen tunic and thick leggings from one of the local weavers, to replace my constrictive cassock, and I moved unencumbered from then on. I cut myself a thick, straight, heavy sapling, too, to use as both a walking stick and a makeshift quarterstaff. On one of my walks I had a recollection from boyhood, of emerging from a swimming hole with my cousin Will and seeing for the first time the clean-cut muscles that were starting to fill out his body after months of training with our boy-sized quarterstaves. I found myself smiling at the recollection of how mercilessly our tutor, Ewan Scrymgeour, had driven us in those early days, and I saw no reason why those selfsame exercises could not benefit me now. It had been several years since last I swung a quarterstaff, but I knew I could quickly recapture the skill. Now, swinging my stick with more and more confidence as my arm, chest, and back muscles remembered the once-familiar disciplines, I belaboured trees and standing posts wherever I found them in my travels, enjoying the increasing control of those fighting techniques that came back to me quickly as I practised. A full five weeks of such activity reshaped me and gave me back my strength and stamina, but I felt no urgency now to return to Glasgow, being content for the moment to remain in Lanark, in what had become my sanctuary.

Then, on a bright, warm morning at the beginning
of June, a visitor arrived at our priory doors, and his
tidings left me in no doubt of where my duties lay. I was
invited to join Prior Richard in his quarters to meet with
his guest, and I recognized the newcomer immediately.
Father William Lamberton was the youngest canon of
Glasgow Cathedral, appointed to the post soon after his
return to Scotland three years earlier by Bishop Wishart
himself, in recognition of the young priest's brilliant
academic prowess in Paris, where he had attended
university for several years. We knew each other,
having met several times when he and Bishop Wishart
had come to Selkirk Forest to visit Will in his outlaw
days there, but I was flattered nonetheless when he
greeted me with evident pleasure. He had come
expressly to see me, he told me, to ascertain the state of
my health and, provided I was able, to summon me
back to work. Bishop Wishart, he said, had need of me.

I assured him I was well enough and improving
daily, and he cocked an eyebrow.

"What about talking, though? Is it very difficult?"
He raised an open palm as though in apology. "I know
it must be greatly *different*, of course, but that's not
what I mean. I am speaking of forming actual words,
given that you have lost all your teeth."

I pursed my lips as I thought of how no one else
had dared—or thought—to ask me such a question. I
had always liked Father Lamberton, and I liked him
yet, particularly now that his direct question had
disarmed me.

"I didn't lothe them all," I said. "I thtill have a few on each thide. It'th only in the front tha' I have trouble."

He smiled. "And not too much of that. You sound much as you did before—though a bit more oothy than toothy."

I asked him at once for news of Will, and he told me the same news that Prior Richard had related earlier—that after his daring raid on Lanark, Will had marched south to join forces with Sir William Douglas, who was out again in open defiance of Edward and had reportedly threatened to drive the English out of Scotland. I could see from the set of his face as he spoke, though, that there was more to the story, and so I probed gently, and he told me that Will and Lord Douglas had left Douglasdale some time before and marched northwest, leading a large number of men towards Ayr and Irvine, where they had been joined by Bishop Wishart and James Stewart, the hereditary Steward of Scotland, one of the most powerful magnates of the realm. That surprised me greatly, because the Stewart, as he was known, was a very significant personage, and I could not easily see him choosing to align himself publicly with such an ill-regarded ruffian as William Douglas, whose knightly ranking was, if anything, an affront to the order of chivalry. There in Ayr, Lamberton said, in the Stewart's home territories, everyone was awaiting the advent of Edward's new enforcers for Scotland. I asked him why he had used that word *enforcers*, and he eyed me sombrely. "Because that's what they are," he said, his voice low and level. "Enforcers. Edward is furious and not merely angry and enraged, but vengeful. And, by his own reasoning, not without cause. He has declared Scotland to be in a state of revolt—against himself, its overlord and lawful liege."

I looked at Prior Richard in disbelief, expecting him to refute what Lamberton had said, but he merely stared back at me from beneath raised eyebrows, and I understood that such matters were beyond his humble purview. I turned back to Lamberton.

"But that is ridiculous! Its lawful liege? *Scotland's* lawful liege, the King of England? That is utter nonsense. How can he even—?"

Prior Richard quickly raised a hand, and both of us turned to look at him. We had matters to discuss, he said, that held no allure for him, and he would feel far better returning to his duties and leaving us alone to pursue ours. Neither of us objected, and the moment the prior had closed the door behind him, I turned back to Lamberton.

"Revolt? Rebellion? That really is—"

He swept up a hand to cut me short. "Ridiculous. Aye, you said. But you speak as a Scots priest, Father James, sitting here in Scotland in all humility. Edward, on the other hand, speaks as the Plantagenet, the King of England—and he speaks *from* England, where his word is law. And there, at least, none dare to disagree with him. But why would they even wish to do such a thing? What he is saying is what his barons want to hear, and he needs them to hear it."

"But why stoop to such infamy, in God's holy name? How can Scotland rebel against England? Why would Edward say or even suggest such a thing? We are a sovereign kingdom, unbeholden to him or to England. Has he no shame? No fear for his immortal soul?"

Lamberton chewed at his lips pensively and then sat down slowly, motioning me towards the small room's only other chair, close by the work table.

"He is a king, Father, driven by a king's needs, and as he sees it, his immortal soul must wait upon his mortal obligations. You, as an honest priest, may perceive no difference between a king's needs and those of an upright, God-fearing man, but some men believe those differences exist—particularly men like Edward of England. His barons are in a state of near mutiny against his demands in raising an army to fight in France, and he is close to losing control of them. Thus one of his kingly needs is for a rebellion in Scotland. That gives him the means to bring the barons back to heel, by catering to their greed and their lust for conquest close to home. So what does it really matter if the morality of that rebellion is indefensible? Scotland has provided him with the excuse he needed."

"But it's not rebellion. You know that. Will's uprising is in *defence* of Scotland."

"I know that, Jamie, as does every Scot in this land today. But try telling it to England. All they'll hear down there is 'uprising,' and that's all they'll need to hear. The sole purpose of your cousin's uprising is to sweep the English out of Scotland in the name of our King, King John Balliol, and in our eyes that might be noble, even patriotic. But in Edward of England's eyes, and in the eyes of his people, it is rebellion, plain and simple. As Lord Paramount of Scotland—and that is his indisputable title, awarded to him by the people of Scotland—Edward, in his own mind at least, already outranks a mere Scottish king. He has demonstrated that, by arraigning and dispossessing Balliol as a disloyal vassal, stripping him of his kingship. Thus any rising in Balliol's name can only be perceived by Edward as rebellion against his overlordship."

"But that is—"

"Specious logic. Of course it is—to us. To Edward it is but common sense and straightforward kingcraft. And thus he is greatly angered, publicly so, and determined to stamp out these rebels and their leaders. Hence his decision to dispatch enforcers to do his royal bidding."

"Stamp out their leaders. Do you mean Will and William Douglas?"

"No, not at all. Your cousin and the Lord of Douglas are but two of dozens. The entire country is up in arms, with Lothian alone remaining relatively peaceful. The leaders Edward is referring to are the nobility of Scotland."

I sat mulling that. Lothian, in which I had been raised, was the eastern portion of the country, stretching north from the English border to Edinburgh and the Firth of Forth, and it was the largest English-speaking area in Scotland. It had been taken and settled by the Norman French more than two hundred years earlier as part of William's conquest, and it lay on the principal invasion route from England, which made its folk more vulnerable and, in a minor way, slightly more amenable to English ways and customs. Elsewhere in the country, the dominant language was Gaelic and the predominant view of England and things English was one of distrust if not detestation.

"So he intends to invade again?" I asked.

"No. Not this time. He has too many other things to fret over. He needs to get to France with an army, to finish the war there and put Philip Capet firmly in his place. That's far more important to him than the nuisance of what he perceives as a few rebellious Scots. He sees us as little more than vermin, incapable of offering serious threat to his plans. He defeated us in battle last year at Dunbar, and he has the greater part of the Scots nobility in his prisons, so he considers the problem of Scotland, such as it is, to be largely solved, save for a few local outbreaks of resentment. Edward won an engagement and earned himself a temporary respite, but I suspect he will not recognize that he failed to cut the heart out of Scotland's proud people. Nonetheless, he has made arrangements to clean the place up. Have you heard of Sir Henry Percy, or young Robert Clifford?"

"I know of Percy—at least, the name is familiar.

Isn't he the fellow Edward knighted in front of his whole army at Berwick, before he began the attack there? He's a minor baron, is he not?"

"Hardly minor, but yes, that's the man. Henry, Baron Percy of Alnwick in Northumberland. He is grandson to John de Warrenne, the Earl of Surrey and a close crony of the Plantagenet, and that has done the young man no great harm. He made a name for himself as a fire-eater, a bit of a hothead, during the war in Wales, distinguished himself several times— sufficiently to bring himself to Edward's favourable notice."

"And this other one, Clifford?"

"Clifford is of the same ilk, cut from the same cloth—eager and ambitious, brash and hungry for glory. Edward has named them joint commanders in Scotland, charged with the responsibility to defeat and imprison all Scots rebels. The latest word we heard is that Edward has enjoined the northern sheriffs of Lancaster, Cumberland, and Westmoreland to raise levies from their territories with all dispatch and send them into Scotland to aid in the suppression."

"Damn! That is invasion, whether Edward be there or no. So what will Wishart and the Stewart do now? Will they continue to support Will?"

"Aye, and Douglas. Don't lose sight of Sir William. He is a knight, of noble birth, so he carries more weight than your cousin Will, in name at least. For Douglas, a nobleman, to raise his voice and his hand against his peers is a grave matter, never taken lightly by those peers. This is a man of rank and substance, defying his own kind, and he cannot be hanged like a common felon. Will is a different matter altogether. He could be hanged out of hand as an outlaw, though that's unlikely now, I think. His Grace of Glasgow and the Stewart will stand by both of them, and their combined support could achieve miracles. I imagine they will send your cousin and his followers north before the Englishmen arrive, though that is pure conjecture on my part. I have not spoken with His Grace for nigh on a month."

"You said they'll send Will north. North to where?"

"To Moray, to lend support to the uprising there."

"What uprising?"

He blinked at me. "Did you not know? The whole northeast is up in arms, under your old friend Andrew Murray of Petty."

It was my turn to blink. "Andrew Murray? The one who escaped from Chester? He came to us for help on his way home, months ago."

"That's the man. His father, may God watch over him, remains in London, in the Tower."

I had known the elder Murray was still held prisoner, but this news of his son's uprising was unexpected. I had an instant recollection of myself as a boy, with Will and this same Andrew Murray, sitting, naked and shivering, around a smoky fire on a chilly spring day in the woods surrounding Paisley Abbey while we waited for our sodden clothes to dry after a frightening misadventure.

"I have to get back," I said. "Will you come with me?"

Lamberton shook his head. "No, I'm sorry, I can't. I'm bound east myself, to Fife and St. Andrews, where I must represent my lord bishop at a gathering. I stopped by here on the way solely because His Grace wrote to me in Glasgow asking me to come here and send you to him, were you well enough. And you are, so you should leave immediately. Have you a horse?"

"No, but I'm growing stronger every day. I'll walk. It will take but two good days from here."

"No," he said emphatically. "The bishop is supposed to be at Ayr with the Stewart, and that's half again as far from here as Glasgow is, but by this time he might just as easily be at the Stewart castle in Ardrossan on the Isle of Bute. Either way, there's no high road westward from here, so you'll be following the lie of the land for most of the time. You'll need three days, perhaps even four, and it's June, so you might be ploutering through wind and rain and mud and mire the whole way."

I grimaced, for I had indeed lost sight of the fact that Wishart was not in Glasgow, but then, spurred by Lamberton's evident urgency, and anxious anyway to take possession of my life again, I immediately set about planning in my mind my journey to the coast. Lamberton was right; June could be the foulest, wettest month of the year in Scotland, and if the previous month's weather gave anything by which to judge such matters, this year showed no signs of being different.

I knew I would need heavy, well-made foul-weather gear to keep me warm and dry, as well as a sturdy tent and bedding, basic cooking utensils and rations, a strong pack, and a pair of heavy boots if I were to walk for fifty miles across trackless moorland in a matter of days. Yet I had no such equipment. My entire store of clothing had been lost with everything else I owned the day we fell afoul of the English knight Redvers and his men-at-arms. I looked at Lamberton.

"Can you give me some money?" I asked. I explained my situation to him and told him that I had purchased the leggings and tunic I wore with the only money I had.

He produced a small purse from inside his robes before I had finished talking, but paused in the act of passing it to me and withdrew it. He reached instead into the scrip at his waist and pulled out another, slightly larger one, which he tossed to me. "That will be more useful than the other. The coins in it are common, silver and copper. I nearly gave you gold." He smiled. "Too rich for your purposes in dealing with Lanark tradesmen."

"My thanks," I said, pocketing the purse. "I'll see to it you're reimbursed in Glasgow."

He waved my thanks away. "God's work, God's purposes."

I went into Lanark that same afternoon and made my purchases. Everything I found was of the highest quality, including a pair of boots that fitted me perfectly, though they had been made for a man who had died before he could collect them from the boot maker. I saw no irony in the fact that this unknown benefactor had died the night my cousin Will had raided Lanark.

I took the road to the west early the following morning, while Canon Lamberton struck off towards the east road to Fife, and the rain started almost before I had passed beyond sight of Prior Richard's small community. It began as a steady drizzle, but as the day advanced the clouds overhead thickened and drew lower, and the rain grew ever more sullen and heavy until everything blended into a grey blur within which distances were unfathomable. I slept that night in an ancient stone shelter built by some long-dead shepherd in a hillside gully, and primitive though it was, it kept me dry and warm enough to sleep well.

The morning that followed was no better, revealing a sodden panorama of drenched grasses and water-logged meadows. I dismantled my small camp quickly, then headed steadily westward while I broke my fast on some of the food supplied by the priory kitchens, a dried mixture of grains, chopped nuts, and finely diced dried fruit that was both delicious and highly nour-ishing. I walked all day, eating another handful of the ration mixture around noon, and as the sun began sinking towards evening I met a farmer who directed me to a small monastery less than a mile from where we met.

I was made welcome by the tiny community of Franciscan brothers there, the first members of that order I had ever encountered—they were foreigners and new to Scotland in those days—and I was more than simply glad of the opportunity to strip off my sodden outer garments and dry myself thoroughly by a fine, generous fire of well-dried peat. After a night of warmth and comfort in a padded straw bed that left me feeling mildly guilty over what felt like shameful self-indulgence, I stepped out again into the unchanged world of sullen, unrelenting rain and resumed my journey, concentrating grimly on my daily prayers as I trudged, ankle-deep and far from anything resembling a road, through the mire that served as my cross-country path.

CHAPTER FIVE

ST. DOMINIC'S IRISHMAN

I reached Ayr just before noon on the fourth day. I had somehow managed to travel all around the town for years without ever actually setting foot in it, and when I finally did arrive there, I went directly to the parish church in the faint hope of finding Bishop Wishart. Faint hope, indeed; I could tell by the overall stillness and lack of traffic that the town held no great men that day.

The church itself, as I had known from hearsay, was finer and more substantial than many another in similarly sized towns the length and breadth of Scotland, because it was the family church of the man all Scotland knew as the Steward or the Stewart. The Stewart family had been the hereditary High Stewards of the realm for a hundred and thirty years, since the days of King David I, and Sir James, the current chief whom my employer had come here to meet, was the fifth of his august line. His status as one of the realm's greatest magnates was reflected in everything that represented his authority, including the great new cathedral that had been under construction for years by then in Glasgow, which lay within his territories, and this lesser, more mundane parish church of Ayr, which housed the remains of many of his ancestors.

Unsurprised at finding the place deserted, I hitched up my travelling bag and made my way around to the presbytery behind the church, where I knew I would find someone in residence, even if it were no more than a caretaker. I stopped short of the house, though, and stood in the rain when I found myself being scrutinized by a tall, black-clad priest in the presbytery doorway who appeared to be leaning sideways, holding the wide single door open with his body as he watched me approach. I gazed back at him, seeing what I took to be suspicion and a hint of open contempt in his expression. I was more amused than offended by that, for I knew that had I been he, watching me approach the sanctum that was his charge, my own lip would have curled as his had.

Even through the solid downpour, from more than twenty paces, I could see he was a Dominican, though whether monk or priest I could not discern. The order, sometimes called the Preachers, contained both and was characterized by its mendicant status, its brethren travelling the land in poverty, preaching in the local tongues and living on the goodwill and charity of the inhabitants. Ordinary folk everywhere spoke of them as the Black Friars, the name derived from the black cloak that they wore over their white habits, and the triple-knotted white rope girdling this one's habit provided the final confirmation. I knew that nominally, at least, he would have recognized me as a cleric of some kind, from the muddy skirts of the ankle-length cassock beneath my heavy travelling cloak, but apart from that I could have been anyone, even an outlaw who had killed a priest for his cassock and was bent on further plunder.

Beneficent theory and the platitudes of sanctimony both dictate that priests should treat all men as children of God, deserving of love, respect, and compassion. Pragmatic reality in sudden encounters with strangers, though, has a far more human focus. Four days of trudging over the hills in the worst weather Scotland could produce had done nothing to enhance my appearance, and I was well aware of how I must look to his eyes. Drenched and bedraggled, gaunt, wildly bearded and covered in mud from booted feet to waist, I stood and waited for him to acknowledge me, and he did not keep me waiting.

"If you turn and look up at the sky over your left shoulder, you'll see a wondrous sight."

The words were unexpected, yet spoken in Scots, and his tone was friendly, so I turned to look back as he suggested. And there, several miles away, beyond the grey rain that continued to fall all around me, was a rent in the clouds from which shafts of golden light spilled straight down. I watched it in silence for a few moments, then turned back to him.

"Wondrous is right," I said. "Strange how the most common things can appear miraculous, depending upon circumstance."

"Do you have a name, friend?" His voice, even across the distance separating us, was pleasantly modulated but definitely not Scots. I guessed him this time as being Irish, and the intonation of his next words proved me right. "For if you do, and if I recognize it, I might let you come in out of the rain."

"Wallace," I said. "Father James Wallace, secretary and amanuensis to Bishop Wishart."

"Aha! Then you're the very fellow I'm waiting for. His Grace bade me wait for you here and bring you to him. Come away in."

He stepped back, holding the door open for me as I crossed the threshold, where I propped my staff in a corner and set my heavy pack down beside it, then stood dripping in the entranceway.

"Wet out there," he murmured, and he reached for my cloak. "Give me that," he said.

I gladly shrugged out of it, and he reopened the door and, grunting with the effort, shook the garment hard, scattering a storm of water drops from the waxed wool. "There," he said eventually, and kicked the door shut again. "We can hang that to dry for a while. How long have ye been walking?"

"Four days."

"And rained on all the way? That might make some men doubt their own sanity, wondering why they did not stay at home in the first place."

I wondered if he was twitting me, but he was smiling gently, his face empty of guile. "It might," I agreed, and then added on the spur of the moment, "Or even lead them to doubt the goodwill of the superiors who set them to the task."

It was a risky, even a dangerous thing to say to an unknown priest. He might use it against me afterwards, in pursuit of his own ambitions, or he might simply pass it on unthinkingly, unwittingly condemning me as deficient in my regard for authority. And yet some reckless urging had prompted me to test the man. His response, though, could not have been better designed to put my mind at rest about his motives.

"Superiors who must have known long in advance how foul the weather was to be," he agreed, straight-faced and soberly judicious.

"Absolutely," I concurred, grinning. "I'll make sure to take my lord bishop to task on that when I catch up with him. Where is he, by the way? You do know, I presume?"

"Of course I know. At least I hope I do. I've been waiting here to take you to him, so would I not look the fine fool did I turn out not to know where he is? But come and warm yourself," he said. "There's a grand fire in the hearth, in here."

He led me into a large, open room off the entrance-way and waved me towards the leaping flames. I made directly for them, stretching my hands gratefully towards the heat. Then, simply because the words came into mind, I said, "I doubt I've ever met an Irish Dominican."

"I'm sure of it. There's only me, I think, because I entered the order in France and I met none of my ilk even there."

"France, eh? And how came you to France, from Ireland?"

"I was sent, right enough. God be praised." He blessed himself with the sign of the cross. "My tutors saw something in me when I was a lad that they said must have been planted there by God Himself, since none of my clan at home, fine men though they be, were capable of breeding it into me. They told my lord about it, and he singled me out for special teaching, which took me to France eventually."

"Whereabouts? I hear France is a wonderful place."

He grinned. "It is. I was in Paris. Where else? They sent me to study at the university there, and there I stayed, lodged with the Brethren of St. Dominic, at the Priory St. Jacques."

I made a *phew*-ing sound with my lips. "Had I a tooth in my mouth to make it possible, I'd whistle at that, for I'm much impressed. Who was your lord in Ireland?"

"He is my lord still, and the greatest in all Ireland. Sir Richard de Burgh, the Earl of Ulster."

"Ah, now that's a name worth naming. And what about you, my learned friend, do you have a name a man might call you? And are you priest or simple monk?"

He grinned again, displaying a fine, surprisingly white set of sound-looking teeth. "I am both. Martin is the name my mother called me, and by it I have been christened, confirmed, and ordained."

Close to him as I now was, I could see there was no doubting his Irishness, even had his speech not betrayed it. He had thick, unruly black hair and a high forehead suggestive of a keen intellect. His ears were almost comically big, and the corners of his brown eyes were creased with laughter wrinkles.

"Will you tell me, then, Father Martin, where you think my bishop might be?"

"They set out for the Isle of Bute, Sir James and him, four days ago. D'ye know Bute at all? Lord Stewart has a castle there, at Rothesay. Since then, though, they sent back word that they had had to change their plans and were bound for Castle Turnberry, in Carrick. That's Bruce territory."

"What prompted this change of plans, did they say?"

He shook his head, no trace of levity visible now. "They neglected to say, so I've no idea. But I imagine it's in Turnberry we'll find them."

"And how far to there from here?"

"Ayr to Turnberry? Fifteen or so miles in all, so six hours at a brisk walk, I'd say—and all on good roads, which you'll enjoy."

I shivered despite being dry for the moment in the warm house, depressed at the thought of taking to the road again. "Then we had best be on our way, before they can change their minds again and make for Bute. Are you ready to leave?"

"I am. But sure, there's no need to trip over ourselves. His lordship took the trouble to send word that they were changing plans. It makes no sense, then, that he would change his mind again and not let us know that, too. Otherwise we'd never find him at all, and he *wants* us to find him. Remember what the Romans used to say: *Festina lente*. Go slowly, if you would make quick progress."

He crossed to one of the room's two windows, where he pushed open the shutters and bent to look out and upwards. "The clouds are scattering and the sun is shining. Praise be to God, the storm is over. It won't grow dark until near ten o'clock, and it's not long after noon now, so we are in no hurry." He turned back to me, his eyes alight with mischief. "Father Malachy is the parish priest here in Ayr, and he is avoiding us because he thinks I may be less than respectful in the way I show my gratitude for his hospitality. He's here in the house, somewhere, but he is absolutely scandalized by what I was doing before you arrived, and so he is registering his disapproval by hiding from us and insulting you."

"I see … And what, exactly, were you doing before I arrived?"

"I was exercising my initiative and preparing a welcome for you."

"And that scandalized the good father? I am almost afraid to ask, but what kind of welcome were you preparing?"

"A hot bath, Father James, what else? Knowing you had spent days on the road in a howling storm, and having heard from the bishop himself about your love of hot baths, I asked myself what could have been more welcome to you upon arrival here. I had one myself, three days ago, soon after my own arrival and after but a single day in the storm. But the mere thought of such a thing sent poor old Father Malachy into a fit of nervous prostration. He had his annual bath at Easter, he informed me, and had considered his duty done for the year. But now, forced to tolerate the abomination twice in but one week beneath the roof of his own presbytery, he might never recover."

"Wait," I said, waving a hand to silence him. "You prepared a bath for my arrival, when I myself had no idea when I would be arriving?" I looked around me. "And I see no signs of any bath."

"Hah!" I swear he performed a little jig. "You see no signs of it because it's in the kitchen. I've had it ready since this morning, for *I*, at least, knew you would be coming—if not today, then tomorrow—and it is a simple thing to keep water hot, once you have it heated in the first place."

I was entranced at the thought of climbing into a tub of hot water, a luxury I would not have dared to imagine even a single hour before. "So," I said, attempting to conceal any trace of the excitement I was feeling, "this bath is prepared, now?"

"Aye, if you're ready for it. And in the meantime, we'll get your cassock washed and your boots cleaned up. We'll need to leave by three, if we're to get to Turnberry before ten, but that gives us two hours to dry off the worst of things in front of a roaring fire, and if the weather stays fine, to blow the smoke out of what remains. So, are you ready?"

Two hours thereafter I was a new man in almost every respect, scrubbed and shaved and wrapped in fresh, warm clothing, the nethermost of which had lain clean and dry in the deepest recesses of my pack as I trudged through the four-day storm. My transformation was completed with a quick meal in the presbytery kitchen: a slab of succulent salted, spit-roasted pork between two thick pieces of bread still warm from the oven and a vast tankard of foaming, home-brewed ale, dark and rich textured, tasting of hops, nuts, and some kind of berry. Then, bolstered and rejuvenated, I took to the road again in the middle of the afternoon, happy this time to have Father Martin by my side.

"Do you know Carrick?" he asked me as soon as we had passed through Ayr's main gate.

I glanced at him sideways. He had spoken in Latin for the first time since we'd met, and I wondered, because of that, what the question really entailed, for I doubted that a simple yes or no was what he wanted.

"Which Carrick?" When he looked at me, clearly baffled by my question, I continued, "Do you mean Carrick the place or Carrick the earl?"

"Oh," he said, and shrugged. "Both, I suppose. I don't know much about either one."

I thought for a moment. "Well then, I'm sure you know already that the name of the place comes from the old tongue, from the same word as crag, and means 'the rocky place.' And from what I've seen, it couldn't be better named. You couldn't farm there, even if you wanted to. You can raise sheep, but that's about all."

"No goats?"

"Aye, hordes of them, but goats don't count. They'll keep a man and his family fed and mayhap clad, but milk and meat's about all they're good for. Sheep, on the other hand, have wool, and you can sell wool profitably. That's what all the folk in Carrick do. They're all sheepherders."

"And what about the earl?"

"He's an earl. He probably wouldn't even recognize a sheep unless someone told him what it was. And atop that, he's a Bruce. Robert Bruce. But they're all Roberts, the Bruces. He's the seventh consecutive one."

From the corner of my eye I saw him nod. "I knew that," he said, "but only because I overheard it somewhere. And I was told that the Bruces have been Stewart vassals since the first Steward was appointed. Is that not right?"

"I suppose it is—right enough, at any rate. But the whole thing's much more complicated than a simple liege-and-vassal relationship. It's not plain tenantry and patronage. Nowadays there's blood and kinship involved, too."

He looked surprised. "Then they're related, the Bruces and the Stewarts?"

I laughed. "Aye, that they are, and closely, nigh on incestuously, some might say. Close-knit by blood and marriage."

"Incestuously?" He had stopped walking the moment I uttered the word, and now he was staring at me with genuine horror. I remembered that he was very young and therefore naive, and a priest, to boot. I waved my hand dismissively, realizing I had gone too far.

"No," I said emphatically. "It is sinfully untrue even to suggest such a thing in jest and my tongue but ran away with me. I wanted no more than to emphasize the closeness of the bonds binding their two houses."

His expression cleared and he began to walk again. "No matter. Tell me, though, about this blood-and-marriage relationship. You used the word 'nowadays,' and that suggests a kind of newness to things. How did that happen, and when?"

"A while ago. You know the Stewart family name was originally Norman, do you not?"

His eyes widened. "No, not a bit. I thought they were all Highlanders, from north of the Forth. They're Norman, you say?"

"Aye …" I paused, remembering something I had heard years earlier. "But that might not be absolutely true. According to Bishop Wishart, the family's ancestral name was fitz Flaad, and they were reputed to be, as he put it, Norman by culture and training, but Breton by birth. Anyway, the first one we know of over here in Scotland was a man called Walter Fitzalan, and his son was Alan Fitzwalter."

"And how came they here, to Scotland?"

I grunted, wryly wondering how many times that question had been voiced these past two hundred years and more. "The same way all the others came. They were sent north to settle here by William of Normandy when he became King of England after his conquest. They arrived about two hundred years ago, and sixty or seventy years later one of them became king—King David the First of Scotland. It was he who appointed Walter Fitzalan to be High Steward of the realm, in return for his services to the Crown. The two were friends, of course, and had probably grown up together, but the new Steward, Walter Fitzalan, must have been a formidable man, because the King made the appointment hereditary, granting the stewardship to Walter's sons in perpetuity. Lord James, the current Steward, is the fifth consecutive holder of the title."

"Aye, but how did the name change? You know, from Fitz-whatever it was to Stewart?"

"By word of mouth, how else?" I smiled at him. "From the moment of their appointment, the entire family became known as 'the Stewards,' and since we Scots invariably turn d's into t's at the ends of words, they became the Stewarts. Three generations later, they made it official."

"I never knew that."

I hitched my pack higher. "Not many people do nowadays, even here in Scotland. The Stewarts are the Stewarts. Who cares today what they were called two hundred years ago?"

"So how did the Bruces become involved with them?"

I stopped and looked about me before I answered that question. I was astonished to realize that I had no idea of how far we had walked or even of where we were. "Are we lost?" I spoke half to myself at first, but then raised my voice to include my companion. "We should be close to Maybole by now, but I don't see any signs of life, do you?"

He, too, looked around. "No, but we can't be lost. We haven't left the road, and it's the only one there is. It goes right into Maybole, to the crossroads where we'll turn for the coast. It can't be too far ahead … You were going to tell me about the Bruces." We set off again.

"Carrick was once a part of Galloway," I began. "A hundred years and more ago, a prince of Galloway called Duncan lost his claim to the Galloway lordship, and to compensate, his family gave him Carrick as an earldom. The earldom passed eventually to his son, Earl Neill MacDuncan, who then married Lady Margaret Stewart, the sister of Lord James's father, the fourth High Steward. Neill and Lady Margaret had a daughter, Marjorie, who became the Countess of Carrick in her own right upon her father's death, and *she* married Robert Bruce the Sixth, the son of Bruce the Competitor. Their son, the seventh and youngest Robert Bruce, is the Earl of Carrick today, and he is the grandson of Lady Margaret Stewart. Lord James, on the other hand, is nephew to the same Lady Margaret, so the Steward and the young Earl of Carrick are doubly kin."

"The Bruces live in England nowadays. Why?" The question, naive as it sounded, surprised me, and it must have shown on my face, for he continued, "Oh, I know some of the tale. I have heard stories and rumours and bits of explanation, but I'd like to hear what you have to say about it. You are not afraid to say what you think, even if some might think your opinions ... indelicate."

I saw the expression in his eyes and laughed out loud. "Aye, well, in that spirit, Father, I'll tell you what I think. Mind you, I'm swearing to the truth of none of what I'll say, for much of it is conjecture and the rest is a mix of things overheard and suspected that strike me as being feasible.

"Now, as you no doubt know, there hasn't been a Bruce visible in Scotland these past five years and more. And for good reason, I would say. Not since the conclusion of the Great Cause. You know what that was, don't you?"

He stiffened. "Yes, I know what that was," he grumbled. "I might be Irish, but that doesn't mean I'm stupid."

"Of course not. I was not suggesting any such thing. You may remember that in the end, the search for Scotland's legitimate king came down to two qualified people: the Fifth Robert Bruce, the Lord of Annandale who claimed through the maternal line, and John Balliol, Lord of Galloway, whose claim, while one degree of separation greater, extended through the paternal line. Edward of England was invited to judge the affair, and he and his magistrates awarded the throne to Balliol, citing the law of primogeniture."

My companion stopped walking again and gazed at me quizzically. "Primogeniture. Inheritance through the male line. Since when has that been the accepted way among the Gaels?"

"Since then, five years ago. It is a recent development, brought to us by way of the Pope. It is directly opposed to the ancient tanic law of Scotland and Ireland, which permits accession through the female line. But in recent years, male descent has been increasingly upheld throughout Christendom by the Church, though it has never been proclaimed here. Bruce's claim was tanic, and predicated upon his having served as tanis, or heir elect, before the young King Alexander sired an heir of his own. Edward and the English bishops elected to adopt the primogeniture approach, as recommended by the Holy Father."

"You sound as though you disagree with their finding. Were you a Bruce adherent in this issue?"

"No," I said, "I was a priest. My sole adherence was to Holy Mother Church and my duties on her behalf. What I thought about such an important matter had no importance. Petty priests have no say in the affairs of kings."

"Perhaps not, but they can hold opinions."

"Hah! Presumably they can. And some of them might even do so. But that is irrelevant in this instance."

"It's relevant to me. I would like to know what you personally thought about it all."

I faced him squarely. "Why? It doesn't matter, and besides, my opinions are no concern of yours."

"But they are," he said, unrepentant and grinning, "because I have a need to know, mainly because I am a newcomer. Everyone I meet nowadays—ever since I joined the cathedral chapter—wants me to learn, or at least to subscribe to, his version of what is true and untrue, what is relevant and not so, what is important and what is dangerous nonsense. I had heard of you from Bishop Wishart and he holds you in high esteem. There are few of whom one can say that. His lordship is sparing in his praise and even more cautious of bestowing his trust. And so I am curious about your thoughts on this Great Cause affair. I know your cousin Will was happy with the result and remains a loyal follower of King John to this day, but I have the feeling that you were less than happy with the choice of Balliol over Bruce. Is that true?"

"If it were true, and if I were to admit such a thing openly, I could be held liable of treasonous utterances."

He cocked an eyebrow at me but did not slacken his pace. "That is not entirely accurate, Father James. John Balliol is no longer King in Scotland."

"Ah, but he is, and shame on you for saying such a thing. King John may stand humiliated and dispossessed in English eyes and according to English feudal law, but as a priest you know that God's law is immutable and that, in accordance with that law, John Balliol is the anointed and crowned King of Scotland. He may not *be* here in person, but he remains the King of Scotland in the eyes of God."

"Aha! Then you're a Balliol man."

"No, I am a Scot and a priest. I have no preference in such matters."

"But you dislike the King of England."

"I do not know the King of England, so how could I dislike him? But I will admit I would not trust him with anything of import to me or to my church or, for that matter, to this realm."

"Why not? Why do you mistrust him?"

I was aware that he was baiting me, yet I sensed no malice in his probings. "Out of cynicism, perhaps. And yes, I am fully aware that no priest should ever be a cynic. But Robert Bruce of Annandale was an old man, well past his seventieth birthday, at the time we are discussing. An ancient man by anyone's reckoning, but no less formidable because of that. He was a giant, without peer anywhere in Scotland or in England—or anywhere else, for that matter. Bruce of Annandale had done everything and been everywhere. As a young man, he fought in the civil war in England on behalf of young Edward's father, Henry the Third, against Simon de Montfort and his upstart barons when they rebelled, and later he rode out on crusade to the Holy Land, representing the old King and accompanying the Crown Prince, Edward."

"He fought in England, for England's King?" the Ulsterman said. "Why would he do that?"

I shook my head, making a show of pitying his ignorance. "Because it was his duty," I said.

"How, duty? He's a Scots magnate, not an Englishman."

"And you are wrong again, Father. Bruce has always been a true vassal to the Plantagenets, recognizing them as his feudal lieges. That loyalty has never, ever been in doubt. The Bruces, like the Balliols, the Comyns, and almost all the other noble Scots houses, own vast estates in England, but without exception such estates are held by grace and favour of the English monarchs. It has always been thus, and that, my friend, is the feudal way, honoured by the Bruces. The old traditions are less strong today, and the claims of feudal loyalty and duty appear, at times, to be growing weaker and less valid. But not, to this point, in the eyes of Bruce."

The Irishman nodded. "I see ... The old man's dead now, is he not?"

"He is, God rest his soul. He died last year, at eighty. But even in his youth he was known for his good character and probity and for the sterling soundness of his given word. Throughout his life he took great pride in always speaking truth, no matter what the cost, and no one ever called him liar. The blood of kings flowed in his veins—pure Norman French through his mother, who was directly descended from the first David, the Norman-born Earl of

Huntingdon—and he served as regent to his young cousin Alexander the Third during the King's minority. Robert Bruce of Annandale inspired awe in all who met him. And I suppose that is the cause of my cynicism."

"How so?"

"Because of what happened at the time of the choosing, amplified by what has happened since. Edward chose Balliol. Oh yes, I know it was the auditors who chose him, after eighteen months of harrowing debate, weighing the pros and cons of each man's claim judiciously and openly. But let us be truthful here, just between we two: Edward Plantagenet is England's King, and he lacks neither power nor influence, particularly when he deals with lesser men on matters of discretion. He and his judges had two alternatives from whom to pick Scotland's King, each of them sufficiently wealthy in his own right that neither one could be suborned by the promise of riches. One of those two was a towering giant of a man whose physical courage and moral probity, integrity, and honour were irreproachable and whose nature and character dictated that he could never be coerced into bowing the knee to anyone with whom he disagreed.

"The other, though it was not yet widely known, was made of less solid stuff—equally valid in the strength of his claim to the kingship, but less … inflexible, let us say, in his other attributes. Might I suggest that a slightly cynical, less than naive person like myself might conceivably be tempted to believe that a man like Edward Plantagenet, steeped as he was in kingcraft and the necessities of protecting and augmenting his own interests, might have been induced to tip the scales of judgment favourably in his own direction by making it known to those around him that he would prefer the weaker man over the stronger?

"Pah, you might say. You might even cry foul, slander, and infamy. But what has happened in the years that have elapsed since John Balliol was crowned King of Scots?" Martin met my eye squarely, and I held up one hand, ticking off the points on my spread fingers. "One, since the day of his coronation, John Balliol, King of Scotland, has been a puppet and a catspaw for Edward of England, Lord Paramount of Scotland. His every legal decision and disposition has been questioned and dismissed, he himself summarily ordered to England to defend his own verdicts in English courts—verdicts, mark you, that he had delivered in Scotland, as King of Scotland, on matters concerning his Scots subjects.

"Two, and mainly the outcome of the first, the Plantagenet has consistently defied John Balliol as King of Scotland, and by thus confounding him, time after time throughout his years as King, has actively undermined his authority and made him an object of ridicule.

"Three, the entire disgraceful fiasco was brought to a conclusion by the public shaming, humiliation, and ritualized stripping and denuding of one sovereign nation's king by the lackeys and lickspittles of another, when Antony Bek, a prelate of God's Church, defied God's own law, in the name of an earthly king, by humiliating and publicly abusing another one of God's own anointed Christian monarchs. No man should have the arrogance to defy God openly as Bek did that day.

"And now, point four. This land of ours, this Scotland, after near a hundred years of peace, is plunged into war with England in order to protect itself from the designs of a rapacious, renegade king whose ambitions have overstretched themselves and fallen into madness.

"Now there, my friend, is gross cause for culpability and penitence from one end of shameless England to the other."

For a long time he said nothing, and we walked on in silence until he confounded me again.

"So why," he asked, "did Bruce do nothing all that time? He must have seen what was transpiring from the start—must at least have guessed at the outcome."

The question, so baldly phrased and so direct, left me wordless, for of course it was evident immediately that every nuance, every suggestion contained in it must be true: Bruce must have known what was coming and he must have perceived it clearly, long before anyone else in Scotland, if not in England. Why, then, had he done nothing to intervene on behalf of his own tenants and dependents in Scotland?

"I'll need to think on that one," I conceded, and he nodded in acknowledgment. Our pace slowed to something approaching a toddler's crawl, and Martin, thanks be to God, said nothing more.

"He couldn't have done anything," I said eventually. "He was cut off on all sides at that time, ensuring that no matter what he did or said, or tried to do or say, he would be decried and denigrated by his enemies."

"You have just finished telling me he had no enemies," Martin said gently.

"Don't pretend to be naive, Father Martin, for we both know you are not. I told you no such thing. Robert Bruce was one of the most powerful men of his day, so of course he had enemies. They were everywhere, swarming like maggots on a carcass. What I said was that not even his enemies could call him liar or accuse him of anything shameful or reprehensible.

"The two most powerful noble houses then in Scotland, Bruce and Comyn, had been rivals for generations, and by the time of King Alexander's death, the Comyn faction had grown to be the stronger, more numerous of the two. Each house detests and resents the other to this day, but the Comyns gained supremacy with the coronation of Balliol, for the new King was wed to Margaret Comyn, sister to the Earl of Buchan, who is chief of that side of the family known as the Black Comyns. The other branch of the family, the more powerful of the two, is the Red Comyns, whose territories are ruled from Badenoch by Lord John Comyn of that ilk. Between the two branches, once Balliol was enthroned, the Comyns had the power to stamp out the Bruces as a political force, and they would have done so at once had not Bruce of Annandale himself confounded them."

I looked at the Ulsterman sidelong, lengthening my step and seeing him adjust his own without thought or effort. "D'you know how he did it?" He shook his head slowly, and I continued: "He somehow contrived to find out how the final vote would go. I have to assume that our dear Lord Jesus alone knows how he managed to achieve that, for I have never had time to ask our beloved bishop about it. The vote had not yet been taken, mind you—the balloting would not take place for several days at least, and nothing had been decided, officially speaking—but Bruce learned that the decision would go to Balliol."

My companion pursed his lips in a silent whistle. "So what did he do then?"

I smiled, happy with myself for the ease with which I had come to see the truth involved. "He demonstrated his greatness," I said. "He proved that, at the end of a long and honourable life, he was more far-sighted, more pragmatic, and more solicitous for his family and his bloodline than any of his contemporaries. And he proved it in ways most men have not yet begun to see, even after his death and the passage of five years."

"I don't follow you."

"I know you don't. You can't, because I have only now discovered for myself what your question has brought me to see."

"And what is that? Can you tell me?"

"Yes, I can. I now believe that Robert Bruce of Annandale may have been the greatest man of his age. He certainly laid claim to that title by what he did when he discovered he would lose the Crown of Scotland."

"How?"

"Think about it, Father. He discovered he had lost his bid to secure the throne, a lifetime dream, and that his political enemies had had the best of him. Most men would have despaired at that point, especially men of his advanced age, faced with the prospect of losing everything and being too old to begin again. But not Bruce. What does he do? He sidesteps everything and steals the victor's laurels right from the dragon's mouth.

"In rapid succession he approached King Edward, reminding the monarch of his lifetime loyalty and humbly requesting permission to withdraw his claim to the Scots throne, on the grounds of advanced age, and to withdraw into England to live out the final years of his life in peace and quiet. At one thrust, he disarmed all his opponents by providing Edward the perfect answer to the only problem yet facing him: with Bruce's voluntary withdrawal from the race, no one could ever afterwards accuse Edward of using undue influence in the election of Balliol.

"Of course, there was a price for such a sweet piece of collusion, should that be what you wish to call it. In order for Bruce to be able to retire to England and remain there at peace, he must be able, in good conscience, to reassign his Annandale holdings, and his responsibilities to his Annandale folk, in their entirety, including his yet-valid claim to the Scots throne, to his eldest son, the younger Robert Bruce, Earl of Carrick. Edward was glad to accede to that, and Bruce's plan for eventual triumph was in place."

"What triumph? The man is dead, and he died in exile."

"Not so. He died in England, on his own family estates. And his legacy is safe. Certainly, his Scots estates were taken over by his enemies of Comyn, but that's a temporary thing to be remedied any day now that the Comyns have fallen from power in the aftermath of Dunbar. Nearly all of them are in jail in England, defeated and disgraced. Besides, the ordinary Bruce folk, the commons, did not suffer by the confiscations. They had nothing to lose, other than the name of their masters, and the Comyns are not tyrants to the folk they rule. So Bruce lands will soon be returned to Bruce, and the family's claim to Scotland's throne remains valid, passed on to the old man's descendants, who are well situated to make use of it someday, now that the kingship is in dispute again.

"On becoming Lord of Annandale, the first thing the younger Robert Bruce did—and he was clearly acting upon his father's instructions—was to bestow his own earldom of Carrick upon *his* son, the seventh Robert Bruce. So now the Bruces hold vast tracts of southwest Scotland—Annandale and Carrick—and with their old enemies neutered, they flourish under Edward's benevolence. The current Lord of Annandale is Edward's loyal governor of Carlisle, and the young

Earl of Carrick is treated by England's King like a favourite son. Believe me, Father Martin, men have not yet even begun to perceive, let alone understand, the brilliance of that old man's evasion of what should have been a disastrous situation. He out-thought and outmanoeuvred everyone, friend and foe alike, and took care of his own magnificently. As I said, an admirable man, in every way. Perhaps *primus inter pares*."

"Think you his son is capable of the same?"

There was little now in evidence of the young, brash, thoughtless Irish priest. "That remains to be seen, my friend. But thanks to his father's actions he will, at least, have the chance to demonstrate his fitness, one way or the other."

"I'm told that the youngest one, young Carrick, is a worthless fop," he continued. "A prancing popinjay was the description I heard."

"Is that right? And where did you hear that, Father?"

"I don't remember," he said, not looking at me and sounding elaborately casual. "Someone spoke of it, and those around agreed with him."

"Of course they did. And they all knew young Bruce well, of course, considering that he has not been seen in Scotland these eight years. He went to live and train in England two full years before his mother died, and was still a beardless boy when last he was seen north of Berwick."

He turned and looked at me, his face showing, I

thought, a trace of discomfort. "I didn't ask about that," he said. "I didn't know about it."

"Just as well, perhaps. But although the elder Bruce's reputation in Scotland did not suffer much overall, the grandson is another matter, I'll grant you that. I, too, have heard that young Carrick has grown into a feckless English fop, spoiled beyond recognition by the King, who seems to dote upon him like an addled grandsire. I find that hard to believe, but the boy had lived at the English court in Westminster for years before the family moved there, so there might be something more to it than spite and jealousy. On the whole, though, I do not really care. I would rather concern myself with the memory of a truly admirable old man than waste my time wondering about a young dandy I've never met and am unlikely to meet any time soon."

We lapsed into a silence broken only by the sounds of our progress: the hard, crisp clack of the heels of my new boots and the papery shuffle of his sandals' soles. I began to pay attention to my surroundings and to think more carefully about my rapidly approaching meeting with my mentor and employer, Bishop Robert Wishart, and as though by magic, the mere idea of meeting him again had the effect of loosening my bowels. There was no reason why it should have, for I had no fear of the bishop and my conscience was clear, so it might have been mere coincidence that the stomach spasm hit me when it did, but there was no doubting the urgency of the summons. I quickly lowered my pack and dashed into a dense clump of shrubs.

A thought occurred to me while I was alone, and I was mulling it over as I made my way back to the roadway to collect my pack and my staff.

"Forgive me, Father James," Martin said, "but you look … preoccupied. Is something wrong?"

"No," I said, surprised that my distraction had been so easy to see. "No, there is nothing wrong." And I had to laugh, thinking of the comical way in which the mind could make connections. "It's merely that in doing my business I was reminded of something Edward Plantagenet supposedly said to Antony Bek after having—again supposedly—conquered Scotland last year."

"*Supposedly* conquered Scotland? Why would you say that? He *did* conquer it."

"I said it because it's the truth. They were returning, victorious, to England, and it was last August—less than ten months ago. Yet now, with the majority of the Scottish leadership safely shut up in English jails, English armies are being ordered back to Scotland. Had Edward's conquest last year been as real as he supposed it to be, there would be no possibility of uprisings this soon. Edward's armies beat us in a sore fight at Dunbar and took many nobles prisoner. But the truth is they came nowhere close to conquering the Scots people, the ordinary folk. That's why this whole country is in an uproar now—because Edward failed to make sure that the task he thought was done had really been completed. He left a crew of ruthless, venal cutthroats to administer his interests, and now he's paying the price of underestimating his enemy."

Martin had been listening closely, his brow furrowed. "That makes sense," he said. "And I believe you're right ... So what was it Edward said to Bek?"

"Oh, that. They had been discussing the conduct of their campaign and the success of their banishment of Balliol, delivering all of Scotland into the absolute power of England's rule. 'A man does good business,' Edward is reported to have said, 'when he rids himself of a turd.'"

CHAPTER SIX

REBELS AND MISCREANTS

Father Martin and I walked in companionable silence for a long time after that, and several miles elapsed as the landscape surrounding us changed gradually from a sparse scattering of hawthorn and hazel, more shrubbery than trees, to hardy, dense clumps of shallow-rooted gorse and broom. These we watched die away completely within about an hour to leave us walking through a pale green countryside of low, rolling hills coated in short, sheep-cropped grass scarred by moss- and lichen-covered outcrops of the underlying rock that rendered the place unsuitable for any kind of agricultural activity other than the raising of sheep.

Some time after that, I noticed that my companion was craning his neck to look around us, where nothing had changed within the past few miles. "We really should be drawing close to Maybole by now," he said. "But clearly we have not come as far as I thought we had. I see a farmhouse, though, so we have at least reached civilization."

I grunted my disdain. "Habitation I will accept, but I would balk at *civilization*, in this part of the world." I looked about me, taking in the rolling sweep of the surrounding craggy hills and the paucity of trees. "No signs of settlement that I can see, but I have no doubt Maybole will be here somewhere, and when we find it we will be in the very heart of the Carrick earldom. Pardon me, then, if I walk in silence for a while, preparing myself for the sight of its glories."

We walked on for another half mile until we rounded a bend in the road and came to the so-called town of Maybole. It was a hamlet: a cluster of buildings with two undistinguished taverns and a scattering of people who eyed our priestly robes incuriously. We considered stopping at one of the hostelries, but only briefly, deciding that we would be better to keep going for the remaining few miles to Turnberry. We turned right at the crossroads and kept walking, and the road led us along the bank of a narrow, noisy, fast-flowing brook.

Martin had been walking with his head down, mulling over something, but now he glanced at the roadside stream. "Lots of water around here," he said. "Is this the same burn that we crossed in Maybole?"

"Your guess would be as good as mine," I said. "Running water is everywhere in these parts. There are dozens of these burns, all flowing into one another until they reach the sea as rivers. Some of the rivers have names, others don't. It depends on how close they come to places where folk live."

"I've noticed that," Martin said. "There's one comes out right at Turnberry, forming the spit of land that holds Bruce's castle, and I know it has a name, but don't ask me what it is because I couldn't tell you."

"And how far remains to Turnberry? I have enjoyed your companionship, Father, but our loving Saviour knows I'm ready to reach journey's end this day, pleasant as it has been."

"Six miles, I'd think, something like that. Less than two hours, at any rate."

"Two hours to kill, then. So what will we talk about now?"

"You tell me," he said pleasantly. "It should be my turn to talk, in fairness. What?" he asked me, frowning quickly. "What did I say?"

"You said almost nothing, Father. I've been talking. For hours."

"I don't understand," he said as I felt my face break out in a wide smile.

"Nor should you," I said. "How could you?"

"What on earth are you talking about, Father?"

"I'm talking about anything and everything, it seems," I said, and then laughed aloud. "Martin, you've cured me. I'm talking as easily and fluently as I did before my injuries, and I haven't been aware of it until this very moment."

'What injuries?"

"My mouth, my face."

"What's wrong with them?"

"Nothing, obviously, and for that I thank the Lord God. You have no difficulty understanding me?"

"Why should I?"

"Because—" I realized that I was being foolish. The young priest had never heard me speak before today, so he had nothing against which to judge my prowess. But I had, and I was exultant. I had no doubt I was taking greater care with my enunciation, but I was doing it with ease and confidence. "Because I did not always speak, or sound, the way I do today," I finished. "But so long as you can understand me without difficulty, then I am content. You were about to take over the talking for this next part of our journey, so tell me about France and the university at Paris. I have never been in France but I've heard great things about Paris and its university."

"Ah! Well," he said, "if you've never been to France, that makes Paris difficult to describe, for there's nothing here in Scotland, or in Ireland for that matter, that comes close to matching it."

We conversed on that subject for some time, and I gently twitted Father Martin for his rhapsodic devotion to the beautiful city, to which, apparently, there was not another town in the entire world that could withstand comparison.

"I have a friend who was there for years," I told him, "and he, too, speaks of it much as you do."

"Oh? What's his name? I may know him."

"I have no do doubt you do. He's a canon of Glasgow Cathedral."

"Canon Lamberton! You are a friend of Canon Lamberton? Then you are fortunate indeed." His tone, verging on reverential, left me in no doubt of his sincerity. "What an admirable man he is. You'll be surprised to know I owe my current post to him. I met him there, in Paris, several years ago. We came to know each other slightly, and for some reason he decided I might do well in Scotland. Not too long afterwards, he wrote to me saying he had prevailed upon his bishop to offer me a clerical position on the chapter staff in Glasgow."

"Aha! And what, precisely, is your function on the staff there, apart from representing the adherents of St. Dominic?"

He treated me to the full glory of his engaging smile. "Well, Father James, to tell the truth, I've had no time for staff duty, for I've been filling in for you while you have been away. I arrived in Glasgow while you were in the south with your cousin, and when you were unable to return, the bishop set me to completing the assignments you had been working on before you left."

"I see," I said. "So you have replaced me ..."

"Heaven forfend! No, Father." He had the grace to look horrified. "No, no, don't say that. Bishop Wishart has been champing at the bit like a warhorse, waiting for you to climb back into your saddle. He believes that you and I together might make a worthwhile team, if you could bring yourself to work with me, but I swear by all I believe in that the thought of my replacing you has never crossed his mind—or mine. He thinks too highly of your skills and talents."

I confess his oath of truthfulness set my mind at ease, and I was now more curious about this young priest. Whatever his gifts might be, they must have been prodigious to earn the sponsorship he had won from William Lamberton in Paris. "So," I asked him, "have you met my cousin?"

"I have, several times now. A fine, big man he is."

"Is he with the bishop now?"

"No. He was, for a while, but about a week ago he took off back to his forest den."

"That does not surprise me. Will always was a forester at heart. When did you first meet him?"

"About a month ago, when he returned from Perth."

Once again the Irish priest confounded me, for the town of Perth lay far to the north of Glasgow, in the waist of Scotland, close to the Abbey of Scone, which had housed the Stone of Destiny, the sacred stone upon which the Kings of Scotland had been crowned since time immemorial, until Edward had seized it and had it removed to England.

"Perth?" I repeated inanely, as though I had never heard the name before. "What was Will doing up there?"

That earned me another of Martin's flashing grins. "Why, Father Jamie, you must be the only man in Scotland who would ask that question, for I swear everyone else knows the answer. You know the fellow

Ormsby, William Ormsby?"

"That odious man of Edward's, the fellow he appointed justiciar of Scotland last year, after dethroning King John. I have seldom met a man I disliked so heartily."

"That's the very man, instantly and eternally lovable. He established himself in Perth, making it the seat of his justiciary. His prime task was to administer English justice in Scotland and to see to it that all Scots who had not already done so would swear allegiance to Edward."

I nodded, remembering the outrage that requirement had occasioned. "Swear it not, as they had before, to England's king as Lord Paramount of Scotland, but to Edward Plantagenet the man. And worse, *in person*."

"Ormsby was authorized to use any means at his disposal to achieve that objective," the Ulsterman continued, "and he quickly made himself detested by everyone who encountered him."

"Detested in Perth, you mean."

"Aye, in Perth. He set himself up there because it was within easy reach of all that he wished to plunder. It took no time at all for him to make himself widely loathed."

"In the north," I insisted. "His infamy was not so widespread to the south. I heard of what he was doing, but I heard little to convince me he was the kind of devil you describe. Mind you, in those days I was spending much of my time carrying messages to and from Selkirk

Forest, and that gave me enough to fret about without being distracted by the outlandish behaviour of another of Edward's malicious officeholders."

"You were fortunate to be so well removed from him, then," my companion said. "Those nearer to him felt the wrath of Hell about their ears."

"Aye, including Will, it would appear."

"Including Will, though only indirectly. What I heard was that, just as the fighting ended on the night your cousin overthrew the English garrison in Lanark, someone brought him word that another English force was close by, besieging Sir William Douglas in Sanquhar Castle. Wallace knew the castle was an easy march to the south, and since he apparently admired the Lord of Douglas and the timing seemed right to him, he led his men there, knowing they would feel invincible after their victory at Lanark. They surprised the English from the rear and rescued Douglas, who immediately placed himself under your cousin's orders and declared himself to be a Wallace man. When they returned to Glasgow together, word of Ormsby's most recent excesses had everyone agog with outrage, and a short time later they departed on horseback bound for Perth.

"Of course they were unexpected, and the raid was a complete success. Ormsby barely escaped being taken and had to flee, leaving all his possessions and his entire baggage train behind as booty for the raiders. Your cousin's reputation grew greatly with that exploit."

I was confused. "On horseback?" Will, I knew, was a fair horseman, trained by the stablemen on our uncle

Malcolm's estate in Elderslie, but his men were rough forest outlaws, bowmen, mostly, and all ordinary peasant folk, none of them wealthy enough ever to have thought about riding, let alone owning, a horse. "How was *that* accomplished? And who on earth could have paid for such an expedition?"

"Now there I cannot help you, Father. You'll have to ask that of the bishop when we find him, for he's the man with all the information you're seeking. All I know is that Ormsby needed to be stopped, dramatically and publicly, and the Perth raid achieved that. But I have only the vaguest understanding of the politics involved. I know they were as much religious as they were regal. Bishops and princes, Church and state all intermingled. Edward wants to make Scotland's Church answerable to York Minster, just as he wants to see all Scotland under the heel of his tax collectors. And to defeat those aims, William Ormsby, justiciar of Scotland—the King of England's hated functionary—was sent packing, ingloriously. But without your cousin there as leader, the raid would not have had anything near the same effect.

"The ordinary folk," he went on, "have no trust in the magnates. They never have."

I slowed my pace gaping at him.

"Why should they?" he continued. "How *could* they? The magnates—earls, barons, lords, or knights— have no time for *them*, the ordinary folk who live on their lands and keep them fed. The commoners are given no consideration at all, other than how they might be used and squeezed harder and farther to the benefit of their betters. It has been that way for hundreds of years—so much a way of life that no one has ever thought to question it. Until now. The people—the common folk—are growing aware of themselves and of the power that lies within them— power to say aye or nay, in one united voice, when they so wish."

I was shaking my head even as I listened. "This is nonsense, Martin."

"Is it? Is it nonsense that when most of the noblemen of Scotland are in English jails, your cousin Will's name is on the lips of every man, woman, and child in Scotland? Is it nonsense that the people flock to him from everywhere, shouting his name and willing to risk their lives for him—ordinary men who would never have dreamt of taking up weapons in their own cause before he came along? Is it nonsense that this man, your own cousin, holds no knightly rank but yet commands an army? That has never happened within this realm since the Normans first came north from England, and believe you me, Father James, it is a development of great significance for every living being in this land, for it must mean that nothing can ever be the same again. The Scots folk have found a leader they can follow willingly—William Wallace. One of their own kind, from their own ranks. And they are raising a collective voice in his support that no man has ever heard before."

"That is …" I began.

"That is God's own truth," he said. Then he stopped suddenly, and held out a hand to stop me, too, as he gazed at something ahead of us. I peered into the distance and tried to make sense of what appeared to be a dead man lying in our path, some hundred and fifty paces away.

"Mother of God," I whispered, my mouth suddenly gone dry. "What have we found?"

Father Martin's arm stretched out to stop me as effectively as an iron bar. "Don't move," he breathed. "Stand absolutely still."

CHAPTER SEVEN

LOAVES AND FISHES

"Are you hungry, Father James?"
The words were jarring to my ear. Here we were, faced with a corpse, perhaps murdered, and my companion was speaking of being hungry. Appalled, I turned to look at him and felt my mouth drop open when I saw the smile on his face. He was not looking at me, though. His eyes were fixed on the body on the ground ahead of us. I looked back, just in time to see the "dead" man move, and at once felt light-headed with the relief of recognizing that I had been mistaken.

The man lay on his side more than a hundred paces from us, surrounded by rough tussocks of grass at the very edge of the riverbank we were following, and now I saw that he was fishing, peering fixedly down into the stream that flowed within a foot of his lowered face. His right arm was bared to the shoulder, its ample sleeve pulled high up to his neck, and his arm hung motionless, stretched down into the water beneath the bank. At the end of that arm—and I knew this as surely as I knew my own name—barely within reach of his stretched, caressing fingers, lay a fat-bellied trout, being lulled and cozened towards sudden death as its would-be killer prepared, with great patience, to snatch it up and throw it onto the grass at his back.

Martin spoke quietly. "I wonder if he has had any luck."

"Pray the Lord he has," I said reverently. "Allied to a kind and sharing nature."

At that moment, the motionless form convulsed in a sudden heave and a spray of upflung water that caught the light of the afternoon sun and scattered like beads of glass. My eyes fastened upon the silvery form of the large fish at the centre of the commotion as it soared through the air, scooped up and tossed to the grassy bank by its successful stalker. As soon as the creature landed, the fisherman pounced upon it and gripped it firmly in one hand while dealing it a solid rap on the head from a short cudgel that he had held prepared.

Martin gasped. "Sweet Jesus be praised—that's his lordship!"

It was indeed. Within the space of two heartbeats, the unknown fisherman had been transformed. The head now bared to the sunshine bore the unmistakable square tonsure of holy orders, and the nondescript, brownish robe the fellow wore was revealed as one of the rich brown, green-edged cassocks that were the chosen garb—some said the episcopal livery—of our employer and superior in Christ, Robert Wishart, Lord Bishop of Glasgow.

I hurried forward to offer him my hand. The sprawling man, clutching a glistening fish in one strong hand and his cudgel in the other, looked up at me with surprise and dawning recognition on his face. He was utterly without dignity in that moment, his legs kicking beneath his cassock as he struggled to regain his balance and sit up without using his hands, and as I looked down at him, a voice warned me to pay heed and take care at the same time, or I would be crushed by what this most powerful and dangerous prelate in Scotland would bring about. Now, six and forty years later, I recall that never-again-heard voice as being oracular.

"Jamie," he said, dropping the stunned fish on the grass and stuffing the cudgel into his cassock before wiping his hands on his green scapular. "Welcome, laddie. I've been waiting for you. Help me up."

He grasped my outstretched hand in his own and I leaned back against his weight as he pulled himself easily to his feet, casting a sideways glance at my companion as he did so. "You found him, then," he said in Scots. "Good man. Now here, take this." He bent easily and lobbed the fish so that Martin could catch it. "There's a stake on the edge o' the bank there wi' two lines attached to it. One o' them is tied around the neck o' a goatskin full o' fine German wine that I rescued from Lord James's custody—it should be near perfectly cooled by now—and the other is threaded through the gills of three more o' thae trout. None o' them as fine as that beauty, mind you, but the four o' them thegither should fill three hungry bellies.

I've a fire going over there by that big tree, and you'll find a griddle already on the coals. There's fresh bread and some salt in a bag there, and even some fresh-churned butter. Make yourself busy and start cooking while I talk with Father James here, for if you're like me, we're a' three famished."

I watched as the Irish priest quickly crossed to the edge of the bank, where he pulled in the attached cords hand over hand until he retrieved the wineskin and the other three fish. When I looked back again to the bishop, my hand went automatically to my mouth, to hide my missing teeth.

"Don't bother," he said in Latin, and not unkindly. "It's not really noticeable. I had expected much worse. What about your voice, though? Has it affected your ability to speak?" He waited, and I blinked at him. "You're going to have to say something to me sooner or later, you know, so why not now?"

"What would you have me say, my lord bishop?"

He laughed, and raised his hand in a gesture I remembered well as being a sign of pleasure. "No more than that, lad, no more than that. I understood every word of it, and that's as much as I need to know. Aye, well. I'm glad you're back, Jamie, for God in His Heaven knows I've had need of you these past few months. The world we have known appears to be going to Hell, in accordance with the wishes of the enemies of our realm."

I assumed that by "enemies" my employer was referring, though perhaps not exclusively, to the

English Archbishop of York, whose goal it was to have all of Scotland subjected to the authority of York. If he had his way, the Church in Scotland would be flooded with English clergymen at every level. The case had been argued before the papal curia for a hundred years, and Scotland's cause had been supported every time. But now, with Edward Plantagenet reigning as King of England, it took on new life. Though the King had no love for the Archbishop of York, he supported him wholeheartedly in his designs for Scotland because they fit hand in glove with his own. With English priests and bishops preaching the King of England's will along with Holy Scripture from every Scottish pulpit, the folk of this realm would be deprived of hope as well as salvation.

"You knew we would be coming this way, my lord?" I asked him.

"What other way could you come from Ayr? I warned Father Martin to waste no time in bringing you to me, and I hoped that, weather permitting, you would be here this afternoon. Besides, I was at loose ends, Sir James being much preoccupied today with matters to do with his own territories and tenantry. I would have been bored to death, sitting around listening to such things. And so, it being a fine day for a change, I decided to come out to the riverbank and wait for you. And here we are."

"Indeed." I looked around me again, seeing nothing but the beautiful, rolling meadow stretching for miles and becoming more heavily wooded as it progressed.

"Turnberry Castle is nearby, then?"

"Near enough. It's about two miles over yonder, on the coast." He waved vaguely towards the west. "Have you ever met young Lord Bruce?"

"No, my lord. I've heard of him, of course, but who has not? The Earl of Carrick has made quite a name for himself since his grandfather quit Scotland and took the family with him."

His lordship was looking at me askance, one eyebrow cocked high. "Do I hear disapproval in your voice, Father James?"

"No, sir. I but speak of his reputation ... of how men speak of him."

"Aye, I know. Tell me, do you remember how you felt when first you tried to speak through your new-lost teeth? Did it not cross your mind that other men might laugh at you and talk about you for sounding different?"

I was slightly bewildered by his sudden change of topic until his next words showed me what he was thinking.

"For if it did," he continued, "and if you thought such a thing even for a moment, I would take that as ample cause to disregard what ignorant men might say on anything of import. None of us has any real control over what other people think or say about us, Jamie, and none but a fool would believe that men, being men, are always charitable. Young Lord Bruce is his own man, I now believe, and fashioned in the manner true to his lineage."

"*Now*. Does that mean you have met him recently?"

"It does. Two weeks ago, to be precise, and then again last night, here."

"In Turnberry?"

"Does that surprise you? It is his home, you know, and was his mother's before that. He was born here."

"Aye, but ... I thought he was in England."

"And so he was, for years. But now he is here, with us."

"With *us* ..." Something about the way he said the words made me wary. "Your pardon, my lord, but if I may ask the question, who is *us*?"

"Us, the members of our fellowship here in the southwest, united in the cause of Scotland's realm."

If there was such a fellowship, I thought, it was one I had never heard of, but he was already carrying on, unaware that he had said anything unusual.

"For the moment we. are myself and Lord James the Steward—the last two of the Council of Guardians still in residence within the realm. But we also have Sir William Douglas of Douglasdale, Lord Robert Bruce the Earl of Carrick, and a host of others—lesser nobles, knights and churchmen, and burghers and commoners, including your cousin."

"Will's here? I thought— Father Martin told me he had gone back to Selkirk last week."

"And so he did. He was with us in Ayr until last week, but he is now back in Selkirk Forest, on our behalf." He tilted his head to one side, squinting at me because of the sun at my back. "You knew he went to Perth, did you not?"

"Father Martin told me."

"Aye, well, that expedition did him little harm in the eyes of the people. He came back with more than three times the following he'd had before he left, all of them from the territories he'd crossed on the way north. They're willing enough, but they're raw and untrained and would be worse than useless against English footmen. So I sent him back to the greenwood with them, to meld them with his own folk there and train them sufficiently to send them into a fight without feeling like a murderer. He was loath to go at first, but then he saw the sense of it."

"I see. And how long will he remain there?"

The bishop shrugged. "For as long as may be required. He has a rabble now. What he needs is an army, or at least a force capable of putting up a fight. And so he'll train them, in the forest and in south Lothian, harassing the English garrisons there, most of which are small enough to goad to the point of fury and folly."

"And what about here? Canon Lamberton told me about the new English appointees named to restore the peace here, Percy and Clifford. Where are they now, do you know?"

"Aye." He wrinkled his nose. "They were in Galloway last week, at the new abbey, resting their men and horses, but I heard word yesterday that they're coming this way."

"To Ayr?"

"Mayhap. They are in search of us, after all."

"And when they find you, what will you do? You'll need Will's people with you, unless you have an army of your own at hand … Have you?"

He eyed me calmly, showing no offence at the familiar way I had been addressing him. "We have some men," he said quietly. "A force of kinds—large enough to present an impression of strength, but not a real or efficient army. As for what we will do if Percy arrives? We'll talk to him."

"Talk to him? Forgive me, my lord, but he might be in no mood for anything but slaughter, and if he talks at all it's unlikely to be of anything other than complete capitulation to Edward's authority. Percy is a warrior, from the little I know of him. He's a firebrand, hungry for glory and reward. Such men set little stock upon talking."

The bishop's nod of agreement was slow and deliberate. "True," he said, "that is true … So if the man wishes to discuss capitulation, that is what we will discuss, for as long as may be necessary."

I gaped at him, and he smiled at me. "Come, Father, as a son of Holy Mother Church you should be well aware that wars may be fought with words as well as with weapons—and sometimes more effectively." He stepped closer to the riverbank and picked up a capacious-looking leather bag with a bronze buckle and a long shoulder strap. He passed the carrying strap over his head and adjusted it across his breast so that it hung comfortably by his side. "As a priest, Jamie," he said, switching smoothly into Scots, "ye should ken never to underestimate the power o' words. They may no' hae the cuttin' edge o' a steel blade, but they can turn aside the wrath o' an angry man, an' they can draw the sting frae a wound quicker than a poultice will." He nodded to me to accompany him as he started walking towards the fire and Father Martin.

"While we talk here in the southwest," he continued, speaking Latin again, "holding the English in prolonged debate, others elsewhere may prosecute their designs in greater safety, free of the fear of being harassed by Percy's helots. To be talking with them at all will make us look like cavilling poltroons, but that is of little matter if it leaves our forces elsewhere free to do what they must do."

"What forces elsewhere? Andrew Murray?"

"Among others, yes. Careful there, mind your feet," he said, and I stepped carefully around the edge of a large burrow of some kind, half-obscured by nettles. "Andrew is among them, and he is one of the best, a natural leader, a trained knight, and a born strategist, every bit as popular and successful in his own territories as Will is here. But I meant *everywhere*, Jamie, rather than *elsewhere*. The entire country is up in arms in a way that it has never been roused before, particularly in the Highlands and the Isles. And this time it's not arrayed behind the magnates, for most of the magnates, as you know, are shut up in English jails. The uprising this time is in the name of the folk and on behalf of the folk, and it is driven by generations of hatred and resentment of the English and their arrogance, from the time of the first Norman invasions. It has little to do with the nobility, in any sense. There has never been anything like it in all our history."

We had reached the fire beneath the ancient elm tree by then, where Father Martin was stooped over the coals, tending to the fish that he had spitted carefully on willow twigs and placed precisely on some broad burdock leaves atop the iron griddle, where they would be able to cook perfectly, mere inches above the heat.

"Martin," the bishop said, "the blessed Peter himself could not have made a cooking fish look better—or smell better, for that matter. Are you near done?"

"I am, your lordship. You came well prepared. I've set out the bread on the burdock leaves there, and there's some salt to bring the flavour from the fish itself. I'll be but a minute more, and then we can eat."

"And so we shall, but first we need to drink." He collected the plump wineskin from the base of the tree and poured into three horn cups that Martin had placed beside it. "Here, Father James," he said. "Take your own and mind not to spill it, for it's liquid gold. Father Martin, here's one for you, and then you need to hear what we are talking about."

We drank together, and then the bishop and I made ourselves comfortable while Martin served the meal and his lordship offered a grace. The fish was magnificent, and for a long time there was nothing to be heard from any of us but the sounds of blissful satisfaction.

Finally, though, the bishop sat up and belched quietly. "That was wondrous," he said quietly. "Now, Father James, if you'll clean up here and see to dousing the fire, I'll tell Father Martin about what we were discussing while he prepared this magnificent meal."

By the time I finished putting out the fire and disposing of our refuse, his lordship had told Martin all he needed to know and was talking about the uprising he had mentioned to me.

"And who is leading this uprising?" I asked. "The Church?"

"Yes, led by our bishops."

"Not *all* our bishops, my lord," I demurred. "De Cheyne of Aberdeen has always been Edward's man, has he not?"

"True, but de Cheyne is but one voice. A solitary bishop whose flock disapproves of his personal loyalty to the English King."

"His flock? The Aberdonians?" I heard the scorn in my own voice, remembering something I had overheard an admired teacher say when I was a student at Paisley Abbey. "Forgive me, my lord bishop, but the Aberdonians are not seen by other Scots as being Scots. They're universally distrusted, regarded as aliens. Even their speech is unintelligible to anyone not born and raised there."

His eyebrow rose noticeably. "Ah," he breathed. "Expertise, I see. Have you met many folk from Aberdeen, Jamie?"

"No, my lord. I've met but a few. But they're a

strange and different breed."

"Strange, perhaps, and different sounding I will grant you. But they are Scots, Jamie, as much as we are, and they detest England and the English just as heartily as does your cousin, though for different reasons. What do you know of the history of Aberdeen, or Aberdonians, for that matter?"

"Less than nothing," I said.

"Well at least you admit it," he said quietly. "I myself was unwilling to do that, and I fear my feelings were much the same as yours until I had a long and frank discussion, no more than a few days ago, with a priest from those parts. He overheard something I said and took me to task for my mistaken beliefs, and I was greatly impressed by what he had to say."

He was looking at me expectantly, and so I asked, "Was he from Aberdeen?"

"No, but he was from Petty, in Moray, which is close by."

"And what did he tell you, my lord?"

"Well, to begin, he pointed out that for hundreds of years, in the course of trade and commerce, the people of our east coast have intermarried with the traders and sailors from the Low Countries, and over the generations these incomers have been absorbed into the general populace, so that they are marked now only by their 'foreign'-sounding names. No one questions their origins now because they are Scots, plain and simple. But that was never the case in Aberdeen." He saw my brows crease at that and nodded, forging ahead. "It was hundreds of years ago, but from the outset, for whatever reasons, and most probably because of its location, Aberdeen attracted a far larger settlement of Low Country merchants and traders than any other place did. It was remote, it had a fine harbour, and it was easily accessible, offering great advantages in access to overseas ports and trade. And so the incomers stayed there and prospered. But where their fellows elsewhere intermarried with the local Scots, the populace in Aberdeen were numerous enough to keep to themselves, and because they were forever receiving new immigrants from the homelands, they never had the need to marry outside their own kind. And so they became the folk they are today, isolated, insular, and different from other Scots in many ways, speaking in their own fashion and living as they do. But they are Scots nonetheless, after hundreds of years of living here."

"And they disapprove of Bishop de Cheyne's adherence to Edward of England?"

His lordship shrugged. "I cannot speak to that, but Father Murray seemed convinced of their deep dislike of the English."

"Murray? From Petty? Is he related to Andrew Murray of Petty?"

"Aye, close kin. He is currently pastor of Bothwell, which is owned by Sir Andrew's wealthy brother William, whom men call le Riche. Aha!" His eyes widened slightly as he saw Martin nod. "Do you know the man, Father?"

"Familiar name, my lord," Martin said. "And not merely to me. William le Riche is spoken of throughout the land, and I even heard of him in France. There's nothing like being wealthy beyond the dreams of men to get your name well known."

"That, I fear, is one of the great and unjustifiable truths of life in this vale of tears," the bishop said, and then looked all around the spot where we were sitting on the riverbank, beneath the massive spread of the ancient elm. Then he sighed and bent forward to pick up the wineskin, which remained more than half full despite our best efforts to deplete it over the previous half-hour. "You know, I hate to leave this beautiful spot, but I think we should be moving on. Is there anything else that either one of you wishes to talk about before we go?"

It was a polite question, born more of courtesy than anything else, but it reminded me that I had, in fact, something important that I wanted to discuss with him.

"If it please you, my lord, I do have a matter to raise with you, but I would prefer to do so privily, whenever you might find it convenient."

"Will it take long?"

"No, my lord, not at all."

"Then it would be convenient now. I have no doubt Father Martin will excuse us if we take a stroll together."

Martin was on his feet in an instant. "No need for that, my lord. You two stay here and talk and I'll walk on ahead and wait for you along the way."

Neither of us offered any argument, and he picked up his shoulder pack and walked away, leaving the bishop looking at me and waiting for me to broach my subject.

CHAPTER EIGHT

THE PERTH RAID

An hour later the three of us were together again, walking side by side as we followed the path towards the coast and Castle Turnberry. We walked in silence for the most part, though Martin and the bishop spoke to each other quietly from time to time.

For my own part, I was content to walk with my own thoughts, reviewing my conversation with the bishop on the matter of my employment. I had been anticipating that discussion for weeks by then, acutely aware of my long absence from Glasgow and the consequent loss of familiarity with his lordship's immediate affairs, and growing increasingly afraid that I might have been gone too long and could therefore have been supplanted through necessity. I need not have worried, as things turned out, owing in great measure to Father Martin's diligent attention to my uncompleted duties.

The bishop quickly made it clear that he had been aware of the gravity of my physical condition from the moment Ewan Scrymgeour had delivered me to the priory in Lanark. Ewan, a hairless giant whom I had known since I was ten, was the half-Welsh, half-Scots archer who had taught both Will and me to shoot an English longbow, though my career as an archer had not survived my initial attraction to the priesthood. Ewan was now one of Will's senior and most trusted lieutenants, and after seeing me safely delivered to the priory he had sent a full report to the bishop before he returned to join Will.

The entire southwest, his lordship told me, had quickly plunged into chaos in the aftermath of the events surrounding my own injuries: the deaths of Mirren Wallace, her unborn child, and her young son Will at the hands of the English, and the glaring, violent savagery of my cousin Will's bloody revenge. But even before the word had had time to spread—and it did so with the speed typical of such tidings—it seemed that all of Scotland, both north and south of the River Forth, had erupted in simultaneous outrage against the English and their lawless hypocrisy. The bishop recounted for me the events that Father Martin had described—how, even before the atrocity of Mirren Wallace's abduction, Sir William Douglas, Lord of Douglasdale, had been in armed rebellion against what he perceived to be intolerable English tyranny and had found himself besieged in Sanquhar Castle by an English force dispatched from Berwick by Sir Henry Percy to capture him. He told me, too, how Will had raised the siege and rescued Douglas, after which they had headed north towards Ayr, to acknowledge the authority of Sir James Stewart as the senior Scots magnate left in the country, and how the Steward had immediately sent word to his fellow Guardian, Bishop Wishart, to join him at Ayr.

The bishop fell silent at that point, clearly believing he had told me all I needed to know, but I was far from satisfied with what I had heard.

"You and Father Martin have both told me about Will's raid on Perth, my lord, and I know that he and Douglas very nearly captured Ormsby, Edward's justiciar for Scotland. But I confess I don't yet understand the reason for the urgency. What triggered it?"

My employer blinked at me in astonishment. "You mean the raid itself? Abuse, Jamie," he said quietly. "Abuse caused it. Ormsby and his English ravens were stripping the countryside of everything that could be gathered up and shipped to England. Will and his party rode a-purpose to stop the thefts. They moved quickly, across country, taking care not to be seen, and they almost captured the man himself."

"But they took Perth?"

"No, no, they did no such thing—and you need to be careful about saying things like that. Perth is a Scots town, so there was no need to *take* it. But they certainly entered it and saved it. What they did was to repeat your cousin's feat at Lanark. They surprised the English garrison and drove them out, and they reclaimed Ormsby's plunder before it could be shipped to Edward. It was done at my insistence, and under the auspices of the Lord High Steward." He gazed at me keenly. "That surprises you?"

"It does, my lord, for it must have entailed great risk for the Steward. Why would he commit to such a course of action, openly declaring himself in armed opposition to Edward and England, after maintaining his neutrality so carefully and for so long? From all I know of Lord James, he is a thinker and a planner, not a man of precipitate action."

"I have no quibble with your description of his lordship's temperament, Father," the bishop answered, "but I think your fundamental view of his neutrality is wrong. Ask yourself now, afresh: is neutrality really what the Steward has been practising?" An eyebrow raised high in scorn accompanied that question. "You'll agree, I hope, that neutrality entails a refusal to identify with either side in a conflict. That is *not* what is happening here. Lord James is no third party, refusing to take sides in a fight between others. He is one of the leading victims being bullied in an unconscionable program of aggression and intimidation by an invader. Do you really believe the English consider Lord James to be a neutral party in their plans for Scotland?" He paused, waiting for me to respond, then asked again, "Do you believe that?"

Again he waited for a response. "No, I thought not. James Stewart is one of the greatest and wealthiest of all Scots magnates—and he is also one of the few not languishing in English prisons. His ancestral blood is Norman French, but it is sufficiently fortified with Erse strains by now to make him sympathetic to the ancient Celtic ways. Today he is a Scot, one of this realm's greatest and most powerful sons, bred in the bone and long since purged of any English sympathies. And he is being harassed daily by base-born upstarts, unlettered English louts who treat him and his lands and holdings as their own, as though they hold some God-given right to flout him and maltreat him solely because they are English and he is not. They accord him no recognition, acknowledge no rights of his, and treat him as a lackey. The Lord High Steward of the realm! There is no cause for wonderment, Father James, that when it fell to him, he seized the opportunity to retaliate. What is amazing is that he put up with an intolerable situation for as long as he did."

He reached down to the scrip that hung from his waist, clearly thinking he must now have dealt with the explanation to my satisfaction, but I imposed myself again.

"Forgive my persistence here, my lord, but Father Martin told me Will was in charge of the raid—in command—and yet Sir William Douglas was there, far above Will Wallace in both rank and station. That makes no sense to me at all. Why would not Douglas command? It was a mounted party, and it struck far to the north and at top speed—hard-riding, hard-fighting horsemen. Will can ride, if he must, but he's no horseman. So why was he even there? Why did you send him?"

My employer straightened up abruptly, his face registering astonishment and perhaps anger at my presumption, but then he gave me a tight, almost reluctant grin. "Because I needed to send him," he said. "I needed him there and I needed him visible— more than William Douglas, whose name is less than stainless, as you say, or Sir John Stewart, or any other knight I could have sent, and more than any magnate in all Scotland—more than all of them together, in fact. I needed the folk to see *William Wallace* and to know that Wallace would go wherever he was needed in the fight against the English. The folk needed a champion in Perth, and *I* needed that champion— No, *Scotland* needed that champion to be William Wallace, a man of the folk. And so I sent him. It was the right thing to do."

"That may be so, my lord," I said, determined to make my point even if it earned me the bishop's displeasure. "But I can't see Will Wallace agreeing to do that—leaving his followers behind and striking off on his own, so far out of his own territory—without long and convincing persuasion. I know my cousin well, I think, and the behaviour you are describing is out of character for him."

"Aye," the bishop said, "just as this dogged questioning is out of character for you."

"Then I ask for your indulgence, my lord. My concern may have made me over bold, but I have not seen Will since the moment he entrusted me with the lives of his family, and I failed him. He has seldom been far from my mind since then and I find myself fretting over him, even though Heaven and all the saints know he is more than capable of seeing to himself."

The bishop raised his hand in an absent-minded blessing. "Be at peace, Father. You have done nothing wrong and you ask for no more than is your due. Were I unwilling to speak of this I would not, and there would be an end of it. You are perfectly correct in your judgment. Will had no wish to go riding off into unknown parts without good reason. It took me a long time to convert him to my way of seeing things, and I confess that at first I thought I would fail." He hesitated. "Truthfully, though, I am afraid that much of his initial reluctance was born of a thoughtless approach— or at least an ill-considered one—by Lord Stewart, who set about things awkwardly and created an impression I found hard to overcome afterwards."

"How so, my lord?"

"Why, simply by being himself. The Lord High Steward of the realm is not—" He half smiled. "Let me say simply that Lord James is a courtier, unaccustomed to dealing with the kind of solid bluntness your cousin brings to all his dealings. And being somewhat ... isolated by his exalted status, he had no knowledge of William Wallace's scandalous and widely noted dislike of magnates in general."

"Oh dear. What did Will say to him?"

"It was what Lord James said to him, at the outset, that set the tone of what followed. The Steward and I had been discussing what we ought to do about Ormsby, since we bore the responsibility of being the last two Guardians remaining in the country, and we had gone in search of Wallace to petition his advice and enlist his support. We found him talking with the Earl of Carrick, and Lord James spoke up, flatteringly, about Wallace's prowess as a horseman."

"A horseman? Our Will? The Steward said that?"

"He did. Why would that surprise you?"

"Because I would never have thought to say such a thing," I said. "Will can ride, as can I, but I would never call either one of us a horseman. In fact Will thinks horses are a waste of time, because he's a bowman ahead of all else."

Wishart smiled. "That is almost precisely what your cousin said to Lord James. 'No, my lord,' he said quietly. 'I am no horseman. I am a longbowman—an archer. You cannot use a longbow on the back of a horse.'"

I nodded. "That's Will," I murmured, but the bishop was already moving on.

"I was regretting not having warned Lord James to let me do the talking," he said. "For he was completely unaware of the nature of the man with whom he was dealing and he kept on. 'But you can ride,' he said—a statement, you understand, not a question.

"I could see Will frowning, but I did not want to interrupt too quickly for fear of offending the Steward, so I held my peace. 'Aye, after a fashion,' Will said. 'Why does that interest you, my lord?'" The bishop sniffed suddenly and fumbled in his scrip for a kerchief, and I waited while he blew his nose noisily. "Now," he said afterwards, tucking the kerchief back where it belonged, "I've known your cousin long enough to be able to tell when he is unhappy, and I could see he did not like the way the Steward was talking to him, so I intervened and explained that we needed him to ride.

"'To where?' he said, glowering at me. 'And why?'

"'To Perth,' I told him, and I asked if he knew where that was. He didn't like that. He scowled at me, and there was no doubt in anyone's mind that he was feeling insulted.

"'Of course I know where Perth is,' he said. 'It's north of Stirling, and a long damned way from Selkirk Forest—a hundred miles, at least. Too far for me to want to go there.'

"'It's that far easily, Will,' I told him, and said that was why we needed him to ride there, and ride fast. I remember he turned to look at Bruce, who clearly was not going to be able to help, then back to me. 'Why me?' he asked. 'And why Perth, of all places? To what end? It sounds like madness.'"

The bishop sighed. "Of course, the way he was hearing it, it *was* madness, for until then he had heard no reason for such a thing. But you should have seen his face when I told him next that we needed him to raid it, as he'd raided Lanark." He looked down at the blackened embers of our fire. "I don't know what I had expected him to say next," he mused. "I hadn't really considered it before then. But all he did was grunt and shake his head. He knew nothing of Perth, he said. His men were forest outlaws. They had no horses— wouldn't know how to climb up on one, let alone ride such a distance. And that was when Lord James spoke up again. 'We are not speaking of your men, Master Wallace,' he said. 'Only of you yourself.'"

The bishop smiled suddenly. "I tell you, Father James, I was hard pressed not to laugh out loud, for if your cousin had been surprised when the Steward started talking about his horsemanship, he was utterly dumbfounded now. 'What?' says he, and I swear he was nigh gasping in disbelief. 'You want me to go alone and attack Perth town by myself?'

"Sadly, though, the Steward was not amused. 'Of course not,' he snapped. 'You will ride with Sir William Douglas and fifteen of his men, accompanied by a score more of my own Stewarts, all well armed and mounted on strong beasts. But we must move quickly.'

"Will stood up at that point and turned his back on Lord James to face me, and his expression was grim. 'Tell me, if you will, my lord bishop, what is so urgent, so far north, that it demands this kind of speed?'"

The bishop raised his hands in the air, as though to bless an absent congregation. "That, at least, I could tell him," he said. "I told him about William Ormsby and his mandate to extract an oath of *personal* loyalty and fealty to Edward. Will already knew the bare facts, but I explained how Ormsby was levying fines, in the form of seizure and forfeiture of goods and specie, as penalty for lateness in signing the oath. And how those who did not sign found the penalty was death and forfeiture of all possessions. Accountable to no one but Edward himself, I told him, Ormsby was playing God, hanging and jailing folk and spreading terror far and wide with his burning zealotry for England's ungodly cause. It was high time he was stopped, I said, for the good of the realm."

I was fascinated, because this was all new to me. I had heard bits and pieces of talk about the upheavals caused by the man Ormsby, but most of it had been rumour and hearsay, and before this moment I had heard nothing of any real substance about the justiciar's activities near Perth. Now, I felt myself growing angry after the fact.

"So how did Will react to that?" I asked.

His lordship grimaced. "He agreed with me that something needed to be done," he said. "He called Ormsby an unholy monster, and I confess I was glad to hear him say it, for to me that meant he was starting to see the need for what we were asking of him. But then the Steward spoke up again, just when I had least need of it. 'We have it on good authority,' says he, 'that the fellow has devastated the whole region around Perth, seizing livestock, coinage, goods of various kinds—anything of value on which he can lay his hands—claiming that all of it is owed in taxes to England, and that he is acting on behalf of the treasurer himself, Cressingham. The word we have is that the plunder he has amassed will be shipped south to Cressingham in Berwick, and thence to England within the fortnight.'"

"That must have captured Will's attention," I said.

"Oh, it did. Right away he asked if we knew what route the wagons would take."

"And did you?"

"No, but Lord James and I had talked about it at some length, just before that. There were five possible routes they could take, and three of those were open tracks over rough terrain, making the odds against waylaying them unacceptable. Besides, with the value of what they were transporting, we knew they would take great care to keep their movements secret and unpredictable, and the wagons would be heavily protected. That meant that the only way we could be sure of capturing the prize was to catch them in Perth before they could leave." He hesitated.

"And I presume he agreed with you, my lord?"

"No. As a matter of fact, he didn't. He heard what we were saying, he said, but why did we have to send *him*? Why not Douglas, or Bruce, with horsemen ready to ride?"

"Forgive me, my lord, but his question seems logical."

"Logical to you, perhaps, but not logical in any political sense—and politics was what we had to deal with there. The Steward spoke up again and explained that Perth is in the heart of Comyn country and no Bruce would be welcome there, especially when all the Comyn lords were locked up in English jails and Bruce was known to be beloved of England's King."

"But Bruce was there, was he not, my lord? Did that statement anger him?"

"No, he took no note of it. Besides, it was the truth. But he responded as though his name had not been mentioned. 'Wallace is right,' he said. 'He is an archer, best suited to standing erect among his peers and killing armoured men efficiently from great distances. Why send him all the way up there alone, and mounted on a horse?'

"That answer was mine to make, and no one else's." The bishop looked at me as though expecting me to contradict him, but I remained silent. "And so I jumped in with it before Lord James could say a word. 'Because we need his *name*,' I said, and both Bruce and Will stared at me in surprise. I said, 'We need William Wallace to be seen right there in Perth, taking the fight to Ormsby and delivering a public judgment and a punishment on behalf of all the folk of Scotland.'"

He stared at me for several moments, once again awaiting a reaction that did not occur, then grunted and wiped the palms of his hands down the length of his face. "You really are more like his twin than his cousin," he said mildly. "That was about the same reaction I got from Will."

"What?" I said. "You mean he disagreed?"

"No, more ignored me altogether. His thoughts had already jumped ahead. 'What about the treasure?' he asked me instead. 'Will we return it to its owners?'" The bishop shrugged. "What could I have said to him then? Would we return the treasure to its owners? It was not a question I had expected, Jamie—though I see now I should have—and so I had no answer ready for him. None that would have pleased him, anyway. As God is my witness, I had not even thought, at that point, about what we might do with it if we ever recaptured it, for finding it, let alone taking it, was the longest of long shots. But Will was looking me straight in the eye and I had no choice but to give him an answer. 'We can't,' I told him. 'Not right away. We will, eventually, when we have time and opportunity, but in the meantime we will have to hold it in trust for the people.'

"'Hah!' he roared in that great voice of his, leaping to his feet and putting the fear of God into all of us. 'In trust! And who will we *trust* to make sure it is kept safe? Who will we *trust* to keep it and hold it in good faith without dipping a single, greedy, needy finger into it? Who will stand forth in such sterling, imperishable honesty? Tell me that, my lords.'

"'We will,' I told him, though not with any great amount of confidence in the face of his doubt. I explained that the Church would safeguard the treasure in Glasgow, under lock and key in the cathedral vaults, under my own care. That quieted him, I'm glad to say. 'But we cannot simply return it, Will,' I pointed out again. 'Not easily, at least. No records have been kept of what it contains, because there has been no intent of returning any of it to its owners. That means it would take even longer to redistribute, even were we sure of who owned what. But by seizing it ourselves we will stop it from being shipped away to England, to swell Edward's coffers for his war in France.'"

I nodded. "A very reasonable, logical response, my lord," I said. "And how did Will react to it?"

My employer spoke through a smile. "I remember he grunted again," he said. "He was in a grunting frame of mind that day. 'Well,' he said after a while, 'the Earl of Carrick is right—you don't need me for that. Anyone can capture loaded wagons. And as for my name, I think you're wrong there, too. You don't need it, or me, because nobody up in that part of the world knows me. But if you think it's really necessary, then pick some big, rough fellow and have everyone call him Will Wallace while he's there in Perth. He'll serve your purpose up there just as well as I would.'

"Then and there I had to cut Lord James dead, for I could see he was angry, and it was plain to me that he was about to say something that would do none of us any good, so I waved him off, and he froze in astonishment." He chuckled. "It might well have been the first time in James Stewart's life that anyone had dared to silence him. 'Pardon me, my Lord High Steward,' says I, before he can even close his mouth, 'but I need to speak to this.'

"Of course, as you can imagine, after that everyone was waiting to hear what I had to say. 'Will Wallace,' I said in Scots—for we had been talking Latin to that point—'you and I hae known each other for a lang time now. In a' thae years, have I ever asked you for aught that made you uncomfortable, or caused you any real concern?'

"'No, Bishop,' says he, 'you never have.'

"'Then I willna start now,' says I. 'I need you to go to Perth, Will. *Scotland* needs you to go to Perth.' I saw him start to glower again and held up my hand. 'Wait now, before you say anything. I swear to you, I wouldna ask this if I didna believe it was necessary. Your name has ta'en on a new significance to folk since your foray into Lanark. And you were gey well kent afore that, for a' the reasons ye're well aware o'. Ye've become a leader now, and folk dinna think o' ye as plain Will Wallace these days. Ye're *William* Wallace now, whether ye like it or no', and ye'll be William Wallace frae now on. And the word out there is that ye've laid down your bow and picked up a sword—the biggest sword in a' the land.' I could see the sword at his back, propped hilt-upright where he'd left it in a corner by the fire. 'And there it sits,' says I, pointing at it. 'The very blade. There's no' another like it that I know of in Scotland. And for that reason if nae other, folk everywhere are talkin' about it now, and talkin' about you as the man who wields it in their cause.' He didn't like that, I could see, for he's not the kind of man who cares for flattery, but flattery was the furthest thing from my mind at that moment. 'Dinna look so fierce, man,' I told him. 'I'm no' tryin' to fash you. I speak but the plain truth, and in that same spirit o' truth I am telling you that Scotland—this country an' its folk—needs a leader like you here in the south. There are others in the far west and the northeast, young Andrew Murray foremost amang them, but there's only you, Wallace, in these parts. And these parts, a' the way up frae Berwick on the border, to Perth and Scone and includin' Stirlin' and Edinburgh, are the parts bein' hardest hit by Cressingham's tax collectors and that godless creature Ormsby.' I could not tell what he was thinking and so I charged on as though I was running in a race. 'And so I'm asking you,' I said, 'as your bishop, as your auld friend, and as your troubled countryman, to lend your name and your repute to stopping Ormsby while he is yet in Perth. Will ye do it?'"

The bishop sniffed. "I swear to you, Jamie," he said, "that was the longest silence I've ever had to endure, but I didn't dare to break it. It was so quiet I could hear a knot of resin spluttering in a burning log in the grate. And all the while Will stood frowning into space, seeing nothing but what was in his mind. And just as I was beginning to grow desperate, he looked at each one of us in turn, from Bruce to the Steward and finally to me, and then he stepped to the fireplace, picked up his sword one-handed, and brought it close to his eyes, peering at the cross formed by the junction of hilt and quillons. Then he lowered the point to the floor and swung around to face us. 'I'll go,' he growled to me. 'When will we leave?'

"I swear, Father James, I felt at that moment as though something had burst inside me. The relief I felt was so overwhelming that I was afraid I might fall down. I looked to the Steward for confirmation, and when he nodded I said, 'Daybreak tomorrow. Douglas is making the arrangements as we speak, and he'll be glad to know you're joining him.' They would make a mounted party of fifty, I told him—two and a half score. Seventeen Douglas men-at-arms under le Hardi himself, and a score and a half of Stewarts under Sir John.

"'Who will command overall?' he asked.

"'You will,' I said. 'This will be your raid.'

"He was to move quickly and in secrecy, I explained, insofar as secrecy was possible, keeping to the open country and avoiding contact with anyone else. Some of my own priests had mapped out a route that would allow them to travel north unnoticed by the English. 'But if they should see you,' I told him, 'don't stop to fight. Press on and make for Perth, and if you can, bring Ormsby's plundered treasure back here with you.' The weather had broken, so we were hoping for fifteen to twenty miles a day, putting them in Perth within the week.

"'I'll send my men back, then, to the forest?' he asked me.

"'Aye,' I told him. 'They'll be better off there than here.'

"'Fine,' he said, 'I'll see to it.'"

"And so Will rode to Perth," I said. "Thank you, my lord, for taking the time to tell me that tale. It means much to me, and now I understand why I did not understand before. But ... they failed to capture Ormsby."

The bishop shook his head. "That was no failure. He was forewarned of their arrival and escaped ahead of them. But capturing Ormsby was never in the plans. It was his plunder we were after—taxes, according to England, but plunder by any honest man's description."

"And how was he forewarned?"

"I'm told Will and Douglas's men met a force of mounted English archers unexpectedly, close to Perth itself, and in the skirmish some of them escaped into Perth and raised the alarm. Ormsby surrounded himself with a bodyguard and fled."

"And Will made no attempt to catch him?"

His lordship shrugged. "I doubt Will even knew which way he went. He had more important matters on his hands at that time: capturing the baggage train and making sure the English garrison was isolated and disarmed."

"How big was the garrison?"

"A hundred men, give or take a half score, according to your cousin."

"And what happened to them?"

"Will gave them into the keeping of Sir William Douglas, who stripped them of every weapon and piece of armour they wore and marched them back south under close guard until they reached England, where he ordered his lieutenants to strip them again, naked this time, and set them free to make their way home."

"To fight us again, in the future ..."

The bishop looked at me askance. "What would you have done differently, Father? That is the way of warfare. We could not imprison them, and God knows we could not murder them. We had no choice but to release them."

I nodded reluctantly, aware that he was right. "And what did Will do, after he relinquished the prisoners to Lord Douglas?"

"He spent some time among the burgesses of Perth, letting himself be known and seen as I had instructed him, and then he rode back here, directly."

He met my gaze squarely and I nodded. "As you had instructed him … So William Wallace is your agent nowadays."

I almost expected him to grow angry at that, but he answered without raising his voice. "No," he said. "You know better than to say that. William Wallace is not the kind of man that any other man may safely or conveniently use to his own ends." He stopped and smiled. "And I have just realized I was wrong in what I told your cousin that day. He may be forever *William* Wallace, but most folk speak of him simply as Wallace now, as though that were his single given name. He has become an agent of destiny—of history, if you like. He has outgrown ordinary folk like you and me, I think, and my master in Heaven has taken him under His guard. I now believe, with all my heart, that your cousin Will belongs, in the truest, grandest sense, to this land of ours, this Scotland."

It was the first time I had ever heard my cousin spoken of as a man who was larger than life and greater than the common run of men. That comment from Bishop Wishart was my first glimpse of what God had in mind for my cousin William Wallace; the first hint of the fame and fortune that would raise him up to glory, for a time at least, in the eyes of all who fought with him and all who knew him.

"You look gravely concerned, Father," the bishop said. "What are you thinking?"

"About Will, my lord, is all," I said. "I feel great need to see him. To ask for his forgiveness."

"His forgiveness?" That idea brought a furrow to his lordship's brow. "For what do you need forgiveness?"

"For Mirren's death. She was in my care when she was taken."

"That may be." The tiny frown was still in place. "But there was not a thing you could have done to change anything that happened that day, Father James. It was the will of God, else it would not have come to pass, and for any mere man to feel guilt in such case is to come close to hubris."

"I know that, Your Grace," I replied, hearing the misery in my own voice. "At least, my head and my heart know it, but a part of me feels guilty nonetheless." I waited for the acknowledgment I knew would come, and when he nodded I lapsed into silence, feeling, above all, helpless. But there was one aspect of my life, at least, in which I felt I could still make a useful contribution. "May I presume, my lord, that you will continue to have a need for my secretarial services?"

"Your *secretarial* services?" His jaw dropped. "Good God, man," he said in plain Scots, "I hae a glut o' *secretaries*. A chapter *full* o' them! I canna turn around wi'out trippin' ower one. Why would I need anither? No, Jamie, I hae nae need of you for that, and I'm surprised you think I would."

I was hoping that my face did not reflect the extent to which his answer had shaken me.

"No, Father James," he continued in his usual churchly Latin, "I need you for your mind and your insights. For your long head and your gift for reading men and seeing what lies beneath their smiles and posturings. And to that end I have been sitting here awaiting you these three days, impatient to put you to work."

If his first words had almost overwhelmed me with something akin to terror, my reaction to this last swung me almost as hard in the opposite direction. "To work on what, my lord?" I asked, making every effort to sound calm.

"On whom, not what. Young Bruce, the Earl of Carrick, first and foremost."

"The Earl of Carrick? But not an hour ago you said you believe him to be his own man. I took that to mean you now approve of him."

"Aye, and so it did, when I said it." He had switched back into Scots, as he usually did in order to deprecate himself and his opinions in front of others. "So it did. But I jalouse I might yet change my mind once I've heard your take on the chiel. I hae been wrong a wheen o' times afore now, bishop though I be, an' so I hae nae great expectations o' bein' right a' the time."

I smiled, but kept my response in Latin. "Nothing much to fret over there, my lord. I will meet and speak with the earl as soon as I can arrange it. Is he approachable, or does he hold himself aloof?"

"Och, he's easy enough to talk to." My employer had no intention of being shepherded anywhere, even in matters of language. "Ye'll hae nae difficulty there. It's what ye'll see when you look ahint the surface o' the man that I'll be waiting to hear about. I dinna expect you to find any grim secrets under there, but some men hae great talents when it comes to hidin' things about themsel's, an' sometimes the last thing ye can do is tell that frae lookin' at their faces or listenin' to what they say. But that's what you're best at, seein' what's there under the surface, where maist men canna see."

"How old is the earl, my lord?"

"He's about an age wi' you, I'd say. Mayhap a wee bit younger. You're what now? Five and twenty? Aye, well, he'd hae been three and twenty in July. The two o' ye will get along fine, ye'll see."

He peered up at the sky, where most of the blue had been obscured by banked clouds. "It looks like rain," he said. "And Father Martin will be thinking by now that we've abandoned him. We'd best stir our stumps and be awa, for it's still a good two hours frae here to Turnberry." He stood up and reached down to gather up his bag and walking staff.

"One more question if I may, my lord, before we go? It has to do with the English force you mentioned,

Percy's people. I have never met Lord Douglas and know nothing of him other than by repute, but he is a known troublemaker of notoriously ill repute, not only to the English but even here in Scotland. He has been a chronic source of irritation and dispute to the Council of Guardians for as long as I can remember, and you yourself are acutely aware of that. So the fact that he is here now, siding openly with you and enjoying the support of the last two remaining Guardians in Scotland, will not go unnoticed by the English commanders."

The gravity of my remark tipped the bishop back into Latin. "We will deal with that when it arises, Father. If it ever does. It is my duty to care for my flock, especially when they are troubled. Sir William Douglas is a troubled man and I will minister to him as I would to any other in my care. And that is a matter between me and the God to whom I must answer. It has nothing to do with Henry Percy or his masters, and I will not be dictated to by any Englishman in the performance of my pastoral duty."

There was nothing I could say in response to such equanimity, and so I set about gathering up my own few belongings in preparation for the last stage of our journey to Turnberry.

CHAPTER NINE

INSURGENCY

Turnberry Castle overwhelmed me when I first set eyes on it, and I would have stopped right there at the forest's edge to examine the place more carefully, but Bishop Wishart had seen the view before and it held no mystery for him, and so he kept walking directly towards the drawbridge, and I had to hurry to keep up. Turnberry was a massive fortification built of local stone and situated on a rock promontory that thrust out into the Firth of Clyde, with the Isle of Arran in the distance and beyond that the indistinct shoreline of the Mull of Kintyre. The side of the castle that we approached was a high, unbroken wall penetrated by a single central entrance tunnel reached only by crossing a drawbridge over a wide, steep-sided moat. I saw a strong-looking, circular tower with a pointed roof at the northeast corner, and opposite that, at the southwest corner, I could see the roof of a lower but more substantial-seeming tower, which I assumed to be the keep, housing the Bruce family.

We had to wait for the portcullis to be raised, even though the guards had clearly been expecting us and allowed us to pass without comment. The portcullis was enormously heavy, and its lower edge was lined with lethal, keen-edged spikes, yet it rose smoothly and almost noiselessly to allow us to pass beyond it to the bailey, the open space inside the curtain walls. We followed meekly as his lordship led us through the yard, between and around the various buildings that well nigh filled the place, until we came to the keep. There, the first of what turned out to be a small army of supplicants came running to claim the bishop's attention.

I gazed around while the bishop dealt with the most urgent matters being thrust at him, and I noted most of the facilities to be found in castles everywhere. I saw a cooperage and a carpentry shop, as well as several smithies, a bakery with rows of outdoor ovens, a number of granaries, an ox-powered mill, and even a brewery. There was a leather tannery, too, and a fuller's pond farther away, for though I could see no sign of either one, my nostrils told me they were both close at hand. I was still taking stock of our surroundings when his lordship called us to his side and informed us that Lord Bruce had gone hunting but was expected to return soon, and in the meantime someone would show us to our quarters. The bishop himself had several pressing matters to attend to.

As soon as we were inside our quarters—a long, narrow room containing eight cots and little else— Martin dropped to the hard surface of the bed he had selected and closed his eyes, and something about the beatific smile on his face told me he would not easily rise up again. I made my way back to the bailey yard to continue my exploration of the castle, where I found myself largely ignored by the locals, all of whom appeared to have a great amount of work to do and very little time in which to do it. While everyone around me bustled busily, I meandered aimlessly.

I recognized a familiar noise that had been growing gradually louder as I walked, and I quickly found its source, a large enclosure in an angle of the curtain wall that was obviously set aside as a training area. Two men were fighting there with quarterstaves, watched by a small group of spectators who were shouting and jeering at both men in that manner that marked them all as friends. By the time I arrived they had been going hard at each other for some time. Both were big, tall men, one of them even bigger, it seemed to me, than my cousin Will, and they looked even larger than they normally would because they were wearing practice armour made of pads of densely felted wool strapped over boiled and hammered bull-hide coverings for their arms, legs, and torsos, while their heads were protected by large, heavy-looking war helms.

No one paid me the slightest attention as I made my way towards the fighters, and the moment I sat on one of the upended sections of log that served as seats for spectators, someone among the watchers yelled, "Go on, Rob! Into him!" and both fighters redoubled their efforts, so that the whirling staves were barely visible at times, and the breathing of the combatants became louder and more ragged.

The larger man feinted a high blow to his right, then changed direction in mid-thrust and whipped his staff down and around to the left, checked it, and pivoted tightly, slashing backwards with a short, savage jab that the other man could not counter quickly enough. The blow landed solidly beneath the fellow's sternum, driving the wind out of him in an explosive gasp, and he dropped his quarterstaff as he staggered backwards for two steps, then fell to his knees and pitched forward onto his face to lie gasping and whooping for breath within three paces of where I sat watching.

The spectators and the victor were already celebrating and exchanging wagers, paying little attention to the downed man, since he was no more than winded, but I stood up and moved quickly to help him because I knew, from experience, precisely what he was feeling. Will had once downed me the same way, with an identical sleight, driving the wind from me with a crippling, well-aimed jab, and I had never forgotten the pain and the surging panic of not being able to draw a breath. I bent over the man, seeing how he was convulsing but unable to turn his body because of the constrictive bulk of his padded armour. I flipped him over to lie on his side, and he immediately curled into a ball, whooping and cawing in agony. I left him to it, knowing he would soon recover, and went to pick up his fallen quarterstaff.

The staff was a plain, unadorned thing of dried and hardened ash wood, virtually identical in weight and thickness to the one that had been mine a decade earlier, when I still sparred with Will. In recent times

I had seen more elaborate staves, some crowned with metal to make them even more lethal than nature had intended. I had even seen some that were longer and heavier than this. One of those, I recalled, had been more than six feet in length, and I had wondered at the time why its owner should have felt he needed anything that long, because the added length, to my eyes, made the weapon cumbersome and unwieldy. But swords and metal weapons had been hard to come by in Scotland since Edward had confiscated all the weapons lost at Dunbar, and many men had reverted to the comforting heft of a solid, well-cured quarterstaff, metal-shod or not. I hefted this one myself, gripping it with the ease of long familiarity, and swung it tentatively, left and right, before gliding into the traditional, rhythmical pattern of disciplined exercises basic to the use of the weapon. I ended by twirling it vertically in what had once been one of my favourite moves, with my arm outstretched to bring the weapon's butt end up to slap gently and comfortably into my waiting right armpit.

"Now that is impressive. Where would a priest learn to do that?"

The voice snapped me back to awareness of where I was, and I swung about to find the fallen warrior sitting up and looking at me, his spread elbows resting on his upraised knees and his face invisible behind the cheek guards of his helmet.

"I wasn't always a priest," I said, extending my hand to pull him to his feet.

He swung himself up smoothly and released my hand. "Who are you?" he asked, his voice muffled by the helmet.

I lay his quarterstaff against one of the nearby seats. "Father James Wallace, of Glasgow Cathedral."

"Wallace? Are you any kind of kin to the outlaw?"

"He's my cousin," I said. "But I'm a priest, as you can see, not an outlaw. I'm here with Bishop Wishart, to meet with Lord Bruce."

The metal-covered head tilted towards me. "Lord Bruce of Annandale?"

"No, the Earl of Carrick."

"Ah! They're father and son, you know."

"I did know that," I said.

"Good, then. Help me off with this damned helm, will you?" He had been tugging uselessly at the thing for several moments but it was showing no sign of movement, and now he bent towards me, pushing against its lower rim. I grasped the crown and heaved twice before I finally pulled the helmet off his head.

"Ah! Thanks be to Christ," he said, blithely uncaring of taking the name of the Lord in vain. "There's so much padding in that thing, I come close to suffocating every time I put it on. And there are times it feels so tight I doubt I'm going to get it on at all." He spun the helm in the air and held it towards me for my inspection, showing me that its interior was, indeed, very tightly padded. He was young and pleasant looking, one of those men at whom it was easy to smile.

"You should probably be grateful for that," I said, "because the stuff looks thick enough to serve its purpose. Had that big fellow hit you on the head, you probably wouldn't have come back together as quickly as you did, even with all that padding. That's a big man. Who is he?"

"Our Rob?" He swivelled around and looked across to where his former opponent stood watching us among the other men, and raised a hand in salute. "Rob is the biggest instigator of fights and the greediest manipulator of wagers in Turnberry. He's Sir Robert Mowbray, and he's our master-at-arms."

"Ah," I said. "I heard someone call him Rob, and so I thought he might be Bruce, but then it came to me that here in Bruce country there might be no name more common than Robert."

"And right you are. We have no shortage of Robs and Roberts and even Rabs around here. I'm one myself."

"And what about the others? They must be knights, too, judging by the ease with which they speak to him."

"They are, and two of them are Roberts, too. All knights of the Bruce household, as am I." He grinned at me then. "So, what think you of Turnberry?"

I turned to look up at the lofty tower on the far side of the courtyard. "It is … impressive," I said. "That's the word that keeps occurring to me. I had some time to fill before I meet again with Bishop Robert—"

"There, you see? Another Robert. They swarm like rats around here."

"Aye, well, as I said, I had some time on my hands and so I decided just to take a look around the castle. I was not expecting anything so grand."

One eyebrow rose slightly. "Grand? How, grand?"

"How not? For one thing, I doubt I have ever seen anything quite as well made as that portcullis at the entry."

"Hah! If you think *that* portcullis is grand, you really must go down and see the other one. Now *there* is a portcullis on the epic scale."

"You mean there are two?"

"I do. One at the front and one at the back, over there, facing seaward." He pointed towards the south wall. "Just follow the main track through that arch over there and you won't go far wrong. And now I'll leave you to yourself again, because I need to get out of this damnable armour before I melt like a candle in the sun." He raised a hand in salute and walked away to join the others, who had clearly been waiting for him, since they all trooped off together, laughing and bantering.

If I had been impressed before, the remainder of what I saw that afternoon left me with a feeling of awe approaching reverence, for I had never seen anything to compare, even remotely, with Turnberry. The high, square tower I had guessed at earlier as the probable Bruce family quarters rose behind me to my left, but another rectangular tower filled one entire corner of the fortification, and it was far bigger than the one at my back. I followed the main roadway, which sloped gradually downwards deep into the dim bowels of the huge building.

There were noises in the air all around me now, and the heights of the ceiling over my head were lost in darkness, but I was nevertheless stunned when I realized that I had entered a huge cavern, that I was listening to the unmistakable sounds of water, and that the strange shape I could see moving ahead of me was the mast of a large, oared galley. I went forward slowly, my eyes growing larger with every moment that passed, and came to a point where I could look down and see the entire vista below me. The galley was huge, its sides lined with oarlocks, thirty to a side. It was unmanned and unguarded, safe behind a huge portcullis, and it floated peacefully alongside a man-made stone jetty that must have stretched for thirty, perhaps even forty paces on either side. Above and beyond me soared the sea gate, with its lowered portcullis vanishing beneath the waters.

I had admired the portcullis we had entered under, but this leviathan construction must have been three times the width and four times the height, with pairs of immensely strong-looking ropes attached to its top at either end, each rope the thickness of a grown man's calf. I could do nothing but gape at it in wonder.

I heard a sudden sound close behind me, and I swung around to find my injured companion from earlier watching me. "Forgive me," I said. "You startled me."

He grinned. "So, are you impressed?"

"I am. And I am amazed, too. I've never seen anything like it. And where did the galley come from, do you know?"

"It came from Bute, yesterday. That's the island just up the firth from here. It is an astounding place, I agree. How old it is, I have no idea. It's been in the Bruce family for years. It's a mormaer stronghold." He hesitated. "D'you know what that means?"

"Aye," I said. "The old Gaelic nobility."

"That's right. The ancient Earls of Carrick were all Islanders. Seafarers. And it was they who built all of this, a long time ago."

He was greatly changed from the young knight I had encountered earlier. All of his fustian and felt padding had disappeared, along with the dust and mustiness that went with it, and a very striking man had emerged, tall and well made, with broad shoulders and a narrow waist. His shoulder-length dark hair had been brushed, and I noticed his eyes for the first time, dark blue and sparkling above wide, high cheekbones. He was close to my own age, nobly born, beyond dispute, and clearly very wealthy. He wore a floor-length coat of rich, dark blue brocade with a filigreed yoke of silver wire woven across the shoulders, and a trailing length of bright yellow silk hung down his back on one side, pinned at his left shoulder with a broad, circular clasp of worked silver. A black belt of supple leather circled his waist, with a long-bladed, sheathed dagger hanging on one side and a black leather scrip on the other, and his feet were encased in finely worked boots of what looked like black kid skin.

"I know your name is Robert," I said to him, "and that you are a knight, but that's all I know. So who are you, exactly?"

He bowed from the waist, quickly and self-disparagingly, though that interpretation did not occur to me until long afterwards. "I'm Robert Bruce, Earl of Carrick, but don't let that confound you. I would have told you when you spoke of being here to meet Lord Bruce, but I saw you had no notion who I was and I had no wish to embarrass you." He held up a warning hand. "No, don't say it. You're here, and you're a guest in my house, and I enjoyed meeting you. You'll be having dinner with us, so you can call me Lord Carrick when we meet again. In the meantime, when there's but the two of us, please call me Rob. Now come and walk with me and I'll show you the quickest way of finding your bishop."

I spent the remaining few hours of that late afternoon and much of the evening looking forward to spending more time with the young Earl of Carrick at dinner, and so I was greatly surprised to find I had little time for him that night. I had liked him from the moment of first speaking with him, and had sensed that the amity I felt was mutual, but from the very start of the evening, when the guests began to assemble, the flamboyant and personable young man, despite his proprietorial right to preside there, was quite simply eclipsed by the effulgence of two of the others present.

The first of these, James Stewart, the fifth hereditary Steward of Scotland, was the personification of most people's idea of a great lord. Tall, broad-shouldered, richly dressed, freshly bathed and barbered, and subtly, delicately scented, he radiated both authority and amiability—seldom an easy mixture to achieve in any company. He also enjoyed an ability to put awkward, tongue-tied strangers at ease in his august presence, and I watched in admiration as he set out, effortlessly and with convincing sincerity, to make even the least of his table companions feel more comfortable, encouraging them, without ever appearing to do so, to overcome their natural awe and reluctance at sitting down to dine with him.

He must have been about forty years old, and there was something exotic about him—a hint of foreignness despite the fact that his family had never left Scotland since arriving there from France some two hundred years earlier. And then it came to me that he resembled someone I had once met, a bishop from the Basque kingdom of Navarre, who had visited us in Glasgow a few years earlier. He had been sent to Scotland on a diplomatic mission, to entreat King John's assistance in the war against the Moors who threatened to overrun the Iberian peninsula, and he was the only Spaniard I had ever seen—though when I said so to him he grew offended, insisting that he was a Basque, possessed of a proud, pre-Roman heritage that precluded any possibility of his being Spanish.

I could see the Navarrese bishop clearly in my mind, and he had had the same physical attributes as the striking Scots magnate across from me. James Stewart was as dark skinned and *different* looking as the Basque bishop had been, with a long, narrow face framed by straight, perfectly coiffed dark hair and neatly trimmed beard and moustaches. Large, dark, expressive eyes gazed straightforwardly at the world, and the teeth that gleamed frequently in his smiling mouth suggested strength of character and quiet determination. He was soft-spoken in that way of strong men who know they have no need to raise their voice, and his entire bearing exuded self-assurance and the great confidence of being high-born and wealthy beyond the ken of ordinary men.

This was not the first time I had seen Sir James, of course. He was the Stewart, the chief of all his namesakes, liege lord to all us Wallaces as had been his father before him, and even the Noble Robert, the Earl of Carrick's grandsire and former Lord of Annandale, had bowed the knee in fealty and service to him and to his father before him. This was, however, the first occasion on which I had sat at table with the great man, and it was also the first time I had had the pleasure of being able to watch him at my leisure without appearing to be ill-mannered or impertinent.

There were fourteen people present, and although I did not realize it for some time, being newly arrived and abysmally ignorant of recent developments while I had lain convalescing, the occasion was a meeting of some of the principal figures directing the general uprising that was on the point of erupting throughout Scotland that summer of 1297. The gathering was held in the great hall of Castle Turnberry, which had been partitioned to fashion a room a quarter of its size, and the attendees, myself among them, were arranged casually along the outer rim of a grouping of tables that formed three sides of a rectangle, the open side permitting access for the serving staff.

The Earl of Carrick presided at the meal as nominal host, since Turnberry was his even though he had been away from it for years, and he was flanked by the Steward on his right and Bishop Wishart, the mastermind behind what I was coming to think of as the general insurrection, on his left. The fourth place at the head table, on Wishart's left, was occupied by Sir William Douglas, the Hardy as he was known, a dark-faced, glowering man who spoke little and frowned constantly.

The remaining diners sat at the two flanking tables and consisted of five clerics and five knights. The man on my right, closest to the head table, was Alpin of Strathearn, the recently consecrated Bishop of Dunblane. I knew him well by repute, though I had never set eyes on him until that day, and I knew that Bishop Wishart held him in high regard. I also knew that he had only recently returned to Scotland to take up his episcopal duties and was therefore one of the few Scottish bishops who had been able to avoid swearing fealty to Edward the previous year. He had been in Rome, being consecrated as bishop, when John Balliol was robbed of his kingship and the land first felt the weight of Edward's iron-shod heel. I spoke with him several times in the course of that dinner—he was hugely intelligent and immensely likeable—but I never saw him again after that day.

The three remaining clerics in attendance were priests—Father Vincent, who had been chaplain at Turnberry since the time of Countess Marjorie, the earl's mother, Father Martin, and another newcomer to Turnberry like myself, who, I quickly discovered, was renowned and far more accomplished in all manner of things than I would ever be. His name was Father David de Moravia, and until very recently he had been the pastor of the rich estates of Bothwell, which were owned and administered by his first cousin, William de Moravia, a magnate so wealthy that he was commonly spoken of as William le Riche. I had met the priest briefly on my arrival and liked him immediately, for although he had been introduced to me as Father de Moravia, he had quickly waved the name away as though sweeping it behind him. "Call me Davie," he said quietly, adding with a wink, "Plain Davie Murray, but Father in front o' the servants and the high mucky-mucks." He was a tallish, brisk-looking fellow, heavily muscled, with an open, friendly face and an easy, engaging smile. Had I met him under different circumstances I would have taken him for a soldier far more readily than I might have a priest. Priest he was, though, and, as Bishop Wishart had quietly observed to me, his living in Bothwell was one of the wealthiest in Scotland. But he was also a lively and amusing companion, with much to say on a wide range of topics, and I felt sure he and I were destined to become close friends.

Across from us, at the facing table, sat five knights, two of whom were followers of Sir William Douglas and were, like their employer, dour, taciturn, and generally unfriendly. The other three, however, were of greatly different stuff, and one of them, to my utter astonishment, turned out to be related to me.

When Will and I had first arrived in Elderslie, more than a decade earlier, Malcolm Wallace, the eldest son and namesake of my boyhood benefactor, Sir Malcolm Wallace of Elderslie, had been a squire, and would later become a knight in the service of Lord Robert Bruce of Annandale. Years later, after Lord Bruce's withdrawal from public life and his departure to England, Sir Malcolm had transferred his allegiance to Lord James Stewart. He was four years older than me, and though I had, of course, known all about him since the age of ten, he and I had never met each other. A four-year difference in age is a far wider gap during boyhood, of course, than at any other time in life, and our differing duties and responsibilities while growing up and working had kept us far apart. He knew me as well as I knew him, of course, and so our first meeting, unexpected as it was to both of us, was amiable and mutually cordial, even while we had nothing in common beyond shared blood.

Senior as he undoubtedly was by then in Lord James's retinue, however, Sir Malcolm was by no means the senior of the group at his table. That status was held by Sir John Stewart, who sat to Malcolm's right and was the Steward's younger brother, renowned as something of a hothead but generally acknowledged to be brave, chivalrous, and loyal and honest in his friendships. He, too, I had liked instinctively on first meeting. Beside him sat another young knight who, like me, had met the Earl of Carrick for the first time that day. He was Sir Alexander Lindsay, another liegeman to Lord James.

Thus we were a small party, and because of that the conversation was much more general and far more equally shared than would have been the case otherwise. Everyone listened openly to what was being said at the head table, and aware of that overt attention, Bishop Wishart and the Steward responded graciously, speaking out more loudly and more frankly than they might have in other circumstances. While his companions addressed themselves to their listeners in general, speaking candidly about the events of the previous weeks and the forthcoming arrival of the English force under Henry Percy and Robert Clifford, Sir William Douglas, to no one's surprise, said nothing. He merely scowled ferociously and incessantly, fulfilling everyone's expectations of him.

To that point at least, the Steward remarked, no

physical contact had been reported between the approaching English and any of the militant bands of Scots that were roaming the countryside. That led one of Douglas's two adherents, a knight called Thomas of Lariston, to ask the Steward what had become of Wallace, claiming that no one seemed to have seen or heard of the former forester since his return from the raid on Perth. It was the bishop who answered him, though, after a single, swift glance at Lord James. In a low, clear voice he explained that Wallace had returned to Selkirk Forest and his people there, where he was busy training the hundreds of new followers he had attracted to him in the aftermath of the Perth escapade. Wallace would be ready, the bishop said, when next Scotland had need of him, but as to when that might be, he would say no more than that it would be soon and that it greatly depended on the behaviour of the approaching English army.

"Are we to fight, then?" Lariston's question was truculent, but the bishop demurred, glancing towards the Steward before responding.

"We have talked much on that," he said noncommittally, "and our feeling is that the time is not yet right for fighting. We will not surrender, though, nor will we disband our army and scuttle meekly to our homes to disappear."

The surly questioner was unimpressed. "So, gin we dinna fight, and we winna quit the field, what's to be done? Your Englishry winna thole that, us shufflin' aboot like folk that hae lost their wits."

"We will talk, negotiate."

Lariston scoffed. "Negotiate? Wi' yon crew? Ye'll hae high hopes, I jalouse. I dinna ken who this Clifford is, nor where he bides, but I've heard much o' this other yin, this Percy, an' ye'll no' get him to gie up, meek an' mild, an' walk awa."

"I think we might, Lariston. I know Percy." There came a deathly silence as every eye in the room turned on the Earl of Carrick. He sniffed the air, as though detecting the evident skepticism and hostility, and then smiled tentatively, the tips of his ears growing red in the only sign of discomfiture he betrayed. "Henry Percy and I have been friends for years," he continued. "Close friends, I can say with confidence. We trained for knighthood together in more settled times, as joint protégés of King Edward. He is a good man, Percy— hard-headed, stubborn in his beliefs, but just and reasonable nonetheless. I will talk with him."

"Hmm." Lariston's voice dripped sarcasm. "Be sure ye tak a long spoon wi' ye, gin ye dine wi' the Auld Beast."

Bruce merely looked back at him, one eyebrow quirked slightly, and the youngest knight, Sir Alexander Lindsay, changed the subject smoothly.

"To what ends will you negotiate with them, my lord bishop?"

The bishop shrugged. "To the ends of time," he replied, and smiled broadly. "Time being all-important at this point, ye'll understand. We'll keep our army in the field for as long as we may, holding the English in debate over our terms, and every day we can debate will allow time for our allies in the north and the midlands to broaden their activities against the English." He held up a hand. "And before you ask who our allies are, I'll tell you they are many. MacDuff, the Earl of Fife, has roused his people on the east coast, and here in the south and centre we have Wallace and his army—"

"*Army?*" Lariston spat out the word as he sneered at the head table. "Wallace has nae *army*, my lords. *Percy* has an *army*—knights and mounted men-at-arms supported wi' archers and siege artillery and trained, well-equipped infantry. We here dinna hae an army that could face them. Wallace has a rabble o' thieves and outlaws like himsel' and nary a hope o' fieldin' any o' them against a well-trained army."

Lord James raised a single finger, as though seeking permission to speak, and when the silence that followed had become profound, he asked mildly, "Tell me something, Sir Thomas, if you will. Why is it, think you, that William Wallace, single-handedly, has been the only man in all this region of Scotland to win any kind of substantial success against the English?"

He waited, watching as angry colour flooded Lariston's face. "Can you answer the question? No? Then I shall tell you. It is because the fellow is a natural, inspiring leader whose men—that rabble of thieves and outlaws, as you so aptly name them—will follow him gladly wheresoever he chooses to lead them. That willingness of theirs—that blind trust, if you will—stems from one simple, fundamental truth: they believe he offers them something that none of us here, the magnates and knights and nobles in this room, ever has."

The High Steward paused, allowing that thought to settle. "The folk who follow Wallace so loyally regard him as a commoner, like them, but *we* know—much as some of us may dislike it—that he is rather one of us, bred of knightly stock. But Wallace offers them something of which we have never considered them worthy or deserving: basic dignity and the right to fight, as free men, for themselves and their families."

He paused again, then repeated his last point. "For *themselves*, Sir Thomas. Not for their liege lords or the magnate who owns and controls the land on which they live. For themselves, the folk of Scotland. Now I know that *sounds* appalling—treasonous and threatening. I am completely aware of that. We in this room are bound to find that idea offensive, for at first sight it threatens our privilege and everything we stand for. But I, for one, after long hours and weeks of discussion of this very point with Bishop Wishart here and several of his colleagues, as well as others of my own rank and station, have come to believe that there is no such threat. There is a *seeming* threat, but no real peril, I am convinced, in according common men the respect they earn and deserve. And for men like those who follow William Wallace, such consideration is a gift beyond price. And in return for that consideration—something new and unthinkable to folk like us—they will follow Wallace into Hell itself."

Lord James produced a kerchief from his sleeve and wiped something fastidiously from the corner of his left eye. He peered at the kerchief, inspecting the result, then tucked the cloth back whence it had come. "So sneer at him and his followers if you will, Lariston, from the eminence of your knighthood, but he has put more fear into the English this past half year, and more defiance and spirit into his *rabble*, than all of us assembled here have been able to achieve together."

Lariston sat wordless, his face flushed and sullen.

The Steward cleared his throat. "I would ask you, Sir Thomas, to consider the alternatives to the negotiation his lordship proposes. There are two, as I perceive things, the first being merely to disband our army at once and melt away into the hillside mists as though we had never been here. We *have* been here, though, and with an assembled army, and that has caused Percy and his expedition to be sent against us. I suggest to you we would be foolish to hope that, finding us dispersed, Percy would return to his royal master and report that all is well in Scotland.

"The second alternative open to us if we do not negotiate is to fight, and that is precisely why we will negotiate. We will talk and hold our army ready for as long as we may, because those of us whose charge it is to know such things know that we face an absolute certainty: if we confront Percy in war today, or next week or next month, and come to battle with them as things stand, we will be destroyed."

His eyes moved from face to face among his listeners. "We will be slaughtered because we have no hope of prevailing. Because we lack the horseflesh that the English have in such abundance. Because we lack the armour and fine weaponry that the English have in such abundance. Because we lack the manpower that the English have in such abundance. Because we lack the trained longbow archers that the English have in such abundance. Because we lack the hundreds of thousands of fresh-made, long-shafted arrows that the English produce systematically, as required by law, and so have in such abundance."

He leaned back in his chair. "And believe me when I tell you, Lariston, that those reasons are but the first few of the dozens that swarm in my mind as a Guardian of this realm and the commander of our Scots forces. What you said about our army earlier is correct. We would be slaughtered were we to fight Percy's host—no, we *will* be slaughtered, like sheep. That is an absolute truth, and one that I have no desire to test.

"One more question," he continued, appearing to relax slightly, "and it is one for you to ask yourself, Sir Thomas, before we leave this topic. Had you been in command these past three months of this same army that we have here today, could you have achieved what Wallace achieved in Perth, or in Lanark?" He gazed levelly at Lariston. "Yes, you'll say. You could have.

Well, I disagree. And so would you if you but thought about it logically, without feeling insulted."

The Douglas knight opened his mouth to protest.

"With an army at your back," the Steward said, ignoring him, "you would have had to lay siege to Perth, and the English would have known of your intentions—or mine, or those of anyone leading such an army—a week and more before you passed Stirling and entered their territory. They would have had time to entrench themselves, provision the town, and prepare for your attack, and Perth is a strong place, with stout walls built to withstand a siege. You would have failed—any of us would—and Ormsby's treasure train would have been spirited away while you were yet days distant to the south.

"But Wallace's rabble captured Lanark, and he it was who commanded the raid on Perth. That raid succeeded because it *was* Wallace who led it, and because he has a reputation for fighting in a way no one else fights. It is common knowledge today that he and his folk know the land they live on and fight on, and they know it better and more intimately than any of those who come against them—they use it as a weapon, effortlessly, without having to think about it. The enemy they fight can do nothing to counter their kind of warfare, because Wallace's folk behave like water, fluid and practically impossible to attack to any lasting effect. They go where they can by the simplest route, whereas English armies are like rock formations, inflexible and massive. But a stream of water, if it is strong enough and properly directed, can wash away the largest boulders and bring down the stoutest walls. To my way of thinking, William Wallace is like a river, harnessed while in spate. He is a force of nature, unlike any leader this part of Scotland has seen to date."

For long moments after that no one spoke, and it was the young newcomer, Sir Alexander Lindsay, who broke the silence.

"You said, my lord, unlike any leader in this part of Scotland." He cleared his throat nervously. "Forgive me if I seem foolish or ignorant, but there are other leaders elsewhere, I've been told. One in particular in the north, beyond Forth, the young nobleman Andrew de Moray, or Murray. I know the name, of course, for he is heir to one of the great estates in all Scotland. But the tenor of all that I have heard—although that be garbled reports from people who have heard tales from other people who have been told by others—is that this young man is something of a paragon, single-handedly putting the fear of God into every Englishman north of Forth." He looked from one to the other seated at the head table. "Is there anyone here who can speak knowledgeably about this man?"

The Steward laughed, a booming, wholehearted sound, and waved a hand in invitation to Bishop Wishart, who smiled almost as broadly as he leaned forward to address the knight of Lindsay.

"You are fortunate to have asked that question here, Sir Alexander, for there is one among us who can speak with certainty and familiarity about the man you have named." He pointed down to where I sat with my four clerical companions. "Father de Moravia there has been pastor of Bothwell these past few years, but he is uncle, godfather, and mentor to the very man of whom you speak, young Sir Andrew Murray, the heir to Petty in Moray. Father?"

Father Murray nodded around the gathering. "De Moravia," he said, "is Murray nowadays, the old name changed, like that of the House of Stewart, to reflect our Scottish identity today. I know not if I might honestly claim to be a mentor of any kind to young Andrew Murray, but I think highly of him and I know he holds me in equal regard. I met with him a few days since, and I will be glad to tell you all you want to know of him. But it will take time, and I think we might do well to pause and stretch our legs before I continue."

I saw agreement written plain on several faces, for we had been at table by then for more than two hours, and the idea of an interruption, however brief, was a welcome one. When Lord James rose from his seat moments later and began to make his way towards the latrines at the rear of the house, I followed him, along with several others, and, in the way of such things, ended up standing shoulder to shoulder with the young Earl of Carrick as we voided our bladders thankfully.

When we had finished and were adjusting our clothing, he walked out with me into the gloaming and looked at me with amicable curiosity. "Bishop Wishart has asked me to make some time to talk with you, Father, and I admit to being a bit perplexed. Am I permitted to ask what it is you wish to talk to me about?"

I smiled, hoping to put him at ease. "You are, my lord. I had the privilege of meeting your grandfather when I was a boy, and he told me then he had a grandson my age—a grandson who shared his name and was to be the seventh Robert Bruce. I have been curious about you ever since, for no other reason than that, and so when His Grace the bishop told me you were here I said I hoped to be able to meet you and talk with you, to still that curiosity, I suppose."

"I see. And how came you to know my grandsire?"

"Through my cousin William Wallace."

"Of course! The bishop told me that, but I had forgotten." He shrugged. "I doubt we'll have much time to talk tonight, the way things are transpiring, but perhaps tomorrow?" He hesitated. "Do you hunt, by any chance?"

"No, my lord, I do not," I said. "But I can ride a horse adequately well, and I can beat the bushes in a good cause as well as any man."

His lips twitched in the start of a smile. "Good. We are riding out in the morning. If you would care to come with us, you and I might find time to talk between stalks. More chance there than anywhere else that I can see."

Moments later we were back at our separate tables, preparing to listen to what Father Davie Murray had to say about his nephew.

CHAPTER TEN

THE PRIEST
FROM BOTHWELL

As we took our seats again, it occurred to me once more that this group with whom I was dining was no mere accidental agglomeration of passing strangers. I suspected—and the impression was growing steadily stronger—that I might be the sole outsider in the assembly, but I had no awareness of what the group represented other than a fierce resentment of England and all things English. I knew I should not have been there, strictly speaking, and I could feel Bishop Wishart's patronage hanging over me like a protective canopy.

Father Murray looked about him unhurriedly, an easy smile on his lips as he acknowledged each man there, and I felt a stir of admiration at his complete lack of nervousness or self-consciousness. When he started to speak, he addressed us in Scots, which surprised me at first, because I had been expecting a priest to speak in Latin. But then I acknowledged that some of the knights among us, and in truth probably all of them, spoke little or no Latin.

"Bishop Robert has asked me to tell you about my nephew Andrew," he began. "But I'm not quite sure where to start. The beginning's always a good place, of course—makes developments far easier to understand in the normal run of things. But once in a while I find a situation where I can't simply point and say, 'There! It started there.' That's what we have here. How many of you have ever been north of Forth?"

The group was surprised by the unexpected question, and three of his listeners raised their hands—Lord James Stewart, Bishop Wishart, and Alpin, the Bishop of Dunblane. Father Murray nodded. "Well," he said cheerfully, "that makes things easier. I'll start by telling you a wee bit about my home in Moray, and then you'll have a better idea of what life is like up there. Of course, the first thing you need to understand is that everyone there speaks the Gaelic." He pronounced it the Highland way, making it sound like *garlic* with no *r*. "You'll find no other languages in use up there at all, except English, and the only people who speak that, as you might expect, are Englishmen.

"What you probably do not expect to hear is that there are more Englishmen in Moray at this time than there are in all the other regions of Scotland combined. So, let me tell you what is happening up there." He drew in a deep breath. "There are three great firths on Scotland's east coast, the southernmost being the Firth of Forth, which as you all know divides the country into north and south and which you may not know the English call the Scottish Sea. Above Forth, some fifty miles farther up, is the Firth of Tay, and north of that, eighty miles across the mountains as the crow flies, or a hundred and more miles along the coastline afoot, lies the Moray Firth, the homeland of us Murrays.

"Don't be confused by the names. They may sound the same, but they are not the same at all. Our family name, as you have heard, was originally de Moravia— some of us still call ourselves that. But we settled in Moray many generations past, and our family name changed, over the years, to Murray, taking the name of the region, so that we are now called the Murrays of Moray and the two sound identical. As they should, for they are identical in our minds and hearts.

"We have two towns worthy of note: Inverness and Aberdeen. Both are seaports and both are wealthy and prosperous. Which means that both are very attractive to England and its masters. Inverness is a small town, as towns go, but it is dominated by a very large castle that looms over it." He added dryly, "Ye'll note I did not say it's *protected* by a very large castle. It is not, because the castle is garrisoned by England."

His bushy eyebrows shot up high on his forehead. "'Oh,' you say, 'they even have a castle up there!' Let me tell you, my friends, about some of the castles up there." He held up a hand and began counting off names on his fingers. "Urquhart, Auch, Nairn, Forres, Elgin, Lochindorb, Boharm. They're all castles in Moray. And they're all as big as anything in Lothian.

"They are also," he said, knowing his words would shock, "all held and garrisoned by England. And I should mention, while I'm talking about them, that most of them belong to my eldest brother, Andrew … Sir Andrew Murray, Lord of Petty in Moray and father to the Andrew Murray I am here to talk about. My brother Andrew, more than twenty years my senior, is a patriot in the finest sense of the word—a true lover of the land that nurtured him—but I fear his day is done. He is an old, ill-used man now, and his lengthy confinement in London's Tower will do nothing to better that.

"His son, though, the younger Andrew Murray, is a worthy son to the brother I've known and admired all my life. Young Andrew was arrested with his father, of course, during Edward's last campaign against us. But where the father was hauled all the way south to prison, the son was sent to Chester, in north Wales. Young Andrew had recently been married, though, and a young man in love will stop at nothing to avoid being separated from his mate. So he broke free last winter and came north to find his wife, and he stopped in Bothwell on his way, to ask for my advice."

"And what did you advise?" The question, low-voiced and growling, came from Sir William Douglas.

"I advised him to keep moving north, avoiding contact with anyone until he was back in Moray."

"And was that last you've seen of him since?"

"No, I saw him again ten days ago, before I returned here."

"Returned from where? You've been in the north, in Moray?"

Instead of taking offence at the surliness in Douglas's voice, the priest gave a half smile. "I have. Why should that surprise you, Sir William? It is my home, and I had time to visit family there for the first time in years once my recent tenure as pastor of Bothwell ended."

"So tell us, then, what's happening up there."

"Chaos. There is panic and confusion everywhere, except, thanks be to God, among our own folk. The English are in turmoil throughout the entire region because the people there—the folk they thought were easy prey—have turned on them. They're sickened and outraged by the abuse they've had to suffer from England's arrogance for years now, and so they're fighting back, killing Englishmen anywhere they find them. And as a result, faced with hostility on a scale they never imagined, the English don't know where to turn for aid. They are too far away from home to summon support easily. And as if that were not discouraging enough, they have no confidence that their messengers are even getting through our lines."

Everyone, including me, was leaning forward, listening avidly.

"And *are* they getting through?" Sir William Douglas asked in his rasping, intolerant-sounding voice.

"No, to the best of our knowledge. But it's only a matter of time until someone breaks through our lines and manages to summon help."

"Wait! Wait a moment, if it please you." It was Sir Alexander Lindsay interrupting, his brow deeply furrowed. "This is disturbing." He glanced around at the others. "Was everyone here but me aware of this?" It was plain, though, from the blank faces looking back at him, that everyone else was as ignorant as he was, and he turned back earnestly to the priest. "We have heard nothing of this, Father—nothing credible, at least. We hear the odd rumour about stirrings in the north, but nothing solid, nothing of this magnitude. How long has this been going on, and how did it begin?"

The Highlander shrugged slightly, making no effort to disguise his lack of surprise. "It's been going on since the beginning of May, though it could have started earlier. God knows everything was ready to erupt long before then, but matters lacked a spark to set the grass afire. It was the homecoming of Andrew Moray that set flint to steel. That and his meeting with Sandy Pilche. Both of those happened at the start of May."

The Steward spoke from his seat at the head table. "Who is Sandy Pilche? Should we know this man?"

"No, my lord, you should not—not yet," Murray said. "There was nothing to know about him until these past few weeks. But you'll come to know the name well now, if I am any judge of things. Alexander Pilche is a burgess of Inverness, an important and influential one. He is a successful merchant, a free and well-respected citizen and, from what my nephew tells me, a natural leader of men above all else. Fate threw him and young Andrew together on the last day of April this year, and nothing has been the same in all of Moray since that meeting."

By merest chance I was looking at Lord James
at that moment and I watched him turn and look
inquiringly at Bishop Wishart, who shrugged in
response and mimed wide-eyed ignorance. The
Steward waved an urgent finger at the bishop and
jerked his head.

"Your pardon, Father Murray," Bishop Wishart
interrupted, "but I think this is something we should
pursue, this matter of the man Pilche. If he's to be as
prominent as you suggest, we'll need to know as much
as we can about him, and the sooner the better. You
said that nothing in Moray has been the same since he
and your nephew first met, but you said nothing of
whether that be for good or ill. Did they fight? Is there
ill blood between them?"

"Between Andrew and Sandy? Heavens, no." The
priest made it sound as though the very thought was
ludicrous. "They are the best of friends, and I'm told
they became so within days."

Wishart was frowning slightly. "You'll forgive me,
I hope, but close friendships, in my experience, are
seldom spontaneous."

Father Murray dipped his head. "I gather that, in
truth, they had not been complete strangers to each
other. Pilche had a sister—a twin named Meg—who
had been a lifelong friend to Andrew's wife, Eleanor,
and so when Andrew returned home to Inverness,
knowing of course that his wife could no longer be
living in Auch Castle, he sought out the town provost
in search of trustworthy information. It was there, I

believe, in the provost's home that night, that he first encountered Sandy Pilche. I gather that the spark between them worked from that first meeting, because Andrew told me that he went the following day to Pilche's warehouse, where they talked further and formed the bond that exists today. That is all I know. The history of their friendship did not appear important to me when I was talking with Andrew. There were other elements, like the uprising itself, that struck me as much more significant at the time.

"I know not what else I might tell you. I know they spoke of many things that day, because Andrew told me how impressed he had been by Sandy's attitude to the situation in Moray. And Sandy went to great lengths to try to keep Andrew from going anywhere near his family home. Auch lies a mere seven miles away from Inverness, across the firth on the promontory known as the Black Isle. And like every other castle in Moray at that time, it was held by the English, in this case, a knight called Geoffrey de Lisle. In Sandy Pilche's opinion, de Lisle was the most dangerous and vicious Englishman in all of Moray. Intolerant and ruthless, unpredictable and universally detested—even, it was said, by his own garrison troops. The man had held the local populace in a state of terror since his arrival the previous year, when he quickly established a pattern of hanging men and women for no discernible reason other than whimsy, as though for his own amusement, since he invariably attended all such executions. The word of these atrocities had quickly reached Inverness, of course, but nothing could be done to stop them. De Lisle was all-powerful within his own fiefdom of Auch, and not even Sir Reginald de Cheyne, the military governor of Moray, could raise a finger against him from Inverness when de Lisle claimed to be following his orders and dealing harshly with rebels.

"Even worse than the murders committed, though, Pilche deplored the other effects of the terror. Distracted by fear of losing their own lives and their families, some of the local people had begun informing on others around them, selling their friends and neighbours in the hope of purchasing their own safety. Under such conditions, Sandy Pilche believed, it would be more than merely difficult for Andrew to go undetected. He doubted that the young nobleman would be able to live openly in his home country, let alone survive there.

"But Andrew merely laughed. Auch Castle was his home, he said. He had been born there, and he would take it back as his birthright. His father's holdings were enormous, he pointed out, and he could live anywhere within their borders, with the support of his people. He would be safe with them, he said. The Inverness provost had assured him that his wife had been living openly among them since Andrew's capture, her identity unknown to the occupying English. He did not yet know what he might be able to achieve, now that he had come home, he told Pilche, but he had not returned all that way to sit around idly and do nothing, and it was obvious to him that the first thing that needed to be done was remove de Lisle from Auch Castle. He told Sandy he doubted that his folk would be content merely to hide him. They were Murrays, like him, and they would want him to lead them, too. He was sure they would follow him wherever he chose to go."

Hearing Father Murray say that, I looked across to where the young Earl of Carrick sat listening. According to the reports I had heard from Bishop Wishart, the younger Bruce had been in similar case to Andrew Murray very recently, but he had lost his young wife mere weeks before my cousin Will had lost his Mirren, and he had received very little support from his father's tenants in Annandale when he returned to Scotland afterwards. On the contrary, they had viewed him with great suspicion because of his purported relationship with Edward of England, and had pleaded loyalty to his absent father. If the earl was making comparisons, however, it did not show on his face.

"He did do *something*, though," Lord James said. "Is that not so?"

The priest smiled again. "Oh yes, indeed so. And it was something noteworthy, as all Moray knows today. Within a week of his return, he organized three score of the youngest and strongest of his men into a mounted fighting force, taking them into the wilderness of the Moray uplands to train them. Their mounts were mountain ponies, though, not English warhorses. Andrew had no intention of riding into battle against English cavalry. He set out from the start to use the land itself, its natural features, as a weapon, and so he trained his mounted corps to move quickly and attack swiftly, then withdraw and disappear into the hills before any organized pursuit could be thrown after them.

"He returned to Auch two weeks later, and late on a Wednesday afternoon his mounted men attacked the scheduled train of supplies and provisions bound for the castle. The attack, within view of the castle walls, was brazen, calculated to achieve precisely what it did. The raiders hit the supply train hard and fast. They inflicted heavy casualties and scattered what was left of the escort, who had numbered less than fifty to start with, most of them on foot. They then led the wagons away with much ado towards the woodlands half a mile to the north, taunting de Lisle and openly defying him to follow them if he dared. And of course he did. He turned out the entire garrison and led them against the raiding party."

The priest looked about him, meeting the eye of every man there. "What de Lisle did not know, of course, was that the raiders he rode after were not the sole enemy on his lands that afternoon. They were the only enemy he had *seen*, and their impertinence had outraged him because it was the first overt sign of defiance to his rule that he had encountered since his arrival in Auch more than a year earlier. And so, as he led his men through the main gates of the castle on a wild chase after the brigands who were fleeing with his supply wagons, another hundred men, who had spent much of the night climbing the precipice of the motte and were led by Andrew Murray and

Wee Mungo, entered the fortress by the postern gate.

"No Englishman knew of it, but beneath Auch's postern gate is a secret passage that passes beneath the castle walls from a small cave close to the summit of the motte. The entrance to the cave cannot be seen from above, and the passageway, even though unknown to any but the immediate Murray family, was sealed by a pair of heavy iron padlocked gates beneath the walls. Andrew knew all that, having used the passage many times during his boyhood. He entered the cave alone, unseen by the others, whom he had left behind to wait for his signal, and he carried the keys to both padlocks in his pouch. Minutes later, he opened the postern gate to his men from within."

Sir Alexander, wide-eyed, whistled quietly.

"That incident," Father Murray continued, "announced Andrew Murray's return home to Auch and marked the beginning of his uprising, along with his solemn, public oath, sworn beneath the battlements of Inverness Castle in the town itself, to sweep the English out of Scotland north of the Forth and eventually to cleanse the entire realm of their presence. And people paid attention because Auch Castle had fallen, that easily, and it is still in friendly hands. Geoffrey de Lisle led an army to besiege it soon afterwards, but he was waylaid in the hills on his way to join the attacking force and sustained wounds from which he subsequently died. I am pleased to say that since his death, no one has seemed keen to re-establish the siege."

He waited until the buzz of voices had died down. "The most interesting aspect of all of this, however, is that within days of the recapture of Auch, Sandy Pilche crossed the firth from Inverness to the Black Isle at the head of more than a hundred well-armed men, all of them free burgesses, to throw in his lot with Andrew. And since then, the Scots cause, and the Scots folk, have prospered, with people coming to join the rising in Moray from all over the north and north-east. Andrew commands overall, of course, but he retains responsibility for the mounted component of his force, which is now several hundred strong, and Sandy Pilche has become his most trusted lieutenant, the commander of the foot forces of Moray."

"How many men does Murray command now?" Sir Malcolm asked.

"I can't answer that," Father Murray said. "Ten days ago, when last I saw my nephew, he told me he had a thousand men at his back, but even that number was nearly two weeks old by then, and the incomers had been increasing daily, sometimes by as many as a hundred a day. So who can say? It might be two thousand or more by this time. They've had no reversals, and every skirmish they win draws new volunteers to their ranks. The English are demoralized, and they're impotent for the time being, but Edward is not renowned for appointing incompetents. They have some capable commanders up there—de Cheyne of Inverness is no sluggard, and his subordinate, William Fitzwarren, constable of Urquhart Castle, is every bit as formidable. For the time being, however, they simply cannot seem to come to grips with the damages Andrew's folk are inflicting on them." He shook his head dismissively. "Frankly, I believe that my nephew is a better general than all of them together."

"How so?" Lord James asked. "He's very young for such an accolade, is he not?"

"Perhaps so, my lord, but he has consistently remained one step ahead of everything the English try to do to stop him. Immediately after taking Auch Castle, he came close to capturing Castle Urquhart, wresting it back from Fitzwarren. He might have succeeded, too, had he had more men at his disposal. But that was at the very start of his campaign, when he had only a hundred or so men at his back, and the Comyn Countess of Ross complicated matters there. She had heard about what was happening and marched from her castle at Balconie to offer assistance to Fitzwarren, in hopes of winning favour for her husband the earl, who is imprisoned in London.

"With the Countess of Ross's army outside Urquhart, Andrew could hardly conduct the siege he had planned, and so he withdrew his men without further incident. That he was able to do so easily, without being counterattacked, was a wonder, but it was possible only because the English themselves were not convinced that the Countess of Ross's offer of assistance was genuine. Suspecting an intricate plot either to lure them out of the castle or to permit a Scots army to enter it, they chose to do nothing, and so Andrew was able to march his army away uncontested.

"The Countess of Ross's own fortunes were less happily resolved, because Andrew marched directly north from Urquhart into Ross and captured her own castle. At one blow he rejuvenated the fighting spirit of his men by besting, quite brilliantly and unexpectedly, the very enemy who had thwarted them at Urquhart Castle, while at the same time, by getting behind her army and cutting her lines of communication with her home base in Ross, he taught the Countess of Ross that he was an enemy to be feared, and that armed adherence to England's cause was a dangerous course to pursue in Scotland. Her interference in his affairs had cost her dearly. She could not go home to Ross, and she could not safely remain in Inverness-shire."

He paused. "My nephew himself mentioned another advantage that sprang from what he did in Ross. By seizing Balconie he established an additional safe, easily defensible stronghold for his growing army and a well-known gathering point for all the hundreds of volunteers streaming to join him from throughout the north.

"Setting all that aside, though," he continued, "the point to be made here is that my nephew always uses the land itself as an ally and a weapon. It is a *sine qua non* of his campaigning. He is more than willing to fight against whatever forces the English bring to bear against him, but he always contrives to command the high ground and he always has rising woodland at his back—woodland and bogs into which he and his men can withdraw when necessary, but which render English heavy horse useless, ploutering helplessly through mud and mire. Fitzwarren and de Cheyne have both learned that to their cost, but so far they have been unable to develop countermeasures to deal with it effectively. Andrew and his people know the land as they know their own bodies. The English do not."

Sir William Douglas looked up with a sneer. "So let me ask this again. Do we or do we not know whether word of all these goings-on has reached Edward in England?" The provocation in repeating his question was deliberate, but Father Murray refused to rise to it.

"We don't know, Sir William. We *suspect* that no messengers have managed to get through with word, but we cannot be certain. The very success of such an effort, after all, would ensure that we knew nothing of it. We can but hope, but we must also be prepared to have those hopes dashed at any moment. One thing is certain, though. The moment Edward does become aware of the true state of his affairs in Moray and elsewhere, the response from England will be immediate and, in all probability, enormous."

"Aye, it will be all of that," said Sir John Stewart, speaking for the first time, "but we have more immediate matters to concern us here. This campaign in Moray may be successful beyond its leaders' wildest dreams, but will it have any effect upon us and what we have to deal with here in the south and southwest?"

He looked quickly around the assembly, addressing himself to everyone. "Even were a miracle achieved up there and all the English driven out tomorrow, leaving the men of Moray free to join us as soon as they could be here, would that affect our situation here today, with Percy fast approaching? I think not. Percy could be about our ears within days. Murray might take months to get here." He turned to look at his brother the Steward. "That's really why you intend to negotiate, is it not? To give Murray time to organize?"

Lord James smiled tightly. "Aye, it is. Murray and others, elsewhere in the country."

"And are these others all in touch with one another?"

The Steward glanced towards Bishop Wishart, who answered in his stead. "Not quite. Not yet. But that will be taken care of very soon now. We have plans in place."

"Awaiting what, might I ask?" The Stewart knight was not trying to sound skeptical, but the question begged to be asked.

"This gathering," the bishop said. "Or the other, some might say lesser, gathering that accompanies it." He did not need to look my way. Knowing my employer as well as I did, I knew instantly that I had been correct: my attendance at this dinner was incidental to my true purpose here in Turnberry. I was predestined to be a participant in that other, "lesser" gathering.

Afterwards, when the guests had dispersed, the bishop beckoned to me with fluttering fingers as he bade Lord James a good night, and I went to him as the Steward left him.

"You have work for me, then, my lord," I said quietly, not even attempting to conceal my smile. "Some lesser gathering I'm to attend."

"Don't be impertinent, Father. You're attending it already."

"And how tight is the time frame?"

"Tight enough. Why do you ask?"

"Because Lord Bruce invited me to hunt with him tomorrow morning."

"To hunt with him? *You*, Father James?"

"To talk with him, my lord. He thought there might be more time for talking between kills than at any other time. Should I inform him I cannot go?"

"No, don't do that. This might be the best chance you get to observe him. Besides, we are not all gathered yet. I'm still awaiting two more men. If they arrive tomorrow—they should have been here by now—then we'll all meet tomorrow night and set things afoot the following day. So go and speak with the earl, but be sure to be back here in time for supper. I shall look forward to hearing your impressions."

CHAPTER ELEVEN

BRUCE—FIRST BLOOD

I was up hours before dawn and celebrated Mass by myself, or so I thought until I heard a stifled cough behind me and turned to see a bareheaded figure kneeling just inside the tiny chapel I was using. I was conducting the rites with the ease of long practice, in darkness relieved by the flame of but a single candle, so I could not see who it was who shared the Mass with me. But when it came time to eat the host and drink the sacrificial wine of Communion and I turned and offered to share the Sacrament with my companion, I discovered, to my surprise, that it was the Earl of Carrick himself.

He waited for me afterwards as I packed my vessels and removed my robes, leaving aside my priestly cassock for the day since I was going hunting, and replacing it with the tunic and leggings I had bought when I was recuperating at the Lanark priory. I took my walking staff, too, surmising I might need it in the event I was called upon as a beater, and when I was ready, the earl and I made our way together to the castle kitchens.

It was still night, the quiet, moonless blackness showing no sign yet of an approaching day, and a startled cook, wide-eyed at seeing the Earl of Carrick in his kitchen, offered to feed us on the same fresh bread and duck eggs, whipped and fried in cream and butter, that he had been preparing, probably illicitly, for his own morning meal. He set out a plenitude of cold meats, both flesh and fowl, from the previous night, but both Bruce and I were intrigued by the sight and smell of the eggs the cook had been making when we arrived, and as we ate them we were happy to have arrived when we did.

By the time we finished eating, each of us had grown comfortable with the other, a condition facilitated, I had no doubt, by the intimacy of the private Mass we had shared earlier, and we were perfectly at ease, talking comfortably of trivial things. So when we stood up to leave the kitchen and the earl whistled to catch the cook's attention before tossing him a silver mark in thanks for the meal, I followed my companion out into the darkness, talking away to him as he made his way towards the stables, along the route indicated by a succession of guttering fire baskets.

The eastern sky was still black, but the stables were abuzz and bright with lanterns, with grooms and ostlers bustling everywhere, preparing animals and carts for that morning's hunting party. Some of the more eager hunters were conscientiously preparing themselves and their mounts for the day ahead.

Bruce turned to me. "How good a horseman are you, Father James?"

"Adequate," I told him. "I don't need a spavined, sway-backed nag, if that's what you mean. I can ride and I have no fear either of horses or of falling."

He smiled and beckoned to one of the senior grooms, then told the man to take me out and let me pick my own mount. "Come back when you're ready," he told me. "I'll be here until we leave."

By the time I had picked my mount for the day and had adjusted all the necessary saddlery to my size and riding style, close to an hour must have elapsed, and when I returned I found the earl surrounded by the other nine members of the hunting group, five of whom were the knights we had dined with the night before. They were all in high spirits, even the two from Douglasdale, and no one showed any sign of curiosity when I rode up to join them. I was accepted as one of the party from the outset, and if anyone wondered about the shabbiness of my clothing, he kept his curiosity to himself.

We left soon after that, more than two score of us all told, counting the huntsmen, butchers, cooks, wagoners, and beaters who accompanied us, and from the moment we passed beyond Turnberry's main gates all levity vanished, replaced by the gravitas of the hunt.

We made our first kill in the early light of dawn, having waited on foot in an open dell while a ring of beaters drove a small herd of deer towards us. Bruce held a surprisingly large, laminated bow as his favoured weapon, and while it was by no means as powerful as a yew longbow, it was a solid weapon nonetheless, and he used it well when a proud buck and three does bounded into the clearing where we waited with two of the other knights, both of them armed with crossbows.

The deer came quickly, in almost total silence, materializing almost on top of us, and Bruce raised and drew in a single, graceful movement, loosing his shaft effortlessly and catching the soaring buck at the apex of his spring, the missile striking it behind the shoulder in a perfect, lethal heart shot, so that the beast landed and died at the same instant. It was a magnificent shot—would have been so even for my cousin Will—and I acknowledged it as such, drawing an appreciative grin from the earl before he strode forward to kneel beside his prize. One of his two companions, Sir Alexander Lindsay, had killed his doe, but the other, Sir John Stewart, had missed his animal completely, and I could hear him cursing under his breath.

An hour or so later, we had another opportunity under similar circumstances, and again the earl was successful in his kill, though not with the spectacular brilliance he had shown the first time. This buck drove straight towards him, head on, leaving Bruce less than a moment to aim and fire, but his shaft sank to the feathers in the hollow beneath the beast's neck, cleanly loosed and cleanly delivered. The animal swept on, driven by its own momentum as though oblivious to its injury, knocking the earl aside and driving every vestige of air from his lungs while it continued for four bounding leaps before it fell dead.

It was almost mid-morning by the time we left that clearing, leaving the carcasses to the butcher's crew. The earl had recovered his breath and his composure, and the time for early hunting was long past, but the butchers who had accompanied the main party had been doing their work for long enough by then to ensure that the camp cooks had several choice cuts and delicacies to grill for the hungry hunters. And so we collected our horses—we had, of course, been hunting on foot—and prepared to make our way back to the central encampment where the fires had been set up, about a mile and a half back along the riverbank.

When Bruce tried to mount his horse, though, it whinnied and reared away from him, almost pulling him over, and we quickly discovered that it had somehow been lamed: its right rear hoof was split and the poor beast was unable to place any weight on it at all. Yet none of us could remember any incident that might have caused such an injury on the way out from Turnberry. All three of us remaining with the earl—myself and the two knights, Stewart and Lindsay—offered him our horses, but he would have none of it. He was extremely gracious about the situation, and even jocular in his acceptance of it. He had invited me to join him that day, he explained to the others, in the hopes that we might be able to find sufficient time for me to catechize him about some information Bishop Wishart needed for episcopal reasons, concerning matters in England and details of his previous life there as a liegeman to King Edward. Therefore, he pointed out, since we were in fact about the business of God's Holy Church, it was plain that God Himself had intervened to see to it that we should have as much time as we required for it. He waved away the two knights' protests and sent them on ahead with our horses, leaving the two of us to walk together back to the campsite. I freed my heavy walking staff from where I had secured it to my saddle and handed my beast's reins to Sir John Stewart while Sir Alexander Lindsay took the reins of Lord Bruce's injured animal.

I clearly remember the stillness once the sounds of the four horses had died away ahead of us. We were walking through a grove of majestic beech trees, on a thick carpet of dead leaves from previous years, and the smooth, grey skin of the trees' massive trunks reminded me of the soaring, vaulted heights of the cathedral nave in Glasgow. Somewhere off to the east a thrush was singing, and ahead of us, a pair of linnets were competing with each other in a struggle for melodic supremacy. It was a profoundly peaceful moment, and even as I became aware of it, it was shattered.

Out of nowhere, I saw four men—or rather a blurred impression of four large, armed men—running towards us, and I saw a long, bare, pointing blade. At the same moment I was aware of Lord Bruce dropping into a crouch as his hand swept down for the sword at his waist. But of course no sword was there. We were on a hunting expedition within the earl's own lands, and it had not occurred to any of us that we might need to defend ourselves. I saw Bruce flinch, then start away, his hand now at his other side clawing for the dirk that hung there. But the first attacker was already between us, thrusting at me stiff-armed to knock me aside as he swung up his sword, left handed, against Bruce. He had clearly judged the earl more dangerous than I because he was bigger, broader, and more brightly clad.

The attacker's stiffly outstretched arm came close to hitting me, but I knocked it aside with my elbow, deflecting his charge easily as I grasped my staff two-handed and drove its heavier end into his exposed armpit as hard as I could, knocking him heavily sideways and off balance. As he fell sprawling, his sword spun from his grip, and Bruce pivoted, bending as he went, to snatch up the fallen sword, gripping it awkwardly by the cross-guard as he drew the dirk at his waist with his other hand. Someone crashed into me then from my side and sent me flying.

Armed but yet helpless, the earl spun away from the new attacker in a full circle, changing his weapons from hand to hand as he went. His legs flexed and he straightened, dirk in his left hand and the long English sword in his right, and parried the wild swing launched at him by the fellow who had knocked me down. The sword flashed, metal clanged, the attacker's arm flew up, and the dirk in the earl's hand flickered forward and stabbed deep into another exposed armpit. I heard a choking grunt of pain, but already Bruce was spinning away to confront yet another charging assailant. The long blade in his hand swung up and around and down, hissing with speed and power until its arc ended suddenly in a jarring, meaty sound.

Behind me, I heard fleeing footsteps and knew, without having to look, that a last assailant was running for his life.

Bruce and I stood staring wild eyed at each other, both of us panting for breath, although his exertions had been far greater than my own.

"You saved my life," he said eventually. "That whoreson would have killed me if you hadn't hit him."

I looked down at the man who lay at the earl's feet. He was English—they all were, no doubt of that—a foot soldier by the light leather armour he wore. He was easily as tall as Bruce himself, with long, greasy hair and surprise-filled eyes that stared down disbelievingly at the swaying hilt of the sword that Bruce had just released. The dying man's eyes travelled down the length of the blade for as far as they could, towards the spot he could not see, where the edged steel, driven by all Bruce's strength and anger, had sunk deep into the join of his neck and shoulder.

I turned away from the bloodied forms on the ground at my feet to look at the first man who had fallen; the one I had hit. Relief hit me like a splash of

cold water as I saw he was alive and whole, with no
trace of blood on him anywhere. But he was writhing
on the ground and grimacing, one hand clamped
tightly beneath his armpit where I had struck him.
Bruce crossed the distance to him in one step and
hauled the Englishman to his feet, gripping him by the
arm-holes in his leather armour. The fellow took heed
of the fact that his dead weight was being lifted as
though it was nothing, and blinked up at the man
holding him.

"Who are you?" he slurred, in Scots.

"Carrick." Bruce's response was a feral snarl. He
hitched the sagging man higher, so they were face to
face. "This is my land. Who are *you*? And who sent
you?"

The Englishman was blinking rapidly, beginning
to regain his senses, and he suddenly thrust himself
upright and made to shrug off the earl's grip. Bruce let
go one hand and smashed him hard across the face
with a clenched fist, knocking his head sideways and
drawing a gush of blood from his nose. He then spun
him with both hands, grasped him anew by the nape of
the neck, and swept his feet away with a swift kick,
dropping him heavily to his knees next to the sprawled
corpse of his erstwhile companion before thrusting
him forward to look directly down at the ruined body.

"Look at him, fool. You can be as dead as he is
before you draw another breath, if you so wish. It's
your decision to make, so make it now if you ever
hope to stand on your feet again. Live or die, here and

now, where no one might ever find you until your bones are picked clean by the crows."

At that moment, the other downed man, the one Bruce had dirked in the armpit, began to cough, and we could tell, from the gurgling, painfully laboured sounds of it, that he was close to death.

Bruce wrenched the kneeling man's head around to face the sound. "Your friend there's dying, too," he said. "Deservedly. Four of you, and two of us, and us unarmed while you held the surprise. And now two of you are down, dead and dying, you're next to go, and your fourth man is running for his life into the bogs to the south. He'll die, too, in there." He tightened his fingers on the prisoner's neck. "Now tell us. Who sent you?"

The kneeling man straightened his back and began to speak in a breathless, high-pitched voice. Alas, I could not understand a word of what he said, for he spoke now in a language—or a dialect—that I had never heard before. Fortunately, it was one Bruce was evidently familiar with, for the two jabbered at each other for several minutes before Bruce grunted in disgust. Still holding his captive by the neck, he dragged him bodily to where he could bend down and retrieve the sword he had used earlier. I felt a surge of horror, believing he was bent on killing the prisoner, but before I could even begin to protest he straightened up again and smashed the Englishman behind the ear with the sword's pommel, knocking him senseless and releasing him to fall face down.

"Percy's people," he said to me. "They're closer than we thought—less than ten miles from here but more than five. These four are part of a larger group sent out to scout the countryside. They've been coming north since last night, and the main party—two hundred of them, this fellow said—is about six miles behind them."

"Headed to Turnberry?" I tried to keep the thrill of fear out of my voice.

"No. They're going from west to north, towards Lanark. They'll miss Turnberry."

"Not if the one who escaped finds them again. He'll bring them back this way."

He looked me in the eye. "Why do you say that?"

"Because it's logical. They found us here and the only place we could have come from is Turnberry, or failing that, Irvine or Ayr. There's no other habitable spot to the east of here for miles ... Too many miles for us to be here by accident."

"Damn. You're right. Though they'd never dare tackle Turnberry with only two hundred men. But that would be a wise man's decision, and we're dealing with Percy, so we'd best be ready for folly. Come on, we'll have to move quickly and get ready."

The dying man had fallen silent and the third was unconscious, and there was nothing more that I could do for either of them apart from reciting the Prayer for the Dying over the wounded man, breathing a final Act of Contrition into his ear while Bruce waited, tapping his foot but making no attempt to hurry me. I made the sign of the cross one last time over the man, who no longer appeared to be breathing, then stood up, nodding to indicate that I was finished and we could go. We had nothing to take with us, apart from my walking staff and the English sword, which Bruce thrust beneath his belt, and so we struck off immediately for our hunting camp.

As soon as we were safely out of the glade and were once again moving through familiar countryside between vast, dense stands of hawthorn bushes, I asked, "What language was that fellow speaking?"

Only after I had asked the question did I become aware that my companion might have taken exception to my tone, or to the lack of any honorific, but he merely shrugged and answered the question as asked.

"It was English," he said. "English as the English themselves speak it, that is. They all speak different languages, just like us up here with our Gaelic, and the Norman-French version of English spoken by much of the nobility, and what we call Scots, though that's a bastard thing, born of people's need to trade with one another. We have our dialects, but it's nothing like as bad as in England. The common folk down there can't even understand the languages being spoken in another part of the country, or some-times even the next town. These fellows here are from Sussex, on the south seacoast. My family has lands near there, so I learned to speak their local language as a boy. We were lucky in our choice of prisoner, simply because of that. *I* could talk to him, but he wouldn't be able to talk to someone from Devon, say, or York."

"But he spoke Scots at first, when he asked you who you were."

"He did. That's true. But that might have been all the Scots he knew. He said he came from Sussex."

"So Percy's men are from Sussex?"

"No, not all of them. But they are raised in groups, in local levies, with their own officers, and they generally keep to themselves. They have people whose job it is to stand as interpreters, translating English speech into English speech for different Englishmen, which sounds really strange to us. But they manage to keep themselves informed, nonetheless."

"Hmm. Part of a group. D'you think their friends might have found our camp?"

He shook his head. "I doubt it. We're not that far away and there's at least a score and a half of our people there. Had anything happened, I think we would have heard the noise."

I doubted that, but since I had no more reason for my doubt than he had for his certainty, I said nothing to gainsay him. We lapsed into silence, and relieved of the need to be ready to fight or flee, I muttered a few grateful prayers as we walked, Bruce now a few paces ahead of me.

Suddenly he stopped, and I almost walked right into him. He turned, unsteadily, his face deathly white, and he gazed at me blankly for a moment before looking back in the direction from which we had come. And then he dropped to his knees like a felled bullock, and lurching forward onto his hands, vomited violently.

Stunned, I moved to aid him, though I could do little besides lay my hand on the back of his neck and mutter sounds of encouragement. The paroxysm passed quickly, and after one more long, agonized spell of dry retching, he crawled to a patch of longer grass where he rolled onto his back and lay with his bent elbow covering his eyes. I sat down beside him, wanting to ask him, as people always do at such times, if he was feeling better, but I could see for myself that he was nowhere close to being himself, and so I held my peace and sat there quietly, waiting for him to recover.

A short time later he exhaled deeply and sat up, hitching himself backwards on straightened arms until he could cross his legs beneath him. Then he placed his hands on his knees, hunched forward, and stared at the ground between his legs.

"All my life I've trained for that," he said eventually in a quiet voice. He raised his eyes to look directly at me. "But no one ever told me how personal it is ... It went as I always thought it would," he continued, frowning gently, "almost exactly as I expected, but faster. I *saw* it develop, though, fast as it was, and I suppose my training took over. It must have, for otherwise I can't explain what happened. I don't think there was anything deliberate in what I did—at least, I wasn't aware of doing anything deliberately." He fell silent for a few moments, then continued in the same, slightly bemused voice. "It seemed for a moment as if I were standing aside watching myself and what was happening."

His gaze sharpened suddenly and his voice grew stronger, more like the Bruce I had spoken with earlier. "I'd have gone down in the first clash if it hadn't been for you, and believe me when I say I'm grateful. But after that I was in control at all times. And then out of nowhere, right here on the path, I saw what I had done to that first man with my dirk, and then to the other ... that hacking sword cut. The sound of it. The blood." He closed his eyes tight and shuddered. "I didn't know it would be so real, so personal ... Didn't know I'd see their eyes as I killed them."

I sat thunderstruck, awed by the realization that the men he had just killed were his first, and that probably he had never drawn blood in anger, either. Who would have suspected that, being who and what he was, he had managed to live for as long as he had, during a time of war, without ever having killed a man. I stretched out my hand and helped him to his feet.

"Will you hear my confession, Father?"

"Of course I will. You wish to do it now, here?"

He looked around the spot where we were standing, and it was as quiet as any church. Even the birds had stopped singing. He nodded. "Here and now, yes. I think I need to."

As soon as we arrived back at the campsite, Bruce announced the English presence in the woods, and instantly the mood of the entire assembly changed from celebration to urgency. Everything was packed up and on wagons in no time, the horses readied, the fires put out. Bruce and I wrapped some dripping slices of fresh-roasted meat between new-cut slabs of bread and ate on horseback as we retraced our route to Turnberry, the earl riding on a fresh horse while his injured mount was led by one of the camp attendants.

Within half an hour of our arrival the entire place was seething with urgent, last-minute preparations as the army assembled by the Steward and his friends and allies was made ready to march. The plan was to march northwest, towards Irvine, where Lord Stewart had identified a high-ground site strong enough to discourage any head-on attack by Percy's force, which was generally assumed to be stronger and more battle-ready than our own.

I had gone looking for my employer as soon as we returned, but he had been in conference and had merely nodded to indicate that he would send for me when he was free, and so I was standing in the castle yard, off to one side, watching all the activity when one of his young acolytes came to summon me. I was to go to the chapel, he said, where his lordship would join me presently.

The bishop, who had a horror of wasting time—his own as well as other people's—did not keep me waiting. I had been in the chapel no more than a minute when the door opened and he swept in, glancing around the small space to make sure we were alone. He went straight to the front of the altar and seated himself on the right side of the narrow aisle without genuflecting, waving me to a seat opposite him where we could talk without raising our voices.

"We may be interrupted at any time," he said in Latin, "but there's no other place that's safer from being overheard. How was the hunt? I hear you and Lord Bruce shared an adventure."

"Aye, my lord, you could say that."

"English scouts?"

"Apparently. Ranging a few miles ahead of their main force."

"And one of them escaped?"

"Aye, ran away, rather than escaped, but reported back to his masters either way."

"Unfortunate."

"Very, my lord, but there was nothing we do to prevent it. There were four of them to two of us and they caught us by surprise. We were a hunting party, and no one thought to send out scouts. No one had dreamed the Englishmen might be there."

"Clearly, in hindsight, someone *should* have dreamed they might be there. We've known for some time now that Percy is drawing close."

"Close, my lord, but not yet here. A matter of days removed, it was said last night."

"Aye, and wrongly said, as things transpired. That encounter could have been disastrous."

"It could, sir, but thanks be to God and the Earl of Carrick, it was not. Lord Bruce did well to best them as he did. He was unarmed, except for a dirk, but he managed to wrest a sword from one of them and saved us both."

The bishop eyed me askance, then grunted. "And did you have a chance to speak with him before this happened? For long enough, I mean, to have arrived at a considered, solid opinion before the onset of the earl's heroics?"

"Yes, my lord, I did."

"And? You judge him trustworthy?"

"I judge him innocent of the traitorous perfidy of which some men accuse him. Whether that makes him trustworthy in other matters would depend greatly upon your expectations of him. But I saw no malice in the man, no reason to mistrust him or his motives. He struck me as being honest and straightforward in his dealings with everyone around him, and I like him for himself, which is more than I can say for many another you have asked me to evaluate. And all of those conclusions I had formed before our encounter with the English scouts. What happened during that encounter merely reinforced my view. I would trust the Earl of Carrick, my lord bishop."

"And his ambitions, would you trust those?"

"I would. Why not? He is a Bruce, and makes no secret of it, and offers no apology. What else would you expect of him? As heir to his grandfather's and his father's legacy, he sees the realm as being his by right, and I would wager that when he judges the time is fit, he will step forth and claim it, given the support and backing of men like yourself and the High Steward. That is ambition, by anyone's definition, but it is forthright. There is nothing about it that is underhanded or deceitful. And should it come about that he does claim the Crown someday, I think by then he will be old enough to hold it fast and wear it well. As I said, my lord, I like the man. I believe he will distinguish himself with great honour someday."

I hesitated, considering whether I should tell him about Bruce's reaction to killing for the first time that day, and about how he had made a formal confession to me afterwards.

"You have more you wish to say, Father James?"

"No, my lord. I think I've said all I had to say on the matter of Lord Bruce." The Earl of Carrick's inner peace was his own affair, and I had no doubt he would deal with it satisfactorily.

"Good. Then let us move on. I need you now to go and find your cousin in Selkirk Forest." He knitted his brow and concentrated his thoughts. "He'll need to be ready to move out within the week. With all his men—as many as he can muster. By then, unless I'm sore mistaken, we here will be deep in the discussion of surrender terms with Percy and his minions."

"Clifford, you mean."

He cocked an eyebrow at me, impatient as always when someone missed his point. "Clifford be damned—as I'm sure he will be. I said *minions*, meaning all of them—knights, barons, the entire cavalcade, including Clifford merely incidentally. Our so-called English masters will be expecting a quick solution, the usual profusion of expressed regrets for hasty, ill-considered actions, couched in the customary assurances of future loyalty—all in return, of course, for royal generosity in the form of land grants and fresh revenue sources in England. The true reward, though, after all the tedious talk is over, will lie in the perception that we can all then go home.

"I want Wallace to harry Lothian as the English would, while we delay Percy here. He and his crew must spread utter havoc among the English, and God our saviour knows there's no shortage of them there to wreak havoc upon. I want it known that William Wallace and his army are attacking English garrisons throughout that region, creating chaos and spreading terror, and I need them to keep at it for five to six weeks before they strike inland to cross the Forth at Stirling. We here in the southwest will use the reports of their prowess to our advantage, and our drawn-out negotiations will ensure that Percy can't go charging off to counter them. He would not dare leave an enemy army at his back, no matter how cowardly he might think us.

"No sieges, though, and I'll require you to make that very clear, not only to your cousin but to every other Scots commander you meet. We cannot afford to waste time and men besieging castles. Better to raid them hard—them and their surroundings—and burn the crops meant to feed them in the coming winter. I want Will to harass the garrisons, pen them up inside, and make them afraid to ride out of their gates. I want him to hit the outlying settlements at every opportunity, stripping the manor houses and estates of workers, as well as men-at-arms and foot soldiers. I want him to enlist the local folk and lay waste the whole of Lothian, stripping everything. His prime purpose, you'll tell him from me, will be to put the fear of God into every Englishman north of the border."

"Will should enjoy that, my lord," I said, "if what I've heard of him recently is true. How many men follow him now, do you know?"

"A legion, folk say, but not yet enough. He'll need far more if he's to dislodge the English grip on Lothian. I hope he has his new folk, the ones he brought back from his Perth foray, trained by now, for we can't afford to waste another precious hour. We are out of time. *Scotland* is out of time."

"And why, if I may ask, my lord, is Will to head towards Stirling in six weeks?"

There was steely determination in the look my bishop turned on me then. "Because that's all we have," he growled. "It will take you more than half that time to deliver my message to Wallace and then get north into Moray, where you will contact Andrew Murray and make sure he brings his army south, as fast as he can travel, to join Wallace. It is now mid-June, and Murray must be on the march by the end of July, so you'll waste no time between now and then. England will send a real army north within the next few months, and if we're to be able to stop them, it will have to be at Stirling, as always. So Wallace and Murray must have their combined hosts at Stirling in advance of that, by the last week of August at the very latest. And that means every single hour that passes between now and July's end will be crucial to the well-being of this realm."

My jaw must have dropped as I listened to what he expected of me, for he nodded grimly. "Aye, I ken," he said in Scots. "What I'm asking of you is damn near impossible, but believe me, Jamie, if it doesna get done, Scotland will go down into slavery under Edward's heel."

I shook my head. "It's not impossible, my lord. I'll do it, somehow. But why need it be me? You must have others who could undertake the journey faster that I can. Someone could be halfway to Moray by the time I find Will in Selkirk Forest."

"I know that, Father," he said, reverting to Latin. "I could send another more quickly, as you say, but none who would be more trustworthy. You will be carrying information in your head that can't be set on paper, lest the paper fall into hostile hands. And when you deliver my instructions, you'll have the understanding and authority to change them, if need be." He smiled slightly. "My old teacher Father Aloysius used to say, 'Do right, and you need fear no man. Don't write, and you need fear no prying eyes.' You'll carry word to both principals, Wallace and Murray, on a matter of great import—*crucial* import."

"And what is that, my lord?"

"You tell *me*, Father, for the evidence of it is all around you, frightening in its absence. What is the most precious commodity lacking in this realm of ours today?"

I racked my brain, rejecting everything that came to mind as being less than the most precious thing I could imagine. "You have me, my lord," I finally said.

"Iron, Jamie. Plain old rusty iron."

For some reason I had an instant vision of a coiled pile of rusted chains that I had seen lying in a corner of the castle yard a few days earlier. "Iron?" I said, hearing the incredulity in my own voice. "Iron is *precious*?"

The craggy old face smiled at me. "It is indeed, indubitably so. Especially if you suffer from a lack of weaponry and armour. Look about you, Father, when next you go among the folk. Look at our army, how poorly our men are equipped. It is something we seldom think upon as priests, but our country has been stripped of weapons. All the weapons captured at Dunbar were shipped away to England, and since that time we have been scrambling to deal with the rapacity of Edward's tax collectors. They've bankrupted the realm and destroyed the sole industry that brought us wealth—the trade in wool—and we have been so busy trying to protect ourselves that we have had neither the time nor the materials to fashion new weapons. And because iron is perennially in short supply here in Scotland, we have always had far fewer skilled smiths and armourers than England has."

He grunted as he rose to his feet, then twisted his torso back and forth. "I will explain, but there's little bodily comfort in a hard pine pew," he murmured. "I'm thirsty."

He stepped towards the altar and bent forward to open the tabernacle that surmounted it. When he turned back to me holding two jewelled goblets in one hand and a matching flagon in the other, I could not conceal my shocked surprise. He grinned conspiratorially and pointed his chin towards the red-glassed sanctuary lamp by the altar's side, saying in Scots, "There's nae light burnin' there, ye see, though I'd have thought ye'd see that earlier. Nae consecrated host in the place, nor nae blesst wine." He hefted the flagon. "This stuff here's for drinkin'. I come here when I need to be by mysel'. Ye'd be surprised how hard it is to find a place that's private aroun' here."

He poured two goblets full of wine and handed one to me before replacing the flagon in the tabernacle. "To the realm," he said in Latin, raising his cup, and I repeated his toast as he sipped deeply. He smacked his lips appreciatively.

"I had a letter from Andrew Murray some time ago," he said, "when first he threw the English out of Auch Castle. In it he begged me for assistance in equipping his men. He was training them to fight using wooden weapons, he told me, because the only real weapons they have are those they take from Englishmen they've killed, and it is difficult to kill a man—indeed even to fight against him—when all you have is a wooden club and he is armed with a sharp-edged sword or a steel-tipped spear."

"It must be, my lord. What is to be done about it?"

"It is already in hand, Father, with orders being filled all over Christendom, save only for England. Within the year we will have replenished our armouries completely. In the meantime, we have chartered two ships expressly to relieve our immediate needs, one out of Oslo and the other out of Lübeck. Both vessels will be laden half and half—ingot iron, together with finished weapons and chain mail. Each ship will call into a different port. The Lübeck vessel will sail to Aberdeen, where Murray will receive it. Wallace will meet the one from Oslo at Dundee."

"But—are there not English garrisons in both those places, my lord?"

"There are, but what would you have me do? Instruct the captains of both ships to leave their cargoes on some shelving beach along the coastline, in the hopes that they'll be found intact when our fellows eventually reach them? Andrew and Will will have to exercise their wits in order to achieve what must be done, but that's why they're our leaders. Wouldn't you agree?"

"I suppose so, my lord. As you say, every day is precious. I'll waste no time delivering your word, I promise you."

"I ken that, Father, and we'll do what we can to mak it as easy as may be for ye. Ye'll ride, and ye'll be on official church business, so naebody will meddle wi' ye."

"No Scot, you mean," I said, more to myself rather than him as I thought about the English who swarmed everywhere.

"No Englishman either," he replied, reverting to Latin. "You'll have a letter of safe conduct signed by the King of England himself."

I could not mask my amazement. "How can that be, my lord?"

"Because we have such a letter," he said proudly. "A personal guarantee of safe conduct signed by the Plantagenet and, shall we say, borrowed from a royal English courier less than a month ago. Ask me no more about it, but I assure you the document is genuine, signed by Edward himself and bedecked with a sufficient wealth of waxen seals and brightly coloured silken ribbons to overawe any who set eyes on it, no matter what their rank."

"And will I ride alone?"

"You will. Providing you with an escort would have defeated our purpose, which is to get you from south to north and back again without attracting notice. An unescorted priest, even though he be well mounted and therefore noteworthy, will invite no questions. Your status as an important church courier, summoning the Scottish bishops to an assembly in Glasgow, and backed by formal documentation as it is, will stand up to all but the most malignant curiosity. And I am sure, from what I know of you, that you are astute enough to elude that kind of curiosity."

I nodded.

"There's a sound horse ready for you, and a pack horse has been readied with the usual things you'll need to take with you. Oh, and you'll have no trouble finding your cousin. The last we heard, two days ago, was that he's back at his favourite old encampment in the forest, close to Selkirk town."

I nodded again, then knelt in front of him, facing the altar as he raised his hand over me and blessed me and my mission.

CHAPTER TWELVE

FORGIVENESS

"Will? Are you in there?"

I knocked and waited, but there was no reply, and I frowned, because the guard with whom I had left my horse had told me my cousin had gone inside mere moments earlier. I lifted the latch and pushed the door open, calling Will's name again as it swung back noiselessly on stout hinges of layered leather. I stooped to avoid the lintel as I stepped inside and closed the door gently behind me, feeling an instant, stabbing pain of regret as I breathed in the atmosphere and the suddenly remembered scents of what had been Will's home with Mirren.

To my left, the brightly painted screen of reeds separating the sleeping area from the rest of the single chamber was as brilliant and new-looking as it had been the day Mirren first painted it, and a faint trace of dried lavender, her favourite scent, seemed to waft out towards me from the unseen sleeping space behind it. In front of it, glowing in the light from a single, late-morning sunbeam, sat the rocking cradle of birch wood that Will had made for young Will before the child was born. To my right was a small, plain table with four wooden chairs, and beyond that, in the corner by the stone-built hearth, sat the large, padded armchair that was the first thing my cousin had built for his new wife—a small couch, really, big enough and deep enough to hold both him and Mirren in the comforting glow of an evening fire during inclement weather.

Of my cousin, though, there was no sign, and I remembered a previous occasion on which Mirren, too, had vanished inexplicably in the same manner. That was when I had learned that this single-room building had two exits, one of them sufficiently well disguised to blend perfectly into the rear wall and be next to invisible at first glance. I had questioned the need for such a thing when I first saw it, and my cousin had grinned and shrugged his massive shoulders, saying merely that strange things happen in the world of men and you could never tell when an extra way out of any place might be a blessing. I started to cross to the concealed door, but then I thought again of that first occasion and turned to look behind me, into the corner behind Will's armchair.

The sword was there, where I had last seen it, leaning in the angle of the walls, and it was every bit as impressive and imposing as I remembered. From its large, acorn-shaped pommel to its pointed tip, it was as tall as I am, just slightly less than six feet long. The hilt was a foot and a half of that length, made for a two-handed grip and bound in leather tightly knit with spirals of bronze wire. The slender, twisted, downward-curving cross-guard, made of the same gleaming metal as the blade, was as wide as my shoulders but no more than a 'thumb's breadth in section, turned and worked throughout its entire length to give it the appearance of a length of corded rope, with decorative quatrefoils at each end. Hilt and cross-guard were both made and added to the weapon here in Scotland, Will had told me, by a Highland smith called Malachy whose brother was Will's friend Seumas, known as Shoomy. But Malachy believed the blade itself was forged in Germania, for one of those Teutonic knights you sometimes hear about, the order founded by the Orthodox Christian emperor Frederick Barbarossa.

The first ten inches of the blade below the guard were flat-sided and edgeless, hammered flat to provide a guiding grip for fighting at close quarters, permitting the wielder to use the weapon as a stabbing spear rather than a slashing blade. Lower down, though, the cutting edge was lethal, three and a half feet of tapered steel with an unmistakable, twinkling look of razor sharpness.

A conversation popped instantly into my mind, perfectly recalled from the days when my cousin had first come into possession of it. He had been happily married then, with Mirren expecting their first child.

"What do you need a sword for?" I had asked him, after seeing the huge weapon for the first time. "To enable you to be killed more easily?"

He had smiled at me, knowing I was really chiding him not so much for thinking of giving up his great yew bow, but for what I considered his reckless endangerment of himself and his young family. I had made no attempt to conceal my disapproval of his public acknowledgment, a short time earlier, that he considered himself an outlaw, if that was what physical opposition to the increasing and illegitimate presence of English soldiery in Scotland entailed. His smile was tolerant and genuinely amused, though, warming his eyes.

"No, Cuz," he had said quietly. "If I ever wear that thing at all, it will be as a symbol."

"A symbol …" I pondered that for a moment. "Very well, then, let's accept that a sword such as that could be a symbol. Heaven knows it's big enough. But a symbol of what? Outlawry?"

His smile did not falter. "No, of leadership. Bear in mind, though, that I said *if* I wear it at all."

"Is there doubt that you might?"

"Enormous doubt, Jamie."

"Enormous is more than merely large, Will," I had said, with more than a small measure of cynicism. "What causes such great doubt, may I ask?"

"Aye, you may ask. It's caused by the fact that I'm about to be a father. I'm to have a son, Jamie, or perhaps a daughter. I don't care which it is, but whatever the result, it'll be a thing I've never known before. It frightens me when I think about it: a wee, small person, wide-eyed and alive and hungry for knowledge, and completely dependent upon me for his or her existence." He crossed his arms over his chest and peered at me. "For that reason alone I'll be steering well clear of leadership in future. God willing, I intend to stay here safely in the greenwood with my wife and child from now on, providing for them and getting more of them."

God, though, for reasons known solely to Himself, had not been willing.

I had not set eyes upon my cousin since the deaths of his family, but I had heard much about the aftermath, and I felt my soul quail inside me. By killing Will's loved ones, the English had removed the single impediment to William Wallace's rising up against them, the sole consideration restraining my cousin from seeking bloody, brutal, and merciless vengeance against them and theirs. They treated him as an ordinary man, tragically unaware that no man alive at that time could have been more extraordinary, and then they treated him as a Scot, beneath their lordly notice until it came time to swat him like a fly.

My imagination shied away from thoughts of what Will's vengeance might entail in the times ahead. I loved him deeply and admired him greatly, but I had known Will since we were children together and I had shared with him the unspeakable shame and terror of being sexually violated by the drunken English soldiers who had murdered his parents and decapitated his baby sister while he watched. Perhaps because of my vocation, I had eventually forgiven the benighted souls who had abused us, but my cousin never had. The wounds inflicted on William Wallace's soul that day had been deep and grievous, and he had never forgotten a single detail of what had happened. Nor had he ever considered, even for a moment, forgiving either the crime or its perpetrators, whom he had classified thereafter as "the English." And now, two decades later, he had been deprived again, by other, equally rapacious Englishmen, of his nearest and dearest loves, the wife and children who had, within his own mind, been his sole reason for living.

I had no doubt of my cousin's unquenchable capacity for vengeance, and none at all about the single-minded, implacable ferocity with which he would set about inflicting revenge upon those he believed had wronged him.

Now, I turned away from the concealed door and stepped to where I could reach out and touch the weapon. Though superb, it was simply too large and too heavy for an ordinary man to use. It had stood here unused, in the corner by Will's fireplace, from the time Shoomy had claimed it for Will until Will learned of the murder of his wife and children. From that day on, the sword had gone wherever William Wallace went, and its fame was spreading as rapidly as was his own.

"Jamie, welcome!" I leapt with fright at the sound of Will's voice, for I had not heard the door opening at my back, and I spun to face him. He was holding something in his hands, something draped in a cloth. "Arnulf told me you were here. It's good to see you, Cousin," he said in his deep, rolling voice.

I was watching his eyes, trying to gauge his mood and fighting to conceal my apprehension. It had not really been a long time since he and I had last seen each other, a mere few months, and the last words he had said to me when we parted had been instructions on protecting and safeguarding his family. Within hours of that conversation, though, both our worlds had changed forever.

Mirren's mother had been identified and taken into custody by Sir Lionel Redvers, a knight from Yorkshire who had been charged by the sheriff of Lanark, William Hazelrig, to find and detain the wife and family of the notorious outlaw William Wallace. We— Will's family and I—had encountered the arresting party by purest accident. Mirren had recognized her mother and gone to her assistance. In the melee that followed, I had been left for dead by the side of the road, my responsibilities grossly unfulfilled and my precious charges ripped from my care. Will's two-year-old son, William, had died soon after that, fatally injured in the skirmish—whether by accident or not we will never know—and callously thrown aside to die among the bushes lining a forest track, and Mirren, with her unborn child, had died even more brutally the following night, kicked to death by a drunken, oafish lout of a jailer who had fed her stillborn baby to his pigs.

Within a week of hearing those tidings, Will had killed both Redvers and Hazelrig, before attacking the garrison at Lanark and marching south to Sanquhar Castle to savage and destroy another English force.

William Wallace had unleashed his fury and given notice to Englishmen throughout southern Scotland that they could no·longer ride roughshod over the people here without suffering dire consequences.

I saw the changes in him at first glance and felt the shock of seeing them, even as I wondered whether he was being similarly taken aback by the ravages in my own face.

He was as big, as broad, and as strong as ever, and perhaps even larger—wider in the shoulders and deeper in the chest than he had been before. But there were deeply chiselled lines in his face that were new and cruel looking. His eyes looked feverish, brighter than was natural, I thought, and they seemed to flicker and pulsate with nervous energy. The most striking change, though, was in his hair, now shot through with silver. It was not old-man grey—he was not yet twenty-five, after all—but it was greying nonetheless, individual strands of silver standing out clearly in the haloed light from behind him.

"Wait," he said, "let me put this down." He went to the sideboard by the hidden door, where he carefully set down what he had been carrying, a large jug of some kind. "Fresh buttermilk," he said, smiling as he turned to look at me again. "New from the churn."

He came back to me then and reached out a hand to cup my chin, digging thumb and forefinger into my cheeks and tilting my head towards the light as he peered closely at my face. "They made a mess of you, Cuz," he murmured, "but at least there's no scars. And you were too pretty anyway. I always thought a face like yours was wasted on a priest ... You haven't said a word. Can you talk?"

I managed to find a smile at last. "Yeth," I said, exaggerating wildly. "I can thpeak and thay nathty thingth to people that they don't underthtand, and thometimeth I even thing with the monkth at Thunday thervitheth."

He laughed, and I cannot recall ever hearing a more welcome sound. "Dear God," he said, "it's good to see you again. I've missed you this past while. Come, sit down, for we've much to talk about, even if Wishart hasn't sent you here to put me to work of one kind or another." He stepped back to the sideboard and removed the cloth covering from the jug, then held the jug up to me. "Will you join me? It's cold and it's fresh."

"Pour two, then," I said, hooking a chair from the table with my foot and preparing to sit down. "And I do have instructions for you from his lordship, but they can wait until later."

"Fine, but don't sit down yet. There's a well-built fire in the grate and a live coal in a firebox on the mantel there. I just brought it from the main fire outside, so it should flare up easily. And there's tapers in that long tube beside it, so you light us a fire while I pour us our drinks. And keep talking while you do it. Do you know how long it's been since I last spoke Latin?" He paused. "How long has it been since we two last spoke? Because I'll swear I haven't said a Latin word since then. No one around here speaks anything but Scots."

For the next half-hour, while the fire grew stronger and the buttermilk lasted, we sat together and enjoyed each other as amicably as we had when we were boys, and not until we had been conversing for at least half that time did I become aware of strangenesses in his way of speaking.

I had brought up the matter of his loss and my own feelings of guilt over what had happened, talking about how I had been unable to help Mirren and the children in all the awful consequences of our encounter with the English knight Redvers. It was not a subject I would have willingly confronted, but I was aware of its being there between us, like an open wound, and I knew I would never be able to look Will directly in the eye until I had admitted my fault in the whole thing and laid bare the guilt that had been haunting me ever since. And so, despite the fear that clutched me like an icy fist, I acknowledged my dereliction and asked my cousin if he could ever forgive me.

He sat up straighter suddenly and bent towards me, his eyes filled with concern. "Jamie," he said, "in God's holy name, how can you believe that what happened that day had anything to do with you? You are a priest—you've always been a priest, even before you were ordained. You were never a warrior, and no one ever expected you to be one, so what nonsense is this you're babbling? What could you have done against such odds, even had you owned a sword or a bow? No, Cousin, put your mind at rest on this matter. It was no fault of yours that the woman and the wee boy died that day. That was the Devil's work, done by the Devil's minions, Redvers and Hazelrig, and they have died for it."

In the brief silence that followed, two things became startlingly clear to me: he was being completely truthful, and he had not once spoken either Mirren's name or young Will's, referring to them only as "the woman" and "the wee boy." Was he aware of what he was doing, working so carefully to avoid naming them? Had he lost his mind in his grief? Mayhap he had simply decided it was better and less painful for him not to call them by their names, thereby avoiding the pain and distress of contemplating them too freshly.

He rose up then and crossed in front of the fire to place his mug on the tabletop by the empty jug. "So, Wishart has instructions for me. I'm surprised it has taken him so long to send them, for I've been expecting them since I left him in Glasgow last month. How is the old warlock?"

"He's well, Cuz, but he's not as young and spry as he was when we first met him."

"God's blood, is anyone? He was old even then, and that was a half score years ago at least."

"Closer to three-quarters. I was ten, I think—perhaps eleven."

"But he's hale, eh?"

"He is, thank God, and as curious as ever. He wants to know how many men you have with you now. I do, too."

"Altogether? I couldn't tell you. I've made no attempt to count them recently. They're here aplenty, but there's been no need for an actual tally, though I suppose that's a stupid thing to say. There's always a need for such things. But I came back from Perth with close to two hundred new men. God knows I never sought them out or asked them to come with me—they just followed me back. They wanted to fight for King John and the realm, and they were willing enough. But they would have been worse than useless in a real fight—farmers and labourers, shepherds and swineherds, many of them with no weapons other than a wee knife or a heavy stick, and some with not even that much. Made Ewan and Shoomy near sob with sorrow when they saw them.

"We've been training them since we got back—them and others like them—though we're sorely lacking in weapons, even for training. But at least they all know the difference now between the dangerous end of a club and the end they have to hang on to. And a very few of them can even use a bow. So they're getting better all the time, but not fast enough to suit Long John and the others. What we need to do now is to take them raiding somewhere. That's when they'll really start to learn in earnest, when they're pitted against folk who are fighting back, for their lives."

"So how many actual fighting men do you have, can you guess?"

He inhaled deeply. "Let's see … perhaps five hundred, ready to fight. There are three other camps here in the forest, with two or three hundred in each."

"That's nigh on twelve hundred men."

"Aye, give or take a hundred or so. Do you have a use for them?" He laughed again. "And am I being the fool even to ask? Of course you have a use for them. Or Wishart does. Come on then, Cousin, for I think the time has come. What does the old hawk want?"

"He wants the English out of Scotland, above and beyond all else. I know you spoke with him at length before you came back here, but how much do you know of what he plans to do?"

Will eased himself back in his chair and narrowed his eyes, gazing at me with an expression I found hard to read. "He was talking of holding his army in check at Irvine … to dance a pavane with Percy and Clifford's force but not to fight with them. I think that's worse than foolish and I told him so to his face, but he wouldn't listen. Nor would Stewart."

I nodded. "Do you know what he hopes to achieve by doing that?"

"Let me guess. A lingering death from old age?" His voice was heavy with sarcasm. "No, I don't know what his hopes are. But I know what Henry Percy is likely to do, once he has figured out a way to—"

I spoke right over him. "He's playing the doddering old fool and poltroon, as is the Steward, fussing and fretting and refusing to commit their army—though he's keeping it safe against attack—because he is attempting to buy sufficient time for you and Andrew Murray and several others in the realm to unite the folk in a general uprising and act decisively."

He grunted. "So now we come to it," he said. "Go ahead, then. Tell me what he wants me to do."

I drew a deep breath and told him, speaking words that I had never imagined I could ever say: "He wants you to behave like the Plantagenet at Berwick: to raise the dragon banner against the English garrisons in Lothian with fire and sword and no quarter."

"Does he, by Jesus?" He pursed his lips as he sank back into his chair. "Fire and sword in Lothian, eh?" He pondered that for a moment longer, then nodded slowly. "Aye, it makes sense. My first thought was to refuse, because we'd be waging war against our own. But *are* they our own, these Lothian folk? Or are they Edward's? They've made no effort to rise up against anyone, and God Himself knows that Lothian is a hell-nest of Englishry, right enough."

"Aye, it is, and most of those are safe behind high walls much of the time. Which leads me to something else he bade me tell you. You are to harass the garrisons in any way you can—to coax them out into the open and then smash them—but he doesn't want you wasting any time in sieges. There's no time for sieges. He said to tell you that you need to savage the lands outside and around the castles and garrisoned towns, burning crops and killing livestock to keep them out of English hands and bellies."

"And the folk who live there? What happens to them?"

"They suffer. And that's regrettable because they're Scots, but you yourself just said that of all the folk in Scotland's realm, those in Lothian have been more tolerant and supportive of the English. So now they must pay the piper for being too friendly to the enemy. Just as the townspeople of Lanark did when you went there."

He stared at me, his eyes narrowing, but I did not look away, for I knew the truth of that story, as witnessed by Harald Gaptooth.

"And what will Wishart and the Steward be doing while that is happening?" he asked me.

"Keeping Percy and Clifford away from you for as long as may be, preventing them from striking at your back. They won't dare march against you if it means leaving an undefeated army intact at their own rear. I can't speak for Clifford, but I know not even Henry Percy would be that foolhardy."

"So be it, then. Tell me exactly what their lordships want me to do."

Half an hour later, he professed himself satisfied and went to the door, where he shouted to someone outside to summon his lieutenants to meet him at the command centre in one hour.

"So," he asked me, coming back and sitting down at the table again, "how will you find Murray when you arrive up there? From what I've heard, his territories are vast beyond comprehension and mainly trackless, and he could be anywhere among them, high or low. Where will you even start to look for him?"

"I don't know, to tell you the truth. I know his home is Auch Castle, on the promontory called the Dark Isle, but if he is campaigning as well and as widely as his uncle David of Bothwell says he is, I don't expect to find him there. What I do hope, though, is to find someone there who knows where he is and will take me to him."

"That makes sense," my cousin growled, "but by the sweet Jesus, Jamie, that's a long way to ride, all by yourself and in a hurry and through inhospitable lands. You'll never make it in time."

"I have to. I've no option. If I don't reach Moray in time to send Andrew south to meet you at Dundee at the appointed time, then what the bishop said is likely to come true: all of Scotland will go down into slavery under Edward's heel."

I saw his eyes darken and his brow wrinkle as he absorbed that, but before he could comment I continued: "It's not as bleak as it sounds. We've calculated the total distance from Selkirk town to Inverness, erring always on the side of caution, and it's close to twelve score miles. That is the farthest it can be."

He stared at me as if he thought I had lost my wits. "Twelve score miles? Is that what you said? *Twelve score?* That's nigh on two and a half hundred! Who did the calculation?"

"I did, with the help of some priests who know the terrain up there. If I leave here tomorrow morning, I'll have three clear weeks to find Murray and ensure he can gather his people and meet you in time. Twenty-one days, to travel two hundred and forty miles. That's less than twelve miles a day."

He opened his mouth to protest, but I cut him off. "I know, twelve miles a day would be nothing in England with good English roads beneath my horse's hooves, but there are no good roads north of Stirling. Depending upon the weather, among other things, twelve miles a day over open moors and mountains and up along the coast might turn out to be difficult, but I'm sure it won't be impossible. And coming back south with Murray to Dundee will be more straightforward. According to his uncle David, the shortest route for him would be directly south from Inverness, using the mountain passes through the Highlands of Badenoch and the Mounth until he reaches Perth, and from there it's scarce twenty miles east along the Tay to Dundee. He could do it easily in thirteen days and be waiting for you when you arrive in Dundee."

Will was frowning at me. "Why Dundee, Jamie? Why would we meet up there? It's a nothing place."

I told him then about the supply ship full of armour and weapons that would be waiting for him there. "It's a quiet place, too, don't forget, away from normal traffic paths, and it has a garrisoned castle, a legitimate target for an attack. Taking that will give you and Murray time to blood your armies as a united force, to renew your friendship, and to become familiar with each other's forces. All without too much attention or distraction from the English, who will have other things to occupy them elsewhere. The bishop expects the entire southwest to be crawling with English armies by the middle of August. Percy and Clifford's group are already there, of course, and they'll stay there, but there are rumours of another force being sent north to reinforce them, a levy raised from the northern sheriffdoms of Lancaster, Westmoreland, and Cumberland and commanded by Cressingham. Three hundred horse, according to our source, supported by ten thousand foot. A rumour, as I said, but not unreasonable and more than likely probable."

"How strong is Percy's group, in terms of horse and foot?"

"That's uncertain. The likeliest estimate I heard was two hundred horse—knights and mounted men-at-arms—and three thousand foot."

"Hmm ... You said *rumours*, as in more than one. What else is there?"

"Another almost certain to have substance. John de Warrenne, the Earl of Surrey, still holds command in Scotland although he detests the place and its climate and has not set foot here since last year. According to our friendly clerical sources close to Westminster, he will be coming back to do his duty, under threat of Edward's great displeasure. And he will not come unattended."

"Invasion strength, think you?"

"Invasion strength, for a certainty, the bishop believes."

Will nodded. "Fine, so be it. I'll go to Fife when I leave Lothian. But this route you named for Murray, straight south to Perth, why don't you go up that way, instead of adding twice as much again by going along the coast?"

"Too hazardous to try alone, I'm told. There'll be folk along the coastal route if I get into trouble."

"Aye, and those folk along the coastal route could *be* trouble. Never trust anyone but yourself when you're on the road, Jamie. You should know that as well as anyone by now. Besides, it's summertime. The snow's all out of the high passes by now, and that's most of what makes that route hazardous for a man on his own. I think you'd be better off striking straight north and following the passes. Save yourself a hundred miles that you don't need to ride." He smoothed his shaven chin with thumb and forefinger — a beard wearer's mannerism. "You can cover *ten* miles a day easily, with a sound horse under you and a good pack horse. Either way, what if you run into trouble?"

"From whom?" I replied, smiling to disguise my own misgivings. "Only two kinds of people might cause a travelling priest trouble: Scots and Englishmen. If any Scots attempt to interfere with me, I'll tell them you're my cousin and threaten them with your vengeance, as well as with excommunication. And if any Englishman contests my passing, I'll show him my letter of safe conduct from the King of England himself." I had shown him the captured document earlier. "But nothing will happen to me while I'm on God's business, Cousin," I continued. "And this is most assuredly God's business, so put your mind at ease. I'll leave first thing in the morning, as soon as I've said Mass. If I can do ten miles a day north from Perth, it'll take me but a fortnight to reach Inverness and start looking for Murray."

He grunted. "And if you can't, you'll never be able to make up whatever time you've lost. Your plan leaves you no breathing space, Jamie. I think you should go by sea."

"By *sea*?" The mere suggestion left me open-mouthed. The idea was so far removed from the reality of my life that it made no sense to me. I had *seen* the sea, of course—living in Scotland it was almost impossible not to, at some point—but I had never *been* to sea, afloat upon it in a boat.

"Aye, by sea. How much baggage are you carrying?"

I blinked at him. "Baggage? Not much. Not even enough to merit a pack horse."

"What specifically?"

"Some clothing and a few personal belongings. My sacramental things. Oats and nosebags for the animals, and basic food and utensils to feed myself. Why?"

"What about vestments? Are you taking priestly robes with you?"

"No sacerdotals, no. I'll celebrate my daily Mass alone in the dark before I take the road, and only God and I will know what I'm wearing."

"What else would you absolutely need to take with you, if you were to travel by ship?"

"*What* ship, Will? We're far inland. What are you—?"

"Just tell me, Jamie, what else?"

I thought about it for a moment. "Nothing, I suppose. Some underclothes, my cloak and staff. That's all."

"Are you sure?"

"Of course I'm sure. Were I mad enough to contemplate such a journey, then yes, that's all I would need. But I really have no idea why we're even talking about such a thing."

He gestured towards the sword in the corner. "D'you remember who made that?"

"Aye," I said, glad to have the topic changed. "Shoomy's brother, Malachy the smith. He finished it, anyway."

"That's right. And until Shoomy came back from the north that time, bringing the sword with him, I hadn't even known he had a brother. Or certainly not that the brother had a grown son called Callum."

I blinked at him, wondering where this was headed.

"Young Callum is here right now. He arrived from Aberdeen yesterday morning. His father, Malachy, is dead and Callum was brought south to his uncle Shoomy for his own protection."

"Wait, wait!" I raised my hand to silence him. "Why would this lad come *here*? And how would he know where to find you?"

Will dipped his head in a slow nod. "Excellent questions. He came in the first place because he has been proscribed—he is an outlaw with a price upon

his head. It seems that his father fell afoul of one of
the English garrison commanders in Aberdeen—
some dispute over smithing Malachy was never paid
for. He was angry about it and, being Malachy, he
made no secret of it. So the Englishman, Mowbray
I think his name was, sent some of his garrison lads
to have a word with him. Four of them went into his
smithy and started throwing things around, and
when Malachy picked one of them up and tossed
him onto the fire in his forge, they didn't like that at
all. The noise brought young Callum running at the
head of a crowd, just in time to see his father being
murdered in his own smithy. The boy snatched up a
pitchfork and killed one of the soldiers. The angry
neighbours took care of two more, but the last of
the four escaped and ran back to the castle. And
there, of course, he reported things to suit himself,
and a manhunt was launched to find the murderous
young Callum."

"So how was he able to get away?"

"Because he was fortunate. A man called Sven
Persson—some call him Big Sven, I call him Finn—
was in Aberdeen that day. Finn is, or was, brother to
Callum's mother, who died a few years ago, and he's
a seagoing merchantman out of one of the Norse ports
across the sea, well connected among the burghers of
Aberdeen and other coastal towns. In late spring every
year, Finn takes his ship to Aberdeen, where he seems
to be related either by blood or marriage to half the
folk in the region, and picks up a relative, a cloth

manufacturer and merchant, and takes him down to the Firth of Tay, where the merchant drops off finished woollen goods all along the Fife coast, ending up in Perth. He then picks up a fresh cargo of raw winter wool from the warehouses in Perth and takes it back to Aberdeen for processing.

"Big Sven is no fool—I've met him a few times—and when he found out what had happened, he smuggled the boy aboard his ship as soon as it was dark and kept him out of sight until his crew could load their cargo and put out to sea again. He took the boy with him to Perth, then sent him here with an escort of four of the fighting men he employs to guard his ship. Those four will be returning to Perth come morning, and by the time they get there, Sven should be ready to head back to Aberdeen. I think you should sail with him. That's why I asked you about baggage. There's not much room for extra baggage aboard a seagoing ship."

"But I can't go by sea!"

"Why not? If there's a ship available and willing to take you, of course you can. It'll be a lot faster than going by land."

"But what good would it do?" I asked. "I'd be in Aberdeen with another sixty miles and more ahead of me and no horse to get me there."

"At worst, you could buy another horse, but you won't need to, because you'll continue north by sea, still with Finn, all the way to Inverness. With favourable winds, you'll be there in days, not weeks."

"But … how can you know that? This Finn fellow, or Big Sven or whatever his name is, might be sailing back to wherever he lives as soon as he returns to Aberdeen."

"No, he won't. His next port of call is in fact Inverness. It always is. He has merchants up there, too, who rely on him from year to year—him and others, I mean—to ship their goods to market. As for why he should agree to take you, he'll be glad of the passage money you'll pay him. I'll write to him and tell him you're my cousin and under my protection."

"But how do you come to know this man, Will? How do you meet a sea captain from across the eastern sea when you live as an outlaw in the depths of a great forest?"

He shrugged his huge shoulders. "I meet a lot of people nowadays, Jamie," he said modestly. "And sometimes they arrange for me to meet other people. I know a lot of folk."

"Evidently so," I said, impressed in spite of myself. "And do you really think you can arrange this?"

He grinned. "I'll go and see to it now. You can come with me, if you like."

CHAPTER THIRTEEN

THE BURGESS OF INVERNESS

God smiled upon me in the weeks that followed, blessing my northern journey with the best of weather, so that I sailed up the eastern coast of Scotland aboard Sven Persson's ship, *The Golden Gannet*, in a blaze of dazzling, sun-gilt beauty, seeing the land on my left in its true but savage glory, and reiterating my sincere gratitude in prayer, time after time, that I was safe aboard the vessel that bore me, with no need to attempt that journey on land.

The *Gannet* was a fine ship, sixty feet in length and broad in the beam, with sufficient cargo space below decks to generate revenue for her owner and crewmen year-round. She carried a crew of sixteen, eight of whom were armed guards—mercenaries whose primary task was to protect the vessel against attack by pirates. In the absence of pirates, though, the guards worked beside the remaining crewmen, manning the twin banks of oars that powered the ship when there was no wind. Never having been on board a ship before, I was endlessly impressed by the compact efficiency of the vessel. Not a single inch of space was wasted or lacking purpose, and I understood why Will had insisted on knowing exactly what baggage I was carrying.

How different, I realized, this sea journey was from the land route I might have followed, where every turn, every hillside, involved the possibility of change of direction or purpose. Aboard ship, there were no such possibilities, and the more I thought about the differences between where I found myself and where I might have been, the more grateful I became that I was aboard the *Gannet*. It was one thing to admit that, lacking roads, the Scottish terrain could be difficult to cross. To see that same terrain from shipboard at a distance, however, knowing that there simply *were* no roads traversing it, provided a daunting lesson in the realities of overland travel and the impossibility of progressing with any hope of sustainable speed from day to day. It took me less than a single day after leaving Perth, having journeyed out into open sea, to be able to see for myself how dense and impenetrable were the forests that covered the land, and how its high, rolling hills crested occasionally in majestic, craggy tops that thrust up like breaching whales from the uniform blanket of trees that covered their lower slopes.

Later that first day, before nightfall, the captain and I were eating together with the sole other passenger, huddled in his tiny cabin, when the lookout screamed a warning from above us and sent us running out onto the deck.

I spoke just now of hill crests breaking the surface of the forest like breaching whales, but until that day, I confess, I had never seen a whale. My awareness of the creatures was based solely upon the scriptural tale of Jonah and the Leviathan. That evening, though, I witnessed a gathering of the creatures when we found ourselves sailing northward in the very midst of a large group of them—immense, terrifying monsters from beneath the seas, some of them even larger than the *Gannet*. I froze when I saw the first of them, my eyes directed to the sight by the frantic screams and pointing finger of the lookout on the cross-tree of the single mast. I turned and saw the most frightening sight of my life—a black behemoth leaping clear out of the water less than a hundred paces away and appearing to hover endlessly before it crashed back to the surface and dived. The sight of its mighty, high-held tail remained seared into my memory after it vanished.

I saw how tiny was the ship that I had thought so large, dwarfed and threatened as it was by giant, moving bodies all around us as they rose into view and vanished again beneath the black waters that swirled around our keel. I felt sudden, scalding heat as my bladder gave way with fear. By then, though, everyone aboard was soaked with seawater and so no one noticed what had happened to me. I thought that everyone else aboard the ship must be as terrified as I was, but I soon realized that what I had taken to be their fright was no more than surprise at finding themselves so suddenly among the whales, in imminent danger of being capsized. I was, I later discovered, the sole person there on the deck who had never seen such things before and thought them supernatural.

Afterwards, when the whales had vanished back into the depths and order was restored, the ship making steady headway northward, I asked Big Sven what he would have done had one of the creatures collided with the ship. He shook his head abruptly. "They wouldn't have," he said. "They make no accidents like that. They saw us more clearly than we saw them. They made sport with us, I think, but not war."

I was astonished. "You mean they knew what they were doing?"

"I think so. They are not stupid, these creatures. And the deep water is their home. They make no accidental bumps … they do not get drunk and fall around like people. So if one collides with us, it would be because he attacked us." He dipped his head and shrugged. "And in a fight like that, I think we would lose. He would drown us all."

The captain's fatalistic observation, and the way he made it, reminded me of a long-forgotten conversation I had had with Andrew Murray the last time I saw him, and remembering it, I felt a sudden rush of gooseflesh and a tightening in my chest at the prospect of meeting the man again and seeing for myself how serious he had been in what he said on that occasion. He had stopped in Glasgow to visit Bishop Wishart on his way north to his home in Moray after escaping from

Chester Castle in Wales a month or so earlier. I had asked him a provocative question, one that should never have been asked, since there was no precedent for the possibility I was proposing, but it had simply popped into my mind and I blurted it out as it came to me. What would he do, I asked, if King Edward, for reasons of his own, were to decide that he wanted to make an example of young Andrew Murray of Petty and had him arrested again and executed out of hand, as a lesson to his father and others?

Andrew had looked at me in much the same speculative way that Big Sven had, and then he, too, had dipped his head and shrugged. "I don't know," he said, "but I would fight him to my last breath—and I intend to do that anyway, no matter what he does. My family's lands, in Moray and elsewhere, are vast. And if Edward of England wants to seize them, or me, he will have to come and do so in person, and I will not be standing idly by, watching him from some far mountaintop. I've had a bellyful of sneering English pigheadedness and I'm going home to raise the men of Moray and stir up Hell itself against these arrogant overlords, as they like to call themselves. Overlords! Faugh! One of them's living now in Auch Castle, in the house where I was born. But he'll be leaving once I reach home, and all his people with him, one way or another, and I care not whether they be dead or alive when they go. I am sick to my soul of strutting, overweening English arrogance. Scotland is *ours* by the grace of God—it always has been, and the English have no place in it. And I swear to you that if God spares me, I intend to teach them that, though I have to write it in their blood."

His eyes were flashing, but strangely his voice had grown quieter as he grew angrier, falling to a near hiss as he continued, almost spitting the words. "It's high time someone taught them what they are, these strutting, ridiculous bantam cocks. Who gave this benighted, self-deluding King of theirs the belief that he has a right to come up here and impose his will upon free folk who have no need of his interference, no desire to suffer his attentions, and no intention of lying down and allowing him and his thieving, ignorant bullies to trample them and their rights? My father, Sir Andrew Murray of Petty, is ten times the man England's King could ever be, and he is an old, old man. But he has lived a life any man could be proud of, a life more honourable and upright than anything to which the Plantagenet can lay claim. But now, at the petulant whim of this self-righteous King of England, this posturing, impious popinjay, my father is locked up in London's Tower and like to die there. I swear to you, Jamie, by the living God, that if no other man in Scotland will stand up against this aging, braggart crusader from a bygone day, I, Andrew Murray, will defy him alone and die, if I must, with my bloody spittle soaking his grizzled beard."

Remembering that rant, and the grim-faced, implacable determination of the young man who had uttered it, I grew impatient again with the slowness of my journey, despite my certain knowledge that I was making far better time than I had ever imagined possible. And so, while Sven and his crew worked all around me, I fell to pacing the deck anxiously, though there was scarce room enough to walk four paces before having to turn back and retrace them.

It took us three days to make the voyage to Aberdeen from the mouth of the Tay, and we spent three more in the town, unloading and reloading. The other passenger had vanished with his cargo of raw wool as soon as it was unloaded. I knew no one in Aberdeen, and so I stayed aboard the ship, roaming the harbour during the days and watching, fascinated, the thousand and one activities that go on in such places all day, every day.

A merchant came aboard on the third day, his cargo of heavy, square-sawn lumber already loaded and secured, and our captain—who had invited me that day to call him Finn—introduced us to each other. I disliked the newcomer immediately, and despite knowing I should not judge a man without coming to know him at least slightly, I felt justified in my dislike. The fellow glowered constantly, radiating distrust and hostility, so that among the first words that occurred to me in assessing him were *suspicious*, *taciturn*, *shifty-eyed*, and *surly*. I quickly decided that, having lived for as long as I had without being aware of his existence, I could easily live as long again without a need to be reminded of it. I had no desire to speak with him, or even to remember his name.

I wondered about his cargo, though, since raw, heavy lumber seemed to me to be a strange material to be shipping within a country that was largely covered in forest, but my curiosity did not survive the first two days of sailing farther up the coast. The forest appeared to continue unchanged north of Aberdeen, but on the few occasions when we approached close enough to land to be able to discern such things, I could see that the size of the trees was diminishing rapidly as we progressed northward, and by the time we rounded the Cape of Buchan and turned west to sail into the Moray Firth, the landscape south of us, in the great lordships of Buchan and Badenoch, was mainly treeless—immense, rocky expanses of low hills, covered in scrub and heather, with only stunted bushes and shrubs laying claim to the name of forestation.

Making that turn and sailing west, it seemed to me that we had sailed the length of Scotland and nothing lay northward of us there. That impression, though, lasted less than a day, quickly belied by the reappearance of land to the northwest, which Finn told me was the territories of Ross, Sutherland, and Caithness. He drew me a crude picture with the point of his knife, scoring two shallow lines in the dampened wood of the deck at our feet to show how, like two sides of a triangle, the southern coast on our left and the one coming down from the northeast formed the great funnel-shaped bay that was the Moray Firth, sweeping inland and narrowing dramatically to the town of

Inverness, hard by Loch Ness, at the entrance to the great glen that divided Scotland's Highlands north and south.

As we continued westward, past the small towns of Banff, Elgin, and Nairn on the southern shore, the countryside grew ever more bleak and barren. There were mountains ahead of us in the west and to the south, hulking shapes shrouded in the mist of great distances, but there were no large trees to be seen, and it rapidly became clear to me that the value of the lumber aboard the *Gannet* had increased greatly since it was loaded in Aberdeen.

There were castles, too, visible from the water on both sides of the firth; enormous castles, several of them built of stone and still being fortified, to judge from the scaffolding surrounding them.

"Where is the Black Isle?" I asked Finn on my last day aboard the *Gannet*.

We were proceeding under the power of oars alone by that point, the firth having narrowed between Nairn on the south bank and Cromarty on the north, and Finn was leaning indolently against the railing at the rear of the ship, by the tiller, idly watching the efforts of the rowers. He waved ahead, towards the northern coastline that was now less than two miles from us and growing closer.

"You're looking at it."

I peered more closely at the land he had indicated. "That's an island?"

"It's the Black Isle."

"Well, I would never have known. It looks like part of the mainland."

"Aye, but it's an island nonetheless. There's a wee channel runs all the way across it, isolating it from the land behind. You could jump over it in places, but it's there."

I could see two castles over there, one of them close, on a great stone motte overlooking the south-eastern shore of the island, the other farther off, only its shape visible as a large and obviously man-made block against the skyline to the north and east, beyond the hump of the island's shoulder.

"Which of those is Auch?"

"That one," he said, pointing at the closer of the two. "And now that I see it, I should tell you this is the closest we will come to it, on this or any other voyage, so if it's Auch you want to reach, we can put you ashore over there right now, within easy walking distance of the castle. That would save you from travel all the way to Inverness and back here again by land. Would save you two days, at least. It's your decision, my friend, but if you want to go ashore here you had better decide quickly."

I gazed at the distant fortress, debating with myself, then asked him if Murray had retaken it or was it still in English hands.

"You tell me," he said with a grand shrug. "But I can tell you, Andrew de Moray has been in revolt for two full months and more. Everyone knows that. And he started here, evicting the garrison from his father's castle. I would be surprised if the English have returned since then."

"I would be too," I said, remembering Murray's grim determination. "Can you put the *Gannet* in that close to shore?"

"Not close enough without a long swim." He grinned at me. "But we can row you ashore in a small boat. How long will you take to make ready?"

I stood at the top of the shelving, pebbled beach where Sven's men had dropped me dry-footed, staring up at the castle the de Moray family had built on the summit of a barren, sheer-sided rock. This was Auch Castle, the seat of the de Moravia family, and the very look of it gave warning that its owners were not to be trifled with. It was a classic motte-and-bailey castle: a central, defensive keep built of local stone atop a high motte and surrounded by a bailey, a walled courtyard, that housed other buildings and provided shelter for the people of the surrounding countryside in time of danger. As was the case with many of Scotland's greatest fortresses, though, the motte upon which Auch was built was natural—a large crag thrusting vertically to a height of more than a hundred feet, and the steepness of its sides—sheer cliffs, for the most part—made it easily defensible. Its sole potential weak point, the approach road winding in a series of steep switchbacks up bald rock hillside to the summit, was vulnerable at every stage of its ascent, overlooked and threatened from above. All in all, Auch's was an impressive and intimidating site, and even though I knew the trick by which Andrew de Moray had been able to penetrate the castle and win it back from the English, I could not help but be awed that he had been able to capture the place.

As I stared up towards the distant summit I saw movement on the heights as a file of men emerged and lined the edge of the road above, looking down at me. I was unsurprised. *The Golden Gannet* would have been closely watched since it first became visible to the guards on the walls, long before Finn Persson altered course to set me ashore. Sure enough, I saw movement on the road down from the motte, and I picked up my pack, swung it into place at my back, and went to meet my new hosts.

They treated me with adequate civility from the outset, correctly judging that I posed no threat to anyone. The man in charge of the group sent to meet me, a corpulent, sallow-faced fellow wearing half armour, asked me to give my name and state my business on de Moray land. I told him who I was and that I had been sent north by my bishop to find Sir Andrew the Younger and to speak with him on a matter of some urgency.

"He's no' here," the big man said. "But ye'd better come up to the keep. Bring him!"

The six men who had accompanied him now arranged themselves about me, not in the disciplined way that formal military guards would, but nonetheless effectively, leaving me with no shred of doubt that I was under guard, and we followed their captain as he led us back up the hill. I asked whom I would be speaking to when we reached the keep, but no one gave any sign of having heard me and so I decided to say no more and wait until my question answered itself.

As we approached the top of the road, I could get a better view of the outer wall surrounding the bailey, and I realized it was far stronger and more substantial than I had thought it to be when I was gazing up at it from the beach. I had known it would be massively thick at the base, for it was built on the solid stone summit of the motte, which meant it could have no entrenched foundations, but I had underestimated the scale of the thing.

All curtain wall fortifications are double structured, built with an empty space between two parallel stone walls. The outer wall confronts the enemy and, for obvious reasons, is built of heavier and larger stones than the inner one, and the space between the two is filled with packed earth and rubble. Some curtain walls I had seen were dizzyingly high, towering above the ground to provide the defenders with the advantage of height and inaccessibility. It was not so with the walls of Auch, though, for the monolith that was the motte already gave its defenders both of those advantages, and the curtain walls that topped it, which were no higher than thirty feet, had been built right to the edge of the cliff, offering no foothold or rallying space to any attacker.

The outer wall could be described as roughly circular, following the outer edge of the crag, and its ends overlapped to form a killing ground, a passageway four good paces wide and more than fifty long that led to the main gate and was wide open to attack from overhead at every step. The gate itself, I saw to my amazement, was an enormous and cumbersome thing, built of ancient, square-dressed logs, iron-bound and hinged at the top to form a gigantic, hanging curtain. This gate could be raised and lowered by chains and pulleys, though the lower end could be released to crash down devastatingly in time of need, and once it was down it could be locked in place, secured by a brace of iron bolts each as thick as a man's thigh. That gate, I decided, eyeing the device as I passed through, exactly captured the meaning of the word *impregnable*.

As I slowed below and peered up at the hinged apparatus that topped it, one of my guards, walking too close behind, bumped into me, whereupon he threw himself violently sideways with a curse and drew his dirk as though I had tried to attack him. Seeing the leaping fury on his face, I thought I might die right there in that narrow space between the walls.

"A God's name, Maitland," one of his companions snarled. "Are ye daft? Put up yer dirk."

"He tried to—"

"He tried nothin'. He looked up at the gate is what he did, and had you been awake instead o' stumblin' ahint him like a bleary-eyed tosspot, ye'd hae seen him do it and no' tripped ower him." His voice was heavy with disgust that I knew had little to do with me. "The man's a priest, for Christ's sake! And there's six o' us here guardin' him, so what would he try to do? Ye think he's like to turn on you?"

"What's going on here?"

It was the half-armoured captain, and my defender looked at him almost defiantly, it seemed to me. "Nothing much," he said, looking back at the red-faced dirk-wielder, who was putting his weapon away and looking sheepish. "Maitland here tripped ower the pr—the priest. That's all."

He had been on the point of saying "the prisoner," I knew. The captain looked from him to me, ignoring the man called Maitland, and then sniffed. "Aye, well, we're here now. The rest of you can go back to work. You," he said, pointing at my defender. "Take this one up to the keep and put him under guard until he's needed." He scanned me from feet to head with a scowling glance. "Tell whoever ye leave him wi' that he needna be shackled, but he's to be locked up and kept out o' mischief until he's sent for." With that he turned his back on us and walked away, followed by five of the six guards.

I raised an eyebrow at my guard, and he shrugged one shoulder. "You heard the man," he said.

"Aye, I did." I looked straight up and pointed to the device overhead. "I've never seen a gate like that. Are they common in these parts?"

"What?"

He clearly had not understood the question. "The hanging gate. I've never seen the like. Are there others like it in other castles?"

He, too, looked up at the unusual gate, then shook his head. "I don't think so. That's the only one, as far as I know. And before you ask me anything else, I ken nothing more about it."

"Sir Andrew might know."

"Aye," he said, "Sir Andrew might. You should ask him about it."

"I will." Only when I saw his eyebrow quirk did I realize that he had meant his remark sarcastically, never dreaming that I would, in fact, ask such a trivial question of Sir Andrew de Moray.

He jerked his head in a signal for me to start walking again, and I turned obediently into the yard that opened up at the end of the curtain wall passageway. We walked together across a courtyard that had been chipped and chiselled from the raw rock; the ground was uneven and dangerous to walk on without watching where you placed your feet. In the short distance we covered I saw a well-equipped smithy with several forges, a cooperage with new barrels stacked outside, several storage houses of varying sizes including a strong barn, and a small, squat building with several chimneys from which wafted the mouth-watering aroma of new bread.

The keep dominated everything else, and in the defensive tradition of such buildings, it had but a single entrance, high up on the sheer stone wall and fronted by a long drawbridge. A steep, open-sided flight of steps rose up from the courtyard to the end of the lowered drawbridge, and as we approached it I could see that the bottom of the drawbridge was protected with sheets of iron, so that when raised, it would protect the door in the wall from fiery arrows and other missiles.

We climbed the steps and crossed the narrow bridge—I kept rigidly to the centre, since there were no railings on either side and it was a sheer drop to the uneven rock twenty feet below. The guards at the far end allowed us to pass through into the keep with no more than a curious glance at me. I had to keep my eyes on my feet as we climbed several flights of wall-hugging steps leading to the floors above the main entrance of Auch Castle.

The family quarters of the castle's owners occupied the third floor and were separated from the common stairway by floor-to-ceiling wooden walls, affording a degree of privacy. The floors directly below and above the family's rooms were used by garrison and administrative staff, and it was to the quarters of one of the latter, on the fourth floor, that my escort delivered me. By the time we arrived there, I was growing sure we were headed for the open roof of the keep, for my legs had pushed me up at least a hundred steps and I knew there could not be many more left to climb. Before we reached the roof, though, my escort stopped at an open door and cleared his throat loudly.

The room beyond was surprisingly small—barely larger than a horse stall—and crowded, with a low ceiling that barely allowed its single inhabitant, a man several inches taller than me, to stand upright without stooping. The fellow was leaning against the rear wall, peering through a tiny window that was no more than an arrow slit. He straightened up and turned, and as he took in every aspect of me from shoes to tonsure, I took note of his own appearance, from thinning, reddish hair and blazing blue eyes, to a lean, fit-looking frame. I was wearing my travelling clothes, dark woollen tunic and leggings beneath a heavy cloak, and he was similarly dressed, save that his clothes appeared to be made of finer, less durable stuff than mine and were coloured in varying shades of brown, from walnut dark to palest tan.

He sniffed—disdainfully, I thought. "Right," he said, as though I wasn't there. "Who is he?"

"Priest," my guard said before I could get a word out. "Frae the south. Wants to talk to Sir Andrew." He pronounced it *Surrandra*.

"Who sent you?" the other man asked me.

"My bishop, Wishart of Glasgow," I replied.

"Hmm." His eyes flicked back to my escort. "Right, then. You wait outside, at the head of the stairs. I might hae further need o' you." The fellow waved me inside, and I stepped through the doorway, stooping to avoid the lintel.

Neither of us spoke for a moment, but then he stepped forward quickly—I stepped back instinctively—and removed a high-sided box of documents and tightly wound scrolls from a stool at the side of the room's work table and placed it on the floor at his back. "Here," he said in a voice that now contained no hint of suspicion or distrust, "sit ye down, for then I can sit down, too. I've been on my feet all day and my legs are weary."

Surprised by the signal change in the tone of his voice, I remained where I was. He had an unusual voice, light and high pitched but not unpleasant, and a distinctive manner of pronouncing certain words and phrases that I presumed to be the dialect of Inverness.

He cocked his head and looked askance at me. "Will you not sit?"

As I obeyed, he turned the small room's only other chair around to face me and sank into it with a sigh, stretching his legs out in front of him and scrubbing at his thinning scalp with the palms of both hands. Immured as he was in a small, cramped room filled with books and written records, I assumed him to be a scribe, if not a cleric.

"Do you speak Latin?" I asked him.

He smiled for the first time and shook his head. "I have but one tongue, and this is it. Now then," he said. "I'm Alexander Pilche. But folk call me Sandy. Who are you?"

Pilche! Some scribe! I knew the name well, from having heard Father David de Moray speak of him, but hearing this man lay claim to it surprised me. The reports I had heard of Sandy Pilche had led me to imagine a fierce, warlike man, grim and humourless and bent upon driving the last surviving, wounded

Englishman back over the border to die in England. I had pictured him to be physically large and intimidating, with a loud, commanding voice, but here was a soft-spoken man, and not much older than I was myself.

I now took in the "scribe's" wide, muscular shoulders and big, strong-looking hands. There was a litheness about him, too, that bespoke both speed and grace; a subtle, inherent threat I had acknowledged when he moved to pick up the box from the chair. And then I saw the armour tree behind him, in a dim corner of the room. It was sturdy and functional but bare, save for the long, sheathed sword that hung from one of its pegs on a heavy, supple belt. A dangerous man, then, although the overall impression he gave me remained one of clerical benevolence.

"Master Pilche, of Inverness," I said. "A face, at last, to go with the name. Well met, Master Pilche. Your name is known where I come from. I've heard it mentioned several times in recent weeks, and always admiringly, as one of Andrew's most valued associates. I am James Wallace, and despite my appearance I am a priest, just as the other fellow said. Bishop Wishart is my employer, has been for years."

"Aye, the redoubtable Robert Wishart ..." The high-pitched voice sounded amused. "Rab to his friends, and 'yon holy whoreson' to those less kindly inclined towards him. Andrew speaks very highly of him. But—Wallace?" His eyes narrowed to slits. "Yon's a weighty name, especially down where you come from. Are you any kind of kin to the big fellow?"

"Close kin," I said, smiling. "He's my cousin and my dearest friend."

"Ah, then you'll be the Jamie Wallace I've heard Andrew talk about, the one who saved him from drowning in Paisley when he was a lad, squiring King John."

I found it easy to laugh at that. "Aye, but the man he was squiring was a *lord*—not yet King John. And the reason Andrew was in the water—and believe me, we reached him fast enough to be sure there was no chance of him drowning—was that Will had knocked him off a log, and he had hit his head in falling. But yes, that's me, the same Jamie Wallace, grown up a bit and ordained in the doing of it. Where is Andrew, can you tell me?"

He shook his head. "No, I canna, for nobody really kens whaur he is. But I can send you to him. Brendan out there"—he jerked his head towards the doorway—"will take ye to him, and even not knowin' where he is, he'll find him quicker than anybody else could."

"The guard? He's a tracker?"

"He is. He's Irish, and he's one o' the best we hae. Fights like a man possessed when need be, and has a brain, forbye … *And* he kens how to use it, which maks him different frae the run o' folk about here. He'll see you safely to wherever Andrew might be. He's on the move constantly, you understand— Andrew, I mean, no' Brendan. The English are turning the country upside down tryin' to find him."

"What are you saying? He's out there alone, a hunted fugitive?"

"Of course he's hunted. He's Andrew Murray, heir to the lordship of Petty and fugitive frae an English prison. Every Englishman in Scotland is looking for him, hoping to claim the price on his head, for it gets bigger every day. But I'm no' saying he's alone—nor is he in any danger of being ta'en. There's nae chance o' that ava. He's so far ahead o' them, they canna come close to him. I think of what he's doin' as playin' the lame hare, temptin' the hounds to chase him, and they aey do. And when they find him, of course, they hae nae other choice than to fight him, on ground that he chose and on terms he has dictated."

"Hold now," I demurred. "How does a fugitive dictate terms?"

Pilche laughed outright. "By thinking longer and harder than them he's up against, afore he commits to anythin'. Andrew aey knows what he's about and where he's goin'. He arrives nowhere by accident, and his folk are aey in place, weel hid and ready to fight ... What's the biggest advantage the English have over us in fighting?"

"Other than having ten times the men we have? Horses, I would think. They have bigger and better horses, and their horsemen are better armed and armoured than we are."

"Right you are. And so they harry us on horseback, chasin' and chivvyin' us, snappin' at our heels like dogs, until they round a corner or turn the flank o' a hill somewhere and find themselves where Andrew wants them."

"And where would that be?"

He barked a laugh—short, sharp, and humourless. "Some place where their horses and their mounted men are useless—in a bog, or thick woods, or a steep, narrow ravine. Andrew maks the land work for him all the time—for him and against them. When he turns to face them, he'll usually hae a wooded hillside at his back, or a peat moss bog underfoot, or heavy undergrowth ablow an owerhangin' cliff. Some place where he an' his canna be outflanked and the English canna fight the way they like to. He'll hae bowmen waiting on both sides, forbye, above and ahead of whoever's huntin' him. And he'll be waitin' wi' his main force drawn up in schiltroms, long spears bristling like hedgehogs, so the English riders canna get at them. He wins every time—canna fail." He shook his head slowly and barked that laugh again, a strange sound that was part snort, part scoffing derision. "You'd think they'd learn, but they don't. They aey think to catch him on his own, and when they find themsel's outnumbered and outflanked, outwitted and outfought, they can never believe what's happened to them."

"Surely they must have learned his tricks by this time." I could hear the disbelief in my voice. "I mean, I can understand that kind of ruse working once or twice, but all the time? No one can be that stupid, that much lacking in … what would you call it, common sense?"

He snorted again. "I care no' what you call it, Faither James. I'm too busy thankin' God that it keeps happenin'." He saw the expression on my face then and shrugged his wide shoulders, dipping his head to one side. "If you're really asking me what I believe, I think they're just boneheaded. It's nae mair than stubborn pride, bred o' their ain arrogance. The English commanders here winna even talk to ane anither. They're weeks and months awa by sea and road frae England, and frae their ain overlords, and so ilka man o' them, be he in charge o' a castle or a garrisoned toun, thinks that his wee bit o' Scotland is his ain fiefdom for him to rule or govern as he sees fit."

"Under the rules set out for him, you mean."

"No, I mean what I said. *As he sees fit*. If there's rules set out, they're bein' ignored." He threw up a hand. "Dinna look at me like that, man. I hae naught to dae wi' it. And I ken how daft it sounds to say they take nae heed o' what the high folk in England think or want, but it's what I mean when I talk about their arrogance. And though it seems daft to the likes o' us, it's the truth for a' that, and it'll keep on bein' true until somebody puts a stop to it in Edward's name. An' ye'll pardon me if I sound as though I'm hopin' somebody *will* put a stop to it, for that's no' what I mean at a'. I like it just fine the way things are. It makes the English easier to kill, and I'm glad o' anythin' that does that.

"But aside frae anythin' else, the dunghill cockerels wha rule the roost up here ken fine that Edward has ither things on his mind right now, this war wi'

France the biggest o' them. But that state o' affairs winna last, though they canna seem tae see that. One o' these days, some clerk will tak note that there's no' as much money comin' in frae north o' the Forth as there's supposed to be, and when that happens some high an' mighty body will be sent up here to clean the shite out o' the pigsty and set things in their proper English order, to make sure that Edward gets every siller groat out o' us that he thinks is due to him. There's going to be a wheen o' whey-faced, sorry-lookin' English knights and lordlings in these parts when that day comes."

"You may be right, Master Pilche, but we've changed tack here."

"Call me Sandy, if you will," he said. "When ye say Master Pilche like that ye mak me feel as if I wis guilty o' somethin'."

I grinned at him. "Sandy. So be it. But tell me this: how does what you've said explain the English leadership's not talking to one another, or not combining to fight Andrew's people?"

He looked at me as though I had missed some important aspect of what he had been saying. "Precisely because o' what I've just finished tellin' you." He managed to sound pedantic, despite his Highland way of speaking. "The Englishry here—the knights and lordlings in charge—hae nae trust in ane anither. Ilka man o' them sees a' the ithers as a threat to *him*—to his plans for the future. And so they avoid ane anither, keepin' to themsel's and sharin' neither secrets nor information. That's why Andrew keeps movin' a' the time. He's keepin' them off balance, spreadin' confusion an' unrest an' leavin' them wi' nae time to organize themsel's or to plan a campaign against him. The only bad part o' that is that him movin' about so much sometimes maks it hard for us to know exactly where to find him gin we need to. How quickly do you need to talk to him?"

"Today is the most honest answer. But urgently." I hesitated. In the few months since Andrew Murray's return home, all Scotland had come to know of the remarkable bond formed between him and Alexander Pilche of Inverness. Within days of their first meeting, it seemed, Pilche had earned the young lord's absolute trust and loyalty in a fusion of wills and mutual intent that no one seemed inclined to doubt. I decided to be completely open with him. "I'm carrying instructions for him from the Council of Guardians," I said.

He looked at me quickly, his eyebrows rising. "What council? There's nae *council*. There's but twa Guardians left in the entire realm."

"Well, yes and no ..." I was acutely aware at that moment of my status, not merely as a priest of the Church but as the personal representative of my bishop in his official, political capacity as Guardian of the realm, and so I spoke in my most priestly voice as I continued, while trying to avoid offending my listener by pontificating too much. "It's true, as you say, that there are but the two Guardians left in the land nowadays. But between the pair of them,

Wishart and the Steward, they now embody the full power of the council at its peak capacity of twelve. Four earls there were not so long ago, plus four barons and four bishops, two of each rank from north and south of the Firth of Forth. Bishop Fraser of St. Andrews and Lord John de Soulis are in France at the court of King Phillip, negotiating on the realm's behalf, and eight others are imprisoned in England. All of them retain their status as Guardians but, in effect, they are unable to function. Nevertheless it is the two remaining councillors who have sent me to make contact with Sir Andrew and to bring him south into Angus and Dundee."

"And why," my listener asked me, "would Andrew de Moray leave his home lands at anyone's behest when he has a war to wage here?"

I deliberately put an edge of impatience into my voice. "Because the fight for Scotland is bigger and more important than the local upheavals in Moray, no matter how much import those appear to have to the folk who live here. Sandy, I am the direct representative of the Council of Guardians. They deem the presence of the army of de Moray in the south to be essential to what has become a struggle for the very existence of the Scots realm."

He sat still for a few moments, digesting that, then asked, "What do they have in mind, Wishart and the Steward?"

"They want to drive Edward and the English out of Scotland for good. I can say that with certainty.

How they intend to achieve it, what their plans are, I have no idea. I know as much as they have told me, certainly not enough to encourage me to guess at probabilities. But I will tell you what I know to be true."

I launched then into the tale of how I had come to be in Moray, including what the bishop had told me about the plans he and the Steward had to hold the enemy in negotiations in the hope of gaining sufficient time for Wallace, Murray, and others like them to consolidate their activities against the English.

When I finally fell silent, Sandy Pilche nodded and sat thinking for a while, then rose and looked about him as though wondering where he was, turning his body from side to side as he scanned the room and the welter of papers and parchments it contained, and looking as though he had forgotten something and expected to see it appear by magic at any moment. But then he stepped across the floor and took down the belted sword I had noticed earlier. He hefted it wistfully in his hand before replacing it and turning to peer out through the small window.

"Ye're right," he said over his shoulder as he gazed out through the narrow slit. "Ye need to see Andrew right away. I'll send you wi' Brendan and his four friends. They're all Irish, an' they hae noses like hounds. They'll find him afore I ever could. I'd come wi' you mysel' but I need to be here for the next two days at least." He rose on tiptoe, leaning farther forward into the embrasure and peering up at the sky, his voice pitching upwards with the strain of it. "Mind you, it's gettin' late in the day to be starting for anywhere. There's nae mair than six hours of daylight left. But we havena much choice."

He pushed himself back from the wall and turned to me, rubbing the dust off his hands. "Ye'll no' have eaten yet, eh?" I shook my head, heartened at the thought of food, for I had eaten only a handful of roasted oats bound with honey aboard ship at dawn and now discovered that I was famished.

He grunted. "I thought so. We'll get some food into ye, then, and ye can be on the road within the hour. Can ye ride a horse? Ye can? Good. Ye'll make better time on a horse. Brendan an' his crew dinna ride. They run everywhere, an' I jalouse that wi'out a horse ye'd be hard pressed to keep them in sight for more than a minute at a time. Well-mounted, though, ye'll be able to keep up wi' them.

"Ride north and west for four or five hours and ye'll come to Balconie. That used to be the seat o' the Earl o' Buchan, but Andrew took it after the countess sided wi' the English against him at Castle Urquhart, and now we use it as our base in Ross. That's where Andrew was goin' when he left here last, but that was a week ago and I don't know if he'll be there still. Brendan'll find a place for ye to sleep. Ye winna be able to light a fire, though—there's too many Englishmen out there. Come mornin', God willin', ye'll find word o' Andrew's whereabouts. Now, let's go and eat."

We could not have timed our arrival in the kitchens better, for the household steward fed us freshly baked bread and a brace of roasted rabbits, fresh from the spit, with flagons of cool ale from a newly broached cask. While we were fortifying ourselves in the kitchen, the Irishman called Brendan was gathering his companions and making ready for our journey.

I found myself liking Alexander Pilche increasingly as I grew more familiar with him. We talked easily and openly and, in the course of sucking the flesh off a rabbit bone, I asked him about the friendship that had sprung so quickly into being between him and Andrew Murray.

He grinned and bobbed his head. "You're the first person ever to come out and ask me that directly," he said. "It's been near three months now since Andrew an' me started workin' wi' each other here, and folk still canna believe it. And I canna say I blame them, for even I can see that the odds are long against the likes o' me an' him ever comin' to be allies, never mind friends, and in sic a short time. There's mair rumours goin' around about it than about anything else I can think o'. You say ye've heard o' me, and that surprises me, but I believe ye. I hae nae idea what's being said down there where you come from, but I ken the story spread up here like a fire in summer grass. A jocose pairing, eh, the Inverness burgess and the high-born lord? The merchant and the magnate? Come on now, I'm serious, how do you think it happened?"

"I have no idea," I told him straightforwardly. "But I think I'm glad it did happen …"

He pushed away his platter and wiped the corners of his mouth with his thumb and forefinger. "I'll tell you, then. What few folk ken is that Andrew and me have kent ane anither for years. Ten year at least. And at the start o' that time we was close for a while. But then we grew up. Andrew went away to be a squire to some knight down near Edinburgh, to get ready for his ain knighthood, and my da, who was a wool merchant, apprenticed me to a trader in Inverness."

"And now you're a prominent merchant burgess. You've done well, in a mere ten years."

He waved my comment aside. "I liked the work and I was good at it, an' I wis lucky, forbye. I wed the trader's dochter near five years ago, and her da died o' an apoplexy the year after that, liftin' a bale o' hides. I took ower the place and we did weel. Until the English came."

"How old were you back then, when you first met Andrew?"

"That was ten years ago. I'd hae been fourteen, thereabouts. The same age as him. Mayhap fifteen."

"Still an unlikely pairing. And what brought you together in the first place?"

"Love." He smiled mischievously. "No' that kind o' love, Faither. There's nae need to be scandalized."

I coughed and swallowed awkwardly, trying to pretend that I had not really been thinking anything untoward, but he ignored my reaction.

"I had a twin sister, Meg. She was older than me by an hour, and she and Andrew liked each other frae the first time they met. And once they had met, they kept on meeting, nigh on every day after that, and I aey had to be there wi' them, to keep them …" He laughed. "I don't know *what* I was supposed to keep them. Respectable, or chaste, I jalouse. But there was never any need, for friends was all they were—close and affectionate, but nae mair than that. But that's how Andrew an' me came to ken each ither. An' then he met Meg's other friend, a lass called Eleanor. That was the end o' whatever o' man-to-woman love might hae been atwixt him an' Meg. But they a' stayed friends, that was the strangest bit o' it. Andrew finally was wed to Eleanor just ower a year ago, afore he got captured an' sent to Chester."

"Where is Meg now?"

He dipped his head to one side. "She's deid." He said it flatly, his voice devoid of emphasis.

"Ah. Forgive me for asking."

"No need, Faither. She died last year, while Andrew was away in the south. She'd got wed, ye see, to a young blacksmith. Kenny MacFarlane was his name, an' for a while they was happy. She soon got pregnant, which was nae surprise, but as the months went by she swole up like a mare in foal, and Kenny started frettin'. Twins run in our family, ye see, and frae the size o' Meg's belly anybody could see that's what she was carryin'."

He lapsed into a silence, then cleared his throat fiercely. "Well, that winter came early and it was the worst we'd had in years. There was a bad snowstorm early in November, and the day after that, it froze hard and stayed like that for weeks. Meg collapsed early on in that cold spell, nigh on three weeks afore she was supposed to hae the bairns. Kenny had been frettin' for months that somethin' bad might happen, and so he had arranged for some midwives from Inverness, an old woman and her dochter, to come an' stay wi' them and see to the delivery. But the women werena due for another week, so everythin' went wrong and Kenny was at his wits' end. He made Meg as comfortable as he could an' then went for to fetch the midwives. He left her wi' his young brother Tam, who was just sixteen but was able to keep the fires burnin' and see to it that she and the animals was well fed."

He fell silent again, staring into nothingness, and finally, when I became convinced that he had forgotten I was there, I prompted him. "What happened then, Sandy?"

His eyes moved away from me, focusing on a point somewhere beyond my left shoulder. "Well," he said, his voice flat. "Kenny met an English patrol on his way to Inverness. They tried to stop him, but he wouldna stop, and so they chased him. When they caught him, they accused him of stealin' the horse he was riding. He still wouldna listen, for he was frantic, hell-bent on reachin' the twa wifies in Inverness, and when he wouldna tell them his business they beat him senseless. And then they left him hanging, upside down and naked, from the rafters of a burnt-out cottage at the side of the road. He froze to death …"

I felt a coldness settle around my chest.

"A farmer found him sometime after that—a day or two, it might ha' been—an' cut him down," he continued in that same flat voice. "But nobody knew who he was."

I did not want to ask, but I had to. "And Meg?" ·

"The bairns came … Or one o' them did, or tried to. Poor Tam was terrified out o' his wits, demented wi' her screamin', an' he ran back to the farm, twa miles up the glen in the storm, to get help." He gazed at the tabletop. "When they got back to the smithy, Meg was dead, and so wis the unborn bairns. Young Tam disappeared soon after an' hasna been seen since."

I sat there, appalled. "How … how do you know what happened, Sandy?"

"What?" His brow knitted in a frown.

"You say he met an English patrol, and they accused him of stealing the horse, then beat him and left him for dead. How do you know that? How can you be sure Kenny didn't simply fall among thieves?"

"Because I ken the men wha did it. I ken their names. Made a *point* o' learnin' them all. They boasted about it back in their barracks in Inverness, ye see, an' they brought the horse back with them, to sell it. No' a trace o' shame in any o' them. They crowed about what they had done, catching a Scotch horse thief and servin' him the justice he deserved, leavin' him hung up to live or die according to God's will."

"I see. And did you make a formal complaint against them?"

He looked at me as though I had spoken gibberish. "A complaint? To the English, about English sodgers? No, Faither, I didna complain. I had the men wha did it killed, is what I did. Ten of the whoresons an' the sergeant who was wi' them that day. I broke the sergeant's neck mysel', forbye I slit the throat o' the whoreson who boasted o' haein put the rope round Kenny's neck. And if that was mortal sin, then I'm ready to burn in Hell for it, an' I winna complain there, either."

"Have you confessed that to a priest since then?"

He looked sidelong at me. "Aye, to you. But I havena been to confession, if that's what you're askin'. I'm no' a hypocrite, nor a liar. For confession to be real, ye hae to feel regret—contrition's the word, is it no'? Ye hae to feel contrition for what ye did. I don't. I'd dae it again this minute if I thought one o' thae whoresons was still alive."

He shrugged. "A month or so after that, Andrew Murray came home after escapin' from England. Afore he went on to Auch he went to the provost's house in Inverness, to find out where his wife was an' what was happenin' on the Black Isle. The provost's an auld crony of Sir Andrew of Petty, the Auld Laird as he's kenned here, and Andrew knew he'd get the truth frae him no matter how bad it was. I heard he was there and I went there an' waited for him to come out. We went to a howff for a jug o' ale, and I telt him what had happened to Meg, and what I had done. And then he said he was on his way here to throw the English out of Auch. He didna hae a soul to stand beside him then, but I never doubted he would do it. First they'd be out o' Auch, he said, and then out o' the Murray lands everywhere.

"We got drunk together that night, him and me, and we mourned Meg. And afore he left the next day, he asked me to go wi' him an' help him fight the English. I said I would but that I had affairs to settle first. And so I sent my ain wife awa to live wi' her mother's sister in Elgin while I was out wi' Andrew. She wasna happy, but she went, and then I spent a week shuttin' down my warehouses and raisin' volunteers amang the other burgesses in Inverness. By the time I was ready to leave, we had near a hundred fightin' men—every one o' them well armed and angry and sick an' tired o' bein' treated like dirt. I marched them here, and we've been workin' an' fightin' together ever since."

"One more question, if you'll permit it, and then I'll ask you no more. Why you, a successful merchant? You'll pardon me, I hope, for saying so, but it's a big leap, from warehouseman to warrior. I am having difficulty understanding why it would occur to Andrew de Moray that you could be a comrade-in-arms to him."

"You have a point," he said. "I wasna always a merchant, though. When Andrew first kent me, I was wild. Him an' me fought a wheen o' times, a couple o' dunghill cocks crawin' an' flexin' their wings, and I won every time. That's why my da set me to watchin' ower him an' Meg. He knew she wis safe as lang as I was there wi' her. So Andrew kent me as a fighter, and a better one than him, man to man—or boy to boy. But even then, when we wis young, he'd never get angry when I'd beat him. He'd want me to teach him what I did instead, to show him how I did it. And so I would. But it wasna even that, no' really. What made him decide to ask me to join up wi' him was somethin' that happened that mornin' afore he left here to go back to Auch. It had been happenin' for days, in fact, for I was in the middle o' takkin' stock in the warehouses when he arrived.

"There wis folk comin' and goin' a' the time Andrew was there in the yard and I kept expectin' him to get angry, for we'd had a lot to drink the night afore an' I knew he must be feelin' it as much as I was, and now we kept on gettin' interrupted an' couldna hear oursel's think. But instead o' that, he just sat there listenin' to what my folk was sayin' to me, leanin' on his hand wi' his elbow on the arm o' his chair, no' missin' a bit o' what was goin' on. And then, at the end o' one long talk I had wi' a clever young loon frae Elgin, he looks at me and says, 'You understood all that?'"

His face quirked into a grin. "An' of course, when I said I did, he wanted me to teach him all about it, then and there—everythin' I'd spent the last ten years learnin', one step at a time frae dawn through dusk, maist days. An' yon's really why he wanted me to join him."

I blinked at him. "You'll have to pardon me, Sandy. I don't understand."

"He wanted me because I'm an *organizer*. I deal every day in a' the stuff he kens nothin' about an' hasna the time to learn. You're a priest, but you work for a bishop, do ye no'? And your bishop works for an archbishop, who likely works for a bigger archbishop—what are they called, the high-ups? Cardinals, aye, that's them. And the cardinals work for the Pope, who's the highest o' them all. It's the same in an army. Ilka high chief, ilka man in charge, whether they cry him general or commander, has a quartermaster—Andrew had a fancy Latin word for it, if I can remember it … *factotum*, that's it. Every commander, he said, needs a good factotum to see to the details o' what needs to be done, somebody whose job it is to make sure a' the people an' their gear—weapons, armour, food and supplies, horses, wagons an' kine an' swine for slaughter—reach the right place at the right time. And he had nobody, he said. His father's folk were a' scattered, kicked out o' Auch when the Auld Laird was sent to jail, but they were all too old anyway, and they had aey treated him like a bairn because his father wis their god. He needed someone he could trust, he said, someone he could rely on to stand behind him and tak care o' a' the details—someone that he knew was loyal to him an' no' afraid o' crossing folk who needed to be crossed an' put in their place.

"And so that's what I am now, Faither James. I'm a factotum. I mak sure that men an' supplies are in place and ready whenever and wherever Andrew wants them to be. An' when I can, I fight. And now I'm thinkin' we've been sittin' here too long. Brendan an' his lads will be waitin' outside, so ye'd best be away, and I'll get back to my work."

CHAPTER FOURTEEN

ANDREW
DE MORAY

I arrived in Andrew de Moray's camp at dusk that same evening, which was a development I had not expected. It lay on the upper slopes of the rolling hillsides between the firth's end and the northern tip of Loch Ness, not far from Inverness, and the chief's sanctuary lay at its very centre, in a steep-sided ravine carved into the downslope on the far side of the ridge we had climbed to reach it. As my two guides led me down into it—they were really guards, but deferential and considerate—the brush-filled walls rose above us on either side, closing us in and creating an illusion of isolation even while, at the very least, there were upwards of half a thousand men camped all around us.

I could see the glow of firelight ahead of us as we descended the ravine, and as we drew closer the light from leaping flames reflected from the sides of several large tents. My guards steered me towards those tents until I could make out the forms of half a score of men seated on logs around a fire. Although I was still too far distant to be able to pick out individuals, I had no doubt that I was witnessing a council of some kind. One of my guards reached out to halt me in the shadows between two of the tents, while the other, who had told me his name was Fergus, stepped forward to talk to a man who was hovering watchfully, his attention focused tightly on the group around the fire.

This camp steward—for that was plainly what he was—turned to peer at me, his expression unreadable, and then he moved away and bent to whisper in the ear of one of the group seated by the fire. The man to whom he spoke, whose body radiated displeasure at being interrupted, straightened and twisted around on the log that was his seat, peering back to where I stood in the shadows. I could see his face in the firelight, but it was clear that he could not see me well, for he leaned forward and squinted into the dimness. Then he rose to his feet and began to come towards me.

"Jamie!" he roared, silencing everyone around him. "Jamie Wallace. It *is* you!" He spoke to me in Scots, a great courtesy, since the language he normally spoke was the Gaelic. "Welcome to Moray! I swear I thought I must be hearing things when Angus said your name." He threw his arms wide as I approached him and we embraced, watched by perhaps a hundred pairs of eyes. "You are welcome here, my friend," he said more quietly. "It delights me to see your smiling face. I know there's no need to ask if you are well, for I can see you are." He cocked his head. "You've changed a bit about the mouth, though. It looks as though you might have been talking about politics with English soldiery," he said admiringly, for the sake of his audience. "But I didn't think priests were permitted to brawl like ordinary folk. Is that why you're up here? Have you been exiled to the north, an excommunicated fugitive?"

I was grinning at him by that time, recalling how he loved to banter. "No, Sir Andrew," I said. "I'm here looking for you, no more than that."

"Then your task is done. I'm here and you've found me. But I'm plain Andrew Murray. No king has yet had me kneel at his feet to endow me with the grace of knighthood. Come, sit down and have something to drink." He swung around, placing a hand on my shoulder and raising his voice to address the men gathered around the fire, all of them so watchfully quiet that I could hear the crackling of the fire.

"Hear me, all of you. This is my good friend Father Jamie Wallace from Glasgow. Mark ye that name, Wallace. He is cousin and close friend to William Wallace, of whom all Scotland talks today, and he once saved my life when his wild cousin tried to kill me. If you treat him well, he might tell you about it sometime. But in the meantime he must be nigh famished for the lack of strong drink, so someone fetch him a jug, and you, young Furness, may have the privilege of giving up your seat by the fire for him when we return. First, though, we have matters to discuss between ourselves, Father Wallace and I, so we'll remove ourselves for a spell to where we can speak privily. Come, Jamie, they'll bring us to drink over there."

He led me to another fire some twenty paces away and asked the men seated there if they would leave us alone to talk, and in the time it took for us to settle by the fire and toast each other's health in the ale that quickly followed us, the others moved away, leaving us in the middle of a fire-lit space too large for anyone to approach unseen or to overhear what we were saying.

Of course, the first question he had to ask, after being assured that Will and Bishop Wishart were both well, was how I came to be in Moray, afoot and alone. He evidently had some notion that I might have walked all the way from Glasgow, so I told him about my sea voyage aboard *The Golden Gannet*, my landing in Auch, and my meeting with Sandy Pilche.

"Aye," he said quietly when I had finished. "I was fortunate to find Sandy, though in truth it was he who found me. He's a fine man and a miracle worker when it comes to organizing things. But now's not the time to talk about Sandy Pilche. You're the one who is important here—you and your mission, for I know you would not be here without a mission. And as you came by sea, I assume there's urgency involved."

"There is," I said. "I fear God's work—which means the bishop's work—demands some haste from time to time."

"You're not the first to tell me that," he said, speaking almost to himself. "And you're not the first

to arrive from Aberdeen by sea in the past few days."
His face settled into a scowl. "It seems the need for
haste is greater on all fronts nowadays. And everyone
who's hurrying, no matter what his heading, believes
God is on his side." That was followed by a disdainful
sniff, and he looked at me squarely. "So I think we had
best speak right away of what brings you up to Scotia
for the first time in your life."

"Aye," I said. "But first I need to know how much
you know. Have you heard anything of what's afoot in
the south?"

He shook his head. "Nothing of worth," he said.
"We've heard talk of risings there, and I hear Will's
name mentioned from time to time, but no more than
that. Someone said the Steward—Stewart himself—is
in the southwest, but that would suggest Wishart is
with him, and I've heard nothing of that. Is he?"

"Aye, he is. I'll tell you everything I know—or
everything I *knew* before I left Carrick, two weeks
ago. Since then, of course, anything could have
happened. There was an English army in the offing
when I left, marching towards Ayr. A well-commanded
army, apparently, under Sir Henry Percy and Sir
Robert Clifford, both, I was told, highly ranked among
Edward's Welsh veterans."

"I know of Percy" Murray said. "And you're right.
From all I hear he is no man's fool. Won his spurs,
quite literally, in the Welsh wars and is highly regarded
by everyone who counts, including his own men. The
other one—Clifford, you say? Him I don't know."

"Hatched from the same clutch, reared in the same brood. Not so well born, perhaps, but even more ambitious."

"Then we'll hear more of him, no doubt. And do the bishop and the Stewart intend to fight these two?"

"No," I said slowly. "They have no plans, per se, to come to blows. They have a strong defensive position, which they intend to hold, and they intend to negotiate with Percy, to buy time for forces elsewhere in the realm to organize themselves."

"That sounds foolish. If Percy is half the soldier they say he is, he'll dance around them until they grow dazed and then he'll cut them down at his own speed."

"I doubt that. The bishop assured me that the Steward's defensive position at Irvine is unassailable."

"Hmm." He managed to express a world of cynical disgust in that single sound. "No place is unassailable, Jamie. That's a priest's foolish talk."

I shrugged, unable to dispute that. "Accurate or no, that's what I was told: that the place is in the hills close by Irvine town and the enemy won't be able to assail it without sustaining heavy losses. Whether that be true or not remains to be seen."

"Aye, you'll get no argument from me on *that*." He hesitated, frowning a little. "You said you left from Carrick to come here. Not Glasgow? What took you to Carrick? That's on the southwest coast, is it not?"

"It is. I went there to join the bishop. And he was there to meet with the Steward, who was meeting in turn with Bruce, the Earl of Carrick, at Bruce's castle of Turnberry."

I saw his eyes go wide, and he jerked a hand up to stop me. "Wait. Bruce is here in Scotland? *Young* Robert Bruce?"

"The Earl of Carrick, aye. He has thrown in his lot with the bishop and Lord Stewart. He and my cousin Will and the knight Sir William Douglas. They are up in arms against the English."

"But that can't be! The others I can understand, but Bruce has lived in England these past five years at least. They say he spends all his time in Westminster, where he is one of the King's spoilt favourites. They say he has become an English parasite."

"I think you may have been misinformed on that," I replied. "You have been misled on his whereabouts at least. I assure you Bruce is here in Scotland, and under arms. I spoke with him in Carrick a fortnight since, at his castle."

"So you know him, Robert Bruce?"

I smiled. "I would not say that. I met him briefly, on church business and at the bishop's instigation. It was no more than that."

"But you spoke with him, the Earl of Carrick, two weeks ago."

"I did."

"And does that have anything to do with your presence here?"

"Nothing at all."

"Hmm … All right, what *does* bring you all this way?"

"Your need for weaponry. I'm told you are short of weapons."

He snorted something that might have been the start of a bitter laugh. "Short! Aye, you might say that. My sergeants-at-arms are training my recruits with wooden swords—quarterstaves, to be sure, and ages old in honour and tradition, but there comes a stage in training when the practice weapons have to be replaced with the real thing, and we have none other than those we take from dead or captured Englishmen. So yes, you could say we are short of weapons."

"Well, that is about to change. I am instructed to tell you that the agents of Mother Church, under the aegis of the See of Glasgow, have arranged for a cargo of ingot iron and finished weapons and chain mail to be delivered to you at Aberdeen harbour within the month. I have the papers you will need to claim the cargo—no names attached to them, for reasons of maintaining secrecy, but I have all those in my head. How you will take delivery, of course, is for you to determine, since I understand there will be an English garrison to contend with."

Andrew had stiffened as I told him this. "The garrison will not present a problem," he said. "But there are other difficulties. Within the month, you say?"

"Aye, aboard the vessel *Poseidon*, out of Lübeck."

He drew in a great breath and stared at me for

several seconds longer, then grunted and stood up, twisting around to look back towards the other fire. "D'you recall my saying you were not the first man off a boat from Aberdeen this week?"

"I do. Who were the others?"

"One other." He raised an arm and pointed. "The dark-haired fellow over there, wearing the blue cap with the silver badge and the bright yellow feather. Do you know him?"

I stood up and looked where he was pointing. The man he described was some distance away and the light was untrustworthy, but he was yet close enough for me to recognize had I known him. "I don't," I said. "Should I?"

"Probably not. His name is Garnat MacDonald, but he's most often spoken of as Gartnait of Mar, heir to the earldom of Mar, by Aberdeen."

"I recognize the name. His sister Isabella was Bruce's wife."

"*Was?*"

"Aye, sadly. She died last year, birthing a daughter. They had been wed for less than two years. Bruce was—still is—distraught."

"God! I knew naught of that … I'm newly wed myself, did you know that?"

"Yes, Sandy told me. Your wife is well, I trust?"

"Aye, and lovely as a spring morning. We are expecting our first child by year's end, thanks be to God, though the last thing a woman needs is to be big with child while her man is fighting a war, risking death with almost every day that comes." He inhaled sharply. "That must have ripped the guts out of Bruce, for I cannot imagine how I would feel to lose my Eleanor … And he is here in Scotland now, you say, and out with Stewart and Wishart in defiance of the Plantagenet? That's a turnaround. I wonder if it had aught to do with Edward?" His eyes narrowed. "He's not here as Edward's man, you're sure of that?"

"I'm sure of it," I told him. "He claims, in fact, to be here as *Scotland's* man. Not Balliol's, not King John's, but Scotland's."

"By God, I confess that surprises me."

"I can see that. But why should it surprise you, really, Andrew? The man's as Scots as you are. Both your ancestors, de Moray and de Brus, came to this realm around the same time, two hundred years ago, sent here by the same Norman king, William Rufus."

"That's true, but …" He hesitated, then gave a dismissive shake of his head. "No matter. But I thought he was in England."

"Until you pointed him out, I thought Gartnait of Mar was in England, too, as Edward's captive."

"And so he was. His father remains there as a prisoner, hostage to the son's attendance in support of Edward's war in France. It's a long story, but Gartnait arrived at Inverness a few days ago, sent up from Aberdeen by his associates, to warn me off and convince me to stand down and disband my army."

I had felt a deep pang of anxiety as he spoke the words. "Which you have no intention of doing, I hope?"

"What think you?" He sat down again, waving me down, too, then raised his mug and sipped at his ale, the first time he had done so since toasting my arrival. "I could be offended that you even ask such a question."

"Don't be. It was an observation, if you like." I drank from my own mug and set it down again. "Who are these associates of Gartnait's you spoke of, that they could dictate to him within his own earldom and send him all the way up here to make demands of you?"

He drew air through his teeth. "An astute question, Father. And appropriate, too. They are friends and relatives of mine, as is Gartnait himself, but senior in rank and title to both of us. Edward convinced a number of Scots magnates to exchange imprisonment in England for service in France and Gascony. Hardly a difficult choice for any of them, I suspect, after spending the best part of a year in captivity and facing more to come."

"That makes perfect sense," I said. "Perfect sense for Edward, too, for he would have them under his thumb thereafter, their sworn paroles the guarantee of their fidelity. But no word of this arrangement has reached us in the south."

"It affects me ill, though, in this matter of collecting the bishop's cargo from Aberdeen, because according to Gartnait there's an army coming north from Aberdeen right now, to stamp me down."

He set down his cup carefully, then gripped his knees and swayed effortlessly to his feet with barely a grunt before stepping over to a supply of logs that lay ready for the fire and selecting a couple that were to his liking. He thrust them into the coals in the fire pit, pressed them home with the thick sole of his armoured boot, and returned to sit again as they began to burn.

· "When the magnates with Mar were released from London, they agreed to return home and make ready to embark for France come August. It seems, though, that on the very day they set out northward, a man called Andrew de Rait, a Scottish knight loyal to Edward, arrived in Westminster from the north—from here in Inverness, in fact—with word for Edward about the nuisance we've been causing here in Moray. He carried letters from Reginald de Cheyne, the commander of Inverness Castle—the first official notification Edward had received of our rebellion. That, incidentally, is Edward's word, not ours. It's an English word with an English meaning. Ours is an uprising, not a rebellion. We have risen up in protest against his tyranny, but the English use the term *rebellion* because a rebellion gives an appearance of support to Edward's false claims of ruler status."

"How did you learn," I asked him, "about Andrew de Rait and the letters from de Cheyne?"

"Gartnait told me. In return for de Rait's loyalty, Edward endowed him that same day with all the lands that had been forfeited after Dunbar by his brother. He then turned de Rait around on his heels and sent him chasing after the party that had left for Scotland that morning, with new instructions."

"And who were these travellers?"

"John Comyn, the Earl of Buchan, for one, although there's no surprise in that. He was the leader, accompanied by the other John Comyn, his cousin, the Lord of Badenoch—the Black and the Red branches of Comyn together. Also among their number was Edward's lickspittle toady, Henry de Cheyne, the Bishop of Aberdeen—as God is my witness, I detest that loathsome, unctuous man. Sir Edward de Balliol, the king's brother, was with them, too, as was Malise, Earl of Strathearn, and Gartnait himself. There were others, but those are the principals."

"And de Rait obviously overtook them."

"He did. Instead of preparing to leave for France, they are now ordered to remain here in Scotland and use all the resources at their disposal to stamp out the so-called rebellion in Moray and Ross-shire—that's me and my folk. Bishop de Cheyne and Gartnait are ordered to proceed immediately to the relief of the Constable Fitzwarren in Urquhart Castle, and that's a waste of time, since Urquhart has been unthreatened these past eight weeks. The Comyns, for their part, are to remain in the north, and in the field, until the rebellion be completely quelled."

"Well, there's nothing there that's hard to understand, is there?" I said. "Stop Andrew de Moray by any and all means. So why would they send Gartnait to talk to you?"

One side of Murray's mouth twitched in a half smile. "Because it would have been the most straightforward means of achieving their objective, were it successful. It was the most logical way to begin, and certainly worth the effort."

"But why try at all? They must have known you were unlikely to simply give up and go home. And now you know they're coming to find you, so they've sacrificed whatever surprise they might have achieved by marching here directly."

"No surprise was possible, Jamie. I've known since I set foot again in Moray that someone, someday, would be sent to remove me. The biggest bother in my mind now is that ship. I won't be able to meet it until I've dealt with Buchan and his army."

"The ship is unimportant at this point," I said. "That's weeks away, and will resolve itself when the time is right. In the meantime, you will have time to outface the Buchan crew."

"I hope you're right. They'll come soon, though, and they'll come northwest, through Mar and Badenoch to the Spey river. That's the eastern border of Moray. They'll have to come by the Ingie and the Bog of Gight, and that's where I'll be waiting for them."

"The bog I can guess at, but what's the Ingie?"

That won me a smile. "It's a place, or rather a region. It's the biggest of the royal forests in the north, and it lies on the far side of the Spey. It's dense and trackless—which means completely impenetrable to a marching army. Inside its western boundary, bordering the Spey itself, there's a huge, mud-choked tract of impassable mire called the Bog of Gight. Not good country for heavy horsemen, believe me. But any army coming north and west has to follow the outer edges of both the forest and the bog. It's the only route there is, and I was brought up near there, so I know every inch of it. I'll stop them there."

"And what about Gartnait? You can't let him go back to Aberdeen. Will you hold him here?"

"No," he said. "He'll be leaving in the morning. There's a ship waiting for him in Inverness."

I was stupefied. "You're letting him go?"

"What else am I to do, Jamie?" he asked with a broad smile. "He is my friend, and he is in a nasty predicament, but he came here openly to explain his situation to me."

"And all credit to him for that. But he's an avowed enemy, Andrew. He's Edward's man, bound by parole. He'll destroy you if he can and hand what's left of you and yours over to England."

Andrew Murray smiled again. "Mayhap," he said. "You might be right, but not unless, as you say, he destroys me. And I have some views of my own on that matter. Besides, his enmity's a passing thing—a politician's enmity, enforced by England's aging King."

"Enmity is enmity, Andrew, no matter how it's painted. No one ever confuses it with friendship."

"Then we must be very different in this part of the world." He stood up again—rather angrily, I thought—and moved to stare into the fire, his brows compressed in a frown. "Listen to me now, Jamie," he said, and his voice was soft and serious. "And mark what I'm telling you. The greatest sadness of this war—a war we neither sought nor thought to have to wage—is that the men we actually have to fight, chin to chin and eye to eye, are, in the main, our own countrymen. That is the most damnable part of the pervasive rot that festers in our realm these days: the English use us against ourselves, for their own ends. And here in the Highlands it appears to be more true than anywhere else. Most of the commanders who hold our royal castles against us are Scots, at least by birth. The garrison troops are all English, but the men commanding them are Scots. Edward controls their purse strings, with the threat of denying them their English lands and the income from those lands, and that means he controls their behaviour and obedience. That is the truth of life here in Highland Scotia. But it is not the entire truth, for Comyn, who has no real need of English lands or money, is marching north to lay waste to Moray. Tell me now, why do you think that is the case?"

I was gaping at him, unable to respond.

"I'll tell you why it is. It's because we've done it to ourselves—we, the magnates of Scotland, myself included. We have deceived ourselves and deluded our own people and now we are being made to pay the price. Edward Plantagenet, the all-high King of England, has proved himself to be the great manipulator of the ages, setting us all at one another's throats for gifts of English land and titles, baubles that bind us to his will and to his whims while he steals our realm from us. He holds each man of us hostage against ourselves, in one way or another.

"Look at Sir Reginald de Cheyne, the Scots castellan of Inverness. He is one of the most eminent Scots in the land, nephew to John Comyn of Badenoch and baron of both Inverugie and Strabrock, with their huge estates. The man was King Alexander's Chamberlain of Scotland in his youth! But now he fights for the Plantagenet because Edward holds his first-born and dearest son, young Reginald, prisoner in England. The Countess of Ross, who brought her people out against me when I sought to besiege the Englishman Fitzwarren in Castle Urquhart, did so because her goodman the earl is close held and under threat of death in one of Edward's jails. It happens everywhere nowadays, and all the time.

"And now the Comyns, Red of Badenoch and Black of Buchan, are in similar straits, under Edward's orders to destroy me. They have no wish to fight against their own. They are Highlanders and they know themselves how great the hatred of the English is among their folk. But they can see no way out from the bog into which they have floundered. They hate and fear Edward, but they won't stand against him now because they don't believe they can beat him. He proved that—to their eyes at least—last year when he crushed Scotland's finest army at Dunbar and imprisoned more than half of all the Scots nobility."

"Do you really believe the Comyns will march against you?"

"I believe they have no wish to, but I believe equally that *they* believe they have no choice. They're my close kin, my family, blood of my blood, and though they might be cursing me today for putting them in the case in which they find themselves, I'm reasonably sure they have no wish to kill me or slaughter my followers. That's why they sent Gartnait to talk to me. They believe this will be settled the usual way, by discussion and compromise and *quid pro quo*. That's the way these risings and disturbances have always been settled. From time to time tempers grow frayed, some blood is spilt, there is much rushing around and rattling of spears and bows, and then an agreement is reached, oaths are renewed, titles and rewards and concessions are dispensed, and everyone goes home again."

"But not this time," I said.

"No, not this time, and never again. The world has changed, Father James. Edward of England changed it with his dishonesty and perfidy, his betrayal of our trust and goodwill, and now the folk of Moray are changing it again, and as long as I remain alive it will not change back in England's favour. My Comyn cousins have yet to learn all that, but it is not their fault that they were away in England's jails while new realities took hold up here in Scotland's north, in the aftermath of the Dunbar disgrace. For me, and for the folk who follow me, the time for compromise and submission, aye and for deep-staining shame, is over. My father is a prisoner in London, too, but I'll no longer be bullied into letting an English madman trample me and my folk into the dirt through fear for my father's life. My father would die of shame if he thought I would do so.

"So now I am committed and will not be deflected from my path. I'll fight until England is beaten or I am dead. Gartnait will tell Buchan and Badenoch that when he returns to Aberdeen, and in the meantime I'll be working to make sure that nothing they might do on Edward's behalf thereafter can surprise me or my army. And when I've dealt with them, I'll go to Aberdeen and take possession of my cargo there."

He picked up a short length of charred-end wood and peered at it closely. "That is as far as my planning goes," he continued. "I talked with Gartnait for hours last night, and I made my decision near dawn. This morning I sent out the word for the rest of my folk to follow me eastward to the Spey and to join me at my father's castle in Boharm. Once my army is there— and we'll leave all Moray stripped of manpower—we'll wait and see what the Comyns do, for there's no point in planning anything until we see what their intentions are." He threw the stick back in the fire. "Would you like to talk to Gartnait?"

"Not if he's siding with the English," I said. "I care not what his reasons are for that, but I can't ignore the fact that the friends with whom he rides are Comyns, for they are no friends of me or mine. They have made no secret, these past years, of their disdain for us Scots who live south of Forth and follow the House of Bruce. Besides, did you not say he will leave in the morning for Inverness?" He nodded. "Well, then, there's little point, I think, in spending time with him that would be better spent with you."

He shook his head, half smiling. "I always liked that about you. Direct and to the point. It really is grand to see you, Jamie. I've often wondered what you have been doing, knowing the good bishop and how he drives his people. I could scarce believe my ears when I heard you were here. But I confess, the fact that you *are* here has me concerned. Wishart sent you. I know that because he is the only one who could have, and he is also the only one who would have sent *you*, in particular. Not even Will could send you all the way up here to me unless Wishart gave his permission. Let us talk then, you and I, of Bishop Wishart's urgencies. What else does he want of me?"

I plunged in. "Your presence," I said. "In the south, after you have armed your men."

His eyes were veiled and unreadable. "Where, exactly, in the south, and when, and why?"

I did not know what I had been expecting at that point. Surprise, certainly; disbelief perhaps; refusal in all probability, possibly combined with a measure of anger; even complete outrage would have been understandable in response to such a blatant demand, but the last thing I would ever have anticipated was this absolute calm. This man, for all his youth, was more mature than many another twice his age or older.

"Wallace will be in Dundee in mid-August," I said, "to take delivery of a cargo of weapons from a Norwegian ship that should arrive soon, about the same time as the one you'll meet at Aberdeen. The bishop wants you to meet Wallace there, to meld your armies unseen by the English, and then march together to Stirling. That's where matters will come to a head."

He continued to watch me, and I went on. "Everything depends upon timing, you see. It always does, of course, but in this instance more so than any other. Wishart and the Steward are holding Percy and Clifford in debate—probably now, as we speak. Their intent is to buy time and occupy the English, to enable you to march south without interference.

"An English army is already marching from the northern counties of England to reinforce Percy's unit, but we expect more to head northward once the news of what is really happening here sinks home with Edward. When I left Turnberry it seemed plain that he was considering the risings here as local outbreaks—an irritating annoyance, to be swatted casually by whatever English force was nearest. We now know he has revised that opinion. That's why he sent de Rait running after Buchan and Badenoch with changed orders.

"By now, for all we know, all England might well be in uproar, for once Edward Plantagenet is goaded to snap at an annoyance, he snaps like a dragon, all fire and fury and implacable resolve. His main concern, *Dei gratia*, will continue to be his venture in France— the bishop says he has too much invested there to be able to back away from it now—but I swear he will move heaven and earth to bring about an end to all uprisings in Scotland."

"This army marching to reinforce Percy in the southwest," he said. "When should it arrive?"

"Soon, if they are not already there."

"And you expect there will be other armies?"

"Almost certainly, yes, though whether they will be newly requisitioned or rearranged from existing resources, I cannot say. I heard a rumour at Turnberry that Hugh de Cressingham had been recalled to duty from Lancaster, where he had been negotiating with the northern barons. Word was—though unsubstanti- ated, of course—that he was to return to Scotland with three hundred heavy horse and ten thousand footmen— Why are you looking at me like that?"

"I mislike that—Cressingham coming back."

"I said it's but a rumour, Andrew. But mislike it or not, it should hardly surprise you. He is the treasurer for Scotland, after all. Our sources close to him have made it clear to us that Cressingham's mission to the northern barons on Edward's behalf is strictly secondary to his main responsibility, which is to raise revenues from Scotland for Edward's war in France. And to do that, the man must be in Scotland."

"Aye," he said, "I understand that, but I still dislike the thought of it. I have never met the fellow, but neither have I ever heard his name mentioned other than in tones of hatred and loathing."

I nodded. "You and I have that in common, then. His title is Treasurer, but the folk in Glasgow and elsewhere call him the Treacherer."

"Not up here, they don't, not yet. But the name does not surprise me, after what he did. He single-handedly destroyed the wool trade and came close to bankrupting this entire country, the grasping, thieving bastard. Treacherer indeed."

Every man in Scotland, and every woman and child, too, was familiar with Cressingham's treachery. But they were equally familiar with the other, fouler traits attributed to him—his gratuitous cruelty and the extreme and sickening pleasure he derived from watching people suffer and often even die, hanged or callously cut down for simply bringing themselves to his attention in the performance of his so-called duties.

Andrew Murray was still scowling at the thought of him. "And now he is coming back," he growled.

"The rumour has it that he has been ordered back, at the head of a large contingent from the northern baronies."

"Do you believe that?"

I shrugged. "I see no reason not to. Were I Edward, I would send him back."

"And de Warrenne is to be with him?"

"That is what our sources in Westminster tell us."

His eyebrows rose. "Wishart has spies in Westminster?"

I grinned at him. "No, his lordship has episcopal friends and colleagues throughout Christendom."

"Aye, as a good bishop, he would. But he has spies in Westminster, too." He touched the tip of a finger to the end of his nose, a mannerism of his that I had forgotten but one with which I had grown familiar when I knew him as a boy. It was an unmistakable sign that he was thinking deeply. "De Warrenne is old, is he not?"

"He is, at least as old as Edward and probably older, nearing seventy. He lost his only son last year, killed in a jousting accident, and the loss appears to have sapped him. He has two daughters still alive, the elder of whom is mother to Henry Percy, the fellow facing Bishop Wishart as we speak. The other, of course, you know."

"Do I?" He frowned. "I think not, Father James. Who is she?"

I thought he was jesting, but he was looking back at me in sublime innocence. "She is your queen," I said. "Isabella, wife of King John Balliol."

"Damnation," he said mildly. "I must have known that, of course." He waved the topic away impatiently. "No matter. So this Warrenne fellow is powerful, with connections everywhere, it seems."

"Aye, but bear in mind, he hates everything about Scotland, according to Robert Winchelsea, the Archbishop of Canterbury, who is an old and close friend of his. De Warrenne hates our climate and our lack of roads and generally everything about us and our realm. So he has no enthusiasm for coming north of the border again, even with an enormous army. All he wants to do, according to his friend the archbishop, is to stay at home and enjoy his dotage and his grandchildren."

"But he will come north with the Treacherer despite all that … Together or separately? One army or two?" he asked. I shrugged, and he grunted. "Probably two," he concluded. He fell silent for a moment, then straightened his shoulders and flung up his hands. "Enough," he said. "This is pointless speculation, so a pox on Cressingham and all his ilk, for now at least. What else have we to talk about? What of your cousin Will?"

"Much of great interest," I said. "He's up in arms like you, having raised the dragon banner in Lothian, harrying the English and burning crops to deny them to the English garrisons in the towns and castles there. He is under strict orders, though, from you-know-who, to stay well away from sieges and the like and to keep his men doing what they do best—hit-and-run raiding. Strike, disrupt, and disappear to strike again somewhere else. But he's under strict orders, too, with regard to timing. He'll raid widely in Lothian until the end of July, then head west to cross the Forth at Stirling before striking east again into Fife. He'll pick up his cargo in Dundee and wait for you near there in mid-August."

"Hmm. How many people does he have now?"

"He himself said the number was more than a thousand, with more coming in every day, sometimes hundreds in a single day."

"The middle of August," he said. "That might not be easily done. As I've explained, I can't leave here until this Comyn situation is resolved."

"Of course you can! If the Comyns arrive here and find you gone, they'll claim victory and send word to England that you fled in advance of their arrival, and that should make them all happy. They'll have carried out Edward's wishes without bloodshed, and they'll also have avoided any need to antagonize friends and neighbours by appearing to be too zealous in their support of England. In the meantime you will be free to march to Aberdeen and take possession of the weapons aboard that ship."

He turned his head slightly and gave me a look to which my mind applied the word *mocking*. "Do you expect me to take pleasure in that thought, Father, that I would flee ahead of them?"

"No, not really, I suppose, but it would resolve the situation you were so concerned about."

He twisted his mouth into a humourless smile. "If I believed that for a moment, I would do as you suggest. But it would solve nothing. If I leave my lands before the Comyns come, I'll forfeit them. Buchan or Badenoch will annex them as soon as it's known I'm gone, and they will claim Edward Plantagenet's authority to do so."

"How can they do that? There is no rebellion if you are not here openly under arms."

"Not so, Jamie. They don't need *me*. They'll claim that *Moray* is in rebellion—not Andrew Murray, but the region itself. Every man in Moray has stood openly and steadfastly with me in open defiance of England these past two months and more. That makes Moray a nest of rebels by England's definition. They'll claim, with authority, that they were expressly ordered by the Lord Paramount to stamp out rebellion here by whatever means necessary.

"But Buchan and Badenoch are not only Edward's representatives, bound to obedience by their paroles. They are also our neighbours, land-hungry neighbours whose lands abut ours, and with Edward's mandate they will snatch up my lands the moment I disappear from sight. And that means they'll spill blood among my folk, because my Murrays will not meekly submit to having their land stolen from beneath them. And if that happens, then nothing will have improved since before we started to fight in May." He shook his head. "No, I won't countenance that, will not accept it."

"So what will you do?"

He grinned, a fleeting thing but cheering to see. "I'll do what I'm on my way to do now. As soon as Gartnait leaves for Inverness in the morning, I'll form my men up and march them south to the Spey."

"But he'll warn the Comyns that you're coming, and they'll be waiting for you."

"D'ye think me daft, man? Gartnait doesn't know what I intend to do. He thinks I came this way with him simply to see him safely aboard his ship in Inverness before we return to Auch to regroup. He thinks we'll head northwest into the mountains in search of safety as soon as he is gone. But by the time he reaches Aberdeen, we'll be set up on the bank of the Spey, in the Bog of Gight. We'll wait there for Buchan and his crew to come to us through the Ingie and hope to lure them into fighting in the bog."

"Is Buchan likely to do that?"

He shrugged with one shoulder. "I have no idea, but we'll find out. One thing is certain. If he does commit to a fight under our terms, he's finished. So let's pray he feels strong and confident. In the meantime, we should go back and join my other guests. But listen, as far as anyone else is concerned, you have brought me up-to-date on the situation in the southwest and delivered the letters you were carrying from Wishart and Lord Stewart to my attention. Apart from that, we have been sitting here by the fire reminiscing about our times together when we were boys, before the world went mad. Shall we go?"

In the hour that followed, I spoke briefly with Gartnait of Mar. He was a pleasant fellow, a few years older than I, and I commiserated with him over the death of his sister, Bruce's wife, whom he had loved dearly. It was evident to me, too, that he thought highly of his goodbrother Bruce and set great store upon their friendship, for he asked after him eagerly when I told him of having met the earl, and I detected no hint of malice or envy when he spoke of him; indeed, the topic of Bruce's defiance of Edward and his rejection of the King's favours occasioned not a single word of criticism, and I tucked that information away for future consideration.

The remainder of the evening passed quickly and pleasantly, with a wonderful meal of fish, meats, and kale steamed in a covered pot with herbs and some exotic spice, and we were entertained with pipe music performed by a visiting bard from the Shetland Isles whose sole purpose in travelling all over the northern parts of the realm was to play the ancient, plaintive music of their people for his audience to enjoy. The night approached early for July, and the entire camp was abed by darkfall.

CHAPTER FIFTEEN

TRAVELLING SOUTH

T hree days later we were moving swiftly eastward to the River Spey, where we would lie in wait for the Comyn army. We had skirted Inverness without incident, keeping out of sight of the castle town. The army that accompanied us, which Bishop de Cheyne of Aberdeen would later describe in writing to England as "a very large body of rogues," comprised the combined strengths of Andrew Murray's twin strongholds of Auch and Balconie.

From Inverness we had struck directly east, paralleling the south shore of the Moray Firth a few miles away on our left. But, in contrast to what I quickly gathered was the normal run of things in Andrew-led expeditions, this journey was a restrained and joyless thing, because Andrew himself was restrained and joyless. He rode from the outset in a scowling silence that had an unsettling effect on his people. As the sole outsider there, I was probably the person least affected by his mood, for I had nothing against which to compare it. To his friends and intimates, though, the young leader's withdrawal was a matter of great concern, and each man there, at least as I saw it, was busy questioning himself and his recent behaviour, hoping that it had not been some action of his that had triggered such a prolonged and uncharacteristic reaction from their leader.

Eventually, after two whole days of brooding silence, he drew rein at mid-morning, in the middle of nowhere, and sat motionless, staring off into the horizon ahead. The people following directly behind him came to a milling, disorganized halt. He stood up in his stirrups and turned to look north and northwest. Then, after barely having spoken a word to anyone for forty-eight hours, even when questioned directly, he raised his right hand above his head and rotated it three times before pointing down at his own helmet and barking, "Captains! To me!" He turned then to the trumpeter who rode at his side. "The summons."

The fellow raised his bugle at once and blew the call to summon all the captains within hearing, and there was an immediate surge of movement as those commanders began to move towards him. I kneed my mount away to one side, to make room for them, but Andrew waved to stop me. "Father James," he called. "A word with you, if you will."

He trotted his mount towards me, pointing as he came towards a clear space in the bushes off to one side of the track we had been following. "We can talk over there without being heard," he said when he was beside me. "I want you to know what I intend to do next, because I might not have the chance to talk to you about it again. Your bishop's business must be first in your mind, as it should be, and I don't want you to think I've lost sight of it."

I had no idea what he meant, but I followed him until he reined around to face me, far enough away from everyone else for privacy. "What do you intend to do?" I asked him.

"You don't know where we are, do you?"

"No, I don't." I waved a hand at the head-high brush and bushes surrounding us. "I know I'm lost. I know we are on the south side of the Moray Firth, heading east to Elgin, where we will turn south towards the River Spey. Should I know more?"

He smiled gently. "No," he said, "not really. But over yonder"—he pointed northwards—"over yonder, less than two miles from here on the sea coast, across easy terrain, lies Castle Duffus."

"Very well," I said. "I've never heard of it, but it's clearly important to you, and so I shall ask why."

He grinned, but it was a savage, short-lived thing, showing no hint of amusement. "Because it is garrisoned by Englishmen."

I restrained myself from shrugging. "From what I understand, all the castles hereabouts have English garrisons. Why is it noteworthy in this instance?"

"Because the English had no need to seize this one. Its owners were already in Edward's pocket." His face was grim. "Castle Duffus is my ancestral home, Father James. The original stronghold was built two hundred years ago by my first ancestor in Scotland, a Flemish knight called Freskin. From the day it was built, it was the seat of what became the de Moravia family. The folk who lived there until recently, the Murrays of Duffus, were close kin of mine and good, firm friends. But a few years ago one of them, the eldest daughter, married Reginald de Cheyne, the traitorous whoreson who governs now in Inverness in Edward's name, calling himself the governor of Moray. He's an outlander, Scots-born but English in all else, and he has long since outlived his welcome." He fell silent again, but it was clear he had not finished, and so I waited.

"In the clear but foolish hope of justifying his indefensible conduct," he continued, "he claims to be a victim of coercion in everything he does, forever bleating about how Edward holds his son, young Reginald, in custody somewhere in England, supposedly as surety for his father's obedience and good conduct. But in truth there is too much evidence against the arrogant, unthinking oaf for that claim to be credible. He works too hard on Edward's behalf, performs his tasks too eagerly to be able to claim duress. He is a traitor to his own folk, pure and simple, and I have decided to make an example of him."

"And how will you do that?" I could see no point in protesting. His mind was clearly set on whatever he had decided to do.

"By rooting him out and destroying him. Duffus is his today, part of his wife's dowry, defiled forever by the stench of his treachery. I think I've taken it. Today,

I mean. I should have, by this time. So now we're going to go and make sure of it."

"You're making no sense, Andrew."

"Ah, but I am, Father." He grinned. "I couldn't tell you sooner, couldn't tell anyone at all, for fear word would get out, but it's all done now, for better or for worse. I've had men inside the castle's gates since early yesterday—half a score of my best by the end of the day."

"Great Heaven! How can you be so sure of that?"

"Because I had men watching what went on. Had anything gone wrong, I would have heard of it last night. But I heard nothing, and so they have entered safely, in ones and twos throughout the day, and found places to hide. As I said, they're my best men and it's a Murray castle—they all know the layout of the place."

"But what can ten men do against an entire garrison?"

I saw a feral flash of bared teeth. "My ten *best* men, Jamie, each one worth ten more. They can wait until the darkest hour of night, then dirk the guards and throw open the gates."

"For whom, in God's name? Not for us, surely. We're more than two miles away and it's mid-morning already."

"No, not for us. For Sandy Pilche."

When I closed my mouth, my few remaining teeth came together hard. "I had no idea you were planning such a thing."

"That pleases me, for if you have guessed nothing of what was going on, then no one else has, either. Sandy and I planned the operation before we left Auch. We skirted Inverness carefully, as you know, keeping out of sight. But I had to be sure we would be seen and followed, and attracting their attention while seemingly attempting to creep by without being seen was the best way of achieving that. We have been under close watch ever since."

"But why?" I felt myself frowning. "And why do I think I'm going to feel foolish when I hear the answer to that question?"

Andrew spread his hands wide, his elbows tucked in against his sides. "As long as they were watching us, they knew that we were marching directly east, through Forres to Elgin, staying well south of the coastline and going nowhere near Castle Duffus, which meant we therefore posed no threat to de Cheyne there."

"And Sandy Pilche?"

"Sailed last night from the Black Isle in the dark with two hundred men, and was waiting outside Duffus when the gates fell open."

"Dear God in Heaven! So you *have* taken Duffus!" I was shaking my head. "One part of me can see the satisfaction in that, but another part entirely is asking why. What will you do with it now? Having taken the place, you'll have to hold it, and in the meantime there's an army coming against you from the south."

"Not so," he said. "I have no further need of Duffus. The place means nothing to me. It's far more valuable to the English, now that they've lost it. I'll sack it, free any prisoners, then burn the damned place down and leave it useless to de Cheyne and everyone else. And then, to add insult to their injuries and make the lesson even more pointed, I'll raze the whole damned region. The folk are all gone, anyway. Their lands were stolen from them. I will show the English that they have outlived whatever welcome they imagined existed for them here in Moray."

He glanced over his shoulder, to where his captains were now assembled. "They're ready for me over there, so now I have to tell them what's been happening and what they are to do over the next few days."

"Can I come with you?"

He hesitated, then looked me square in the eye. "You're a priest. Are you sure you want to do that? We'll be spilling blood."

"Then you'll have need of a priest."

"So be it, then," he murmured, sounding slightly doubtful. "Come with us, and bring the Holy Sacraments with you."

And so I rode to war, not as a combatant but most certainly as an observer and a comforter, and as such I was sometimes involved as Andrew and his followers destroyed Castle Duffus and its surrounding estates and outlying farms. He turned his army loose, more or less, with orders to burn or otherwise ruin growing crops before they could be harvested, and to confiscate livestock and destroy anything that might be deemed in any way useful to the occupying

English. He took care to tell his men that the folk among whom they would be marauding were all Scots like themselves, with no say in, and no responsibility for, the behaviour of the occupying English, so no abuse of them personally would be tolerated, and punishment for transgressions would be swift.

I was called upon to serve as one of a large number of observers sent out with the raiding groups and charged with making sure that they adhered to the spirit of Andrew's intent. I was more than glad to learn afterwards that not a single instance of abuse had been reported. In the meantime, though, I had been sickened by the whole experience of having to sit idly by as the very stuff of the life of the countryside—growing food, fine pastureland, and thriving livestock—was utterly destroyed. I returned to camp on the final day of the campaign reeking of smoke from burning crops and buildings, my throat raw from the helpless retching caused by the smoke itself and the roiling sense of disgust that had haunted me since the expedition began.

The Duffus garrison had turned out to be smaller than anticipated, numbering fewer than forty men, and the men of Moray had been merciless in dealing with them, but Andrew left two wounded English commanders alive, to relay word to Sir Reginald de Cheyne that his days of trampling Moray underfoot were at an end, that his remaining castles and holdings would soon be taken and destroyed, and that de Cheyne himself now stood proscribed by the Murrays of Petty, a bounty offered for his capture or death.

Duffus Castle was a valuable asset—a strongly fortified castle surrounded by an arable estate—but it was a Murray fiefdom, and it was unprecedented at that time for a Scots leader to destroy his own possessions in order to deny them to the enemy. The sacking and destruction of Castle Duffus, more than any previous action had, made it perfectly plain to the Scots populace and to the occupying English forces in the region that nothing was to be held sacrosanct from that time on.

A few days after leaving Duffus, during a marching break late in the forenoon, I sat on a large stone in a grassy, sunlit hollow on the bank of the River Spey and listened to Andrew Murray as he spoke to his assembled army. To one side of me, one incautious man must have swallowed a fly or a bee, for he erupted in a sudden fit of noisy coughing, to the great annoyance of those around him, who cursed him roundly.

I was immediately struck by the fellow's facial resemblance to a priest I knew in Glasgow, whose name was Ignatius. Father Ignatius, though, was soft-bellied and overweight, notorious among his peers for his sweet tooth and his self-indulgences. The disparaging thought sprang instantly into my mind, and irrelevant as it was, it made me aware that there was not a single fat man in the army that surrounded me. All around me, everywhere I looked—and I searched keenly—I saw lean, hard faces surmounting lean, hard bodies.

They were tall men by and large, these Highland mountain dwellers, and noted for that height in southern parts, where they were known disparagingly as caterans by people who believed that a cateran was a rogue, a vagabond. In fact the name was simply the Gaelic word for a landsman, a peasant farmer. But neither the northern land nor the way of life of the folk who lived on it permitted the luxury of extra fat on any man's frame. Highland Gaels, from the time they were born, had to claw their way doggedly towards survival, day in and day out. They lived on barren lands that blunted and rejected ploughs, and they survived mainly on a sparse, unvarying diet of ground oats and goat's milk, leavened very seldom with infusions of venison or mutton. Theirs was a life of constant hardship that stamped the evidence of their privations into the very fabric of their bodies. There was a gaunt, spare sameness to them all—a long-legged, watchful, catlike grace to their movement that suggested danger, coiled tension, and a barely muted threat of explosive violence should they be crossed or displeased. Even their clothing had a sameness to it: hard-wearing garments of durable, tight-woven homespun wool, dyed in a range of drab, natural browns, dark greens, and shades of grey that leached the differences out of their wearers, reducing them, from a distance at least, to indistinguishable, featureless clumps of ... *folk*.

That drabness, that sameness, brought home to me that day a sudden understanding of one of most noticeable differences between the Celtic Gaels and their southern Scots counterparts: the Gaels loved colour, the more vibrant the better, and their adornments and jewellery reflected that love, probably because their clothing could not; brightly coloured feathers in yellow, red, pale greens, and brilliant whites and blues flashed in the July sun, pinned to men's caps and to the breasts of their tunics and plain leather jerkins. And the jewellery that they wore was even more distinctive, fashioned mainly of heavy silver, though I had seen a few pieces made of gold, and studded with big, brightly coloured local stones: blood-red garnets, lozenges of polished jet, pale purple amethysts, and the flashing, glassy yellow stones called cairngorm, with here and there a glowing blob of precious amber marking a man as being wealthier or more fortunate than his fellows. Set against the dullness of their clothing, the sparkling highlights on brooches, pins, belt buckles, and the hilts and sheaths of dirks and swords drew attention to the men's strutting, cocksure self-awareness, the strength and natural arrogance of males in their prime who knew they would not easily be bested. And now here they were, held rapt, drinking in a younger man's every word.

A single glance at the man addressing them established his pre-eminence instantly, for his dress, his armour, his weapons, and his bearing all set him apart. Tall and wide shouldered, he exuded confidence and good breeding, and his voice rang with the strength and authority of a man bred to leadership. He wore a simple but richly woven dark brown woollen tunic and matching close-fitted trews tucked into thick-soled boots that were reinforced with strips of steel to protect his ankles, and on his upper body he wore a heavy shirt of burnished mail covered with a light, sleeveless linen surcoat of bright blue, bearing the three white stars of the ancient House of de Moravia. A fine, heavy sword hung by his left side, and a long dirk in a handsomely chased sheath balanced it on his right.

I had never heard Andrew speak publicly before, and I admired the way he held himself, gazing down calmly and solemnly at these wild men who were his followers—I estimated that there were between five and six hundred of them packing the hollow—and waiting for them to grow silent. When they did, he reached behind him to unhook the battle-axe that hung at his right hip. It came free smoothly and he raised it high above his head to a roar of approval that made me smile, remembering what Will had told me about it.

Despite what men now thought, Will had said, Andrew Murray had never had much regard for the battle-axe as a weapon, preferring the more knightly sword and lance, but he had used the weapon to great advantage on one occasion, albeit without intent. It had happened at a tournament hosted by some English nobleman years earlier in Aberdeen, when Andrew, newly knighted, afoot, and disarmed in the heat of a melee with a group of heavy horse, had snatched up a fallen axe to defend himself. He had been fortunate when the trailing edge of the blade had caught firmly in the links of an English knight's mail, allowing Andrew to use his weight to unhorse the fellow and cause him to be adjudged dead by the tourney judges. The incident had been much talked about by Murray's men, all of them unaware of its accidental nature, and Andrew had become famed as an axeman of great ability. Since then the battle-axe had hung from his hip at all times, a visible symbol of his prowess and abilities.

When the roar began to fade, he released his grip on the axe's handle and caught the heavy head as it fell, then swung it behind him and replaced it smoothly on his hip, and as he did so he began to speak, stilling the crowd instantly. He spoke in Gaelic, and he spoke in short, easily understood sentences, and again I found myself admiring his control of himself and his audience.

"I'm taking you to fight," he began, and paused to wait out the upswelling of muttered comments. "Against our own." This time there was no audible reaction, but he paused again, scanning the faces staring up at him.

"Against our own," he repeated. "Not Englishmen this time. Scots like ourselves. Think on that. Think on it and be sure you know what is at stake before we go on."

Again he scanned the faces watching him. "I could tell you tales and cozen you, to anger you. I could denounce and curse the men we go to fight—Comyn of Buchan and his cousin of Badenoch, Malise of Strathearn, and Edward de Balliol, the King's own brother. I could decry all of them, the leaders, magnates, and mormaers of Scotia who bring their men against us now in the name of Edward Plantagenet."

He allowed the names to hang naked in the air as he looked around the gathering.

"I *could* do that, but it would not change the fact— it *will* not change the fact—that the men who follow those leaders are our own kin, men bred and raised in these very parts. They follow because they must. Remember that. They have no other choice. Some of them will be known to us, some loved by us, blood of our blood. Kinsmen, coming against us because they have to follow those who lead them. Kinsmen who will kill some of us—will be killed *by* some of us— because their leaders choose to stand with England. I want you all to think on that, to know what it means, before we move from here."

This time the silence seemed to me to hold a different quality, an element of solemnity.

"Be clear on this, above all else," he said, his voice now loud and strong and clarion clear. "The enemy we are facing is England. Edward Plantagenet. No other. That these are Scots who come against us is a ploy—a lesson Edward hopes to teach us about power and politics. Buchan and Badenoch, along with their friends and all the men who follow them, are but an English weapon in this fight—a weapon swung against us. That they are Scots, and kin of ours, merely makes the weapon heavier and sharper, deadly enough to crush and maim us if we stand still from guilt and let them cut us down.

"And bear in mind, too, that Comyn stands for Comyn first and last when blood is spilt and lands are up for grasping. Buchan and Badenoch are our neighbours. That is fact. So is Malise of Strathearn. But they are drooling neighbours who have long been covetous of our lands in Moray. Will we stand by and give those up because we fear to spill Comyn blood when it comes against us?"

"No!" The roar was deafening, and a distant echo returned it to our hearing moments after it had faded.

"So be it, then. I have thought long about this, and here is what we will do. Spey lies at our backs—that's why your feet are wet." A ripple of laughter ran through the crowd. "I thought about waiting for them back on the other side, forcing them to fight their way across to meet us. But that would have been folly. The time of year is wrong. The river is too low and easy to cross, no barrier at all to heavy horse. And Buchan will have heavy English horse with him, be sure of that."

He stretched himself up to his full height and looked out over his men to the lush growth at their backs. "We're better off on this side of the Spey. There's only one road up to here from Aberdeen, and they have to take it, through the forests of the Ingie and along the edge of the Bog of Gight. I know that country inside out and so do you. And that's where we'll wait for them. Inside the forest where their heavy horsemen will be useless, and in the bog itself, where they'll be even worse off. We're all afoot, and that's the way we fight." His eyebrows rose in a wildly exaggerated expression of alarm. "All except me, that is, so make sure you don't mistake me for an Englishman!" Murray held his smile until the laughter began to flag, then became serious again.

"And so we will fight them *our* way. On *our* terms. In the woods and in the bog—in mud and water, where they can't deploy their horsemen, their armoured men-at-arms, or their ranked archers. We'll lure them off the road and into the woods, and we'll kill them.

"You might find that some of them will say they have no wish to fight you. But be careful. They might be feigning friendship. Better to be sure they're really harmless than to die from a stab in the back." He raised a hand high, fingers spread. "The English are the English, straightforward enemies. Kill them as you find them. But be careful of the Scots you face. Make sure they're weaponless before you turn your back on any of them."

He looked around the throng again.

"There's one more thing to say," he said, in a slightly quieter voice, "though it alters nothing of what I said before. I swear, I have no idea if this will come to pass, but there is a chance that they truly might not want to fight us. They're under oath to Edward, true. He holds their paroles. But these men have been in prison for a year, and they were there for defying Edward and thumbing their noses at England. They can't be strong after a year in prison. And above all they are Scots. They'll have no real desire to fight for England against their own realm—against their neighbours and cousins." He paused again. "If they want to fight, we'll fight them. And if not, we'll wait and see. Now, are there any questions?"

"Aye, I have one." The speaker was a forceful-looking character, unsmiling and dour. Like most of his fellows here, he wore no armour, though he was well equipped with a long, plain sword and matching dagger, the hilts of both polished to a shine from years of daily use. "Tell me this," he rasped. "If Buchan and his folk *do* fight, and I catch hold of the old earl, who gets his ransom money? Me or you?"

Again the crowd erupted in laughter.

"Alistair," Andrew said when the noise died down, "you bring old Buchan's bony arse to me in person and I swear in front of everyone assembled here that you'll have every silver groat we can squeeze out of it in ransom for him." A loud cheer greeted that. "And now it's time to form up and be on our way again."

As the assembly began to break apart, Andrew beckoned me over, grinning. "Well," he said, "I'm glad that's out of the way. It went as well as could be hoped for, don't you think?"

"I agree," I said. "And I'll pray the gentle Jesus proves you right about Buchan's reluctance to fight against his own."

"We won't know until the time comes," he said quietly, then looked at me sidelong. "Look, I'm going to have to leave you on your own for a while, perhaps for several days, for I must attend to a number of things in a very short time."

"Oh, don't worry about me. I'm a grown man and I've spent days on my own before."

He smiled again. "Good! That's excellent. Walk with me, then, to the horse lines. I wasn't hungry before, but I could eat something now. With any kind of fortune we'll scrounge some trail food from the cooks."

"No complaints from me," I said, and fell into step beside him. "Who was that man Alistair? He seemed very … different."

"Different?" He chuckled. "Oh, Alistair is that and more." But then, instead of explaining, he asked, "How many men would you guess were there altogether?"

I shrugged. "At a guess, five to six hundred."

"Six hundred and thirty-four," he said quietly in his sibilant Gaelic. "Sandy Pilche counted them before we left Duffus. And among all of them, including my own Wee Mungo, Alistair Murray is the one you least want to have angry at you."

I had suspected as much, purely from the fellow's appearance.

"He'll guard you while I'm away." Andrew saw my reaction. "No, I'll hear no objections. You need a good man at your back, Jamie, so humour me and don't argue. You are a stranger here and don't know who you can trust or who you can't. Neither do I, in truth, apart from my close friends and captains. Alliances change overnight in times like this, and friends are being suborned every day by Edward's

spies and toadies. And you are not only a stranger but
also a messenger from the south, from Wishart and the
Steward. Take my word, Jamie, your life will be in
danger all the time you're here, so whether you like it
or not, Alistair will be your guardian angel henceforth.
Trust him as you trust me, for he is my cousin and one
of my oldest friends—we were raised beneath the
same roof and shared a bed for years as boys. He will
look after you as well·as I could, mayhap even better."
He looked about us, and his face broke into a grin.
"Here he comes now, so let me make you known to
each other."

CHAPTER SIXTEEN

A SHOW OF PRUDENCE

It was to be four days before I laid eyes on Andrew Murray again, for he vanished into the Bog of Gight shortly after introducing me to his cousin Alistair, at the head of a scouting group of half a hundred men. The rest of the army, including me and my new shadow, Alistair Murray, followed them hours later at a far slower pace and eventually reached an encampment that had been partially prepared for us.

I was surprised to see it at first, but I quickly learned that it was typical of Sandy Pilche's thoroughness. And it made me realize once more that Andrew Murray had planned far ahead. Six spit-roasted deer ensured that everyone ate well that night once the work of setting up camp and posting guards had been completed, and afterwards, as the dusk was deepening to night, the sergeants and captains moved from fire to fire, sending their various charges to their beds.

I was astir and celebrating Mass in the open air, at an altar made from a folding table, long before dawn the following day. The night had been warm and calm and the pre-morning air was motionless, and I was gratified to see how many men joined me there in the peaceful darkness by the flickering light of a few torches. As the Mass progressed, I was aware of increasing activity all around us, and by the time the brief Sacrament was over, the morning sky was pale and birds were singing in the surrounding trees. I blessed my congregation and dismissed them, and soon after that the daily drills began.

I spent the next few hours watching the men, for what I was witnessing was far from the kind of disciplined drilling I had seen the English soldiery practise on the few occasions when I had been close enough to study them. There, squads and groups of men had marched in solid blocks to the commands of petty officers, all uniformly moving according to long-established procedure.

The Moray men I watched that morning were made of different stuff. Highlanders all, they scorned the rigid formations that formed the building blocks of English military prowess. They took pride in being warriors, and the tactics used by the English invaders were alien to them, to the extent that whereas the common English soldier went to fight protected by effective armour, whether of boiled, hammered leather or linked mail or both, the Highland Gael was frequently known to plunge into battle completely unclothed, discarding the toga-like garment in which he habitually wound himself, because it was too restrictive for armed combat.

I remember I laughed when first I heard that, thinking it a lie concocted to gull fools, but Sandy Pilche convinced me it was true, telling me, in all seriousness, that the Scots Highlander preferred to fight naked, armoured only in his own righteousness and protected by a round shield called a targe and the keenness of his own steel. The Gaels were not soldiers, he insisted; they were not militarily disciplined; they were warriors, each one unique, a law and a force unto himself, and their training methods reflected that. The disciplines they pursued in readying themselves for battle were mostly concerned with stamina and bodily strength. I quickly became accustomed to the sights and sounds of them competing with one another in great feats of strength, hurling massive stones one-handed and hoisting and throwing entire tree trunks, besides running for hours at breakneck speed across terrain that would daunt even my cousin Will's forest outlaws.

Even so, I spent the greater part of the days that followed sitting alone in my tent, compiling a report on my progress to Bishop Wishart. I knew I would probably deliver it into his hands in person, since no one else was likely to reach him before I did in mid-August, yet I was glad to get to work and enjoyed the challenge of capturing the details of my journey before I could forget them.

The solitude was mental rather than physical, because, like the poor in the Scriptures, Alistair Murray was always with me. When I went outside he hovered around me like a hunting hawk, his eyes scanning our surroundings high and low for signs that anyone was watching me too closely or thinking about harming me. He was constantly fingering the hilts of his weapons, too, gripping them and twisting them, easing them in their sheaths as if he were afraid of finding them too tightly seated should he need to draw them quickly. I was impressed by his dedication, but I found his fierce-eyed presence disconcerting and wished he were less intense.

I tried speaking to him, when first we found ourselves alone together after Andrew left, but my attempt at cordiality rattled off the armour of his indifference like hailstones off a slate roof, and for a while I was determined not to speak to him again. I found it difficult to remain angry at him, though, for it was plain that he was focused on protecting me, and so I spoke to him whenever he was nearby, hoping to break through his indifference. And slowly but surely he began to thaw, though it was alien to his nature to be garrulous or demonstrative. By the end of the third day he would answer me, sometimes even civilly, but it was always I who initiated the conversations, such as they were.

On the morning of the fourth day, I had broken my fast with a handful of salty roasted oats and chopped hazelnuts and was washing them down with fresh spring water from the hillside above our camp when I saw him across the communal space fronting the fire pit outside my tent. He had been gone for mere minutes, probably to relieve himself, and as he moved fluidly back towards me, idly twirling the heavy quarterstaff he carried, I snatched up my own walking staff, a stout and useful one as heavy as his, and stepped forward to meet him. He halted immediately, eyeing me speculatively: no doubt the warrior in him recognized the threat I posed in stepping forward boldly as I had, while the good Catholic in him balked at the prospect of challenging, perhaps even having to fight, a priest in holy orders.

I hefted my staff across my chest and stretched it towards him, holding it with my hands about a foot apart. "A challenge," I said, and spun the weapon quickly with my right hand. "To pass a little time. I'm trained to it, so you needn't be afraid of hurting me. And even if you do," I said with a grin, "I promise I'll absolve you of the sin of it. Guard yourself."

I dropped into a fighting stance and advanced towards him and he reacted instinctively, raising his own weapon and sidling away from me. His face, though, still betrayed his confusion, and I leapt at him, swinging my staff hard towards his head. He countered with a solid block and a counterstroke, his reflexes taking him instantly where his piety would not permit, but before the blow was fully released I was already on one knee, my staff scything towards his ankles. He leapt back nimbly, avoiding my sweep and launching himself back at me in a driving blur of whirling wood that ended with a sudden sharp, one-ended thrust that might have cracked my sternum had it landed.

We went hard at it for a full quarter-hour, neither conceding anything to the other, and eventually he threw down his staff and raised both hands.

"Enough," he gasped. "Enough. I keep waiting for you to remember you're a priest, but you need no reminding, do you?"

I dropped my own weapon beside his. "No," I said, "I don't. But from time to time, especially when I take a hard rap, I have difficulty remembering not to blaspheme." I drew a deep, shaky breath, then let it out. "I enjoyed that … and in truth I think I even needed it. It has been some time since last I fought."

"Is that a fact?" he said, in a voice both wry and dry. "Well, ye'll be glad to know it was barely noticeable. You fight well for a man who has no business fighting."

"Oh, I might argue that," I said. "Remember, even our Lord Jesus took a whip to clean the money lenders from the Temple. Priests are men above all else, Alistair, and any man will fight, given sufficient provocation."

From that time on, he and I were comfortable with each other.

It was later that same day that I was working outside in the sunshine, at a table in front of my tent, and had completed the fair copy of my report to Bishop Wishart moments earlier. I was, in fact, waving the final written page from side to side to dry the last few lines of ink, when I glanced up to see a lad of ten or eleven scurrying towards Alistair, who sat in the shade of a nearby hawthorn tree. I guessed as soon as

I set eyes on the boy that he came bearing tidings, and I knew I was correct when he half turned and knelt on one knee, carefully presenting his back to my gaze, and bent forward to whisper in my guardian's ear. Alistair, who had seen the boy approaching and obviously knew him, had risen to his feet and moved forward into the light to meet him, and now he knelt beside him, one elbow resting on a raised knee and his head cocked as he listened, his eyes finding mine over the lad's shoulder.

I remained at my table, watching them. Unlike most of his fellow Highlanders, who wrapped themselves in the single voluminous garment called a plaid, Alistair Murray chose to wear the southern style of clothing, a knee-length tunic over trousers or leggings and heavy, thick-soled leather boots that laced up almost to his knees. He also wore a loosely belted sleeveless jerkin of tanned leather that did nothing to disguise his heavily muscled shoulders. A gleaming torc—the intricately carved collar of heavy gold that marked its wearer as a Gaelic chieftain—encircled his neck, today left bare by the single tight-braided queue that pulled the hair back off his face to hang behind his head.

He stood up, keeping his eyes fixed on me as he patted the young lad roughly on the back and dismissed him with a word of thanks. I watched as came towards me, hitching the sword belt at his waist until it hung comfortably again.

"Andrew wants us" was all he said, passing by me on his way towards the horse lines.

I scooped up my report and my writing materials and carried them quickly into my tent, where I tucked them beneath the thin mattress on my cot for safety before hurrying out to catch up with him.

"What does he want?" I asked when I caught up with him. "Did the boy say?"

We had reached the horse lines by then and I saw the boy himself watching us from the back of the horse he must have ridden on his way to find us. Beside him, on one of the few truly black horses I had ever seen, sat Fillan de Moray, the young chieftain whom Andrew had left in command during his absence. Alistair nodded to the chieftain, then glanced at me briefly before taking his horse's bridle from the wooden frame that held it.

"It's not the boy's affair," he answered. "He was sent to fetch us, that's all. We'll find out the rest when we reach Andrew." He set about bridling and saddling his horse then, and since I was similarly occupied, we spoke no more.

We rode in silence until we reached our journey's end, some six miles farther south, for the so-called road we were following was no more than a winding, beaten track that wound haphazardly around and between, and sometimes up and down, the contours of the land. On a particularly narrow stretch through a press of springy saplings, the boy turned sharply right into an unseen junction and went ahead of us along a narrower and even more serpentine path that climbed steadily upwards. Again we rode in silence, our attention on the narrow, treacherous, stone-littered track beneath our horses' hooves, until our flagging beasts struggled up a final steep incline to a cairn of stones, where our guide drew rein and pointed to a bush-covered crest higher than any we had encountered until then.

"Up there," he said. "I'll mind your horses."

We dismounted and climbed the last forty or fifty paces on foot, making heavy going of it until we arrived at a small plateau where two guards waited. They stopped us, and one of them vanished into a cleft in the hillside, to reappear a short time later followed by Andrew Murray himself.

"Welcome," he said. "I had you stopped here because there is a need for caution farther along the path." He beckoned with his fingers. "Come and see."

We followed him for a short distance, along a track no wider than a goat path, until the land ahead of us disappeared without warning, swooping away beneath our feet, and we found ourselves standing on a rock-strewn crest among head-high clumps of the wild broom that was known up here as whins, gazing down a precipitous hillside towards the continuation of the road we had been following earlier.

"What do you make of that?" Andrew asked.

No one answered him, for we were all three trying to make sense of what we were looking at. The winding road far below us was obscured by a solidly packed mass of men and horses that was obviously the English army we had been expecting. But it was far from being what we might have thought to see. An army on the march—*any* army on the march—formed a long, disjointed train, strung out along its route, and most particularly so when that route was tightly restricted, as was the one below us. What we were seeing, though, appeared to be massed formations of foot soldiers, flanked on the side nearest us by ranks of heavily armoured cavalry, all apparently proceeding slowly in line of battle, as though defying an enemy. But our own force, some six miles behind us, was the only other army in the region. Who, then, were the English facing? I looked at Alistair and saw at once from his frown that he was as much at a loss as I was. It was left to Fillan, Andrew's lieutenant, to ask the necessary question.

"I can make nothing of it, Cousin, for it makes no sense. They're expecting to be attacked, clearly, but who by? There's no one there."

Andrew grunted. "I've been watching them since they came into view this morning, and I kept asking myself the same question because I didn't believe the obvious answer. Straight away I sent for you three, wanting you to see the truth of it."

"The truth of what, Cousin?" Fillan was frowning, too. "What is Buchan's army *doing* down there? Making ready to fight off an attack from us? If that's so, he's plainly mad. Unless—unless it *isn't* Buchan's army."

"Oh, it's Buchan's," Andrew drawled. "There's no mistaking that. If you squint into the sun you can see

his standard at the head of the first rank of cavalry—
three golden stooks of corn on a blue field. As for what
you are looking at, well, I think we're witnessing
something altogether new."

We all looked at him.

"What that spectacle down there means, my
friends, is that John Comyn, the Earl of Buchan, is
prepared to spend a long time on the road to Elgin. A
very long time. He is marching in full battle order,
making very little progress—his men are practically
standing still—but keeping his formations absolutely
safe from attack, by us or by anyone else who might
come along."

"Name of God!" Fillan spluttered. "Why would he
do that? It's sheer folly."

"Prudence," Alistair said, more to himself than
anyone else, and Andrew grinned at him.

"Aye, prudence, Cuz. A bit of fear, a bit of wisdom,
much of common sense, but prudence in the main.
You can see he has the forest on his right, at his
back. And we know how dense it is there. It's impenetrable, in fact, so he's safe from attack in that
direction and free to front all his strength towards
the left. He must have been marching like that since
they entered the Ingie."

"So they're expecting a fight," Fillan growled.
"Then I say we give them one."

Andrew looked at his cousin and smiled. "And
how should we attack them, Fillan? What would you
propose?"

"We'll—" He stopped abruptly and stood frowning before he muttered, "We can't, can we?"

"No, we can't. Not down there, and not while they're drawn up and waiting for us. We would be slaughtered. So you're right. We can't attack them. And what does that tell us?"

Fillan looked back at his commander and, for the first time since we had arrived on the crest, showed some good judgment, for he said, "It tells me nothing, but I'm not as clever as you, so why don't you tell us what you think?"

"Right," Andrew said, looking at each one of us in turn. "I will." He half turned away from us and stood looking down at the army of Comyns as he spoke on. "It tells me that my cousin down there, John Comyn, might have learned a lesson from his past defeats, even before his downfall at Dunbar."

"What past defeats?" Fillan asked him. "Dunbar was his *sole* defeat."

Murray nodded gently. "That is true, I suppose ... But would you not agree, Cousin, that a long series of inconclusive fights and a complete lack of victories, even small ones, amounts to overall defeat?"

Fillan made a face. "Mayhap ... I might ... I would, in fact. So what are you saying, Andrew?"

"I have already said it, Fillan. Buchan has learned from experience, and I now suspect that he really might not want to fight us—and I don't simply mean here on this road. I think he might not want to fight us at all."

"But he's here, is he not?" Fillan said. "And with an army big enough to kill us all. How can you say he doesn't want to fight?"

Andrew looked at him and wrinkled his nose, sniffing loudly. "Say I can smell it in the air, Fillan. Look," he said, "there are two ways to consider this situation. The first is to see it as it appears to be, plain and simple and seemingly straightforward. The other, though, is to look beyond what appears to be, and see what is really happening here. The truth is that Buchan is here with an army because he is under oath to Edward, but I think that is open to challenge. His oath was taken under duress, as a quid pro quo, paroled freedom in return for a commitment to fight in Gascony.

"To fight in *Gascony*, Cousin. Understand that clearly. In Gascony, but not here, not in Scotland. I would stake my life—and in fact that is precisely what I intend to do—that there was no mention at the oath-taking of fighting here in Scotland. The world is aware that an oath sworn under duress has no validity, but that's of little import here. The fact is that we have had no indication to this point that Buchan wants to fight us."

He paused, surveying the road below. "He is also down there with an army because his orders were changed, brought to him on the road by Edward's messenger. Those changes required him to march north from Aberdeen to Inverness and relieve Castle Urquhart. That was not necessarily an order to *fight*, for in Edward's mind, a sufficient show of strength might have been adequate to win the day. But the fact remains that the road my lord of Buchan is on right now is the sole route that would permit him to discharge that obligation. The fact that we are here on the same road, waiting for him, is incidental. He's a Comyn, born and bred up here in the north, and he has known from the outset that we would be waiting for him somewhere along the way.

"Then again, that he is moving with such obvious caution tells me something more, for he is using far more of it than I would ever have expected him to. It tells me he has been listening to scouts, informants, perhaps spies, and taking note of what they report. He'll have a good idea of our strength as being close to his own or perhaps even greater, and so he's taking no chances." He quirked one eyebrow and looked at each of us in turn. "Be sure of this, though: that has nothing to do with fear—either of us or of his situation. It simply means that he's a veteran campaigner. He knows this country as well as anyone, including me, so he's aware of the dangers of the Ingie for an army like his. And believe you me, he will take no chances in the Bog of Gight. The Earl of Buchan is more likely to sprout wings and fly away than he will be to let us lure him off the road and into the bog where we can destroy him."

Alistair blew out a breath of air. "D'ye mean we're no' goin' to fight him at all?"

Andrew answered without looking at his cousin, his eyes fixed on the spectacle below. "I would have scorned you had you asked me that last night, Alistair," he said. "But what I've seen this morning makes me wonder what we have to gain from forcing a fight here.

We can't fight them there on the road, where they can dictate the terms of fighting. We'd be slaughtered. We know that and Buchan knows it, too, and it's going to stay like that because His Grace cares nothing for the time he wastes in avoiding being attacked. The same goes for the bog—I had hoped to lure him into there, but it's clear now we have no chance of that. For now I'll watch him and wait. And I'll let him see us watching him at every step along the road from here on. He won't come against us from the roadway, for he can't. He has no room for his army to deploy. All he can do is keep them huddled close for safety, and what's safe for him and his, in this particular place, is safe for us, as well."

But Fillan had other thoughts. "What happens once we cross the Spey? The country opens out up there. He can spread his forces into ranks anywhere up there."

"Aye, and so he might. But he's not likely to, if what I suspect is true. I believe he'll rest content to march in defensive order all the way to Elgin. And if he does that, then in all probability he will turn west and continue all the way to Inverness."

"Without a fight? Once we're across the Spey, we could force him to fight anywhere we choose."

"We could, Fillan. Of course we could. But if we do, his men will kill a host of ours and we will kill a large number of his and all we'll end up with will be hundreds of dead Scots. And the more I think of that, the less I like it. Hundreds of dead Scots. All killed for England's cause. That makes no sense at all. Especially when they'll soon be fighting by our side anyway."

Fillan blinked in bewilderment. Perhaps we all did. "What d'you mean, fighting by our side?"

"Buchan and all the other magnates will join us, Fillan, sooner or later. That's why he doesn't want to fight us at this stage. He's waiting to see how matters develop. And when he's grown convinced we will prevail, he'll cast off his false oath to Edward and declare for us and for the realm."

"He will?" Even Alistair seemed stricken by Fillan's obtuseness, for he turned his eyes away to study a giant clump of gorse far below.

"Of course he will," Andrew said. "They all will— all the Comyns and their ilk, forbye all the MacDougalls and MacDowells, the MacDonalds and the Stewarts, the Campbells and the Grants—all of them will come together for Scotland. You wait and see."

"I will," Fillan said. "I'll wait and see. But why should they? They never did before."

I saw the consternation that sprang into Andrew's eyes at the simple truth of that statement.

But the amiably witless Fillan was already nodding vigorously. "Of course," he said, bubbling with enthusiasm, "we're going to win easily."

Andrew Murray's eyes, unreadable in his emotionless face, swivelled to meet mine, and he closed one eyelid in a conspiratorial wink that I construed as a warning to say nothing that might discourage Fillan's enthusiasm. Then he led us back down the rear of the ridge to where we had left our mounts.

CHAPTER SEVENTEEN

SILVER STARS AND GOLDEN STOOKS

Andrew was right: John Comyn, the Earl of Buchan, along with his namesake and marching companion John Comyn, the Lord of Badenoch, and their assorted allies, was being careful to provoke no confrontation. The group clearly had no wish to alienate their own people by appearing to align themselves too blatantly with the hated English and their rapacious King. At the same time, no open rapprochement between the supposed antagonists was possible, for fear of reprisals against those hapless captives remaining in Edward's prisons in England. And so an appearance of hostility had to be maintained.

From the moment the two armies first came into view of each other, it was evident that the contest to be played out would be one between a hedgehog and a tortoise. The Highlanders of Moray had developed a technique for defending themselves against English heavy cavalry, using dense infantry formations they called schiltroms. These tapering, double-ended wedges were safe from even the heaviest-massed cavalry, because the defenders presented bristling walls of extremely long, thick-shafted spears against their attackers, whose mounts balked at impaling themselves. The English footmen, on the other hand, took shelter from attack beneath a protective roof of upraised, interlocking shields that the ancient Romans had developed almost two millennia earlier, and they were equally impregnable.

I watched the developments from the outset, though as a non-combatant and a diplomatic observer I had nothing to contribute. I merely held myself available to be consulted should anyone show interest in my opinions, and, as I had expected, no one did. The English advanced doggedly, steadfastly keeping to the road and refusing to be coaxed off the beaten path, and the two equally matched armies lumbered awkwardly around each other at every stage of the journey north to Elgin, neither one daring to attempt an attack in the face of almost certain failure and defeat. The result? Not one drop of blood was spilled on either side.

Late on the evening of the second day of these manoeuvres, immediately after the evening meal, a visitor arrived in our camp demanding to speak with Sir Andrew Murray. Even muffled and cloaked to the eyes as he was, his clothing made it obvious to the guards who first challenged him that he was a nobleman, and so he was taken directly to the command area, where Andrew was relaxing with some of his commanders. I was there, too, minding my own business by the fire, when the stranger arrived. He stood stiffly between two escorting guards and uncovered his head. I was astonished to recognize, once again, the Earl of Carrick's goodbrother, Gartnait of Mar.

"Come and sit," Andrew said, rising to embrace him. "You'll have a cup of wine, I hope?"

Gartnait looked about him quickly and shook his head. "No," he said, his voice hard-edged. "We need to talk privily, Cousin. You and I, alone."

"Of course." Andrew turned to the assembly and gently waved us all away. "My friends, leave us now, if you will. I wish you all a good night's sleep, and may tomorrow's morning be as bright as this day's was."

I was probably no more disgruntled than any of the others around that fire at being so effectively excluded from what was to pass between our leader and the envoy from the enemy's ranks. I returned to my own tent, where I lay wondering what the two were saying to each other. I must have dozed off, though, because I was startled awake by angry voices, and I had swung my legs out of my cot and onto the cold ground before I understood that I was hearing but a single voice, and that it belonged to Andrew Murray, summoning his guards.

I was crouched over on the side of my cot, my arm outstretched in search of my sandals, when I heard Fillan's voice.

"Name of God, my lord Murray, what's amiss?" Something about his tone held me in place so that I stayed still and listened, not even bothering to draw back my hand.

"Nothing's amiss, Fillan—save for this sorry world and the English folk who pollute it." His voice was loud and angry. "Our guest here, the young lord of Mar, has outstayed his welcome and will now return to report to his masters." He stopped, ominously, then continued, slightly louder. "To report *failure* to his masters, both in Scotland and in England."

His voice changed slightly as he addressed Gartnait of Mar directly. "Tell them, though they should know full well by now, that Murray is not for sale. Not for English silver, nor for rich grants of English lands. And tell them, too, they have no place here in Scotland and no right to *be* here. And as for surrender, they will have no such thing from us until we are reduced too far and bled too weak to stand and fight them longer." His voice changed again. "Fillan, see his lordship to the edge of the camp and on his way to Buchan, and instruct your guards to bar him from any camp of ours from this time on. I'll have you out of here now, my lord of Mar, without the need to see your face or hear your voice again. Fare ye well, among your English brethren."

I listened as the guards formed up and led Gartnait away, but no one spoke after Andrew's parting words, and soon I heard the slow, muffled footsteps of people drifting away quietly. Eventually I lay down again and made myself comfortable, listening to the silence. It took no great mental effort to know that Andrew would be in no mood for pleasant conversation for the remainder of that night.

On my way back from saying Mass the next morning, soon after dawn when the camp followers were busily engaged in breaking down our overnight camp, I caught sight of Andrew headed for the latrine pits below the campsite, and though he was a long way from where I stood, I could tell, simply from his bearing and the way he strode, stiff-legged, that he was still angry. When we took the road again he rode ahead of everyone else for much of the morning, so that long before noon the word had spread throughout the entire host that the chief was in a foul frame of mind and should be avoided. By the end of the afternoon, by which time he had found fault, ill temperedly and loudly, with what appeared to be every single detail of the day's march, people were audibly cursing Gartnait of Mar, John Comyn of Buchan, their entire army, and their damnable English arrogance.

The morning after that, as I was preparing to mount my horse, he came striding in my direction, resplendent in a fresh white surcoat with his crest of three white stars against a field of deep blue on his chest. He was frowning deeply, unaware of me, I thought, but then he stopped and dipped his head to me in greeting, eyeing my mount as he did so. I returned his nod and he flipped a hand, beckoning me.

"Come, ride with me a while," he said, and so I stepped up into my saddle and followed him slowly to where a groom stood waiting for him, holding his horse's reins. He took the reins from the boy and pulled himself easily up into his saddle. I rode behind him in silence as he led me around and between piles of baggage rolls and groups of wagons until we had left the camp and its people behind us and were cantering almost side by side across a stretch of open heath. He looked back at me over his shoulder.

"You look as though you want to ask me something, Father James," he shouted over the thumping of our horses' hooves.

I kicked in my heels and pressed my mount forward until we were side by side. He turned and looked at me squarely, and I was surprised to see him smiling.

"Well?" he shouted. "Have you been stricken mute?"

"Not me," I shouted back. "But you've been quiet yourself ... for a while now."

He reined in his mount, slowing it to a walk and standing in his stirrups to peer all around before he settled back into his seat. "So," he said then, turning to look at me directly. "Ask your questions."

"There's but one. What did Gartnait of Mar say to make you so angry?"

He smiled. "He said I must make sure that everyone believed I was angry at him. I have to assume I was successful."

I hauled back on my reins, pulling my horse to a standstill, and he stopped beside me. I stared at him. "That—that was all a ruse? It was! Of course it was. A nonsense, all of it. You're not angry at all."

"Not a bit." He grinned. "But Gartnait was right and I knew it. We had to make the whole encampment think he had insulted me past bearing—past friendship and kinship."

"Why?"

His eyebrows shot up. "You need to ask me *why*? I thought it was obvious. We had no choice, Jamie. We needed everyone to think there is bad blood between us and the Comyns now. Having seen and heard for themselves what was said and done, none of our folk would ever imagine for a moment that there might be anything *friendly* going on between us. And that means we don't need to worry about any unguarded word or drunken slip of the tongue that might betray to the English in Inverness that we acted in collusion to defeat Edward's purposes."

"And are you?"

He quirked his mouth into a lopsided grimace. "We are. That's why Gartnait came here—to propose a compromise dreamed up by Buchan and Badenoch and to work with me to hammer out the details. A truce of kinds, though none of us can ever let it be known such a truce exists. That knowledge would vex Plantagenet, and once vexed sufficiently, there's no telling what that man might do to those of our countrymen left in his prisons. He's supposed to be a civilized and Christian King, but I've seen the man up close and he frightens me. By my lights there's little in him that's Christian, Father, and I would not want to cross him and remain within his reach. I doubt we've seen the worst of him yet."

He broke off, his gaze distant, then seemed to shake himself. "Be that as it may, the truth of the matter is that I was right. The Comyns have no wish to fight on Edward's side here in Scotia. So they sent Gartnait, and we arrived at an agreement. We will proceed as we are now, equally on guard and alert for treachery and attack, until we reach Elgin and turn west for Inverness."

"And what will happen then? Surely once the Comyns are safe in Inverness, they'll have to fight you. They'll be surrounded by their bloodthirsty English allies, all of them clamouring for your blood."

"Let them scream their heads off." He grinned. "I won't be there."

"You won't? You mean you'll let them do whatever they want then, free of threat?"

"God, no, man! What d'you take me for, an idiot? *They* won't know I'm not there. Sandy Pilche will bring his garrison the seven miles from Auch to Inverness under cover of night, and I'll move off with a strike force, including you, that same night. When the sun comes up, no one in Inverness Castle will be able to tell that the army in front of them is different from the one that was there the previous day. It might seem a bit smaller, but they'll have no wish to test it. Mark my words."

"And where will you be?"

"I'll be where you said I need to be! On my way to Aberdeen." He laughed aloud, almost crowing at my slowness in understanding what he had said. "They've left the place defenceless, Jamie, in their rush to get up here. They brought most of the garrison with them, never

thinking that we might jouk around them and go there
ourselves. Aberdeen lies undefended. Gartnait let that slip
when we were talking—I don't think he even knows he
said it. So we'll purge the castle like a dose of salts, and
once we have the town in our hands, we'll claim the cargo
waiting for us in the harbour. We'll load it into wagons,
distribute the weapons, and then head south, towards
Dundee, where we'll join up with Will and his group."

"And what about the rest of your army? D'you
mean you'll leave them here in Moray?"

"Not at all." He peered at me from beneath lowered
eyebrows. "You really have no high opinion of my
strategies, do you? The folk I leave in place will threaten
the English in Inverness for another week, then they will
disengage and head directly south through Badenoch
to join us at Dundee for the march to Stirling."

I allowed myself to smile. "In fact, Master Murray,
I have the greatest admiration for your strategies. It's
merely in my nature to ask questions. But what about
Auch Castle? Will you leave it sitting empty?"

"Never. We'll leave a holding force to man it,
though I think we may leave Balconie empty, as a gift
for the Countess of Ross. An unmerited gift that might
remind her where her loyalties should lie."

"I see," I said, and I did. "You have thought everything through."

"From start to finish, with Sandy." A smile twitched
at one corner of his mouth. "Have I earned your
approval?"

"You have," I said. "And my blessing."

A fortnight later, on the Friday of the first week in August, we arrived in Aberdeen to a welcome none of us would have imagined. The Earl of Buchan had indeed stripped the garrison of nine-tenths of its manpower when he set out northwards, and he had apparently done so in complete ignorance of the extent to which the native Aberdonians detested all things English. Whether or not that decision reflected irresponsibility on the earl's part was debatable, and a capable lawyer could have made a strong case on Buchan's behalf, claiming that the earl's ignorance of local conditions was natural and wholly logical, since he was newly returned from having spent an entire year in prison in England—a year, moreover, the advocate might point out, throughout which the earl had been informed, time and time again by his captors, of how completely vanquished and subdued Scotland had been since the battle in which he had been captured at Falkirk. What reason might such a man have, then, the advocate would ask, to suspect that there was any peril in leaving a formidable, English-held fortress such as the one at Aberdeen in the care of an adequately armed and provisioned holding crew in the temporary absence of its garrison?

That same advocate, of course, would have been praying fervently throughout the proceedings that no one on the opposite side of the court would bring into evidence the fact that the Earl of Buchan, having grown to manhood in his family territories north of, and abutting, the Aberdeen region, must have a lifelong familiarity with the peculiar and illogical but nonetheless spectacular hatred that the folk of that region felt for the English, whom they regarded as gibbering foreign devils and unconscionable thieves.

Be that as it may, and whatever the folk of Aberdeen might have thought of John Comyn of Buchan, there could be no doubt of how they perceived the young man who rode at the head of the two-hundred-strong attack force we brought to their town. As soon as the word began to spread that Andrew Murray of Petty had come south, the people of Aberdeen rose up. The report I heard, once everything was over, was that the castle gates had been standing open at mid-morning, the marketplace outside them thronged with people, when the word of Murray's approaching army first was heard. A group of citizens and merchants had exploded into action and attacked the gate guards, throwing their lifeless bodies off the causeway leading to the gates. Others surged through the castle gates, taking the remaining occupants unaware and killing all of them. Thus Aberdeen had been ripped out of England's hands before Andrew Murray even entered the town.

There was quite a grand celebration that night, to mark what folk were calling *the liberation*, but the festivities were largely confined to eating and drinking, with the local provost and members of the various town guilds making speeches in honour of their liberator,

Andrew Murray. There was not even any music or
dancing, and though it seemed strange to me, everyone
was abed early that night. We were in Aberdeen, when
all was said and done, and grateful though they might
have been for our "deliverance," the folk of the town
were as insular and circumspect as ever in their distrust
of outsiders, particularly when those outsiders were
warriors, lacking women of their own.

The next morning, fresh from celebrating my daily
Mass in private—Aberdeen was the seat of a bishop and
therefore had no lack of priests or churches—I stepped
outside to find a brilliant, beautiful summer's morning,
the marketplace already bubbling with activity. I was
alone, for Alistair de Moray had been relieved of his
duty to watch over me weeks earlier, once Andrew had
returned to camp after a brief absence, and I had grown
re-accustomed to being shadowless. I broke my fast
with a mouth-wateringly fine meat pie from one of the
market vendors and made my way down to the harbour,
where I amused myself counting the boats at anchor and
trying to identify the vessel from Lübeck.

I identified six possible vessels, then disqualified
four simply because they looked too small, and I could
read their names and understand the language spoken
by the men working aboard and around them. Of the
two remaining, I had no idea which was the one we
sought, so I walked back up the hill to view them again
from a greater distance. One of them was moored to a
side wharf, its prow pointed directly towards me so
that all I could see was the front of the ship. I stood

gazing down at it, vaguely troubled by something.

"Which one is ours?"

Startled, I turned to see Andrew, at first surprised that he should have come to look for me, but realizing at once that he had not. A few paces behind him stood his entourage, a gaggle of Highland leaders, peacocks all, resplendent in their Gaelic savagery. I nodded to Alistair and Fillan.

"I don't know," I answered Andrew. "Maybe it isn't even here yet. How far is Lübeck from here?"

He turned towards his group. "Does any man know how far it is to Lübeck?"

They looked at one another, shrugging, and a man standing nearby, wearing the clothing of a seaman, said, "Eight, nine days' sail. Straight out from here, north of east for six hundred miles to Gothenburg, then due south along the coast of Denmark for four hundred more. Lübeck lies on Germany's north coast."

"Which is it, then?" Andrew asked. "Eight days or nine?"

"To a seaman?" said the fellow's friend. "Who can tell? Might be half a score, mayhap longer. It's a' up wi' the winds."

Andrew blinked at him. "What?"

"The winds, loon," he growled, explaining as he might to a child. "Gin they blaw fair, ye'll fa' shin. Gin they're no', ye'll no'."

Andrew turned to me. "Did you understand that?"

I was about to shake my head when a third voice spoke up, one of Andrew's group. "He said that everything depends on the winds. If the winds are fair, you'll make good time and have a swift voyage and a fair landfall. If they are not, you will not."

Andrew surveyed the boats in the harbour. "I don't think our ship has come in yet, Father. When did you say it was due?"

"It must be here," I said. "Bishop Wishart said it would be here by July's end, the first week of August at the very latest. So no one is late—not us, not them. The first week of August yet has two days to run."

"Well, we'll soon know." He raised a hand and signalled to Alistair, then instructed him to take his fellow officers down to the wharf and find out which of the vessels there had sailed from Lübeck.

"No point in my going down there until we know something," Andrew murmured to me as the others left. "Why run the risk of looking ignorant, impotent, or indecisive when there's no need?"

"I agree, now that you mention it," I said.

Soon Fillan de Moray was gesturing widely to us, waving and pointing towards the vessel moored at his back, the one I had been looking at prow-on. It was the largest ship at the wharf, which is not to say it was very large at all, and I felt apprehensive, eyeing it. It looked old, with a general air about it of having been battered and beaten beyond endurance.

"That's it?" Andrew sniffed. "It doesn't look like much, does it?"

"Not at first glance, no." I hesitated. "Something is not right with it, though I don't know what it is …"

He tilted his head, frowning. "What are you talking about?"

"I don't know. But it looks wrong, somehow. We're too far away to really see it, though, and the angle is bad."

"So let's go down and look at it from the viewpoint of the owners of its cargo."

As we moved down the hill towards the wharves, I recognized what had struck me as being "wrong" about the boat, and when we reached its moorings alongside the wharf, we could see a splintered stub projecting upwards from the deck well that had held the rear mast.

One of the crewmen standing close to us on the wharf was a Scot, I decided from his dress, and while Andrew went to talk with the captain, I asked him what had happened. He told us that the ship had made harbour mere hours before, struggling in on the morning tide after encountering an unseasonable series of storms and squalls far out on the North Sea. They had lost part of the mast, with all its sails and rigging, in the most savage squall, and had come close to capsizing, he said, dragged down by the wreckage with the seas breaking over the stern and threatening to swamp the ship.

"Stay well clear, lads, and let the crew have their way!" Andrew had finished his colloquy with the captain and rejoined us, and the crewmen were already clambering aboard the ship, some of them preparing to open the hold while others worked to prepare the gin hoist that would lift the cargo from the hold. Someone on deck shouted, but not urgently, and then came the sound of the hatch covers being removed. The captain beckoned to Andrew to come on deck.

Andrew glanced at me. "You brought the word and all the documentation, so you had better be the one to check the cargo's appearance."

I followed him up the short, sloping ramp that led to the deck until we both stood looking down into the cargo hold. It was filled almost to the level of the deck itself with carefully stacked crates of varying sizes.

"I see nothing out of place," I said quietly to Andrew. "But since I have no notion of what we should be expecting, I can say no more than that."

"What we are expecting," he answered in a matching tone, "is weaponry. And it looks to me as though that could be what we have here. Spears in the long cases, I'd say. Swords and axes in the shorter ones, and who knows what in the others." He stepped back and raised two fingers to the captain, indicating that he was satisfied and the unloading could proceed.

"Alistair's folk should have horses and wagons here by now to carry the crates up to the castle. We'll unpack them there, distribute weapons as needed, and then we'll send an escort with the things we don't need right away—the ingot and sheet iron—back up to Auch. Our smiths there are waiting for them, hungry for work. The remaining weapons and armour we'll take with us to Dundee, for Sandy's people."

He crossed in front of me, between me and the ship's hold, then bent his knees slightly and peered down. "There," he said, pointing towards a corner below the deck. "Can you see back there? Shields, stacked up like coins, and lots of them. We need as many of those as we can get, God knows." He straightened up again and made his way back to the wharf, with me following close on his heels.

"Axes," I said as we stepped back onto the dock. "You said there would be axes in some of the crates. Did you ask for those?"

He grunted. "Ask for them? I didn't even know these things were coming until you turned up and told me. How could I have asked for axes? I told the bishop we needed weapons, but I had no hope that he might actually provide them. If anything, I would have asked for swords, though. Not axes."

"Well," I said, "we'll find out what we have when we open the crates."

He turned away from the busyness on the wharf. "Let's get back up to the castle. There's much to do and I want to be on the road south the day after tomorrow."

"Do you think that's feasible?"

He looked askance at me. "Why would it not be?"

CHAPTER EIGHTEEN

TROLLS AND TRIALS

I t had been a long day's march and I was more than glad to reach the end of it, for I had spent much of it slouched in my saddle, paying little attention to anything while I mulled over my report to my employer and the analysis it would contain of our march down along the coast road from Aberdeen towards Fife. When we reached that day's campsite, as soon as I had taken care of my horse's needs— always the first priority for a rider at the end of a journey, the necessary half-hour ensuring an uneventful day to follow—I delivered him to the horse lines and went looking for a comfortable seat beyond the smells of horses and stables. I was fortunate, finding a pleasant spot far enough removed from the odour of dung and the hubbub of setting up the camp. I sat on a mossy, comfortable mound at the base of a sturdy young elm that would support my back, and dug into my satchel, retrieving my ink flask and pens, some of my precious paper, and the plain thin wooden sheet, two handspans long and nearly the same wide, that I carried as a makeshift writing surface, supporting it on my knees at times like these when I had no table.

I knew by then exactly what I wanted my report to say, but I began by making a *nota bene* list of memoranda, some precise and others less so, on thoughts and events that had come to mind earlier in the course of my journey. I soon lost all awareness of my surroundings, and as I scribbled there, locked up in my own little world of recollections, the new encampment took shape around me and the noise and bustle gradually died away as the army began to settle down after the exhausting ten-hour daily grind.

I was brought back to the present by Alistair de Moray. Startled by his voice, unexpectedly loud and close by, I looked up to see him lounging against the bole of a large beech tree a few paces from where I was sitting.

"I asked you if you know what a troll is."

"Of course I do," I answered, mystified. I set my writing materials carefully aside, using the ink pot's base to secure the papers against an errant gust of wind. "It's a mythical monster from Norse legends. A giant, misshapen, manlike creature of immense strength, but lacking a human soul."

He nodded. "And are they bald?"

"I believe they are. Hairless. Why?"

He grinned. "Because there's one of them outside the camp, surrounded by half a score of guards, and it's asking for you."

It took several moments for my mind to make the connections, but as soon as it did I sprang to my feet with a most unclerical whoop of delight. "Ewan Scrymgeour! Where is he?"

"You know him, then," Alistair said, no trace of surprise in his voice.

"I do indeed. One of my oldest and dearest friends, with a face that frightens children and grown men and a nature that delights God Himself." I was already looking down at my feet, eyeing my writing materials. "I have to clean up here first, before I go anywhere," I said. "If I leave these things here, they'll be gone when I come back."

"I'll help you." Alistair sank onto one knee in front of me, reaching for my ink pot and the stained wooden box that held my pens. "Here, hand me your bag. I'll hold it open, and you put these inside, since you know how. Careful ..." He held my sheaf of written papers in one hand as he plied the other, and we quickly had everything loaded into the large shoulder bag that accompanied me everywhere. I stood up and looped the carrying strap over my shoulder to let it hang across my chest, and Alistair led me quickly to where Ewan waited for me on the camp outskirts.

I saw the big archer before he caught sight of me, and I felt a surge of affection. Clad in his perpetual Welsh archer's green, he towered head and shoulders over the men around him, none of whom would have been small in any company. The sheer width and bulk of Ewan's shoulders astounded me again, though, no

less than it had on the day I first saw him, when I was
a ten-year-old boy. But I saw no sign of his bow, and
that made me frown, for even in the safest of company,
among friends when he had no need of a weapon,
Ewan carried his precious unstrung bow shaft with
him at all times.

"Ewan!" I shouted. "Over here!"

He spun towards the sound of my voice and
threw out his arms, and his ruined face sank into
what only those who knew him well would recognize
as a great grin of happiness. What I had said to Alistair
earlier about Ewan's face frightening children was no
exaggeration, and if children were around, the big
archer often wore a mask to hide his disfigurements.
Any sane person knows that a battlefield is no fit place
for any twelve-year-old boy, but there are always boys
in the middle of battles, hauling supplies and running
with messages, bringing water to the fighting men,
and, if they are trainees and apprentices, assisting their
masters in the field. Ewan had been twelve at the time
of the battle of Lewes, newly apprenticed to an archer
with the army of King Henry III. He had been struck
by a heavy war club, and the blow had crushed his
right cheek and jawbone and completely destroyed his
right eye. The appalling extent of the damages had
grown more noticeable as he aged.

Ewan reached me and snatched me up in a huge
embrace, swinging me high into the air with utter
disregard for my priestly dignity, just as I had known
he would. Three times he swept me around in a circle,

then carefully set me back on my feet and pushed me away to arm's length, scanning me with a single, keen eye that I knew to be eagle sharp. He was the only one-eyed archer I had ever known, and I had never known more than two normally sighted men who could match him, shaft for shaft. I smiled and endured his scrutiny, wondering how anyone could ever think him frightening, and soon he grunted and stepped back slightly, his ruined face settling into itself again.

"Ye look well," he said in that gentle, careful voice that I had quickly grown to love as a boy.

"You, too, Ewan," I said, blessing him with the sign of the cross and aware of the eyes of the surrounding guards. "But you look naked. Where's your bow?"

His eye gleamed and his face shifted again into what was, for him, a grin. "Times change," he said softly. "Your cousin carries a sword nowadays instead of a bow. So I'm considering doing the same."

"Go and tell that to someone who will be more likely to believe you. I doubt if you would even know which end of a sword to snatch up. Now, where's your bow?"

He sighed, a gentle sound, before eyeing the guards who crowded around us. "It's back there," he said, jerking his head in the direction from which he must have come. "Safe hidden. When folk around here see a big bow like mine, they tend to think 'Englishman' and behave badly."

He looked at big Fergus, the man in charge of the guard that afternoon, picking him out as leader as easily as though Fergus had been wearing a sign. "I am a Scot," he explained. "Or my father was, so I'm half. My mother was Welsh and I was trained in Wales as a longbow archer. I fought for Edward of England once, years ago, but when he turned to steal Wales from beneath our feet, I left and came here."

I picked up where he left off, for I knew he was too modest to finish, and I spoke for all to hear. "And since he came to Scotland, more than a decade ago, he has been the closest thing to a brother and a father that my cousin William Wallace has ever had. This is the man who taught Will Wallace how to string and use a longbow."

Will's name was nowhere near as well known in these northeastern parts as Andrew Murray's was, but it was known nonetheless, and I knew the mere mention of it in connection with the towering newcomer would be enough to accord Ewan a high measure of respect among the battle-hardened men who heard me.

"Now, let us go and collect your bow before we do anything else."

We barely spoke as I followed him back along the path, because I was scanning the land ahead of us all the way, watching for either a dense clump of bushes or a patch of boulders and rank grass. We were looking for a longbow case, a solid, four-fingers-wide tube of highly polished, waterproofed bull hide, six feet long and arrow straight, and there are few places where you can hide such an unnatural thing effectively in open country. In the end, about eight hundred paces from the camp, we came to a spot that featured a profusion of hazel bushes—they were too small to deserve to be called trees—growing among a jumble of rocks that had fallen at the foot of a low, much-eroded cliff of soft shale and now mostly obscured by tall grasses. I was faced with a choice: where would Ewan have concealed his precious bow? In the ranks of straight hazel saplings, or in the mix of boulders and long grass? I opted for the stony ground and long grass half a heartbeat before Ewan stooped to reach into the grass, moving a few heavy boulders out of the way and retrieving the long case, wrapped in a loose sleeve of old, dirty, grass-stained homespun cloth. Beside it, no more than two paces away, lay another shrouded shape, containing the case that held the longbow's yard-long arrows.

"I was wondering if you would still have those old clouts," I said. "Are they the same ones? If they are, they must be close to falling apart by now."

"Same ones," he murmured, stretching them out individually before folding them carefully and stuffing them into his shoulder bag. "Only ones I've ever had."

"That is amazing," I said, shaking my head in wonder as I watched the care he bestowed on such old and insignificant rags. "How old must they be, then?"

"Old enough to look the part and do the job I ask of them, though I can't say how long I've had them. I'm surprised you'd remember them."

"Ah, but I've never forgotten them, Ewan. I especially remember how when you wrap one around your case like that, and place it on the ground among stones and long, rank grass, both clout and case disappear completely. The loose cloth blurs the case's edges, and the old, green-stained colours blend perfectly into the long grass. In fact I had a wager with myself that we'd find the case here."

He grinned that sunken grin of his. "Then you're still as clever as ever you were, boyo." He picked up his arrow bag and slung it across his back, the feathered ends projecting high above his right shoulder, and then stooped to pick up the longbow case. "Will we be able to talk at your camp without being overheard, or should we go for a walk first?"

"Let's walk," I said. "It's a grand summer evening and we have an hour and more before dinner is anywhere near being ready. So tell me, what brings you here? Have you tidings from Glasgow? Has anything changed in the southwest?"

He seemed about to say something but then frowned and shook his head. "No," he said, "nothing's changed and nothing's different, as far as I know." He looked about him. "I passed an open meadow on my way here, about half a mile back," he said. "There was a thin dead tree in a patch of open sward and I took note of it as a place to practise. I've barely drawn my bow in more than a week, with all the running around I've been doing. So I can practise there and we can talk without being overheard."

"Lead on, then," I said, and he turned away without another word.

Less than half an hour later I lay back on a grassy knoll and watched him string his bow, admiring the practised ease with which he did it, for it was a task that would have defeated most men. But of course, as with all such things, there was a knack to it, and Ewan had learned that knack as a young apprentice, a decade before I was even born. When he was satisfied with the feel of the weapon, he set the bow down and removed the arrow bag from his back, then selected six yard-long bodkins—the arrow of choice for target practice because of their smooth, tapering, cone-shaped heads. Originally designed to pierce armour and mail, they had been so successful that armourers had laboured for decades afterwards to develop steel plate thick enough and smooth enough not only to deflect a bodkin but actually to repel a direct hit. The bodkin might no longer be an effective tool against heavily armoured knights, but it was as fearsome as ever to less strongly protected men, punching cleanly through all but the most expensively wrought mail and plate. The newer broadhead arrow, on the other hand, was useless for target practice because it was triple-bladed and wickedly barbed and so could not be retrieved from a target without risking significant damage to both target and warhead.

Finally, satisfied with the straightness and fletching of the bodkins he had selected, Ewan stuck them points down and side by side in a row in front of him and turned his single eye on me. "Ready?"

We had paced the distance from the dead tree together and it was one hundred and eighty long paces from where we now stood, so that the hand's breadth of space between the two green bands spanning the narrow tree trunk—Ewan's green clouts again—was now barely visible to me, and I had two good eyes. That narrow strip was Ewan's target, and any damage to the bordering cloths would be unacceptable.

I nodded. "Go ahead. Let's see if you can still impress me."

He did. His first arrow struck the side of the tree and glanced off. His next three landed side by side within the tiny band between the cloth strips. He didn't even bother to use the last two missiles. He simply put them back into his quiver and quickly unstrung his bow, handing the string to me to wind for him. I watched him go through the familiar motions, admiring, as always, his economy of movement and the concentration with which he worked. No true archer ever left his bow strung for a moment longer than was necessary, for the very resilience that made the yew bow such a formidable weapon could be leached out of it by leaving it arched into its bow shape for too long. The wood "learned" the arch of its shape and consequently lost the tension necessary to retain its strength.

He polished the shaft lovingly with the soft cloth he used solely for that purpose and slid it carefully back into its carrying case, closing the lid securely before slinging the case to hang by his side. I handed him back his bowstring, wound precisely the way he had taught me years earlier, then walked with him to the target to collect his arrows and precious cloths.

"Do you feel like talking to me yet?"

He looked at me sidelong, saying nothing, and I continued, "You will admit, I hope, that I've been very patient. Especially because I am a priest, after all, and therefore naturally curious. But it's nearing time for us to head back to camp and you still haven't said a word about why you're here. Or about what's bothering you, and something plainly is."

We reached the target and he flicked a finger down and to his right. "See if you can find that first one," he said, pulling one of the three bodkins from the narrow strip of bark that showed between the strips of cloth.

I found the arrow by sheerest accident, sticking up almost vertically from a tussock. I brought the missile back and handed it to him, and he held it up to the light and peered along its shaft.

"Warped," he murmured. "Just enough to throw it off." He snapped the shaft across his knee, surprising me. Then he glanced at me, almost furtively. "It's Will."

"What is?"

He dropped one of the pieces into his scrip and threw the other aside. "Can't waste a good warhead," he said.

"*What's* Will, Ewan?"

"Will's what's bothering me."

Even though I had used the word first, it sounded alien coming from him. I had seldom known anything to bother this big man unduly.

"*Bothering* you … Very well, then, what is it about him that is … *bothering* you?"

"His behaviour." The natural softness of Ewan's voice and the whistling sound of his slight lisp made the words close to inaudible. "He's changed, since we left Selkirk to come up here."

"Well, of course he has changed," I said, perhaps just a little relieved. "Who wouldn't have changed after all that has happened to him?" I hesitated, struck by his expression. "But that's not what you mean, is it? You're not talking about Mirren and the children. You're talking about something else …"

He shrugged his shoulders hugely but said nothing.

"Ewan, you have to tell me *something* more than the little you've said. I have no idea what you're talking about and I can't even begin to guess at it without some clues. Was it Lothian? Did something happen there? Or did something happen after you attacked Lothian?"

"We didn't go to Lothian."

That left me floundering for a moment. "But— but the instructions I took to Will from Bishop Wishart were to raise the dragon flag and harry Lothian with fire and sword. He was to spend a month doing that and then come northwards across the Forth from Stirling."

"Aye, well, the Bishop changed his mind—him and the Stewart. Don't ask me why, for I don't know. All I know is it had something to do with all the talk at Irvine, between them and the English under Percy and Clifford. What was the word they used for it? It wasn't surrender … Something like cap …"

"Capitulation?"

"Aye, that's it. What does it mean?"

"It means surrender. Just another way of saying it."

"Ah! Well anyway, something came up there, in their discussions of that … capit-what-you-said, and Wishart sent word to us, just before we left the forest, to back away from the assault on Lothian, for the time being at least. We were still to head up here at the appointed time, but we were to keep the peace until then."

"And how did Will react to that?"

He looked at me sidewise, his good eyebrow raised in mild surprise. "How did he *react*?" He shrugged dismissively. "He didn't react. He was fine. Glad he didn't have to risk hurting his own folk, I think. Scots folk. He had never felt right about that, even when he raided Lanark, for he felt that even if the townsfolk were helping the English, it was because they had no choice, and he thought Wishart and Stewart were wrong in what they wanted to do in Lothian. But then the word came to hold back and I think we all felt better. Will spent the time training his new men, but harder than before, now that they knew they were close to coming face to face with England."

"I see," I said, though I truly did not. "And what has that to do with what you're fretting about now?"

He looked at me sharply, as though I had said something outrageous. "Nothing," he said. "Nothing at all. As I said, we were glad."

"Then what *are* you fretting about now, Ewan? Am

I supposed to read your mind? You're concerned about Will, you say, but you have shown me no slightest reason for saying that." I stopped, abruptly aware of my mounting frustration, and drew a deep breath, willing myself to remain calm. "Please, then, Ewan, if you will, and if you can, tell me what is going on."

"Ach!" He turned on his heel and began to walk away, back in the direction of our camp, and I walked quickly to keep pace with him. He did not go far, though. He stopped suddenly in the middle of the narrow track we were following and turned to face me almost defiantly. "It's not me, Jamie. Will's the one who is fretting," he said sibilantly, his Welsh intonation suddenly very pronounced. "I'm just upset because I am unused to seeing him this way—unsure of himself and doubting his own judgment."

"His judgment on what?"

"On this excursion to Dundee, for one thing, and on Stirling and Andrew Murray for another."

"In God's name, Ewan, he's going to Dundee to collect a much-needed shipload of weapons and armour. What could be dubious about that? By his own admission he stands in dire need of weaponry. And what nonsense is this about questioning going to Stirling? Wishart's instructions were clear: collect the weapons, meet up with Murray, and head together towards Stirling."

"Aye, but it's the meeting with Murray, after so long a time, wi' so much having happened in between. Will is wondering if he should be lending him his support."

I was aware of the silence that stretched out before I heard myself asking, "Will is having doubts about *Andrew Murray*? They've been friends since we were boys together."

"Aye—and that's what has him so upset. Is the man Andrew Murray the same person as the *boy* was? Or has he changed, growing up?"

I was hearing far more here than I wanted to, and it was not merely unnerving me, it was actually frightening me. I could completely understand why Will might have grave concerns about being so far north of Forth. To the best of my knowledge he had never been in Fife before, nor in Dundee, and so he might well have reservations about being so far removed from his own territories and among people whose language was barely intelligible to him and his folk. It was another thing altogether, however, to hear that Will might be considering abandoning the task set him by Bishop Wishart and returning home to Selkirk Forest. Such a decision threatened not only our own personal endeavours—mine, Andrew's, *and* Will's—but the welfare of Scotland's realm.

My heart was thumping against my breastbone and I knew I was gaping. "This will not do," I said. "I can't talk about this here, standing in the woods like a witless goatherd who has lost his kine. Both of us need to think, and with great care, about what we are discussing. Because whether we like it or not, we could soon be talking about treason."

He nodded, and we walked on together in silence until we came to a place where our path crossed another, wider and deeply rutted by wagon traffic, and we stopped there, hesitating as we heard noises from the encampment close ahead of us. We had barely paused when an errant puff of wind wafted the aroma of fresh spit-roasted meat to where we stood, and Ewan sniffed deeply at it and turned to look at me, cocking his head as he waited for me to make a decision. The area around the crossing itself, while not extensive, was bare of vegetation, and someone had rolled an ancient log close to an equally ancient fire pit. I nodded towards the spot.

"This will do," I said. "Close enough to camp that we won't miss dinner, and we won't be interrupted because everyone else will be eating."

We seated ourselves quickly, and then sat looking at each other. I knew it would be up to me to start the conversation, and so I plunged straight ahead.

"Right," I said. "Andrew Murray ... Why is Will suddenly doubting him after all these years? You must have some idea."

Ewan shrugged. "He's doubting him not so much for who he is as for *what* he is ... or might be," he added quietly.

I waited, but there was no more forthcoming and I snapped back at him in frustration. "And what is *that* supposed to mean? You make no sense, Ewan."

"Of course I do, Jamie." There was no trace of argument in his voice. "You know Will even better than I do. When has he ever been comfortable around magnates?"

"He never has." I threw the answer out without needing to think. "Doesn't care for them as a breed and doesn't trust them."

"There you go. And Andrew Murray is a magnate."

I opened my mouth to scoff, but the words died on my lips.

"Aye," my friend murmured, nodding sagely. "That's right. He is. One of the most powerful in the land. Or he will be, once his father and his uncle die. He is sole heir to both of them, and they are old men now, locked tightly away in London's Tower. Since he came home to his northern lands, he has been acting in his father's stead, as Lord of Petty, and the whole of Scotland knows that de Moray of Petty is one of the proudest, strongest, and most powerful houses in all this realm—bigger, perhaps, than Bruce, and easily as strong as Comyn. And that, vast as it is, is merely Petty," he continued, unaware of any irony. "But Petty is dwarfed and beggared beside the estates of Andrew's uncle, William de Moray of Bothwell, William the Rich." He raised a single finger in warning. "Once Andrew comes into his own, ruling the estates of Bothwell *and* Petty, there won't be a magnate in Scotland who can come close to him in wealth or power. And *that* is what is worrying your cousin. Will doesn't know whether Andrew Murray remains true to what he believed in when he was younger. He wonders whether he should consider the possibility that even great men tend to grow corrupt with power and riches."

I knew, even as I listened to Ewan saying the words, that the archer had captured the heart of Will's problem. No one—no bishop, lord, or savant—could have expressed it better. And hearing it expressed so simply and cleanly, I knew at once how to deal with it.

"I need to see him. Now," I said. "Where is he?"

"Now? Well … I suppose he's where I left him this morning, close by Dundee, about twenty miles south of here."

"Damn! That's too far. A four-hour ride, at least, and I need to be here. You'll have to go for me."

"Already? But I came to speak with you, about Will and what he is thinking."

"And we've done that, Ewan. And I think the problem is resolved."

He looked at me, his single eye exaggerating his astonishment. "It is? It's been resolved? Why didn't I know that?"

"Ewan, d'you think Will trusts me?"

"Of course he trusts you, more than anyone else in the world."

"Good. Then I beg you to remind him of that trust, even though you think he needs no such reminding. Point out how deep and old it is, how reliable it is, and really how reliable *I* am in the whole scape of his life. You think I'm talking nonsense," I said. "But I'm not. If there's any nonsense involved here, then Will himself is the one to blame for it, with all this twaddle about not knowing whether or not he can trust Andrew Murray.

Well, Will needs to know—to *accept*—that he can
trust Andrew Murray twice as much and twice as
far as he would ever dream of trusting me. I have
been here for weeks, Ewan, spending time with
Andrew Murray, and I know, beyond question, that
Will is fretting over nothing. Andrew de Moray—
Andrew Murray the *man*—is rock solid, Ewan. He is
sound in everything he does, and I judge him honest,
upright, noble, and without pretension. And he
considers William Wallace his close friend, simply
because of the bond they forged as boys together.
Not only would I stake my life on that being true, I
would stake—no, I *will* stake, I *am* staking—the
welfare of this kingdom, of the realm of Scotland
itself, on the truth of it."

I paused, looking Ewan straight in the eye. "I trust
him, Ewan. I trust him absolutely. And my cousin will
trust him, too, as soon as he meets him face to face
again. And so that's what we must achieve within the
day ahead of us, you and I. We must bring them
together tomorrow, alone."

"You should be there, too. You have a place there
with them. Always have had."

He was right and I nodded. "And I can be useful to
both of them. Good."

"So how will we arrange this?"

"I've no idea, but it will be done. First, we'll go and
eat because we're both starved. Then we'll talk about
details, and then we'll sleep. You'll be up and away by
dawn and I'll follow you by noon with Andrew … Did

you make any friends in Dundee? People you would trust?"

"A few," he said as he rose to his feet. "One in particular, a half-Welsh archer by the name of Olwen. I'd trust him."

I stood up, too, adjusting my satchel to hang comfortably. "Does he know the Dundee countryside?"

"He's lived here for twenty years."

"Good, then get him to suggest a meeting place close to the road we'll come down, then make sure Will is there to meet us when we arrive. I'll talk with Andrew tonight. And now we should find some food, before the smell of fresh bread renders me too weak to walk."

CHAPTER NINETEEN

THE ROAD TO DUNDEE

The man sent to meet us on the road the next day was an old friend from my days as a young, newly out of school lad in Paisley. He was known as Long John of the Knives and had been one of Will's most trusted followers since those early days. He was extremely tall—one of the few men I had ever seen who towered several inches over Will himself, which explained the "Long" part of his name. The heavy belt around his waist explained the last part: it supported a collection of sheathed knives, and anyone who knew the man knew, too, that he could sink any one of them into any target and from any distance with astonishing speed.

He was waiting for us as we breasted a sharp rise in the road, sitting at ease on a roadside stone at the edge of a deep gully on the right of the path, and enjoying the bright warmth of the summer sun. He might have been dozing as he waited, but his hearing was keen and as soon as he heard us he stood up, smiling at me in welcome and nodding in greeting to

Andrew, recognizable in his half-plate armour worn over a close-fitting suit of mail, the whole covered by a loose, brilliant blue surcoat emblazoned with the three white stars of de Moray.

I was very glad to see Long John, for it had been years since we had last met. I moved to dismount, but as was ever the case, John had little time to waste on niceties.

"No," he said in Scots and held up a hand. "I'll no' keep ye. I ken ye need to meet wi' Will, an' he's waitin' for ye." He pointed down the hill at his back. "There's a wee glen doon there, ahint the scree," he said. "An' a linn, forbye. The linn's no' much to look at, but it's deep enough to haud the two o' ye an' ye'll likely be glad o' it on a hot day like this. There's a fire doon there, and a nice brace o' hares simmerin' in a pot wi' ingins an' garlic, an' some fresh-baked bannock to go wi' it. Ye'll see Will there, so I'll be on my way and leave ye to say what ye hae to." He tilted his head towards Alistair. "Ye're welcome to come wi' me, unless ye're privy to what's to be discussed."

Alistair cocked an eyebrow at Andrew, who waved him gently on his way.

"Right," Alistair said, hoisting his pack again. "I'll join you again later."

"Grand," said Long John. "I'll see ye again later, Jamie. Maister Murray." He nodded gravely to Andrew and then walked away, accompanied by Alistair.

"Do you know," Andrew mused, "if I didn't know for a fact that no friend of Will Wallace's could ever be such a thing, I might be tempted to think yon fellow could be a dangerous man."

"Who, Long John of the Knives?" I said, smiling. "What could possibly make you think that?"

"I have no idea," he murmured. "Save, perhaps, for something in the way he walks. He's like a big cat."

"He is. He and Alistair are two of a kind. There's something feline about both of them."

"Aye, but Alistair is just a plain, grey Highland wildcat. Long John there is like a great cat from Africa that I once saw at King Edward's court. Some kind of leopard, it was, spotted as they are, but this one was lean and tall, long-legged like a hunting hound, and lightning fast. Anyway, let's go and find Will."

"No need. I'm here."

The voice, coming from directly at our backs, made us both jump, and we stood up simultaneously in our stirrups, twisting around awkwardly to look back. Will smiled a little, his mouth quirking upwards as he noted our surprise, but it was not the grin I would have expected from him after such a trick. My first reaction was a kind of regret that Long John should have lied to me, but then I realized that he had done no such thing. He had said only that we would see Will by the fire down at the linn. He had not said Will was already there.

That momentary twinge of misgiving I had felt on seeing Will's restrained smile persisted through the greetings that followed as we exchanged the normal, banal pleasantries and small talk. I had never known

Will to be as ill at ease as he was in those first moments. Andrew noticed it, too, much to my chagrin, for when Will turned away to lead us down into the ravine, the Highlander glanced at me with a raised eyebrow.

And it was Andrew, blunt and forthright as always, who settled the matter as well, tackling it head-on in his own inimitable way as soon as we arrived at the concealed meeting place. He bent over the fire and lifted the lid off the pot that sat nestled on a bed of cooking stones, sniffed deeply and appreciatively at the cloud of fragrant steam that swirled up and around him, then stood up to gaze towards the six-foot waterfall, and the deep pool beneath it.

"A beautiful spot," he said to no one in particular, but speaking Latin because he knew Will's Gaelic was less than fluent. "Cool, clear, deep water to refresh a fellow on a hot and sunny, sweaty afternoon, and pot-roasted meat to fill his belly afterwards. A sane man could scarce ask for more on a day like this … Unless it were an understanding of why the friend he has come so far to see is being so damnably unfriendly." He looked Will square in the eye. "What think you, Will Wallace? Is there a valid reason for your reluctance to smile and welcome us honestly, or are you merely showing me a side of you that I never suspected was there? Something is stuck in your nose, I think. So blow it out. How have I offended you?"

Will, who had been leaning on his walking staff, did not quite step backwards, but he reared up to his full height and, to my dismay, answered Andrew's question with another, adding to the overall impression of disdain that radiated from him. "Why would you think you have offended me?"

"Wrong word," Andrew snapped. "I do not *think* I have offended you. I am *hoping* I have offended you, for then I would know it was unwitting and I have no reason to be angry. Failing that, though, I would have to take your treatment of me to this point at face value, and that would be unfortunate, for to say you have been less than friendly would be understating the truth."

I was appalled. I had anticipated, at most, some minor difficulty in smoothing Will's ruffled feathers and cajoling him into acknowledging his lifelong bias against magnates. It had never occurred to me that I might find myself facing the very real possibility that these two men, my two closest friends in the world, would refuse to bury their differences—differences I was fully aware Andrew Murray had not known about. I knew too, beyond doubt, that the Highlander would not back down and would not be bullied, even by William Wallace. And for once in my glib-tongued life, at a time when I really needed to be eloquent and persuasive, I found my tongue stuck to the roof of my mouth.

Andrew turned his back on Will and took one long step across the distance that separated him from where I stood holding the reins of his horse and my own. He bent forward and around his animal to pull his heavy quarterstaff from where it hung securely beneath

the skirts of his saddle, then sprang away before either
Will or I could react. He flipped the heavy quarterstaff
up and caught it in a two-handed grip.

Will watched, one eyebrow rising high on his forehead. Andrew kept moving, with exaggerated stealth
and slowness, looking about him carefully until he
found a spot where he could stand and fight easily.

"Well?" he said. "Are we to fight, you and I, or
merely stand here all day staring at each other?"

I thought I detected the first flickering of a smile
at the edge of Will's mouth, and my relief was
instantaneous.

"You hae no more chance of beating me today than
you did the first time we fought," Will said.

"That was years ago and we were boys. But remind
me about it when we are done." And with that Andrew
attacked, crossing the space between them in two swift
strides and launching a lightning-fast series of thrusts
and strokes. Few of the moves he made were like
anything I had seen before. He was using his staff more
as a short lance or a two-handed stabbing sword than as
the standard flailing-broadsword quarterstaff, and it
was clear to me from the outset that Will thought the
same, for he fell back at once and snapped into a classic
defensive pattern of block and parry. He responded to
Andrew's new moves with great caution, and I was
hugely impressed, for I had never before seen Will
Wallace being less than fully committed in a fight.

Will was narrow-eyed in concentration, refusing to
commit himself to an all-out fight before he had

gleaned some kind of understanding of the tactics being used against him. After a time, though, I saw the tension start to drain from him as he began to grasp the elements of Andrew's strategy, and after that the tempo of the bout increased appreciably. The clacking rattle of heavy staves of seasoned oak and ash hammering against each other grew faster and faster until it was almost impossible to say which of the two opponents was working harder.

Andrew took the first blow, a hard sideways rap to the outside of his thigh. It almost felled him, but he swung sharply out of the fight zone, throwing himself into an elaborate spinning dance on one leg that whirled him close to a boulder. There he dropped his staff and braced himself against the stone surface while he sucked air harshly through tight-clenched teeth and massaged his thigh with one hand until life returned to it.

Moments later, when the whirling reel was at its height again, Will took the brunt of a hard-swung shot that must have come close to breaking his arm, and probably would have shattered the bone had it not been for the spectacular layers of archer's muscle that transformed my cousin's upper arm and shoulder into a limb that not one man in a thousand might possess. That caused another break in the proceedings, but no one made any suggestion that the trial might have gone far enough.

The two opponents faced off to each other for a third time, and this time there was no question of either man going for a quick victory. They circled each other warily, filled with obvious respect for each other's prowess, and I could not remember ever having known it to take so long for the opening blow to be struck in a two-man contest. Once that opening blow was struck, though, the rest followed quickly, and the air was filled again with the rushing sounds of whirling quarter-staves and the staccato clattering of attack following retreat and circling to renewed attacks, with neither combatant showing the slightest sign of flagging.

The end came suddenly. The two men came together, as they had so often before, their weapons windmilling but under tight control, and then it seemed to me that Andrew swayed or dipped somehow and stepped in closer on one foot before switching away on the other, bypassing Will as he went. But as he went he bent to his left from the waist and braced himself on the ball of his outstretched left foot to sweep his right leg backwards, catching my cousin behind the knees and knocking him off balance precisely at the moment when the right end of Andrew's trailing staff, firmly held in a cross-chest, levered grip, swept up and out to catch him square beneath the jaw. Will staggered and spun, cross-legged and cross-eyed, trying valiantly to remain upright, and as he did so Andrew pivoted tightly and swung his staff up and over to crash down across Will's shoulders, smashing him to the ground, face down.

Even as I opened my mouth in shock, though, Andrew spun towards me, raising a finger to his lips and bidding me with an outstretched hand to stand still. He stepped nimbly away, back towards the pot simmering on the nearby coals. Once again I watched a cloud of fragrant vapours swirl about his head as he lifted the lid.

"This smells really good," he said to me. "And the bannock looks freshly made. Come on over here and let's eat before our quarrelsome friend wakes up and adds his hunger to our own."

"Let me see to the horses first," I said, only then beginning to marvel at how quickly things had developed here, for tending to our mounts would normally be the first priority of any rider at the end of a journey. I led the two horses away cautiously, for the ground was uneven and littered with sharp-edged, flinty stones that could easily split a hoof. As I did so I heard Will groan, and I looked back just in time to see him thrust himself up onto one elbow.

By the time I had finished tending to the horses and returned to the fireside, the two erstwhile combatants were sitting side by side, Andrew staring thoughtfully into the fire while Will glowered morosely into the bowl from which he was eating. Neither of them spoke to me as I rejoined them, although Andrew glanced up at me and winked, tacitly indicating that he had the situation in hand to his liking, before looking back into the fire. And so I ignored both of them and went about helping myself to some food. I split and spread a slab of bannock and drenched it in the delicious-smelling gravy from the stewpot on the firestones before adding a plump thigh and other pieces of meat from the hares. I then moved to a spot close by the fire, keeping carefully upwind of it, and made myself as comfortable as I could before I started to eat. And still neither man so much as looked at me.

I ate in silence, consuming everything on my plate until I could mop up the last remaining traces of gravy with my last piece of bannock. When I was replete I stood up and carried my plate to the stream, where I used some sandy grit and a piece of cloth to scrub away the congealed grease carefully, without scratching the metal unduly. I then rinsed it again and dried it meticulously before replacing it in my travelling bag. The platter, my own personal salver, was in all probability the most valuable possession I owned at that time. It had been given to me, with a matching cup, by Bishop Wishart a few years before and it was made of pewter, a rare and precious alloy. It had been made in France and was quite literally irreplaceable, since no one in all Scotland knew the secrets of making pewter.

Will groaned, loudly enough that I thought immediately that he was doing it for effect rather than out of great discomfort. Sure enough, as I turned to look over at him, he flexed his right shoulder dramatically and raised it above his head, bringing his hand down to cup the back of his thick neck.

"Holy Mother of God," he said. "Did you have to hit me that hard?"

"Don't play the fool," said Andrew. "You know damned well I did. And even so, I wasn't sure I had hit you hard enough. Have you seen yourself recently? Anyone hoping to put you down for long has no choice but to hit you with everything he can muster."

"Hmm."

"Hmm?" Andrew said, his eyebrows raised. "Is that all you have to say? What does 'hmm' mean?"

Will sniffed. "I suppose it means I hope you won't hit me again, for a while at least," he said.

Unnoticed by either man, I resumed my seat by the fire.

"Where did you learn all those fancy moves?" my cousin asked.

"In England."

"They're … elaborate. Flamboyant, even."

Andrew shrugged. "Aye, mayhap. But effective, too. That was you face down on the ground there, not me. In England nowadays they're using techniques that were brought back from France and other places overseas. The German states are very enthusiastic about all that, and very thorough in their studies of the tactical uses of what was formerly a simple wooden staff but has become a wooden sword and sometimes a lance."

"Hmm. Teutons."

"Aye, Teutons. They started it, or the Emperor Barbarossa's Teutonic Knights, but that was a long time ago. Barbarossa has been dead for more than a hundred years and matters have come a long way since then. Warfare has changed. Armour and weapons are different and better. Even steel is harder and holds a better edge. And why were you being so evil-tempered and foul-minded when Jamie and I arrived?" The unexpectedness of the question made me blink. "Are you really angry at either one of us?"

"No," he said, frowning more in perplexity than anger. "Of course not."

"Well then, what's wrong with you? *Something* is stuck in your craw."

Instead of answering, Will surged to his feet and looked about him, carefully avoiding eye contact with either one of us. His gaze settled eventually on our horses, hobbled nearby. I had seldom seen my cousin so ill at ease. He was even shifting from foot to foot.

"You're not angry at me," Andrew said. "I know that because I have done nothing to anger you. But you are angry at something *about* me. Am I right?" He raised a hand to stop any response before it could emerge. "It's clearly not the smell of me, for after that fight we must both stink like goats, so it must be something else, something more subtle. Could it be … my rank?"

"Your what?"

"My rank, I said. My status in this land and among its people. As heir to Bothwell and to Petty, I rank highly among this realm's nobility, both Scots magnate and Gaelic mormaer. You don't like magnates, I know—that's one of the things *everyone* knows about you—and while I doubt you might ever have known a Highland mormaer, I would guess you hold them in the same contempt. You don't trust *noblemen* and you never have, not since you were a boy. That's why you are the William Wallace you've become today." He looked Will straight in the eye. "I am not saying you are wrong. Your opinions are your own and you are entitled to hold them. But now your lifelong attitudes are bidding you look at *me* with jaundiced eyes, purely because of where and how I was born and the parents who produced me. And you judge me solely by your prejudices."

"That is not true."

"Nor should it be, I agree. And I agree as well that it is equally true, and every bit as evident, that horses ever shit."

The silence that followed seemed as though it might stretch forever. Andrew stood up, the white stars of his crest bright even in the shade of the hollow. He looked every inch the magnate.

"Ask yourself this, Will Wallace," he said at length, his voice emphatic. "Why are we two here, in this place and at this time?" He held up his hand again. "And don't tell me it's because Robert Wishart called us here, because that, too, is horseshit. We are here, today and together, because we are the sole leaders in all this realm who still have fighting men in the field and are capable of stopping—or even attempting to stop—Edward Plantagenet from usurping this realm we call ours. Am I right?"

Will's frown was still in place, but it was altogether different now, keen and intent rather than bearish. He nodded minutely.

Andrew nodded, too, but fiercely. "Right," he said. "There is no one else but us, Wallace and Murray, and the folk we lead between us. We are all that stands in Edward's way, and as soon as he is rid of us, he'll conquer all of Scotland. When Balliol led the realm to war, not two years ago, he raised the standards and called the armies out and all the land responded—all the magnates and the mighty of Scotland who thought it unimportant that no Scottish army had fought a battle of any kind in more than ninety years, who assumed that, simply because they were Scots and under arms, they would emerge victorious. And at Dunbar the English armies smashed them beneath the hooves of their horses like baskets of eggs. More than half of all the realm's nobility imprisoned after that debacle. All the weapons from the battlefield and from the captured men, along with every remaining weapon that could be found in Scotland, impounded by the English for use against us. All hope lost. All pride abandoned ... save in Selkirk Forest and in Moray these past few months."

One side of his mouth curved up into a half smile. "I know your feelings about magnates, Will Wallace, and I even agree with them to an extent, though for reasons different from yours. But I'm not here today, leading the men I lead, because I am a magnate. I am here because I'm a Scot and it turns my stomach to have to grovel to some ignorant, uneducated English lout for permission to live and breathe the air in my own land— *on* my own land! I would rather die than put up with that, and the men who follow me know that and march with me because of it. Those among them who followed me from the start did so because they are my folk, but now there are hundreds at my back who are not my folk and never were. Those men, and their families, follow me because they have chosen to do so. *Chosen*, William Wallace, of their own free will. And that's why we are who we have become, you and I. We lead the *folk*, the people of Scotland, and they trust us to lead them and to speak for them. And that, old friend, is something wondrous and new in this land of ours: the folk trust *us*, you and me, to lead them. And that is as frightening as it is new, for *where* are we to lead them?" He paused, though only for the briefest of moments. "Have you any ideas? For I confess I have none."

Will inhaled deeply, then reached down blindly to grope for the stone on which he had sat earlier, his eyes never leaving Andrew's. His outstretched fingers touched the stone and he sat down on it. "To freedom," he said eventually, his voice pitched low so that I had to lean forward to be sure of hearing him. "We need to lead them to freedom."

"*Freedom*'s a big word," Andrew said slowly, speaking as though he were musing aloud. "It calls for a whole new world. But what does the word even mean? I've thought about it, and I'm sure you have, too, and to me it is a condition, a state of existence. And I believe, too, that it means something different to every man who dreams of it. Freedom. Men love the thought of it, the idea of it, and they will fight and die in the hope of winning it. And yet, even though you can know it and enjoy it, you can't touch it. You can't caress it and you can't buy it. Nor will it sustain you physically, for you can't eat it or drink it. It's an abstraction, and one that invites questions: Freedom from what? Freedom to do what?"

For a moment Will's mouth pursed into a pout, but then he answered, "Freedom from threats, to start with. From Edward of England or anyone else who might think to threaten us again."

"*Again?* We're being threatened *now*, Will. Our land is occupied by invaders. And so far, we have achieved nothing in the way of united resistance, let alone counter-threat."

Will flicked a hand impatiently. "We are not being threatened. We're being persecuted—and invaded. But that will pass, once we've killed a few more hundreds of Englishry."

"I see, or I think I see, what you're saying." Andrew tilted his head. "But what if we can't do that?"

"Can't do what?"

"Kill a few more hundred Englishmen."

Will's frown deepened. "We can, and we will. We have no choice. We have to kill them, and keep killing them until England accepts that we won't be trampled on."

"And do you think England will stand meekly by while we do that?"

Will shrugged. "They'll be like us—they'll have no choice."

"Perhaps not, but d'you think that will suffice?"

Will cocked his head. "I don't follow you. Will what suffice?"

"The kind of killing that you've been inflicting on them."

"Killing is killing. And forbye, I thought there were two of us, that you were playing this game, too."

"Oh, I am, have no fear of that. But nearly all the men we have killed until now between the two of us have been foot soldiers."

"Englishmen, every one."

"Aye, but insignificant Englishmen."

"Insignificant? What does that mean? They're dead, and they were all Englishmen, bone deep. They bled and died as all men do, and they were English."

"Aye, they were and they did. But they were not knights, or barons, or dukes. They were not men of *substance*, Will, and we won't impress Edward Plantagenet until we start damaging his men of substance. He could watch every last foot soldier in his armies fall in a single battle and he would be unmoved, because foot soldiers are less than human in his eyes. They are not real people."

"That's nonsense." Will threw a glance at me. "And blasphemous, to boot."

"No, it is not, not from the viewpoint of the King of England, and his viewpoint always originates within the royal treasury. Edward can afford to lose five hundred foot soldiers a day without even noticing the cost of replacing them. We cannot afford even to think about losing that many men in a month here in Scotland, but to Edward, with ten times our populace to draw upon, such losses are negligible.

They are nothing. But a knight of repute lost in battle, or a baron, or even, may God forbid, a duke? Now there would be an enormous loss, its cost scarcely calculable.

"There are no more than a dozen dukes in all of England, Will, and each one of them is directly related by blood to the King himself: his brothers, sons, uncles, and first cousins. Among them they share the entire land holdings of the realm. Ask yourself what the loss of one such man in battle would be worth to England, not merely in terms of money, but in loss of prestige? How would a loss like that be seen, a death inflicted by an enemy in an armed conflict? How would it affect people's perceptions of the safety, welfare, and even the stability of the kingdom? To anyone ignorant of how to begin calculating such a thing—which would include every person I know and probably everyone you know, too—I would point out that even a well-horsed man-at-arms, an armed and armoured mounted soldier of no significant rank, is of incalculable value if you weigh him in the balance against ordinary foot soldiers, taking into account the costs of his horse, armour, weaponry, equipment, and years of training. And I fear that example alone, modest as it is, illustrates Edward's perception of the damage that you and I combined have inflicted upon his forces in Scotland to this day."

"You mean he'll ignore us. Or swat at us as he would a horsefly."

Andrew's mouth twisted into a bitter little grin. "That's a good comparison. And yes, that's exactly what I mean. His lesser men, the ones we attack and fight, will pay attention to us, but as far as Edward the King of England is concerned, we are a minor annoyance to be brushed aside in passing."

"Then we have to change his perceptions."

I was on the point of chuckling at the naivety of that, but I held my peace when I saw that Andrew did not look amused at all.

"Agreed," he said. "That is *precisely* what we have to do. But I hope you have some strong ideas on how to go about it, for once again, I have been thinking about ways for months now, and I have nothing to suggest. Nothing."

"It's obvious," Will said. "We attack his knights."

Andrew's entire tone of voice changed instantly. "Of course! That is exactly what we have to do. So how do you suggest we do it?"

Will noticed the heavy irony in his voice at the same moment I did and his eyebrows shot high on his forehead. "You're mocking me."

"No, I swear I'm not." Andrew raised both hands, palms forward. "Edward won't fight us, Will. Not you, and not me."

"He will if we force his hand hard enough, or fly in his face until he can't ignore us."

"No, believe me, Will, he will not. The laws of chivalry forbid that. To fight us head-to-head would be to acknowledge us as a bona fide enemy force. It would grant us a legitimacy that Edward could never concede. In his eyes we are rebels and outlaws. You are a proscribed brigand, to be stamped out like vermin or hanged immediately if captured alive. In addition to which, your knightly family notwithstanding, he deems you a base-born commoner. Edward would never field a military force to meet you face to face in a straightforward fight." He shrugged. "As for me, I'm but a landless boy, not even a bannered knight. No more than a hopeful heir and hence, for the time being, of negligible import."

"Fine. So be it. Then we will go after his knights and men-at-arms, one by one if we have to. We've killed a few of those already."

"Aye, you have. But it has done your cause little good, proving merely that the charges of brigandage lodged against you are justified."

"Then we'll …" My cousin was beginning to look angry. "We'll enlist some of our own Scots knights to aid us and lend us legit—"

"No, Master Wallace, you won't do that, either."

Will blinked at him in astonishment. "Are you suggesting—?"

"I am suggesting—I am *insisting*—that such a thing is not going to happen. Not as matters stand today. Think about what you're saying, Will, and think who you are saying it about. Do you believe Edward and his English nobles are the *only* people who resent you for being a commoner whom other commoners respect and admire? Think you only

Englishmen are envious of your success in spite of your low birth?"

"They won't help us," Will said. "The Scots magnates. Is that what you are saying?"

Andrew gave a slight shrug. "Some will, but many won't, I fear. And most of those who won't will withhold their support through simple fear and jealousy. They see you as a threat to their way of life, and until you convince them otherwise, they'll ignore you as an upstart and a fomenter of strife and trouble. Wishart and the Stewart are the two main exceptions, the two sole Guardians left in Scotland. The others ... well, I doubt the others will do anything to help you."

"It's not me who needs their help, Andrew. It's the realm!" Will turned to me for the first time. "Isn't that so, Jamie?"

"Leave Jamie out of this, Will. He's but a messenger here, and powerless to change a thing. You talk about the realm as though it were a living thing, and so it is. But no living thing can survive without a head. And our realm lost its head when John Balliol abdicated from the kingship."

"He didn't abdicate! It was forced upon him, by Edward."

Andrew dipped his head as if in agreement. "When he was first deposed, yes, that was true," he said. "But I know Lord Balliol well, Will. You know that, for you fought a clash of staves with him at the abbey when you and I first met. I was his squire then and I served him for years. I liked the man. I still like him, if truth be told. But he was not the king this country needed, and Edward knew that when he named him heir to the throne. He abused and flouted him thereafter as he would never have been able to use Bruce, and he finally stripped the man completely of his outward powers. But anyone who understands a shred of canon law knows, too, that the humiliation John endured was nothing more than that—humiliation. Not true dispossession. No earthly king has the power to un-king God's anointed.

"Since then, though, Balliol has fled to France, and there, unthreatened by Edward's claws, he speaks of voluntarily resigning his kingship, with the assistance and concurrence of the Pope and the King of France. John Balliol is no longer our King. He will not be coming back, and that means he is not the king that Scotland needs today. That is the truth, whether we like it or not, and it means that the *realm* of Scotland, as it once existed under King Alexander, and briefly under John, is headless again until a new, strong king comes along to revive it."

He gazed narrow-eyed at Will, who looked deflated. But as I watched my cousin anxiously, alarmed at the curious uncertainty that seemed to have overcome his natural buoyancy, I saw him straighten up.

"They'll fight for Scotland, though," he said, his voice fierce and defiant.

"Aye, that they will," Andrew agreed. "The magnates will fight to win it for themselves. But they won't fight on behalf of Scotland in the way you imply.

They'll fight *over* it, for ownership, because in their minds, as magnates, they *are* Scotland, and Scotland is theirs. So they'll be fighting for themselves, each and every one of them.

"You mark me, we are about to see the buildup to the Great Cause all over again, with each house vying for supremacy, and we'll see Bruce and Comyn rise up to face each other again. And believe me, too, when I say they'll have no place in any of their schemes for you or me." He paused, then added, "And that is where I share your views on the magnates in general."

"How so?"

Andrew shrugged. "They are my peers and my brethren in chivalry, but I distrust them, to a man, with few exceptions. They are all too self-absorbed and self-important, and it is plain to me they have no sense of patriotism."

"Patriotism," Will repeated. "You mean they have no love of their country?" He shook his head. "No," he said. "I think you're wrong there. God knows I have no love for them, but even I would not accuse them of that."

The white flash of Andrew's grin caught me by surprise. "Oh," he said warmly, "the chorus of plaints would deafen all of us were that opinion of mine to be heard spoken. They would all be outraged at the mere suggestion, but that's their weakness and their folly and, in the end, their undoing. They'll fight to demonstrate that they love their country, and they'll fight among themselves for any advantage that might give them dominance in the struggle for the empty throne, but they'll join hands and present a united front to prevent you, a commoner, from waging war on any of their knightly class, be he English or Scots. That kind of thing lies beyond the bounds of patriotism and invokes self-interest and self-preservation."

He held up both hands and clenched and unclenched both fists twice. "I doubt if there's a score of magnates in all Scotland who do *not* hold more lands in England, and draw more revenues from them, than they have here at home. And that is why I say they are not patriots. As long as they take profit from their holdings in England, they'll be dependent upon the King of England's goodwill to retain those revenues, and they'll suffer from divided loyalties. No man can serve two masters, and not a man among them, whether he calls himself magnate or mormaer, can honestly claim to be a patriot, or a Scot at all, until he has surrendered his obligations to the King of England. *All* his obligations, including his lands and properties in England. I believe that only then, impoverished as he may be by English standards, may a man of conscience in this country claim to be a patriot.

"We Murrays held few possessions in England, but I wrote to Edward when I came home last year, renouncing all of them on behalf of my family." He smiled diffidently. "It was not difficult to do, and we will scarcely feel the loss of what we have resigned, but there was principle involved, and that was what dictated my actions."

He held up one hand in mock penitence. "I know what I have said flies in the face of centuries of usage and tradition, but times change and customs change with them. The old feudal ways are no longer suited to this world in which we live. I have examined my conscience with great care and I can find no good reason for believing, in the depths of my heart, that Edward of England has even the slightest, most minute claim on my fealty—not on my personal life, not on my life as a free-born Scot. And that entirely spurious question of ancient feudal loyalty is the cause of our country becoming mired in this politically engendered swamp in the first place, when our noble families, my own prominent among them, recognized the Plantagenet as feudal overlord and Lord Paramount of Scotland, according to arcane and obscure criteria unused for hundreds of years. In doing that, they jeopardized their own future existence and gelded our land's new King before he was even crowned. And we all know how things have progressed since then."

Will stood up and walked away, but took no more than three paces before he stopped and drew himself up to his full, imposing height. I watched, wondering what he would do, while he stood unmoving. Then he swung back, and stepped forward to confront Andrew de Moray with his outstretched hand. And when he did, he was the other William Wallace, the one of whom men spoke in hushed tones.

"I ask your pardon, Andrew Murray," he said. "For doubting you. Doubting your good faith in spite of what I knew in my heart."

Andrew grasped the outstretched hand. "Freely granted," he said, smiling. "But don't ever doubt my prowess with a quarterstaff again. For as long as you promise to do that, I will promise never to hit you again as hard as I did." He threw open his arms, and my cousin stepped into his embrace.

They had not yet finished their colloquy on tactics, though, and it continued in the newly rekindled warmth of their friendship.

"So, then," Will said, "we are agreed between us that from this day forth, we will focus upon destroying knights and men-at-arms ahead of foot soldiers. Is that correct?"

"It is. But how will we do that? The footmen are there to protect the others, to throw a screen between them and do casual harm until the horse are ready to attack. If the mounted men should be our targets, how will we reach them?"

"Any way we can," Will said. "We'll use the land itself against them—to entrap them. We'll dig holes, set snares, burn the forests and the countryside around them. Whatever we need to do, we'll do, and Edward of England can roast in Hell for all we care. We'll stalk his knights and kill them any way we can."

CHAPTER TWENTY

BERSERKER

We walked slowly along the hillside after that, all three of us leaning to our right against the slope, Andrew and I leading our horses for the couple of miles taking us back to Will's camp. It was probably awkward and uncomfortable walking, now that I think of it again, but our mood was lighthearted by then and we were fit young men, so we barely noticed any discomfort. We had the luxury of time in hand, for once, with no need to hurry, and so we dawdled along, enjoying our fleeting freedom from responsibility, and reminiscing, as friends do, about bygone days. And as we went, the mass of Andrew's army overtook us in good order, spilling along the hillside track below us in quick-moving, disciplined divisions of about a hundred men apiece. Their path was wide in places, and reasonably level in others, after hundreds of years of foot traffic. On their left, as they went south, the slope fell steeply to the sea, which stretched away, empty of visible life, to the eastern horizon.

"They don't even know we're up here," Will said. "But they're moving well."

"Aye, their morale is good," Andrew said. "As for their not knowing we're here, that's not surprising. The sun's at our back." He turned and squinted up, over his right shoulder. "Our scouts found us quickly enough, though." It was true. The flanking scouts ahead of the march had found us, but since they could see who we were, they had not come close enough to interrupt our talk.

Will hawked and spat, then pointed down the hill. "Look at that. You were saying earlier that the magnates will join hands wi' the English nobility to keep the likes of you and me from threatening their way of life."

"Aye, what of it?"

"You said they wouldn't … what was it you said? They wouldn't deem us worthy of recognition as a fighting force, for fear of granting us legitimacy."

"Nor will they."

"Ah, but they will. You're wrong for once, Andrew de Moray, and I'm glad to be able to tell you that here, so I can rub your nose in it."

"Excellent, then. It pleases me that I can make you happy." Andrew's grin was wide. "But rub my nose in what?"

"In your lack of insight. You're looking too closely at the one aspect of this thing—the magnates' self-centred need for self-protection—and you are not seeing the other sides of it at all." He nodded towards the men moving on the hillside below, most of whom had overtaken us and were now rapidly leaving us behind. "Those are your men down there, on their way to join mine. Between the two of us we have, what? Five thousand men? Six? Perhaps even as many as seven thousand, though I would be surprised at that. We should take the time to count them one of these days. And now they're all heavily armed and freshly supplied, thanks to Wishart and his sailor friends. So which of your self-interested magnates is going to turn us away in the face of the coming fight?"

"What coming fight?"

"The fight that's going to happen when Percy's army marches north to the Forth and the remaining Scots magnates realize that you and I have the men to stop them going any farther." Will had stopped walking again and was watching Andrew's face, and when he saw the doubtful look in the Highlander's eyes he grinned exultantly. "They'll want to lead them, won't they? They'll demand to lead our men, because they're magnates and they will assume that gives them the right to take any men available. Am I right? And so we won't object. We'll let them take command. And once they think they are in command, they'll come to fight as magnates, armed and armoured and mounted, all bright in their knightly colours and flapping banners, and we'll line up behind them, against the English."

"What? And sacrifice all our folk?"

Will shook his head pityingly. "Listen to yourself, Andrew de Moray. D'you think me completely mad? Who do you think our men will listen to, once the fighting starts? The magnates, or you and me?"

"They'll listen to their commander—the senior man present, whoever he is."

"And he will be a buffoon like all the rest of them, who won't think twice about throwing our folk to the wolves, pitting them head-on against the English horse to be slaughtered while he and his cronies plot to surrender and negotiate more lands and money out of Edward. You might listen to a fool like that, but you were born and bred in that tradition. The men who follow you today would shake their heads over your foolishness. They'd think you crazed. This time, for the first time ever, our men will be *ours*, under our command. We'll tell them, well before the fighting starts, exactly what we want them to do. And then we'll do it. Have you ever been to Stirling?"

The young lord of Moray cast a quick look at me before he answered, as though to gauge what I was thinking. "I was there once, as a boy, at the castle with Lord Balliol."

"And what do you remember of it?"

"Almost nothing, apart from the castle itself, or the view from the battlements. It was a long time ago, about when I first met you and Jamie. In fact it *was* then, during that same excursion. We had travelled down from Aberdeen, through the mountain passes of the Mounth to Scone Abbey, and then to Perth, and from there all the way to Glasgow Cathedral and Paisley Abbey, by way of Stirling."

"And what do you remember about Stirling Castle?"

"The height of it," Andrew said, "up on that massive crag. It was the most wondrous thing I had ever seen. The rock itself is astounding, and at its base, hundreds of feet beneath, the bright, broad miles of land that stretch eastward to the sea are like a carpet spread at its feet."

"Did you ever go down and look at that bright green carpet?"

"What? Go down there? No. What reason would I have had for doing that?"

"Did you cross the bridge as you continued south from there? You must have."

"The bridge … Oh yes, you mean the bridge across the river there, the Forth. Aye, we did. I remember thinking it was a strange place to build a bridge, for the river was neither deep there nor swift flowing. And I recall it was very narrow, the bridge. When we reached it, a wagon, a farm cart, was crossing towards us and we had to sit there and wait for it to pass because the farmer could neither turn his cart around nor back his horse off with safety."

"What season of the year was that, do you remember?"

"Hmm. It was early spring, because we had waited in Aberdeen for the snow to melt in the mountain passes."

Will nodded. "Aye, I recall. And the grass around the bridge at Stirling that day, was it green?"

"Of course it was green. It was springtime."

"Aye. Bright green?"

"Very bright," Andrew replied, frowning a little at this odd line of questioning.

"It wasn't grass," Will said. "It was new-sprung water weeds." Andrew de Moray gaped at him. "We've been standing here too long, and we should get down to the road. We'll talk as we walk. You might have already heard some of the things I'm going to say next, for there's nothing secret about them, but just listen."

We made our way diagonally downhill for several hundred paces before he spoke again.

"The English have never had great difficulty invading Scotland south of the Forth," was how he began. "The road across the border at Berwick is wide open, even when the castle there isn't occupied by an English garrison, and smaller forces—raiding parties— can cross farther west, fording the tidal flats of the Solway Firth, north of Carlisle. That is not always easy. In fact it's difficult most of the time, but it's far from impossible. No matter which way they come, though, through Berwick or Carlisle, once the English armies are north of the border they may come and go as they please—south of the Forth.

"North of Forth, though, it's another matter, different in almost every respect, and that is because of Stirling." He turned to address Andrew. "Nowadays you have English garrisons everywhere up there, from what I hear."

"We do," Andrew said. "All over the north. When I arrived home last year, there wasn't a castle north of Forth that wasn't garrisoned by Englishmen—even my own was in English hands." He flashed a grin. "That's not the case today, for we took some of them back. But there are still too many foreign garrisons up there that need to be thrown out. But what point are you trying—?"

Will suddenly lurched to one side, spun around, and half fell. He only stopped himself from falling by clutching at my horse's stirrup leathers. He half hung, half stood there for a moment, holding one foot raised behind him. His head was down, and he was sucking air loudly through his teeth.

"Are you hurt?" I asked.

He released his grip on the stirrup leathers and straightened up. "No," he said, "I don't think I am." He grasped his ankle in one hand and probed deeply at it with his forefinger. "I think I'm fine. The way my ankle twisted under me, I feared at first I had wrenched it badly, but I think I've been more fortunate than I deserve." He stood erect again, testing his weight on his foot. "It's fine," he said quietly. He glanced at me. "I wasn't looking where I put my feet, and it might have cost me dearly. I could have broken my ankle or worse, and endangered our entire venture." He faced downhill again and stepped forward resolutely. Andrew and I fell in on either side of him. "What was I talking about before that happened?"

"About the situation in the north," Andrew answered. "The occupation up there."

"Aye … What has happened up there is an entirely new situation, as you know, Andrew. It's important to

understand that, and how it came to be. What happened
was … unconscionable." He looked quickly at me. "I
remember that word from our school in Paisley. Is it
right?"

"Of course," I said. "It means neither right nor
reasonable and, by extension, morally blameworthy."

"Aye, I thought so." He turned back to Andrew. "It
was unconscionable. The English garrisons were
allowed to march into Scotland, north *and* south,
uncontested and in good faith, in order to hold the
royal castles safe until the succession was resolved.
That was misguided optimism, of course—sheer
stupidity. There's no disputing that now. But it was
done in good faith, nonetheless. That the English were
in fact invading the northern half of the realm that had
always been closed to them was a truth that no one
witnessing the events at the time could have imagined,
let alone suspected, because Edward Plantagenet had
not yet shown any signs of the duplicity that is now
recognized as his standard behaviour."

He stopped walking and stamped his foot down
hard on a slab of stone beside him. "Good," he said.
"No pain at all. That's hard to believe." He started
walking again. "But now let's think back again to
Stirling. The last thing I heard, and that was two weeks
ago, before we left the south to strike into Fife and find
Dundee, was that Percy and Clifford were at Ayr,
awaiting reinforcements from England. Don't ask me
what became of the nonsense with Wishart and the
Stewart, for I've no idea. We have heard nothing from

anyone on that topic for nigh on two clear months. But the reinforcements for Percy are our main concern, because two weeks have passed since then. As soon as those reinforcements arrive, which should be any day now, Percy will take them north to reinforce the garrisons in Moray and elsewhere, and recapture the castles that you took back from them, Andrew. And that's where we may have our opportunity."

"What opportunity? To do what?"

We reached the flat surface of the road as Andrew asked his question.

"To beat the whoresons," Will answered. "To stop them and savage them and send them running home with their tails between their legs."

Andrew's eyes opened wide. My cousin seldom used profanity, and each time I heard him do so I was struck by the potency he achieved by using it so sparingly.

"Now there is a feast I would like to attend," Andrew said admiringly. "Would you be willing to tell me how you think it might be achieved?"

"Happily," Will said. "If you are content to let me dream a little."

"Dream away."

Will grinned. "D'you recall that beautiful carpet of green grass at the foot of the castle rock in Stirling, the one that reaches all the way east to the sea?" Andrew nodded, cautiously. "Well," Will said, "it is my understanding that all that lush greenness is no more than the fragile skin of a giant bog. There are a few cultivated fields and meadows in places, mainly on the outskirts of Stirling town itself, but for the most part that green plain, so pleasant from above on the castle crag, is a muddy wilderness, and filled with dangers. They call it the Carse of Stirling, and it bars the way north from there to the Highlands. It's a huge area, the valley of the River Forth, which twists and turns all the way through it like a great, looping serpent, flooding with each heavy rain and keeping the surrounding ground almost liquid throughout the year. There's no drainage there at all, I'm told, because the whole region lies on top of a bed of clay and the ground is so low that there's no place for the water to drain into. So you have one enormous, horse-devouring bog." He turned to me. "Did you know that, Father James?"

I noted the use of the honorific. "I did," I said, "but solely because I have read some of the records of the Abbey at Cambuskenneth describing some early efforts of the monks to reclaim arable land from the carse when the abbey was built, more than a hundred years ago."

"That's my cousin Jamie," Will said fondly, smiling at Andrew. "He has never been there, but he knows everything there is to know about the place." I had heard this song before and knew it was useless to attempt to contradict him. "He carries so much knowledge in his head that I am constantly expecting it to overflow, but it never seems to fill up.

"Anyway," he continued. "Thank God for a level road underfoot, eh? But what I wanted to say was that the most important section of the carse is what the locals call the Yett, the Gate. It's a narrowing passage, like a funnel, that runs south to north between the two big crags that flank the river there—the one the castle's built on, and Abbey Craig, about a mile and a half west. That mile-and-a-half-wide space is, quite genuinely, the solitary gateway by land to the Highland north. Any army—no, *every* army—marching north has to pass through it, crossing the carse, with the Forth River in the middle of it. Once through the Yett, the entire country opens up ahead, so if an invading army is to be stopped at all, then it's there, in that narrow gap."

Andrew's expression was thoughtful. "So all the English garrisons in the north today came up that way?"

"They did. Every last man of them. But no one disputed their passage."

"What difference would that have made?" When Will did not reply, Andrew's eyes narrowed. "I asked the question hoping for an answer. Would it, could it, have made a difference?"

Will shrugged. "Beyond question. As I've said already, I've never been there, but there's not a doubt in my mind. Had the right man been at the Yett to meet them, the English would never have passed the Forth."

"None of them? That seems like wishful thinking, Will."

"Mayhap it does, but I know what I'm talking about and it's the truth."

"Hmm … The right man, you said. And who would that have been? You, William Wallace?"

"No," he said quietly. "I told you, I've never been there. The right man would have been a man determined to deny them passage—a local commander, with followers who know and understand the nature of the place, who know and understand that the carse is the valley of the Forth River. So we ought to talk about the river, you and I. That bridge you crossed? Well, it's the only means there is of crossing the river and the carse in safety." He stopped suddenly. "No, pardon me, that's not quite true. You can cross on foot. It's muddy and difficult, and dangerous in places, but the local folk do it all the time. What you can*not* do, though, is cross the carse on horseback, unless you do it by the road that crosses the bridge. That narrow bridge. One farm cart at a time, or two mounted men side by side. The bridge will hold no more."

"Of course it will hold more," Andrew said. "How long is the bridge deck? Two mounted men abreast, and say six more pairs behind them, would make fourteen men and horses on the bridge at a time, plus those behind them, waiting to cross, and those already across ahead of them. That's a fair strength."

"That it is," Will said, nodding judiciously. "But going where?"

Andrew blinked at that. "Why, going across the bridge, of course."

"And what then?"

Andrew threw me a look of pure exasperation and spread his hands. "What *then*? Then all the others follow behind them and they've crossed the bridge."

"Why, so they do," Will said, grinning broadly like a man who knew a juicy secret. "And they find themselves on the path on the far side. I'm enjoying this, so be patient with me … And so they find themselves on the far side, on the causeway that's the same width as the bridge deck and stretches for half a mile in front of them, just as it did for half a mile behind them. A long, narrow roadway, built up to keep merchants, farmers, and honest travellers safe above the deadly bogs on either side."

Andrew nodded slowly. "All right, I understand that," he said. "What I do *not* understand is your insistence upon talking about it."

"I'm saying nothing other than the simple truth," Will said. "Think about it. Once they have crossed the bridge, they will still be on the causeway, two by two abreast in the middle of the carse. You might recall, my young lord of Murray, my mentioning that the bog is not impossible to cross, because the local people do it all the time. They follow pathways where the mud is firmer."

Andrew had his head cocked now. "Go on," he said quietly.

"Remember that I am speculating here." Will glanced at me again, his eyes twinkling. "Now I know *that* is the proper word," he said, then turned back to Andrew. "I am speculating … imagining possibilities."

"Yes, yes. Continue."

"I was saying that *people* can cross the carse on foot, Andrew. But horses and mounted men cannot. Once on that causeway, horses and mounted men can go nowhere but forward along it to the end ... even should they be under attack from all sides."

"Sweet Jesus!" the young Highlander said. "Are you actually proposing such a thing? An attack while they are on the causeway? It would be murder."

"No, it would be legitimate warfare, a trick to cut down the outrageous advantages cavalry has over foot soldiers. Of course, the trick would be to lure them into committing themselves to crossing the causeway in the first place. But if they remain unaware that men on foot can cross the bog, that should cause us little difficulty. If they even suspected we might be able to reach them across the mud flats, they'd never risk an unguarded crossing. They'd find a ford somewhere upstream, then send an advance guard to secure the ground on the far side of the causeway, so we would have to find some way of concealing our presence on the northern side until they commit to the bridge crossing ... But it's an interesting idea, is it not? Since we were talking earlier today about the need to damage Edward's men of substance." He reached behind him to draw the big blade that hung at his back and he held it out, point towards us, in a two-handed grip. "Were we able to carry out some such attack, it would take us far along the route towards that goal, do you not agree?"

Andrew released an explosive breath. "It would, beyond a doubt … But it's no more than a dream, is it? You don't really believe anything resembling the situation you describe is possible, do you?"

Will shook his head. "No, I don't. I would pray for it on my knees all night and all day from now until then if I thought there was the slightest chance that any army would be so suicidal as to put itself in that kind of peril, but it is no more than wishful thinking at its worst."

"Then hold! Let us accept that and dream a little longer, if you will, because now I am curious. What *would* it take to get those horsemen up onto that causeway?"

"Idiocy on their part, pure and simple," Will said. He looked over and waved a hand towards me. "Ask Jamie. He knows more about what it would need than I do, for it involves his specialty, as a priest. You are asking about miracles, my friend, and not merely one of them, because one alone would be of little use to you. To bring about what you're imagining would require simultaneous miracles of incompetence, stupidity, gross carelessness, and military neglect amounting to dereliction of duty. That's four miracles we need already, and we've barely begun to count. But we'll be facing an army commanded by Henry Percy and his cohort Robert Clifford, both of them knighted for their prowess in battle during Edward's Welsh wars. They are young men, young paladins, eager, ambitious, and hungry for glory, and

I can't see either one of them being guilty of any of
the weaknesses I named."

Andrew sniffed, looking slightly crestfallen. "I
suppose you're right. And it's a great pity. I would
have enjoyed storming that causeway … So, it seems
we have no other option than to find another *modus
operandi*."

"And we will, in time," Will answered.

We had turned inland about an hour earlier, striking
southwestward, and the coast was now a good three
miles behind us, the hills ahead of us gentler and more
rolling and well treed. Will waved to where a knot of
men had emerged into view on the crest of the ridge
we were climbing.

"There's Ewan, with Big Andrew and Long John,"
he said. "I knew we must be getting close by now. The
camp's just over that rise, in what used to be an ancient
forest. There's plenty of space for both our armies to
stretch out and be at ease for a day or two. There's
more fresh water running down from the hills than we
need, and there are enough old shade trees to make it
a comfortable place. The first thing facing us right
now, though, is the matter of melding your men
smoothly with mine." He glanced sidelong at Andrew.
"D'you foresee any difficulty there?"

Andrew turned down his lips and shook his head.

"Well, I wish I could say the same for myself," Will
said, "but the truth is I can't. I'm told that most of your
men are ordinary folk, evicted from their homes and
deprived of their livelihood by the English—a common

story throughout Scotland nowadays. So they're all honest men and women, not outlaws at all except in English eyes." He cleared his throat noisily. "And so I need to tell you this: most of the men who follow me *are* outlaws. There's nothing wrong with that today, God knows, for I am one myself, outlawed like hundreds, mayhap thousands more, by the English." He grimaced. "But I have some wild and ungovernable wretches among my ranks, hard men who need a hard hand on the leash that holds them. A few among these men are beyond salvage, in this world or the next. They keep their heads down out of my sight most of the time, but I know every one of them, and when they do come into view—and they always do, sooner or later—I show them no mercy. I've warned them all I'll take no stupidities from any of them when your folk arrive, and if anyone causes trouble I'll take an eye for an eye, regardless of whose eye is involved." He dipped his head to one side. "So what I am saying is, don't be surprised if you see the odd man hanged while you're here. It's the only language some of these people understand."

"I see," Andrew said in a quiet voice. "So how, in fact, do you normally maintain order within your host? Do you have deputies?"

Will released a sharp bark of laughter, then raised a placatory hand, smiling. "Forgive me, my friend, but that struck me as being laughable, considering who and what we are here. We are forest outlaws, Andrew— broken men, they call us, which is another way of saying we are proscribed criminals with prices on our heads … my price outstripping any other's."

"Forgive me. I spoke without thinking." A flush of colour had infused Andrew's cheeks.

"I know you did," Will said. "But to tell you the truth, besides the occasional brawl or falling-out, the men are normally well behaved, just as they would be were they at home in civilized surroundings. It helps that they all look up to Wallace, and that some of them have to tilt back their heads to do it. It helps, too, that I'm bigger than most of them. The rest tend to fear me, and I encourage that. I take no disrespect, and I extend no favours. So they heed me."

"Aye, I can see that." Andrew was looking up the ridge, at the group watching us. "Well, will we join the throng?"

As matters transpired, the two armies blended peacefully. Both armies knew what they were hoping to achieve together against the English, so there was a sense of shared expectations from the start.

There was, however, one incidence of violent disagreement that marred the melding, and I was there to witness it, as, indeed, were all the principals of the gathering. It began innocuously, with a collision that I knew beyond a trace of doubt was accidental, because I had watched it happen.

It was mid-afternoon, and we had been in Will's encampment for perhaps an hour, finally beginning to accept that our long march was over, our supplies of arms and armour had been replenished, and we were finally free to start to unwind. I was anticipating a hearty meal and an evening of music and song before we moved to the quarters set up for us on the edge of Will's main camp. While we were still on the road, we had sent a magnificently large, freshly killed hart to Will's camp ahead of us, and Will's own hunting parties had been busy for two days, roaming far and wide throughout the surrounding country and gathering enough meat and fish—both salmon and mountain trout—to feed the multitude, and the mouthwatering aroma of baking bread filled the air everywhere. The initial greetings and speeches of welcome were over, and the men had been dismissed to mingle and meet one another.

Being a priest with nothing to contribute to the discussions of strategy and tactics that were unfolding all around me, I had been left to my own devices and I was having a fine time. The men of the two armies surrounding me were all deeply involved in trying to assess the knowledge and experience of the strangers with whom they would now be associated, and no one was paying a jot of attention to me as I sat in solitary splendour, perched on a high stool I had found by the fire in front of Will's tent. I was enjoying the novelty of reading my daily breviary in comfort for once, as opposed to crouching in a stiffening huddle in my saddle, straining my eyes in the gathering dark at the end of a long day's march and trying to complete my dutiful reading before the oncoming night blinded me completely and ensured that I would have to finish my reading by candlelight later, when I ought to be sleeping.

The danger in the daily reading of the breviary, for every priest in every land, is that familiarity breeds the temptation to idle and to gloss over the content of the prayers, and that temptation grows increasingly potent as the years slip by and the daily exercise grows more and more familiar.

On that particular occasion, I was floating on the narrow margin separating conscientious reading from the much more worldly pastime of daydreaming. I was paying no particular attention to what was happening around me, but at the same time I was aware that Will and Andrew were talking together in the open space off to my right, surrounded by a number of their lieutenants. I was vaguely aware, too, that opposite them on my left, on the other side of the fire, there was a raucous gathering of some of Will's men, close by Will's tent. There were nine of them, and they appeared to be English archers, for they all appeared to have that unmistakable archer's bulk of chest, broad back, and heavy shoulders. I was mildly curious about how a group of English archers might end up in the middle of an army of Scots outlaws. The probability was, of course, that they were there because of the love of archery shared by Will himself and our early teacher and mentor Ewan Scrymgeour. I guessed, therefore, that they were either Welsh mercenaries or deserters from some English baron's entourage. But that reminded me of a harrowing experience Will and I had shared together as mere boys, and remembering his violent aversion to English soldiers, and to deserters in particular, I decided these men must be Welsh mercenaries.

I had noticed them originally because of their boisterous laughter. It was loud, unrestrained, full of good humour, and impossible to ignore. But then three other men had come to join their group, and within a quarter-hour the laughter had dwindled and died, and several of the original group of nine had drifted away in search of other company. Curious, I had looked at the newcomers more closely, and had not liked what I saw. They were clearly Scots from Will's following, for their dress and bearing showed that they were not Highland Gaels. Where the archers had been noisy and plainly enjoying themselves, these newcomers had brought a silent, menacing threat with them, standing shoulder to shoulder and glowering with sour disapproval at everything around them. I could tell that the archers knew who the trio were, and also that they wished the newcomers had gone elsewhere. There was no laughter now. No one was even smiling.

I was on the point of returning to my breviary when someone came running towards the knot of men. I recognized him as one of Alistair Murray's men, a close-mouthed but likable young fellow called Callum who was Alistair's favourite courier, gifted with astonishing speed and stamina. I had once heard someone joke that the young man had been born running and had never learned to walk. Now, as he came closer, I could see that he was not merely running for the enjoyment of it. He was lightly dressed, bare legged as always, and his feet were encased in well-worn brogans. He carried no sword, and I knew he never did, for he considered the weapon to be a hindrance to his running, but he wore a long-bladed dirk in a sheath at his belt, and I could see he carried his two-foot-wide targe across his back, made of studded, hard-boiled leather stretched over dense ash wood.

Now he swerved to pass the archers' group, but as he did so, one of the three newcomers, the largest and most truculent looking, stepped away from his companions and directly into Callum's path. I was amazed that Callum managed to avoid hitting the fellow, but he did, thanks to an admirable combination of reflexes and alertness. He swayed sideways and passed smoothly by the stranger, less than a hand's breadth separating them, and ran on directly to the fringe of the group surrounding Will and Andrew, where he stopped and grasped Alistair by the elbow.

Alistair swung around to savage whoever had dared to touch him, but the instant he saw Callum's face, he frowned, took Callum firmly by the arm, and propelled him urgently away from any danger of being overheard.

I noted the urgency of the encounter even as my attention was transferred to what was happening with the fellow Callum had almost run into. The scowling ruffian was now behaving as though he had been hit and was glaring towards Callum, while Callum, completely unaware of the fellow, and propelled by Alistair's grasp, was coming directly towards the fire where I was sitting. Alistair was practically pushing him along, gripping his arm tightly above the elbow and walking close beside him, his head bent to one side to catch what the young man was saying. He stopped, sensing his nearness to the fire, and I saw his body tense.

"Go and find Fillan and bring him here, quick as you can. I'll talk to Andrew and Wallace. Quick now!"

Fillan de Moray was scouting on our left flank, far out ahead of our line of march, and hearing Alistair's instruction intrigued me. Eager as a hare, Callum spun on his heel and broke into a flat run. But he had gone just five paces when the angry stranger lunged towards him, pivoting his entire upper body to smash his elbow square into Callum's face, felling him instantly. Alistair had seen nothing; he was striding back towards Will and Andrew, oblivious.

I gaped down at Callum, shocked at the amount of blood gushing from his broken nose and mouth and stunned by the swiftness of the attack, and then I looked at the man who had done this to him. A single word, *berserk*, sprang to my mind. It was an ancient Norse word, used to describe the fighting madness, supposedly inspired by the gods, that sometimes consumed Viking warriors in battle, and I knew that this man was berserk. He was hopping from foot to foot, clenching and unclenching his big hands as he grimaced and growled deep in his chest, radiating hatred and malevolence towards the man he had attacked so treacherously. He muttered something just as I looked at him, but I did not hear what it was. A moment later he repeated it more loudly, and a third time he screamed it. It was gibberish to me, a crazed outpouring of guttural noise.

Callum had somehow begun to collect himself and was attempting to stand up. I bleated something sympathetic and moved to help him, but before I could reach him he regained his feet and stood swaying, gripping his legs above the knees and looking at the ground between his feet, his head drooling ropy skeins of blood.

I stopped then, apprehensive. Turning my head no more than a fraction of an inch, I saw that the madman had backed away. But as I turned a bit more, to look at him directly, I saw him draw weapons, and I looked quickly back at Callum, still swaying and dripping blood. And still I made no move to touch him, for I dared not take that risk on his behalf unless he asked me to. Then, as now, the unwritten law governing witnesses to men in single combat was absolute: no spectator must ever touch a man fighting another for his life, unless requested so to do. The reason is obvious: the most innocent, unthinking interference might distract a fighter and cause his death.

Callum held no weapon, and I turned to point that out to the other man, who grinned at me as evilly as he had glared at Callum, with the same hatred in his dead, black eyes. I opened my mouth to speak and he spat at me, a mouthful of mucus that he had clearly been nursing for that purpose. The spittle hit the front of my tunic and hung there, but I was too busy looking at the madman's weapons to care about that. They were common enough, but both were half the size I would expect. In one hand he held a single-bladed battle-axe, with a long blade no more than three fingers wide, but the other end of it was a heavy, flattened hammerhead, a bludgeon designed to shatter skulls. His other hand held a short flail, made from a net of tightly woven leather strips twisted around a thick handle, with a heavy, fist-sized pebble, or perhaps it was an iron ball, securely bound inside the net. And then I heard the unmistakable slither of Callum's dirk leaving its sheath.

There are moments in life that announce themselves, with absolute authority, as being catastrophic, and our minds accept them instantly, aware that we are utterly powerless to influence the outcome of whatever is about to happen. I saw young Callum, upright now, his face and neck slick with appallingly bright blood, advancing to confront his attacker with his long-bladed dirk in his right hand and his small, circular targe in front of him, covering his left breast. He never had the chance to raise his weapon. The other man whooped some kind of battle cry and sprang forward, high into the air, his flail whipping over and down to crash into Callum's temple, sending the young man reeling, already dead. But before he could even fall, the war hammer in his attacker's other hand swept over and smashed in the other side of his skull, driving the eye on that side out of its socket to hang by a length of something unspeakable. Callum fell sideways like a log.

My mind was empty. I saw the broken corpse at my feet, and I saw the crazed, grinning face of the killer leering at me. Then I felt myself hurled aside as Alistair de Moray straight-armed me out of his way, his long-bladed sword in one hand and his dirk in the other. He did not make a sound; he simply threw himself towards the three men now confronting him, because the other two had advanced to flank their friend as soon as they saw Alistair approaching. His long blade flickered out and across, too quick to follow, and the man on his right sprang back, barely in time to avoid being cut. And as he moved, so too did his companions, sidling backwards and moving apart to present a larger target and to give themselves room to fight.

Alistair straightened slightly from his fighting crouch and moved forward, ignoring the men on either side of him now, all his attention focused on the killer, who was still grinning insanely, still muttering to himself, and still brandishing the weapons he had used on Callum. He took a short step backwards, then another, and then sprang, leaping high into the air towards Alistair with another of those blood-curdling screams, swinging both axe and flail. But Alistair leapt backwards, too, avoiding the other's rush, and instantly launched himself forward, that long blade thrusting ahead of him.

I thought it strange that the madman's arms flew up and apart a moment before the Highlander's blade plunged into the soft flesh beneath his sternum, sinking in for half its length before its point jarred against the fellow's spine. It all happened very quickly, and then, just as quickly again, it was all over. The assassin dropped to his knees like a spike-hammered bullock in a sudden, dead silence, then pitched forward full length, face down, and I saw the black metal handle of a knife projecting from the base of his skull. I raised my head to look for an explanation, and was unsurprised to see Long John approaching from behind the dead man. On either side of him, the madman's two supporters were being close held, their arms pinioned to their sides.

My cousin was suddenly there, looking down at the two corpses. "Berry," he said, almost to himself. "I always kent it would come to this." He raised his eyes to Andrew. "I hae to ask your pardon, my friend, for lettin' anythin' like this happen at our first meetin'. I never knew the young man wha died here, but I can see he'll be sair missed."

I knew, because he was speaking in the broad, rural dialect called the Doric, that he was highly aware of the silent, gawking crowd that had gathered. He turned then to the two prisoners. "As for the pair o' you," he said, pitching his voice to be clearly heard, "d'ye no' mind my warnin' ye on what would happen gin ye didna mend your ways? Are you too stupid to ken a threat of death when ye hear it?" He shrugged. "It's clear ye are."

He turned back to Andrew. "Master Murray, you'll nae doubt hae arrangements to make for your young man there, I suppose. Would you care to do that now?"

"Aye, and I thank you." Andrew turned to Alistair, who was sheathing his sword after cleaning the blade. "Will you arrange a burial for Callum," he said in Gaelic, "and tell Sandy you'll need money to send to his wife. Someone will have to go and tell her, but it will wait until we get home. That will save the poor woman months of mourning." He nodded his thanks to Will.

Will nudged the dead man at his feet with the toe of his boot. "Hang this filth," he said to Long John.

"There's a knife wound in his neck, Will," Long John said. "A rope would cut right through him."

"Then loop it under his shoothers, but hang the whoreson. Hang him high, where everyone can see him. And hang these two aside him. They stood at his side when he was alive and murdering folk, now they can hang at his side when he's dead and danglin' frae a rope.

"The rest o' ye!" His voice rose dramatically, ringing out clearly to the encircling crowd, which had grown larger with every passing moment. "Hear me now! Pay heed! This foolery is finished"—he pronounced it *feeneesht*—"it's a' done an' there's naethin left to see. We've had murder done here an' justice rendered, blood for blood and a life for a life. So awa ye go now, back to what ye were daein afore a' this started."

Someone murmured to me, asking me to move aside, and a pair of men with a stretcher crouched in front of me and covered poor Callum's mutilated corpse with a grey blanket before they lifted him onto the stretcher and carried it away, and as I watched them go I heard Will call my name. I looked in the direction of his voice and saw him standing with Andrew in the middle of a large group of their captains and lieutenants. Surprised at their numbers, for I had so far paid them no real attention, I estimated that there must have been close to two score of them surrounding their leaders.

Will was looking at me, frowning. "Are you well?" he asked.

We both knew I could not be well after witnessing such horrors as I had seen, but there was genuine concern on his face, and I nodded wordlessly, acknowledging his solicitude.

"But?" he said. "What's wrong?"

"Nothing's wrong, Will, except for what we've seen here. But I need to talk to the two men you've condemned. They deserve an opportunity to confess their sins and be forgiven in God's eyes."

He drew himself up, and for a moment I thought he was going to refuse me permission to visit them, but he scowled and shook his head. "You think they deserve that, Jamie? You saw what they did. They knew Berry was raving mad, perhaps possessed by demons, and yet they chose to help him murder an innocent boy."

"I know. I was there and watched as they did it."

"And you can still say they deserve forgiveness?"

"In God's eyes, Will, every man deserves forgiveness. I would never attempt to tell you they deserve forgiveness in yours, for your nature, like my own, is human and demands satisfaction. But I must offer them the solace of confession and last rites. That is my duty."

"Then it's a damnably foolish duty. But go ahead and do it if you must—later, though. After I've done speaking here."

He strode to the stone-ringed fire pit and leapt up onto the largest of the upright seating stones surrounding it. From there, where he could both see and be seen by all his captains, he beckoned them to come closer, and beckoned to me as well, and when we were all gathered, he stood looking down on us for a time, his gaze moving from man to man, eyeing Andrew's Highlanders as squarely as he did the familiar faces of his own men. Then he spoke into the profound silence surrounding him, in plain, intelligible Scots.

"Master de Moray's scouts behind us in the southeast report that there's a fleet of English ships headed up the Tay to Dundee." He made eye contact with each man as he spoke. "We don't know what they intend to do—whether they even intend to land—and neither Master Murray nor I have any wish to wait around here to find out. So we'll break camp in the morning and be on our way west again come noon."

"What about Dundee?" The question came from one of his own captains.

Will nodded. "Those of you who joined us today know nothing of what has been happening here these past nine days, and you should know. Because many of you speak only the Gaelic, I'm going to have your commander tell you what you need to know. And those of you who follow me and speak no Gaelic, there will be nothing said here that you don't already know. Master Murray, will you come up?"

Will jumped down from the stone and Andrew exchanged places with him. He went straight to the meat of things, his Gaelic liquid and beautifully rippling.

"As many of you know, a ship similar to the one we met at Aberdeen arrived at Dundee for Master Wallace a few weeks ago. Unlike Aberdeen, though, which contained a mere skeleton force, Dundee is strongly garrisoned and the English are well supplied, in case of siege. Wallace's army, thousands strong, reached the town nine days ago and set about besieging the castle—the sight of their numbers served to keep the English penned up inside the place. But Wallace's main reason for laying siege to the castle was to distract the garrison from the activities down at the wharf, while his men were unloading the cargo of the ship that had been waiting for them. That cargo of weapons and armour is now safe beyond

Dundee and distributed where it will do most good. But the siege, which is hopeless at this time, since we lack the proper siege engines, remains in place.

"That is what prompted the question you heard asked, 'What about Dundee?' And the answer to that question is that word will go out within the hour to the besieging force to abandon the siege works and evacuate their positions before morning. They will then march westward, following the coast road, and meet up with us there."

"And these English ships," someone asked, "what about them?"

"What *about* them?" Andrew dismissed them with a wave of his hand. "Were we to remain in place, besieging Dundee, they could land and assault us from behind, but they can do nothing to us as long as we keep moving. And so we will leave here and keep moving until we reach Stirling. That is all I have to tell you, so you may split up now and tell your men whatever you need to. Eat well tonight and then sleep well, and tell your lads to do the same, for we'll be up and away come the dawn. Dismissed!"

He looked directly at me and smiled, extending his hand because I was no more than two paces from him.

"Father James," he said. "Will you help me down?"

CHAPTER TWENTY-ONE

CHANGES AND
CHALLENGES

From the moment we turned our backs on Dundee the following day, to strike west towards Perth and the Tay crossing, the pace of events picked up visibly for all of us. I overheard Will and Long John talking quietly together, on our second day on the road, about how, after long weeks of trying to conceal an army on the sixty-mile march from Lanark to Dundee, everything had changed, and concealment was now the last and least of anyone's cares.

The same held true for Andrew and his Morayshire men; they and I had come south from Aberdeen and had hardly seen a living soul along the way, but now we were being overtaken daily by new recruits who had followed us southward. They, of course, had the advantage of travelling in small groups, which meant that they could move quickly and without attracting attention. We could not, because an army can travel no faster than its slowest component, the all-important baggage train. The distance from Aberdeen to Dundee, for a crow in flight, was little more than seventy miles, but for an army travelling on foot over mountainous terrain, as we were, that distance was hugely multiplied by many factors, some of which, like the trackless four-mile stretch of sheer-sided ravines and deep gullies we encountered near Kincardine, resulted at times in a daily progress of less than five miles.

Some of the recruits and volunteers who overtook us in those days after Dundee came alone or in small groups, but there were also several substantial contingents of ordinary men from some of the Highland districts, Forfar in the Mounth being one such place, who marched under the supervision of trusted men selected by their local sheriffs for their steadiness and dependability. These levies were raw and untrained rural folk for the most part, but all of them carried a weapon of some description, even if it were no more dangerous than a hay fork. In addition to the locally raised levies, three groups of well-armed and well-disciplined fighting men under the command of experienced commanders also made their way to us, the smallest of the three consisting of thirty-two mounted men. It was after one such surprising arrival that a discussion among Will, Andrew, and their senior lieutenants threw some light on what was happening.

Forty-four armoured men, well equipped and mounted and wearing uniform surcoats of pale brown linen emblazoned with a black boar's head, had joined us that afternoon, to the alarm of our forward scouts, who thought them English at first. They turned out to be men from the ancient abbey town of Dunkeld, raised and equipped by Matthew de Crambeth, the bishop of that see. Their commander, Sir Iain Crambeth, was the bishop's eldest nephew, a soft-spoken knight with a highly pleasant disposition and sufficient education to converse intelligently on a wide range of subjects.

It was after dinner on the night he arrived that the subject of his uncle arose and led to a wide-ranging discussion of the changing realities of Scotland. The food had been cleared away and the army's high command—though none of the ten men present at that gathering would ever have thought to call themselves by such a title—were seated around a roaring fire, talking freely but drinking sparingly because supplies of ale had run low and the last small cask of good wine had formally been declared dead by Andrew's cousin Alistair two nights earlier. Will had been in good form throughout the meal, playing the gracious host and keeping his guests amply entertained, but it was Andrew Murray who drove any thoughts of after-dinner music and minstrelsy from the minds of the gathering.

"Sir Iain," he said, during a lull in the talk, "I am curious about the device on your surcoat, that black boar head. Knowing that Bishop Crambeth himself is responsible for your joining us here, I would presume it to be the bishop's own emblem, save that it appears to be a remarkably savage image for a bishop of the Holy Church. And besides, I am sure Father James here told me Bishop Crambeth was in Paris. Has His

Grace recently returned? Forgive me if I seem to pry, but it seems to me it would be difficult for the bishop to raise a body of men as well equipped and organized as yours without being here in person."

I raised an eyebrow, for I could have told him otherwise and I was genuinely surprised that Andrew should not know that for himself. But then I realized I was being naive. Andrew had spent far too much time around senior prelates to be in any doubt about what a bishop could and could not do.

Sir Iain, however, took not the slightest offence at Andrew's questions. In fact he laughed aloud. "You are in error in both cases, my Lord of Petty. In the first place, the black boar head is our family emblem, not my uncle's alone. It is the crest of Crambeth and has been since from before the days King David sat upon our throne. The pale brown of the surcoat is my father's and will be mine one day, and it sets us apart from other septs of our house, which use white, grey, and pale blue." He smiled engagingly. "As for the need for His Grace to be at home in Dunkeld in order to furnish monies in the cause of the realm, it seems clear to me, Lord Murray, you have not spent much time around the servants of Holy Mother Church. Our Lady Church has a long and puissant arm and can achieve great things with no apparent effort. My uncle Matthew remains in France, at the court of King Philip, where he works incessantly with the good Bishop Fraser of St. Andrews on Scotland's behalf, to achieve the reinstatement of King John."

Twice now the newly arrived knight had misnamed Andrew, according him a title he did not possess, and I waited for Andrew to correct him. Instead he looked directly at me, as though divining what was in my thoughts, and winked one eye slowly. He had started people thinking, though, and a fresh question quickly followed.

"Where are all these new people coming from?" The speaker was one of Will's lieutenants, a newcomer. "Nobody seems to be trying to stop them reaching us."

"No one is even pretending to try, Cormac, so you needna feel confused." All eyes turned to Will. "It's a sign of the times we live in—a sign that folk are taking note of what we're doing. The only folk in all Scotland today who would want to stop us are the English, and they are all too much in disarray to do anything. You might expect the magnates and the mormaers to try, but they are holding their breath instead, watching each other sideways and waiting to see what becomes of us and our wee uprising."

His gaze turned in my direction. "Isn't that the truth, Father James? You know me, and so does everyone else here, and you all know my lack of esteem for the magnates of our land. But that lack means that when I say things like that, folk shrug and think I'm but venting spleen."

He turned back and raised his voice, indicating with a sweep of his arm that he wanted everyone there to listen to what he was saying. "Father James here is my cousin, for those of you who don't already know that, and even though his clothing and appearance might not tell you so at first glance, he *is* a priest, attached to the chapter of Glasgow Cathedral. Jamie disagrees strongly with my views on our noble families, and we have argued over that since we were boys. And so I'm asking him, in front of all of you, for his opinion on what I said about the magnates and mormaers holding their breath. Father James, on your honour as a priest, am I wrong?"

Every eye was fixed on me. "No, Cousin," I said. "In all conscience I cannot but agree with your opinion. Based upon the evidence we know about— the events of the past few weeks in general since we left Aberdeen, and the last few days in particular since we left Dundee—I have to agree that it looks as if the entire nobility of Scotland is biding its time." I looked around at the faces watching me, and I saw no trace of doubt.

"And why should they not?" I continued. "Politically, they would be fools to do otherwise at this stage. They have nothing to lose by waiting, providing they don't commit themselves one way or the other. If they do nothing and we fail and go down in the face of England's armies, they will provide a hundred different reasons to Edward of England for not having been able to come to grips with us before we met our well-earned ends. On the other hand, if we should win, they will claim equally to have supported us all along, since they made no move to interfere with our patriotic efforts. And even should we do no more than bring about a stalemate, why, then they will have won again, by gaining time to lick their wounds and sniff the air and guess which way the cat will jump next time."

"Aye, thank you, Father James," Will said. "I ken how it must gall you to agree wi' me on sic an arguable point." That won him a laugh from his listeners, and he switched out of the dialect to the more formal language he used with his lieutenants. "It is true, nonetheless. That's why we have seen no signs of opposition from the Earl of Buchan and his crew. Even the Balliols, those few of them who remain in Scotland today, have made no move to interfere with us, and nor have the Bruce supporters in Mar or Lennox. The earldoms of Atholl, Strathearn, Menteith, and Lennox all lie ahead of us as we march, but we have heard no word of anyone seeking to resist our passage, have we?"

No one answered him, so he rose to his feet and looked about him. "I'm told we've drunk all the ale we had," he said. "That's a disgrace. But on the other hand, we are close enough to Perth that we'll be able to send a wagon in tomorrow night and resupply ourselves." He waited until the wave of raillery subsided and then raised a hand for silence. "Think of this," he said. "And that means you, too, Cormac. No one will be attacking us until we come to Stirling, which should be within the week. We'll come towards it from the northwest, looping down and around through the Ochil Hills, and with the grace of God we'll get there before Percy and his lackeys show their noses. Now get ye all to bed and sleep well, for we've a hard day ahead of us. I bid ye all a good night."

"Before we go, Will, one more question?"

He smiled. "Always another question, Father James, eh? Ask away, then."

"Why would you come down through the Ochil Hills? Surely it would be faster and easier to go directly to Stirling from the east?"

"It would be. But it would also be more public. I don't want to set people talking about the Scots army being on the move, for then the English will hear about it. If we keep our presence unknown, we can approach at our own pace and set up camp in the woods at the base of the Abbey Craig, facing the end of the causeway across the Forth. We can be in hiding there before Percy and Clifford reach Stirling." He had watched comprehension dawn in my expression as I listened, and now he nodded. "Good, then," he said, glancing around him. "That's settled. Now, all of you, go and get some rest."

The crowd around the fire dispersed slowly after that, the men chatting easily among themselves before drifting off in ones and twos, until eventually there were but six of us remaining: Will, Ewan and myself, and Andrew, Sandy Pilche, who had caught up to us that very day, and Alistair Murray. The talk was desultory for a spell, until Will sat up straight and turned to Andrew, frowning slightly.

"I've been sitting here thinking about the Comyns being out of prison, Andrew, and I'm reminded that there is something I've been meaning to ask you for a few days now."

"Then ask, anything you like, though I doubt I can tell you much about the Comyns. We are relatives, and they have always been our neighbours, too, but none of them have ever been close friends to me or mine."

"In truth," Will said, "there was only one Comyn in my head—John, the Earl of Buchan. He's the one who should have challenged you before you ever got as far south as Aberdeen, if he had ever meant to fight at all. And that made me wonder, what *was* Buchan's intention? Did he ever intend to attack you and commit himself to being Edward's man against a Scots uprising? And *that* question set me to wondering about this whole liege-and-lackey situation that exists between Edward and our noble magnates. Common folk like us—and I know you are not really one of us, being one of *them* by birth and station, but I include you as a tried and trusted friend—folk like us will never really understand what is involved in all that, because that system of lieges and vassals and ancestral fealty, of ancient, formal loyalties, doesn't affect us one whit. It belongs up there"—he waggled his fingers vaguely in the air over his head—"with them, the magnates, somewhere over and above our base-born, ordinary heads. It has no significance to us in our day-to-day lives.

"And yet the truth is that it *does* affect us, does it not? It affects every single one of us, man, woman, and child, in ways we can't begin to imagine, for it's the biggest weakness in this realm of ours. It threatens our very existence as a separate people." He stopped himself and frowned. "That is the truth, mad though it sounded even as I said it. It's the single biggest weakness that this country has. It threatens our very status as a folk."

He spoke now to Ewan Scrymgeour. "Look at what has happened to the Welsh, to your mother's folk. Wales, the land where you were born, is part of England now, and the folk there, who were there before the Romans came—and I've heard you say this yourself— are being treated like a lesser kind of English peasant, inferior by birth and not worthy of the name of Englishman. That's what Edward is trying to make happen here in Scotland. And in keeping with his overall plan, that's why he tried to use the Comyns of Buchan and Badenoch to rid himself of you in Moray, Andrew. If he can use the Scots to keep the Scots in order, he need not expend a single Englishman. But fortunately for all of us, the Comyns stayed their hand, for sufficient time at least to permit you to come south."

Andrew nodded slowly. "I understand what you are saying," he said. "And it makes much sense, despite the valid arguments that every titled family in Scotland will put forth against it in favour of the hallowed customs of feudality. I've heard your argument that speaks of changing times and changing needs to fit those times, and I've been told it's a viewpoint you share with some of our exalted bishops, and even, rather surprisingly, with the young

Earl of Carrick. And it is also an opinion with which I am inclined to agree, in principle at least, even though all my training and my traditional beliefs are based firmly on the side that disputes such viewpoints."

He bent forward and picked up a half-burnt twig from the ground at his feet, blowing the dead ash from the end of it before holding it up for everyone to see. "Dead," he said. "No spark of life in there." He flicked the unburnt portion into the fire, where he watched until it burst into flames. "It galls me, though, that I can see no way to change things, other than by throwing the entire thing into the fire. The magnates need their estates in England. They need the revenues they gain from them because their revenues here at home are so small and unreliable. The English seize and tax everything in Scotland, from wool to herring, taking the stuff of life right out of our magnates' coffers and making them more and more dependent on their English rents." He flicked a finger towards me. "We've been through all of this before, Jamie and I, and the sole remedy we could dream up would require that every noble house in Scotland resign its entire holdings in England, returning them to the Crown." One side of his face twisted into a rueful smile. "I fear that finding a spark of hope in that, as things stand today, might be as faint a hope as was finding a spark of life in that cold twig, before I threw it back into the fire."

"That may be true." Will's response was immediate and firm. "But as things stand today, we are the sole remaining force of any strength in Scotland committed to Scotland's cause, and we are in danger of being defeated by Scotland's own noble families because of their need for English gold and lands." He barked a short, bitter laugh. "That is beyond shameful, and if it is really true, mayhap we deserve to be conquered."

There was no response to that, but after a few moments Andrew spoke again.

"You started that by saying you had a question to ask me, Will, but you went off into the question of Buchan's intentions. What did you want to ask me at the start of this?"

"Aye, it was about this matter of parole and obligations and your family's role in what is going on. Would it offend you if I ask you about that?"

"Not at all. Ask away."

"Well, we know Edward has been releasing highborn prisoners who agree to join him in his war in France. That's why Buchan and Badenoch and Gartnait of Mar and the rest of that crew were marching up from Aberdeen, and I'd wager there are others like them, scattered across the country—prisoners who would rather fight in France than rot in English jails. But I've been wondering why your father and your uncle of Bothwell have not been similarly freed. They're both rich beyond belief, so each of them could easily raise a private army of his own to take to France, particularly if he had no other choice. It's not like the Plantagenet to ignore such opportunities, and we know he is in sore need of money, with all the resistance to his French war from his barons. Do you have any thoughts on that? Or is there something I don't know?"

Andrew Murray grinned. "They locked me up in Chester Castle," he said. "Do any of you know the place?"

We all shook our heads, except for Ewan Scrymgeour. "Aye, I know it," he said. "It's in Wales. I was there once, when I was younger, as an archer with King Edward. Prince Edward, he was then. It's the biggest castle I've ever seen."

"I thought the same when I first laid eyes on it," Andrew said. "It's gigantic, one of the oldest castles in all Britain, built by the Romans over hundreds of years. It was the fortress of the Twentieth Legion, the Valeria Victrix, for more than three hundred years, and in all that time, it's said, no prisoner ever escaped from it."

Will raised a pointing finger. "Yet you escaped from it."

"I did … but solely because no one expected me to try." He shrugged. "Everyone believed escape was impossible, and so I simply walked away one day. I was one of six prisoners taken there after our defeat at Dunbar, and the other five are still there, living in comfort and treated well."

"If they're that well cared for," Will said, "why did you feel the need to break out?"

Andrew grinned again. "I thought you were never going to ask me that. I broke out because I believed that Edward had no intention of ever setting me free. He meant me to die in Chester Castle. To understand why that should be, we must go back to what you said about my father and my uncle William. Both of them are, as you say, rich beyond belief, but do you know how rich that really is?"

He looked at each of us, as if expecting someone to say they did. "Well, lads," he said, "there are rich men—and you've all seen a few of those, if merely from afar—and then there are *wealthy* men. Most people will tell you there's no difference between being rich and being wealthy, since both are beyond the reach of ordinary men, but I swear to you, on my father's honour, that those people are wrong." He looked around him, and then he clicked his fingers. "Think of a new-growing tree," he said. "A healthy, thriving, two-year-old sapling, and imagine it stands for riches. Well, here is the difficult part of understanding the difference between the words 'rich' and 'wealthy.' If that green, healthy sapling is riches, then wealth, real wealth, is an ancient, majestic oak so vast, so overwhelming, that the sapling doesn't even see it as being a tree, doesn't know it is growing in the oak's great shadow. It simply believes that the shade surrounding it is the way the world was made.

"I fully understand the differences between that sapling and the oak tree looming above it. And I understand it because I know that if I survive my father and my uncle, I will be the wealthiest man in all Scotland, seigneur, as the French say, of all the enormous territories of Bothwell in the southwest and Moray in the northeast." He looked askance at Will, who was frowning slightly. "I am not attempting to make myself look grand, Will Wallace. I am trying to make my answer to your question understandable. So, why have my father and my uncle not been freed?"

He stood up and shrugged out of the woollen shawl that covered his shoulders against the cool evening air, and folded it upon itself four times before placing it carefully on the log he had been sitting on. Then he sank down to sit on it, sighing appreciatively. "There," he said. "A cushion between me and the hard realities of a soldier's life. That's much better. Believe me, all of you, when I say that, of all the cushions in the world, none is more comforting than the privilege accorded to great wealth. And among the wealthy noblemen of Scotland, none were more closely aligned with Edward Plantagenet when he was first crowned King than were my father and his brother William the Rich. Even then, forty and more years ago when they were very young indeed, each one of them already outshone the greatest of the English dukes and barons for wealth and possessions. The brothers were so wealthy that Edward could not influence them with offers of land or holdings in England, and he never tried to. He borrowed easily from them instead, and he numbered them publicly among his closest friends, always taking care to repay the loans before asking for renewals. I knew that as a boy, and I know exactly when it stopped and matters changed." He gazed into the fire.

"Well, man?" Will prompted him. "You have us all holding our breath."

"It was six years ago, in the early summer of ninety-one, several months after the death of Eleanor of Castile, the truly beloved wife who had kept Edward on a tight leash for more than forty years. Her death was sudden, the illness that took her unknown, and Edward appears to have lost his reason for a time because of it, his mind unhinged. He went into mourning and remained in complete seclusion for more than three months, during which the entire country stopped functioning. For three whole months, all governance in England simply stopped: no laws were enacted, no treaties were signed, no courts were convened, and nothing that required governmental approval was approved. Edward had always been a conscientious taskmaster, who would brook no laziness or inefficiency in his subordinates, and because of that, through sheer fear of the consequences of an inadvertent error, the entire government ground to a halt."

He made a tutting sound as he shook his head slowly. "But the time passed, the country survived, and Edward eventually emerged from his self-imposed exile from the world. And yet the man who came out of seclusion was no more than a bitter, twisted shadow of the King people remembered. The changed monarch of England was forever angry and contentious, suspicious of his lifelong friends, and convinced, deep within himself, that he had forever lost the destiny of which he had been so sure all of his life.

"Everyone was aware of it, though few dared comment upon it. But among those few were my father and my uncle. They had earned the right as his friends, had known him close as kinsmen for more than forty years. And yet, because they *were* close friends, they held their peace for a long time — held it, in fact, until they could, in good conscience, hold it no longer."

"And when they did speak up, how did Edward react?"

"Not well," Andrew said with a grimace. "I remember hearing my uncle say, on many occasions, that princes *are* predictable, despite what most folk like to say, because they will all react angrily to anything that does not immediately fall into line with their wishes. Well, Edward proved that to be true. Their criticism marked the beginning of my family's fall from grace in the eyes of England's King."

"The beginning, you say. And what marked the end of it?"

Andrew made a snorting sound. "The day they told the King that they knew what he was doing. That would have been about three months later, in the high summer of that year."

Will was nodding. "That was the summer when the court of auditors convened to judge the claims of Balliol and Bruce."

"It was. My father was the first of the brothers to notice that something was wrong. I have the impression that it was something Edward said in an unguarded

moment that alerted him, some minor lapse of judgment, or perhaps a mere slip of the tongue. Whatever
it was, my father came to understand its true meaning
in the weeks that followed. A month or so later, when
he was sure of his own conclusions, he summoned his
brother from Bothwell and told him what he suspected:
that Edward had a close-held, secret agenda and
intended to add Scotland to England's Crown as he
had Wales.

"My uncle agreed with my father's interpretation,
and together they confronted Edward in a private
meeting and told him what they had divined. At first
he pretended good-natured amusement, denying
everything with laughter and trying to cajole them into
believing they had been mistaken. They were unconvinced by his protestations. They warned him that the
House of de Moray would oppose him, beard to beard,
if he ever tried to gain control of Scotland. And they
offered him a means of avoiding embarrassment at the
same time. If he did nothing further to advance these
plans he said he did not have, then they, in turn, would
remain silent about those beliefs they could not prove.

"And so a truce was struck and time moved on, and
John Balliol was crowned King of Scotland. And my
father and uncle lived on, too, unmolested and protected
by their wealth and privilege. Last year, though, they
went to war with King John against Edward and were
captured at the Dunbar fight and imprisoned in the
Tower." He shrugged. "I doubt they will ever see
freedom again, for they have the power—the will and

the wealth—to denounce Edward publicly and oppose him actively. And had I chosen to remain in Chester Castle, I would probably be conveniently dead by now, through some obscure accident, for why would Edward free me, knowing I would inherit both estates?" He brought his hands together slowly, resting them beneath his chin. "So that is why I chose the path I have taken. My public denouncement of the King of England in what I do now from day to day is far more effective than any other that my father and uncle might make from where they are."

My cousin had been looking at Andrew strangely for some time by then, his eyes narrowed almost to slits and his head tilted slightly to one side as he listened. "So," he said now, "the House of de Moray is for Scotland?"

Andrew Murray looked back at him directly and scratched idly at his right shoulder. "No, and yes. There has never been a time when the House of de Moray was *not* for Scotland, and such a day will never come. But today, in this war in which we are engaged, the House of de Moray acts in its own defence, as well as in Scotland's, for we share a common enemy."

"So be it, then," Will Wallace said, and stood up, extending his hand to the Highlander. "You have killed the last of my concerns. I will follow you now."

Andrew rose to his feet, eyeing the other man levelly. "No," he said. "I think not. I want you beside me, Will Wallace, not following me. We are friends, you and I, blood brothers these ten years past, so march with me as an equal, sharing command. And if we are to die in this Carse of Stirling, then let us die together."

We came to the old bridge that crossed the River Tay at Scone just before noon the next day and spent most of the remainder of the day watching our forces cross it in good order. I was one of the first to cross, well ahead of the main body, and I went directly to the abbey to pay my respects to the abbot, Thomas de Balmerino, and to request his permission for our host to make camp for one night in the large riverside meadows belonging to the abbey. It was, of course, a request that the good man could not refuse, but I went out of my way to present my request courteously, in the names of both William Wallace and Andrew Murray of Petty, and he extended his permission graciously. But Abbot Thomas's reception of me surpassed mere graciousness. It may have been because he deemed it necessary, aware that an entire army, commanded by the man Wallace who had raided Perth, a mere five miles down the road, was about to come knocking at his gates, but he was kind enough to receive me in person and in private, in his official quarters but without observers, where he offered me refreshment and a comfortable chair near a crackling fire.

I had met him six years earlier, at his official installation as abbot in 1291. He did not remember me at all, and neither did I expect him to, since mine had been but one strange face among the hundreds assembled to wish him well on that day. But when I told him I had been part of the entourage surrounding Bishop Wishart of Glasgow, Abbot Thomas seemed to hesitate, then looked at me differently, through narrowed eyes, as if he were attempting to recall something that lay just beyond his reach.

"Of course," he said, almost musingly. "It was a long time ago, but I remember you now. Not your face, of course, but I recall your name, and your unusual gifts. We spoke of you at length that night, His Grace and I, and he pointed you out to me the following day before you left to return to Glasgow."

I made no effort to conceal my surprise, but he smiled kindly and waved my splutterings aside. "I recall the incident clearly now," he said. "We had been indulging ourselves, I fear, passing verbal judgments, though privily, on some of our so-called betters and the divergences between what they claimed to do and what they actually did, and we were deploring the duplicity of powerful men in general and political duplicity in particular. This was at the time, you may recall, when the court of auditors was yet in session, assessing the credentials of the various claimants to our throne—and His Grace mentioned that he had a young priest who was gifted with what he called an astounding ability—and I recall his words quite clearly now—an astounding ability to see beyond the facade and discern men's true intentions and motives. He would give anything, he said at the time, to be able to find a score of others like you, but he had to be content that he had found you. And obviously he has been able to retain your services."

I smiled, flattered and delighted to be remembered in such a gratifying manner. "He has, my lord abbot, and I am happy in the work he assigns me."

"Praise be to God." The abbot sighed. "I hope he is well, for he is no longer a young man and he will be sore missed while he is gone."

So profound was my shock to hear those words that I forgot my place and spoke roughly. "What ever do you mean, he will be missed? Are you telling me he is in danger?"

Abbot Thomas blinked at me, his mouth falling slightly open. "You do not know? How can this be? His Grace is imprisoned in Roxburgh Castle, arrested by Henry Percy."

"But—! We knew of the bishop's plans to hold Percy in negotiations at Irvine, and we heard of the capitulation, but we knew nothing of Bishop Wishart being imprisoned." In my agitation I had stood up and begun to pace the floor. "Percy has been busy, it would seem," I snapped. "But no matter how large the army at his disposal, my cousin Will and Andrew Murray are on their own way south to put the English upstart in his place."

Abbot Thomas's eyes went wide. "To put him in his place? Sir Henry Percy? How so, Father James?"

"Firmly and finally, my lord abbot. By defeating him in battle."

"But …" Abbot Thomas was clearly bewildered. "But he has no authority now, no military status other than as subordinate to his father-in-law, Sir John de Warrenne, the Earl of Surrey. He rides with the earl, according to what I have been told, but in a subordinate capacity. The earl himself is coming north at this time, at the head of a large army, and I have no doubt Sir Henry Percy rides with him."

"No," I said, shaking my head with conviction. "That cannot be true. De Warrenne went home to England in disgust last year, claiming to be too old for Scotland's climate. He made no secret of the fact that he hates it here and he had no intentions of *ever* returning."

The abbot grimaced. "I remember that well. But since that time England's King has sailed for France and left his senior barons to keep peace in Scotland. I am told he reminded the Earl of Surrey of the meaning of the title he had bestowed upon him last year— warden of the kingdom and land of Scotland—and warned him of the consequences of inaction while his monarch was in France. And so de Warrenne is coming, with a mighty host, they say."

"How mighty might that be, my lord abbott? Do you have any knowledge of their numbers?"

The abbot shook his head. "No, my son, I do not. But I do know that they are being augmented by a second army from Berwick and the lands of Northumberland, under the command of Hugh de Cressingham."

"Great God in Heaven! Forgive me, Father Abbot, but I must take this news to Wallace and

Murray at once. They know nothing of any of this." I froze as I remembered the initial purpose of my visit. "Pardon me again, Father, but I came here to ask for your permission for our forces to make camp in your water meadows overnight."

He waved me to silence. "Of course you have my permission, and my blessing. How long will you remain?"

"Only this night, Father. This information makes it vital that we proceed to Stirling with all speed. Would you happen to know where the enemy is now? How far north have they come?"

The abbot shook his head sadly. "Even were I able to answer that, Father James, the 'now' I speak of would have been a week ago, and probably longer. I heard only that the armies were assembling and coming this way. The wandering brethren who deliver our tidings walk, and their information travels at the same pace." He raised his hand and blessed me. "Go now in peace, and tell your commanders all of you will be in my prayers from this time on."

I thanked him and left, escorted by a monk he had summoned to see me safely on my way, and as I headed back to look for Will and Andrew I had much to think about.

We had come here anticipating a fight with manageable numbers, under Percy and Clifford. Now, instead, we were faced with the prospect of meeting two far larger armies, rich in heavy cavalry and disciplined men-at-arms supported by large numbers of massed archers, and commanded by Hugh de Cressingham himself, the widely detested "Treacherer" of Scotland. Cold comfort there, I thought, for a temporary camp at the end of a long, hard march.

The two leaders took my ill news remarkably well, all things considered. Neither of them appeared to be in any hurry to speak up when I had finished what I had to say, and each of their faces remained unreadable as they digested what they had heard. After a time, though, Will turned to Andrew.

"What do you think?"

Andrew grimaced. "We should have been in Stirling yesterday," he said very quietly. "Tomorrow might be too late."

Will sucked a deep, quick breath. "You might be right," he said. "But I doubt it. De Warrenne will be an unwilling traveller and the Treacherer's a fat, lazy slug. Neither one will be racing to reach Stirling. They think they're facing nothing more than a rabble of outlaws and serfs—no horsemen, no discipline, no archers, and no magnates to command them. So they'll be in no hurry, and they'll be expecting to swat us out of their way like flies."

Sandy Pilche, who had been sitting with them when I arrived, cleared his throat. "Can we be sure they're going north?" he asked. "Right away, I mean. What if they decide to stay in the south for a while instead and destroy everythin' there afore they move on? If what we've been telt be true, and there's that many o' them, it shouldna be much trouble to them to mak sure they leave nothin' ahint them that might be a threat at their back."

"They won't do that, Sandy." Andrew's voice was firm. "They have the south in hand, for now. Or so they think. If we in Moray think our northern lands have been stripped of their leaders, the situation in the south is twice as bad. England's jails are full o' high-born southern Scots." He shook his head resolutely. "No, no. It's in the north where trouble is brewing fastest for them. And that's where their eagerness for victory and plunder will take them directly. They'll be wanting to stamp us out, because they still believe we're all up there fighting yet, and they'll be looking to burn and plunder everythin' they can lay hand to once they've dealt wi' us. Believe me, they'll have no interest in staying south o' Stirling. Will, what say you?"

"No argument from me," Will said. "They're bound for the Highland Line, and to get there they'll need to cross the Forth at Stirling, so that's where we should be waiting for them." He shook his head. "It's not just a matter o' bein' there. It's a matter o' bein' there first and bein' ready to stop them. I agree with you that we should hae been there yesterday, and failin' that, we should be marching this minute. But it's too late in the day now and the men need to sleep. So we'll be up and away come dawn and we'll no' stop until we reach the Carse o' Stirling from the northwest, around the back o' the Ochil Hills. That way, if they're there before us, they'll no' see us comin'."

His brows wrinkled in thought, and then he looked at me. "Jamie, I'll need you to ride for me again. Find that fellow Lamberton who impressed you so much and hae a talk wi' him, quick as you can, and then come back here wi' whatever information or instructions he can give us. He'll be in Glasgow, I jalouse, at the cathedral, for he seems to be the one deputizing for Rab Wishart during his absence, and he'll no' be far from the centre o' things. You'll be bringing back the only reliable information we might have about what's going on wi' Warrenne and Cressingham."

I nodded. "I'll leave before dawn. Can you arrange for me to have a couple of good horses?"

He frowned. "That's too dangerous. You'll attract attention riding on your own and wi' a spare horse. You'll need an escort."

"Fine," I said. "But not a large one. I still have the letter of safe conduct signed by Edward, and the documents attesting that I ride on church business, so I'll need only two well-armed men to discourage thieves."

"You'll take four men. I'll have Sir Iain assign his best to see you safely there and back."

"Go with God, Jamie," de Moray said. "And gin He smiles on us, we'll see you again in Stirling."

CHAPTER TWENTY-TWO

THE PATH TO STIRLING

I remember how keenly aware I was of the emptiness of the countryside as we rode that morning, for being part of an army changes one's view of everything in every way, and it seemed to me like a very long time since I had gone anywhere without being surrounded by a multitude. Our journey south was uneventful, and we made excellent time, riding openly and travelling the entire distance from Perth to Stirling without seeing a single sign of English presence. The plain truth was that our little jaunt to Glasgow would not have been worth more than passing mention in this tale had it not been for one unexpected encounter that resulted in an unprecedented opportunity to acquire information about the enemy's plans.

I went directly to the cathedral when we reached Glasgow. Father Malachi, the oldest member of the cathedral chapter, scuttled away, wide-eyed, to tell Canon Lamberton that I wished to speak with him, and mere moments later Lamberton himself came striding out, smiling widely, to greet me in person. He shook my hand warmly and took me by the arm to walk back with me across the cathedral precincts to the bishop's residence, where he was staying while Wishart was imprisoned in Roxburgh, and there he permitted me to exchange greetings and pleasantries with all my old friends and colleagues on the diocesan staff. Before long, however, he dismissed everyone and took me into the bishop's sanctum, where he ushered me into a chair by the welcoming fire in the hearth, and I was reminded that even on the hottest summer day in our land, large houses are dark and dank inside, for sandstone blocks are impervious to sunlight and warmth.

At ease in his role as the bishop's deputy, the canon poured a cup of wine for each of us and came to sit across the fire from me, and as the questions began I quickly discerned that he was as starved for reliable information here in the southwest as were we to the north. Fortunately, however, each of us knew enough about the other's lack to permit us to put each other's mind at rest.

He had heard rumours of failure out of Moray, the most worrisome yet least substantial of those being that Andrew Murray had been taken and hanged by the hapless Reginald de Cheyne, the English-appointed governor of Moray. According to the report he had received, he told me, Murray had been hanged and drawn—a barbarous, scandalous death for anyone, let alone a nobleman—after Pilche, his

rebellious accomplice, had betrayed him under torture
before dying himself.

I listened in disbelief, and as soon as he had
finished speaking I said, "Believe me, Canon, Will and
Andrew will be much impressed by that tale when
they hear it, and so will Sandy Pilche, unless these
events took place yesterday, for all three men were
alive and well the day before that, when I left them."

Moments later, he was able to dispose of my own
concerns in much the same way, but far more emphatically, shaking his head decisively when he heard me
say how afraid Will and Andrew had been that they
might not reach Stirling ahead of the English.

The English were nowhere close to Stirling, he told
me. De Warrenne was being stubborn—had been since
the outset of this supposed invasion, dragging his
heels at every step along the road north from his home
territories in southern England in a manner that
Lamberton described as being dangerously close to
open defiance of his King's wishes. It was a stubbornness reinforced, Lamberton opined, by the knowledge
that Edward was safely overseas in France, with more
important things than the dilatory antics of the Earl of
Surrey to occupy his attention. De Warrenne had
crossed into Scotland with his army a mere four days
earlier, he told me, and was still encamped at Berwick,
supposedly consolidating his supply train before
venturing farther north.

In the interim, according to other reports, the earl's
recently appointed co-commander, the treasurer Hugh

de Cressingham, had been evincing a seemingly equal reluctance to set about subduing the so-called rebellion in Scotland, though his concerns were more conscientious and defensible, based solely, it seemed, on the fiscal aspect of his responsibilities. He appeared to be holding his own forces in check south of the border until he could see an irrefutable need to commit them to action, with all the concomitant expenses entailed in that decision. In light of that, Lamberton said, Will and Andrew had all the time they might need to prepare for the enemy's arrival.

I asked him how he could be so sure of his information.

"Why, it came through Lionel," he said. "Lionel has assured me of the truth of everything I've told you."

"Who is Lionel?" The name meant nothing to me, though I had met hundreds of people in the course of my work with Bishop Wishart.

"Forgive me," Lamberton said quickly. "You know him by a different name. His real name—his family name—is Lionel Cunninghame, and his father and my own are twins, so he has always been Lionel to me." He paused, smiling as some recollection occurred to him. "Lionel has always had a—" He hesitated, searching for the right word. "Shall we say a rather *different* sense of humour? He took the name Father Thomas, appropriately, he believed, when he was finally ordained in France, after years of self-doubt and much questioning. Père Thomas de Clermond, the Doubter."

I made no attempt to mask my surprise. "Thomas
Clermont, of course," I said, using the Scots name
by which I knew my old friend. "I had no idea he
knew you."

"How could you have? When you knew Lionel, I
was but a newly ordained young priest. Older than
both of you, but junior to you both in service."

"But how …? You say *he* told you these things? I
thought he was back in France. It must be five years
since I've seen or heard of him."

"More than that, Father James. He returned to
France in 1291 and lived there for three years. But
then, in the summer of ninety-four he was sent to
England, ostensibly, perhaps even genuinely, as an
interlocutor for a man called Bertrand de Got, who
was vicar-general at that time to his brother, the
Cardinal Archbishop of Lyon, with whose name you
must now be familiar."

"I have never heard of Bertrand de Got."

"Yes, you have. But you would not have recognized him by name. Pope Boniface recently named him
Cardinal Archbishop of Bordeaux in recognition of the
valuable work he had done during the years when
Lionel worked with him fighting King Philip's determination to impose taxation on the Church in France."

"Oh!"

"That means nothing to you?"

"I knew nothing about it."

"No matter. But Lionel was in the cathedral
chapter of Lyon when he came to the vicar-general's

attention as an English priest. In very short time thereafter, Lionel had become a member of the vicar-general's personal staff and was subsequently delegated to act as the Archbishop of Lyon's official liaison with his brother in Christ in England, the Archbishop of Canterbury. You may remember the archbishop's opinions were being widely scrutinized at that time by everyone concerned about the potential taxation of Holy Mother Church, not only in France but in England."

He paused, but when I gave no sign of being aware of this, he merely nodded, accepting my ignorance, and continued: "In fact, his voice had become the foremost in Christendom protesting King Edward's declared intention of taxing the Church in England. And so he was being widely watched and heeded, since all Christendom knew that if the Church were forced to pay taxes in both France and England, it would soon be paying taxes everywhere."

I nodded then, remembering. "It never came to pass, though."

"No, it did not. Mainly because, in the following year, Philip Capet of France enacted a law forbidding the transfer of money or goods from France to Rome. He cut off the Church's funds from France entirely and forced Pope Boniface to back down and permit a limited degree of taxation of the Church in times of national emergency. By that time, though, de Got had distinguished himself for service to the papacy in the dispute.

"His detractors—and he has no lack of such—claim he is naught but a glorified clerk with delusions of greatness, but the fact remains that he is now the Cardinal Archbishop of Bordeaux and therefore one of the most powerful clerics in all of France, a friend and intimate of the Pope himself."

He paused, and then went on in a softer, musing tone. "Not all men are awed by the power of the papacy, though. And Edward of England ranks high among those who believe themselves stronger than any mere Pope. He saw the advantages of having influence over a weak pontiff, and he set out to assert his own inimitable will and, using Philip of France's methods, to apply taxation measures of his own against the Church in England. Of course, in the meantime everything has changed. England is now at war with France, and Philip won his right to tax the Church in France. In return, he made peace with the Pope and enlisted his aid and support, as an arbitrator, in his war against Edward and England. So now Edward is negotiating with the Church and Boniface, but from a position of weakness, and the matter of taxing the Church in England is yet unresolved."

"He'll never win there. Despite what happened in France, no Pope could accept such a proposal. To tax God's work? The thought is ludicrous."

"Not to Edward. He sees the Church's revenues and wants a part of them—a large part. But you are right. Boniface will never again submit to that."

"And so Thomas remained in England, with the Archbishop of Canterbury?"

"He did. But Archbishop Winchelsea has been divorced from royal favour for a long time now, and though Thomas was left high and dry by the changed circumstances of his principal, he remained effectively in the employ of his master, the new Archbishop of Burgundy. And as such, he was transferred to the Diocese of Winchester, because the bishop there, John of Pontoise, is French-born. Thomas has been there ever since, as some undefined form of papal ambassador."

"But he's a Scot! And he's a rabid, anti-English one."

"Aye, and so is the young Earl of Carrick, I've been told. But that did not disbar him from Edward's service or from his royal patronage."

"What has Bruce to do with this?"

Lamberton dipped his head. "He is an earl of Scotland, and he has chosen to defy Edward of England. I would say that puts him on a par with your cousin and Andrew Murray."

"Perhaps." I was unconvinced of the canon's accuracy and unimpressed with the earl himself, for I had heard nothing worthy of note about Bruce since the brief time I had spent with him months earlier, and I had seen more than a few lips curl, either up or down, at the mere mention of his name since then. "But how has he defied Edward? I heard he was involved in the negotiations at Irvine, but I have heard no mention of heroic deeds on Scotland's behalf."

Lamberton was frowning slightly. "But he led the army of his earldom, all the men of Carrick, to the support of the realm in time of great need."

"Not all his men," I said quickly, and his eyebrows arched.

"*All* of them. I said Carrick, Father James, not Annandale. The men of Annandale are loyal to the elder Bruce, and he remains loyal to Edward as his liege lord."

"Aye, Edward's loyal servant, the former governor of Carlisle. That's the same old loyalty problem that Will is always talking about. Scots lords with English loyalties."

"May I continue?"

"Of course."

"My thanks. I was saying he brought his earldom's army to the defence of the realm. In doing so, he demonstrated his commitment to the *community* of the realm."

"How so, if I may ask?"

"By taking a stance that few seem willing to adopt today. He joined the other leaders of the rising to complete the three rankings of guardianship required by ancient Scots law to constitute a legitimate council of leadership in the absence of a king—a bishop, Bishop Wishart; an earl, himself; and a baron, the Lord High Steward—and in doing so he aligned himself clearly against England."

"And where is he now?"

For the first time, Lamberton looked uncertain. "I don't know," he said.

"Why wasn't he arrested with the others after the Irvine affair?"

"I don't know that, either. He managed to remain free, somehow, along with the Steward. Lord James, I presume, offered the English some form of guarantee of his good behaviour and obedience, and it seems reasonable to me that the Earl of Carrick did the same. His Grace of Glasgow, I fear, was arrested for reasons of church politics, more attributable to the insistence of the Archbishop of York than to the displeasure of the English King."

"Aye, mayhap, but Bruce's vanishment perturbs me more than Bishop Wishart's banishment." I must have sounded more bitter than I really felt, for the canon frowned again, quickly this time.

"What is wrong, Father James? You had no difficulty in thinking well of Robert Bruce the last time we spoke of him."

"I know," I said. "But that was before he became invisible again."

"Bruce was never invisible and never could be. It is not in his nature. I may not know where he is at this moment, but I have no doubt he will show up soon and will still be true to the decision he made before he came here. You do know how he came to be here in the first place, do you not?"

"Of course I know. He came in the hope of enlisting

his father's men in Annandale on Edward's behalf, and when he could not do that, he crossed into Carrick and raised the men there."

"And what of the oath-taking?"

I felt my eyes narrowing to squint at him as I absorbed that question. "What oath-taking? He made them take an oath, his own men?"

"No, the English made *him* take an oath."

I stared at him.

"Bear with me, Father James, and imagine this, if you will: a young man, born and bred of one of this realm's oldest and most distinguished families, is suddenly uprooted and dispossessed, effectively banished to live in exile in another country, his patrimony confiscated and redistributed among his enemies as recompense for merely being who and what he is, the scion of a noble house whose enemies perceive him and his as political threats. He transfers all his loyalties to a new King, who receives him and his family with honours and privileges, and he eventually becomes that King's favourite young knight, enjoying royal patronage and high esteem. His family prospers, too, and his father is appointed to the prestige-filled post of governor of Carlisle, one of the land's most important towns. And then one day, without apparent reason, the young man forsakes all that and casts his lot, deliberately and without forethought, it would seem, with the very people who have wronged him and dispossessed his family." He stopped short, watching me with his head cocked.

"Does that strike you as logical? Or even natural? Or might you suspect there could be other things at work herein, other unseen, unenvisioned things?"

"Like what? What happened?" I had lost all awareness of speaking to a cathedral canon or an acting bishop; I was speaking as one ordinary man enthralled by the tale being spun by another.

"He lost his wife, whom he loved dearly. She died in childbed, though the child, a girl, survived. And then the King he admired treated him poorly thereafter—for what reasons, no one knows, but there are indications that the King's true displeasure was with the father, and the son merely suffered by association. Be that as it may, word spread quickly that he had lost the King's esteem, and the resentful and envious predators who always note such things were quick to react."

"What did they do?"

"They acted by being themselves in England as they would had they been Scots in Scotland. Such people swarm in every society, maggots thriving on the unseen, corrupt aspects of the life around them. Edward gave young Bruce a task to perform, and before he set about it, he went to Carlisle, to visit his father. While he was there, though, he somehow fell afoul of the Bishop of Carlisle, John de Halton. Do you know the man?"

I shook my head.

"He was here in Scotland for the conclusion of Edward's court of auditors when Balliol was named

King, and later he returned and stayed for three
years—until the war broke out last year, in fact—
charged with collecting the Pope's crusading tax. He
went back to Carlisle and he's been there ever since.
I've met him several times. Strange man, not one of
my favourite people. Anyway, it is plain that he did not
like young Bruce. He even wrote to the King about his
distrust, and generally treated young Bruce with
disdain and suspicion until—" He cut himself off, but
then went on.

"Mind you, we do not know if this was his own idea
or if it was ordered by the King, but the Bishop of
Carlisle eventually arrested Bruce and threatened him
with imprisonment unless he swore an oath of allegiance, of personal allegiance, to Edward. Now that
must have been intolerable for Bruce because he had
publicly sworn precisely such an oath less than two
years before that, at his wedding in Westminster Abbey,
and then another last year, when Edward rubbed the
noses of all the Scots nobility in their own mess by
forcing them to swear personal allegiance to him at the
gathering he convened after winning the war, the
humiliating ritual they call the Ragman's Roll."

"My God," I whispered.

"Aye, it seems scarce believable that any
Englishman, particularly a bishop, should require any
such oath after two such public declarations. But
Bruce swallowed the insult, took the oath, and rode off
to perform the task Edward had set him, which was the
arrest and abduction of Lady Douglas of Douglasdale."

"But he set her free instead. I've heard the tale. But I have no idea what caused him to do such a thing. Given the realities of his former situation, it makes no sense at all."

Lamberton nodded, his face grave. "I agree with you. It makes no sense at all. But you left out a very important word: *apparent*. It makes no sense at all, given the *apparent* realities of his former situation. What happened was that when Bruce arrived in Douglasdale, he discovered, very quickly, that his presence there was an elaborate pretense. He realized that instead of being in charge of the expedition to arrest Lady Douglas, he was there solely in order to be *seen* there, as a Scots lord dealing English justice to a Scots rebel. His English troops, his so-called *subordinates* from Berwick, were really there to ensure he behaved himself properly, and they held royal authority to carry out the King's wishes should they deem Bruce to be incapable or unwilling. He knew he had been duped, used for political effect and nothing more.

"That realization completed the young man's education on the loyalty and friendship of kings and princes. And so, mindful at last of his grandfather's teachings, he went home to Annandale, to his family's seat, and spoke to the men who had followed the old nobleman. He told them that his experience in Douglasdale, coupled with the insult of the Carlisle oath-taking, had forced him to examine his own beliefs in the light of his grandfather's, and he deemed it unacceptable that he, or anyone else, should be

forced to swear an oath. An oath rendered under
duress is no oath at all, he said—and he is correct—
and his oath, with all others like it, is thereby rendered
invalid and untenable. He swore, too, on his grandfather's memory, that he believed no man should ever be
forced to turn against his own folk. He is a Scot, he
declared to them, his birthright above and beyond the
political disposition of others, and Scotland is his
home and his patrimony. *That* is why he turned on his
English watchdogs, rescued the Lady Douglas, whom
he did not know, from beneath their noses, and went to
join the bishop and the Steward. And Edward of
England will one day come to rue his own headstrong
malice in bringing that about."

"I knew nothing of most of that," I said. But then
another thought occurred to me. "Think you he has his
eyes on the Crown?"

Lamberton pondered the question, then shrugged.
"I would be greatly surprised if the idea has never
entered his mind," he said. "He is a Bruce, after all,
and his family has a valid claim, as Edward himself
made clear with his court of auditors." He sipped delicately at his wine. "But then you have to consider his
intellectual position. Bruce is no fool, and he is well
aware of the situation as it exists today. The decision
of the court of auditors demonstrated quite efficiently
that the Balliol claimant had the stronger claim over
Bruce of Annandale. Most people in Scotland were
happy with that verdict at the time, glad to see what
they perceived to be an end to doubt and indecision

and a return to order and the rule of law under a duly crowned king.

"Of course, much has changed since then," he went on, "and people look less kindly on Edward and King John than they did. But one fact is unaltered and unalterable: John Balliol remains our lawful, anointed King. And the Earl of Carrick is well aware of that. If he has designs upon the throne, as you suggest he might, I believe him clever enough, and sufficiently patient, to rest content for the time being and await an opportunity to press his claim legally at some future time. If he is to emulate his grandfather, he has sixty years and more ahead of him. He would be a very foolish young man to betray any signs of such ambition prematurely."

"Aye, but if he has the thought in mind, it would provide a reason for his defiance of Edward and his return to Scotland."

"It would, and it might well be that he has returned precisely to establish himself in residence here again, with an eye to the future … And come to think of it, we might not be the only folk thinking along those lines. Part of the terms imposed upon him by Percy and young Clifford after the Irvine affair was that he must hand over his infant daughter, Marjorie, as hostage for his good behaviour thenceforth. I had all but dismissed that as being unimportant—a minor nuisance imposed as part of the overall penalty—but now it appears as something utterly different, far too subtle and complex for those two young firebrands to have thought of by themselves. That stipulation must have come from Edward himself—a threat to the daughter's safety as a curb on Carrick from now on."

"So the English now hold the child as hostage? That is infamous. She can't yet be two years old."

"No, not so. I mean it would be infamous, of course, beyond dispute, but they do not yet have the child. And there, I would suggest, is the real reason for Bruce's disappearance after Irvine. He consented to the terms, to ensure he would remain free, and then he took the child and went into hiding."

"You mean he broke an oath."

"Aye, presumably. Another oath." The canon's face remained expressionless, but his voice nonetheless conveyed his weariness. "I fear the world in which we live today takes little note of oaths and oath-taking. Instead of being what it truly is—a personal promise to God in the cause of achieving salvation—the sacred oath has been debased in recent years. Oaths are now become a tool of politics and policy makers. The King of England has much to do with that, being among the greatest offenders in what amounts, when all is said and done, to the subversion of God's will to the earthly benefit of his own." He shook his head. "It pains me to say that, remembering the paragon that he once was, but it is true. The man administers oaths with the abandon of a drunkard, all of them under duress and all of them invalid therefore. So who among us can condemn the men who swear the oaths because they have no choice, then disregard them afterwards? It is the way of this world today, and as such it is damnable, in the true sense of damnation."

"But in the meantime, Edward appears to be convinced that Bruce represents a future threat to his well-being—sufficiently convinced to try to take the child away from him. No wonder Bruce is defying him yet again. Suffice that he did so once, over the Carlisle oath-taking, but this threat of losing the child must have been beyond bearing to force him into taking the stance he has taken."

My companion looked at me, waving my words aside with extended fingers. "No, no, no, the Earl of Carrick is doing far more than you perceive, Father James. I believe you are missing a significant point in all this. Bruce's defiance of Edward is less telling than his defiance of his own father, Annandale."

I was shocked. "I don't follow," I said. "What d'you mean?"

"Think about it. Bruce's father is still alive and hale and employed in Edward's service in a position of great trust. Whatever the young earl's motivation may be, he must have taken his father's situation into consideration before deciding to change sides. He must have been aware that his defection would imperil Annandale's position as governor of Carlisle and put him in an untenable position. And yet he went ahead and crossed over anyway. That tells me there was more than pique and injured dignity involved. There was a deliberate commitment in doing what he did, and his choice was not made without profound soul-searching and deliberation. It was a premeditated declaration, a political decision, taken with great forethought in the knowledge that he was breaking, possibly forever, with his own father. That is nothing like the behaviour of a rash young man whose pride has been hurt."

I had listened to this with growing amazement, recognizing the truth of his words as he spoke them, and when he had finished it took me several seconds to articulate the new and disturbing perspective he had suggested.

"So," I began, "you believe that Bruce had made up his mind to change sides long before he ever reached Castle Douglas that day."

"Something of that nature," Lamberton concurred. "I have come to believe that, though perhaps not conclusively. Prior to the fact, he himself might not have decided consciously to defect, but there is no doubt in my mind that he had given the matter great thought. What he realized at Castle Douglas probably served to confirm his conclusions and precipitated his decision."

"So what has happened to his father?"

Lamberton shrugged. "Nothing, as far as I know. Nothing yet, at least. And I can say with some certainty that I would have heard by now had Edward lashed out at him in retaliation for Carrick's actions."

"So he still governs in Carlisle Castle?"

"Apparently so."

"Hmm. This casts the Earl of Carrick in an entirely new light. And I accept your opinion unreservedly on this matter of the threat to the child. If we can guess at Bruce's motives, however dimly, so can Edward of England ... which makes it easy to see why Bruce has vanished." I shook my head. "You may think me addle-headed, Canon Lamberton, but I can't remember how we came to talk of Bruce here."

He grinned, amused and, I thought, relieved. "We had been talking about my cousin, Father Thomas, and how such a rabid, anti-English Scot might have found himself in England's court working, even at arm's length, for the Plantagenet. He is there because he caught the eye of the King himself and managed to impress him. And that is, I suppose, what he has in common with Bruce. It is important to realize, Father James—for most people do not—that Edward deals in men. I once heard you say he studies kingcraft and that may be true, but *men* are his primary interest, his stock-in-trade. Their place of birth—even their station in life—is irrelevant to his designs, and he can afford to ignore their former loyalties once they come to his attention. When Edward Plantagenet decides he wants a man, he buys him, loyalties and all, and treats him like a jewel of great worth. Once he has the man entrapped, though, he ignores him, save when he needs something from him. This seems to be how it was with Bruce, who was once his great favourite. And my cousin Lionel, Thomas to you, is most definitely a Scot. And a zealous one, emphatically, by birth and temperament."

"So where is he now, this cousin of yours, that you have such access to his knowledge?"

That earned me an open smile. "He is here in Glasgow, conducting business with the Bishop of Durham's clerks on behalf of his current patron."

"The Bishop of Durham? Antony Bek, the King-breaker? Pardon my frankness and lack of charity, if you will, but I thought that sacrilegious, pontificating hypocrite long gone from these parts."

Lamberton's eyes crinkled at the corners. "Ah! I see you are yet another of the Prince Bishop's admirers. He was gone for a while, but now he is back as part of Edward's administration."

"And he is Thomas's employer now, his patron?"

"No, no, no, no, not at all. Thomas is merely dealing with his clerics, who cannot, in charity, be held responsible for their superior's shortcomings. No, Father Thomas's current patron is Sir John de Warrenne."

I sat gaping. "Thomas is part of the Earl of Surrey's *entourage*?"

"Household chaplain. He's part of the earl's household, not merely his entourage. His Grace of Surrey is a pious man, I'm told—genuinely so, I mean. I am not mocking him. He is no longer young, as you probably know, and in his later years he has found consolation for many things, including the loss of his beloved wife, in the observance of the Church's teachings. He is generous in his donations, and in return his diocese—not coincidentally Winchester— takes great pains to ensure that his daily spiritual needs are well looked after. And to that end Bishop

John of Winchester appointed Father Thomas as his chaplain and liaison with the diocesan chapter. It seems the earl had met Lionel a year or so earlier and liked him greatly, apparently because my cousin bears a strong resemblance to his favourite son, who died years ago. And when his old confessor died, he asked for Lionel by name."

"And Thomas is now his chaplain. Dear God! Do you have any …? That is …"

Lamberton's lips quirked into an off-centre grin. "Were you about to ask me if I know how significant that is? Because I do. I know precisely what it means to this realm of ours. Quite apart from the sacrosanctity of the confessional, which will of course remain inviolate, it means that we have free access to all information relating to half of the invading English forces, along with the very strong possibility of complete access to information about all of it, once the two armies meet up. How fluent is your French?"

"It's not," I said. "Why do you ask?"

"Curiosity. Here's another question, but think carefully before you answer it. Has anyone ever identified you as a Scot from the way you speak Latin?"

"No," I said. "Can you?"

"My opinion's not to be trusted. I'm a Scot myself, so I might not notice a distinctive element in your voice."

"Is that important?"

"It could be, were you to live and move among Englishmen for a while."

"And why might I choose to live among Englishmen?" The question sounded sheepish even to my own ears.

"Because the realm requires you to, Father James." I heard the words clearly, but my comprehension had not quite caught up to my premonition. "Thomas—my cousin Lionel—has been living a very lonely existence recently. I feel sure it would be beneficial both to his spiritual and his physical well-being had he someone with whom to share his duties, someone dependable and trustworthy whom he has known for years."

I met his gaze squarely. "That might be true, Canon," I said. "But where would he find such a man, so advantageously?"

"Within the tabernacle that sustains us all, Father James—within God's will. In a more worldly sense, though, he could easily meet him here in Glasgow when he comes to visit me within the week—a fortuitous reunion with an old friend and fellow student from his days in France."

"I see," I said. "And can you tell me how it would benefit the realm if, as you say, I were somehow able to join Father Thomas?"

The canon smiled. "I remember the way your eyes opened wide when I told you where he was—entrenched as a member of the Earl of Surrey's household. You saw the possible advantages at once—the value of our having sympathetic eyes and ears in the enemy camp. The only thing missing now is the presence of an organizer who can take what he sees and hears and pass it along to us. Father Thomas can't do that, at least not safely, and he is far too valuable to risk endangering him."

"And I am not."

"You said that, Father James, not I. Your value is equally great, but differently allocated. God's ways can be obscure and known solely to Himself."

And so it was that my mission took an entirely different turn, putting me, for the first time in my life, in the position of a spy.

Instead of returning to Stirling after my meeting with Canon Lamberton as I had been instructed, I took the time to write a long letter to Will and Andrew Murray, explaining what had emerged in the course of my discussions with the canon, and the opportunity that had arisen to give us access to confidential information inside the enemy camp. I closed with a promise that they would soon be hearing from me with information drawn directly from the horse's mouth. There was an element of danger involved in setting down such information in a letter, of course, but every travelling priest carried letters with him wherever he went. That was a commonplace of clerical life. Information and the dissemination of it were the lifeblood of the religious world, and one undistinguished letter among so many others would attract no attention from anyone I had to fear—more so, I thought, if the courier delivering it had no knowledge of its importance. And so I enclosed my letter inside another, this

one addressed to my recent benefactor, the abbot of
Stirling Abbey, requesting that he pass on the enclosed
missive as quickly as possible to "my cousin Will." I
entrusted the package to Canon Lamberton with a
request that he send it to Stirling with the next courier
heading that way.

With that safely taken care of, I travelled to
Berwick with Father Thomas, who introduced me to
Earl Warrenne's clerical staff there as an old friend,
Father Jacques de la Pierre, whom he had known when
he was a seminarian in Paris. He explained that I
hailed from the Basque region in the far south and that
I spoke no English at all, in addition to which my
French was so heavily accented that it was virtually
indecipherable even to Frenchmen. I had been sent to
him, he claimed, bearing messages from the Bishop of
Paris, who was himself a Basque speaker and a close
friend of Pope Boniface, and such was the tone of
mysticism in which he spoke of those unspecified
messages that everyone believed I had been sent
because my way of speaking was something of a papal
code in itself.

I enjoyed being reunited with Thomas, for our
earlier friendship, though fairly brief, had been a close
one, born of the necessary intimacy of hard times
shared in far-off places as penniless, hard-working
students, and our first meeting after a long gap of years
was an occasion for sharing nostalgic memories. The
pleasure lasted beyond the reminiscences, though, and
we soon fell to talking easily about the ramifications

of Canon Lamberton's plan for us. I was surprised afterwards, I recall, by how easily I set aside my own misgivings and committed myself to a course that involved deceit on a grand scale. I—or we, since Thomas was included with me—had absolutely no reason to fear being caught, he assured me, because priests were anonymous and faceless, and nowhere more so than in a military camp, where we were tolerated as being there to serve as interlocutors between fighting men and their God. Beyond that we were ignored, as we were unnecessary to the successful prosecution of warfare.

All my friend's assurances notwithstanding, though, I was thoroughly terrified during my first few days among the English, acutely aware that I was in the very belly of the beast. I had not known what to expect on first arriving there, but the reality had been both striking and disconcerting, because until that time I had never associated the word *alien* with any specific person or society. Yet *alien* was the word that came to me on my arrival in the English camp and stayed with me for a long time afterwards, because *everything* about the place was unfamiliar to me. Even the clothing people wore was different, influenced by Earl Warrenne himself, who was a stickler for deportment and decorum. Commanders could be distinguished from their subordinates at a single glance, set apart more by the quality and colours of their clothing than by any other visible sign of rank. But I noticed the general conduct of the camp's inhabitants was different, too. Things like morale and confidence varied widely from unit to unit, and language differences could be so radical that the rank and file of units from different areas of England were often unable to speak to one another.

In those first days I was constantly waiting for someone to address me in the Basque tongue and expose me as a fraud. No one ever did, and my fears faded rapidly once I found I was accepted without question and then—as Thomas had predicted—generally ignored.

Much of my new-found sense of well-being undeniably sprang from the fact that I felt safe again in a religious community, where the politics of God and His Church took precedence over all else and where the racial origins of the community members were of no real significance. All such human differences were nullified by the common language of Latin, so that French *curés* spoke easily with their German, Dutch, Spanish, or Danish counterparts.

Within two weeks of joining the chaplaincy of the Earl of Surrey's camp, I had spoken with the earl himself, or rather been addressed by him, on three occasions, and on the third of those he was accompanied by Hugh de Cressingham, King Edward's treasurer for Scotland, who had newly arrived from Newcastle. Earl Warrenne had come to speak to Father Thomas, of course; I was permitted to be present because I was a priest, known to be working closely with Father Thomas on business for King Edward and Pope Boniface, who were, at that time, engaged in secretive diplomatic negotiations having to do with the highly sensitive business of Church, state, and taxation.

Lord John greeted me with a curt yet courteous nod and thereafter ignored me—he had been told I spoke no English. He introduced Cressingham to Thomas before grasping my friend by the elbow and leading him aside by two paces to speak quietly into his ear. Cressingham stood watching them, content merely to wait, and I, knowing myself unobserved, made use of the opportunity to look closely, and I will admit critically, at the man who was so wholeheartedly detested by everyone in Scotland.

He was not an attractive man, in any sense of the word. Tall and grotesquely corpulent, he was cursed with a sallow, much-spotted complexion and pendulous, clean-shaven jowls that weighed down the lower half of his face and drew attention to the slackness of a loose, pendulous lower lip. He wore his hair to his shoulders uncombed and tied with a white ribbon, the only spot of brightness that he wore. I paid particular attention to his clothing, for I had been told that he spent inordinate amounts of money on rich and sumptuous clothing, all of it black and all of it especially made to disguise his obesity and supposedly to render him less physically repulsive. The man seemed completely oblivious to the reality that it was not his corpulence that made him so widely detested. The hatred and disgust he inspired was due entirely to his offensive, repugnant personality and his rapacious, merciless dedication to bankrupting Scotland and everyone who lived therein.

As I stood observing him, I felt my skin crawling with an intense dislike akin to loathing. It was a sensation new to me at that time, and the recognition of it shocked me deeply, for my lifelong training had taught me to abhor such feelings towards my fellow men. Though I was to remember it many times over the years afterwards and seek to absolve myself of the guilt I felt because of it, I was never able to renounce it completely. Hugh de Cressingham was the most instantly despicable man I ever encountered. There was no single element of his being that offered a hint of redemption.

I heard my name, and I looked quickly towards Thomas, who was waiting for a response to whatever he had said.

"Forgive me, Father Thomas," I replied, broadening my vowels ludicrously and slowing my speech in what Thomas had assured me was the speech pattern used by residents in what he called *le Pays basque*. "I was at home in the Pyrenees."

He grunted in acceptance, then said, still in French, "I was saying that Lord John here is dispatching a delegation to Paisley Abbey to collect some valuable documents from the archives there, documents relating to King Edward's status as Lord Protector of the Realm. He wants us to accompany them as far as Paisley, for safety's sake, and then to carry additional dispatches onward, on his behalf, to Bishop Bek of Durham, who is presently believed to be in Glasgow."

I shrugged, glancing at Earl Warrenne as though I were almost disinterested, and added, "So, we go?"

"Just so," Thomas agreed. "We go."

"Today?"

"No, tomorrow morning. Lord John's people are copying the dispatches we are to carry, and they will have them ready for us by tonight."

I shrugged again, taking great care to avoid looking again at the hulking figure of the Treacherer. Within a few moments the earl finished his business with Thomas and dismissed him with a wave of the hand before striding away, followed by Cressingham and leaving me with the distinct impression that his tolerance for the King's treasurer was no greater than my own.

"So we are bound for Glasgow," I said as soon as we were out of earshot. "What brought that about?"

"I have no idea. The man simply came striding by—have you noticed that he strides, by the way? He doesn't simply walk, like other men. He strides."

"I've noticed, yes. So he came striding by … and what?"

"He saw me, stopped in his tracks, and told me he was sending me north with this delegation bound for Paisley."

"But I can't go to Paisley," I said. "Not if I'm to remain a Basque. I trained there, in the abbey, and my cousin Malcolm is still the librarian and archivist there. I'll be recognized the minute I set foot in the place, and no doubt the others in your delegation would be very interested to learn that I'm a Scot after all."

"Peace, Jamie. The man said we were to travel *as far* as Paisley with the others, and then we are to strike on past to Glasgow and Bek."

"And what if Bek is not *in* Glasgow?"

"Then we'll have to find him."

"That could take weeks. And we haven't got weeks to waste. We need to get to Stirling. That's our first priority."

"Then make a special plea in your prayers that he be elsewhere when we reach Glasgow, for if he is there, he might well answer Warrenne's letter directly and send us straight back here with it. And if it turns out he is elsewhere, we'll be able to send someone from Glasgow to find him, without going ourselves."

We went about our business for the remainder of the day until it came time to take delivery of the dispatches for Bishop Bek. And the next morning we travelled north obediently.

We parted company with the other delegates before we reached Paisley, and we made our way directly to the cathedral in Glasgow. We had barely settled ourselves at the table in the room we had been shown to when, greatly to my surprise, for I knew that he must be busy beyond belief with diocesan affairs, with little time for unexpected guests, Canon Lamberton himself swept in. He welcomed us both warmly, expressing his own surprise to see us there when he had thought us safely lodged with Earl

Warrenne. The first thought that had crossed his mind, of course, was that our illicit activities had been detected and we had been banished, but then he realized that had we been caught spying in the enemy camp we would have been hanged—after being tortured to find out what we had learned.

I quickly set his mind at ease and told him why we were there, that we had brought confidential dispatches from the earl himself to Bishop Bek, and he frowned, though whether from displeasure at our mission or at the mere mention of Bek's name I could not tell. Bek was not in Glasgow, he told us, and he did not know where the man was.

"We have to find him, Canon," I said. "Have you no slightest notion where he might be?"

"None at all. He barely spoke to me in all the time he was here. He could be back in England by now, for all I know. Though I doubt that. He has work to do on his master's behalf, and he'll be here until it's done. You will simply have to wait here for him to return, or for someone to come along who can take you to him."

"You know we can't afford to simply sit around idly waiting, Canon. We should be in the English camp, doing what you sent us there to do."

"You could leave the dispatches here for him and go back."

"Someone might be curious why we did not wait and complete our task. If he has responses to anything, we'll be expected to deliver them to the earl."

"Hmm." He had been holding a folded letter in his hand when he entered the room, and now he held it out to me wordlessly. I took it from him and held it towards the nearest light, peering at the inscription.

"This is my letter," I said, surprised. "The one I asked you to send to Stirling. Why didn't you send it?"

"I did. The priest who carried it collapsed and died within a few miles of here on the very day he left. Sadly, he was not found for more than a week, and then the discovery was accidental. It was the smell that was found, in truth, for the man himself was not known to be missing before his body was discovered. The wallet he was carrying was returned to me, since I had sent him out on his last journey." He grimaced. "I was looking at it this very afternoon, wondering what to do with it—send it to you or await your return—when word came to me that you were here. Was it important, your letter to the abbot?"

"No." I had been fingering the letter, squeezing it, and now I tore it open, exposing the other one inside it. "*This* was important, though. It's to Will, explaining what I've been doing among the English—or what I was about to start doing." I held it up now between finger and thumb, brandishing it gently as thoughts began to click into place in my mind. "Now I really have to find Bek—but not too soon."

Father Thomas gave me a puzzled look. "What does that mean?"

I turned back to Lamberton, still shaking the letter in my hand. "I have to talk to Will. I need to explain this to him. He has not heard a single word from me in weeks, so he'll be wondering what's wrong. How long will it take to get to Stirling in a hurry?"

"It's about thirty miles. Two days, mayhap three, depending on the weather and your own strength and stamina."

"Good, then I'll need a week. Three days there, three days back, and one day with Will and Andrew. In the meantime, we'll have to make a show of hunting for Bek. Where is he *least* likely to have gone?"

"God alone knows," Lamberton muttered. "Edinburgh, St. Andrews, Scone, Paisley—he could be anywhere. What are you driving at?"

"Priorities, Canon Lamberton. I need to talk with Will, face to face. To do that, I need to go to Stirling, where he's headed. So I'll say we went to Stirling looking for Bek at the abbey. He didn't tell anyone where he was going, so he can't expect to be easily found. As soon as I've seen Will and Andrew, I'll come back here. If Bek's back by then, so be it. If he's not, then I might wait, depending on what Will and Andrew have to say about it. By that time, we'll have been away from Earl Warrenne for about two weeks, and he'll be the first to see the folly of simply sitting around waiting and wasting any more time than we've already lost."

CHAPTER TWENTY-THREE

THE ENEMY CAMP

No matter how many times I see the castle at Stirling, it always leaves me with a fresh sense of wonder, due in no small measure to the changes I have noted over the years since I saw it first. When I was a young lad barely out of boyhood, the place was already formidable, perched atop its great, towering crag and overlooking all the land below. But in those days its main fortifications were wooden palisades of heavy logs—enormous logs, to be sure, but logs nonetheless—backed with ramparts of packed and hardened clay. King Alexander, an admirer of Edward Plantagenet's prowess and opinions on all things military, had already begun replacing those with walls of stone, copying the new castles the English King had started to build everywhere, and that task has been continuing ever since.

Now, five decades later, the incessant construction has brought about changes that would have seemed incredible in those earliest days. The wooden palisades are all gone, replaced by massive walls of sculpted stone that announce the place, even from afar, as being impregnable, and those walls continue to increase in height and bulk from day to day even now, fed by an unending stream of labourers and masons, so that, after an interval of mere months, a returning visitor may perceive great changes in the sweep or shape of a certain wall, or the height of a flanking tower, signs of growing strength adding to the aura of invincibility that surrounds the place.

Father Thomas and I rode into Stirling village from the south, riding our mounts openly beneath the slopes of the great crag and relying on our obvious religious trappings to suggest to anyone curious enough to look that we were on our way east to Cambuskenneth, the abbey that had graced Stirling's name for nigh on two hundred years. The English garrison was pent up within the castle's walls that day and no one appeared to take any notice of us as we passed by, making our way along the road that led out north from the castle crag towards Stirling Bridge and the causeway that Will and Andrew and I had talked about a few weeks earlier. As I crossed the bridge this time, my faculties were on high alert, and I took careful note of all the details that I had never thought to look for in times past.

I looked eagerly for the bright green water weeds that Will had spoken of, but saw nothing of the kind. Instead, I was vaguely disappointed to see that much of the land on both sides of the narrow causeway appeared to be firm and solid, some of it even culti- vated. I looked farther afield, comparing what I saw to what I remembered of Will's description of the terrain. The causeway was just as he had described it: long and straight and built up above the surrounding land, but so narrow that only one wagon, or two men riding abreast, could cross at a time, and there were slightly widened sections at both ends of the bridge, fashioned to permit one wagon to wait while another crossed towards it. Below the causeway, on each side, the land was flat, featureless, and largely dry, with what appeared to be sluggish, shallow channels of water meandering among low, reed-covered rises. *Marshy* was the word that came to me as I looked at it, but from what Will had described, I had been expecting wide expanses of wet, glistening mud flats offering transit solely to the intrepid local folk.

The causeway rose slightly as we approached the bridge, and the clattering of our mounts' hooves on the wooden deck was amplified by the low wooden walls on either side. Halfway across, I kneed my horse to one side and looked down into the river beneath us. It was fairly narrow, a clear channel less than twenty paces wide, I estimated, its waters black and seemingly still and bordered on either side with long, trailing weeds.

Thomas had stopped when I did, and now he kneed his mount forward until he could see what I was looking at. He sniffed loudly and looked at me from beneath a raised eyebrow.

"So that's the mighty Forth," he said. "It looks cold. And deep. An armoured man would vanish quickly, falling in there."

"Any man would," I said, surprised by his comment. "Unless he could swim."

"Can't swim in armour," he said, and swung his horse's head away to move on, leaving me wondering, despite the obvious inference, what had provoked him to think of drowning armoured men. I had not told him about Will and Andrew's discussion on that very topic.

We rode for a mile or so in silence after that, following the causeway to its end and then leaving the road to head overland towards the jutting upthrust of the Abbey Craig, the pillar of rock that lay across the Forth from its twin, the giant crag that was crowned by the castle itself, which was visible at our backs, a mile and a half away. Behind the Abbey Craig, the swell of the Ochil Hills was clearly visible, and we steered our mounts towards them, keeping the heights of the Abbey Craig on our right.

I had been hearing the raucous cawing of crows and rooks in the distance for some time, and the noise grew louder as we approached the far edge of the carse, prompting me to draw rein and stand in my stirrups, scanning the skyline ahead of us for a sight of the birds, but there was nothing to see.

"Trees," my companion murmured. The word was barely audible, more for his own ears than mine, I felt.

"What about them?"

His eyes widened and he sat up straighter. "What about what?"

"*Trees*, you said."

"Ah! Forgive me, didn't know I'd spoken aloud. Trees fascinate me. Especially the ones that grow in places like that." He waved a hand towards the great crag. "Look at the trees at the base of the crag over there. It's all shut in—a damp, fetid place, nurtured by the swampy valley of the river, so everything's always green and moist, the rocks and the moss and even the trees. No one ever cuts down trees in there, because they cling to the rocks of the cliff sides, their roots exposed and moss-grown like everything else. In fact the roots sometimes look thicker than the trees themselves. I lived near a place like that when I was in France, and it was like having my own personal cathedral—a dark, steep-sided ravine with light filtering down through trees that grew above a wide, running stream, clinging by their outstretched fantastical roots to the vertical slabs of fractured stone that formed the sides of the nave."

I was gazing at him in astonishment, leaving my horse to pick its own way forward over open ground, and Thomas glanced at me and grinned, evidently delighted by the shock he must have seen on my face. "It's true," he said. "I spent months trying to decide if I should become a priest or run from the seminary and live the life of an anchorite in my favourite ravine among God's beautiful trees."

Unable to think of a single word to say in response to that, I turned my eyes away to look again for the birds, for the noise they were making had grown intolerable, and I was surprised to note that we were no longer on the flat surface of the carse. A quick turn of my head told me that we had left the flats and our horses were following a faintly defined track that was little more than a game trail.

"We're climbing," I said.

Thomas looked around, almost furtively, before answering, "We are. Probably because we're going uphill."

I shook my head at his obtuseness, then decided to ignore him and concentrated on the path ahead. I was still trying to locate the source of the noisy birds, but the trees above and ahead of us continued to conceal them.

The path we were following was rising rather more steeply here, curving discernibly to the right as it went, and I nudged my horse forward, moving in front of Thomas and increasing my speed to a canter. A copse up ahead seemed to move away from me as I approached and began to skirt it, an illusion created by my own speed and the curve of my approach, but as the open space behind the copse came into view, it exposed a sight that was no illusion. I heard Thomas's indrawn hiss of breath as he saw it, too, and I hauled on my reins, pulling my horse back hard enough to make it rear in outraged complaint.

On the hillside above us, two naked men, recently hanged, dangled side by side from the single outstretched limb of a dead tree. There was no slightest breath of wind where we were, and yet the corpses above us turned slowly on the ends of their ropes. We exchanged glances and Thomas nodded, and we made our way cautiously forward.

The birds were visible now, their noise deafening as they gyred and swooped around the dead men like black leaves swept up in a whirlwind. And I was appalled to see that on the hillside directly below the two dead men, capering about like a man possessed, was a third man, wearing a startlingly bright green jerkin and wielding a long, leafy branch or sapling that he was using to beat the corpses above his head.

"What in God's holy name is happening here? What kind of madman flogs dead men?"

"He's not flogging them," Thomas said. "He's fighting off the birds. He must have known the men. But you're right about him being a madman. He must be mad even to try that. What can he hope to achieve? We had best offer him some comfort."

"He won't hear you, Thomas. They must be newly hanged, those two."

"Aye, within an hour or two. He's kept the birds off them thus far."

As he spoke I sensed a sudden stillness and looked back to see the man poised motionless now, peering down at us like a startled deer. Before I could even open my mouth to call to him, though, he bounded down the slope away from us, gaining speed with every running leap until he vanished from our sight, concealed by the swell of the hillside.

"We should go after him," I said half-heartedly.

"Why? You'd never catch him," Thomas said. "And even if you did, what then? Let's take a closer look at his friends, if that's who they were. What could they have done, I wonder, to be hanged naked? As if mere death by hanging weren't bad enough."

Moments later we were within ten paces of the hanged men, and could see that not only were the men naked but they had been mutilated, their genitals severed. Their thighs and legs were coated with dried blood.

"This is Will's work," I said.

Thomas swung towards me, wide-eyed. "Your cousin? How can you even say such a thing without knowing what happened?"

"It was Will. These were Will's men."

"Fine. I'll believe you. But how can you be so sure?"

"Because these two were condemned for gross sexual sins—for brutal, mindless violation of some unfortunate soul. Will has no mercy for such creatures."

"This outlawed cousin of yours disapproves of outlawry? Does he then deem himself to be some kind of godlike being? Is he on some divine mission?"

I looked at him with reproach. "No, Thomas, he does not think himself a god of any kind. Had you ever met him you would know that he is the last person who could be accused of such a thing. And if he has a mission, it is to save our realm."

"But we don't even know Wallace is here. We've

seen neither hide nor hair of him or any of his men."

I gazed about me, studying the grass. "He's camped close by, judging by the way the ground's been trampled here. We'll find him soon, or he'll find us."

He found us, or his people did, less than a mile from the scene of the hangings. We had climbed several hundred feet, and the track we were following had changed dramatically, growing steeper and more dangerous as the hillside became more mountainous. At one point, a shoulder of rock thrust out from the side of the hill, forming what appeared to be a flat wall as we approached it, and our path narrowed and almost pinched out around the base of it, the ground beneath our horses' hooves dropping away precipitously to our left. I estimated the drop to be perhaps twice my own height, hardly sufficient to strike terror into anyone's soul, but nonetheless dangerous enough to inspire caution in those who had to travel this way. I was happy to see the gentle slope that lay on the far side, falling down and to our right again. And there we saw four men who were struggling to restrain a fifth.

"That's the fellow who ran away," Thomas said. "The crow fighter."

The bright green jerkin was unmistakable, and even as I took note of it his captors subdued him and two of them began to lead him away, holding him tightly by the arms. One of the others came towards us, smiling broadly.

"Father Jamie!" he shouted. "Well met! Will'll be right glad to see ye."

"And I him," I said. "It's Rab, isn't it?"

He looked pleased that I remembered him. "Aye, Faither, that's me. C'mon, I'll tak ye right to him."

"My thanks. Tell me, who was that fellow you were struggling with?"

"Och, him? That's Daft Danny. He's no' a' there, ye ken? Maist o' the time ye'd never see or hear him, he's that quiet, but we hung his brither Geordie this mornin', alang wi' a right wild whoreson cried Henderson. Geordie wisna much cleverer than Danny, but he fell in wi' a bad crew when he met the Hendersons, and it got him hung. An' poor Danny canna handle it."

"They ravaged a woman?" Thomas asked.

Rab turned to him with a look that said plainly, "And who might you be?"

"This is Father Thomas, Rab, a friend of mine from long ago."

Rab nodded. "Aye. God love ye, Faither Thomas, it wis worse nor that. A wild laddie might ravage a nest frae time to time—herryin' it, we say here—until he's telt no' to do it again. This wasna the same kind o' thing at a'. There was five o' them, an' they found a woman and twa young lasses a' their lane in a farmhouse no' far frae here. They herried the women, then butchered them and stole everythin' they could carry. And they burnt the hoose."

"How do you know all that?"

"Twa monks frae Stirlin' Abbey was nearby and saw what happened. They came straight to Will as soon as it was safe, and they had five guid descriptions o' the men. We kent the five o' them, an' fower o' them wis nae surprise. The fifth was Geordie Miller, though. He hardly had the wit to ken what they were doin' wasna right, but he was there an' he was part o' it. Henderson himsel' and Geordie was the only ones that came back. But the ither three are dead men already, nae matter where they went. They'll turn up someday, an' when they do …"

"So these men were tried and hanged on Will Wallace's orders?" Thomas asked.

"Tried!" Rab said, his voice dripping with scorn. "Naebody had any need to try anythin'. Henderson was drenched in blood and he was carryin' a bag fu' o' weemin's stuff, pots an' needles and stuff he could sell. Will took one look in the bag and asked the monks if Henderson was one o' the men they'd seen. They said he was the leader, an' that was that. Will said we was to hang them right then and there."

I asked him, "What will you do with the brother?"

"Nothin'," Rab said. "There's nae harm in him. He'll forget it ever happened and he'll settle himsel' again, and we'll look out for him in the meanwhile."

"Good," I said. "Now take us to my cousin, if you will, for I should have been here days ago and he's probably wondering what's happened to me."

"I don't like that at all. It's dangerous and it's foolhardy."

"What's foolhardy about it? We're there by invitation, Will."

"No, you're there by tomfoolery, and someone's going to discover that sooner or later. I want you out."

"Why? Because I'm your cousin? Would you be as angry if Thomas was in this alone?"

Will was as angry as he had ever been with me, but I was equally upset at him. He sat glaring at me from across the table, radiating hostility and displeasure, and the others present—Andrew Murray, Sandy Pilche, and Ewan Scrymgeour's cousin Alexander, who appeared to be permanently attached to my cousin nowadays—were all being unnaturally silent, afraid, I had no doubt, of interrupting and thereby incurring Will's wrath. But my blood was up and I was beyond caring about Will's displeasure, because all I could see was his stubbornness and his lack of imagination.

I bit back on the bitter words in my mouth and restrained myself from banging my fist on the tabletop. "Will," I said, hearing the impatience in my own voice, "there's very little danger here. We are on the Church's business, on the business of the Pope himself, and no one in England, from the King on down, wants to risk of offending the Holy Father at this time. There is too much at stake, with King Edward suing for papal judgments in his favour against King Philip in France, and in Gascony, as well as here in Scotland. The Archbishopric of York is trying yet again, despite a hundred reversals, to win the Pope's permission to appoint English bishops to Scottish sees. All of these judgments are pending, so all the noblemen of England who find themselves in Scotland today are scurrying

around on tiptoes whispering, for fear of doing or
saying anything that might upset the Church, the Pope,
or the cardinals and influence the outcome of Edward's
plans. Besides, Thomas and I are in a position of trust
inside the enemy camp, so no one is going to question
us or what we do. We are churchmen, and no one
attached to the armies cares what we do."

"Aye, you are in a position of trust," Will growled,
his voice quieter, though the anger still bubbled in his
throat. "And what you are proposing is a breach of that
trust, the more heinous because you are both priests."

"Oh, listen to yourself, Will Wallace! That is
ludicrous! *Heinous*? A heinous breach of trust? For
counteracting the breach of trust that brought an
invading English army across our borders? They have
gone far beyond threats, Will. God knows I never
thought to have to tell *you* that. You were the one who
brought it home to me. And Thomas and I, as priests
and patriots, have been given an opportunity to learn,
for your benefit and for the good of all of Scotland,
foreknowledge of how they intend to proceed with
their military campaign to steal our realm from under
us. I see no sin in that, and certainly no shame."

"Jamie is right, Will."

This was the first time anyone else had spoken up
since Will and I had begun our altercation, and it was
not surprising that it should be Andrew. Will turned his
head slightly and looked at him through narrowed
eyes, though he said nothing, and Andrew stared right
back at him and continued.

"If it were anyone else coming to you with this information you would not be able to believe your good fortune. Eyes and ears in the enemy camp! And not merely in their camp but in the command centre itself, and privy to the very thoughts and musings of the enemy leaders. Admit it, Will. This is an undreamed-of advantage. But you don't want to accept it because it entails a risk to your cousin, your closest and dearest relative. Your emotions are blinding you to the advantages the situation offers all of us."

Will was glowering at me again while Andrew spoke, and when the Highlander had finished he answered him with his eyes still on me. "Jamie could be killed. His priestly rank would not protect him if he was caught spying."

"He's a grown man, Will, and a trusted and respected cleric. Think you he has not thought about the risk involved?" He turned to me. "Father James, have you considered the possibility that you might die in doing what you might be able to do here?"

"I have, and I think it's unlikely," I answered. "All we would do is pay heed to what we hear and pass on the information through our usual clerical channels. Besides, if the information I supplied were to save the life of even one man in battle, then I would gladly go to God as a martyr for the cause of the realm."

Will's clenched fist hit the table with the force of a hard-swung axe, spilling ale from a nearby tankard, but when he spoke, it was not the angry roar everyone had expected. "You're right," he said, his voice sounding choked and tight. "Damnation, and may God forgive me, you're right."

"So now what?" Andrew said. "How do we make the most of this opportunity? And how do we make sure that any word from Thomas or Jamie reaches us as quickly as possible?"

I had the answer to that question before it was ever asked. The most obvious way was to entrust the delivery to the priests and monks who were always moving throughout the countryside, but I had concluded that that was not the most efficient way of doing things, for most of those monks and priests went everywhere on foot, which made them too slow. The other deterrent in my eyes was an uncharitable one, but no less valid. Priests and monks were men who spent most of their lives alone. It was a reality of our calling. When they did foregather with their peers, therefore, they tended to talk unguardedly, particularly if they were speaking in Latin. I do not mean they were knowingly careless in their speech, for most of them were aware of a need for confidentiality when carrying messages. They tended, nevertheless, to be free in their normal parlance, uncaring of being overheard among their equals, and trusting in the natural goodness of mankind to guarantee discretion regarding what might be overheard. In my mind, that disqualified most priests from consideration as clandestine messengers, particularly now, when the Scots and English armies were almost cheek by jowl and there were as many English priests as Scots in any gathering of clerics.

Instead, I suggested—and it was agreed—that we would maintain a small team of six trusted young Scots priests, chosen for their stamina and fitness, and infiltrated into the enemy camp as primary messengers. Priests and monks came and went constantly to and from the army encampment, generally being so ubiquitous that the camp guards rarely challenged them, so the odds were in favour of our six priests escaping notice. The six would work in pairs, with one man, a "walker," on duty in the enemy camp while his cohort, a "runner" dressed in layman's clothing, would be camped nearby, yet far enough removed—a mile or so away—to be safe from discovery by English patrols. The walker would walk each day to where his companion waited and pass on whatever information we had gathered since the day before, and the runner would run with it to a team of mounted messengers who would be camped roughly three miles from the enemy encampment. Andrew's riders would then carry the dispatches to the Scots commanders, working in two-mile relays should speed and necessity dictate such a need.

It was not a perfect scheme, and we had little time to implement it, but we were hopeful that once the six messengers were in place in the enemy encampment, our plan would quickly bear fruit.

Three days later, Father Thomas and I were on the road again, moving quickly. First we made our way back to Glasgow, where we found the ill-tempered and

abrasive Bishop Bek in residence and resentful that we
had not awaited his return instead of rushing off to
look for him. I endured his abuse with patience, since
there was no point in attempting to deflect it, and
eventually took possession of his response to Earl
Warrenne, that being the original purpose, of course,
for our excursion to Glasgow. From there, we travelled
south and east again under threatening, lead-coloured
skies to Lanark, there to rejoin the earl, who had
finally brought his army up from Berwick. We were
not permitted to rest, though, for the army was
preparing to march again the day after we arrived. And
so I called a somewhat hurried gathering of our people
and alerted them about what to expect in the next day.
We allocated duty times for our runners and walkers,
but we could do no more than hope that Andrew's
riders were being vigilant out there, anticipating what
might happen once the army began to move.

The next day, when we set out from Lanark, was
the second-from-last day of August, and the sun had
sunk without being seen at all the day before, leaving
everyone edgily aware that bad weather might well be
in the offing. Sure enough, the heavens opened in the
darkness before dawn and the rain poured in torrents
until long after darkness fell again that night, inun-
dating the entire countryside.

De Warrenne's people had considered postponing
the march that morning, but the decision was not theirs
to make, and the earl, having belatedly decided to
move northward, was not now disposed to be dissuaded,

so the order was soon given to set out, in the belief that the storm was too violent to endure and would therefore pass quickly. That was a disastrous decision, and its consequences became more and more obvious throughout the day in the degenerating condition of the terrain through which the army struggled. After hours of unremitting downpour, wagon wheels were sinking to the axles in freshly churned mud, and men and horses were slipping and floundering and falling helplessly everywhere I looked. We covered less than four miles that first day, and the entire effort amounted to a punishing, debilitating study in futility that infuriated everyone from the Earl of Surrey down to the meanest groom among the horse lines.

Summer, in the sense of sustained periods of fine weather as enjoyed by the English and French during July, August, and September, is never a reliable phenomenon in Scotland, but if there is to be a spell of warm weather in any given year, the probability is high that it will occur at the end of August or in the early part of September. The year of our Lord 1297 was an exception. The weather turned foul on the penultimate day of August and it rained incessantly for seven days, with never the slightest sign of sunshine. Conditions along the route of the English march were dreadful, and the army floundered despairingly, men and beasts soaked to the skin without hope of relief, battling their way across broken, hostile terrain and through swollen, dangerous streams, and often wallowing in deep mud on softer ground, making little forward progress at even the best of times. The Welsh archers who provided the main strength of Warrenne's unmounted contingent would have been helpless in the face of an unexpected attack during that entire week, for their bows were useless. Every man among them had his precious bowstrings carefully rolled up and tucked away in the driest, warmest hiding places they could devise—usually in tightly wrapped wax-coated packages of oiled cloth carried next to their skin—since nothing could be more useless than a damp bowstring on a Welsh longbow. The archers themselves were no more or no less miserable than anyone else on that hellish march, and I include myself and my religious brethren among that number, but at least the other marchers could have fought, had the need arisen. Rain is no great deterrent to using a sword, a spear, or for that matter a mace or an axe. Of course, any enemy force foolhardy enough to attack would have faced the same hardships, and so everyone dismissed the thought of human enemies. The sodden countryside and the ceaseless rain were enemy enough throughout that journey.

The score of us in the clerical detachment attached to the Earl of Surrey's entourage travelled in five large, solid wagons, each pulled by a team of four horses and covered with a sturdy roof of double-thick sailcloth for the protection of the valuable documents contained within the carts. For this reason we were able to sleep in relatively dry comfort each night, but we quickly learned that in times of adversity there are disadvantages to match every advantage. The wagons were ours, and we had to handle them and care for them ourselves, for no one else had either the time or the inclination to assist us with our opulent transport. And so we spent most of each day manhandling horses and wagons—both of them heavy, awkward, and recalcitrant—until we were so exhausted that we could scarcely keep our eyes open, despite our misery. And yet we knew that we were fortunate and truly privileged, because it was plain that we, among all the varied elements of Surrey's army, were set apart from the misery and tribulations being suffered by everyone else.

For the rank-and-filers of Surrey's army, the most mundane tasks associated with setting and breaking camp each day quickly became torturous. The pitching and dismantling of tents was a nightmarish struggle, every evening and every morning, with slimy, water-soaked leather panels or equally heavy sodden sailcloth tenting and rough, thick hempen ropes with wet, obdurate knots. For that reason, very few tents were pitched on that march, most of the knights and men-at-arms and all the footmen preferring to find whatever shelter they could by themselves, since they could be no wetter or colder than they already were. None but the senior commanders slept under tents, the large, high-peaked rectangular kind known as pavilions, and that was more a matter of convention and dignity than one of warmth or shelter, for the very fabric of their roofs and walls was saturated with rain,

and the ground on which they were erected was heavy
mud. And while it was true that fires could be lit
beneath the soaring roofs of the great tents, nothing
could be dried effectively there, and worse, the tents
themselves trapped the heavy smoke from the wet
wood burning in the braziers, making the atmosphere
almost unbreathable. Even the sleeping cots were wet,
their covers heavy and cold with dampness. And in
consequence of that general misery and squalor, there
was little talk at night before men slept. Men ate in
grumpy silence, unhappy with whatever food the
hapless cooks had managed to prepare, and then they
sought oblivion in sleep, hoping the rain would stop
before they woke again.

I heard the weather change finally, in the small
hours of morning on the sixth day of September,
because I was already astir, preparing to assist Father
Thomas in celebrating a pre-dawn Mass, and the abrupt
stillness when the rain stopped thundering on the
leather roof of the tented pavilion we were using as a
church caused both of us to look up. We looked at each
other with raised eyebrows—we were the only two
people there—smiled quickly, and returned to the sacrifice under way, but I know that I, at least, was unable to
focus completely upon it thereafter. Too many thoughts
and possibilities were now swirling in my mind, and I
wondered, not for the first time, how my friends had
fared in Stirling throughout the week-long deluge.

I had already been out of doors for an hour before
daybreak, enjoying birdsong for the first time in many

days and breathing deeply the fresh, clean air, and when the first rays of the sun lanced into a blue and cloudless sky, I imagined that everyone else would be as happy as I felt. I was soon disillusioned on that count. After a week of unrelenting rainfall, everything—clothing, bedding, tents, provisions, supplies, weapons, and livestock—was not merely soaked, but much of it had begun to grow mouldy. I realized that it would take much more than the promise of a bright, dry day to lighten the loads—both physical and emotional—of the bedraggled host that surrounded me.

By then, though, couriers had arrived from Stirling Castle, reporting the presence of "a large host of Scotch rogues" in the vicinity of the town, and the English commanders knew they had run out of time. And so the woebegone army took to the road again, hauling their rain-sodden possessions with them.

More than a week had passed since we had organized our system of messengers to ferry information from our camp to Stirling, but we had not sent out a single word in all that time other than that we had nothing to report. Our situation in the English camp, which had seemed so exciting and filled with potential for great success in duping the enemy, had produced nothing, thanks to the foulness of the weather.

CHAPTER TWENTY-FOUR

THE INVISIBLE
PRIEST

It was the eighth day of September, a Sunday, before we finally completed an entire day's march without being rained upon, and we arrived in the middle of that afternoon at the spot where we would spend our last night of that particular stage of this campaign. We were perhaps three miles from Stirling town, and the castle, clearly visible atop its soaring crag in the distance, seemed to beckon to us as the feverish activity of setting up another marching camp broke out yet again.

The surrounding countryside, so tranquil when it first came into view, was transformed within a single half-hour as the army spilled out of its line of march and became an amorphous, sprawling multitude of men and beasts and wheeled vehicles of all descriptions. We priests, the score of us, moved as one small part of the enormous mass, for our own role in this diurnal ritual was now as well known to us as the soldiers' were to them. Since it was my turn that day to drive the wagon I shared with three others, I guided my team into place in our five-wagon chaplains' procession to our assigned location and then set about the preparations for celebrating evening Masses in several locations, one for the Earl of Surrey and his personal entourage in the privacy of the big tented pavilion that served as the earl's private quarters, and a number of others throughout the vast encampment that was being created all around us.

We arrived at our allocated spot—always close by the earl's quarters—and quickly settled into our daily routine, drawing our five wagons together in a rough circle that we knew would be left unmolested by the soldiery who otherwise swept everywhere as they searched for the things they needed. While some of us, myself among them, began to unload necessities from the wagons, others of our number dug a central fire pit, while others went searching for stones with which to line the fire bed, and still others went to gather firewood. And writing about that now, I find myself a little in awe, for no one who has never been part of an army on the march can appreciate the difficulties involved in such seemingly simple activities. Unless you have been in such a situation, you might never think to question the ease of lighting a campfire. You dig a pit, line it with flat stones, and gather firewood to burn in it. It all seems perfectly straightforward—unless you are in the midst of an army of five or ten thousand men, with women and children in tow, all arriving in one place at the same time and all looking for the same materials.

We had all completed our various tasks by the time evening approached, and while everyone was waiting for the army cooks to prepare dinner, Thomas and I walked over to say Mass at Earl Warrenne's command centre, easily distinguishable with its cluster of imposing high-peaked pavilions topped with the brightly coloured banners and bannerets identifying the various noblemen and lesser knights of the commander's party. The centre was well sited, pitched on a hillside plateau above a tree-filled valley, with a fine view of Stirling to the northwest.

This had been the first day to pass without a drop of rain since we'd left Lanark, the third consecutive day of intermittently sunny skies, and it had taken this long for the effects of the week-long drenching to wear off. The crowd around the headquarters enclosure, awaiting the summons to table, was noisy and cheerfully animated as we picked our way among the throng, heading towards the earl's pavilion and the altar that had been erected inside it, Earl Warrenne was there in person, I saw, enjoying the sunshine in front of his pavilion and surrounded by most of the people represented by the banners and bannerets atop the surrounding poles.

I recognized the blue and yellow lion rampant banneret of Henry Percy, and I knew that he had arrived the day before from England, having ridden north with a small party of adherents. I had no way of recognizing Percy himself, never having knowingly set eyes upon the man, but I saw the massive figure of Hugh de

Cressingham standing at the earl's shoulder and then realized, disconcertingly, that his dark, glowering eyes were staring directly at me. I looked away at once and said something to Thomas. I told myself that Cressingham had never set eyes on me until that moment and I must therefore have imagined his interest in me, yet I was afraid to look back at him again for fear his gaze might still be following me. I could not quell my curiosity, though, and when I did glance back I saw that Cressingham now had his back turned towards me. I swallowed hard, relieved to be relieved, and put the thought of having been recognized out of my mind.

Only a few moments later, walking by Thomas's side in companionable silence, I became aware of raised voices somewhere in the near distance. I paid little attention at first, but then as the noise continued to grow, I stopped and turned towards the source of the sound, rising on my toes to see what was going on. Everyone else, though, turned to do the same at the same time, and so I saw nothing at all except a wall of broad backs.

Thomas nudged me. "What's happening? What is it?"

As I strained to see between the bodies ahead of me, I heard someone say, "Scotchman" or "Scotchmen." I heard someone else repeat it, and then another voice said something about "come to parley."

I turned back to Thomas. "Did you hear that?" I asked, mangling my French deliberately as any listener might expect from a Basque.

"Hear what? I heard nothing I could understand."

"They're saying there are Scotchmen here, to parley."

"Shit! Are you sure?"

"That's what I heard. Let's get closer."

I can think of few things more difficult than trying to conceal your curiosity and disguise your excitement when you are agog with surprise, when you suspect that matters of great moment are unfolding all around you but you do not really know what is going on, and most particularly when you are agonizingly aware that to betray the slightest sign of your excitement could be lethal. But of course while my inward coward was quaking with guilt and dismay, my outward persona betrayed nothing at all. I moved forward with the crowd, craning my neck and searching for information as eagerly as everyone else in the vicinity, and like them trying to make sense of the garbled scraps that came my way.

When I felt Thomas's hand grip my arm I almost leapt with fright. "Quick," he said. "The earl will need his chaplain." He spun away and I followed him. Within moments we were within hearing range of Warrenne and his coterie, taking a place standing slightly behind them as the crowd in front of them parted and swept to either side, clearing the way for a dismounted party of five to approach the pavilion. They were leading their horses and followed by a vigilant and hostile-looking phalanx of English guards. I immediately recognized these newcomers, for the

High Steward of Scotland, Lord James Stewart himself, was first among them. He was flanked by two of the proudest Gaelic mormaers in the realm of Scotland, both of them known to me by sight because both had had dealings with my employer, Bishop Wishart. They were Maol Choluim, the Earl of Lennox, whom the English called Malcolm, and Maol Iosa, Earl of Strathearn, whom most folk called Malise. Behind that trio, walking no less proudly but maintaining a distance of half a step behind the three leaders, walked two men whom I knew to be kinsmen of the High Steward. The mere sight of them filled me instantly with trepidation, since both were likely to recognize me. They were Sir Alexander Lindsay and Lord James's younger brother, Sir John Stewart, and both had shared a table with me at the Earl of Carrick's castle of Turnberry, the night we had been rousingly addressed by Father David de Moray.

Sure enough, as soon as the Steward's party came to a halt, Sir Alexander looked directly at me. I saw the exact moment when he recognized me and began to smile, then frowned. His eyes widened as he attempted to make sense of seeing me there in the English camp, and he opened his mouth as if to speak, then closed it quickly as the frantic quality of my frown and the furtive shake of my head made him bethink himself. I held my breath and waited to be challenged, sure that some sharp-eyed soul among the crowd must have noted our brief interaction. But no accusing shouts rang out. All eyes were on the two principals, the Earl of Surrey and the High Steward.

It was John de Warrenne, the Earl of Surrey, who spoke first, turning away from Cressingham, who was spluttering with indignation at the effrontery of these rebellious Scots interlopers.

"Lord James," he said civilly, managing to convey his surprise in the two words. "How come you here, to Stirling? My nephew Percy tells me he left you safely abed in Ayr mere weeks ago, so you will understand my surprise to see you here, and in such company." He waved a hand to indicate the two Scots earls. But Lord James was too old a fox to allow himself to be so easily placed on the defensive.

"We would have waited upon you in Stirling, Lord Warrenne," he replied, "but your constable there is much perturbed by the presence of a host of Scots under arms nearby. And so, aware that we, as Scots ourselves, might increase his unease by requesting entrance to his castle, we decided to come to meet you here."

"And how did you know we would be here?"

The Steward smiled. "All Scotland knows you are here, my lord—knows it and regrets it deeply."

"So why are you here? What would you have of us?"

"Words, Lord Warrenne. We come to exchange words, to mutual benefit. And we come alone in demonstration of good faith."

"Words ... On what topic, Lord James?"

"On that topic most important to all of us: the army waiting on the far side of Forth."

His words brought a silence that lasted until Warrenne replied, "Then here is no place to talk of it." He raised a hand in a signal to his guards, indicating that they should look after the visitors' horses, and half a dozen men stepped forward to obey, already reaching for the reins as the earl turned on his heel, his right hand sweeping out and around in an invitation to his guests to walk with him into his pavilion. A sigh of disappointment arose from the watching throng as the command group moved into the tent and a screen of guards stepped forward to safeguard their privacy.

I was about to turn away myself when Thomas plucked at my sleeve, and with a muttered "Come" led me through the entrance and into the pavilion's spacious interior. No sooner were we inside than Earl Warrenne beckoned to Thomas, and we both stopped.

"Father Thomas, I fear we must postpone the celebration of the Mass for now, for we have pressing business here. Will you wait until it is concluded?"

"Of course, my lord. The Sacrament cares not when it be celebrated, provided it be not ignored."

Thomas bowed deeply and the earl turned away, satisfied, and gave his attention to his unexpected guests. There was a period of activity as servers hurriedly cleared away the seats set out for Mass and replaced them with wooden chairs that they set around a heavy, oaken table. Mere weeks earlier, I would have

been astounded to see such a table in such a place, but
since then I had learned much about the Earl of Surrey
and how he went to war. His personal baggage train,
attended by his own retainers, was almost half as large
as the army's own supply train, and it carried all the
outward signs of wealth and privilege he deemed
appropriate to his age and station.

When the servants withdrew, he waved a hand
towards the table. "Sit where ye will," he said. "There
is no ranking here."

Even so, by the time everyone was seated, the
Scots were on one side of the table and the English—
Warrenne, Cressingham, and four more—were on the
other. The remaining people in the pavilion, Thomas
and I among them with three other priests, moved
away and stood lining the walls, waiting for whatever
might develop. I knew none of the four men seated
alongside the earl and the treasurer, but I suspected
that the youngest among them might be Henry Percy.

Earl Warrenne, blunt and forthright as I had come
to know he was, wasted no time but spoke directly to
the Steward. "We should all know each other here, but
since there is one among you I don't know myself, I'll
settle that now." He looked directly at Sir Alexander
Lindsay. "Who are you, sir?"

Lindsay smiled and inclined his head slightly in
salute. "My name is Lindsay, my lord, Alexander
Lindsay of Barnwell."

"Lindsay …" Warrenne's brow wrinkled slightly.
"That name is known to me. Are you kin of any kind

to that Sir David de Lindsay of the Byres, who crusaded in Egypt with Prince Edward?"

"He was my father, sir, but I never knew him. He died on crusade."

"Aye, he did, and I can see him in you now. I was with him when he died, you know. He was my friend, not merely a brother in arms. He was a fine, upstanding man whose name you may bear with pride."

He spoke then to the others on his side of the table. "So, Sir Alexander you all know. As for the others, in the middle you have James Stewart, Lord High Steward of Scotland. On his right is Malcolm, Earl of Lennox, and to his left is Earl Malise of Strathearn. And the man on the end there is Lord James's brother, Sir John Stewart."

He changed his focus to the Scots. "You all will know Sir Hugh de Cressingham, King Edward's treasurer for Scotland. Beside him is my grandson Sir Henry Percy, Baron of Alnwick, and beside him is his teacher and mentor, Sir Marmaduke Tweng. The man beside Sir Marmaduke is Sir Tibbalt de Blount, constable of Tyneside, and he commands our forces from that region. And Prior Anselm of Hexham Priory in Northumberland is a visitor here, newly arrived and bearing letters from the Bishop of Lindisfarne to my attention." That said, he seated himself, leaned back in his chair, and eyed the Steward. "You came to speak, so speak."

I had been staring at the man beside Sir Henry Percy, for his was a name I had known for years. Sir Marmaduke Tweng was a warrior knight of great fame,

a veritable paladin, known and respected throughout
Christendom and named in tones of awed respect
whenever men spoke of tourneys and chivalric prowess.
I had heard many men speak of him, and never a word
of disrespect from any, but I had never expected to set
eyes on him, and I was still sufficiently boyish and
wide-eyed to feel a thrill of wonder at being in his
company, even as a bystander. He was no longer
young, yet far from being either old or failing, but his
eyes sparkled with humour and vitality and he radiated
confidence and calm. He had the broad width of shoulders that bespoke a lifetime practising with heavy
weapons. Beside him, the fiery and much-talked-about
Sir Henry Percy looked young and callow, in spite of
the stern set of his features and his obvious determination to be recognized as a man among men.

A deep harrumph from the Steward interrupted my
musing. "We are here about a task that should be
equally beneficial to both our realms," he said. "We
both are well served should we be able to resolve this
matter facing us in the valley of the Forth without
blood being shed on either side."

"And how do you suggest we might achieve that?"
It was plain from the irony in the earl's voice that he
was expecting some attempt to trick him.

"By suborning Wallace's army. Depriving him of
his best men."

I was rocked to my very soul by what the Steward
had said, and before I could adjust my thoughts he
spoke again.

"You may not be aware of this, but in recent weeks he has attracted a number of knights and men of noble station to his cause, and they now rank high among his followers. That is why we are here now. I have no knowledge of how he enlisted their support—for he is a common outlaw, beyond doubt—but there is no doubt that he did. I believe, however"—he checked himself, then indicated his companions—"*we* believe that those men might still be induced to bethink themselves and return to their true loyalties, which are to the realm and to their natural station as nobles of Scotland."

"As you yourself were induced by Baron Alnwick here?" I was not alone in wincing at the sudden sound of Cressingham's braying, at once both hectoring and abrasive. "You were a rebel recently yourself, Stewart, flouting the King's peace, as everyone here knows. But now you expect us to heed your advice for dealing with rebels?"

"Ah, Master Cressingham," Lord James said quietly, turning his head slightly to look the treasurer in the eye with no sign of antipathy. "What a loss good men everywhere will suffer when your dulcet tones and tactful words are one day silenced in this world … In response to your question, though, I must say yes, I do expect that you will heed my advice, since I propose to offer the men in question precisely what Sir Henry offered me and my companions at Irvine. The logic of it is sound and the acceptance of it is a matter of good sense, since no reasonable, healthy-minded man can deny his own origins. The men of whom I speak have gone astray, choosing to follow a broken man who has gulled them with empty promises of what he calls freedom." His face clearly showed the scornful contempt in which he held the mere idea.

I had barely managed to collect myself to that point, because the words I had heard from this man were heretical. I drew myself up to my full height, anger roiling in my throat, and was about to step forward when the Steward's eyes shifted and met mine, stopping me before I could move. His face was blank, but I knew instantly that he had been aware of me all along and that his acknowledgment of me now was deliberate. As I hesitated, he frowned, still looking directly into my eyes. It was a clear instruction to stand still.

Then, his face still wearing that same frown, which now became one of abstracted attention to some passing thought, he spoke again to Earl Warrenne. "The treasurer may be correct, to a degree, my lord," he said, "but he is wrong nonetheless. I was involved in a recent uprising, but I negotiated an honourable peace with your grandson here, Sir Henry, and have abided by the terms of it since then."

"No, by God, sir, that you have not," snarled Cressingham, causing Lord James to whip up one hand and silence him.

"Yes, by God I have, sirrah!" His voice was savage. "Name me one instance where I have not."

"We have heard nothing from the Earl of Carrick since the day the terms were made."

"Spare me your concerns about the Earl of Carrick! I barely know the man. He has been a favourite of your King for years, and he came out of England last May, uninvited, and aligned himself with us, claiming the right to do so as an earl of this realm. But it is no responsibility of mine if he or any other man reneges upon an oath or fails to honour a promise made in person. That has nothing to do with me, Master Cressingham, and if you choose to impugn *my* honour further by insisting that it is, I will be more than happy to defend that honour in single combat—sword, daggers, mace, axe, or any other weapon that you choose."

Not a sound occurred in the great pavilion. Even the servants were shocked into immobility by the vehemence of the Steward's rejoinder. Not a man around that table doubted his sincerity or his sudden readiness to spill the treasurer's blood.

"Well?" he barked.

Cressingham was widely known to be hotheaded, but even he recognized the implacable nature of James Stewart's anger, and he flushed. "You take me wrong, my lord High Steward. I had no thought to impugn your honour. I was but commenting on—"

"We all heard your comments, sir," Stewart said. "Be kind enough to keep them to yourself in future, unless you have firm evidence upon which to base them." He turned back to Earl Warrenne, ignoring Cressingham thereafter. "I was about to say, my lord earl, that the truce I entered into mere months ago with your King, ably negotiated by your grandson and agreed upon at the time by all concerned, was built upon the logic of sound principles and the accepted canon of feudal law. I could find no fault with the terms as presented to us, and since I am suggesting that we—both you and I, representing the realms of Scotland and England—extend identical terms to these people facing us across the river, I anticipate that they will likewise accept what we will say to them."

Warrenne sniffed. "Some of them might," he said. "I doubt the Wallace fellow will. And it comes to me, too, that the other so-called leader of this rabble, the northerner de Moray, may be as bloody-handed as is Wallace. What will you say to them?"

"Nothing. They are outlaws, both of them. My aim is to win their well-born supporters away from them by appealing to their better natures and their family loyalties and offering them amnesty. And also by pointing out to them the hopeless nature of their situation should they refuse, the certainty that they will lose everything they hold dear when Wallace and his rabble are stamped out."

He waited for de Warrenne to respond, but the earl betrayed no eagerness to speak. Instead he shifted his backside and slid lower in his seat, tucking in his chin and tugging gently at the tuft of hair beneath his lower lip as he stared back at Stewart, the silence stretching and growing and everyone else in the assembly waiting and wondering which man would yield first.

It was the Earl of Surrey who spoke first, showing not the slightest sign that there had been any kind of conflict going on. "Of how many men are we speaking here?"

The High Steward shrugged, but not broadly. "Word of this has come to me but recently from people who know of other people, knights and titled folk, who have joined Wallace, so we do not really know how many of them there are at this time, but there is no question of there being anywhere close to a hundred. A score, perhaps. Perhaps twice that many. And to be truthful even half a hundred would not surprise me. More than that would, though."

"It would surprise me, too. Why are you really here, Stewart? Because this is nonsense. The loss of fifty men would go unnoticed in an army of a thousand. And this rabble-rouser has drawn several thousand to his cause, however foolish such a cause might be."

Lord James rose to his feet, then stepped around his high-backed chair and leaned forward against it on his hands, his chin almost touching the peak of its back as he perused the row of Englishmen across from him. "His cause is simply stated, and to Scottish ears there is no foolishness in it," he said, in firm, measured tones, looking from face to face. "It is to drive the English out of Scotland, root and branch. And there's the pity of it, and the reason why this must be done—because he has set himself a task that is impossible to complete, and all that he can ever achieve will be catastrophic damage to his own folk, in the certain death of the thousands who follow him.

"But the men we will take from him—be they a score in number or half a hundred—are not ordinary men, and their defection will *not* go unnoticed. In fact the opposite is true." The Steward's gaze drifted back to meet mine again, and for a moment he looked directly into my eyes as he continued: "You are correct in what you said a moment ago. Wallace is an outlaw and his so-called army is a rabble, without training, without discipline, and without a hope of surviving their first encounter with your army. He has no means of protecting them against your massed ranks of longbow archers. And he has no horses other than a hundred or so of their stunted mountain ponies, useful for herding cattle but worse than useless against trained and armoured cavalry. The only mounted strength that Wallace has, in fact, is vested in the very men we will take from him, men who know, already, that they have no hope of winning against your mounted knights and men-at-arms, the same men who know, too, that in riding with Wallace they are demeaning and insulting their own families, spurning the very way of life that made them who they are. The loss of them would be a giant blow to Wallace's esteem. It would be seen as a betrayal of enormous consequence, and I doubt Wallace could recover from it. It would destroy his confidence and undermine his self-assurance, but even more, it would destroy the status he enjoys among his rabble."

"Hmm …" De Warrenne sat up slightly straighter. "And you believe, in all honesty, that you can achieve such a thing?"

"I would not be here otherwise."

The Englishman frowned. "How would you go about it? What would you do?"

"We would ride into their camp and simply do it. We're all Scots. We would be welcomed."

"Never! They'd hang you high the moment they got wind of your intent."

"And how would they conceive of our intent?" The Steward indicated the Gaelic earls seated beside him. "We three rank among the senior officers of Scotland's realm. No one would ever think to doubt our good intent. Think about what is involved here, Lord Warrenne—why these men of whom we speak are so important to the rogue Wallace. It is because they represent something the man has never known or had until now—respectability. They are knights and men of rank, of stature and status, even the meanest of them. And thus they offer him and his a kind of recognition, an illusion of valid authority. Acceptance from his betters is something Wallace craves, and something he can never have. He is an outlaw and a criminal, and no one knows that better than he does, so it will never occur to him to turn us away or refuse to talk with us. He will not be able to believe his eyes when we approach his camp, because our presence there will give him what he lacks so sorely: a visible sign of having gained that respectability and recognition that is like meat and drink to broken men like him — the essence of life itself."

Earl Warrenne sat silent for a while then, stroking his nose absently with a long, bony finger, but he finally sat up and gripped the arms of his chair, then bent forward and turned to peer at his companions on that side of the table. "Does anyone have anything to say?" he asked.

His grandson Henry Percy leaned over to whisper in his ear. The older man's eyes grew wider as he listened.

"Quite right," he said, nodding. "Quite right." He raised a hand to the captain of his guards, who had been watching, hawk-like, from just inside the entrance flaps, and then raised his voice to address not just the five Scots but the people lining the walls. "Would everyone go outside, if it please you. We need to speak privily here."

On our way out of the tent I pulled Thomas close. "I need to talk to Lindsay, the one whose father Warrenne knew. He speaks French, so introduce him to me in French, and then go on and speak to the Steward. They all think you're an Englishman, so they'll probably be unwilling to speak with you, but that's good, because it will keep the guards' eyes on you and them and away from me."

He did not even look at me but changed direction immediately and walked to where the Scots emissaries stood isolated from everyone else, under the vigilant eyes of a dozen guards who kept their distance but were evidently ready to move quickly if need be. He nodded courteously to the Steward and the two mormaers, who eyed him suspiciously, but he was soon chatting easily with Lindsay and asking him, in English, if he spoke French. I stood close by him, saying nothing, and Lindsay looked curiously at both of us before nodding and saying that he did. Thomas smiled then and indicated me, and I took the conversation from there, smiling uncertainly and bowing and bobbing and generally playing the fawning, bumbling fool until I was sure no one was watching us.

"We don't have much time before they call us back inside again. What are you people doing here, Sir Alec?"

"I'll ask you the same question."

"I'm spying, for Lamberton of Glasgow. I'm sending out dispatches to Will every day, but because of the foul weather I've had nothing substantial to report yet—other than the obvious information, of course."

"What obvious information? Battle plans?"

"Nothing that grand, I'm afraid. If Surrey has battle plans, he hasn't yet decided to share them with his troop commanders. I've no doubt he will, once he is safely ensconced in Stirling Castle, with dry clothing on his back and a roof over his head and the leisure to think ahead and make plans. And as soon as he does, I'll send the word on to Will. In the meantime, I've been able to send him details on the numbers and disposition of the English army, but the really important information is that de Warrenne has almost ten thousand infantry with him, counting the contingent under Cressingham. He has more than fifteen hundred heavy horse, three hundred of them knights, a few minor barons among them, and the rest well-equipped men-at-arms. And he has more than a thousand Welsh archers, to boot. But they have no siege engines, which means they have no plans to besiege anyone."

"Why should they?" Lindsay was frowning. "We hold no positions worth besieging."

"That's not important, Sir Alexander. What's important is that we *know* they have no siege engines. And we *know* how many men they have, and how they are composed—the numbers and types of weaponry. That's more information than most commanders ever discover about the forces opposing them, so Will and Andrew should be able to put it to good use." I shrugged. "That's why I am here," I said. "So why are *you* here?"

Lindsay's eyes swept around, looking for possible eavesdroppers. "For the same reason you are. In search of information, and hoping to postpone a battle."

"Postpone it until when?"

"Until Wallace is better prepared. As it stands now, he has numbers, but they are all afoot, and that leaves him short of strength overall. He has nowhere near enough archers and no horse."

"And why is James Stewart here? That seems—"

"He's here in hopes of discovering when the English intend to attack, for at this time no one can even guess at their intentions. He is also here to lend his authority to what we are trying to achieve."

"What, undermining Wallace?"

"No! Supporting him, and encouraging others to join us. Lennox stands with us, but Malise is undecided, as are many others. Most of them are dithering, afraid to commit themselves to either side too soon, and so they withhold their support for the rising, unable to see that by so doing, they are endangering the realm. The Steward will speak more of that when we return."

"So he has no intention of stealing away any of Wallace's people, and you are truly here to help our cause?"

The look he threw me, of scandalized astonishment, convinced me of his truthfulness even before he said, "You doubt us?"

"I wondered. But no longer. So what is the Steward planning?"

As I spoke, however, a blast from a trumpet turned every head, and the captain of Earl Warrenne's guard came striding to summon the Scots party back inside. Lindsay nodded tersely and said, "You'll find that out now," before moving back to take his place with the others in his group.

Thomas joined me wordlessly, an unspoken question in his eyes, and I nodded to him, indicating that I was satisfied as I fell in beside him, following Lord Stewart and the others back into the pavilion. The English party were still seated as we had left them, but the expressions on their faces seemed different to me.

Once again, de Warrenne wasted no time. "We have discussed your idea and are prepared to support it. How long will you require to complete what needs to be done?"

Lord James made a moue and spread his hands apart. "That depends upon you, my lord earl. How long can you give us? It goes without saying that the more time we have, the more we might hope to achieve, but we are dealing with small numbers here, and the need for secrecy dictates an equal need for haste. Three days? That seems to me to be a sufficiency."

"Too long. Two days is all you have, today being gone by now. You will have tomorrow and Tuesday. No more than that. We will rest here tonight and be in Stirling Castle comfortably by noonday tomorrow, and my troops will spend the afternoon and the following day preparing to fight on Wednesday. That will be"—he glanced around, as though waiting for someone to assist him—"the eleventh of September, a date the Wallace upstart will rue for the remainder of his brief life.

"So." His face held no expression, and even from the side view I could tell that his eyes were as flat and empty as his tone had indicated. "Two clear days. Can you achieve your aims within that time? I ask merely out of courtesy, because in truth it makes little difference to me whether you can or not. My mind is set on it. We will make an end of Wallace and his rabble come Wednesday morning, and be back in the castle by mid-afternoon."

Lord James inclined his head. "That will work well for us, my lord earl. We will return with the fruits of our labour before you commit your vanguard to the attack. And now we must away, for I would like to gain the Scottish camp before nightfall, to let the word of our arrival spread before we start our work." He rose from his seat, and the others in his party rose with him.

Earl Warrenne turned suddenly to look at Thomas, a questioning look on his face, and when Thomas nodded, he turned back to the Stewards. "We are about to celebrate Mass, Lord James. Will you not stay and pray with us? The ears of our Lord are always attentive to devout prayers."

"Forgive me, but I think not, your lordship. I attended Mass this morning before break of day. Besides, it will take us a good two hours to ride to where we need to be this night, and I have no desire to ride in there in darkness."

De Warrenne sniffed. "Aye," he growled. "Nor would I, in your shoes. But tell me this, if you will, because your actions make little sense to me from one particular point of view. Why would you people act against your own? We expect it of you, but it strikes me as being unnatural, notwithstanding our expectations. You are all Scots, all of a kind, and even though the leaders of this rabble are outlaws, they, too, are Scots nonetheless, resisting us in the name of their realm. And so I have to wonder why you would offer aid to us instead of to them."

The Steward faced Surrey squarely, his jaw jutting pugnaciously. "Out of fear," he said tersely, surprising me yet again. "Not fear of Wallace or de Moray, or even of their folk, but fear of *losing* those folk, of seeing them slaughtered needlessly and tragically. Because Wallace and de Moray, despite the petty victories they may have won, are tyros—they are untested and unbloodied in the realistic ways of war. They are too young, both of them, untrained and lacking in experience, and they have no older, wiser heads advising them. The successes they have won before this point were all accidental, small in themselves and predicated upon the unpreparedness of the men they fought. These two are upstarts, and like all upstarts, they are dangerous to those around them. They are overconfident, overweening, and overreaching themselves. And as surely as the sun rises each day, they will lead everyone foolish enough to follow them into perdition. They will throw good, honest men, deluded but sincere—and they have *thousands* of them following their lead—into certain death in battle against your veterans, against your banks of archers, your companies of mounted knights and men-at-arms, and your formations of armed and armoured footmen. It will be murder on a catastrophic scale, and it will destroy this realm's ability to recover its strength for a generation."

He stopped, still rigidly erect, his shoulders back and his head high as he glared at John de Warrenne as though defying him to disagree. "That is why Wallace and his accomplice de Moray have to be stopped. That is why we have come to you like this.

And every man we can convince to quit his side and sue for amnesty will make this seeming senselessness worthwhile."

He then inhaled deeply, saluted the group at the table with a clenched fist raised to his left breast, and spun around and marched out, followed by the others in his party.

CHAPTER TWENTY-FIVE

THE FORDS OF DRIP

On Wednesday, the eleventh day of September, as de Warrenne had promised, the English launched their attack on the forces of William Wallace and Andrew Murray.

I saw the entire battle from the English side, which is something very few of my compatriots can claim. I celebrated early-morning Mass for the soldiers, then found a vantage point high on the walls above the castle gates, from which I watched them march away, in high spirits, chanting the rough marching songs of their individual divisions as they went. It was soon after dawn, before the new day's sun had crested the horizon, and the skies were cloudless. The English soldiers' morale was high, their confidence absolute, and I found myself muttering prayers for my friends in the valley below as I watched the enemy ranks twisting and rippling sinuously as they followed the narrow winding track downward from the castle gates to the causeway that stretched north towards the old wooden Stirling Bridge.

I had thought it odd to have seen no signs of the Earl of Surrey that morning—he seldom missed early Mass—but when Thomas questioned one of his household attendants, we learned that the earl had been awake for more than half the night and had not yet risen. The information was delivered with a broad wink and one finger laid along the speaker's nose, from which I inferred that his lordship had been the worse for drink when he went to bed, and I thought that strange, too, for the earl, unlike most of his ilk, was an abstemious man, not normally given to excess of any kind. But then I thought that his situation the previous night might well have been less fraught than I had at first assumed. Certainly there was a battle to be fought the next morning, but in the eyes of Surrey and his commanders—indeed in the eyes of his entire army—that battle was already won, since the rabble of untrained peasantry following the outlawed Scots leaders could not possibly compete with a disciplined English army—an army commanded, moreover, by the very man who had crushed the royal Scottish army and its noble but ineffectual leaders at Dunbar the previous year. And thus the wine drunk that night might have been in celebration of the next day's assured victory.

It is a fact, witnessed by many including myself, that when Hugh de Cressingham, enormous in black plate armour and mounted on a massive horse, gave the order to the assembled host to proceed that morning, no one questioned his right to do so. He was

co-commander of the army, with full power in the
absence of the earl, and so the procession moved out
obediently in orderly alternating formations of four
hundred infantry marching in fours, followed by sixty
cavalry riding two abreast. Less than a half-hour after
the first columns had set out, though, Earl Warrenne
emerged from his quarters in a state of undress and in
a towering rage. He had given no orders to proceed, he
said, and Cressingham had had no right to usurp his
authority as commander of the army. He screamed at
his subordinates with a malevolence I had never seen
in him before, and heralds were sent at the gallop to
stop the advance and order everyone, including
Cressingham, to return to the castle immediately. By
the time the heralds were able to catch up to the front
ranks and present their orders, the sun had already
cleared the low hills on the horizon and the leading
infantry column had crossed the old bridge. A deal of
confusion and much milling about followed thereafter,
as the advance formations had to be turned around to
reverse their course on the narrow strip of the
causeway, no easy feat to accomplish. The exercise
was completed, though, and without attracting any
unwelcome attention from the Scots, whose closest
formations were visible less than a mile from the north
end of the bridge.

It was mid-morning by the time the army was
re-formed outside the castle gates, ready to march
again, and Thomas and I were still perched on our wall
above all the activity, waiting, along with everyone

else, for Earl Warrenne to issue his own word to advance. He had summoned Cressingham inside to talk to him privily as soon as the treasurer returned, and that conversation had been brief and, everyone assumed, less than comfortable for Cressingham, who had emerged white faced with anger at the end of it and had not spoken a word since to anyone. The earl had then summoned his senior troop commanders, both horse and foot, to an assembly within the castle yard while the army completed its regrouping, and when they finally re-emerged, all of them radiating confidence and eagerness, someone called out the ancient British war cry that had greeted Caesar's legions when they first landed in England: hip-hip-hip-hurrah!

Trumpets sounded as the last cheer died away, and orders were bellowed into the silence that followed, and then the front ranks lurched forward on command and the army began to advance for the second time. But even as the first ranks began to move, before their shuffling gait could grow into the tramp of marching feet, Thomas jumped up and stood peering northward, one hand shading his eyes from the glare of the sun on his right.

"Somebody's coming," he said. "A large party, crossing the bridge. It looks like the High Steward." He fell silent again, peering, and then said, "It is the Steward, with cavalry. I can see his banner, and they're coming this way." I stood up to look as well, and he asked me, "D'you think he actually did it? Betrayed Wallace?"

It appalled me even to hear the question asked, but I shook my head firmly. "Of course not. He was the man who first put Will up against England, years ago. Betray him now, and at the cost of everything he holds most sacred? Never."

"Then where did all those horsemen come from?"

"They're his, Thomas! His and Lennox's and Strathearn's. They all have followers and bodyguards.":

"Then quickly, tell de Warrenne he has to stop them."

"Stop the Steward?"

"No, his own folk. Stop the march!"

"Why?" I had no idea what he meant.

"Because if the Steward's people meet this army on the road they'll all be killed before they can prove who they are. Stop the march!"

I had already turned to obey him, but I stopped short and turned back, suddenly anxious. "I can't. I'm not supposed to speak English, remember?"

He scowled at me, then pushed by me, taking two swift steps to where he could best see Earl Warrenne below. Then he cupped his hands over his mouth and bellowed, "Your Grace!" at the top of his voice. Twice more he yelled, and I joined him, both of us capering and waving our arms wildly until someone, some officer standing near the earl, looked up and saw us. He pointed us out to Warrenne, who recognized Thomas immediately and swung an impatient arm, beckoning him down.

"Stay here," Thomas said to me and began to run towards the steps. But I was close behind him when he reached ground level and ran to where the earl was waiting for him, surrounded by his mounted officers and commanders and controlling his sidling, nervous horse with a strong hand and tight reins.

"Someone's coming, my lord earl," Thomas gasped. "Across the bridge. The Scotch party you met with. I recognized their colours."

"Stewart." To give him his due, Warrenne grasped the implications instantly, and his eyes met mine briefly and utterly without recognition. "How many men are with him?"

When Thomas said he had seen perhaps three score, the earl swung to face the treasurer. "This could mean capitulation. No need to fight and spend your precious money." He pointed a rigid finger at a heavily armoured knight. "Despencer, send some of your best riders to stop the advance. Immediately. Stop it now, then pull everyone back here. Move, man!"

The knight saluted with a clenched, mailed fist, then wheeled his destrier noisily on the cobblestones of the yard and clattered out through the gateway. Warrenne then spoke to another visored knight close beside him.

"You, Mortimer," he snapped. "Find my grandson. He'll be making ready to depart, to guard the bridge approaches. Send him to meet Lord Stewart and bring him and his people straight here to me in the anteroom beside the armoury. You understand?"

The knight nodded, cuffing up his visor. "The anteroom by the armoury. Aye, my lord."

"Good, then go now. Now, quick as you can."

Mortimer, who wore the gaudy blue and yellow bars of the earldom of March, in Wales, slapped his visor down, then pulled his horse up into a rearing turn and went cantering off at a lumbering trot.

The earl now addressed the remaining knights grouped around him. "Dismount and rest your horses, but don't go far away. We'll be on full alert until I have heard what the Scots lords have to say."

He then swung his leg over the rump of his great warhorse and dismounted, handing the reins to a groom. "You have good eyes, Father Thomas," he said, nodding to me in vague recognition. "Well done, and you were right to summon me. If Lord Stewart brings the word he said he would, we may save thousands of lives today. You know the anteroom by the armoury?" Thomas nodded. "I'll want you in there, with your writing tools, in case we have need of them, so you had best make ready." Someone else spoke to him then, and he stalked away, leaving the two of us standing by ourselves as stablemen, grooms, armoured knights, and bustling messengers moved all around us.

"Do you keep records of his meetings, too?" I spoke in French, in case anyone was listening, but the question came naturally to me, for the earl's request had surprised me.

"No," Thomas said in the same language. "But I am a cleric, and clerics do write things down and keep records. I have done His Grace a similar service once before, solely because then, as now, I was conveniently at hand. So come, then, and help me prepare."

By the time Sir Henry Percy led in the Steward's party, Thomas was set up at a table off to one side of the anteroom, with parchment, pens, and inkwells laid out should they be required, and I sat across from him, prepared to assist in anything that might be asked of me. Sir John de Warrenne sat with Cressingham at the end of a table similar to the one he had used in his field pavilion, and he was flanked by several knights, none of whom had been present at his meeting with the High Steward the previous Sunday. Two of those I recognized as the knights to whom he had issued orders earlier, Sir Hugh le Despencer and Sir Roger Mortimer of March. They sat on opposite sides of the table with their crested war helms upright in front of them, and I was surprised to see that, lacking the bulk and menace of their heavy helms, both men were younger than I had thought them. They sat stiffly, neither acknowledging the other, and it took no great insight to see that they disliked each other intensely.

There came a rap at the doors, which then swung wide, and Henry Percy stepped inside, accompanied by another knight unknown to me and closely followed by Lord James Stewart and the Earls of Lennox and Strathearn. All three were grim faced.

"What is wrong?" De Warrenne spoke directly to Lord James, and the tone of the question was accusatory, while the one that followed immediately made it clear that the niceties of rank and protocol were not to be observed this time around. "Did you do what you promised? I'll tell you bluntly I never thought to see your face here again. And I have to say in truth I never thought, from the very outset, that you would succeed. But you've come back, so you must have been successful—you would scarcely return to report a failure. And yet the three of you look like men who've seen their favourite sons killed. So what is the truth? Success, or failure?"

He was interrupted by a snort of wrath from Cressingham, but he slammed the flat of his hand on the table and raised a warning finger. "Enough, sir! Not one word."

The High Steward looked from one to the other of them before he answered. "Failure. I came back solely because I said I would return before you launched your vanguard. I considered that to be a promise, and I keep my promises."

Warrenne was frowning now. "But if you failed, who are the three score riders who came out with you?"

"They are four score, not three, and they are our personal retainers and escorts."

"And Wallace simply permitted you to leave? All of you?"

Lord James looked at the Englishman with something akin to sympathy in his eyes. "What could he do otherwise? We spent two days within his camp, attempting to dissuade both him and de Moray from confronting you, while my men tried privily, with equal lack of success, to wean away his knightly followers. When it was clear that I could change neither of their minds, I expressed my regrets and took my leave."

"And they made no attempt to stop you."

"No. They had spent the same two days trying to convince us to join them. When they saw that we would not be moved, as we had seen they would not be, we parted amicably."

"I find that hard to believe."

"Why should you? Did you think perhaps they might believe they could force us to fight for them? That is foolishness. They accepted the inevitable, as did we, and when we left they were preparing to confront you."

"Damnation! Then so mote it be. If confrontation is what they seek, they shall have it until they choke upon it."

The Steward smiled a wintry little smile. "That is precisely the sentiment, if not the words, that Wallace expressed to me before we left. He may be a common bandit, but he is far from being a stupid man, and it requires no great intellect to guess that we would be brought here after we left his camp. Your folk control the bridge, the sole way into and out from where he is, after all."

Warrenne frowned. "What do you mean by that?"

"I mean he knew we would be coming here now, to talk to you, because we could not hope to pass by Stirling without being stopped by your people. And so he sent you a message, knowing I would bring it to you. Let me cite his words precisely: 'Tell your English friends,' he said, 'to send us no more olive branches, for we have no need of firewood.' And then he said, 'We are not here to forge a peace. We came here to do battle and to liberate our country. So let them come on, in war, with all their force, and we shall prove it in their very beards.'"

The earl grunted. "He has no lack of balls, I'll give him that for all his folly. Very well, your message is delivered, and its arrogance will be amply rewarded. Now you may leave, and if you have any regard for your own welfare you will take your men south, and quickly, clear of our lines. For I warn you, if any of my people encounter you more than one hour from now, you will be treated as Scotch rebels and dealt with accordingly."

He stood up and beckoned his ever-present guard captain. "Captain Sallis, send a troop of your guardsmen to escort his lordship's group to the rear of our lines in safety. Tell your troop commander to notify our outlying guards to treat the group as enemies should they attempt to return to Stirling. Clear?"

There were no farewells, no more civilities. Lord James's group stood up and left in silence, and as soon as they were outside the earl issued orders to Sir Hugh le Despencer to have the army prepared to move out yet again.

"Wait." This was a new voice, and hearing himself addressed so firmly, the big knight paused in the act of turning away and cocked his head towards the speaker, Henry Percy. "You will pardon me, I hope, Grandfather, but I have a question that needs to be asked. Have you an alternative plan for today's movements?"

The old man glared at him and appeared ready with an angry retort. But he hesitated, and asked, "What d'you mean, Grandson?"

Percy snatched a deep inhalation and straightened his shoulders almost imperceptibly. "I fear we have alerted the Scots. They must have scouts and spies watching our every move, and our activities today have clearly signalled our intention to attack. And now our army stands assembled again, in full public view, prepared to set out yet again—for a third time, sir—to assault an enemy who appears to have no solid line of battle prepared."

"So much the better, then. With no solid line to hold, they'll have no anchor. We'll push them back until we can surround them."

"That may not be possible, my lord earl. They hold the slopes over there, with soft ground below and to their front and thickly wooded hillsides at their back. No place for either cavalry or archers."

"Nonsense! We'll turn the hills at their back into an anvil and pound them flat against it with our horse and infantry. They may fight doughtily, but they cannot prevail against our army. They are undisciplined and untutored."

"But they have numbers, my lord. More numbers than we had thought possible for such a crew. There are thousands of them, perhaps ten thousand."

"Ten thousand walking corpses, then. That's what Stewart was afraid of, why he sought to bring about a truce: he fears a bloodbath that will wipe their manhood out for generations to come. And extermination is a fate that they have earned. But even should they avoid our direct thrust and slip away sideways through the valleys to the north, we will simply pursue them and achieve our ends no matter where they go or how they fight. Once we cross the Forth and penetrate the lands beyond those marshes, all the north will lie open to us."

"They might attempt to stop us at the bridge, my lord. It is discomfortingly strait."

"Nonsense again! How would they do that? By leaving their safe hillside and charging across open fenland for a mile to challenge us?"

"My Lord Surrey, may I speak?"

This was another new voice, unmistakably Scottish, and I turned my head quickly to see that the speaker was the unknown knight who had entered with Percy. I was not alone in failing to know the man, because the earl glowered at him and barked, "Who are you, sir? You are here in my privy council but I do not know your face."

It was Percy who answered him. "Sir Richard is with my household, Grandfather. I invited him to attend me here, in the belief that he has something to offer us. I present to you Sir Richard Lundie, who joined our ranks and entered the King's peace at

Irvine, before we concluded the terms of surrender with the group organized by Stewart, Wishart, and the Earl of Carrick. Sir Richard's lands are near here and he has information that can be of great use to us."

"Has he, indeed?" The earl sounded less than enthused, eyeing the Scots knight from head to foot as though affronted by his presence. "Well, man, speak up. What is this information that we need so greatly?"

Lundie cleared his throat nervously, but before he could say a word Percy spoke up again. "He offers us a means of protecting our advance upon the en—"

"Let the fellow speak for himself. If he is, in fact, capable of speech. We know already he is capable of changing his allegiance with some ease."

"My lord," Percy protested, sounding genuinely outraged, but the older man cut him off with an upraised hand.

"My council, Grandson, my rules." Again he scanned the man from head to foot, scowling. "Well? Can you speak?"

"Aye, er … I can, Your Grace."

"Speak up, then, and tell me why you changed sides. If you were out as a Scot, you could have felt no loyalty towards our King. So why cross over to his peace? That brands you as a turncoat, and no turncoat of any kind is welcome in my council. I have fools enough around me whom I trust. I need no extra mouths I cannot trust. So why the change?"

The Scots knight's face was flushed, his eyes fierce. "I rode oot in the first place to kill Englishry. For Christ kens they had kill't a wheen o' us, wi'out cause ither than they wanted to. So I joined Stewart, thinkin' he was at war wi' you. But he wasna … he wasna there to fight! He just wanted to talk, an' talk, an' talk, an' he would dae nothin'. An' so I took a scunner to the lot o' them."

"You what?"

Lundie glared back at him blankly, and Percy stepped in again. "A scunner, my lord. It means disgust. He was disgusted by the behaviour of the Scots leadership."

"Why so?" he asked Lundie.

"What wey? Is that whit ye're askin'? I'm talkin' about honour here, an' dishonour. An' that's what I saw. Dishonour—Scotland's noblest sellin' their honour again for English coin. It happens a' the time, and I was sick o' it."

"You … took a scunner, and so joined the enemy in protest?"

"Aye, I did." The Scot scowled.

Earl Warrenne sat up straighter and blew out a short, sharp breath. "I see. I mean, I don't really, but I know how it feels to be driven to rebellion. So be it, then, Sir Richard Lundie, I find your sentiment acceptable. Now, if you will, tell us what my grandson wants us to know. Unless, of course, you have now taken a scunner to us …"

Several of the listeners laughed, but it was evident that Sir Richard Lundie was deficient in his appreciation of humour. He merely frowned, then cleared his throat and launched into his explanation.

"There's a ford a few mile upstream frae the auld brig down in the carse there, at a place called Drip. It's broad—broader than here—and it's naewhere near as deep. They ca' it the Fords o' Drip. It'll tak up tae saxty abreist."

"Saxty abreesh?" The earl glared at his grandson. "In God's name, what does that mean?"

"It means abreast, my lord," Percy said hastily. "Sixty men abreast was what he said, meaning that three score men may cross the fords there side by side, at the same time. What Sir Richard is suggesting is that we—he and I—could lead a striking force of horse and foot upstream today and cross the Forth up there in safety and at speed before the sun goes down. That would leave us safe and dry on the far side, to move forward in the morning in support of your advance across the bridge. That would serve double purpose, in protecting your flank against attack as you advance and in surprising the Scotch by doing something they had not expected."

"Aha …" There followed a long pause before Warrenne spoke again, and when he did he sounded less hostile than before. "So we would stand down today and attack tomorrow, with an added margin of surprise. Is that what you are saying?"

"Yes, my lord. Precisely so."

"Hmm … How far is it to these Fords of Drip? How long to get there?"

Percy wrinkled his nose. "With horse and foot? Say two hundred of each? It's slightly more than eight

miles, Lundie says, so we could reach there and cross
over easily in daylight, were we to leave here within
the next hour or two. We would set out again at dawn
tomorrow, and be safely in place across from here,
threatening the rebels' western flank before you are
ready to set out."

Now the earl was nodding his head. "Do you
know," he mused, "I am inclined to think that might be
worthwhile pursuing. In fact, the more I think about it,
the more good sense I see in it …"

I had been watching Cressingham while the earl
was speaking, for I had seen him stiffen and sit up
straighter when the Scots knight started to talk, and
now I could see that he was livid, though I could not
have said whether it was with peevish anger or righ-
teous disapproval. Now he pushed himself to his feet,
his face dark with dissatisfaction.

"My Lord Surrey," he protested. "Surely you cannot
intend to heed this fellow? His idea is preposterous."

Warrenne turned slowly to gaze at the big man from
beneath lowered brows. "Preposterous, Cressingham?
How so?" He spoke quietly and without obvious heat,
but venom dripped audibly from his tone.

"Damnation, sir, the man is a Scot and a turncoat, by
your own word! And he is proposing to take four hundred
of our best men—they would have to be the best, to
undertake a task like this in proper fashion—and to lead
them off somewhere into the wilderness where, not
inconceivably, he could lose them when they are most
needed here. My lord, it scarce bears thinking about."

"Is that a fact? And yet I am doing precisely that, Master Cressingham. I am thinking about it, and I like the sound of it. I am examining the notion and perceiving great merit in what appears to me to be a solid, practical idea based upon clear-headed thinking. And so …" The earl's voice was filled again with the blistering scorn he had used so scathingly towards the Scottish knight mere moments earlier, and no one dared to stir as he fell silent, lest his displeasure be turned on them. "And so I have a suggestion to propose to you."

He thrust himself away from the table and stood up, placing his palms flat against his hips and arching his spine backwards, grunting as he pushed against the restriction of the heavy suit of mail beneath his brightly coloured surcoat of yellow and blue squares. He was sixty-six years old that year, and though he frequently complained of being too old for many of his duties, he yet retained the stamina and the athletic physique of a much younger man and he enjoyed being able to flaunt both attributes. He completed the exercise by throwing his arms in the air and then bending forward from the waist until his knuckles touched the ground in front of him, after which he straightened with a sigh and began to pace the floor, the sound of his heavy, nail-studded soles crunching on the flagstones.

"Let us suppose, Master Cressingham, that we have come to an agreement, you and I," he said, speaking as though he and the treasurer were alone in the ante-room. "An agreement to be truthful with each other in all things. You are a treasurer, defined by your title and appointment. You deal in fiscal things, monies and matters arising from the gathering and dissemination of those monies—taxes, levies, financial arrangements, incomes and expenditures. Is that not correct?"

"It is, my lord," Cressingham responded, his voice conveying the tacit comment, as you well know.

"I thought so. Well, since we are to deal in truths here, why would you not tell me the real reasons for your refusal to consider this plan being proposed by my grandson and his client Sir Richard Lundie? The truth, mind you. A truth that I am convinced will be closely connected, at base, to your fiduciary responsibility. Then, once I am in possession of that information, and speaking to you as a knight, a soldier, and a lifelong student of military matters, I will inform you, in turn, exactly why I intend to ignore all your unsought advice and proceed with what I perceive, from my position as King Edward's deputy, to be the right thing to do."

Cressingham had frozen where he stood, and for long moments he said nothing. But then, just as people were beginning to feel uncomfortable, he spoke up. "You malign me, Lord Surrey," he said in a quiet voice that struck a pang of sympathy inside me that I never would have suspected might be there.

To my very great surprise, the earl stopped pacing and looked back at him, no vestige of his sudden flaring anger now apparent. "No, sir," he said, shaking his head gently. "As God is my judge, I do not malign you. I speak the simple truth, with no intention of defaming or insulting you in person. You are a functionary, as I said earlier, Master Cressingham, and as such you are circumscribed by your own designation as treasurer. Your life is governed, and your actions are dictated, by the responsibilities laid upon you by our monarch, may God bless him. Those responsibilities are onerous, I know, and I thank God that they are yours and not mine, for they entail the constant, unrelenting need to fill the coffers of the treasury and an equally restrictive requirement to detect and account for needless expenses and to curtail them wherever possible. That is why you and I will never be in harmony while we supposedly hold joint command of this or any other army. The very nature of our callings sets us at odds."

Cressingham opened his mouth to respond, but found no words.

"For God's sake, man," the earl said, and his voice was urgent but not angry. "You undercut my strength at every move, or you try to. You sent one-third of our army home—one-third of our strength—before we even reached the border. Men and resources we might need before we are done here. And why? Because some addle-headed fool named them as reinforcements in your hearing. We had no need of reinforcements, you said. They would be a needless expense once Wallace and his rogues were put to death. Is that not the truth? Speak up."

"Aye, it is the truth," Cressingham said, though not defiantly. "It was true when I said it and it remains true. We have had no need of them."

"And pray you to God it remains that way, else I shall be really displeased with you. But now you seek to do the same again, in this matter of the Fords of Drip." He snapped a hand up to forestall whatever Cressingham might try to say. "I know how your mind works, Master Treasurer, and I could almost tell you what you thought when you first heard of this. Expense, you thought, and at once set about calculating the associated costs of sending four hundred men away on a dubious venture while retaining an entire army in the field for a full, extra day—food, provisions, weaponry, supplies, and all the other thousand things that must be bought and paid for every single day of an army's existence. And that, Master Cressingham, is where we differ irrevocably. I see what must be done in terms of duty, fighting men, and objectives, in terms of casualties suffered in exchange for victories gained, and I will suffer damnation before I will allow a man of mine to die because some tight-fisted money counter deems him to be worth less than the cost of saving him might justify."

I have never been a gambler, but at that moment I would have wagered heavily that Percy would be sent out that day with his four hundred men, to cross the Forth upstream and threaten Will's flank the next morning. And I would have lost.

The last words had barely left the earl's lips when the door to the chamber opened and his captain of the guard stepped inside to report that Lord Stewart's party was safely out of the area, as His Grace had ordered. Then, in addition, he volunteered the information that his guards on the castle walls had reported that there were no signs of activity on the Scots' side of the river valley.

Warrenne went utterly still, digesting what he had heard, then swivelled his shoulders slowly towards the guardsman. "Nothing? No signs of activity at all?"

The captain, standing rigidly at attention, spoke to a point somewhere above his superior's head. "Nothing, my lord. According to my man Dickon, who's 'ad 'is people watching 'em since dawn, the rebels 'asn't dared to show their face all mornin'."

"And why might that be? Did Dickon say, or do you know?"

"My lord?"

"I am asking for your opinion, Captain, yours and Dickon's. Do you have any thoughts on why the rebels are keeping out of sight? Speak out, now. I would not ask you if I didn't want to hear what you have to say."

The captain blinked, frowning beneath the rim of his helmet. "Aye ... Well, they might be afeared, my lord, if there was less on 'em. But they's too many to be that afeared." He paused, then plunged on. "I wondered the same thing when Dickon give me the word, an' so I asked him wot 'e thought about it."

"And?" the earl prompted.

Sallis jerked his head in a terse nod. "'E'd been wonderin' what they was up to, too. 'E reckoned they was watchin' us an' saw us turnin' back this mornin'. Reckons they think we've changed our minds an' don't think as we'll be comin' back today. Not till tomorra, an' 'e thinks—an' I do, too—that they'm all gettin' ready for us to attack come mornin'."

"Tomorrow morning … You think that, too, you say?"

The guardsman nodded again, more confidently. "Aye, sir, I do. That's why we're seein' no sign of 'em, 'cause they's not there no more. They's round be'ind the woods down there at the foot o' yon big crag, thinkin' they'm safe out o' sight, an' doin' summat to entrap us come mornin'."

"And you may be absolutely right," the earl said quietly. Then he straightened and nodded abruptly. "My thanks, Captain Sallis, for your opinion. I'll think upon it before I make any decisions."

The guardsman saluted smartly and left, and Warrenne turned back to his grandson, resting his elbow on the high back of his chair and propping his chin on his thumb as he rubbed the side of one finger pensively against the tip of his nose.

"I like your man's suggestion, Grandson, for crossing the Fords of Drip and mounting a combined attack tomorrow, but Sallis is no fool, and his factotum Dickon has been soldiering against King Edward's enemies for almost as long as I have myself. I suspect their judgment may be absolutely right and that the Scots are not expecting us to come at them today. Which means that were we to attack right now—immediately—we might well catch them off guard. What think you, Sir Roger?"

Mortimer blinked and his eyebrows shot up, betraying how shocked he was at having his opinion sought. He opened and closed his mouth twice before he found his voice. "I believe Captain Sallis may be absolutely right, my lord, and if he is, then your assertion, too, is correct. We might catch Wallace unprepared if we strike now, while his people believe that we do not intend to come at them until tomorrow." He paused, then continued: "I like Sir Richard's idea, too, and such a move would give us full protection against a flank attack when we attack tomorrow, but at the same time we would be running the risk of giving Wallace more time to prepare to fend off our attack. There is much to be said, both pro and contra, on both sides, but in truth I favour a hard strike now, when they are least expecting it."

"Henry?"

If Percy was surprised to be addressed by his first name, he showed no sign of it. Instead he cocked his head to one side. "I don't know, Grandfather," he said. "We'll fight one way or the other, and we'll win, but I have a feeling, almost a conviction, that the Fords of Drip offer us the greater advantage. What say you, Despencer?"

It was obvious from his tone that he expected Sir Hugh Despencer to agree with him, and I, too, expected Sir Hugh to support him, if for no other reason than to spite Mortimer. Despencer pushed his chair back from the table and sat staring at the ground between his feet, and when he looked up, it was to Earl Warrenne that he spoke.

"My lord," he said, "I believe you are right in wanting to strike now. I think your judgment is sound in trusting the wisdom of your veterans and their opinions on what seems best for you and for them. On the other hand," he added, raising one hand towards the Scots knight, "looking at Lundie's plan to cross the fords at Drip, I cannot fault it. We could do exactly as he suggests—send men upstream to cross the stream in safety and swing around to outflank Wallace's people in the morning. The logic of such a move is self-evident, and there is no valid reason for not executing it. None, that is, save for one consideration. Is there really any need for such a move? Certainly, it might protect us against a counterattack as we advance, but is a counter-attack being planned? The evidence indicates to me that there is not. The rebels have not set up any battle lines, and therefore, as you said, they have no anchor point, no rallying place. They also have no formal leadership, in the sense that we understand leadership—they have no senior commanders of proven worth and experience, trained in the craft and tempered in the realities of war, to lead and inspire men by example.

"They have two men in charge, as do we." He indicated Cressingham with a wave of his hand. "But theirs are men of straw, unbloodied and untried in formal battle. Even their own Scotch nobles have no faith in either one of them. We heard the High Steward himself say they are too young and too callow to be taken seriously by any man of rank. And to top everything, they have no cavalry—at least, no cavalry that we would recognize as such. I'm told they have a hundred mounted men on Highland garrons, but garrons are hill ponies, not warhorses. So, no cavalry, no archers, and no discipline among their rank and file. In fact, my lord, they have no rank and file!"

That earned him a few grim smiles from his listeners, and as they were nodding and grunting in agreement he rose to his feet.

"I think, Your Grace, that you should strike now. A wiser man than I once said, 'Carpe diem, quam minimum credula postero.' It means seize the day and make the most of it; put not your faith in tomorrow." He paused, smiling, aware of the astonishment on every face around him. Thomas turned to me with raised eyebrows. I looked back at him equally wide-eyed, amazed at hearing a knight, even a well-spoken English knight, quoting Horace, and not merely spontaneously but accurately.

Despencer spoke again into the admiring silence. "We have the strength to win, my lord, and since they think we will not move again today, we have the opportunity. We might not have as much tomorrow."

It was a truly astounding speech for a young knight, and in other circumstances I would have stood up and applauded him, but of course he was advocating a surprise attack upon my own friends and kinsmen, and I felt no enthusiasm. It was not so with the remainder of his audience, though. Every man around the table had been caught up in his sweeping declamation, and there was no doubt at all that he had wholly won their approbation.

The Earl of Surrey spread his arms, commanding silence, and when it fell he looked at Despencer. "Well spoken, Sir Hugh," he said. "I could not have said it more clearly myself. And you have aided me to my decision." He looked around the table. "To your positions, my friends, and rally your charges. We march within the hour to teach these Scotch rogues the error of their rebellious ways. Spread the word and make your preparations immediately."

Within moments, Thomas and I found ourselves alone in a suddenly empty room, staring at each other apprehensively across our table. We could hear voices shouting in the distance, and from even farther away came the sound of trumpets, but otherwise the silence surrounding us was unsettling.

"It's happening," Thomas said, his voice low and strained. "What should we do?"

"We should send word to Will and Andrew faster than a bird can fly, but we can't. It would mean stealing horses and fleeing, and we would never make it through the gates, let alone across the bridge. So all we can do now, really, is wait, and pray that Will has keen-eyed scouts down there watching for signs of activity on the road down from the gates."

Thomas shook his head impatiently, "I know all that, Jamie. What I meant was, how do we get down there? We'll be needed, once the battle starts."

"Aye, but we can't go now. There's no place for us on that road, and anyway no one would make way for us. Until the blood starts to spill they won't tolerate us among them. We'll wait until the way is clear and then go down with the Hospitallers and the other priests. Do you know any of the Hospitallers?"

"No. I met their commander, when the army assembled weeks ago. His name's Reynald, and he has a cadre of about fifteen brethren with him, plus a score or two of ancillaries, I believe. But he would not remember me."

"Probably not, but I'll wager he will not refuse your services today. Nor mine. I think we should align ourselves with them. We'll go and find Brother Reynald now, and travel down with his people."

It was the right thing to do, I knew, for once the fighting started, it would be left to the Hospitallers and their helpers to tend to the wounded. And they would do so with perfect impartiality. There were no enemies among the gravely injured; all were equal in being victims of the evil that is war.

We had no difficulty in finding Brother Reynald and his companions, for the black robes they wore, adorned on breast and back with the eight-pointed white cross of St. John, made it impossible not to recognize them. We found them making their preparations for the fighting that lay ahead, busily loading eight sturdy wagons with equipment and materiel, none of which looked familiar to me.

We told Brother Reynald who we were—I saw no

need to maintain my pretense of being Basque—and asked if he could use our assistance.

"Have you done this kind of thing before, Father James? Have you been involved in a battle?"

"No," I said, "but a priest is a priest and his duties apply under all circumstances."

One side of his mouth quirked slightly upwards. "True," he said. "I merely wondered ... I have found there is no worse place on earth than in the midst of a battleground when there are people dying all around you and you are powerless to influence anyone or anything. That is what you face today, my friend. But as you say, a priest is a priest. And of course we can use your help. Yours and that of everyone else for miles around, could we but enlist them. Pardon me."

He called to someone behind him, and an enormous fellow came towards us.

"This is Frère Etienne," Brother Reynald said. "Brother Steven. Steven, we have two new volunteers, chaplains of the Earl of Surrey's household. They would like to be of help to us, and our Heavenly Father knows how grateful we will soon be for whatever assistance is offered. Will you introduce them to the others and show them what will be required of them?"

Brother Steven nodded and smiled, but said not a word, and Reynald turned back to us.

"I will leave you in Steven's hands, knowing you could not be better served. He will have no shortage of work for you, and he will keep you sufficiently occupied that you will be ready to sleep well by the end of this day. Go with God, and we may meet again later."

Less than an hour later, we were walking behind one of their wagons as we wended our way down the castle hill, aware that we could already hear the rising sounds of conflict in the distance ahead of us.

And so I went to war, real war, for the first time.

CHAPTER TWENTY-SIX

THE STIRLING FIGHT

The most astonishing part of the journey we took at the tail end of the Earl of Surrey's army that September day, wending our way down the steep slope from Stirling Castle towards the Carse of Stirling and the causeway, was that most of us had no notion at all of what we were walking into.

The marching troops were far ahead of us, hidden from our sight by the twisting of the road, and we walked sedately in procession behind the Knights of the Hospital and their wagons as if we were on pilgrimage to some hallowed event. The high ground under our feet was dry and rocky, and there was nothing to indicate that the river valley below might be different, but the truth was that the heavy, sustained rains of the previous ten days had thoroughly soaked the ground on both sides of the causeway, making it too soft to withstand the churning feet of Warrenne's ten thousand marching soldiers, and too dangerous to trust with the weight of mounted men. The army that preceded us down the hill had been in high spirits, moving jauntily along in the expectation of a short fight and a swift victory, and we followed them in silence for the most part, a few of us praying, perhaps, but most of us simply talking quietly and feeling grateful to varying degrees, I am quite sure, that we were non-combatants and therefore not at risk.

Most of us among the hundred or so volunteers that day were priests, forbidden by our calling to spill blood yet driven by our very humanity to minister to those who fought and whose blood was spilt. Our allotted task—Brother Steven had appointed me to be in charge of six two-man teams of stretcher-bearers—was to roam the battlefield, identifying wounded men and taking them on stretchers to the wagons at the Hospitallers' site, where their wounds would be treated.

Anyone who has ever been in battle will already have seen the extent of our naivety, in our failure to ask what was meant by "roam the battlefield, identifying wounded men." But even had we asked, I doubt that anyone would have seen a need to explain the absurdity of the mere thought of roaming anywhere on a battlefield without being killed. That should have been self-evident to anyone with a brain in his head, and so no one saw a need to warn us that we would have no need to roam; that we would literally be surrounded by dead and dying men.

We were aware, at some cerebral level, that men were going to die. We knew, too, again in that same abstract sense, that some of those wounded men were going to be gravely wounded and would require our assistance to reach the care of the Hospitallers. But we were simple priests, sheltered by our blessed vocation from the harsh realities of armies and fighting men. In our stupid, credulous gullibility we could never have suspected that the God-filled, safe, and prayerful world in which we lived and worked was about to be destroyed—set at naught as though God Himself had turned His back on it. We could not possibly have known that Satan and his cohorts, with all their swarming minions, were about to be loosed in havoc on the field surrounding us.

We had no sense of anything being amiss—at least I, for one, did not—until we reached the quarter-mile-long stretch of level plain leading to the south bank of the river and the narrow wooden bridge over the Forth. But when our single file of loaded wagons slowed and then stopped altogether, unable to proceed farther, we were able to tell from the tumult ahead that something had gone wrong. I shifted the knapsack containing all my priestly tools until it hung comfortably at my back, then hauled myself up to perch on the hub of a rear wheel of the wagon in front of me, and from there I was able to see that the brothers driving our wagons were all standing on their benches, peering forward to the north and shouting questions to those in front of them. Behind them—for there was no room to spread on either side—we could see and hear nothing, and so all we could do was speculate among ourselves about what might be happening.

From my vantage point of the wheel hub, I saw Brother Reynald coming straight towards us, leaning slightly sideways because of the closeness of the wagons on his left, and I jumped down from my perch to let him pass. He thanked me with a nod and clambered up onto the wagon's side and thence to the tailboard, and we clustered around to hear what he had to say.

The Scots had taken the initiative, he said gravely, by launching an attack across terrain that the English scouts had deemed to be impassable after weeks of torrential rain and rising water levels. It had proved to be as impassable as predicted, he reported, for both "our" cavalry and infantry formations—he was a Norman-French Englishman, born and bred—but not for the Scotch hordes who ran across it lightly, many of them barefoot and wearing little or no armour. My astonishment grew to awe as he then explained that the road on the far side of the bridge was long and straight, built up above the surrounding flatlands for a full half-mile, and that the Forth River enclosed much of it in a loop to the right of the bridge, forming a spur of marshy land surrounded on three sides by the river. The Scotch attack, swift, unexpected, and unstoppable, had been devastating, capturing that entire spit. Armed with light, abnormally long spears that enabled them to reach their tightly restricted enemies without being reached in return, they had come running from the northeast, down from the woods at the base of the Abbey Craig, in a great, sweeping charge that arced

from right to left to cut across the road at the end of the
causeway and then drive south on both sides of it,
isolating and containing the hapless English cavalry
and infantry units, thousands of men in all, who had
crossed the bridge but remained stranded on the
causeway, far short of its northern end.

The high banks on either side of the road had thus
become a kind of prison, for their height and steepness
ensured that any mounted man seeking to leap or ride
down to the valley floor risked plunging his mount
into soft ground that could swallow his animal to the
chest and break its legs. In similar fashion, though to
a lesser extent, the ranks of heavily armoured men
crowding the road would be hampered and weighted
down upon reaching the flats, their very numbers
churning the muddy ground to the consistency of soft-
ened butter. Thus the people on the bridge were cut
off, Reynald said. They had been stopped and rendered
useless, their front ranks facing annihilation as they
marched four abreast against the hordes awaiting them
at the causeway's end, while the men and horses
behind them, being pressed unbearably from their rear,
were unable even to turn around on the narrow
roadway in order to retreat. De Warrenne had halted
the advance and ordered the remnants of his force on
the south side of the bridge, something close to half his
army, to deploy to each side of the entrance, so that the
bridge itself was now relatively clear.

This was our sole chance to cross the Forth,
Reynald said, and we would have to take it now, before

the hard-pressed army on the other side could turn itself around and render the bridge impassable again. We would cross on foot, and we would carry with us what we needed, for our wagons would be useless on the causeway. Once across, we would set up a hospital directly west of the bridge, on the southward bend of the river where we would be close to both the water and the fighting.

In crossing that bridge, we walked into Hell.

We found ourselves floundering ankle-deep in a sea of blood, slipping and falling and close to drowning in it and surrounded by sundered corpses and dying men, severed limbs and spilled entrails, and gouting fountains of fresh gore from deep-trenched wounds, as though the crimson ocean already spilt by then was nowhere near sufficient. We heard the screams of dying, maimed men mingle insanely with the shrieks and cries and frantic, despairing pleas of wretches who fought in abject terror for their very lives, fought in the crazed belief that their survival lay in slaughtering or maiming every panting, screaming wretch who faced them.

At one point—and I have no idea when this occurred or how long the battle had been going on by then—I remember coming to a halt, sobbing with exhaustion and looking about me in despair, feeling the knotted rope across my shoulders digging into my flesh like an iron rod. My role as supervisor had changed to that of porter when a young Dominican priest called Alaric, one of my twelve charges, suddenly dropped to his knees in front of me with the lethal barbs and bloodied shaft of a broadhead arrow jutting from his shattered neck. He dropped his end of the stretcher and toppled forward onto the man he had been carrying, and the sudden weight tore the stretcher from the hands of the man on the front end. I heaved the Dominican aside and snatched up the end of the stretcher, signalling to the other bearer to do the same, and from that moment on I scarce remember anything. I recall my hands being so sore at one time that I could no longer hold the stretcher, and so I snatched up a fallen length of rope and tied its ends to the arms, with great difficulty because of my bruised and bleeding fingers, then laid it across my shoulders, transferring much of the weight from my arms to my back.

Another time, caught in the middle of vicious fighting between two large groups, I was struck heavily from behind and sent flying. I landed awkwardly, face down and momentarily stunned, aware that I had lost my stretcher and had no idea where or how. I lay there for a while, gasping to regain my breath and quite incapable of movement, though I was being trampled and kicked within what appeared to be, from where I lay, a forest of straining, pushing legs. Unable even to try to roll over, I closed my eyes and imagined that I was covered with a heavy, stifling blanket of appalling sounds: grunts and thuds and smashing, concussive, meat-cleaving sounds; clanging, clashing, slithering sounds of metal blades and the incisive, clean-edged strikes of hard-swung blows; there were spitting, hissing, snarling, keening sounds of human voices in there, filled with rage, confusion, and terror and mingled with panic-stricken whines and unintelligible snatches of half-formed words, prayers, or curses; and one awful, instantly recognizable combination of two sounds close to my ear: the heavy strike of a pointed blade—a spear or a broadsword—piercing mail and driving deep with a squealing noise of metal scraping metal and a gritty rending of flesh and bone, and the instant, chilling scream of agony and grief that accompanied it.

And then, in the blink of an eye, it seemed, all the legs that had surrounded me were gone, moving away from where I lay gasping, and taking much of the deafening noise with them. I was alone for a while then, safe from the madness for long enough to catch my breath, then roll over onto my back and explore myself for injuries. There was blood everywhere, of course, thinning and liquefying the glutinous mud underfoot. I was awash in it, my clothing slick and greasy with it, much of it in clotted lumps and clumps, but none of it appeared to be my own. My right arm and shoulder, where the blow had landed, were numb and lifeless, but even as I probed the area with my left hand, the numbness started to wear off and the pain from the blow began to assert itself, forcibly, so that my vision blurred.

I gritted my teeth, and after a while, squirming and grunting, I succeeded in hauling myself into a sitting position, my back supported by a hard object that I hoped was a boulder and not a corpse, and I sat there

for a while with my eyes screwed tightly shut, fighting
desperately not to think of the carnage around me. I
dug my fingers hard into my damaged shoulder, trying
to focus my mind on the pain there and use it to my
own ends. But then I heard a high, wavering scream
and the approaching sounds of a running fight that
seemed to be coming directly at me. I opened my eyes
and turned my head slightly to see a knot of men
rushing towards me, flailing at one another with
heavy weapons. I could not tell which of them were
Scots or Englishmen, for they were uniformly filthy
and indistinguishable one from another, but within
moments they were on top of me, their blades hissing
all around me. I saw one man go to his knees, blank-
eyed with shock as he lowered his head to look at the
heavy spear that had plunged into his chest and killed
him. Dully, I saw someone standing in front of him
and raising one leg to brace his foot on the dead
man's torso as he hauled on the spear's shaft, but the
weapon's barbs were buried deep in the flesh it had
pierced and would not be dislodged. The fellow
cursed and heaved again, but then a long blade struck
him sideways from the rear, splitting his face wide
open at the junction of the jaw and throwing him
aside like a discarded garment. I did not turn to look
at his assailant, nor did I move to see where the dead
man fell. I willed myself to stay motionless, my eyes
closed again, and some time later, I have no idea how
long, I noticed there was silence around me. The knot
of fighters had all died or moved on.

I managed to struggle to my feet, and then I simply stood swaying and looking around me for a while. The entire landscape, every yard of it, it seemed to me, was strewn with dead and dying men, some of them piled deep in places, and it occurred to me, incongruously, that no army I had ever seen had looked as large or numerous as this battalion of the dead. We tend to look at soldiers, when we see them, in terms of units and formations: densely packed, shoulder-to-shoulder foot soldiers, archers, or men-at-arms. It is not until you see those disciplined units scattered and heaped and piled in banks and rows and swaths of sprawling, stiffening limbs and the lifeless, unnatural attitudes of violent death that you see just how much space they really do take up.

I was alone there, I realized, the only man left standing in a wilderness of death.

I could still hear the far-off noise of the fighting, though there were other, more urgent noises all around me, a chorus of them, all human, all filled with misery, and all demanding my attention. They ranged from quiet whimpers to sustained groans and sudden cries, and occasionally to harrowing, demented screams born of unbearable agony. And then, looking down at one of the whimperers, a disembowelled but still living man who lay at my feet, I discovered one more novelty to add to my growing list of appalling non-clerical realities. I became aware of the stink that filled my nostrils, the stomach-turning stench of battle-slaughter: the sharp and acrid tang of new-spilt, visceral fluids from ruptured entrails and other riven and severed organs, mingled with urine and feces. The smell of hot, fresh blood is in there, too, with its coppery, metallic, almost tangible texture. And all of those are added to the predominant military stink of mouldy fustian; dirt-encrusted, too-long-worn chain mail; rank, sweat-stained leather; unwashed bodies; and rancid human and equine sweat.

The man at my feet was speaking to me, though I could hear no sound from his moving lips. I stooped, reaching out carefully like an old, weak man to stop myself from falling on top of him, and bent forward to where I could hear his words. He wanted me to kill him. I felt mindless panic welling up in me as I stared back into his imploring eyes. He would die soon, of that I had no doubt, for his intestines lay beside him on the ground, trodden into the blood-thick mud. A voice inside my head was telling me that it would be an act of mercy to kill this man and free him from his torment, but I ignored it, knowing I could never kill another human being, and searched my mind instead for some other way I could aid him. The answer shocked me like a sudden dousing with cold water, for in all the disorientation of my surroundings, I had forgotten what I was.

I pulled my knapsack around from between my shoulders, and within moments I was kneeling by the dying man's side with my priestly stole about my neck, administering him the last rites and listening to his confession. He heard my words of absolution and squeezed my hand as he drew his last breath, and for a brief moment I felt exultant … And then I looked about me. I moved to the nearest living soul and began the ritual afresh.

I cannot say how many times I moved from spot to spot, or how many viatica I administered long after my supply of the sacred chrism had been used up, for I lost track of everything save the need to comfort as many of the dying as I could. I had no wine, nor even water, but I had a crusty loaf of bread in my knapsack, and I blessed it and transformed it, then doled it out in pinches as the Body of Christ until nothing remained of it. Fighting men came back and swirled about me from time to time, but intent upon my work I paid no heed to them and, as God protects both drunken men and children, so too did He protect me from being struck down that day.

At last there came a time when all the noises close to me had ceased and I sat there exhausted and unmoving, slumped back on my heels. I knelt among the dead I had been praying with for hours, and I wept as I seldom have, grieving for the senseless loss of life I had witnessed that day, for the destructive and debilitating waste of it all, and, be it said, for my own lost innocence, for never again would I be able to regard human strife and the shedding of men's blood, in any cause, as being either acceptable or justifiable. I felt empty, hopeless and desolate and close to despair, sitting there, but I know I was exhausted, and I lapsed into a kind of waking stupor, dead to all awareness of my surroundings and the passing of time.

But then I heard my name, spoken in a voice that seemed to echo as though it came from a great distance away, and I looked up to see a familiar face frowning down at me.

"Jamie?" he said again. "Father James, in God's name, is that you?"

He spoke in Gaelic, and I nodded. "Alistair," I answered, in the same tongue, and I heard my voice come out a croak. "Where have you come from?"

His eyes widened. "Where have I come from? My God, man, where have you been? Look at you. You're clarted in mud and blood. I've never seen the like. You could not be dirtier if you lay down in the mud and wallowed like a sow." He had been looking about him as he spoke, and now he shook his head and his voice sank to become barely audible. "God's sweet blue eyes," he said, more to himself than to me. "Look at this place. How many men died here? I have never seen this many dead in one small place." He looked back at me. "What are you doing here, Father James? This is no fit place for a priest."

I stopped him with a raised hand, astounded to find myself close to smiling at the outrage in his voice. "It is the perfect place for a priest, Alistair," I told him. "Places like this remind us of why we are priests. I have been ministering to those in need of God's mercy, and if I grew soiled and dirty in the doing of it, so be it. Dirt is no more than earth, and it will wash away in the river." I was on the point of saying I doubted the blood would ever wash away, but I bit back the words and held out my hand to him. "Help me up, if you will."

He reached out and pulled me easily to my feet, and I looked him up and down, content to see that he appeared to be unscathed. He looked clean, which surprised me, and there were no visible signs of blood on his clothing, armour, or weapons, though his round targe bore a few fresh scars and there were streaks of dried blood below his right knee. His legs were bare beneath a kilted woollen tunic, and over that he wore a loose shirt of mail, belted at the waist. A heavy sword belt hung across his chest, and the hilt of a long sword thrust up above his shoulders. I drew a great breath and blessed him with the sign of the cross.

"You have not answered my question, Alistair. How come you here?"

"To find the Hospital Knights. Andrew has been wounded. Stabbed from behind in a melee."

"Dear God! How badly is he hurt?"

His sharp shake of the head told me as much as the grim jut of his jaw. "Who knows? It doesn't look too bad, because there's not a lot of blood, but it's wide and we don't know how deep the blade went. There's no such thing as a good sword wound. The knights will be able to tell us how serious it is."

"A single wound? No more than one?" My relief must have made me sound dismissive, for he frowned quickly.

"No more, but will that not suffice?" He caught himself and shook his head. "Forgive me, Father. That was uncalled for. I know what you meant and, yes, there's but the single wound."

"And what about Will?"

"I have no idea. I've not seen him since we launched our attack. He and his led the right flank of the charge and we the left. Anyway, I must go. Do you know where to find the Hospital people?"

"I do not, but I should. I was with them, working with them, before the fighting separated us, but that was a long time ago and I have not seen them since. Wait!" I turned in a circle, concentrating hard and trying to orient myself by the few landmarks I could distinguish. I found the Abbey Craig in the north with ease, but when I faced south towards the castle crag I gasped. The bridge across the river was no longer there. I blinked, seeing only the ruins of its remains.

"Aye, the old brig's gone," Alistair said. "They pulled it down for fear we'd cross after them."

I stared at him. "The English pulled it down? You mean the battle's over? I can still hear fighting."

"No, you're hearing our men celebrating. The English are gone, fled with their tails between their legs."

"Praise be to God," I said, meaning every word, and then I saw in the distance the high black-and-white standard I had been searching for. "There it is, over there! You see yon black banner? That's where the knights are stationed." I looked about me, my tiredness forgotten and my mind functioning clearly again. "Look you. There's no point in both of us going all the way over there simply to walk back again. I was working near here before I started giving the last rites to dying men. I had a stretcher, for carrying the wounded. It must be close by here somewhere. If we find it, you can use it to bring Andrew to the hospital over there. I'll go ahead of you and tell them Andrew's coming. Now help me find that stretcher. You'll know it when you see it—a plain wooden bier, two long side pieces with crosswise slats."

It was half hidden beneath a pile of bodies, and Alistair Murray carried it away with him, holding it in front of him like a shield while I knelt above the body of my former colleague, whose name was unknown to me. He was entirely encrusted in filth, unrecognizable save by his ankle-length habit and his tonsure. His knapsack was unopened, its contents yet intact. I opened it and placed the stole of his priesthood around his neck, then anointed him with his own chrism, administering the last rites posthumously in the complete belief that he had no need of them. And then I left him there, his hands crossed on his breast, and set out to rejoin Brother Reynald and his Hospitallers.

I found a scene of appalling horror awaiting me when I reached the hospital, but I could see I was the only person there who was aware of it, for no one else had time to look at it. I had thought myself amid the atrocities of Hell out there on the battlefield, surrounded by the dead and wounded, but the hospital was worse, for there in one small place were collected casualties from all areas of the field. Englishmen and Scots lay

side by side, all race and ranks ignored in the reality of
fighting now for breath and life itself. Peasants lay
among noblemen, and common foot soldiers lay
bleeding beside others whose bedraggled finery
proclaimed them to be high-born knights and lords.
And all of them were in extremis, for no man well
enough to walk away from there would have thought
of remaining in such a place. There was surprisingly
little noise, though, there where I would have expected
the screaming from so many throats to have outdone
the worst I had heard earlier. I soon realized that most
of the men there were too gravely injured to make
much noise. Of course there were exceptions, and no
shortage of them, but I tried to close my ears, as those
around me must have done already.

I found Brother Reynald by the largest of the
wagons, surrounded by several of his brethren. He was
standing by a bloodstained table, holding his hands up
in front of him as he watched one of his fellows sew
an open wound shut with a large needle. Blood
dripped heavily from his upraised hands, and I thought
he had cut himself, but as I watched, someone handed
him a ragged towel and he wiped his hands on it,
taking care to clean the clotted stuff from between his
fingers. Two other men moved forward, stooping over
as though about to kneel for his blessing, but they went
to work instead, one of them holding open a large sack
while the other filled it with severed arms and legs that
he drew out of a mountain of limbs that had been
concealed from my sight by the tabletop. It was a sight

that came close to overwhelming me, even after my earlier ordeal, but as I stood there reeling, Brother Reynald looked up.

"Father James! Come over here."

I walked slowly over to where he stood. His companions paid me no heed at all, so busy were they at their work, but as I approached him I could see he was looking at my clothes much as I was looking at his. We were very similar in appearance then, save that his robes were drenched in pure blood, whereas there was more mud in the mixture that coated mine. His eyes narrowed and he nodded at me. "They tell me it is over," he said quietly.

I nodded. "Aye, it is. A man I know, a Highlander, told me it was done."

He turned aside and looked around the hellish scene surrounding us. "They'll be bringing men in here for hours to come and there's little we can do for any of them. May sweet Jesus have mercy on us all ..." He inhaled a great breath and expelled it noisily. "And the worst of it," he continued, "the worst, most evil and satanic part of all of this, is that some arrant, self-important, witless fool—some worthless, prancing, prating, high-born stay-at-home buffoon who thinks he has a right to send his fellow men to die—will proclaim a God-given victory here, as though some great and wondrous thing has been achieved and this foul crime, this slaughterhouse, should be remembered as a signal token of God's favour." He grunted, a bitter, disgusted sound. "They'll say that England won and Scotland lost, or Scotland won and England lost—I neither know nor care which might be held correct—but look around you, Father James, and tell me, if you will, what was won here in this awful place, and whose brow will wear the victor's laurels?"

I had no words with which to answer him, and it was clear that he expected none.

"Where will you go now?" he asked.

I shrugged. "Return to the castle, I suppose, although I don't know why."

"No more do I," he said, looking at me from beneath one raised eyebrow. "What is a Scot doing in an English army?"

"Spying?" I said, and his face twisted in a rueful smile.

"Go with God, then, Father James, but I warn you, don't look for Him out there on the field. Not for a few days. He has too much to do here."

"I came to tell you that they are bringing in one of the Scots commanders, a young man called Andrew de Moray. He was stabbed in the back."

"I see." He looked disappointed. "One of the architects of this debacle, and you want me to have an eye to his wounds?"

I searched for words that would address what he had said without demeaning myself or endangering the outcome of what I was asking of him.

"You wrong him when you name him architect of this, Reynald," I said. "There is but one sole architect involved in this entire debacle, as you call it. Many actors, many participants, and many victims, but no more than one architect. That man is Edward Plantagenet. He alone conceived the elements of all of this when he decided to claim Scotland as his own."

His face betrayed nothing of what he was thinking.

"I have little more to say," I continued. "You are an Englishman, and I am a Scot, and so we may regard the matter differently between the two of us. But we are both priests, and our oaths of fealty and worship are to the God we serve, not to any worldly king with human weaknesses and vices and a lust for foreign conquest. As for the wounded man, Andrew de Moray, I know him well and find him truly admirable—a fine, upstanding, noble young man who knows and understands his God-given duty to his people. He was a leader here today purely because there was a crying need for someone, somewhere, to step forth and raise a hand against the tyranny that threatened him and his and all of Scotland."

When I fell silent he twisted his mouth as though nibbling at the inside of his lip, then dipped his head in the smallest of nods. "Where is he?"

"They're bringing him in. On one of your stretchers."

"He is fortunate," he said quietly, "that you and I share a distaste for the greed of ambitious monarchs. When he comes in, bring him to me here." He turned away without another word and stepped back up to the bloody table.

There were hundreds of people coming and going all around me, and I watched them curiously while I waited for Andrew's stretcher, distracting myself by trying to identify the colours and escutcheons of the various English knights I saw being carried here and there. I saw no Scottish colours, for there had been no Scottish lords present as far as I knew, apart from Andrew de Moray himself, who would be wearing his father's crest of three white stars on a field of dark blue. And as I thought of those white stars, I saw them on a banner in the distance, being carried by a stripling lad who should have been at home with his mother that day. I would have recognized the group without those stars, even had Alistair not been walking ahead of them—eight tall Highlanders, four of whom held their young chief's stretcher while the others walked along on either side of them, ready to relieve them.

I made my way directly to them. Andrew lay motionless on the bier, on his belly, his eyes closed.

"How is he?"

Alistair shook his head. "He was like this when I got back and he has not stirred since. Some English priest dosed him with something, some powder he claimed to have received from a Muslim physician when he was in the Holy Lands. He swore it would ease Andrew's pain and make him sleep. He wouldn't have done it had I been there, I can tell you, for I'd have gutted any Englishman who tried to come near Andrew. But Sandy Pilche told me that Andrew knew the fellow well, from his time in England, and that he drank the stuff down willingly enough. I suppose it's reassuring that the priest made no attempt to flee afterwards."

"Bring your men and follow me."

CHAPTER TWENTY-SEVEN

AFFAIRS OF STATE

We left the hospital compound while Brother Reynald tended to Andrew, walking until we found a place to sit on the riverbank. Alistair cocked his head to one of the younger men, holding up a hand and wiggling his fingers.

"Duncan," he said. "The flask."

The young fellow hitched a knapsack around from where it hung by his hip and reached into it, producing a tightly stoppered bottle made from hard leather. He removed the stopper and handed the bottle to Alistair, who took a sip from it and rolled the liquid round his mouth pensively, then swallowed it and took a mouthful more before offering it to me. I started to wave it away, then changed my mind. I tilted my head back and filled my mouth with the fiery spirits. My entire mouth seemed to explode and I swallowed, feeling the liquor burn its way down to my stomach. It was well named, uisge beatha, the water of life. I had no will to fight it. I simply lay back in silence and let it do its work until Alistair poked me and thrust the bottle at me again.

"So," he said eventually, "what do you know of what's happened?"

"Nothing except what you've told me and what I've witnessed with my own eyes. How much more do you know?"

"No more than you. I saw the Englishry strung out across the bridge and along the causeway, and then we started our attack, running across the flats. After that I saw nothing except what was happening right there beside me. I killed a few men, no more than five or six, but they were all trying their best to send me off. At first, I spent most of my time safely behind a wall of swords, playing the captain and keeping the wall in place against everything the English threw at us. And they were good. Someone said they were young Baron Percy's men, but I don't know if that was true or not. No one really knew. But whoever they were, the whoresons were hard men who knew their business. Their weapons and armour were well made—easily as good as our new supplies—and they had been trained long and hard. As soon as we cut one of them down another stepped right in to fill his place, and they kept coming forward, no matter how many of them we killed. But then the MacDonalds on our right broke through the line and turned their flank, leaving the men against us unprotected on that side. That was the end of them, for once they started to crumble, their entire wall collapsed, and that's when I started fighting.

The next thing I knew, there were no English anywhere around us, and someone brought the word that Andrew had been killed. That's what I heard at first, but no one with a whit of sense ever believes a rumour."

"Where was he?"

"Safe off the field. Sandy had taken charge and he saw to it they carried him away to where he would come to no more harm, back the way we had come, towards the Abbey Craig. But they were thinking clearly. They stopped at the first dry spot they found well clear of the fighting and stayed there, then set up a shelter to keep him out of the sun."

"You mean a tent?"

"A canopy—they had no tent. But the sun was high and the mud was steaming. And flies were swarming, with all the spilt blood."

"And Andrew was conscious?"

"Aye, and clear headed. But he was in great pain."

"So where is Sandy Pilche now?"

He shook his head. "I can't tell you. He wasn't about when I went back to fetch Andrew, and I didn't think to ask where he'd gone."

I paid no real attention when Alistair said that, because at that particular moment, I was more interested in finding out about Will's whereabouts than I was in anything else, and so it was not until much later, days later, that I realized that no one, in fact, had thought to ask where Sandy Pilche had gone. He had simply vanished and was never seen again, one of the uncounted multitude, including my colleague Father

Thomas, whose existence had been unambiguously blotted out in that awful place. They died unnoticed and were gone, either drowned and washed away by the river or coated beyond recognition by the mud that covered the entire battlefield. Days were to elapse, though, before the chaos died down and folk began to realize that they had lost friends and kinsmen they had assumed were safe elsewhere, and that was the case with me, searching for Will and assuming my other friends were safe.

"And you heard nothing more of Will?"

"No, not a word. But he's out there somewhere, still alive, for if William Wallace had been hurt or killed, we would have heard of it by now. News like that always travels fast."

"So how did we turn the English? We were outnumbered in every way."

"We were, but we hit them and cut them off before they could all cross the bridge. That was what did it. We cut them in half at the outset, then kept them pent up where they couldn't fight other than by our rules. We stopped them from using their horsemen, and their archers did them no good, stuck on the far side of the river."

I frowned. "But they had archers on this side. I saw them leave the castle, behind the mounted squadrons who were first in line. There must have been a hundred of them."

"Aye, there were some at first, but they were useless, too closely packed on the road, and we were too fast for them—our front-runners were among them before they could spread out to form their lines, and so they broke and ran for their lives, right into the river. Some of them even swam across, but their weapons were lost or ruined."

"Did we take any knightly prisoners?"

He looked at me, pretending to scowl. "I surely hope so, for before I left to start looking for the Hospital knights I heard Andrew say we'll need the ransom money. We've none of our own left, he was telling Sandy."

Evening was approaching, and I was suddenly anxious to be up and about, an anxiety induced, I have no doubt, by the whisky I had drunk so quickly. "How can we find out what's going on? Who would know?"

Alistair rose to his feet. "We can walk about and ask folk—that's the best way I can think of." He was right, I knew, and so I stood up and stretched, then fell into step beside him.

We walked for almost two hours, stopping to talk to anyone we met who looked as though he might know something worth knowing. But we quickly found that no one did. Everyone else was as ignorant of what was truly happening as we were, completely dependent upon reports from others who had learned things at second hand. We heard early in our quest that a number of English horsemen had escaped, fighting their way through our ranks and swimming their horses across the Forth, and that the treasurer Cressingham had been killed. He had ridden out to battle armoured as a knight, but had apparently been recognized by his sheer bulk when his horse sank to its belly in the mire beneath his weight. He had then been pulled from his saddle and killed before he had an opportunity to defend himself. We heard, too, that he had been flayed after his death, the skin stripped from his flesh, but that detail we assumed to be exaggeration and chose to disbelieve it. And we were told, by someone who had come across the bridge shortly before the English destroyed it, that the English commander, Earl Warrenne, had been seen fleeing south, surrounded by a number of his subordinates. But that, too, was a word-of-mouth report.

In fact it took us a full day to piece together the details of what had taken place on the Carse of Stirling that day, and another entire day would elapse after that before anyone could even attempt to begin assembling an authoritative summary of the developments. And of course the responsibility for gathering and collating the information fell to the clerics of the realm.

I played a part in documenting that report. My association with the English army had ended when Earl Warrenne fled the field; there was no English army left in Scotland after that. I joined a cadre of monks and priests assembled from the Stirling area, and took up residence in the Abbey of Cambuskenneth, beneath the shadow of the castle rock, which remained in the hands of its English garrison. It took the better part of a month to assemble all the information we could glean from a multitude of sources and arrange it into an intelligible narrative, but when the official version of the fight took its final form, it contained a verification that Cressingham's body had, in fact, been flayed and mutilated. No one was ever arraigned for it, though, because, incredible as it may seem even after all this time, no names were ever associated with the crime.

It defies belief that none of Cressingham's detractors ever grew sufficiently drunk or indiscreet to let slip some hint, some clue, about having been involved, or knowing of someone who was involved. But it seems the general hatred of the man was sufficiently profound to guarantee the anonymity of those who defiled his corpse. That would remain a mystery until a credible-seeming tale began to spread, a year or more later, that my cousin himself had used the dead man's hide to make a belt for his great sword.

That rumour tormented me for years, for even though I denied it and defended my cousin against the allegation whenever it came to my attention, I always wondered, deep inside, whether it might be true. Cressingham was reviled as the grossest, most excessive and detested symbol of English tyranny, and every Scot who heard the word of his death at Stirling Bridge was glad of it. It seemed likely to me, then, despite my reluctance to believe such a thing, that the rumour of Will's sword belt might be true. I asked him about it eight years later, when he was in London, waiting to be executed. He denied it and, thanks be to God, I saw the truth of his denial in his eyes and knew him to be innocent of the crime.

As for the report we compiled, its details are now common knowledge, the main points listed fluently by any child in the realm. It was not a massive battle, for the opposed armies were relatively small, but it was a giant victory for us. It was the first occasion in more than two hundred years on which an English army had been beaten by a Scots one. Alone, and without the guidance or battlefield support of any of the great Scottish houses, William Wallace and Andrew Murray, two relatively unknown local men, had defeated and routed an English army in the field—a well-equipped and structured army of professional infantry, cavalry, and archers. These two young leaders had achieved a monumental victory with a following of landless, untitled, and unlettered men whose sole connection was their commonness, their sense of community. They had combined two hosts of undistinguished but determined fighting men—from the south, the men of Selkirk, Galloway, Annandale, Carrick, Lanark, Lothian, and Stirling, and from the north, the free fighting men of Moray, Banff, Aberdeen, Kincardine, Forfar, Perth, and Dumbarton—to crush and humiliate and repel a far larger army so well supplied and armoured that there should have been no possibility of beating them. And they had done it in a single encounter, sending the English High Command into headlong flight back towards England and safety. The victory transformed Wallace and Murray into giants, making them, with one strike, the two most powerful men in all the realm.

The awareness of what they had achieved changed the way the common folk of Scotland looked upon themselves. They had always had a single-minded self-awareness, a form of independence that enabled them to think themselves entitled to speak on equal terms to any man around them, including their crowned kings. Now that they had ousted the English with their own hands, they took delight in their prowess.

One of the earliest English casualties among those cut off on the northern bank of the river when the Scots attacked was the constable of Stirling Castle, Sir Richard de Waldegrave. He had taken a full company of the garrison to the fight with him, but the news of his death, and of the loss of his garrison troops, did not reach Earl Warrenne on the other side of the river until two full hours had passed. And by that time the slaughter on the north side of the Forth had run its course, the day was irretrievably lost, the unblooded English formations remaining on the south side of the bridge were disintegrating to find their ways homeward in disgrace, and the Earl of Surrey was making his own hasty preparations to depart for England.

One of the few English knights who had distinguished himself and behaved with great honour that day was Sir Marmaduke Tweng of York, the renowned warrior who had sat among Earl Warrenne's men at the parley with the High Steward, and whom I later learned to be a former tutor of Robert Bruce, the Earl of Carrick. Finding himself and his mounted company surrounded and close to helpless on boggy ground, being cut down and harried by running footmen with long spears, Tweng rallied his companions and had them form up in a tight wedge-shaped formation. He then led them slowly forward, fighting off attackers on all sides, until they reached the river's edge, where he bade them leap in and swim with their mounts, armoured as they were, across the swollen stream. He gained the safety of the south bank, having lost but six of his group of thirty men, and was on hand at de Warrenne's side when the news of Waldegrave's death arrived.

A short time earlier, the earl had ordered his engineers and sappers to destroy the old bridge, for fear the Scots might come across the Forth to strike at him afresh while his forces were in disarray. So great was his fear of being taken unawares again that he had ordered his Welsh archers to let no one come across the bridge, not even the hundreds of wounded and desperate English survivors thronging the causeway. Thus the messenger who had swum across the Forth bearing the word of Waldegrave's death found the earl close to the bridge's end and was confronted by the astonishing sight of massed Welsh archers aiming above the heads of English sappers labouring to pull down the bridge, and threatening to shoot the English wounded who packed the bridge itself. And upon his arrival the bridge collapsed without warning, trapping and killing some of the sappers who had weakened it and hurling most of the men on the bridge deck into the deep, cold waters underneath. The messenger stood open mouthed for a time, watching with the others, and then when people started moving again he bethought himself and stepped forward to inform the earl of the constable's death.

De Warrenne apparently reacted with nothing more than a distracted nod, and then stood mute for a while, staring off absently into the distance before drawing himself up to his full height and turning to eye the men beside him. He pointed a gloved finger towards Sir Marmaduke Tweng and named him garrison commander of Stirling Castle, bidding him hold and maintain the castle in the name of King Edward. He then seconded the former constable of Urquhart Castle in Aberdeenshire, Sir William Fitzwarren, to assist Tweng. Having attended to the continuance of the state, he then rode away to the south with his personal guards as fast as their horses could bear them.

To their credit, and lacking any guidance from on high, Surrey's lieutenants marshalled the remaining portion of the army—very few of whom had come within half a mile of the enemy that day—and marched them south towards the border as quickly as was possible. Their intent, we learned later, was to avoid the main towns as far as they were able to, keeping to the hills and valleys far from the main roads. An army, though, and particularly a fleeing army, is hard to hide, and Will himself rode off in hot pursuit of them, his victorious followers ravening for blood like hungry wolves, chasing the remnants all the way to the border.

There were other predators out there that September day.

The eighty-strong party of horsemen led by the High Steward and the Earls of Menteith and Lennox had not ridden far beyond the southern limits of the English camp before they turned their mounts eastward and climbed gently for two miles to the high ground that afforded them a view of what was happening both at the bridge crossing and in the area called the Pows, almost below the wooded heights where they were sitting. The Pows was a wasteland, a flat expanse of bog far more perilous than the terrain over which the Stirling causeway had been built. The place was all but impassable save by an uneven ridge of rocky higher ground that formed a so-called road.

That road was the sole southward escape route available to the English. And as the Steward's party watched, it grew more and more crowded and less passable as the fleeing army filed onto it, until eventually it was jammed solid in places where the roadway, such as it was, narrowed dramatically, creating bottlenecks that grew more and more congested, with increasing pressure from the people at the rear of the column who could not see what was causing the delay ahead of them. The men looking down from the hillsides above could see perfectly well what was happening, though, and they could also see, behind the army, the wagons of the English baggage train, haplessly awaiting their turn to proceed. It was a target too rich to ignore.

The High Steward led his men down to attack it, becoming the first of Scotland's great nobles to align himself openly with William Wallace and Andrew Murray. His four score men, hungry for activity now after watching the victory at the bridge, savaged the retreating soldiers on the narrow road, striking them from behind and crushing them against the unmoving press beyond them. Then, having demonstrated their ferocity, they turned around and captured the entire baggage train with little difficulty.

Lord James Stewart's "conversion" to the patriots' cause, as it became known in certain quarters, was merely the opening note of the fanfare with which the Scots magnates now rushed to shower their blessings and congratulations upon Will and Andrew. But unlike the acceptance of Lord James, who had been one of the architects of Will and Andrew's uprising, the thanks and good wishes of the ruck of the magnates were too little and too late, and every soul in Scotland knew it.

I had already joined the secretariat in Cambuskenneth Abbey, compiling the official report of the battle, when I heard that Will had arrived back from harrying the fleeing English, and I sent a messenger to ask him if we might meet soon. I was unsurprised that I did not soon receive an answer, for I had heard reports of how he had been overwhelmed on his return by the amount of work that needed to be done. He had returned as the seasoned, confident leader he had been before, and had had no idea of how greatly his life and all its circumstances had been altered by the victory at Stirling Bridge.

No more had I, I soon realized, for I had assumed, with my normal naivety, that, with the English gone, life for both of us would return to normal. Nothing, in fact, could have been further from the truth, for normal was a word that no longer held any relevance for me, or for Will. My cousin was now the most powerful man in Scotland, a notion that was completely alien to me, entailing, as it did, the thought of his being now superior, in strength and immediate influence at least, if not in rank, to men like Lord James Stewart and John Comyn the Black, the Earl of Buchan. For me to have expected him to make time for me was ludicrous.

Yet send for me he did.

When last I saw my cousin, Will had been staying in a small camp, and he had slept in a small tent to which none of us had paid any attention beyond being aware that it was Will's tent and he might be found in it from time to time. Now, though, he had an encampment—a military camp laid out in blocks and orderly rows of tents, with streets and cross-routes and gated entranceways, as such places had been arranged since the days of the Roman legions—and his personal tent was an imposing pavilion, fully twenty paces long on each squared side, guarded at all times and furnished within with dividing walls of cloth. I stood outside it on the sunny afternoon of the day he summoned me, feeling oddly shy and awkward in a way I had not been for many years, and reluctant to make myself known to the guards on duty in front of the tent, all of whom wore the colours and livery of the

Lord High Steward. My shyness went unnoticed by
the sergeant of the guard, who recognized me as soon
as he set eyes on me and greeted me by name before
summoning me inside. There I found my cousin sitting
at a fine oak table like the one Earl Warrenne had had
in his pavilion, poring over a letter written on fine
vellum and festooned with ribboned seals.

"Jamie!" he cried, jumping to his feet and dropping
the letter to the tabletop, where it sprang back into its
cylindrical form and rolled off the edge. "Come in,
come in. God, man, it's good to see you. Come here
and let me look at you. Are you well? How are the
Augustinians treating you down at the abbey?" He
cocked his head, looking at me and answering his own
question. "Very well, it seems. You're looking grander
than I've seen you in a long, long time."

I knew precisely what he meant. I was wearing a
new full-length cloak that day, over a fine new
cassock with buttons all the way down the front from
throat to ankles. The garments had been issued to me
that very morning by the almoner at Cambuskenneth,
whose responsibility for the provision of alms
extended to the provision of new habits, robes, and
vestments for the members of the abbey community. I
was a guest of the community, not a member, but the
clothing I had worn on the day of the battle had
proved to be beyond salvage, despite the best efforts
of the abbey launderers. The Augustinian brethren of
Cambuskenneth wore plain black habits, but simple-
looking as they were, the clothes I was wearing now

were far and away the finest and most beautifully made I had ever owned.

Now, seeing my cousin eyeing the broad, richly tasselled black belt of plaited silk strands around my waist, I felt myself flush. Determined to change the subject, I moved quickly to pick up the fallen letter from beneath the table.

"This," I said in Latin, "is an impressive-looking letter." I fingered the three separate ribbons dangling from its seals.

"It's from the Comyns," Will said quietly, his voice close to a growl. He resumed his seat at the table and waved me to an empty chair across from him. "Sit down. A clutch of Comyns, in one letter—Buchan, Badenoch, and the Countess of Ross—all seeking to awe me by pointing out how fortunate I am now to have their support."

He made no attempt to hide the scorn he felt for them, and I rewound the scroll and set it down between us on the tabletop.

"Aye," I said. "You'll be getting a lot of that now, no doubt."

"Aye, enough to make me want to vomit. There were a score such letters awaiting me when I got back to Stirling, all of them from folk desiring me to be duly grateful—humbly grateful, they meant me to understand—that they now support my leadership of Scotland's folk. And all wishing me, at the same time, to ignore what they did, holding back and doing and saying nothing that might commit them, shutting their eyes and ears until they could see which way the cat was going to jump. Well damn them all. I never cared what they thought or did before, and I'll not change that now."

"How is Andrew?" I asked, not because I wanted to change the subject but because I had not heard any word of him.

"He's fine, thank God," Will said. "His wound was not as deep as we had feared, and he grows stronger every day." He peered around as if searching for something he had mislaid. "In fact, I'm going to see him now and I want you—no, I need you to come with me."

"For what?"

He looked at me with raised eyebrows. "To help us. There's much to be done, Jamie, a terrifying amount, and I'm not good at that kind of rubbish." He snapped up a hand to quiet me before I could even open my mouth. "I know, I know, it's not rubbish at all. Far from it. It's work that needs to be done, and done well, handled with an eye to other people's certain discontent at what we do. Andrew's better at it than I, but even he is a soldier, not a cleric, and a clever cleric's what we need. There's a wide range of matters that have to be resolved, matters of government and the safety of the realm that can't be put off much longer. I could not be content to leave them in the hands of the same folk who have failed us in the past. I don't trust the magnates and I do not want them taking control again. Not without oversight and supervision from able folk—folk I know and trust.

That's why I need you. You have the critical eye of a cleric trained in such things."

"I can tell you here and now, Cuz," I said, "that's far too much responsibility for me. Matters of state are too important and too complex to entrust into the hands of someone who does not know exactly what's involved."

"And isn't that what I've just said? How do you think I feel when I contemplate what needs to be done now? It frightens me nigh to death, Jamie." He pushed his chair back and stood up again, then walked away to where his sword stood propped in the corner of the fireplace, and I watched as he grasped it by the hilt and swung it towards me, his arms outstretched and elbows locked, sighting at me along its long blade.

"This is what I know, Jamie. Weapons, fighting. And even this with the sword is new to me. I'm an archer, a bowman. I can pick a moving target a hundred paces away, then track it and knock it down before most men can even see what I'm aiming at." His arms relaxed and he stepped back towards me, holding the great sword one-handed and laying it gently on the tabletop. "And I'm learning how to use this, too, more easily than I thought I would. But what I know nothing about, what I can never hope to learn about, is statecraft, the ten thousand things any man needs to know if he is to govern a country, and the thought of having to deal with it is terrifying."

"I believe that," I said.

"You remember Brother Duncan, Jamie?" I nodded, for Duncan had been a favourite teacher of ours at Paisley Abbey. "Well, Brother Duncan once told me that God would set no man a task he was incapable of doing. If the task is assigned to you, and you know that it is truly yours, then that assignment is a token of God's confidence in your ability to do it." He grunted. "No matter that you might not know how to do it at the time. That's not important. What is important, Duncan said, is that you learn how to do it in the time ahead, and that you work at it until the job is done."

"I remember that," I said, "for he was talking to me, about working in the library. I'm surprised you remember it, for it had nothing to do with you."

"It does now, Cousin, for I can't deny the task God has set for me. I worked towards it and reached out for it on the Carse of Stirling. And now I must learn how to deal with it."

The tone of his voice had altered subtly, and I stared at him, suddenly wary of what I heard. "You sound as though you believe that," I said.

"I do, Jamie. What other choice have I? My biggest fear is that I won't be able to live up to it."

"Live up to what?"

"To the challenge." He sighed. "We have an opportunity here, I think, to do something truly fine in Scotland, something that has never been done before—an opportunity to shape something noble for our folk and rid them of the fear of never knowing what to expect from those above them. But the misery of that is that I don't know where to start or, once I do, how to go from there. All I can do is pray to God for guidance, and I'll have to rely on you and your brethren for help with that."

I had never heard my cousin speak that way of God before, but I knew that that was not the time to say so, and so I smiled, and tried to sound unconcerned as I said, "Well, I don't even know what we are talking about yet."

He made a doleful face and started ticking off topics on his fingers. "The magnates, first and fore-most," he began. "How do we handle them? Can we handle them? Will they agree to work with us, mere base-born folk beside their lofty names?" He ticked another finger. "The Church. Scotland's bishops. The three strongest men in Scotland's Church aren't even here. Wishart's in jail, Fraser of St. Andrews is in France on King John's behalf, and Crambeth of Dunkeld's there, too, and like to stay there for some time. We need to address that, and quickly, for the last thing our cause needs is weakness within the Church. We need the support of all our bishops, but of those three most of all, because they control the country and its clergy."

I was nodding before he had even finished speaking. "I know Wishart's deputy in Glasgow, Canon Lamberton," I said. "He's a good man, with the same kind of strength—the fortitude and forthrightness— Wishart has always had. You'll like him. In fact you should make a friend of him as quickly as you can, because he is his own man and will not be dictated to if he is not convinced of the righteousness of the dictator. I know he'll be of great help to you once he knows what you require. I can write to him. What else is on your list?"

"The English." He snorted derisively. "They're right at the very top of my own personal list. We've run them back across the border, and Edward's safely at war in France, but the whoresons still hold all our castles. Here we are in Stirling, talking about governing the country, and the castle above our heads is held by Englishmen! That has to change, and quickly. That will be among my first three priorities, and we'll start by starving out the garrison here in Stirling."

He ticked a fourth finger. "And then there are the Scots. They'll be no easy folk to govern, especially now that they've run the English out, and we won't be able to tackle that until we've decided what to do about the magnates—and *they'll* be determined to cling tightly to the administration of the realm's rules of chancery. The magnates are going to be our biggest problem."

"Which brings us around in a full circle. Is there anything else?"

"Aye," he said heavily, "there is. The biggest, most contentious matter of them all. It overshadows all the others and it influences every aspect of everything we need to do."

"You make it sound like doomsday."

"Close ... close. We have no money, Jamie." He saw the lack of understanding in my priestly eyes.

"*Scotland* has no money. The realm is penniless—bankrupt. This country of ours ran on wool, Jamie. It made us prosperous, after a fashion. It certainly allowed us to survive in comfort. But that fat slug Cressingham destroyed the wool trade, and we are left with nothing in its place for earning revenue. Our barns and warehouses are empty, their contents seized and shipped to England as taxes. The farmers who reared the sheep that supplied our wool have eaten their animals. The English burned our granaries and flooded our pastureland. Many farmers refused to plant crops, unwilling to labour in the fields only to have their harvests ripped away from them at the end of the year. And our trading fleets have gone elsewhere. Add that to everything else the English have plundered from us in the past two years, and then throw in the costs of arming and equipping armies—one for us, to fight the English at Dunbar in support of King John, and now this one to pay for Edward's wars in France—and we're left with nothing, Cousin. You can't feed folk with nothing."

He smiled, a small, bitter, self-deprecating smile. "Think about that while we walk from here to Stirling, and then be prepared to hear the same, with variations, from Andrew."

"Is Andrew well enough to deal with all of this?"

The smile reappeared, slightly broader this time. "He has no choice. We need him on the walls." He picked up the Comyn letter and placed it inside a plain but polished wooden chest that stood on a small table in one corner of the tent's main room. "Believe me, though," he added, "when I heard that he had been carried off the field without my ever learning of it, I died inside at the thought that he might have been killed, leaving me to face this dying world alone. Selfish, no doubt of that, but what I am facing, what I have to contend with, is the ending of the world as I have known it all my life. Would you disagree with that?"

I shook my head. "Probably not, from your point of view," I said. "You have achieved some signal changes in these past few months. My world is much the same as before, but my world is the Church with all its permanence, whereas yours is … the ever-changing world of men, with all its flaws and follies."

He picked up his huge sword and slipped it through the ring that hung between his shoulders, then crossed to take a long cloak from a stand in one corner and swung it out and around to settle on his shoulders with the sword's hilt thrusting up from beneath it. "Come," he said. "We'll talk as we walk. Andrew's expecting us and there is no reason for us to keep him waiting."

It took us the better part of half an hour to walk the two miles from Will's camp to the house in Stirling where Andrew had been lodged. We would have taken him to his own estates in Bothwell, once he was well enough to travel, but the English garrison still held Bothwell Castle. And so we had found quarters for him in a house that had belonged to the former town provost of Stirling, and while far from being grand in the sense of denoting nobility, it was large enough for a family of ten. What made it suitable for Andrew in his convalescence was that it had a separate suite of chambers at the rear, complete with a door leading to the lane behind the house. Mistress Morton, the provost's widow, lived in the main house still with her two plain and unmarried middle-aged daughters, Morag and Marjorie, and she had been happy to make her premises available to the dashing young chieftain from Moray. Andrew's wife, Eleanor, had been summoned from Auch Castle to join her husband, and when she eventually arrived, she would move into Andrew's quarters with him.

Andrew was even happier to see us than Will had been to welcome me, and we spent no small amount of time catching up. He was looking far better than I would have expected, considering that he had had half a foot of steel thrust through his lower back a mere week earlier. He was gaunt, of course, his jaws more sunken and his cheekbones sharper, and the lines running from his nose to bracket his mouth were graven deep. He was sitting stiffly, on a high-backed wooden chair. But his eyes were bright and clear, he was clean and close-shaved, and he bore no discernible trace of sickness about him. He offered us wine when we arrived, but neither one of us accepted, and soon we had come down to business, considering the priorities Will had defined earlier, and tossing thoughts and ideas back and forth from one to another as they came to us.

We had barely started on the topic of the letters from the Comyns and other magnates when we were

interrupted by one of the widow's two daughters, who
tapped on the door and entered timidly, her eyes fixed
in awe upon my cousin Will and her entire demeanour
suggesting she might flee at the slightest sound.

"What is it, Morag?" Andrew said courteously.
"You look concerned. Are we making too much
noise?"

Her eyes shot wide and then she frowned immediately, making me want to smile. "Eh? Whit? Och
no. We canna hear a thing oot there. There's a man
here to see you."

"A man? Did he give you his name?"

"No, sir, but he asked for you."

"What manner of man is he, can you tell me?"

Wide-eyed again, she nodded. "Aye. He's big …
Bigger nor you. And he has armour on, like Maister
Wallace's, but cleaner, shinier."

"Shinier, aye. Is he old or young, though? Does
he have a beard?" I had the distinct feeling that
Andrew was teasing the woman, trying, albeit gently,
to fluster her, but if that were the case he was wasting
his time.

She pressed her lips into a slightly disapproving
pout. "He's young," she said.

"Then be so good as to bring the young man in, if
it please you."

Morag nodded, still with that look of pouting disapproval, and pulled the heavy door shut behind her.

"I wonder who would come calling upon me at this
hour of the day, and in shinier armour than yours,

Will." He sounded facetious, as though he was not really expecting an answer, but before Will could respond the door swung open again and the answer walked into the room and stopped short, gazing at Will and me in astonishment that quickly yielded to a grin of pleasure.

"God bless all here," he said. "But as He is my God and witness, I did not think to find a house full of Wallaces! I but came by to make myself known and offer my respects to Master de Moray." He turned immediately, smiling still, to where Andrew sat mystified, watching him with wondering eyes. "Pardon me, sir, for this discourtesy in interrupting you while you are conferring with your colleagues. No, stay," he said, seeing Andrew gathering himself to rise and greet him. "No need to stand on my behalf." He extended his hand and strode forward quickly to where Andrew could reach it without having to rise. "As I say, I came but to present my respects. I am Robert Bruce, Earl of Carrick, and I am here to place myself at your service." He moved his eyes slightly to include Will. "At service to you both, indeed, if you will have me."

Andrew had not recovered from his astonishment, and looked wide-eyed at Will, but my cousin was gazing fixedly at Bruce.

"Where were you last week," he said bluntly, "when we were fighting at Stirling Bridge? We could have used your service then."

"I was in the Carrick hills," Bruce said, and shrugged. "In my own lands, safe among my own folk. I know you are familiar with the outlaw life, Master Wallace, how it feels when you cannot openly approach folk that you meet for fear of being recognized and taken or betrayed. When you must live in hiding, it grows difficult to stay abreast of things well known to other people. I have been living with my head down these past three months, avoiding the attentions of the English since the surrender at Irvine, because I much dislike the terms imposed upon me there by Henry Percy and his warty familiar, Robert Clifford. I had no part in the discussion of those terms, and they demand that I give up my wee girl Marjorie as hostage to my good behaviour and obedience. They have required three oaths of loyalty from me in as many years, and now they want to take my daughter as an earnest of my honour and good faith. She is not yet a year old, and she is all I have left of my wife, Izzy, who died birthing her. So I removed her to safety, where she will not be found. And that is where I was last week.

"As for why I missed the Stirling fight," he went on, "I was misinformed about de Warrenne's movements—Cressingham's, too—and by the time I discovered the truth, I was too late to join you. I knew you had come west from Dundee, and I knew you would block Surrey's advance at Stirling, but I did not know how quickly it would come to pass. I thought to be here in time to join you. And for that failure, I am regretful, for I would dearly love to have been here with you when you sent them packing."

I had been watching Will all the time Bruce was speaking and I could see he was impressed by the earl's words. I had no doubt in my mind that Bruce had spoken truthfully, and my gut told me Will believed him, too.

"Let me say one thing more, Master Wallace, before you reject my offer to join you." Bruce paused. "The offer is genuine. I know exactly what you think of Scotland's magnates—people like me. We have spoken of it in the past, between we two, and so I am aware of your distrust and your suspicions when it comes to dealing with what the nobles of this realm delight in calling the nobility, with their divided feudal loyalties and ancient ways of doing things. I know all that, and yet here I stand, to face you. I have little doubt you'll be collecting finely worded letters of intent from every noble household up and down and all across the land these days, offering service and assistance whenever you might have need of it. Am I correct?" He was watching Will keenly, and even though his question went unanswered, he smiled. "That's what I thought," he said. "For my part, I believe you might have need of service and assistance here and now."

"Why would you think that?" Will's voice was soft.

Bruce glanced over to where the sweat-beaded metal ewer of untouched wine sat on the table beside its cups, and he turned to Andrew. "Would you object were I to pour myself some wine?" He moved without waiting for an answer, though Andrew was already shaking his head and waving him to proceed. He poured one cup of wine and then look up inquiringly at the rest of us. "Anyone else?"

"Aye," Will said, nodding, and Bruce ended up pouring wine for all of us and taking Andrew's cup to him.

Bruce tasted his, nodded in approval, then sat at the table, close to Andrew. "Why would I think that, you asked. Well, let me try to answer." He sipped his wine again, then set down his cup. "You two have achieved a miracle. You took a ragtag army of ill-equipped and untrained men and led them to destroy an English battle force in its full panoply. And then, having broken and beaten them in the field, you chased them all the way back to England. And you did all of it without help from any of the great houses"—he glanced at Andrew—"with the singular exception of the House of de Moray, be it said. And now you are the two most puissant men in all the realm—victorious, triumphant, and with an eager, loyal army at your backs. The word throughout the realm, I'm being told, is that you have united all the folk, the ordinary folk of Scotland, as they have never been before. That is something unprecedented."

"Then why do you believe that we need help?" Will's tone was dry. He had not yet tasted his wine and was holding the cold rim of the pewter cup against his chin.

"Because I think you have no real idea of what you need to do next." No one reacted, and Bruce's eyes shifted from Will to Andrew and back again, sliding

over me as though I was not there. "I did not say that
to offend you," he went on. "But you have no idea
what is needed to govern a country, and yet that is
what you have condemned yourselves to do from this
day forth—you now need to govern." He threw up his
hands. "Where you may find guidance in doing that is
in God's hands. It is most certainly not in your own."

Will pulled himself to his full height. "Grant us a
trace of wisdom, Lord Bruce, at the very least." His
emphasis on Bruce's name and title was slight enough
to avoid outright offensiveness, but it was there nonetheless. He continued, almost in a growl. "We're not
quite as helpless as you seem to think. We have identified our priorities and we are well aware of what we
need to be getting on with." He nodded to me, because
I had prepared the notes on all we had discussed
before Bruce's arrival, and I read the list aloud.

"How to deal with the nobles," I began. "The
magnates and mormaers. How to deal with the Church,
when the three strongest bishops in the realm are all
absent. How to get rid of English garrisons now left in
Scotland, now that they are cut off and isolated. How
to deal with the governance of the realm, so that the
machinery of government, including the law courts
and the royal court of chancery, keeps working. And
last, but first in overall importance, how to replenish
the treasury and rebuild the realm's economy."

Bruce's eyebrows had risen high on his forehead as
he listened to the litany, and now he placed his open
palm on his left breast and bent forward in his seat in a

mock bow. "Well done, my friends," he said, with no trace of mockery in his voice. "I'm both impressed and relieved, for I believe you have managed to include everything that needs to be achieved in that short list. Achieving it all will take more lifetimes than we have among us all, for that kind of endeavour is never ending, but the fact that you have identified the elements so readily tells me you might be better prepared than I had thought."

"You're wrong on what comes first, though, Jamie," Will said quietly. "Finding money is important, but the most important consideration facing us now is what to do about the magnates and the mormaers, for until we find a way to deal with that, we won't be able to do anything about the treasury." He looked directly at Bruce. "And in that, Earl Carrick, you may perhaps be able to offer us some assistance."

"With the magnates?" The look on Bruce's face was not encouraging. "I doubt they'd pay much heed to me. I've been away too long, and I'm a Bruce now in a Comyn country." He stopped, seeing how Wallace was shaking his head. "What?"

"We don't need for you to go a-preaching on our behalf," Will said. "We need more practical assistance, in the kind of thinking that people of your rank and station use. To begin, you can help us decide what to call ourselves. You were right about the letters from the noble houses. We have many of them and they all need to be answered, but how should they be answered? We are not magnates or mormaers and we have no grand titles. Andrew is of de Moray, but he is not a knight, though he will be soon. And I am a verderer, when not beyond the law. So what will we call ourselves in dealing with the dignitaries of the world?"

Bruce thumped a clenched fist on the table. "Hah! See? At one thrust you have punctured the bladder of empty air that keeps the majority of men from ever achieving anything worthwhile! What should you call yourselves, indeed. You should call yourselves exactly what you are, awarding yourselves the honours you have won and which no one can take away from you, and you should do it by honouring and including those who made it possible—the ordinary folk of Scotland. In all your writings, you should name yourselves Andrew Moray and William Wallace, commanders of the army of the kingdom of Scotland and the community of that realm." He paused, looking from one to the other of them. "You might think it sounds pretentious now, but it is not. It is precisely who and what you are. So say it out loudly, then let the doubters and the sneerers try to fault you for any part of it. Any man who dares to challenge you will be declaring himself to be no friend of this realm or its community."

I was stricken dumb by the beauty and perfection of what he had defined, and I was glad to see that both Will and Andrew were gaping at him.

"By the living God, Sir Robert," Will said, "I openly aver I stand henceforth in your debt. That solution is perfect—you agree, Andrew? Perfect."

Will stopped and gazed at the earl and then shook his head. "You know, I have no wish to like you or admire you, for you stand as an example of all the things I disapprove of in this land of ours. You appear much of the time to be more English than Scots, and your allegiance has, for years now, been freely given to England. But you're a Bruce, and you were driven out when King John Balliol was chosen over your grand-sire. Now, even though you have turned your back on England, there is a voice inside me that wants to ask, 'Will he turn his coat on me?' But for all of that, I cannot seem to help myself from liking you, and I believe we will be grateful for any help you can give us."

The Earl of Carrick smiled. "It gladdens me to hear that," he said. "So let us see about finding something to eat, and then we may settle in and come to grips with the items on your list. There are people, excellent people throughout the land who we can conscript to help." He looked at me again. "Of course, most of them will be priests or monks—clerics of some description—since few others read or write well enough to help us keep the records that will be neces-sary or draft the number of letters and communications we might require."

Will scowled. "What kind of communications?"

"Straightforward ones, explaining to people how you intend to run the country now that it is open to change. I am assuming, of course, that you have no intention of restoring the status quo to what it was before Edward invaded?"

"If you mean leaving all the power in the hands of the noble houses again, then you are correct. I won't do that. Not without some form of accountability. And if that means that we may, in time, need an army of recruits from every monastery in the realm, we'll recruit them. And if we are to have accountability on such a scale, we will need courts and magistrates to enforce penalties for lapses of that accountability. The great houses will continue to administer their own affairs, but they will be held accountable to this community of the realm of which you spoke. Their days of ignoring the laws of the realm and simply riding roughshod over everyone in pursuit of their own ends are over."

Bruce shrugged. "From what I know of such things, the great houses will benefit greatly by all that in the end, no matter how much it grieves them at the start. Accountability will bring stability, and everyone will gain from that. They'll all get over their discontent eventually, one way or the other."

Andrew asked him, "And are you sure you want to be identified with this? Your peers may deem you traitor to your own class."

"I care not for that," Carrick said. "But I will not be a part of it. I'll do what I can do at this time, and I'll help you to set things in motion, but I have much to take care of on my own nowadays. My earldom needs my attention and my father's territory of Annandale has been neglected for too long, so I'll assist you now, say, for the remaining months of this year, but after that I must be about my own affairs."

Will nodded. "So be it, then. Now let us see about finding some food, and then we'll get to work."

CHAPTER TWENTY-EIGHT

THE PERTH ASSEMBLY

Despite his lack of training and experience, Will showed an amazing aptitude for the task to which he had newly turned his hand, and in the course of the ensuing four days he achieved much, mentored and guided by the willing Earl of Carrick. I watched them as their relationship quickly became easy and natural, and they worked together smoothly, with Will spending most of his time listening and asking questions that Bruce seemed happy to answer at length. Will was twenty-seven that year, and Bruce was four years younger, but the mentor-to-student relationship was unstrained despite the disparity. Will was eager to learn, his attention captured and his imagination challenged by the magnitude of the task facing him—and not merely him, but all of us who took part in that exercise, Andrew included. Bruce, for his part, appeared to be comfortable in the task of teaching, and he was more than merely familiar with much of the subject matter, for in his relatively short lifetime he had absorbed a profound understanding of the mechanics of both government and governance, having learned the basic elements of both at his father's knee. And then later, when he had begun to grow towards manhood, he had been shown the finer points from the perspective of his formidable grandsire and namesake, the Noble Robert, Bruce of Annandale who, at the age of more than seventy, had come within hand's grasp of wearing the crown itself.

I served as notary for everything that was discussed among the three of them during that time, and for days my fingers were in a constant state of cramp, black with ink, and painfully tight and knotted from the effort of writing without respite for hour after hour, for the list of things to be addressed grew bewilderingly once we had begun to apply ourselves. The truly daunting part of what we were doing, though, was our awareness that we were merely identifying things that needed to be attended to; we were doing nothing at all to deal with them.

There had been no formal gathering of parliament or governing authorities for years, since the dispossession of King John, and the country was in chaos, close to anarchy and on the edge of famine. All of that was bad enough, but now with the flight of Surrey's army, the English administration itself had come to a halt; local officials everywhere were scrambling to escape and save themselves from an angry and vengeful populace, and there was no one, anywhere, with the authority or ability to step forward and replace them.

With Wishart, Fraser, and Crambeth out of the picture, even the Church was in disrepair, the normally firm grip of the bishops effectively annulled. Alpin of Strathearn, the recently appointed Bishop of Dunblane who was the sole Scots bishop not to have been forced to swear allegiance to Edward Plantagenet, was unable to provide much help, being too new to his post and consequently lacking the power and influence to assert himself sufficiently. And Archibald, the Bishop of Moray, although a formidable presence in earlier days, had held his seat now for forty-four years and was palsied and increasingly infirm. The only other man who might have been expected to contribute to the struggle was Nicholas of Brechin, bishop of the powerful east coast diocese of Dundee, but he, too, was newly consecrated, little known, and reputed to be in ill health.

Elsewhere in Scotland, the prelates were a lacklustre crew, reluctant to take an open stance for or against the English claims, save for Thomas of Kirkcudbright, the Bishop of Galloway, who had never made any secret of his loyalty to the English Archbishop of York, and Henry de Cheyne, the Bishop of Aberdeen, detested by the people of his diocese, who had never concealed his allegiance to Edward of England and anyway was now a fugitive, hiding somewhere in the northern mountains in fear for his life.

After Bishop Wishart's imprisonment, the occupying English had focused upon harassing and oppressing the parish priesthood throughout the realm. As a result, more than half the parishes of Scotland had no priest, an intolerable situation that deprived the people of the comforts and necessities of their religion in their daily lives. Ordained priests are the only people who can administer the sacraments of God's Church, so it followed inevitably that half the people of the realm were therefore forced to live without the blessings of the divine sacraments: marriage, baptism, confirmation, confession, the Holy Eucharist, and the Holy Anointments or last rites. It was a situation that screamed for redress yet was incapable of being quickly resolved, since, without the presence of active bishops, no new priests could be ordained in Scotland.

There was no shortage of priests in England, and the Archbishop of York had already professed, to all who would listen, his devout willingness to provide an unstinted supply of fresh new priests to fill the vacancies that existed throughout Scotland. To allow York to supply English priests to Scotland, though, was unthinkable, tantamount to surrendering all authority to England, since it would permit the unrestricted dissemination of England's wishes, viewpoints, and dictates among Scotland's faithful.

In the hope that Bishop Wishart's deputy would be able to aid us in addressing this dire situation, I had written to Canon Lamberton on the night of our first discussions, inviting him to join us or to send us some assistance. I told him about Bruce's participation, and outlined our concerns and our activities to that point, and I had sent the letter off to Glasgow by fast courier.

What would come of that remained to be seen, but there was no doubt in my mind that the perilous health of Scotland's Church was of overriding import to everything we were discussing.

The layman's world was equally endangered: the land was infested with army deserters, outlaws and thieves who roamed unchecked, pillaging and killing at will because they knew there was no one to arrest or punish them. The law courts were no longer operable, for the English had usurped their function. Scots judges, magistrates, and lawyers had been imprisoned, dismissed from their positions, or in some instances simply made to vanish. In some parts of the country plague and pestilence were widespread, and there were reports of entire communities that had simply disintegrated, their occupants scattered, homeless, and destitute. On the eastern coast, the centres of maritime trade and commerce had suffered widely. Piers and docks, warehouses and storage areas, harbour-works and flood-banks had all been either badly damaged or dangerously neglected, and inland bridges and fords everywhere were largely in disrepair, abused and, in the case of the river fords, almost obliterated.

We were confronting a disaster of overwhelming magnitude, and it seemed that the closer we looked, the more we discovered and the worse the situation appeared. And yet we achieved much within a very short time. We had no shortage of supporters waiting to be put to use, for all of Scotland, it seemed, was flocking to Stirlin' toun. All of Scotland, that is, except those of the nobility too proud or yet too stubborn to acknowledge what had taken place.

At Bruce's suggestion, beginning on the morning of the second day of our talks, and using the copying resources of the secretariat at Cambuskenneth Abbey and the exact inscription of Will and Andrew as leaders of the army of Scotland and the community of that realm, invitations had been sent out to that community by courier to attend a gathering that would be held at Perth on the twenty-fifth day of September. The location of the event would be the Blackfriars Monastery. This was a sometime royal residence and the traditional site of such major events as church councils and national gatherings, since it housed the largest public chambers in the region, dwarfing those of the neighbouring Scone Abbey. Of necessity, the summons was of short notice, but there was no other option, and such a gathering was long overdue. An assembly, they called it, for it could not be called a parliament, lacking a royal command, and the legally required forty days' notice for a convention of the estates was out of the question, given the circumstances in effect. And so an assembly it was deemed to be, convened to examine the immediate needs of the realm in consequence of the recent victory at Stirling. It was agreed that every noble family in Scotland should receive an invitation.

"And what will we do if they don't come?" Andrew asked, and we all looked at him in surprise.

"Who?" Bruce asked.

"The magnates. What if they stay away?"

"Oh, they'll not stay away." Will's voice was a low, rumbling sound filled with disgust. "They'll come running, never fear about that. They'll be afraid not to, lest they miss some chance of profiting from what comes next. The English are gone, but they'll be back, and when they come next time, they'll come in earnest. But that's a year away at least, depending upon how Edward's wars in France progress, and in the meantime there's not a magnate in the land who won't be wanting to know what *we* intend to do to change things between now and then. They won't think to take the responsibility upon themselves, but they won't hesitate to foist it onto us. But that doesn't answer your question, does it?" He made a harrumphing sound, but he was smiling. "If they should fail to come, we will do exactly what we would have done had they been there—we'll get on with addressing the needs of the realm. For it is the realm that is important here, not the hurt feelings and posturing puffery of offended, foolish folk who should know better.

"But they will come, believe me," he went on. "And they'll be no more tolerant or considerate of anyone else than they have been in the past. They'll whine and cavil and carp and complain and try to browbeat one another and everyone else nearby"—he switched to broad, exaggerated Scots in mid-sentence—"but they canna browbeat you and me, young Murray, for we're the chiels wha won the Stirlin' fight, and our army's our ain. They canna touch it or lay claim to it, and God knows they winna daur dispute it.

"This assembly is for the *community*." He flicked a finger towards Bruce. "That same community o' the realm that you're aey harpin' on about, Rob. So it should be open to that community and whaever else wants to come, forbye the gentry an' nobility. The high kirkmen will a' be there, needless to say—the bishops and abbots and priors and deacons o' a' the great kirks—but we should hae the common parish priesthood, too. They're the ones wha stay amang the ordinary folk an' dae maist o' the work, anyway. And then there's the burghs—a' the provosts and councillors should be there, forbye the magistrates. And the trade guilds, as well. And even the minor local gentry, knights and sodgers."

"What about county sheriffs?"

The question came from Bruce, and Will curled his lip. "Are there any left? Scotch ones, I mean? Maist o' them were either Englishmen or English lapdogs." He hitched one shoulder in a dismissive shrug. "I suppose ye're right, though. Gin there's any sheriffs left in place, they should be invited, though the thought o' creatures like yon crawlin' thing Stewart o' Menteith bein' there to thumb his nose at us makes me want to vomit. His heel crushed mair Scotch necks than the English did while he was sheriff o' Dundee."

"Menteith won't come," Andrew said. "Not after what he has done in England's name. He wouldna dare to show his face. They'd hang him."

"Who would hang him? The Dundee folk?" Will's scorn was withering. "I doubt that. There's no' a man among them wi' the balls for that job. Don't you delude yersel'. The man's a barefaced turncoat and a scoundrel, but he isna short o' backbone, and he'll no' be scared by threats. He'll be in Perth, gin he hears o' it in time. But half the counties in the land will need new sheriffs now, so we'll hae to appoint them durin' the assembly." He shook his head tersely. "The truth is that there's nae lack o' people to invite, and they a' *should* be invited. An gin the great lords of the realm come to speak sensibly, their voices will be heard. On the ither hand, gin they elect to stay away, folk will tak note o' it." He continued in churchly Latin. "In the meantime, though, we have little more than a week to prepare, and we have other things to occupy us."

It was true. Word had come that day, from the castle on the rock above our heads, that Sir William Fitzwarren wished to negotiate terms for surrender, claiming he had insufficient supplies of food to sustain his garrison. Will had expected that and was unsurprised; he knew that two large supply trains had been intercepted in Selkirk Forest no more than a month earlier by his own people and that no effort had been made since then to replace the lost provisions. He delegated several of his lieutenants, among them Sir Neil Crambeth of Dunkeld, to dictate *his* terms to the English commanders, and they were blunt and not negotiable: surrender and leave immediately, or stay and die of starvation.

The English hauled down the royal standard over Stirling Castle's keep the following day, and the garrison troops were permitted to depart.

The day after the surrender of the castle, just as the four of us were starting to prepare for the thirty-mile journey to Perth, Canon Lamberton arrived from Glasgow, bringing tidings from France. Bishop William Fraser, who had served the realm of Scotland long and well in many capacities, including years as one of the joint Guardians in the interregnum after King Alexander's death, had died near Paris on August twentieth, and had been buried in the Dominican church there. The news could scarcely have come at a worse time, given the present state of the Church in Scotland, for now, in addition to finding the resources to staff the land's parishes with priests, the realm was faced with an urgent need to replace one of its staunchest and most loyal servants: the bishop of the see of St. Andrews, the oldest and most influential shrine in Scotland.

The unexpected news distressed us all, for when Lamberton was ushered in, we had been discussing what to do about the situation within the Church. Our collective chagrin upon hearing the news of Bishop Fraser's death must have been obvious, for the canon stopped what he was saying and looked around the table, eyeing each of us in turn before he shook his head and held up one hand with two raised fingers, as though he were about to bless us.

"My friends," he said, "remember who you are, and what we are discussing. We are speaking of the continuity of God's Holy Church within this realm, not of the death of some obscure landowner. This news is cause for celebration, not for mourning. It means we have an opening for a new bishop *now*, and right here in Scotland, a vacancy that has been gaping like an undressed wound this past year and more, and would have continued to do so for as long as Bishop Fraser had remained active in France." Again he looked at each of us. "Think carefully upon that, my friends. Bishop Fraser's death is Heaven sent, from God's own hand and to our benefit.

"Can you really doubt God's purpose in recalling him? The Church in Scotland is in dire need of a sure, controlling hand to see it through these current times and troubles. Surely none of you can believe that the Almighty has not already provided that successor? Somewhere within the realm today, the next man to be Bishop of St. Andrews for the greater glory of God is waiting, all unknowing, to feel the hand of God upon his shoulder." He smiled, a great, blazing smile of joy that lit his face like an internal beacon. "Believe me, my friends, we need this man, and we need him quickly. So trust in God to make His wishes known to us without delay. He will not waste our time or His own when so much needs to be achieved so quickly."

I turned idly to look at Will, and to my mild consternation I found him eyeing the canon strangely, his eyes narrowed so that they were almost closed and his jaw set in a way that gave his face a speculative expression. He kept his eyes on Lamberton, his expression unchanged and unreadable as he listened to what the canon was now saying about the need to convene the bishops of the realm to consider who the new Bishop of St. Andrews might be.

We had no time to waste, the canon said, not a single hour, let alone a day, for time was flying by too quickly and the demands upon the Church were already threatening to exhaust its dwindling resources. We needed, urgently, he said, the input and guidance of all the other bishops, whether they were present in person or not, and irrespective of their health and physical capabilities, for the new bishop-elect would have to travel to Rome upon his election, to be personally assessed and endorsed by the Pope himself before being consecrated. That would take months—a long and harrowing sea voyage at the best of times, even without the hazards of running an English blockade and risking interdiction—and Scotland's Church did not have months to spare.

"Tell me, Canon," Will said. "This matter of Rome. Is it truly required? Are you saying that the new bishop *must* go there before he can work here?"

Lamberton nodded. "Aye, Master Wallace. It is traditional, even ritualistic, but it is required." He waved a hand dismissively. "Mind you, though, in the normal scheme of things it is a joyous occasion, the sacramental procession of a successful son of Mother Church to the centre of the Church's existence in Rome and the welcoming benediction of the Holy Father himself. A grand occasion crowned with a magnificent rite of celebration and fulfillment. It is merely our present circumstance that places these constraints of time and need upon us—the fact that we are simultaneously at war with England on one hand, and virtually at war, though liturgically so, with the Archbishopric of York on the other. Neither of our opponents would like to see Scotland's Church being strengthened at this time, and therefore we must forge ahead at speed and, as far as we can manage it, in secrecy."

"Then forge ahead, Father. What will you require of us?"

"Nothing, Master Wallace, but I thank you for your offer. I have already set the thing in motion—even to sending some of my people privily to talk with Bishop Wishart in his jail in Roxburgh Castle and enlist his aid."

He turned then to Andrew. "All of that I would have done on my own initiative anyway, Master Murray."

"So if you would have done all that anyway, why are you here today? Why leave Glasgow at such a time?"

Lamberton's smile included all of us this time. "Because I was invited, by Father James, and I have enough conceit to think I might be able to assist with what you are doing. Everything is in hand in Glasgow and I trust my staff, so I have no concerns there. Here, though, is stronger, meatier stuff. What *are* you doing, if I may ask?"

Andrew laughed aloud. "I believe we are arranging the convocation of bishops you have just described.

We will have them all together and in one place within the week, all unknowing of your need. They will convene at Blackfriars Church in Perth, but they will doubtless all be lodged nearby in Scone Abbey. We sent an invitation to you to attend, two days ago, but you would have passed our courier on the road."

"God be praised," Lamberton said quietly. "Did I not say He would not waste our time or His?"

Will's face was still unreadable. He had lost that look that had so disconcerted me earlier, but he was still observing Lamberton impassively, and I had to fight down the urge to ask him what he was thinking.

From that moment on, though, William Lamberton became completely engrossed by what we were doing, and his contributions were invaluable. Will accepted all of them without reservation or demur, and I set aside my concern over whether or not he liked the canon, for had he not, or had he disagreed in any way with Lamberton's suggestions, he would have said so.

The great and grand of the realm all came to Perth as Will had said they would, but Robert Bruce, the Earl of Carrick, was not among them. On the very day that we were to depart from Stirling, word reached Bruce that his presence was required in Annandale, where the Bruce estates were being harried and laid waste by a strong English raiding force out of Newcastle, under the command of Sir Robert Clifford, the same man who had presided with Henry Percy at the Irvine capitulation. It was obvious to Bruce that the raid had little to do with the English defeat at Stirling the previous week, for the arrangements to launch the expedition must have been in hand long before the Stirling fight occurred. In addition, the fact that the lands in question were not Bruce's own but were yet owned by his father, who remained a loyal vassal of King Edward, suggested that this was a punitive expedition in retaliation for the younger Bruce's failure to produce his infant daughter as a hostage, as stipulated by the terms of the Irvine settlement. He had left immediately for the south, accompanied by the hundred men he had brought with him to Stirling, while we rode north without him.

In the town of Perth, the great lords and officers of state were lost among the mobs that thronged the place, so we avoided the town and went directly instead to Scone Abbey to pay our respects to the abbot in the hope that we might find accommodations there, no matter how mean or Spartan they might be. Of course the ancient abbey was a natural destination for all the senior churchmen looking to attend the assembly, and we arrived to find the place already crowded with bustling, sleek-looking senior clerics, including several priors and abbots and a number of deacons and subdeacons. Much to my own gratification and surprise, though, Abbot Thomas welcomed us warmly, remembering me kindly from my visit weeks before, and insisted that our entire party, including Canon Lamberton, should accept his gracious offer of accommodation within the abbey precincts. The abbey was spacious and prosperous, he said, with ample room for important guests, whereas Perth town was straining at the seams with an influx of people unlike anything he had ever seen, even at royal coronations in the abbey.

Two days later, on the twenty-fifth day of September, the assembly was called to order by William Sinclair, the Coadjutor Bishop of Dunkeld responsible for supervising the affairs of the diocese during Bishop Crambeth's absence in France. He began by offering a prayer of thanks to the Almighty for the recent victory at Stirling, and he made sure to acknowledge the pivotal role therein of the two new champions of the realm and commanders of the armies of Scotland, William Wallace of Elderslie and Andrew Murray of Petty. The acknowledgment was met with cheers from the packed ranks of the commoners at one end of the great hall, which drew frowns and stony silence from the assembled lords.

Silence fell again eventually, and from that moment forward the wrangling began as the various groups and factions began vying for whatever advantages they perceived to be attainable. As a representative of Bishop Wishart, I sat with Canon Lamberton on the right of the great chamber, in the raised section set aside for the bishops and mitred abbots known as the lords spiritual, while below us sat the priors and lesser churchmen in order of seniority. The corresponding section opposite us was filled to overflowing with all the land's nobility, seated in order of precedence, beginning with the great officers of the realm, senior among those the High Steward, James Stewart, and the High Constable, John Comyn, Earl of Buchan. Following those in descending order came the earls and the lords, all of whom were represented, and then the knights and petty barons, with the surviving Scots sheriffs of the counties seated below them, along with the governors of fortresses and keepers of royal castles. The lowest places on that side were taken up by the lairds and minor landowners, and the provosts and magistrates of the burghs of the realm.

The commons stood clustered at the east end of the hall, and Will stood among them, towering above those around him. It seemed strange to me at first to see him there, the acknowledged hero of the day, so far removed from all the seated figures representing greatness, both temporal and spiritual, but it was his proper place according to his birth, as Andrew's was among the lords up on the dais, where I could see him almost directly across from me, looking pale between Gartnait of Mar, newly risen to the earldom after the recent death of his father, and Malcolm, Earl of Lennox.

I spent a considerable amount of time, over the hours that followed, marvelling at the accuracy with which Will had predicted the behaviour of the nobles. The earliest dealings of the assembly were concerned, necessarily, with civic affairs and the needs of the various royal burghs, because until the burghs were returned to functioning normally, little else could be achieved. And so for the first hour and more the floor was occupied by civic functionaries familiar with the things that needed to be done, and accustomed to making such things happen. The nobility quickly became restive with that kind of thing, though, seeing such interminable on-goings among small men as being a waste of their aristocratic time, and they increasingly began disrupting the proceedings, demanding to be heard on, as they said, more important things. The more impatient they grew, the less tolerant they became and the greater the arrogance they showed, each of them seeking to assert his supposed superiority over everyone around him. And precisely as Will had predicted, they carped and cavilled and whined and complained until the entire great hall had degenerated into a scene of utter chaos, with everyone shouting at once and no one paying attention to anyone else.

William Wallace walked from the press of people around him and made his way up to the dais where William Sinclair was trying in vain to make his voice heard over the uproar. I did not see him move, for I was watching an altercation across from me that involved several of the realm's most prominent figures, among them fiery "Red" John Comyn the Younger of Badenoch and the Highland mormaer Malcolm, heir to his father's earldom of Lennox, who looked close to flying at each other's throats. Some difference in the tenor of the general uproar alerted me, and I looked around quickly to see my cousin standing on the chancellor's dais beside Bishop Sinclair. He was simply standing there, looking about him. The chancellor had turned to face him and was gazing up at him, wide-eyed, and at the same moment I heard how rapidly the sound in the great refectory was dying away as others became aware of his presence there. It was a remarkable phenomenon to witness, for in less than the time required to count to ten the awareness that Wallace had moved forward spread throughout the massive room and stilled the crowd, so that the wave of people turning to look as they fell silent spread as swiftly and visibly as the rings from a stone dropped into a calm pond.

The silence that filled the enormous room then was as profound as it was sudden. Everyone, it seemed to me, was holding his breath, for the very air in the place was motionless. Then Will scanned the entire assembly, making eye contact with as many of them as cared to look back at him. He did not speak, but neither was there doubt in the mind of any man there that Wallace would speak first. And then, finally, he looked towards the two highest-ranking officers of the realm, Lord James Stewart and John Comyn.

"The realm is in sore need of repair, my lords Constable and Steward. But I doubt we will repair it if we carry on like this, screaming at one another like angry fishwives and getting nothing done. We need action here. We need to take firm, sure steps for the common weal."

He looked then at the other lords, the earls and barons.

"We have beaten an English army, but is there any man here fool enough to think we have beaten

England?" No one moved or spoke. "They are gone, for now, but they will be back, and next time they will not be so easily drawn out and duped. Next time they will seek to make Dunbar look like a bicker between bairns. The questions that we have to ask ourselves now, though, are whether or not there is anything we can do to change the way of things between now and then, and whether or not we will be ready for them when they come."

Among the gathered lords a few heads began to turn and look at others, though no one said a word. It was the Earl of Buchan who cleared his throat loudly and spoke up, after exchanging glances with his colleague the High Steward.

"We are all in your debt, Master Wallace," he began, then hesitated. "Indebted to yourself and to your ... your associate, young Master Murray. We have all noted that you call yourselves jointly commanders of the army of Scotland ..." It was clear that he could see how condescending he sounded, for he had the grace to be abashed and his voice tailed away.

"Aye," Will pounced, "but there's more to it than that. We speak of being commanders of both the army of Scotland *and the community of that realm*. That wording is important, Constable, for it was that *community*—embracing and including the common folk of the realm—that enabled us to win the Stirling fight. And it was the *common* part of that community—most definitely not the most high-born part."

The words provoked a storm of cheering and unrestrained enthusiasm among the watching commoners—a storm that barely failed to mask the underlying threat within what he had said. The Earl of Buchan understood the implicit challenge clearly, and he was too old a campaigner to ignore it or to try to deflect it. He nodded, keeping his face inscrutable, then spoke again, his tone conciliatory.

"Your pardon, Master Wallace. I had no wish to give offence. I meant, of course, that you and Master Murray call yourselves—and justifiably so—commanders of the army of the kingdom of Scotland and the community of that realm. And so, that being said, what would you have us do from this day forward?"

Another flash of recognition brought more of Will's words back to me: *They won't think to take the responsibility upon themselves, but they won't hesitate to foist it onto us.*

"I would have you all accept that the realm has need of all of us," Will answered. "All of us, from the highest to the lowest, irrespective of rank and station. I would also have you recognize that we have never known a time more dire than today. And I would have you agree that there are a number of things we can do right now to heal ourselves, and then work together to make them happen."

"Can you name some of those things we might do right now?"

"Aye, easily, as can any man with eyes to see and a mind with which to reason. The first would be to

agree that we are on the edge of famine. We don't
have food to feed our folk because the English took it.
We have no stores of grain or meat, and few crops in
the ground, so we'll have little harvest again this
year." There was a rumble of bitter agreement as
those words sank home to their listeners. "North and
south of Forth the folk are starving, but there is something we can do immediately to change that." Utter
silence then as people waited to hear what that something was, but Will out-waited them until the High
Steward asked the question in everyone's mind.

"And what is that?"

"We can begin by conducting a survey of the entire
realm, dividing it into regions and making an inven-
tory of what food, and how much of it, each region
holds and what it requires most. That could be quickly
done, with teams of clerks sent out as soon as they can
be assembled and instructed." There was much
mumbling and sage nodding of heads as folk digested
that, but Will was far from finished with that topic.

"In addition, though," he continued, raising his
voice to recapture everyone's attention, "there is
much more we can do to save ourselves, and our folk,
by acknowledging one simple and straightforward
truth." He turned in a full circle, spreading his arms to
embrace everyone there. "Lothian," he said, and
waited for a reaction.

I truly did not know what he was expecting, for at
first I saw no connection with the preamble and
neither, it appeared, did anyone else.

"Lothian," he said again. "Think about Lothian, about how rich and prosperous it is. It covers all the southeastern area of this realm, from Berwick on the border all the way north to Edinburgh and the Firth of Forth. You all know that, or you have heard it, but most of you know nothing at all about the place because few of us ever go there. We stay away from it, because it's as good as English. It has always been English. The Lothian folk speak English—not Scots or Gaelic. They speak English or Norman French because they deal with the English all the time—English merchants and English traders and English earls and dukes and barons, English garrisons and English administrators.

"For that reason, the English have always taken good care of Lothian. And who can blame them? It's the richest farmland in Scotland and it hasn't been damaged by war at all, not for years. There is no war in Lothian. But—and this I swear by the living God—there is food aplenty: rich, lush farmlands, overflowing granaries, and fine, fat herds of cattle, sheep, goats, and swine, all of it harvested and tended carefully, kept in store for English use. Most of it—most of Lothian, I mean—is Cospatrick country, the fief of Patrick Cospatrick, Earl of Dunbar and March. And that means it's Northumbrian English in all but name, since Cospatrick lives in England and is Edward of England's man."

He raised his voice to a roar. "But Lothian is *Scotland*, whether the English believe that or not. And we should be there *now*, reminding the folk of who they are!" He paused, then resumed in a more moderate tone. "My own people in Selkirk Forest tell me the Lothian farmers have enjoyed a wondrous harvest, so their bins are full. Full enough, I would say, to feed their fellow Scots in this time of need. So I say we should be sending expeditions in force, to encourage the locals there to share their good fortune with their countrymen."

He had to stop then, until the turmoil of response died down, but there was no doubting the tenor of the room: even the assembled lords seemed unanimous in their praise of Will's proposal.

The High Steward raised a hand to Will. "We can put your idea to the vote, Master Wallace, though I believe it already has the approval of all here, but it raises the question of who would be responsible for its execution. Would you wish to see to that yourself?"

"No, my lord Steward, I would not—though many here will think me highly qualified, as a bandit and an outlaw, to conduct such levies." That brought a roar of laughter, and Will waited until it died away. "In the normal run of things, I would be glad to commend my friend and colleague Andrew Murray to you, for he would bring all his integrity to the execution of the task, and speaking as the outlaw and bandit that I am, moral integrity is something I have never aspired to. But Andrew Murray needs time now to rest, having had an English sword blade sheathed in his back, and so on his behalf I must refuse yet again. But nevertheless this task is a knotty one, and the details of completing it will require serious attention from an organizing authority.

"Besides," he added, "that idea was only one of the things I proposed doing right away. There is another."

Again a silence settled over the assembly as people strained to hear every word that would follow. Will looked from face to face, from one side of the crowded hall to the other, and when he spoke he barely had to raise his voice, so intense was the silence.

"I have thought about this one at length," he said. "And I will conduct it myself … We are not simply starving here in Scotland. We are in dire poverty—penniless and ill used. Our coffers have been emptied these two years by England's tax collectors and we have nothing left—we can't refill them. Our traders lack the wherewithal to trade and our merchants lack the goods and storage spaces they would need if ever they were able to restart their enterprises. We have all grown accustomed to the sight of our wealth, our goods and our resources, being shipped away to England, never to return. The wagon trains and their escorts seemed endless, and there were times this past year when the sound of wheels rumbling away into the distance barely seemed to fade before new squeaks and the clomping of heavy hooves announced the coming of the next. My folk in Selkirk Forest seized many of them back as they went by, but nowhere near enough to make the English stop, or even take notice. No matter what we did to try to stop them, the wagon trains kept moving, carrying the riches of our realm down into England, then returning laden with supplies and rations for the English garrisons."

He reached down into the scrip that hung at his waist and produced a tightly rolled and beribboned scroll, brandishing it above his head for all to see. "I have word here," he said, "from people I sent out right after the Stirling fight. They say there will be no more wagon trains bound for English garrisons in Scotland … because there are no more English garrisons in Scotland, or there will be none, within the next two weeks. Stirling and Edinburgh Castles are surrendered, as are—" He had to stop again, for his voice was overwhelmed in the cheering that greeted the recapture of the realm's two greatest fortresses. He waited patiently for it to subside. "The other castles left in English hands will soon follow, for they are all cut off. Lochmaben in Annandale is ours now, and Roxburgh, where Bishop Wishart is detained, will not hold out for long, I am assured." The approving roar swelled up again, but this time he waved it down quickly.

"I have a point to make here, and it is this: roads stretch in both directions. They go and they come, and wagon trains move as easily north along them as they move south. I am told that the roads on the other side of the border are better than ours, so I am going to use them. But I have *not* been told, by anyone, that there is the smallest hint of either poverty or famine in the fat and fertile lands on the far side of the border. It is a land flowing with milk and honey, where the milk and honey both are served in golden cups."

He straightened up and looked around the enormous room again, then raised his voice to a shout. "It's time the English gave back some of the wealth they've stolen from us, and it's high time they learned what it feels like to be invaded and abused, robbed and despoiled. I will ride into England within the next few days with a raiding party of three thousand, all mounted and well armed, and all hell-bent on plunder and the refurbishment of our realm's treasury with funds that were stolen from us over the past few years. We will harry Northumberland, Durham, and Cumberland, hitting hard and often—towns, ports, castles, and whatever else we find. We will mount no sieges and waste no time in conventional warfare. We'll attack targets as we find them and move on quickly afterwards, shipping our plunder northward in as many wagons as we can find."

"Where will you get three thousand horses?"

I did not see the man who shouted the question, but the voice had come from the ranks of the lords opposite.

"I would steal them if I had to, but I have them already. Garrons and Irish ponies. They're not the beasts you and your knightly friends might choose to ride—they're no coursers or rounceys—but they're strong and sure-footed, with broad, flat hooves that will let us ride through places where your dainty-hooved mounts would founder. They're Border horses, all of them, and ridden by Border fighters, from Annandale, Liddesdale, and Galloway. Nothing in England will withstand us."

The same man responded. "Will you take none of your own men with you, then?"

Will grinned at him, though it was more snarl than smile. "They are my own men," he said. "All of them."

CHAPTER TWENTY-NINE

A NATURAL AND PERFECT CHOICE

In the month that followed the sine die adjournment of the assembly, great things were achieved by those appointed to pursue the objectives drawn up by the committees created in the crucible of that gathering. The tasks they faced were daunting, and their completion would take far longer than the single year Will had anticipated as the time remaining before the English returned, but a solid start was made during those first weeks, with priority given to the twin tasks of fighting the famine, by resupplying the realm with food from the wealthy Lothian country, and fighting the darkness of ignorance caused by the shortage of parish priests. Every ordained priest in the land, including many whose lives had been entirely cloistered and monastic until that time, was put to work within days of the assembly, visiting parishes that lacked a priest, to ensure that community life went on as it ought to, with every family having access to the Blessed Sacraments. And as though by magic, both of these programs began to show results within a single fortnight.

Then, with the rapid resurgence of hope and a rejuvenated sense of communal identity, and despite the lack of common funds to pay for such improvements, a determined effort was launched to repair the damage done by Edward's army of occupation. Under the aegis of the Church authorities, and backed staunchly by the support of the High Steward and the High Constable of the realm, who compelled their subordinate lords, under pain of treason, to grant leave to their liegemen to participate in the endeavour, armies of local volunteers were conscripted everywhere and assigned to repair the public works identified as being crucial to the welfare of the realm. Bridges were rebuilt—though not the one across the Forth at Stirling—and river fords were repaired. On the eastern coast, seaboard and port facilities such as piers, wharves, boatyards, slipways, cranes, and warehouses were refurbished. Mills were repaired and in some instances rebuilt completely, with new millstones where the earlier ones had been damaged beyond repair. And granaries, barns, and farm buildings that had been torn down or burnt, or both, were replaced with new ones. And as the work progressed and successes grew, the whole country grew stronger: sawmills and manufactories prospered, stonemasons flourished again, and the associated trades and guilds in every burgh began to thrive ever more strongly. The work would continue for years, we all knew, but the skills of the people organizing the efforts of everyone involved on such a scale would grow in proportion, and everyone knew that, too.

I spent most of that first month completing my secretarial tasks in Stirling, at Cambuskenneth Abbey, and it was there I heard the tale of how Will Wallace, in a triumph of brazen effrontery, had talked the English commander of Roxburgh Castle, which sat on a spit of land at the junction of the Tweed and the Teviot Rivers and was considered impregnable, into surrendering without a blow being given or received on either side. I smiled, on hearing the story, for though people recounted it in tones of awe, I recognized it as being typical of my cousin. He had never been much of a gambler, but whenever he did decide to flirt with the gods of chance, he would study the situation and calculate the odds for and against success. Then, his mind made up, he would proceed with his plan of engagement, never betraying his intentions by the slightest flicker until he had done what he set out to do. He seldom lost his hazard.

In this instance, he had parleyed with the English commander, eye to eye, and convinced him that, as the last surviving English governor of any castle in Scotland, he ran the risk of being flayed like the infamous Cressingham if he was taken. Roxburgh Castle was deemed impregnable, he pointed out, but he pointed out, too, that it lacked its own well and depended upon an underground supply of river water that was about to be sealed off because Wallace himself had hired a local stonemason to dam and divert the river channel. He won his gamble, and within a day had taken possession of the ancient castle, freeing its sole prisoner, Robert Wishart, Bishop of Glasgow.

My bishop was free again, and from the moment I learned of it I could hardly wait to finish the report I had been working on—the accounting of the Battle at Stirling Bridge. The preliminary work had all been completed, much of it while I was attending the assembly at Perth, and so I drove my team of scribes relentlessly to complete the project, and on the fourth day after having heard that Bishop Wishart was a free man again, I was satisfied that it was finished and I could return to Glasgow with a clear conscience. I left the work of producing copies in the capable hands of the Augustinian friars, bade my farewells to their holy abbot and his considerate almoner, and betook myself home to Glasgow in the last but one week of October.

The word had spread by then that Will had been raiding widely in the north of England, and the tales of his exploits were widespread, yet most of them were so lurid that I could take little pleasure from them: offensive and outrageous stories about the excesses of his raiders; about the terror his name now generated in the towns of Northumberland, Durham, and Cumberland; and about the destruction and despoliation of priories, abbeys, and churches by his people throughout the northern counties. It was not the kind of information I enjoyed receiving about my cousin, even knowing his detestation of all things English, and I sought refuge from it by travelling south alone and on foot, avoiding human contact as much as I could.

Most of my favourite, personally loved places are intimately linked to my boyhood years, and the most important of those is Paisley, with its great abbey church. It makes little difference to me today that the church no longer exists. Edward Plantagenet ordered it burned down in 1307, six and thirty years ago in the first year of King Robert's reign, but the abbey church and its magnificent library were indelibly stamped into my most beloved memories long before that infamous date. But my daily loyalty had long since been transferred to the cathedral church in Glasgow. By the time of the Stirling fight in 1297, Glasgow Cathedral had been my home for years, and I always imagined that my footsteps grew lighter and more carefree as I approached it after any absence, no matter how brief.

On this occasion, that was particularly true, for it had been nigh on four months since last I saw my employer. He had sent me off to Selkirk Forest and thence to Moray slightly before mid-June, and already it was mid-October. Now that he was free again, and presumably in good health—for I was confident that I would have heard word had anything been amiss in that regard—I walked in a condition approaching euphoria, my sense of relief and happiness being close to overwhelming.

And so on the morning of Monday, the twenty-first day of October, having completed the thirty-mile journey south from Stirling in two days, I crossed the bridge over the River Clyde and made my way past the wharves and warehouses lining the riverside until I found myself at the Mercat Cross by the town's salt market. Ahead of me, dominating the skyline, was the massive yet unfinished cathedral church that, along with the natural anchorage of the river channel, gave the small town of Glasgow its prominence.

Eight hundred years earlier, St. Mungo had established his small church by the side of the ford there, at the junction of the river Clyde and the smaller, swift-flowing stream known as the Molindinar Burn, in the knowledge that he would have no shortage of travellers ripe for conversion to Christianity. The ford was the southernmost one on the Clyde, which deepened rapidly as it flowed west to the Irish Sea from that point, and Mungo had fallen in love with the location's natural, tranquil beauty, naming it glas gui, which meant "the dear, green place." And it really was a beautiful place, only slightly marred in recent years by the commercial shipping activities of the trading fleet that plied regularly between there and Ireland and less frequently taking the hazardous voyages between the more distant ports of France and Spain. In recognition of its growing importance, the town had been awarded the status of a royal burgh by King William the Lion, and now the burghers, and their town, were prospering. The cathedral had been decades in the building, and would take decades longer to complete, but the glory of God takes no notice of the passage of time.

I entered the cathedral nave almost perfunctorily, not expecting to see anyone I knew there. I genuflected in front of the main altar and then knelt there for a quarter of an hour, curbing my impatience by imposing a penance upon myself and praying for the souls of the unfortunate hundreds who had died at Stirling the month before. Only when I had completed the number of prayers I had decreed for myself did I rise, genuflect, and go outside again in search of my employer.

The residence known as the Bishop's Palace lay at the rear of the cathedral precincts, and it was more of a defensive keep than a house, though no one had ever been able to explain why a bishop should require a castle keep. I made my way directly to the rear of the interior, where the cathedral chapter maintained a suite of offices for diocesan affairs, and I heard my employer before I ever saw him. The door to his inner office was open and his current secretary, whom I had known for years, was seated just outside it, flicking the tip of his nose with the end of a grey goose quill as he peered down at a document held open on his desktop by a quartet of granite pebbles. He looked up, hearing my approach, and his face broke into a smile, but as he started to stand I waved him back into place and silenced him with a finger to my lips, then walked right into the room beyond the open door.

There was a huge old piece of weathered wood in there, an ancient tree stump that sat upright on the stubs of its dried, sawn-off roots. Its bole, a good fifteen inches in diameter, stretched upwards to the height of a tall, helmed man, and its entire surface was scarred and chipped and scored and dented from years and years of being hacked by swords, or more accurately by a sword. It had been in place when I first arrived there years earlier to take up my duties as a junior secretary, and I had asked about it on my first day because I thought it looked grotesque sitting there in the bishop's official pontifical office—an unsightly excrescence on a magnificent, highly polished floor of flawlessly milled pinewood. It was the bishop's aid to meditation, I was told, and my employer would belabour the ancient hardwood mightily as he wrestled with whatever problems were besetting him.

Now His Grace was at it again, and as he came into view I was reminded of my own situation of several months earlier when I had first regained my feet after a long period of being confined to bed. Even though Robert Wishart was no longer young, his shoulders were still broad and square, if slightly hunched, and his back was still wide, though now somewhat stooped. He was working hard, the blade of his sword whistling as he swung it vigorously. He must have sensed someone behind him, for he swung one more hard, chopping blow, then spun to crouch facing me, his blade extended towards me, clutched firmly in both hands. I saw his eyes flare with surprise, and then he straightened up abruptly and lowered his point.

"Jamie," he said, as though he and I had spoken mere hours earlier. "I was beginning to think the Augustinians were going to keep you up there at Cambuskenneth."

"No fear of that, my lord," I said. "I had a task to finish there, and when it was done, I came home.

The word of your deliverance from Roxburgh reached us just before I left, and so I wanted to be here to welcome you back to Glasgow."

He looked careworn, which was not unusual, for he took his duties seriously and always had, and four months away from his seat would have done nothing for his peace of mind. His face, naturally swarthy and weathered, had always been gaunt and lined, but now his cheeks were sunken and the lines in his face were graven deep, emphasizing the hawk-like jut of his great, bony nose and the sharp glint of his eyes blazing out from beneath fierce, grizzled brows.

"They treated you well in Roxburgh, my lord?"

His eyes changed, and then he smiled the little smile I knew so well, the one that told me he had seen through my supposedly innocent question.

"For jailers, you mean? Aye, I suppose they did. They never maltreated me, if that's what you are asking, but neither did they let me forget for a minute that I was a prisoner. They gave me clean clothes once a month—I was due another just when your cousin rescued me—and the food was edible. Not enjoyable, mind you, nor even plentiful, and there were times when it was barely adequate, but it was edible. The governor there, a man called Grey, had nothing much to say about anything other than warfare and the head-aches of running a garrison. A boring man, he was, with little conversation and less humour. Fortunately, I seldom saw him. But I can see from your face you are concerned about me. Do I look that ill done by?"

"No, my lord," I said, shaking my head. "No, you don't … You're merely thinner, I suppose." I nodded towards the tree stump. "I haven't seen you whacking that thing in years. Why now?"

He turned away and laid his sword on top of the table. "I felt in need of the exercise. I had little opportunity for anything of that kind in Roxburgh. They seldom let me out of my room."

I nodded again towards the stump. "I remember that when you used to attack that thing most strongly, it usually meant you had a thorny problem on your mind. You would keep hacking off splinters of tree until you had resolved it."

He smiled again, a small, lopsided grin. "You remember that, do you? I shouldn't be surprised, I suppose. You miss but little."

"I try not to miss anything, Your Grace. May I ask, then, what's bothering you now?"

He pushed his lips out in a pout that I recognized as a sign that he was thinking hard, deciding whether to lie or be truthful, and then he brought up his hand and rubbed his nose hard with his open palm. "Damnation, Jamie," he said. "You never were an easy one to hoodwink, but that's why I valued you so much."

He crossed to the table and sheathed his sword, then collected his scapular from where he had thrown it over the back of his chair and shrugged into it, pulling it down over his head and then arranging it on his shoulders so that it hung comfortably, front and rear. His pectoral cross lay on the table, too, and he slipped its chain over his head, then hesitated in the act of turning back to face me, his eye fixed on the sheathed dagger attached to the sword belt on the tabletop. He reached out with both hands, drew the weapon, and spun on his heel, throwing the blade end over end at the old tree trunk, some eight paces from where he stood. It crossed the room in a whirling blur and struck the trunk hilt first, leaping straight up in the air and clattering to the floor.

"Shite!" His voice was harsh as he crossed to where the dagger lay and picked it up, staring down at it as he tested its edge against the ball of his thumb, and I knew, then and there, beyond a doubt, that he had bad news to break to me.

"What is wrong, my lord?"

"Murray," he said.

I felt the surprise register on my face and in my voice as I responded, "Andrew?"

"Andrew, his father, and his uncle William. All of them together."

"Forgive me, my lord, but I don't understand," I said. "Andrew is here and the others are imprisoned in England."

"No, one of the others is in France." He cut himself short and I could see that he was seething with barely suppressed anger. "Word's been coming in since yesterday. Three separate messengers, the first of them last night and then two more this morning, one from Bristol and one from Westminster. The Bristol message, a brief letter written in haste by Murray of Bothwell himself, William the Rich, says that by the time anyone reads his words in Glasgow, he himself will be in France with Edward, and he does not expect to return to Scotland. No reason given for his being in France or for Edward's decision to compel him to go there. No explanation of how, why, or when. Merely the word, sent privily in a letter carried by an itinerant friar who was five weeks on the road from there to here."

"And the Westminster message?"

"Mere rumour, passed on to me by a friend in the Bishop of Westminster's entourage, who had heard someone in authority—he didn't name names—say that Andrew's father, the Lord of Petty, is dead. Found dead, apparently, of natural causes—or so we are expected to believe—in London Tower. As I say, though, that is no more than rumour. We have no proof of any part of it." He cocked his head to look at me. "When did you last see young Andrew, and how was he?"

The word of Andrew's father's death had stunned me, notwithstanding the qualifier that had been tendered with it, for it meant, among other things, that Andrew might now be Lord of Petty. "Two weeks ago, Your Grace … No, forgive me, it was closer to three, just before he left Stirling to return to Bothwell. He looked well, I thought. As well as could be expected, I mean, after having a sword thrust through his guts. He had lost weight and looked haggard, as you would expect of a wounded man, and he was in no fit condition to ride a horse—in fact, they took him to Bothwell in a carriage—but Will told me he was recovering more quickly than expected. And his condition could only have improved once he reached Bothwell and had access to proper care and rest."

"Aye, and so it might have. Where was Will at that time?"

"On his way to the Borders. He had left Stirling the day before. What did you mean by 'so it might have'?"

"Hmph!" The bishop's grunt sounded disgusted. "I meant had he stayed in Bothwell as he was supposed to, it would have been good for him."

"He didn't stay?"

The bishop scowled. "He was gone again within the week. As soon as his escorts departed for Stirling, he was on the road again, riding south and east to East Lothian to join your cousin, who was in Haddington seeing to the collection of food and grain, as decreed by the Perth assembly. They spent much time there together, generating a spate of letters that they signed jointly as commanders of the army of Scotland and the community of the realm. The letters went out to the Hansa trading leagues of every seaport and trading post on the other side of the North Sea, telling them all that the kingdom of Scotland, by the grace of God, has been delivered from the English, its freedom regained in battle, and that Scotland is once again open for trade. They must have had an army of clerics making copies for days on end, though I'm told the letters were all signed on the same day, the eleventh of October.

"I knew nothing about any of that until I returned from Roxburgh a few days ago. At any rate, Andrew eventually returned to Bothwell, though no one seems to know how or when. That's all we know—and it's all we would have known had we not received a letter from Andrew's uncle, Father David Murray. You remember him, do you not?"

"I do, my lord. He talked to us about his nephew that night we dined at Turnberry."

"That's him. He wrote to say he had gone to Bothwell recently from Moray, whence he had escorted Andrew's young wife, who is with child. Upon their arrival they discovered his nephew to be in dire condition—in extremis was how Father Murray phrased it—and not likely to live for long. It seems his wound, while outwardly appearing to mend, had been festering unchecked beneath the skin and had erupted as the result of the hard riding Andrew had done on the way to and from Haddington. Father Murray, knowing nothing of my recent release from Roxburgh, and not daring to leave the young woman alone, wrote to William Lamberton as deputy bishop here in the hope that he might be able to send word to me of Andrew's likely death."

I have no notion of how long I sat there, speechless and sightless, before he called me back to the present, his voice now filled with concern verging on alarm as he asked me how I felt. Even as anger at the inane banality of the question swelled up in me, though, I knew he could not possibly have known how affected

I would be by these tidings, for though he was aware that I had known Andrew as a boy, he could not possibly have known about the closeness and affection I had recently developed for my Highland friend.

I shook my head, attempting to clear it. There was no point, I knew, in saying anything to upset the bishop further, for I could see he was already greatly disturbed, and I remembered the deep, paternal affection he had always shown towards Andrew, even as a boy. And so I merely asked, "Where is Canon Lamberton now, am I permitted to ask?"

"On his way to Bothwell," he said, showing no surprise. "He'll be there by now, I imagine. I should have gone myself, but I could not. I'm bound here for now, tending to several urgent matters, none of which permit me to leave the cathedral, so William went in my place ..."

His voice trailed away, and then, lapsing into Scots as he so often did, he muttered, "The damned young fool. Ye'd think he'd tell somebody he was in pain! Ye'd think he'd hae the sense to ken somethin' was far frae right, for he must ha' been in agony, these weeks on end. But no, he was that stubborn and he didna want to be a bother to anybody. An' his damned Moravian honour wouldna let him whine. God damn the injustice o' it a'. He was what, twenty-five?"

I nodded. "Aye, twenty-five. He and I are the same age." I sat up straighter. "I should go and see him."

"No, you should not." In the blink of an eye, with the change of topic, he had reverted to his normal Latin speech. "That would be a waste of time. Even William might have been too late to see him, for Father Murray said he might not last out the week, and his letter was written last Wednesday, so he meant the end of the week now past. The wound was foul, he said then, and Andrew was unconscious and raving most of the time and growing worse from hour to hour. The odds are he is dead by now, even as we sit here talking. I know Davie Murray well, and he is no alarmist, but he said it would take a miracle to save his nephew's life."

"Dear God in Heaven, protect us all. Have you sent word to Will?"

"I have, but I've no conviction he'll receive it, for we don't know where he is. There are reports of his men raiding far and wide in Durham and Northumberland, and even farther west along the Borders, but no one knows where precisely he is, and he likes to keep it that way. He knows the sound of his name strikes terror into English hearts and he uses that terror as a weapon, showing himself time after time in places miles apart, and even having other big men pretend to be him, so that he is being sighted several times a day in different places altogether."

"So how many men did you send out to find him?"

"Three men I trust."

"Three? You sent but three, against such odds? Why?"

"Because we need to be discreet. Until we know for sure of Andrew Murray's death—the which may God forbid—we need discretion over and above all else."

"Why, in the name of all we revere, should we need to be discreet?"

He looked at me sternly, a frown ticing at his brows. "Why?" he repeated. "You ask me why? Bethink yourself, man. The entire land is seething with angry, envious men whose power has been usurped by two young upstarts whose names were all but unknown a year ago. Now they are become the most powerful men in all the realm, beloved of the Fates, like Romulus and Remus, Castor and Pollux, David and Jonathan. Not even our Lord God in Heaven knows what might happen if word were to get out too soon that one of the two has been struck dead, but the likelihood is that the surviving one would not remain long in power." He paused, head cocked. "You see that, I hope?"

"I see it now that you bring it home to me," I said, slumping back into my chair. "You are right, of course. Of the two men, Andrew was the one more acceptable to the magnates. His rank and birth made him one of them, whether they liked it or not, and as such, he provided Will with a degree of authority and dignitas, simply by according him the respect and ranking of an equal. The magnates will waste no time in using Andrew's death to their own advantage, undermining Will's authority."

"Attempting to undermine his authority." The bishop's voice was hard as steel. "I believe they'll find Will's position more difficult to undermine than they would have thought possible two months ago."

"Aye, they might, but they'll keep trying. How can we stop them? What can we do if Andrew is already dead?"

"We can conceal his death for as long as we can. At least until we can sit down with Will and make some kind of plan to deal with what we will all have to face."

"Pshaw!" I threw up my arms. "What kind of plan will keep the magnates from reacting? They'll move against Will as soon as they hear tell of what has happened, and there won't be a thing he, or we, can do to stop them."

"No, Father, they will not move, not until they have decided what is best for them to do, and they will not do that without consulting one another as to what would be the best way to proceed. And they'll tread very carefully, believe you me."

"Why would you think that, my lord?"

"Father James, you are Will Wallace's cousin and you should know why I think it. Think, man! Scotland's magnates have had their own little fiefdoms to rule since the days of King David, and each of them sees himself as God within his own domain. They listen to no man in deciding what they may and may not do in their own lands, and for hundreds of years they've treated their folk like cattle. Stirling Bridge has changed all that. Your cousin and Andrew Murray have changed all that, and I, for one, believe they've changed it forever."

He fell silent, fingering the silver cross on his breast, then picked up the old, worn sword belt with its attached weapons and crossed to lean the sword against his tree trunk, lodging its plain steel pommel carefully in one of the old, splintered scars he had gouged long since in the once-smooth surface. When he was satisfied the sword would stay in place, he came back towards me, clasping his hands behind his back, beneath the scapular panel that hung there.

"When I said Andrew Murray and your cousin have changed things forever, I meant every word of it, for I now believe, with all my heart, that the Scots folk will never submit again to the kind of tyranny that the Normans have subjected them to in the past. Let's admit this, you and I, here, between ourselves and as men of God committed to His Holy Church and the salvation of all souls before and ahead of all human endeavours and loyalties: when we speak of the Scots magnates, we don't mean the Scots at all. The magnates are all descendants of the Normans who came over here in 1066 — two hundred and some years ago — with William the Conqueror, and they have been here ever since, ruling this realm for so long that now they think of themselves as Scots and consider the true Scots to be provided by God for their especial benefit." He shrugged. "Is it untrue? The exceptions, of course, are the mormaers, but they were never Norman. They were here when the Normans arrived, the ancient earls and rulers of the Gaels."

He caught my eye. "Why, Father James, you are shocked." His face was crinkled in a rueful grin that contained little of humour, and I shook my head and spoke quickly before he could say more.

"No, my lord bishop, that's not—" I stopped, aware of the lie before I uttered it. "Well, it is true, I suppose, but I am not shocked in the way you think. I'm merely shocked that you would say such things aloud. For you could be hanged for saying them." I hurried on before he could stop me. "And why would you say them anyway, whether they be true or not?"

"They came from what I said directly before, Jamie, when I said Andrew and Will have changed the old ways forever. For the folk will not settle back easily into harness now, to be the way they were before Will Wallace and Stirling Bridge. Think about that, Jamie, about what I've been told your cousin said in Perth, the truth of it: it was the folk themselves, the folk, who won the Stirling fight, and they did it without the magnates." He gestured for me to keep silent, even though I had made no move to speak.

"That's not all of it, though, for what they did, in truth, was to stand against magnates—the magnates of England—and run them off the field of battle. They thrashed them and threw them out. And now they are harrying England itself. Believe me, Father James, our own Scots magnates will think long and hard before they run the risk of prodding and provoking this new creature that William Wallace and Andrew Murray have created from the folk of Scotland."

I felt my jaw sagging open and closed it quickly, but I had seen the truth of what he said.

"That's why we need to plan," Wishart insisted. "That's why we need to meet with Will, as quickly as it can be arranged. We need to strengthen his authority as commander of the army, and to keep the army itself beyond the reach of the magnates. I believe the latter part will be easily achieved. And I believe that, in achieving it, we can resolve the other difficulty—supporting Will against his nobly born detractors. He'll have no lack of those."

His eyes narrowed. "Mind you, hearing myself say such things, I hope I am not committing the sin of pride—what the Greek ancients called hubris—in presuming to guess at the will of God. I really have no certainty at all of what I am saying. I'm but giving voice to what I hope, and what good sense would seem to dictate. And there's a doubting voice inside me asking when I last knew the magnates to do anything according to the dictates of good sense and logic. They'll always look to their own interests before those of anyone else. But that may work to our advantage, for we won't need much time, once Will's back here. We'll simply have to keep Andrew's passing secret for as long as may be possible. That's why I sent William to Bothwell, simply to be there and to keep an eye on things, to make sure no unwelcome word goes out before we want it to."

That made me feel better immediately, simply to know that Canon Lamberton was taking charge in Bothwell, and I said so with sufficient enthusiasm to draw a questioning glance from the bishop.

"I've never asked you for your professional assessment of Canon Lamberton, have I?" It was hardly an ingenuous question, for he knew full well he had not. His memory was flawless on such matters.

"No, my lord," I said. "You never have."

"Well, then, let me ask you now. You are sufficiently familiar with the canon's personality and methods to have formed some judgments, I presume."

"Yes, my lord, I am, and I have."

"And so? Tell me what you think of him."

"I think you could not have found a better or more suitable deputy anywhere in the length or breadth of Scotland. I find him admirable, competent, articulate, compassionate, pious without being unctuous, effective in all that he does, and loyal—to you and to his calling—above all else."

"But." His pounce was catlike. "There's more. I can hear it in your tone."

I sucked in a great breath and blew it out. "Nothing at all to Canon Lamberton's discredit … It's merely something that troubles me, and it is irrational, not really worthy of mention."

"Spit it out."

I shrugged. "Will doesn't seem to like him, and I don't know why. But it concerns me."

"Have you asked Will about it?"

"No, I have not. Mainly because I haven't had the opportunity."

"What makes you think he dislikes him?"

"Nothing … the look on his face …" I told my

employer what I remembered of the occasion when I had first noticed Will looking strangely at the canon, when we were discussing the need to appoint a replacement for Bishop Fraser of St. Andrews.

He nodded. "Aye, he telt me about it," he murmured, this time in Scots.

"About what?" I could hear the surprise in my own voice, and he smiled and slipped back into Latin.

"About that conversation. It was the first time he had ever met Lamberton, he said, and we talked about it at some length."

"And he said he didn't trust him?"

"No, not exactly. He said he believed Canon Lamberton would be a natural and perfect choice as Bishop of St. Andrews."

I sagged in my chair, feeling as though the wind had been kicked out of me. "Will said that?"

"He did." The old face cracked in a grin. "He's a clever lad, your cousin. He always was. He said everything you said, but added one more thing. He spoke of a glow of fiery innocence and purity and great, shining enthusiasm that consumed the man while he was defending God's omniscience in having placed someone in Scotland already—a man ready and willing and fully equipped to take up the required burden of the office."

"William Wallace said all that, in those words?" I could scarce believe what I had heard.

"He did," the bishop said. "And more. Sufficient to convince me he was right, though I will admit I took but little convincing. The man is a natural choice for the position."

I was agog. "That is—wonderful," I said, my voice sounding hushed. "Does the canon know?"

"No, he does not, and nor will he until it has all been arranged. For now, the only ones who know are we three. And that is how it must stay until I can arrange everything to satisfaction. So I command you: not a single word, not even a hint of interest in the vacancy, to anyone from this time forth. You may think the pride of magnates and mormaers is a difficult matter in which to deal, but believe me, Father James, you will never know the truth of such things until you have had to juggle with the pride and wilfulness of prelates. Now away you go and make yourself ready to resume your life here, then come and see me when you are ready to return to work."

CHAPTER THIRTY

THE SIGN OF THE BLUE COCKEREL

To my complete astonishment, Canon Lamberton arrived back in Glasgow the next afternoon, with a small entourage that included an enclosed wagon drawn by a pair of horses and containing the desperately ill and pain-ravaged Andrew Murray, miraculously alive despite the expectations of everyone around him. With Andrew was his wife, the Lady Eleanor Murray, who was visibly pregnant and greatly distraught over her husband's condition. Like everyone else, she had been given to understand that his wound was not life threatening and that he was recuperating well. The greater her shock, then, to reach the end of her journey through roadless and largely lawless lands and discover that she might have to bury her young husband and then return alone to Morayshire as a grieving widow.

I was present at her arrival in Glasgow, but we did not meet or speak to each other; she was too absorbed in her own grief to have time to look about her at people she did not know, and I was too uncomfortable around women in general to think to impose my presence upon her sorrow. I was curious about her, nevertheless, because I knew Andrew was completely besotted by her, forever talking about her wit as well as her beauty. And she really was beautiful, in that strikingly black-haired, blue-eyed Celtic fashion seldom encountered in southern parts of the country. Of course, I saw no slightest sign of the sparkling wit her doting husband had so loved, but I did admire her quiet dignity and the calm self-possession with which she bore her evident grief.

I wanted to visit Andrew immediately upon his arrival, but his physician, Father Henry Tertius, denied me access on the grounds that my friend was far too ill and in too much distress to see anyone. I accepted Father Tertius's decree without demur, for he was generally recognized as the most gifted and highly trained physician in all of southern Scotland. He had graduated from the University of Bologna as a doctor of canon law while still very young, and had then gone on to study medicine extensively at the universities of both Oxford and Paris.

I went instead in search of Father Murray and found him walking in the cloisters on the cathedral grounds, head bowed and hands clasped behind his back as he paced slowly back and forth. As I hovered there, on the point of retreating and leaving him to his meditations, he looked up and saw me and called me by name. I was flattered that he remembered me, and for a few minutes we exchanged small talk, in which I offered him my condolences on his family situation and asked after Andrew.

"Aye," he said. "You were there at Stirlin', were you no'? Then you'd hae been like the rest o' us, ta'en right aback wi' the way he's come doon." I remembered how down-to-earth and plain-spoken he was, preferring to speak the tongue of his local parishioners and countrymen over the Latin vulgate preferred by his fellow clerics. "Nane o' us knew how bad his injuries truly are, though I suppose we should have kent, gin we'd used the brains God gied us. Ye canna take a sword stab in the kidneys then just jump up an' walk away. An' yet, that's what he did, and we a' just believed it …" He shook his head in disbelief, then squinted at me again.

"It was Turnberry, was it no', where we first met, you and me? That night Rab Wishart asked me to talk about my nephew. Aye … Here, come ower here an' sit wi' me, for I could use some company." He indicated a stone bench against an ivy-covered wall, and we sat down together in the full, pale light of the October sunshine. "That would ha' been when, last May?"

"Aye, May it was," I said. "I am surprised you would remember me."

He raised an open palm, half smiling. "And so you should be, had it no' been for Canon Lamberton, and for your name bein' Wallace. I remember your face, now that I see it, but prior to lookin' up and seein' you, all I knew or recalled about ye was what the canon telt me. He said you an' Andrew became close friends, and ye worked wi' the four o' them—him and Wallace, Andrew an' Bruce—on the aftermath o' the Stirlin' fight an' the arrangements afore an' after the Perth assembly. So there's nae magic involved in my kennin' you, Father Wallace. Ye're a member o' the Stirlin' Council, and as one o' them, ye're one o' the people clever men ought to ken."

"The Stirling Council?"

He looked at me askance, then grinned. "Have ye no' heard tell o' it? It's the name o' the organization runnin' Scotland at this very moment. I've just finished cryin' all o' them by their names—Wallace, Murray, and Wallace, wi' a kirkman called Lamberton, an' a nod o' the head frae an earl cried Bruce."

I was not accustomed to hearing my own name included in context with such company, but I had more urgent concerns.

"Tell me about Andrew, if you will, Father, for they won't let me see him and I don't know how bad he really is. Do you believe he is going to die?"

He pursed his lips and narrowed his eyes, then nodded slowly, his expression one of regret and dejection. "Aye," he said, "I fear he is. I saw it in his eyes when I arrived in Bothwell last week wi' his lady wife. I'd sent a sodger on ahead o' us to warn them we'd be there within' the hour, but when I saw Andrew wasna there at the castle yetts to greet her as we drew close, I kent somethin' was far frae right ... And it was. He had collapsed the previous night and wasna even conscious when we arrived."

"Was there a physician with him then?"

"No. There had been one there, but he had left when Andrew insisted on riding to Haddington—said he refused to be responsible for such folly. And he was right."

"And no one had replaced him?"

Murray shrugged. "I was told they wanted to bring someone else in. Ian Balfour, Sir William's deputy and factor here in Bothwell these thirty years, wanted to bring in a Hospitaller knight frae Lanark, but Andrew wouldna hear o' it, an' the time just flew by then until it was too late."

"They should have brought him in, regardless of what Andrew wanted—Dominic of Ormiston, I mean." I saw from his face that the name meant nothing to him. "That's the Hospitaller from Lanark. Brother Dominic is the man who wired my broken jaw last spring. He's very good. They should have brought him in at once. I cannot believe no one looked to Andrew at all in all that time."

"All what time? There wis nae time lost or wasted. The lad was fine when he rode off, and he looked fine—or he was pretendin' to—when he got back. The trouble started after that. One minute he seemed hale, and then he fell down unconscious."

"But surely this—this man Balfour must have seen that something was amiss? How could he not have seen it?"

"I asked the same question," Murray said. "And they telt me there was nothin' to see. Everyone there said the same thing. The stab wound looked clean and healthy. But the damage was happenin' elsewhere, and Andrew himsel' was the only one who could tell. An' of course, he was sayin' nothin'." He looked down at his hands, folded in his lap.

"When I saw him lyin' there in bed that day in Bothwell, I couldna believe my eyes. He was a dead man, lyin' there, but he wis still breathin'. We couldna waken him. By then it was too late to send for the man frae Lanark, so I wrote to Canon Lamberton, hoping he'd send someone, but he decided to come himsel'. He took one look and made arrangements right then and there to bring Andrew here directly, so that Father Tertius could see to him. I wasna too happy about that, for I was feart the lad might die on the road, but Canon Lamberton said it wis in God's hands anyway …" He shook his head dubiously. "I'll tell ye, though, I'll be mair than surprised if it's no' too late by now. He's wasted awa to a shadow o' what he was, and he doesna look likely to recover."

I was so upset by then that I could no longer sit still, so I rose to my feet and began to pace in agitation, my hands clasped tightly at my back and my mind full of thoughts about how Will would react, and how the news of Andrew's death would affect the political situation not merely here in Scotland but in England and France, too. Father Murray watched me pace, his face clearly showing his concern, but he said nothing, content to leave me to my own deliberations. Finally I stopped and faced him, reluctantly asking the banal question that I knew he could not answer any more sensibly than I could.

"What will we do, if he dies?"

Hearing the words as they emerged from my mouth like a bleat of self-pity, I felt a surge of loathing at myself for even voicing such a feckless question. But David Murray shrugged, tacitly admitting that he was as powerless as I to change one whit of anything that had happened or would happen in the future.

"I hate even to say it," he said, looking up at me, "for it's what any tavern tosspot would tell ye. But there'll need to be changes made. In the way we do everythin'. We'll need to adjust, mak allowances for the way things will be down the road. An' no' just you an' me an' Lamberton, but the whole o' the country. The realm itsel' will hae to adapt."

He paused, thinking, and then resumed talking in a different manner and tone, his words more deliberate and thoughtful and the broad Scots of his local dialect muted. "An' let us hope and pray, for the love o' God and the good o' everybody, that we don't go down the same road we took after the death o' the old king, Alexander ..." He grunted and sat straighter. "My nephew was no king, God knows," he said quietly. "And Alexander was no strutting young man, for that matter. But there are similarities in the circumstances of their deaths that might bode ill for all of us: two champions, two proven, potent leaders, one young and one not so, but both victorious and well loved, both responsible for the welfare o' the realm, and both o' them unexpectedly cut down before they could complete what they had planned." He held my gaze. "A bad development, that, Father Wallace, and dangerous in that it could open up the threat o' civil war again. The Comyns, thanks be to God, no longer hold the power they had when Alexander died, and most of them are away, in jail or in France, and the Bruces' prospects arena' what they were, either. But they'll a' come back once word o' what's happened gets spread about. That will be the time of greatest peril for the realm, when some folk will try to twist things to suit their own needs while others will look elsewhere to foster theirs."

He sniffed, then rose and reached out to grasp my upper arm, frowning at me. "It's your cousin who'll need to be the strongest, though, for the fate o' the whole realm will be in his hands now. And he'll have to take control, on his own, before anyone else can move to stop him. And believe you me, there will be no shortage o' folk willing to try. He'll need all the help we can provide for him—you and me and Willie Lamberton and Bishop Wishart. The Steward will back us up, too, I'm sure, for Wallace is his man at root, and a few o' the other earls might stand up wi' us, forbye, but everything will come down to how your cousin handles things. He's the man who'll hae to set the reel for the fiddlers to play in the times ahead. Gin he permits it, gin he so much as falters, them that's jealous o' him will rip the leader's reins out o' his hands in the blink o' an eye and we'll be back into the old ways as if the Stirlin' fight never happened. But if he stands firm and rallies the ordinary folk at his back, he'll be able to thumb his nose at every magnate in the land, for they'll no' be able to put him down, short o' murder … And I wouldna like to be the man foolish enough to try to murder William Wallace."

He pointed his finger directly at me. "You need to go and find Lamberton," he said. "Now. Tell him what I said and see what he has to say."

"Will you not come with me?"

"I would, but I need to stay with my nephew. I'm his closest kin—next to his wife, of course—and I'm a priest, so they'll let me sit with him a while. Besides, you know now what I think, so you don't need me to be there to say the same thing all over again. Go you and talk to Lamberton, and then go with him to Rab Wishart. By the time the two o' ye are finished there, I'll be ready to help wi' whatever might be needed next. Now away ye go."

I left Father David sitting there and went in search of William Lamberton, but I was informed that he was in conference with the bishop, who had issued strict orders that they were not to be disturbed for any reason other than an attack by the King of England in person. His Grace had been absent from his seat for nigh on four months, and I knew there was much for him to absorb, and even more for him to do, now that he was back in Glasgow again. And so instead of fretting and fulminating selfishly as I wanted to, I offered a silent penitential prayer and took myself off back to the cloisters, where I knew I could be alone to think through all the pros and contras of the crisis that Andrew's death would trigger.

It was well that I did, and I have no doubt my Master in Heaven was responsible for my decision to go there, for in the silence of the late afternoon of that single October day, uninterrupted for hours as darkness approached, I confronted the reality of what had happened and of what might happen next, and I came to terms with my own uncertainties, acquiring a new and more complete understanding of all that had been set at hazard in the foregoing few days. I reflected on the motivation that drove my cousin, and the wrongs that had become so commonplace in Scotland that they were ignored by almost everyone except my cousin.

The awareness that I myself had been guilty, even unwittingly, of the same complacency shamed and humbled me, and so I did what I—what most priests—always do at such times. I knelt and prayed for guidance, there in the fading dusk within the cloisters, and as I prayed, the rain began to fall, making me aware that I had not even noticed the skies clouding over. The first sparse drops, icy on my tonsured scalp, quickly increased into an insistent downpour, and I pulled my cowl up over my head, resisting the urge to go in search of shelter before finishing my prayers. But God had already heard me and He answered my entreaties almost before I had finished them.

"Father James? Jamie, is that you?"

The voice was high-pitched, its tone urgent. I had difficulty placing it for a moment, but then I turned quickly, remembering, and looked to where a tiny man crouched by the wall, watching me nervously and clutching a crossbow almost as big as he was, holding it instinctively with one end of the bow tucked into his armpit and his arm extended down along the bowstring to protect it from the rain.

"Big Andrew," I said, and my pleasure must have shown itself in my voice, for he grinned and nodded eagerly, then beckoned me furtively to join him in the shadows.

I stood up and moved to join him, wondering vaguely why he was being so secretive, though more than ten years of living in Selkirk Forest might well have explained it. Now, though, in the aftermath of Stirling, he was a hero, one of Wallace's lieutenants with no need to skulk or hide from anyone in Scotland.

"Where have you come from?"

Instead of answering, he shook his head with that same disturbing air of clandestine urgency and beckoned me to a nearby corner where he crouched down, plainly anxious to avoid been seen. Mystified, and starting to grow apprehensive myself, I went to sit beside him, watching the way his eyes flickered from side to side.

"In God's holy name, Andrew," I said, "what is wrong? What's the matter?"

"Nothin', wi' you," he hissed, baffling me completely.

Andrew Miller was known as Big Andrew because, although the smallest of all Will's followers in stature, he was one of the largest in terms of loyalty and commitment to Will's cause. And now he crouched in front of me, brushing uselessly with his left forearm at the rainwater streaming from his thinning hair into his eyes, blinking and frowning.

My heart was racing. "Is it Will? Is something wrong? Has he been wounded?"

"No! No, no, no, it's nothin' like yon. He needs to see ye. Now!"

"Then take me to him. Where is he?" I started to stand up, but he reached out and pulled me down again.

"No," he hissed. "I canna tak ye. He disna want me seen. Ye're tae gang yer lane—an' tell naebody."

"What?" I felt a sudden surge of irritation and allowed it to overwhelm me for a moment, perversely glad to have an opportunity to vent some of the anger and frustration that had been boiling up in me throughout the day. "For God's sake, Andrew, he's William Wallace! Am I to understand he's suddenly gone into hiding from his own folk, afraid to show his face?"

"Aye, somethin' like that."

That unexpected answer sucked all the anger out of me and left me gaping. An unearthly weight, numinous and unsettling, seemed to press down on my shoulders. "I see," I said, although in truth I did not. "Where will I find him, then?"

"Crawford's howff," he said, renewing my confusion, since Crawford's howff, or tavern, had been our favourite drinking spot when Will and I were students. The owner's son, Alan, had been another of Will's early followers.

"You want me to go all the way to Paisley? Right now?"

"Nah," he said, waving a hand. "It's here in Glesca now, near the Cross. The auld man moved here last year, for the docks and the shippin' traffic. The sign's the blue cock."

I had seen the sign of the Blue Cockerel many times in past years, in passing the Mercat Cross and the salt market, but it was a riverside dive, catering to seamen and the loose women who catered to them, and of course I had never been inside the place.

"And I'll find him there?"

"No' inside. There's a kind o' a shed at the back. He'll be in there. Long John'll be there, waitin' for ye."

"And what about you? Where will you go now?"

He shrugged. "I'll just away, afore somebody sees me who kens me. My job was to find you. Awa ye go, then. Will said ye were to come right away."

"Just tell me why he doesn't want to be seen— doesn't even want you to be seen."

He looked at me, honestly bewildered. "I don't know," he said.

I left him there and made my way swiftly, angrily, through rain that was now torrential, towards the public square known as Glasgow Cross, with its row of taverns and warehouses lining the docks along the river Clyde.

The tall, gangling outlaw known as Long John of the Knives materialized from the shadows like a ghost as I strode towards the place called Crawford's howff, and I veered towards him, raising my voice above the noise of the pouring rain.

"John. Where is he?"

He raised a long, thin hand and crooked a finger, then turned away and moved smoothly towards a squat, dark, windowless, and abandoned-looking building at the side of the Blue Cockerel tavern, where he stopped and waved me forward. I could hear shouts and raucous laughter coming from the tavern on my right, but there was no sign of life at all in the smaller building. The sound of the rain drumming heavily on its roof made it seem even more dismal than it was.

I turned to Long John. "He's in there, really? In the dark?" I had to shout to make myself heard.

John shouted back, "He's in there right enough, but he's no' in the dark. There's a cellar, for storage. He's down there. Just go through the trapdoor. I'll wait out here and make sure you'll no' be bothered by unexpected company. He's waitin' for you."

And so indeed he was, waiting to wrap his enormous arms about me as I reached the bottom of the flight of steps that led down from the trapdoor. He

hugged me tightly for a long time, not saying a word
until he pushed me out to arm's length to look at me.

"You're soaked," he said, needlessly. He had a
tense, gaunt look about him, and his beard was longer
and bushier than I had ever seen it. His eyes were clear
and keen, but the grief in them was unmistakable. "Is
it true? Is Andrew dying?"

"I don't know, Will, but he might be. Did he look
sick in Haddington?"

He shook his head, a deep frown stamped between
his brows. "No. He was fine. Thin, and drawn and
pale, but no more than you'd expect a wounded man
to look."

"Aye," I sighed and glanced around the room.
"Have you any wine here?"

"Of course. Here, sit down by the fire."

He went over to a table by one wall and busied
himself with cups and jugs while I took one of the
chairs that sat facing a fire blazing in a chimneyed
brazier in one corner. The underground room was vast,
far larger than the tavern above it, I judged. More than
that, it was both high-ceilinged and bright, and surprisingly airy, for I realized I could smell none of the
smoke from the fireplace.

"Where does the smoke from the fireplace go?" If
this cellar was secret, as Long John had suggested,
then any smoke would attract curiosity.

My cousin looked up from his pouring. "It goes up
the howff's chimney, cunningly," he said, and grinned.
"That's one of the reasons Matt Crawford bought the

place. This is one of the oldest buildings in Glasgow — so old that no one can remember who built it, or when, but they say there's always been a tavern atop it. Once, long ago, when they set to digging out a cellar, they found a series of caves down here, leading inland from the riverbank, and so they set to work enlarging them and converting them to their own needs. Which suits Crawford fine. It's safe, secure, and weatherproof, a perfect place for storing goods, and he trades regularly with the ships that come and go from here."

He came back to where I was sitting and handed me a cup of wine, holding the long-necked ewer in his other hand. "Here, try that. It's from Germany, and it's been here, waiting for us to drink it, these past five years and more."

I tasted the wine. It was wonderful, and I gulped deeply at it, then held out the cup to be refilled. He topped up my cup, then fetched his own and sat across from me, placing the jug at his feet.

"Well," he said, lifting his cup high. "Here's to Andrew, and to a long life for him."

I nodded and we drank.

"So," Will asked, "what will we do, if he dies?"

I stared into my cup. "We'll do what we have to do," I said, shrugging my shoulders. "We'll bury him, and mourn him, and in due time we'll turn back to what we need to see to — the restoration of the realm. Now tell me, if you will, why it was so important to send Big Andrew to find me in such secrecy. I've never seen him so ill at ease. What did you say to him?"

"Nothing!" Will was wide-eyed with innocence. "I said nothing but that he should find you and send you here."

"But he should not be seen himself. Why was that necessary?"

Something flickered in my cousin's eyes. I tilted my head to one side, examining him carefully, and decided that he was, in fact, red-faced beneath his beard.

"What's wrong, Cuz? Something is troubling you deeply. If I did not know you as well as I do, I might be tempted to think you're afraid of something. So tell me what it is. I might be able to help."

"I think not, Jamie." His voice was close to inaudible, forcing me to lean towards him. "I doubt anyone can help me in this case."

"In what case?"

He lowered his head and gazed at his feet. I had never seen my cousin this way before, and I racked my brain, trying to think what could be upsetting him, but of all the thoughts that flitted through my mind, there was only one that settled, and it unsettled me.

"Will?" I asked him, "Do you mean that no one can help you if Andrew dies?" Again, he would not respond. "What kind of plaint is that? No one can help any of us if he dies. We'll all be bereft, every one of us. We'll all talk of the waste of a young life, and about being deprived, and we'll all rail at God, even me, even while we know His ways are incomprehensible to men. Andrew's wife will be devastated, Will, deprived of his love and companionship after mere months of marriage, and knowing the babe she's carrying will never know its father. How, then, can you believe that you will suffer any more than the rest of us?"

He straightened up suddenly as though I had reached out and slapped him, his eyes flaring wide. "What do you mean?" He sounded as hurt as he appeared to be. "That's not what I meant at all. I wasn't talking about me. I wasn't being personal. I was talking about the realm—about our cause! His death would mean the end of everything we've been fighting for."

Had anyone ever told me that I would one day hear my cousin say such a thing, I would have scoffed aloud. But here I was now, sitting across a fire from him, from William Wallace himself, listening to him admit that he doubted his ability to stand alone without the support of a man who, until a bare three months earlier, he had known only as a boy. The mere idea struck me as ludicrous, but I felt no urge to laugh at it, or even smile, for it was plain that the possibility was all too real for my cousin. I hunched down in my chair and eyed him squarely.

"Why would you say such a thing, Will? Why would you even think it? Tell me, because I want to know."

"I say and think it because it is true. Andrew was the engineer of our success at Stirling. Without him, we would have lost that fight before it began."

"That sounds like nonsense to me, Cuz."

"Then clean your ears, Cousin!" His voice was as startling as a whiplash. "Pay attention and listen to me."

Slightly chastened, I set my empty cup on the floor and listened.

He had always admired Andrew, Will told me, in spite of his briefly held suspicion that Andrew's real intent after escaping from prison in Chester was to claim his heritage prematurely, while his father and uncle were yet alive in England, and to consolidate himself as primus inter pares in the ranks of the magnates. After meeting him again in Dundee, his suspicions had flown, to be replaced with whole-hearted admiration. In Will's eyes, I soon discerned, Andrew Murray had everything that William Wallace lacked: he was high-born, not yet a knight but destined to be knighted in due course, and he was heir to two of the largest, wealthiest estates in all of Scotland. Well-bred and smoothly cultured, he was at ease among the nobility, dealing with them easily and casually as an equal to the grandest, and his immense wealth, or the promise of it, was sufficient to guarantee him their respect, no matter that they might dislike him in person or envy him his good fortune. In addition, he had earned the respect and admiration of his elders by absorbing the rules and disciplines of chivalry, including the techniques of modern warfare, not merely in theory but in their practical applications during training exercises throughout his young manhood. Beside the quick-witted and quick-thinking Andrew, Will confided to me that night, he had always felt himself to be awkward and clumsy, ill mannered and inept.

I had never ever thought of him as being any of those things and I protested strongly. By that time, though, he had begun to enjoy the black mood that possessed him, and I listened, appalled, as he continued his litany of his imagined failings and shortcomings, opening himself gladly to the novelties of self-flagellation and too busy with his mea culpas to have time to heed my protests.

He would have lost the fight at Stirling, he swore, had it not been for Andrew, for it was Andrew's insistence upon choosing the ground for the Scots defences that had ensured the security, and the ultimate victory, of the Scottish army. Andrew it was who insisted on drawing up the Scots host on the slopes below the Abbey Craig, with the wooded hillside at their back and the slopes of the Ochil Hills ensuring that the English would not be able to outflank them. "Pick your ground with care," Andrew had told him. "Fight where the English horse are useless." And so they had drawn up their lines and waited where the English would have to confront them without being able to outflank them. It was only when they saw the English advance proceed precisely as they had prayed it might in their fanciful imagining a week before that they decided to seize the opportunity presented to them by de Warrenne's carelessness, and attack before the English could organize themselves properly.

I held up my hand and waved it in front of him until he stopped and looked at me. "Whose decision was that?" I asked. "To charge the causeway by crossing the flats?" He blinked at me as though he had not understood the question, and so I repeated it. "Who called for the charge?"

"Both of us."

"But who mentioned it first?"

"I did, I think."

"Why? Why did you mention it?"

"Because I could see it, in my mind. It was what we'd talked about before, that night before we reached Stirling. You were there, when we were saying how we would love to see the English make fools of themselves, though none of us believed for a moment that they ever would. And then, on a sudden, there they were, doing exactly what we had wished they'd do."

"And you pointed it out to Andrew?"

"I did."

"And had he seen what was happening before you brought it to his attention? Had he seen the significance of it?"

"He would have, at any moment … I'm sure he must have."

"Are you sure, really? Or do you simply believe he would have?"

"What is the point of this, Jamie?"

"Answer me, Will. Had Andrew noticed anything amiss with the English advance before you spoke to him about it?"

He paused, frowning ferociously, then shook his head. "No," he said. "I remember now. He didn't understand what I was saying the first time. I had to tell him twice, and remind him of what we had talked about."

"You mean you reminded him of all that had been said that night about the English being stranded on the causeway while the Scots spearmen danced around them on the mud."

"Aye, I suppose …"

"And what did he do then?"

"Nothing. He agreed with me."

"And after that you split your forces and led the charge of your infantry down against the causeway."

"We did. Andrew took his men to the east at the bottom of the slopes and I led mine west."

I leaned forward and clapped my palms together. "So," I said, "Andrew chose an excellent defensive base ground for your battle lines—a site you would not have chosen. Is that right?"

"It is."

"But you had no need to use it. You, on the other hand, identified the enemy's weakness and acted upon it, did you not?"

"We both did."

"No, Will, you did. You saw the weakness. You identified it."

He faced me squarely and set aside his cup, which he had not lifted to his mouth since he sat down. "I know what you're trying to do, Jamie. You're hoping to convince me that I'm wrong, and that Andrew's death is of less import than it truly is. But you won't succeed. It's really not of any import that Andrew chose our defensive ground that day—as you say, we didn't have need of the advantages it offered us. But what makes the difference between Andrew Murray and a man like me is that he knew how to choose the site. He understood the strengths and weaknesses with which he dealt—not merely the strengths and weaknesses of the army we commanded and the other facing us, but the strengths and weaknesses of the lie of the land itself—the marshy ground below and in front of us that would impede the English horse, and the dense, wooded slopes at our back that would render their cavalry useless while protecting us at the same time from being attacked by archers from behind. I know none of that kind of stuff, Jamie. I have none of that knowledge. But I am learned enough to know that we can never truly hope to fight and defeat the armies of England without it. Andrew knows it all—or knew it. We talked about it often, he and I, about the kind of force we would need to beat an English army in the field, and he always said we could not do it, that we were too weak—"

He looked at me fiercely as though daring me to contradict him, but when I offered no response at all he went on.

"He didn't mean weak in resolve, or lacking in courage. He meant we lack the physical strength to challenge England nowadays. Scotland is too poor, he said, too lacking in wealth and resources, to field the kind of armies England boasts under Edward and after four decades of unending wars. For while they have been fighting constantly these past decades, building their strength and battle-readiness, we have been at peace and growing fat and slack. We like to talk about being hard and sharp, but we've lost whatever edge we once had because we went for all those years without a need to fight.

"Look at what happened last April, at Dunbar, when we finally went to war. The flower of Scottish chivalry went down to defeat within an hour and were taken prisoners like sheep—Buchan, Comyn, Atholl, Menteith, Ross, the first names that come to mind, all captured. We lost everything at Dunbar, Jamie, except our damnable pride. But Edward confiscated everything we had, and now we have nothing with which to fight back. The bare facts that face us when we even dare to dream of defying him again are staggering. Never mind the leadership, though God knows we need that more than any other single thing. The Comyns, so hungry to seize power, have won us nothing since John Balliol took the throne. But even if we were to find a champion among the magnates, we could not back him, for we lack too much. We lack warhorses for our knights, and because of that our knights are too lightly armoured to withstand their English opposites. But Andrew Murray had the plans to redress all those things. Not by tomorrow, or even by next year or five years hence, but he knew what needed to be done, and he had the means to achieve his ends. He planned to enlist the magnates and mormaers to his cause in organized army-building—cavalry, footmen, and archers. And I truly believe he would have done it. Now, though, if he is dead, it will never happen."

He stood up and turned to stare down into the flames of the brazier, clasping his hands at the small of his back and speaking to me over his shoulder.

"The noblemen would never work with me the way they would have worked with Andrew, one of their own." He twisted fully around to look at me, a bitter little smile on his lips. "I know you don't put much credence in the import of that, because they never have worked with me in the past and without them we won Stirling. But you're wrong, Jamie. Stirling is the past now, and I'm not the man to dictate the future. Not without Andrew, and not without the input of the nobles, for they, whether folk like you and me like it or not, are the men who make the rules by which wars are fought and won. And by those rules, those wars are fought by organized, professional armies, commanded by knights and noblemen and won by strategies tested and proved on formal fields of battle.

"That is the reality of the world, Jamie, and it's a reality I can't change. I know nothing of the crafts of knighthood or of soldiering, and because of that, if for no other reason, because I am no knight, the magnates will not follow me. I'm but a commoner. And yes, I can see you nodding your head and I know what you are thinking: I am an uncommon commoner and the folk will follow me where'er I choose to lead them. But you're the priest, Jamie, so tell me, if you will, as a priest—where would I lead them to?"

He stared straight into my eyes, and when he spoke again, he spoke softly and clearly, in the language of the local people. "They're folk, Jamie. Ordinary folk, wi' ordinary lives to live and wives and bairns who look to them for safety an' protection. Ordinary folk are just that—they're ordinary. They canna win battles against squadrons o' barded knights and men-at-arms, or against ordered regiments o' sodgers supported wi' massed Welsh archers. So where could I lead any o' them but to death? I can fight really well in the woods, wi' my ain men, an' I can marshal them against any groups of sodgery who try to come into my forest, but I could never hae beat Warrenne and Cressingham at Stirlin' had they no' been as bare-arsed stupid as they were. They beat themsel's wi' their ain foolishness.

"But now I'm a giant, it seems. The English in Northumberland and Durham ca' me a deevil, and the Scotch expect me to redeem them, to cure a' their ailments and fling the English out o' this land forever." He grunted, a malformed, self-mocking laugh. "Well, gin Andrew Murray had lived, I would hae tried it, just out o' belief in him. Wi'out him, though?" He shook his head. "Wi'out him, I doubt I could survive for a month."

He fell silent then, and I knew he had nothing more to say. I was searching frantically within myself for words with which to answer him, but I knew, deep in my being, that I had no arguments sufficiently eloquent to counteract the simple truths he had stated.

In the end, I made no effort to change his mind. I simply accepted what he had said, and prayed with him for half an hour, the only way I could believe with confidence that I might strengthen his resolve and ease his mind. But I decided, too, to report his concerns to my superiors as soon as I returned to the cathedral. He knelt to receive my blessing, and then we embraced and parted company.

When I returned to the cathedral, I discovered that the bishop and Canon Lamberton were still in conference. I was astonished, for to my certain knowledge they had been conferring for more than five hours by then, but I was also relieved, to a degree, because I had been determined to rouse both of them from their beds, irrespective of when they had retired.

The bishop's secretary would have prevented me again from disturbing the two, but I was in no mood to be deflected, for I knew neither man would thank me for any delay in telling them about what had happened. I swept past him and threw open the door to the bishop's office.

The large chamber was dark, its walls and high ceiling barely discernible even in the light from the dozen thick and heavy beeswax candles that blazed from the massive candelabrum in the middle of the long, oaken table that Bishop Wishart used as a work desk. The room's two occupants were seated on opposite sides of the table, the entire top of which was littered with documents, some of them rolled up, tied or untied, others flattened and weighted down with pebbles and ink pots.

"Father James?" The bishop blinked at me owlishly. "How come you, here, at this hour of the night? And what hour is it, anyway?"

"Forgive me, my lord," I said. "But I have news you will not wish to hear. My cousin Will believes he is unfit to continue as a leader of the realm."

CHAPTER THIRTY-ONE

THE GUARDIAN

Frowns chased themselves across Bishop Wishart's face like moving shadows as he mulled over all I had told him. At length he sniffed, the sound loud in the silent room, then inhaled deeply and sat straight up in his chair.

"You were right, Father James. This is ill news, and it couldna hae come at a worse time … Where is he now, your cousin? Would he join us if we sent for him?"

"I doubt it very strongly, my lord. He was fretting about having been away from his command for too long, and he intended to be up and away on the road again before dawn. And now that I think of it, I don't even know where he was going. I didn't ask and he didn't say."

"And he didna even try to see Andrew, after comin' a' the way up here? That makes nae sense."

"With respect, my lord, it does to me. He didn't come here to see Andrew, for fear of what he'd find. What he came for was the truth about whether or not the rumours he had heard were true. Knowing Will as I do, I understand that not knowing the truth would be intolerable to him."

"Hmm …" His eyes drifted away from mine, his gaze unfocused. "Damn the man, and damn his conscience, too," he said quietly, speaking almost to himself. But then he looked at me and continued in a louder voice. "Did he say when he'd be back?"

"He did. He said he would return within the week. It will depend on where his raiders are when he gets back to them."

"Aye, of course …" He shook his head. "I want to be angry at him, but that would do us nae good, for in some ways he's right. No' completely right, mind you, but near enough, in some ways. He's upset, an' that's understandable—he's no' a priest an' he's never been the kind o' man wha thinks about God's will and the ways He expresses it. But he is William Wallace, and he's lookin' at the world right now and seein' nothin' but darkness, and that's no' right—there's light out there aplenty, he just canna see it. He must ken the entire Church stands solid at his back, surely?"

"My lord, I don't think the support of the Church ranks high among Will's priorities right now." I saw his eyebrows shoot up in surprise. "It does, of course, but what I mean is that his attention is too closely focused upon the potential loss of his friend and the effect that loss will have on his ability to do what he believes people, including all of us here, expect of him. He fears that if Andrew dies now—"

The bishop quickly raised a hand, its open palm towards me, and I felt a clutch at my heart. "Andrew is dead, Jamie," he said. "God rest his soul, he died about four hours ago." The open hand waved towards Lamberton on the other side of the table. "That's why we're still here, still workin'. They summoned us about three hours ago, but there was nothing we could do by then except pray for him. He'd had the last rites administered long since, and he was in a state of grace at the time of his death. And so we prayed for him and then returned here. We'll bury him the day after tomorrow, in the cathedral cemetery."

I had heard what my employer said very clearly, for I remember the words, but I had not expected to hear it because, somewhere deep inside me, I had not really believed that Andrew Murray would be taken from us. I have no recollection of what was said or done for some time after that, because I was over-whelmed by the reality of what I had been told. The next thing I remember is taking a small horn cup from Canon Lamberton, who was standing over me, a thick leather bottle in his right hand.

"Drink it," he said. "Throw it back. All of it."

I did, and almost choked as the fiery liquor burned its way down my gullet. When it was safely down, he spoke again. "Is it going to stay down?" I nodded, shuddering. "Good," he said, and took the cup from my hand to fill it again and hand it back to me. "One more, then, and you're done."

A short time after that he sat down in front of me, where he placed one hand on my knee and leaned forward, peering intently into my eyes. "Listen to me now, Father James, because this is of great import, much as it grieves me to say it. There is no time now — we have no time now — to deal with the grief of Andrew's passing, for the needs of the realm are such that our personal feelings will have to be set aside until the realm is safe. We need to turn all our attention to this matter of your cousin and what he will do next, for where William Wallace goes, this realm will surely follow. Do you hear what I am saying to you? Do you understand?"

I heard him. His word were annoying, like an insect buzzing around the edges of my vision when I was trying to concentrate, but they did penetrate my awareness and reminded me that I liked this man and that I knew he would not trifle with me. And so I emptied my mind of everything, including the numbness of the shapeless weight in the centre of it.

"I hear you," I said. "I understand and I'm listening."

"Good," he said. He stood up and moved away. "Then come and sit by the fire with us. It's cold and it's late and we still have much to discuss."

Still moving as though dazed, and not yet fully compos mentis, I sat down on the left of the fire, facing the bishop, while Canon Lamberton took the chair between us.

"What must we do, Your Grace?" I asked my employer.

He glanced at Lamberton. "I'll let William answer ye," he said, "for he's thought the matter through, more thoroughly than I hae, and he's the one best equipped to deal wi' it. William?"

"Wallace is right," Lamberton began. "And at the same time, he is as wrong as could be. Every single thing he told you, every point he made, every inference he drew from what he has heard and from what has happened, is essentially correct. But, to varying degrees, all of what he said is incorrect as well.

"But before we go any further, we need to understand, and to agree upon, what we are talking about—what's right and what's wrong and, most important of all, what we can and cannot do to change any or all of that. Because underlying everything we have to deal with here is the truth that we three here, whether we like it or not, will need to make decisions that will influence the welfare, and perhaps even the continuing existence, of this realm as we have known it."

He leaned towards me and held my gaze so that I saw the shadows of the leaping flames against his right cheek. "Do you understand that, Father? Really understand it? Believe me, it is of crucial import that you do, that you understand precisely what your report of your cousin's dilemma has provoked. You may think yourself a simple priest, with dreams of one day running a parish, but here and now, this night, circumstance has thrust you into a position of grave responsibility—the kind of responsibility that few men are ever sufficiently privileged or cursed to be called upon to exercise. This night, acting upon the information we alone possess, and predicated upon the possibilities of all that we know, guess at, and fear, you will determine, along with Bishop Wishart and myself and the guidance and assistance of God Himself, the future course of this realm of Scotland, in the hope of enabling it to survive the tribulations threatening it today."

He leaned back into his chair. "Of course, you can refuse to be involved, but I believe you are here tonight because God sent you here with these tidings, for His own purposes. If you decide you have no wish to be involved, His Grace and I will go ahead and decide what must be done without you. It will be done, though. Failure to decide tonight could mean anarchy and civil war, at best. At worst, it will mean invasion, conquest, and the loss of everything that makes our land the sovereign realm it is, unlike any other in Christendom."

"I understand all that," I said, for his earnestness had made me pay close attention to every word he had said. "I accept the responsibility. Tell me what I need to know, and what I need to do."

Lamberton glanced at the bishop, who wiggled his fingers, bidding him to proceed.

"The rights and wrongs," the canon began, "of Wallace's stance—"

"Stance?" I interrupted. "There is nothing wrong with his stance, Canon. His stance is heroic, the victor of Stirling Bridge. Will's concern is for his future status. We are concerned with his opinions here, not his attitudes."

"Forgive me," he said quietly, nodding his head. "I misspoke and you are correct. So let us say, the rights and wrongs of his opinions about his future prospects. He has the love and the support of the commons. Wheresoever he leads them, they will follow. He fears to lead them to their deaths, though, and that I can understand. But they will stand solidly behind him when he asks them to. So let us accept that and move on.

"The Church. As you so aptly pointed out earlier, the assistance of the Church does not rank high among Wallace's priorities. I understand that, because as a warrior and the commander of the armies of Scotland, his first concern must be for the replenishment of his ranks—replacing the men he lost at Stirling and raising levies of new fighters. Priests and monks, and even canons and bishops, will offer him little hope of sustenance in that endeavour. Eventually, though, once he finds his feet again and can see beyond the pressing needs of the moment, he will come to realize that Holy Mother Church is his strongest and most vigilant supporter. It always has been in the past, and I am quite sure Will has never doubted the truth of that—he has merely lost sight of it among all the other problems facing him. With the active support of the Church, though, he can spread the word of his need for fighting men throughout all Scotland, from the smallest kirks in the land to the great cathedrals, abbeys, and priories. He's not the kind of man to neglect the power of the pulpit for any length of time."

He stood up abruptly and went to the work table, where he bent to look at the documents lying there, passing his open palm over them as though expecting one of them to leap up into his grasp. He quickly found what he was searching for. He came back to the fire and handed me a rolled scroll. It was a letter of some kind, unimpressive and lacking any elaborate seals.

"You wish me to read it?" I asked.

He smiled gently. "No, I can tell you what it says. It is from Robert Bruce, the Earl of Carrick."

I glanced over at the bishop, but his lordship's eyes were closed, the leaping flames now reflecting on his hawk-nosed face, though I doubted he was asleep. I looked back to Lamberton. "And why would you show me a letter from Lord Carrick? Is he still in Annandale?"

"No, he is back in Carrick, having dealt effectively, I understand, with Clifford's raiders. I brought the letter to your attention because he will be here tomorrow. He is coming to consult with me on something that has nothing to do with any of what we are discussing."

I felt a frown tugging at my brow. "And so? Forgive me, Canon, but how is this relevant?"

"It's relevant because it bears directly upon the thing we must talk about next—Wallace's greatest fear, that he will be scorned and shunned by the nobility. There is some truth in that perception. He is a commoner, after all, and the nobility are unaccustomed to regarding commoners as people with minds and opinions, let alone gravitas." He hesitated. "As a vessel for holding a fluid idea, though, his opinion on

that matter is as full of holes as a brazier basket. The
magnates may not like having to deal with him, but
they cannot simply shun him or shut him out,
because he has the trust and support of the common
folk, the source of the fighting men they all need. In
addition to that, given that the Church itself will
demand that everyone in the realm support Wallace
actively, in his capacity as commander of the armies
of Scotland, it will take an arrogant, defiant nobleman
indeed to risk the Church's displeasure. Besides,
there are many among the nobility who will have no
difficulty at all, despite Will's fears, in working with
a champion of his stature. You may start with Lord
James, the High Steward, and throw in several of the
earls and chiefs." He shrugged. "I can't name too
many names with absolute certainty at this point, but
there are many magnates, including Gaelic mormaers,
who will work with him, even if some of them do so
reluctantly. The benefits they stand to gain are too
large and too impressive to permit them to stand off
on principle."

"And what does any of that have to do with the
Earl of Carrick in particular?"

"Nothing at all, on the face of things, though Bruce
is one of the men I had in mind when I said there are
some who will not hesitate to work with Will. But I've
been thinking about Carrick—the earldom, I mean—
from another direction altogether. Politically, rather
than militarily."

The bishop's eyes were still closed.

"Politically," I said slowly, thinking about the word and what it meant in this context. "Can you explain?"

"Of course." He shrugged. "The earl is in a difficult position, I believe."

"With regard to Will, you mean?"

"No, with regard to himself, to who he is and what he represents." He hesitated, cocking his head. "Forgive me, Father, but I have to ask this and I have no wish to offend you. You do know what I mean by what I just said, do you not?"

"Of course I do—is there a man in Scotland who might not? If there is, he must be a newcomer, for the Great Cause left its mark on everyone who was here while it was being debated." I stopped abruptly, on the point of adding something more, something that might have been considered treasonous in some circles, and Canon Lamberton eyed me strangely.

"Isn't it fortunate," he said, "that His Grace should have fallen so deeply asleep? He has had a long day and is obviously overtired." I glanced towards my employer, utterly convinced in my own mind that he was as wide awake as I was.

"Aye, it is," I said with a nod. "It will do him no harm to sleep a little, providing he is comfortable, which he appears to be."

"I agree," the canon said. "Forgive me, though, for interrupting you. You were about to say something further on the matter of the Great Cause, I believe … something about the mark the debate made on everyone who was in Scotland at the time. It would please me greatly to hear more of what you really think of that, in the light of all that has occurred since then."

There it was, an invitation to transgress. I caught my breath, yet barely hesitated before answering him honestly, in tribute to his openness and proven friendship.

"In the light of all that has occurred since then, Canon, I believe a man could present a valid argument in favour of the idea that the King of England acted in bad faith when he decided to uphold the Balliol claim over that of Bruce. What's done is done, of course, and throughout all of Christendom the ruling of Edward's court of auditors in settling the matter of the Scottish succession has now enshrined the precedence of primogeniture over the ancient Celtic laws of tanistry and royal descent through the female side. But I find myself wondering, nonetheless, how the personalities of the two claimants affected Edward Plantagenet's perceptions of what lay at stake in his decision. He was the kingmaker—oh, I know his was an arm's-length involvement and it was the auditors themselves who brought down their verdict.

"But truly, Canon, in the light, as you yourself said, of all that has occurred since then, is it not unlikely that this King, as strong willed and domineering as he always is, could remain aloof and not make some attempt to influence the minds and opinions of the auditors who looked to him constantly for favour and for guidance? And is it far-fetched to consider, knowing what we know now, that he might even then have had plans in mind to undermine and traduce the Scottish monarchy and subsume the realm of Scotland as he had previously done with the Principality of Wales? And if we nod our heads in agreement to even one of those thoughts, must it not then follow that the choice between the claims of Bruce and Balliol must have been, to Edward, one between black and white?

"In the black choice, he had Robert Bruce of Annandale to deal with, a man of seventy years of immaculate probity and iron will, who had never bowed the knee in servility to anyone throughout a lifetime rich in valour, integrity, and flawless honour. The white alternative on the other hand, John Balliol of Galloway, was, and remains, essentially a weakling, a man desperate to please and to be liked, incapable of making a decision without consulting whoever might be around him at that moment, irrespective of their qualifications to advise him in such matters and regardless of what those matters might involve."

I was well aware by then that I had said far more than I intended to say when I set out, but it was the truth, and hearing myself speak the words was exhilarating and liberating, no matter that I might be held to account later for saying them. But even as I was thinking that, I recognized a flaw in my own argument.

"Of course there are folk, even here in Scotland, who will tell you half the auditors were Scots, and that as Scots they could not, and would not, have been influenced to such a great extent by England's King. And I agree, Edward had far less influence upon the Scots auditors than he had over their English counterparts. They might have been open minded and disposed to be friendly towards him, but they were all Scots and loyal to this realm, and he simply could not have bent them all collectively to his will. But he didn't need to browbeat them, because he had help from us. The Church itself was working on Edward's behalf, albeit unwittingly and in all innocence. That may horrify us today, years later, but it is a consideration in light of what we have since learned. At that time it had not yet occurred to anyone other than a few folk to doubt Edward's goodwill, and few would ever have suspected that he might harbour designs upon the sovereignty of our realm. Bad faith on his part was simply unimaginable then. And we, the servants of our Holy Mother Church, had axes of our own to grind." I paused, looking at him, and he quirked one eyebrow, waiting for me to continue.

"You mentioned politics earlier," I said, "in talking about Carrick politically rather than militarily. Well, let's raise that thought of politics again—Church politics in this instance. In the days before this realm's Great Cause, the entire question of primogeniture versus succession claims from the female side—the Salic laws of France, for instance, and our own tanic laws are but two examples—had been disrupting countries within Christendom for decades, and the Church had decided, in the years leading up to the start of the Great Cause, to champion primogeniture in settling matters of royal succession. This dispute in Scotland was to be the defining example, and acting upon instructions from the curia in Rome, the Church authorities in Britain—for the activity took place in England, too, as well as Scotland—decided to militate actively in favour of primogeniture—descent through the male bloodline."

I glanced towards Bishop Wishart and could have sworn I saw his eyes flick shut.

"So there you have it, Canon. We ourselves, the servants of God's Church in Scotland, aided Edward in placing King John on Scotland's throne. And he is now our valid King, duly anointed and crowned in the eyes of God and man. It was Edward of England who proceeded thereafter to change the rules and throw everything into hazard … And I've been talking far too long and have, no doubt, said far too much."

The bishop slumbered on, not moving a muscle.

"Valid," Canon Lamberton said. "You said King John is now our valid King. I could dispute that, were I inclined towards semantics. John Balliol is our legitimate King, no doubt of that, for he was duly crowned and anointed, as you say. Validity, however, is a different creature in this instance. He was deposed and degraded, as all the world now knows, but that was an act of culpable human arrogance on the part of an aging despot who knows better but cares nothing for what anyone may do. It was a humiliation imposed upon one hapless man at the will and express purpose of another man, and it had no effect whatsoever upon the legitimacy of John Balliol's status of King of Scotland." He caught my swallowed comment at that. "I beg your pardon, Father. You said something I did not catch."

"It was nothing, Canon," I said, shaking my head. "A mere reaction to the name you gave him, which was correct: the King of Scotland. I find that offensive, but my dislike of it is purely personal. Our kings have always been kings of the people, not the land. Alexander, our previous King, may God rest his soul, was King of Scots, as was Macbeth, and Malcolm, and David the First. Our current King is the only one, ever, who called himself King of Scotland. But that is neither here nor there."

"On the contrary, Father," Lamberton demurred. "It speaks to the character of the man and to his personality. By naming himself king of the land, instead of the folk, he aligned himself with every other king in Christendom—a transparent attempt to ingratiate himself with his peers. But I was talking of validity rather than legitimacy. Abdication was forced upon John Balliol, as was his imprisonment in London, and there is nothing we can do at this time to change any of that." He shrugged, a mildly distracted, throwaway gesture. "I have it on good authority, from someone I trust, that the Holy Father is moving heaven and earth to secure his release, and that Edward might be induced, given enough in the way of incentives and encouragement, to release the King into the custody of some other Christian monarch. But John himself has lost hope, in his prison there in London, and appears to have abandoned any plans he ever had of returning to Scotland to reclaim his throne. Edward has completely broken his spirit, it seems. But in the eyes of God he is still the King of Scotland and will so remain until he dies.

"In the meantime, though, his absence has created a moral dilemma for all of those who seek to govern Scotland in his name, because this is now a realm without a king. Edward Plantagenet's arrogance has created a yawning hole in the fabric from which this realm is woven, and by so doing he has thrust responsibility for the future onto the shoulders of patriots like your cousin, forcing them to undertake tasks and duties that should not be required of them."

"And is Bruce one of those same patriots?"

"He is. But Bruce has a legitimacy that is all his own. If what you said earlier is accurate, and Edward Plantagenet plotted in advance to usurp this realm—for only a fool would doubt, today, that that is his intention—then everything that Edward did in this matter of the choosing of the new king is rendered suspect and invalid. And that makes Robert Bruce, the Earl of Carrick, a legitimate heir—you'll note I am not saying the sole legitimate heir—to the Crown of Scotland. So let us look at Bruce's situation. He has told me, and I believe him, that he has no wish to seek dominance while John is yet our legitimate King, but he has assured me, too, that he intends to look after his own

interests in this matter, and he will consider advancing
his own claim should the throne become vacant."

"The Comyns will have words to say on that," I
said.

He nodded. "They will, but they will not be crowing
as long or loudly as they did five years ago. They no
longer rule the dunghill as they did then, once the old
Bruce, Annandale, was out of the way. Since then,
for five uninterrupted years, they have had things
very much their own way, and yet for all their
vaunted claims and loud crowing they have failed—
spectacularly failed—to achieve anything in the way of
victory or progress in protecting the realm against
England's bullying. Their record since 1292 has been
one of relentless defeats and failures, culminating in
the fiasco at Dunbar when most of them were taken
prisoner. That record has not gone unnoticed, believe
me, and people are far more dubious about House
Comyn than they used to be."

"They can't all be incompetent," I said. "I hear the
youngest one, Comyn of Badenoch, is an able fighter."

"He is, apparently, though he is young and relatively unknown to this juncture. But have you heard,
too, that he and Bruce—they're of an age—detest
each other?"

"No. I didn't know that … But it is interesting."

"Aye, or it could be, depending on what happens
next. Anyway, Bruce is the greater unknown here, at
least as far as public repute applies. His grandfather
took him to England ahead of John's coronation in

ninety-two and they remained there until Carrick's return here last spring. In the meantime, the old man died in Essex or Sussex—somewhere in the south— and his son, the present Lord of Annandale, became Edward's constable of Carlisle, holding it, nominally at least, against King John, though in fact he was holding it against the Comyns, who had been rewarded with his forfeited lands of Annandale and Carrick. His son the Earl of Carrick, in the meanwhile, had become one of the pampered and spoilt favourites of Edward, who, like many another despot before him, believes in keeping his friends close and his enemies even closer."

"If that's so, why is he here in Scotland now, a rebel against Edward?"

"That, Father James, is the question troubling most of those in Scotland who pay attention to such things, but I have a theory that might cast some light upon it. Edward is Edward and, like all men who wield great power, he enjoys demonstrating his ability to exercise it." He paused. "I was just about to say that I have heard something on that topic from someone in authority, someone I trust, but then I realized how often I say that, and how true it always is, and I felt a sudden surge of gratitude that I am a priest and that, in conse-quence, I have great privileges and unlimited access to information on a vast range of topics, all of which bear upon the Church and its mission here on earth." He smiled again, little more than a grimace this time.

"Be that as it may, the English King, I'm told, enjoys manipulating his puppets. And all who are around him, with remarkably few exceptions, are essentially his puppets. By applying pressure to a variety of his people at any time, he keeps the others on their toes and in fear of attracting royal displeasure. It was as part of one those manipulations, apparently, that he ordered Bruce north into Scotland, to burn Douglas Castle and take Lady Douglas into custody in Edward's name. The order was issued publicly, akin to rubbing a puppy's nose in its own mess, save that Robert Bruce appears to be more his grandfather's offspring than his father's, and is no puppy to be manhandled and publicly abused. I have no doubt there was more to the affair than that, but whatever lay beneath young Bruce's revolt, the order to bring back the woman to Edward's justice was clearly one more thing than he would bear. So now he is here, back in Scotland, and saying nothing about his reasons for quitting England. And naturally, people are suspicious of his presence and his motives."

"But you are not."

"No, I am not. And that's why I think his coming here tomorrow is providential in this matter of your cousin and our need for him."

"You think Bruce will support him?"

"We—" He caught himself and glanced at Bishop Wishart, but the bishop had not reacted. "I believe he has no other choice. Consider: the folk here know not whether to trust Bruce or reject him, and they can see for themselves that his father's people in Annandale will not follow him. That, mind you, is as it should be.

The Annandale folk are his father's tenants and their duty is to his father while the elder Bruce yet lives, but the bulk of the people don't see things quite that simply. To them, the root matter is one of trust—is Bruce one of their own, or is he merely a half-baked Englishman, a spoilt favourite of Edward's, playing the fool and waiting to be received back into the royal favour? That resolution will come only with the passage of time. Bruce will have to show his willingness to earn that trust and demonstrate his worthiness, and in the meantime he will have to wait. And while he waits, he's going to need stability and a calm, lawful environment in which he and his folk can live and prosper. He won't get that if the Comyns come to power again, so he must be reliant upon Wallace." He shrugged and spread his hands. "It's common sense. If Bruce is ever to have an opportunity to claim the throne, he must wait for King John Balliol to die, and while he is doing that he will need security and peace throughout the realm. Wallace will be his best hope of achieving those objectives, ergo Bruce will support Wallace, and enlist his Bruce allies to his cause."

"I see," I said. "And so am I correct in thinking you will speak of this tomorrow with Bruce?"

"You are. Would you like to join us?"

I thought about that for a moment and then nodded. "If you think I might have something to contribute, I'll come willingly, but in the meantime I wish to spend some time with Andrew's widow, the Lady Eleanor. What are her plans, does anyone know?"

"I do. We will bury Andrew here, temporarily at least, and Lady Eleanor will stay here at the convent for the remainder of her term until the baby is born. In the spring she may wish to return home to her family in Petty, and if she does, we will arrange to have Andrew's remains repacked and shipped north to Inverness, there to be buried with his ancestors."

"So be it, then." I glanced at the fire, which had died down to ashes and glowing embers. "I had better get to my bed, for I want to be up and about with my daily Mass celebrated before dawn, so I will bid you goodnight, Canon Lamberton."

"And I you," he answered, rising to his feet. "I'm glad we spoke like this. It was worthwhile … and necessary, too."

I bowed and left him there, and as I went, the bishop said, "God bless you, Father James. Sleep well."

"And you, my lord," I answered, closing the door quietly behind me.

As it transpired, Lamberton did not summon me to his meeting with Bruce the following day, although I was scarce aware of that until it started to grow dark and I realized I had heard nothing from him.

I had spent several hours with Andrew's young widow in the morning, and though there was nothing I could do to console her, I prayed with her and after sat talking with her for a time. She was a beautiful young woman and I estimated her age to be less than twenty years, but she was self-composed and dignified, and once she discovered that I was the same Father James who had travelled to Morayshire to meet her husband, she became avidly curious to know all that I knew about him. She had met Andrew but once, and only briefly, at their betrothal in the autumn of 1295, she told me, and had not seen him again until the day they were wed, in Petty, in March of the following year. That had been a mere five days before Andrew was called away to ride south with King John, to be defeated at the Battle of Dunbar and subsequently thrown into prison in Chester Castle. A few months later, he had escaped and returned home to her as little more than the total stranger she had first met the previous year. They had had three months together then, as man and wife, before his campaign against the English in Morayshire and Ross had forced them apart once more, leaving her alone again but this time with child. From then until now, she told me, she had spent no more than five entire days and four nights with her husband. And now she was a widow. Small wonder, then, that she devoured what I could tell her of my friendship with the man she had married.

I spent the remainder of the day working in the library—always my favourite way to pass whatever spare time I ever had—and it was there that one of the novices found me, late in the afternoon, and told me that Canon Lamberton would like to see me in the bishop's chambers.

The canon and the bishop were both there when I arrived, but there was no sign of the Earl of Carrick. Both men must have noticed the look on my face, for

I was remembering my own words to Lamberton: If you think I might have something to contribute, I'll come willingly. The obvious conclusion to be drawn was that they had decided I had nothing to contribute.

"Earl Robert didna want to disturb ye needlessly," the bishop said. "He accepted that Will winna be back for a few days, and he said there was lots o' time tae make demands on ye." He nodded towards Canon Lamberton. "He left word for ye wi' William."

I turned curiously to the canon, who was smiling at me. "Earl Robert remembers you very well, he said. Something to do with a confession over blood spilt? I confess the way he worded his comment, smiling as he said it, made me curious to know more and I might have questioned him further, until it dawned on me that he was speaking of a confession he had made to you and for which you had absolved him. I was intrigued, I must admit. In any case, the earl requests a favour of you: that when Will returns from the south, you will arrange a meeting between him and Bruce. It will be brief, with none but the three of you in attendance—unless, of course, your cousin wishes to include some of his own associates. Will you oblige the earl?"

"Of course I will."

"He will be here for the next ten days, living within the cathedral precincts—or sleeping within them, at least, since he'll be out and travelling every day, conducting an audit of the region's crops and stores of food. Once you have made arrangements with Will, you can inform the earl."

The next day, we conducted funeral services for Andrew Murray, and installed his coffin, lined with lead, in a raised temporary tomb in the cathedral vaults, where it would stay until the spring, when, depending upon the wishes of the young widow, it would either be interred here in Glasgow or shipped home to Morayshire with the widow and her young child.

Will was waiting for me in my office when I arrived just before the arranged time, and Bruce arrived mere moments after me. We exchanged greetings, with Bruce being more exuberant and Will being more reticent, I thought, than I had ever known either of them to be. When they were seated I immediately turned the proceedings over to Bruce, who scratched his beard, then turned to Will and spoke in passable Latin.

"Canon Lamberton tells me Andrew's death has you upset."

Will shrugged. "Upset is not strong enough to be adequate."

"He says you're thinking of withdrawing from the fight altogether. I think that's unacceptable. What is it that's bothering you?"

"What's bothering me? This from the Earl of Carrick, as if he can cure all ills? Fine, I'll tell you what is bothering me."

And he did just that, unaware that Bruce had already heard all his arguments. Bruce sat silent throughout, saying nothing and permitting no emotions to show on his face, and when Will eventually ran out of words he continued to sit still, saying nothing and simply staring at Will's face, until he grunted and nodded.

"Well," he said, "I've listened, and while I think there might be a few things that are credible among all you've said, I have to say that much of it sounds to me like self-serving, self-pitying pap, and I did not expect to hear that kind of mewling out of you." He raised a hand, as though in a blessing. "Now, if you will, sit still for a moment and let me have my say, and then you can walk away."

Will had been flushing red as he listened, but he nodded deliberately, keeping his face blank. "I am listening," he said, emphasizing the verb's tense very slightly. "Say what you have to say."

"I know you know what duty is, Wallace. You've demonstrated that before, many times, and it's an attri-bute that not all men possess—many of those non-possessors coming from the ranks of the so-called nobility. You have it, though. You understand the concept of duty, and that sets you apart from the ruck of men, giving you a nobility that is all your own. Sadly, though, I fear you've lost sight recently of what your duty is and where it lies."

"My duty?" Will leapt to his feet, his face whit-ening with outrage. "God damn you, Bruce! By what right do you, one of the Plantagenet's favourites for years, think to preach to me about my duty?"

Bruce sat where he was, staring calmly at Will until my cousin subsided into his seat again.

"I would not think to preach to you on anything, Will Wallace," Bruce resumed. "But your duty, for the lack of a better name for it, is to this realm—as is my own, along with that of every other loyal Scotchman. It's not to dead or vanished friends, or even to our dead wives, God rest their souls. It's not to children or to families, save in the widest sense. Our duty, over and above all else, is to Scotland. I have never heard you question that. I've never thought you ever doubted it. I've never seen the slightest evidence that you are unaware of it. But I suspect now that you have lost sight of it, and I won't allow you to do that, any more than I would permit myself to lose sight of it, because I know you would never be able to live with yourself once you saw what you had done."

Will was holding himself rigid, glowering, as Bruce continued speaking. "This realm needs you, my friend. It needs William Wallace, the victor of Stirling. It needs the man who has just returned from carrying war into the English homeland. The man whose very name puts the fear of God into the hearts of every English man and woman and every bishop, abbot, and prior within three days' ride of the Scottish border. So feed me no sorry tales of not being fit to lead. Listen, man, to what you are saying! Not fit to lead? The man who captured Edward's money train and exposed the treachery of York's archbishop in flouting the laws of God and man to smuggle it into Scotland to pay Edward's armies, is unfit to lead?

"Look at yourself, William Wallace, and then shake yourself and try to see yourself through the eyes of those who love and worship you. You say you have no wish to lead them into death? Why not, in God's holy name? If Edward of England has his way, death will be a blessed relief for Scots everywhere. And you, you alone, have the power to defy him because you have the ability to mobilize every man and every true patriot in this realm. And they will follow you because they trust you as they have never trusted anyone before this day. Because God knows they won't trust me, or any other magnate in the land. They'll trust no knight, because all they have ever known from knights is arrogance and disdain, and disregard and abuse. But they trust you, because you have never betrayed them or let them down or broken promises you've made to them. Instead, you offered them dignity and self-respect—the right to hold their heads up high and take pride in their own capabilities. And you would have me think that you are not fit to lead?"

He stopped abruptly, and then continued. "No more talk of unfitness, then. No more self-pity."

Watching closely and holding my breath, I saw Will begin to relax as the meaning of what Bruce had said sank home to him. His shoulders slumped as he sat back into his chair, and there was an almost palpable lessening of the tension that had gripped him.

"There's to be a meeting held within the month," Bruce said, "in Selkirk Forest, to debate what's to be done from here onwards. A meeting of the magnates.

You will be there, with me, although in truth it's I who will be there with you. By then I'll have my friends and clients all lined up as they should be, and we'll name you Guardian of Scotland."

Will stared at him, wide-eyed with shock. "Guardian of Scotland," he said. "Sole Guardian of Scotland?"

"Aye, sole Guardian. Alone. You were joint commander of the armies of Scotland for a while, but God amended that for His own reasons, so now you are sole commander. Who is going to deny you that, after the fact? And so you will be sole Guardian. That sounds reasonable."

Will looked at him, straight faced, for a long time. But then he began to smile, and then to laugh, until he was clutching his ribs in a paroxysm of mirth. Bruce and I laughed with him, I, at least, unsure of why I was laughing so hard but incapable of withstanding the infectious pleasure of simply bellowing with laughter. Will pulled a kerchief from his tunic and wiped his eyes, shaking his head in disbelief.

"My Lord of Carrick," he said shakily, "I fear you may have lost your mind there, so forgive me for laughing at you. But the thought of the Earl of Buchan, or any of his kin, accepting me calmly into their fellowship and promoting me to Guardian's estate was a bit too much to swallow, even for me. Still, the thought was pleasant, while it endured."

Bruce's face was sober now. "What?" he said. "They will accept you. You will be Guardian. I'll see to it."

"And how, in God's name, will you do that? Bethink yourself, my Lord of Carrick. I am a commoner. I have a brother, Malcolm, who was knighted by your grandsire Lord Robert, but I'm no knight. Andrew Murray was not even a knight."

"No, but he would have been, had he lived."

"Aye, he would, and he would have been accepted for his wealth. But I'm not Andrew Murray."

"No, you are not. You are William Wallace, and Andrew Murray is dead … Do you remember the very first time you and I set eyes on each other?"

Will smiled. "Aye, I recall it well. You were having trouble with your spurs."

"Indeed I was. They were brand new, a gift from my father, and I had never worn spurs before. I tripped over them and fell on my arse, and when I looked up you were laughing at me."

"Not laughing, my lord. Not out loud. Smiling, perhaps."

"You know that was the day I was knighted?"

Will nodded. "Aye, my lord, I do."

"King Edward was to have knighted me the summer before, but my mother died on the day of the ceremony. And so, in the final outcome, my grandfather himself knighted me, as was his right."

"And it was appropriate and well done."

"Aye, it was. I could not have fared better or been knighted by a finer man. But I am privileged myself in that regard."

There was a provocative note to his voice, and Will

noticed it at the same time I did. He cocked his head slightly to one side, in the way I knew so well, and said, "How so, my lord? I missed your meaning there."

Bruce stood up, turning as he did so towards the corner behind my chair, where Will had propped his massive sword when he arrived. "I am privileged, Master Wallace, because I am the Earl of Carrick, and Carrick is one of the most ancient earldoms in all of Scotland." He stepped closer to the sword and reached out to pick it up, then turned back to face us both. "I am a mormaer, should I ever choose to use the title, and that means I can knight any man whom I consider worthy of knighthood. So we will go to Selkirk Forest, you and I, Will Wallace, and there, I swear to you on my mother's memory, I will dub you knight in front of all of them, and with this very sword, should that be what you wish. And once you have stood up from where you kneel before me, you may deal man to man and sword in hand with anyone who dares to insult Sir William Wallace, sole Guardian of Scotland's realm."

He turned to look at me, smiling, and then turned back to my cousin. "And now, in God's name, will you stop whining, take this blade from me, and accept your duty?"

The smile that William Wallace unleashed then was a thing of glory.

"I will," he said.

GLOSSARY

a wheen: a few; several

a' their lane: all alone; by themselves

ablow: below

aey: always (pronounced "igh" as in kite)

ahint: behind

aiblins: perhaps

ava: at all; whatever

chiel: child

clarted: caked or thickly coated with dirt

cried: called; named

cry: to call, name, or designate

daur: dare

fash: to anger, upset, or frustrate

forbye: as well as; also

gang yer lane: go alone

gey: quite; rather

gin: if

groat: the most common small Scots coin

ilka: each; every

ingins: onions

jalouse: suppose; guess; imagine

jouk: to dodge or duck

linn: a pool under a waterfall

loon: boy; young man; fellow

ploutering: wading; splashing; wallowing

schiltrom: defensive formation of spear-bearing Scots
infantry
sic: such
siller: silver; money; coinage
thae: those
thole: to tolerate
whaur: where
yett: gate

ACKNOWLEDGMENTS

As has been the case with the first two books in this series, I am greatly indebted to several eminent historians for their sweeping and exhaustive studies of the lives of William Wallace, Robert the Bruce, and in this particular instance Andrew Murray the younger, joint commander of the armies of Scotland with William Wallace at the battle of Stirling Bridge, and heir to the estates of Petty in Morayshire and Bothwell in Lanarkshire. G.W.S. Barrow's *Robert Bruce and the Community of the Realm of Scotland* (Edinburgh University Press, 4th rev. ed., 2005) has been invaluable to me, as have Prof. Edward Cowan's essay "William Wallace: 'The Choice of the Estates,'" in his *Wallace Book* (Birlinn, 2007), and Peter Traquair's scholarly take on the Scottish Wars of Independence, *Freedom's Sword* (HarperCollins, 2000).

There is, however, one additional source whose writing has inspired me during the composition of this book, and I found him almost by accident, having seen his name, Evan M. Barron, cited time and again by those experts with whose work I was trying to famil-iarize myself. It was only when I saw his history of Wallace's struggle cited by Professor Barrow in *Robert Bruce* that I suddenly took notice and went looking for the book, *The Scottish War of Independence* (Barnes and Noble, 1997), which he first published in 1914. What a find that was for me! The man's style, rhetorical and high Victorian, swept me up and plunged me into areas of thinking that I had never even considered exploring until then. He made it very clear to me, from the very beginnings of my reading, that the entire matter of time and travel—the length of time it took to travel anywhere in fourteenth-century Scotland and the degrees of difficulty attached to accurate and timely communication of even the most simple information—was hugely significant to everyone and everything in ways that we, with our cellular phones, social media, and instant messaging services, can no longer imagine. But Barron made me *think* and question my own notions, and his descriptions and interpretation of historical events set my creative juices churning and thrust me towards a point of view that was new and exciting to me. I have no idea, really, how he is regarded by the academic community of historians today, but no one can deny his passion for, and championship of, Scotland's prowess against Edward Plantagenet's England, and he passed that fire along to me as I read his book from a hundred years ago.

There is one other man I have to thank here, my long-time friend and fellow member of the Calgary Burns Club, Jim Osborne, noted peddler there of all things Scottish. Jim is from Aberdeen, and when he wants to, he can turn the accent of his birthplace on so thickly that the words ooze like syrup from a keg. When the time came, therefore, for me to represent the actual way the Aberdonians talk, there was no doubt at all in my mind about whom I needed to consult. Jim read the conversation that I had drafted in English, then translated it into phonetic Aberdonian. You'll find it here precisely as he submitted it to me because I wouldn't dare presume to change a letter of it. Thanks, Jim.

Book I
The Guardians Series

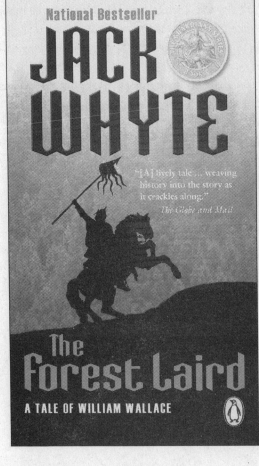

National Bestseller

JACK WHYTE

"[A] lively tale ... weaving history into the story as it crackles along."
The Globe and Mail

The forest Laird

A TALE OF WILLIAM WALLACE

penguinrandomhouse.ca

Book II
The Guardians Series

National Bestseller

JACK WHYTE

The Renegade

A TALE OF ROBERT THE BRUCE

penguinrandomhouse.ca

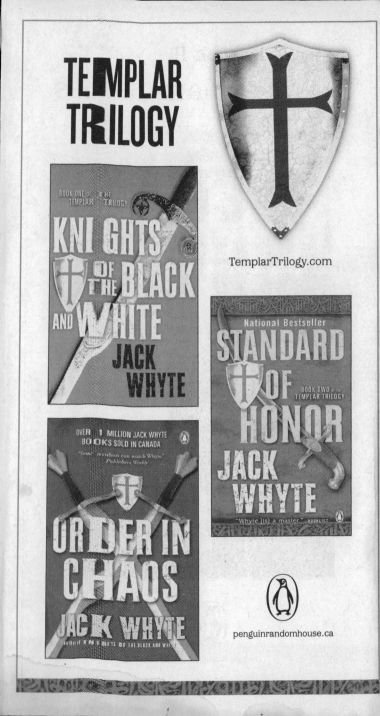

Jack Whyte

A DREAM OF EAGLES *series*